THE SPLINTER KING

First published 2021 by Solaris
an imprint of Rebellion Publishing Ltd,
Riverside House, Osney Mead,
Oxford, OX2 0ES, UK

www.solarisbooks.com

ISBN: 978 1 78108 921 7

A CIP catalogue record for this book is available
from the British Library.

Map by Gemma Sheldrake/Rebellion Publishing
Cover art by Head Design
Designed & typeset by Rebellion Publishing

Printed in Denmark

KIBURU
THE CITY

CATSEYE MOUNTAINS

SUNDAI RIVER

THE HUDANAR

LAKE WOUSOULD

GREAT BOW RIVER

GREEN ISLAND

RIVER IDRA

CROWN ISLAND

N A R I D A

Mountain	Settlement	Marsh	Broadleaved Forest	Rainforest
Hills	Capital	Pine Forest	Mangrove	

1. BLACK KEEP
2. IRONHEAD
3. SMOKING VALLEY
4. DARKSPUR
5. TAINMAR
6. BRIGHTWATER
7. WAYMEET
8. IDRAMAR

9. NORTHBANK
10. GREENBROOK
11. TORGALLEN
12. TORGALLEN PASS (TO MORLITH)
13. GODSPIRE
14. SACRED MONASTERY

15. BOWMAR
16. WOUSOULD HASTE
17. HIGHBRIDGE
18. WHITTING MOOR
19. NORTH MARCH
20. NEW BAYCLIFFE
21. EMERALD BAY

22. EAST HARBOUR
23. WEST HARBOUR
24. KOSZAL
25. TORAKUDO

THE SPLINTER KING

MIKE BROOKS

SOLARIS

This is for anyone who picked up the first one, and came back for more.

SYNOPSIS OF *THE BLACK COAST*

SAANA SATTISTUTAR, CHIEF of the Brown Eagle clan from the islands of Tjakorsha, is fleeing *The Golden*, a body-snatching spirit known as a draug that has broken the clans of her homeland and brought them under its rule. Saana has led her people westwards across the ocean to the land of Narida, where they have historically come as raiders, but now she intends to settle at the small, southernmost town of Black Keep. Opposed to her are the thane *Asrel Blackcreek*, his blood-son *Darel*, and his law-son *Daimon*. Asrel appears to honour Saana's flag of parley and meets her on the marshes in front of the town, but then attempts to kill her. Seeing only certain death for himself and his town if they resist, Daimon betrays his father and brother and agrees that the Brown Eagles can settle. Asrel and Darel are restrained and Daimon assumes the role of thane, but it is agreed that Saana's daughter *Zhanna Saanastutar* will be held as hostage against her clan's good behaviour.

In the Naridan capital of Idramar, the God-King *Natan Narida III* reluctantly agrees to his sister *Tila*'s plan to send more assassins after the *Splinter King* and his family, their exiled relations in Kiburu ce Alaba, the City of Islands. Tila is concerned by rumours that their divine ancestor *Nari* has been reborn, as prophesied centuries ago by *Tolkar, the Last Sorcerer*, and feels that the additional threat of the Splinter King must be removed, especially since Natan has no intention of fathering children, and the succession hinges on the male line of Nari. Tila undertakes the voyage herself in her secret identity of Livnya the Knife, head of Idramar's criminal underworld.

In East Harbour, capital of Grand Mahewa, the largest of the islands, street thief *Jeya* is caught trying to pick the pocket of a wealthy youth, but is allowed to go free. Struck by hìs attractiveness, shé locates hìs house with the help of hér friend *Damau*, but when trying to sneak into the garden at night is shocked to find hìm trying to sneak out. The youth reveals that hìs name is *Galem*, and that hè finds hér as attractive as shé finds hìm. They commence a clandestine relationship.

In the Blackcreek lands, Daimon is forced into fighting the Brown Eagles' champion *Ristjaan the Cleaver*, a close friend of Saana, when Ristjaan is identified as the murderer of the man *Evram*'s brother some ten years before. Daimon wins and kills Ristjaan, which drives a wedge into the fragile alliance between him and Saana. Despite this, both peoples attempt to make the best of their strange situation, with the Naridans under threat of death from the more numerous Tjakorshi, and the Tjakorshi aware that their own lives will be in danger once word gets out of their presence, unless they can prove that they genuinely mean no harm. However, the freeman *Shefal* persuades Evram to sneak away north to the neighbouring thanedom of Darkspur to raise the alarm. Meanwhile, Daimon and Saana clash over cultural issues, since women can rarely hold power in Narida and are sometimes viewed as witches in service to *the Unmaker*, the queen of demons who was driven out of the land by the Divine Nari during his life. The Tjakorshi value the guidance of their witches and see no difference in status between men and women, but unlike Naridans, have taboos against men lying with men, and women with women. Daimon seeks to harbour good feeling by entrusting Zhanna with the raising of a young dragon called a rattletail, which she names *Thorn*.

In East Harbour, Tila uses her connections to find *Kurumaya*, a criminal boss known as a Shark. She provides Kurumaya with details of a family she wants killed, without disclosing either their true identity as the Splinter King, or her own identity as either Livnya the Knife or as Tila Narida. Kurumaya accepts the job and the payment, but the fighting ring where the meeting is taking place is raided by the Watch. Tila flees with her bodyguard *Barach*, and in the company of two other Naridans she met there that evening: *Marin of Idramar*, a thief, and his husband *Alazar Blade* or *Sar Blacksword*, a disgraced sar – Narida's warrior caste – who was fighting in the pits. Tila offers them passage off Grand Mahewa if they can get her back to her ship, which they do. However, she realises after boarding that 'Sar Blacksword' was known to her twenty years ago as Alazar of White Hill, and is the man she blames for her father's death.

Kurumaya entrusts the killing of the Splinter King's family to *Nabanda*, a lifelong friend of Jeya's and, like hér and Damau, a former street orphan sheltered by *Ngaiyu*, an old person who opens thëir home to those in need. Nabanda and a crew of thugs attack the Splinter King's house at night and kill three of the family, but cannot find the last member, an adult masculine youth. Unbeknown to Nabanda, that youth – the Splinter Prince – is Galem, who had crept out to spend time with Jeya that night. The pair of them see Nabanda's crew climb into the garden, although Jeya is not close enough to recognise Nabanda. Galem realises that another Naridan assassination attempt is taking place, and they flee. Hè reveals hìs true identity to Jeya who, guided by an appearance from the golden-maned monkey god *Sa*, leads hìm into the abandoned and derelict Old Palace to spend the night.

In Black Keep, *Aftak*, priest of Nari, finds a curse stone marked with witch's runes buried next to a house where a Tjakorshi woman had died suddenly, and in great pain. Daimon sets his reeve *Kelaharel* to find the witch, but discreetly, so the Tjakorshi do not turn on them. Another Naridan sends the Tjakorshi's corpse painter *Chara* into the woods and Daimon and Saana have to rescue her from predatory razorclaw dragons, and a fight breaks out when the nephew of the Brown Eagles' former chief takes exception to having to treat Naridans as his equals. Daimon and Saana seek to unify their people by having them compete alongside each other in the Black Keep Great Game, a team sport, but in the process one of Daimon's guards attempts to knife Saana, and Daimon is forced to cut off his hand as punishment. In the Festival of Life afterwards Saana gets angry when she discovers that the healer *Kerrti*, one of her witches, has developed an attraction to a Naridan woman, and her attitudes towards this are challenged by Daimon. Saana gets drunk and sleeps with *Tavi*, the Black Keep dragon groom.

Evram has reached Darkspur, and Thane *Odem Darkspur* has sent on word to the Southern Marshal *Kaldur Brightwater*, who arrives with an armed escort. Brightwater is angry to hear of the Tjakorshi settling, but is also angry that Odem has not taken action by himself. Their combined forces head for Black Keep, intent on driving the Tjakorshi away.

Returning to Narida, Tila begins to hear more rumours of the Divine Nari's rebirth, and sees that some of the country believe that her brother's rule is coming to an end. She also hears that he has been taken ill, and resolves to get back to Idramar as fast as possible. In the meantime, she tries to avoid Alazar Blade: partly because she cannot stand him, and partly because she cannot risk him recognising her.

In Black Keep, Daimon comes to the conclusion that only one thing will persuade the rest of Narida that the Brown Eagle clan are genuine, and proposes to Saana that they should marry, despite it not being what either of them would want. Saana is persuaded that it is the best thing to do, but in doing so alienates her daughter Zhanna, who has become attracted to Daimon, and is closer to him in age than her mother is. The wedding is interrupted by Asrel and Darel, who have been freed by agitators including Shefal and Kelaharel. Asrel publicly disowns Daimon and challenges him to an honour duel, which Daimon accepts. When Asrel breaks off the combat and tries to strike Saana down Darel intervenes to protect her, and Daimon kills their father. However, Black Keep then comes under attack from the forces of *Rikkut Fireheart*, a young warrior sent after Saana and her clan by The Golden.

Black Keep and Brown Eagle join together to fight, but Fireheart's forces begin to overwhelm them. Fireheart himself finds Saana and attacks her, and is winning until Zhanna leads a group of Naridan and Tjakorshi youngsters into the battle and stabs him from behind with Asrel's sword. The forces of Marshal Brightwater arrive and turn the tables, sending the remnants of Fireheart's raiders fleeing on their ships. Brightwater accepts that the Brown Eagle clan have made a home in Black Keep and have behaved honourably, but sentences Daimon to death for kinslaying. Darel proves that Asrel had disowned Daimon prior to his death and the sentence is revoked, and when confirmed as the new thane, Darel immediately re-adopts Daimon as his brother. However, Marshal Brightwater tells them of the rumours of the Divine Nari's rebirth, and his concerns about what that will mean for Narida. He instructs Darel to accompany him to Idramar to get God-King Natan's blessing for the Brown Eagle clan's presence, so that he knows the south will be whole and true through whatever may come.

PROLOGUE: CAZIEL

THANE CAZIEL RUMEDELL watched the strange procession wend its way up the valley towards him. Rumours had reached him of the rebirth of the Divine Nari: confused and jumbled rumours, each one seeming to give a different location for the God-King's discovery. Many of Caziel's fellow Westland thanes were gullible fools, who would all too easily accept such a claim. So far as Caziel was concerned, the rightful monarch of Narida was the one sitting on the Sun Throne in Idramar. It was inconceivable that Natan III's divine ancestor could have been reborn without the current God-King knowing of it.

'There are more of them than we were led to believe, lord,' Sar Disman said from beside him. Caziel glanced sideways, but his armsman was sat on his dragon and facing straight ahead, giving no indication of the alarm that his words might have conveyed had they not been delivered in a neutral tone.

'The lowborn ever did cleave to foolishness,' Sar Barlam said stoutly. He came from a long line of warriors, who had served the Rumedell family for as far back as anyone could remember. His lineage was only noble in the loosest sense, but he still had strict views on what separated him from the general populace of Narida: in the main, the lack of intelligence of the masses.

'Do you intend to hold the road against them, lord?' Disman

asked, ignoring his fellow sar's comment.

'This thane cannot allow such blasphemy to pass through his lands,' Caziel declared. 'To do such a thing would be akin to joining our blades to this pretender's cause.'

Disman turned his head to look behind them. 'I fear the men we have with us will not prove sufficient to the task, should these pilgrims choose to press the matter.' They had a hasty muster of two dozen, mainly Caziel's household guards and a few men of fighting condition from his lands. He could have roused far more in the event of a war, of course, but he had wanted to move quickly, and had not anticipated that the heretics' numbers would have grown by so many since he had received word of their approach. There had to be a couple of hundred at least on the road.

'There are the three of us, all mounted on dragons, and two dozen well-equipped soldiers,' Caziel said calmly. 'This rabble have as many old people and children as they do hale adults, and the dragons with them are beasts of burden or wagon haulers, not war mounts like Varrayne.' He slapped his dragon's neck, and it responded with a snort. 'In any case, we are defending the honour of the rightful ruler of Narida, and his divine ancestor will look upon us with favour.'

'This sar would prefer if He were to look upon us with twenty archers,' Disman muttered.

'Disman!' Caziel snapped, irritated by his sar's irreverence. 'Mind your tongue!'

The first of the pilgrims were now approaching the mile marker that served as the boundary between Rumedell and Broadfield, the thanedom through which they had been travelling. Caziel was surprised that Thane Badan had allowed them to pass unchallenged, but he was getting old now, and his sons were far from dutiful.

Caziel drew a long, broad-bladed spear from his saddle rack, and levelled it at the man in the lead: a tall fellow in a robe and a cloak, with a head that had clearly been shaved clear of hair before its time, and with a pipe that gave off a few wisps of smoke clenched between his teeth. 'Halt!'

The man walked on for a few more steps before deigning to oblige, coming to rest with his feet apart some ten yards away. His companions slowed as well, and none moved past him. Unsurprising, Caziel thought. Who would wish to face the wrath of a mounted thane of Narida?

'Who are you, who seek to bar the way of the Divine One?' the bald man called around the stem of his pipe. 'Or do you not yet know what transgression you commit?'

Caziel's temper flared at the man's sheer effrontery. 'The Divine One passed from this world centuries ago, and his descendant sits on the Sun Throne! Your heresy will not be tolerated on these lands, wretch! Return the way you have come, and you may keep your lives in the hope that you will renounce this foolishness! Take another step, and this thane will strike you down!'

The bald man removed his pipe from his mouth and, with a sigh of regret, knocked it out on his boot. He then pulled back his cloak to place it in a pocket of his robe, and Caziel saw a scabbarded sword belted at his waist. And not just any sword.

'Whose longblade do you carry?' Sar Barlam demanded angrily. It was indeed a longblade, the weapon of a sar; a far finer blade than the simple triangular sword that might be carried as a sidearm by a spearman. Caziel had one at his own belt, along with its companion shortblade, both scabbards decorated with artwork depicting his battles and triumphs.

'This priest's name is Mordokel,' the bald man said. 'The blade at his belt belonged to him in his past life, when he was a sar of Oakscar. He presented it to the Divine One when he first swore himself to the Divine One's service, and the Divine One was gracious enough to grant it back to this priest.'

Caziel studied the man anew, with not a little disdain. Priests were all well and good, of course, but to renounce your vows as

17

a sar to become one? And in service to a pretender at that? It did not bear thinking about.

'Regardless of your history, you may not pass,' he said clearly. 'Shepherd your charges away, or face the consequences.'

Mordokel placed his hands on his blade – one on the hilt, the other on the scabbard – and dropped into a slight crouch. His form was good, Caziel noted; it seemed likely that his account of his past was truthful, strange though it was.

'You are not accepting the thane's gracious offer?' Sar Barlam asked, readying his own spear.

'This priest cannot,' Mordokel said levelly. 'The Divine One has instructed us to take this route, and so we shall. You may swear yourselves to His service now, and join us. Otherwise, your bodies will be left on this hillside for the scavengers.'

The priest's eyes were hard, with no suggestion of doubt or fear. Caziel had to give the man credit for that, at least.

'This thane does not wish to draw his blade on fellow Naridans,' he said, hoping that sense might yet prevail.

'This priest has no such compunctions, should his fellow Naridans stand against the Divine One's wishes,' Mordokel replied flatly.

'So be it,' Caziel said with regret. He raised his spear and drew in breath to shout the order to attack.

Mordokel moved first.

The priest drew his blade in a swift, sharp motion that had clearly been performed thousands of times before, and broke into a dead run. His immediate companions came with him, producing their own weapons from under their cloaks, and behind them the snake's body of the pilgrimage began to lurch after them. Caziel was so taken aback by people on foot charging *towards* mounted sars that he hesitated for a moment before applying his heels to Varrayne's flanks, and by the time he did so the onrushing attackers were too close for his mount to build up the devastating momentum that was the reason mounted sars could hammer through foot troops.

Then he was in and among them, stabbing downwards with his spear, and there was no time for thought.

THE DIRT OF the road was warmed by the sun, and the sun itself was beating down with the vigour of late spring, but Caziel Rumedell was cold. He still fought to rise, to take his longblade back into his hands and fight, but to no avail. His body was not responding. He had already been cut down: he just was not dead yet. It was coming, though; the edges of his vision were darkening.

Footsteps approached, moving in the opposite direction to the rest of the faithless heretics traipsing past him without a glance down at thane of the lands into which they were moving. A pair of well-worn but well-made boots came into his view, and the toe of one reached out to tilt his face sideways, to look up at the sky.

A man stood over him, silhouetted. Caziel couldn't make out the face, but the way the sun gleamed off the bald pate gave him all the clue he needed.

'Mordokel,' he whispered, unable to summon any more volume or venom.

'Three of your men saw sense, and their lives have been spared,' the priest declared, in a tone as neutral as if he were discussing the weather. 'One, in fact, has been healed of his wounds by the Divine One Himself. The rest of you will, as this priest promised, be left for the scavengers.'

'Shortblade,' Caziel hissed. 'Let this thane . . . take his life . . .' He had failed in his duty; at the least, he could die by his own hand rather than this extended death. But his shortblade was no longer on his belt, and his longblade was nowhere in his sight.

Mordokel shook his head. 'Your options were made clear to you, and you made your choice. You died opposing the Divine One's will: anything else is an inconsequential detail.'

19

'Mordokel!' Caziel spat, with all the breath he had left. 'You were . . . a sar! You know . . . the Code of Honour!'

Mordokel knelt down, bringing his face closer. Now Caziel could just make out some of his features, even through the darkness cast by the sun and his own failing vision. The priest's eyes were, if anything, even harder than when he led the charge.

'The Code of Honour no longer holds any weight,' he said simply. 'The Divine One is reborn, and all of our old structures can be cast aside.' He tutted. 'The world you knew has gone, thane. It will be changed beyond your recognition. Perhaps this is indeed the most merciful end for you. Die here in the dust, thinking of the Narida you love, and take some comfort from that fact that since you could not accept the truth, at least you will not see what it does.' He stood up, becoming lost in shadow once more, and turned away.

'Mordokel!' Caziel spluttered. 'Mordokel!' He no longer knew if it was a curse or an entreaty, but it mattered not. The priest neither slowed nor looked back, and the daylight faded on Caziel, accompanied by the tread of feet and the creak of wagon wheels.

PART ONE

The tides, they rise and fall, my sweet
When The Dark Father snores
But when Father Krayk breathes in deep
Be not too near the shore

For he will suck the waves away
And show their gleaming bed
But when Father Krayk breathes in deep
He will breathe out again . . .

Tjakorshi children's rhyme, usually sung as a prelude to a chasing game

DAREL

IT WAS A bright spring morning in Black Keep, the southernmost town of Narida. The last of the lowland snows had melted, although the slopes of the distant Catseye Mountains to the west remained coated in white, the town was already busy, and Darel Blackcreek was bidding farewell to his brother in the gardens of their family's castle.

'It is a great shame that you must leave,' Daimon said miserably. At two-and-twenty summers old, Darel's law-brother was two years younger than him, and a hand's-breadth taller. Both of their cheeks were streaked with ash to mark their mourning of the man who had fathered one of them and adopted the other, and in the end had turned against them both.

'You did not do so very badly at being thane,' Saana Sattistutar protested to her husband. The chief of the Brown Eagle clan was taller than Darel as well, as indeed were many of her folk. 'Your wife is sure you can manage again.'

'Saana is correct,' Darel agreed, allowing himself a small smile. 'All will be well. And besides, you have Osred for counsel.'

'How can a man fail to be encouraged by such overwhelming faith in his abilities?' Daimon muttered, glancing from one to the other of them. 'But that is not what he meant, in any case. Our steward probably knows the running of Blackcreek lands better than you, and certainly better than your brother: Osred could be left solely in charge, and everything would likely proceed without problem. But your brother will miss you.'

Darel sighed. 'And your brother will miss you, too.' And he would, there was no doubt about it. The journey to Narida's capital city of Idramar and back, to answer to the God-King himself for the decision to allow the Brown Eagle clan to settle and live on Blackcreek land, would take weeks. It would be, by far, the longest time that Darel had been away from his home, and indeed his brother. And yet . . .

And yet, *Idramar!* The greatest city in all of Narida, supposedly in all of the world. The seat of Natan III, the monarch descended by blood from the Divine Nari, the first God-King who had driven out the great demon known as the Unmaker, slain her witches, and forged a land awash in fear and darkness into a single nation under His noble rule. Darel had longed to walk Idramar's streets for as long as he could remember, but he had never imagined he would get the opportunity. He couldn't deny the excitement in his belly, for all that he was essentially making the journey to plead for the lives of his town.

'Has the High Marshal decided upon a route?' Daimon asked.

Darel grimaced. 'Aye. We are to make for Tainmar and take ship up the coast with a small escort, while his main force returns to Brightwater from there.' He had never sailed before, and the prospect was not an appealing one.

'Take ship?' Saana frowned. 'Your Flatlander ships are slow and clumsy. You should take one of our yolgus. It would be quicker.'

'A Tjakorshi ship might not get the warmest reception elsewhere,' Darel pointed out. The journey would certainly take less time, but Darel could just picture the scene as they attempted to sail into any Naridan port on one, let alone Idramar itself.

Saana shrugged. 'Can you not make the Marshal stand at the front, so everyone knows who you are?'

Darel winced, and glanced over his shoulder at the guest quarters. Tjakorshi humour was somewhat irreverent, and he didn't think that was a suggestion that Kaldur Brightwater, a Hand of Heaven and High Marshal of the South, would appreciate hearing.

'It would be best if we sailed on a Naridan vessel,' he said. 'Besides, we don't know where the survivors of Fireheart's raiders fled to. If they sailed up the coast, another Tjakorshi ship following in their wake is even more likely to be attacked.'

Saana scowled at the mention of Rikkut Fireheart, who had scarred her cheek and wounded her leg, which reminded Darel of something.

'Where is your daughter?' he asked, looking around. Darel and Daimon had agreed that Zhanna could keep their father's sword, and she'd become a familiar sight in the town over the last week doing her best to assist in translations, although her mastery of Naridan was not as good as her mother's.

'She has her crew repairing the wall today,' Saana said dryly. Zhanna had become the unofficial leader of the small group of youngsters, both Tjakorshi and Naridan, who'd followed her into battle. The Tjakorshi among them had all now received the thick stripe of tattoo that ran down from the forehead to the bridge of the nose and denoted adulthood; shockingly, several of the Naridan youths had followed suit. Darel and Daimon had both needed to prevent outraged Naridan parents from starting fights with the Tjakorshi who had 'mutilated' their sons and daughters.

'It is good that they are providing an example,' Darel said, with what he hoped was an encouraging smile. 'Your law-brother is certain that by the time he returns, the whole town will be of a similar mind, and the walls repaired.'

'You are an appalling liar, brother,' Daimon said, shaking his head only half in jest. 'The battle brought our peoples together, but there are still treacherous currents beneath the surface.'

'There always are,' Saana said. 'People argue: it is what they do. In ten Tjakorshi, you get eleven opinions. The chief steps in when arguments get too high, otherwise . . . ' She made a vague waving motion with her hands, which Darel gathered was intended to signify letting people get on with things in their own manner. It was easy to forget, looking at this towering warrior in her furs, that she had been the chief of her clan for ten years. Naridans were different to Tjakorshi, of course, but with his new wife to back him up, Daimon wouldn't be left to cope with the running of things entirely on his own.

'Black Keep is in good hands,' Darel said with a smile, and realised that he meant it. He bowed deeply to Saana, and she returned it somewhat clumsily. Then he stepped forward and opened his arms to embrace Daimon.

Their father Lord Asrel would have frowned on such a gesture of affection: in fact, Darel suspected he would have done rather worse than frown. However, Asrel Blackcreek had been so caught up in his ideals of honour and proper conduct that he tried to kill his own sons rather than accept that Naridans could live peacefully alongside Tjakorshi. Darel used to think of himself as a disappointment to his father, and he knew that Daimon had felt the same way. Now he was starting to realise that his father's expectations had not been as flawless as he had always assumed.

'Take good care of yourself,' he said into Daimon's ear. 'Your brother will be back before you know it.'

'You are still an appalling liar,' Daimon replied with a chuckle. 'Your brother will count the days until he sees you again.'

'Then your brother will keep the number as low as possible,' Darel told him honestly. He relaxed his grip, stepped back, and took a deep breath as he squinted up at the sun. 'Well. We are due to depart shortly. Do try to keep the town in one piece, at least until your brother returns.'

STONEJAW

ZHELDU STONEJAW LOOKED around at the dead Flatlanders, whose small fishing village was being torn apart by her crew as they searched for desperately needed supplies. It had been an easy victory, but it wasn't exactly a triumph about which anyone would be composing a song.

Rikkut Fireheart had set out from Tjakorsha with twenty yolgus, vessels crewed by the islands' finest warriors. They'd sailed with one purpose, and one purpose only: to find Saana Sattistutar and her Brown Eagle clan, to take the belt that marked her as chief from her dead body, and bear it – along with any of her clan who could be persuaded, by whatever means – back across the Western Ocean to their homeland, and to the monster that sat waiting for them.

The Golden. The Breaker of the Clans. The draug that had clambered up out of the Dawn Mountain and then brought fire and death to the entire archipelago, one island at a time. It wore a man's scarred flesh, and it spoke with a tongue that very nearly got all the sounds right, but Zheldu had seen into its eyes. There was nothing human there: nothing but ice and hatred.

The Golden had granted Fireheart command of the largest war fleet ever assembled. They'd crossed the ocean thought to be endless, though their provisions had nearly been exhausted in doing so. They'd landed on a shore they'd never dreamed they'd see, and easily breached the walls of the small settlement where the Brown Eagle clan had settled alongside the locals. It should have been a slaughter. At first, it was.

Then the beasts came.

Zheldu knew the krayk, the great, dark-scaled creatures that swam the ocean's depths. Every Tjakorshi knew them: they were the pureblood children of the Dark Father, Father Krayk, who'd separated the land from the ocean before time had meaning, before Kozhan Lightbearer had placed the two moons in the sky. Rikkut Fireheart, that fearless madman, had killed one of the damned things on the voyage over.

None of them had known that the krayk had kin who walked the land.

Zheldu had still been outside the walls when she'd heard the first roars of the beasts, and the moment that Tjakorshi war cries had turned into screams of terror. And then, while leading a group trying to break down the gate on the far side, she'd been chased back to the ships by one monster erupting from within the town, and more coming down out of the trees to the north, each ridden by a Flatlander. Warriors she had known for years were trampled flat, or impaled on huge, broad-bladed spears. Rumour had it that Fireheart had killed one of the beasts, but had then been slain in turn by a girl of the Brown Eagle clan. Zheldu didn't know if that was true, but it didn't matter. Rikkut Fireheart was dead, and his war fleet was broken. She'd led the remnants north up the coast, but with only scraps of food and dregs of water left to them, they'd risked hitting the first village they'd seen.

'Some of them made it into the trees,' Zhazhken Aralaszhin said in disgust, breathing heavily as he approached her. Zheldu fixed him with a glare.

'And you ran them down?'

'The Dark Father take that!' Zhazhken retorted, spitting on the ground. 'I'm not going in there! What if there are more of those monsters?'

'They'll be running to *find* the warriors that ride the monsters, you fool!' Zheldu yelled at him, and he recoiled. 'Tell me that someone went in after them!'

Zhazhken shook his head mutely, and Zheldu bit her lip until she tasted blood. By Father Krayk and all the ancestors, she had no wish to face down any more of those things! She looked over her shoulder to check how far she was from the shore where their yolgus were beached, then angrily kicked the corpse of a Flatlander lying at her feet.

'Load up!' she bawled, turning in a circle and addressing every Tjakorshi she could see. 'Find their food, fill the water barrels, then get back on the ships!'

'Who're you to be giving orders?' Kulmar Ailikaszhin demanded, straightening up. He was fair-haired and fair-faced, and his blond beard was forked. Far more importantly, he was a captain, and he'd managed to make sure his own ship was one that the remnants of Fireheart's war band had taken as they'd fled the rout in the south. Zheldu Stonejaw wasn't a captain; she was just a warrior.

She punched him in the face as hard as she could.

He went down into the mud, one hand clawing at his belt for his spearfish-bill dagger. Zheldu waited for him to wrench it free, then dropped one meaty knee on his chest and grabbed his hand in hers to pry the weapon loose. It only took a moment – there was a reason she was undefeated in wrist-wrestling – and then she had the point of it at his throat while he wheezed for breath.

'Fireheart's dead!' she called out, as those of Ailikaszhin's crew who'd been with him paused in the act of drawing their own weapons. 'Fireheart's dead, and we're not getting Sattistutar's belt! We're on a land we don't know where the warriors ride monsters, and if we go home empty-handed the draug will skin us! So does anyone else want to argue about getting some food and water on the ships, and then getting back on the fucking sea while we figure out what to do next?'

Silence greeted her words. All around her, Tjakorshi warriors looked at each other, and then at the dark line of unfamiliar trees out of which charging, thundering death might emerge at any moment.

'Good,' Zheldu said, pushing herself up again. She dropped Kulmar's dagger on top of him, then deliberately turned away. 'The *Storm's Breath* is mine. If you'd be my crew, find some food or water, or something valuable, and take it aboard. I'll not spend a moment longer here than I have to.'

The warriors around her sprang back into action as she finished speaking. Even Kulmar did nothing more than shoot her a glare. It was as easy as that for Zheldu to take charge, but, she reflected bitterly, that was hardly anything to celebrate. Those who achieved great things became great heroes. Those who died attempting great things, like Fireheart, were remembered in song. Those trying to salvage something after bloody fools had died attempting great things had a thankless task with little potential for glory and a lot of potential of blame, but it still needed to be done.

She glanced up as another warrior approached her: Korsada the Dry, the daughter of a Tjakorshi father and a Drylands mother, whose skin was darker than any other Tjakorshi Zheldu had ever seen. Zheldu didn't know Korsada well, but she was supposedly deadly with her mother's long, thin steel blade that hung at her right hip.

'You want something?' Zheldu asked, sizing the other woman up. There were whispers that Korsada's parentage meant Father Krayk didn't recognise her as his child. This was evidently nonsense to Zheldu's way of thinking, since, if that were true, Korsada would never have survived the voyage here, but it meant she'd probably not have the support to challenge Zheldu's hastily won leadership of the fleet. On the other hand, these were strange times.

'I may have something of value to you,' Korsada said quietly, coming to a halt three paces away, with her hand on the pommel of her sword.

'Then put it on the ship,' Zheldu told her. Korsada smiled.

'It's not food, or water. It's a thought of where we should go.'

Zheldu eyed her. Korsada was from Sorlamanga, Tjakorsha's northernmost island, and if there was one thing Zheldu had learned recently, it was that the different clans had their own secret ways across the oceans. Sattistutar's people had supposedly been visiting these Flatlands for generations before they fled here, yet Zheldu had never even heard a rumour of this land she now stood upon, across the Western Ocean. It was entirely possible the northern clans had similar secrets.

She raised her eyebrows. 'I'm listening.'

'Have you ever heard,' Korsada said, leaning in a little closer, 'of the City of Islands . . . ?'

TILA

Princess Tila Narida had broken into quite a few buildings in her time, but some challenges were beyond her. Climbing three sandstone storeys of the Sun Palace's central keep would have sorely taxed her even in the prime of her youth, and as she approached her thirty-eighth birthday she was increasingly aware that her prime was behind her. For another thing, even the plainest, least-adorned dress that she could get away with wearing as a princess was far too weighty and cumbersome for such exertions.

If caught, there was also the matter of why she might be attempting to climb through the bedroom window of her brother, the God-King himself, when he was confined to bed with a sickness. Tila knew that many of the Divine Court neither liked nor trusted her – they called her 'the Veiled Shadow' as mockery behind her back, to distract themselves from the fact she knew things she should not know – and she would not have put it past them to suggest she might be trying to ensure Natan's demise. She would have to visit him officially.

The only problem was that she'd been away for months, and Nari alone knew what the situation might be in the Sun Palace, or who might try to throw up obstacles to her seeing her brother. Tila had swept through the Sun Palace as fast as she could, to minimise the chance of anyone important hearing of her return and heading her off before she'd achieved what she wanted, and she bore down on the guards stationed outside Natan's door like the wrath of Nari Himself.

'Is this princess to understand,' she said, slowly and deliberately, 'that you are attempting to prevent her from seeing *her own brother*?'

'Orders of the Grand Physician, Your Highness,' one of them muttered warily, looking at the floor.

'Is the Grand Physician here?' Tila asked, looking up and down the corridor, which was lit by rushlights. 'This princess does not see him lurking in the shadows.'

'He's not here, Your Highness,' the guard admitted.

'And who do you suppose can make your lives more miserable?' Tila demanded, fixing them alternately with a glare that neither was willing to meet. 'The Grand Physician, or this princess?'

Neither of them answered that, but they both looked at each other with the expressions of men who knew that they were not getting out of this one. The guard on her right did make one last effort, however.

'The door's locked, Your Highness,' he managed. 'The Grand Physician has the key.'

'He has *a* key,' Tila snapped, producing her own from her sleeve. 'Stand aside.'

They did so. To lay a hand on the Princess of Narida without her permission was a flogging at the very least, potentially the loss of the hand, or even execution. They both stared directly ahead as she slotted the key into the hole and jiggled it around until it caught and the lock slid open.

'Do not let anyone enter,' she told them as she cracked the heavily carved door open and slipped through. 'Including the Grand Physician.'

It was dark inside. Tila locked the door and closed her eyes for a few moments, alert for the sound of movement, then cautiously opened them again. Her vision began to adjust, and the dim light from the keyhole provided enough illumination that she felt confident about walking forwards without falling on her face.

'Natan?' she called, but her voice came out more quietly than intended. Fear had strangled her; fear that her brother would not respond, either because he was at death's door or because he had already crossed the threshold. Tila found her brother incredibly frustrating at times, mainly due to how carelessly he approached his rule, but she loved him nonetheless. The thought of him wracked by illness, sweating and shivering and coughing . . .

A sound came from ahead of her: a faint rustle of movement from the master bedroom, where Natan slept, but no voice calling out in response. Tila tucked her key away and pulled out a knife instead. The Divine Princess had no familiarity with weapons, of course, but Livnya the Knife had not come by her name by chance. Tila could hit a target the size of a person's head at thirty paces, most times. The one advantage of her gowns was that there were any number of places to secrete small weapons, and no one would ever dare search her.

'Natan?' she called again. 'Are you here?' He had to be here. Where else would he be?

But what if he wasn't alone? The climb to his window would be hard, and the guards in the grounds should see anyone attempting it, but it was not impossible, and Tila knew full well that guards were not always where they were supposed to be, or looking where they should be looking. Natan had no heir: he didn't even have a spouse. Any foreign power wishing to throw Narida into chaos could do so by ending her brother's life . . .

She moved more quickly, relying on memories of her countless visits to her brother's chambers as much as on her barely visible surroundings. She crossed the floor of the small entrance room, skirted the table in the reception parlour, passed the door on her left to Natan's bathing room where he would have heated, scented water brought to his huge copper tub, and reached out to take hold of the latch of his bedroom door. A faint, flickering light was cast beneath it: there was a shuttered lantern or low-burning candle alight within.

There had still been no reply. Tila adjusted her grip on her knife so she was ready to slash with it or throw it as necessary, briefly directed one more curse at her gown, lifted the latch, and pushed the door inwards.

Natan III, God-King of Narida, was standing at the foot of his huge bed with their father's longblade unsheathed in his hands and pointing at her. Tila's immediate relief at seeing him on his feet collided with her utter confusion. 'Natan? What are you—'

'Are you alone?' he cut her off, the tip of the sword wavering.

Tila blinked at him. 'Yes, your sis—'

'Oh, thank Nari.' He let out a breath, sagged against the bedpost, and lowered the sword. 'It is so good to see you, but . . . '

'All the rumours say that you are sick,' Tila said, advancing towards him. She peered at his face, which was heavy with beard stubble, then looked him up and down. 'They say that you have taken to your bed, but you do not *look* sick.'

'Your brother is *not* sick,' Natan told her, his voice low and his eyes darting from side to side as though afraid of the shadows in his own room. 'He has been faking it, waiting for you to return.'

'Faking it?' Anger rose up in Tila's chest, squashing down the relief that had instantly flowered at her brother's first words. 'All the worrying your sister went through? The helplessness? All that, and you were *fine*?'

'Tila,' Natan said, his voice as serious as she'd ever heard it, 'listen to your brother carefully.'

Natan was rarely serious. Languorous, often. Dismissive, sometimes. Sarcastic, more often than she'd like. Tila bit down on the angry words that were still poised on her tongue and nodded. 'Go on.'

'The palace has changed while you were gone,' Natan said. 'The rumours of Nari's rebirth are not going away. It feels like everyone is waiting to find out which way to jump.'

Tila stared at him incredulously. 'You mean people *believe* the rumours?'

'No one will say so outright, of course,' Natan replied. 'Not the Court, at any rate, but neither are they denying them as rigorously as we would want them to.'

'What about Taladhar?' Tila demanded. 'Why has he not stamped this out?'

'The Western Marshal assures us that his men can find no evidence of anyone actually claiming to be Nari reborn,' Natan replied with a snort, 'but your brother does not believe he has been looking hard. You know how pious old Taladhar is: Godspire's shadow practically falls on his home. His loyalty is to Nari's bloodline, not to us, and he is more likely than most to believe that these rumours are genuine. Your brother suspects he is either waiting to see what develops or is actively trying to throw us off the scent.'

'Tolkar's arse!' Tila swore. This was worse than she'd feared. 'But this does not explain your mummery.'

'The Court are scared of you, Tila,' Natan said bluntly. 'They would not move against your brother with you here, but with you absent one of them might have been overcome with religious fervour and made a move.'

'They would not dare,' Tila said instantly.

'Why not?' Natan demanded. 'To whom would they answer? Your brother has no heir, and even if you could defy all convention and take the throne, you could not have done it while you were not present. There would be no incentive for the others in the Court to exact vengeance, no one for them to seek the favour of by so doing.' He shrugged. 'So your brother feigned illness. With him less visible, they are free to scheme without feeling they have to remove him first. Also, any of them who believe your brother should die might just wait for the illness to do the job for them, rather than risk sticking their neck out.'

Tila nodded slowly. 'Your sister must confess, that is a more reasoned approach than she would have expected of you.'

'Your brother is not a total fool, Tila, despite what some people believe,' Natan said with a wry smile. 'But he cannot manage the Court without you here to frighten them into line.'

'What about the Grand Physician?' Tila asked him. 'Does he know the truth about you?'

'If he does, he is at least as good a mummer as your brother,' Natan replied. 'He clucks and sighs, and makes your brother drink all manner of foul-tasting potions. No, no one knows of your brother's pretence, except you.'

'Good,' Tila muttered. 'What do you plan to do now?'

'Recover within a reasonable timescale,' Natan said. 'Suitably reward the Grand Physician for his efforts. And shave,' he added, rubbing his cheek with a shudder. 'Your brother felt that letting his beard grow would assist with his pretence, and to be fair, it does actually make him feel unwell.'

'Very well,' Tila said. 'Your sister will see who has been making the wrong sorts of noises while we have both been indisposed.'

'And what if the rumours *are* true?' Natan asked softly. 'What if Nari has been reborn?'

It was a strange feeling, to have been told all your life that you were divine, that you were the highest of the high, only to encounter the possibility of someone taking that from you. It was not a sensation that Tila welcomed.

'If that has happened,' she said carefully, 'then you will meet our reborn ancestor as a strong ruler secure in his power. If we are satisfied with his claim, we can discuss the transference of authority. But until we are convinced that this person exists, and that they are no fraud, you will continue to rule Narida, and all will pay your proper homage.'

'Except you,' Natan smirked.

'Only when no one else can see,' Tila snapped. She sighed. 'Your sister must sleep now. She has much to do tomorrow, and will no doubt have to deal with many people who consider themselves dangerous. Get some rest. You will need it.'

ZHANNA

THE TATTOO ON Zhanna's forehead still itched.

The battle had been terrifying, but thrilling. She'd snatched up the longblade belonging to Daimon Blackcreek's father, rounded up a few other Brown Eagle Unblooded, and then shamed a group of Naridan youngsters into picking up weapons and fighting as well. They'd turned the tide, and she'd killed Rikkut Fireheart. The fact she'd stuck her sword through him from behind before she'd taken his head off was neither here nor there: the man was just as dead, her mother was still alive, and Father Krayk wouldn't care either way. Battle was battle: if you were foolish enough to leave your back open, someone would stick something sharp into it.

She'd come through the fight uninjured, was cheered as a hero, and then she'd gone and got her Blooded tattoo and the damned thing had *hurt*. She'd never admit it though, unlike the local Naridan kids who'd demanded to have the same thing and had ended up crying about it. Now she was sitting watching her mother and Daimon talk with Osred the steward about how best to manage the town, and trying not to rub at her forehead all the time.

'It's not really an issue with the willingness of the thralls, lord,' Osred was saying. 'So far they have behaved as Lady Saana said they would.'

'Stop calling this man that, please,' Zhanna's mother sighed. 'She is a chief, not a lady.'

'Your husband is a lord, so you are a lady,' Daimon said, and Zhanna dug her nails into her palm. Daimon was still quite young, much younger than Zhanna's mother, and really rather pretty. He was nice, and friendly (at least when he forgot to be all Naridan and stiff), and when she'd technically been his hostage against her clan's good behaviour he'd taught her the basics of how to use a Naridan longblade in exchange for her teaching him some of her language. He'd also given her Thorn, who was currently perched on her shoulder.

And then her mother had gone and *married* him.

She'd said it was all to do with protecting them against the other Naridans, *of course*, but the High Marshal had come and gone now, and hadn't ordered any of the Brown Eagle clan to be killed, so Zhanna couldn't see why they had to keep on with it. It wasn't that Zhanna wanted to marry Daimon as such, but . . . well, he was too young and pretty a husband for her own mother, and that was an end to it.

'Your wife was made chief by her clan's witches, because they thought she would be a good chief,' Zhanna's mother was saying, with a little heat in her voice. 'She has earned that title, and will keep it. She is your wife, but she is not a Naridan lady.'

Daimon stuck out his jaw, and for a moment Zhanna thought he was going to argue with her – she could have told him that wouldn't end well – but then he sighed and nodded. 'Chief Saana to our peoples, then. But you may have to be Lady Saana to other thanes.'

'That is fine,' Zhanna's mother sniffed. 'They do not count.' She looked at Osred. 'Please, carry on.'

'The issue is not with the thralls' willingness,' Osred began again, looking relieved that the issue was resolved. 'They work as directed, and have shown no sign of rebelling. The issue is that we sorely lack people who can actually direct them.'

They were talking about those of Rikkut Fireheart's raiders who yielded in battle. Zhanna didn't know what the Naridans would have done with them, but Tjakorshi custom was that they would serve their captors for a year and a day without complaint, so long as they were treated fairly. Since they mainly yielded to Brown Eagles, this had won out, and now Black Keep had a workforce of healthy adult warriors to help repair its walls and tend its fields.

'This man can help with that,' Zhanna's mother said. She turned to look at her daughter. 'And so can Zhanna.'

Zhanna folded her arms. 'I'm not standing around all day telling a bunch of thralls what to do,' she told her mother in Tjakorshi, and Thorn clucked in what she chose to take as agreement. Across the room, two other young dragons looked up from where they were dozing near the fire pit: Daimon's dragon Rattler; and Talon, who'd belonged to the stable master Tavi before he'd been killed fighting the attackers.

'Zhanna, someone needs to,' her mother replied, switching into the same language and eyeing Thorn dubiously. 'I'm busy. We've put Nalon to work trying to teach everyone the basics of each other's tongues and he didn't much like that, so he won't appreciate us now telling him we want him to do something else—'

'And what about me?' Zhanna demanded. 'What about whether I'm going to appreciate what you want me to do?'

'Well, what do *you* want to do?' her mother snapped. 'We need the fields worked so the crops grow and we all eat when winter comes around again. Do you want to eat?'

Zhanna looked over at Daimon and Osred, who clearly had no idea what was being said, and switched into Naridan. It was a clumsy, clunky language, and she didn't speak it that well, but she thought she knew where she could get support, and it wasn't from her mother.

'This warrior was to Tatiosh talking,' she began. 'He said his mother's clan not down from mountains come.'

Zhanna's mother looked sideways at Daimon. 'Who is Tatiosh?'

'The son of Bilha and Amonhuhe of the Mountains,' Daimon replied, scratching his jaw. 'Amonhuhe is of the Smoking Valley people. And Zhanna is correct: they have always come to trade at the Festival of Life, but they did not this year, else you would have already met them.'

'Tatiosh says his mother wants go to mountains,' Zhanna continued, keeping a wary eye on her own mother. 'This warrior could take her crew and go—'

'No!' Zhanna's mother snapped, dropping back into Tjakorshi again. 'Absolutely not!'

'Are you telling me I can't go as my mother, or as my chief?' Zhanna demanded, and her mother's mouth snapped shut, although her eyes flashed dangerously. Zhanna was Blooded now, which meant she was an adult and wasn't necessarily expected to do anything her mother said . . . Although, of course, it was still considered polite to listen to your parents and take their opinions into account. On the other hand, a chief made decisions for the clan, but wasn't like a Naridan lord. Daimon could tell any of his people to do something and they would be expected to do it: Zhanna's mother would never try the same.

If Zhanna decided she was going to the mountains, there wasn't *really* anything her mother could do to stop her, short of threatening to kick her out of the clan for abandoning them.

'The Smoking Valley people are our friends,' Daimon said cautiously, looking between Zhanna and her mother. He could hardly have misinterpreted Zhanna's mother's reaction, even if Zhanna hadn't taught him (among other things) the Tjakorshi for 'yes' and 'no'. 'Saana, your husband had already been thinking about whether we should send a messenger to make sure no disaster has befallen them.'

Zhanna pointed at him and looked at her mother triumphantly. 'See?'

'To the mountains?' Zhanna's mother demanded of Daimon.

'She doesn't know how to live in mountains!'

'Amonhuhe does,' Daimon replied. 'If she wishes to go, she can guide anyone we send with her. Also,' he pointed out, 'Tjakorshi are better dressed for the mountains than Naridans.'

Zhanna's mother couldn't argue with that. Their clan's clothing was wool beneath thick furs taken from the sea bears that hauled out on the beaches of Tjakorsha's islands, and more than enough to deal with the winter in a land where Long Night apparently never happened.

'And who would we send?' Zhanna's mother demanded.

'This warrior's crew!' Zhanna replied immediately. 'They want to come,' she added, when her mother glared at her. Of course, the Brown Eagles were all adults now, like her. She wasn't sure about the Naridans, but Tatiosh would certainly be going with his mother.

'If your servant might suggest,' Osred put in. 'To send a strong youth away would make life harder for the families left behind.'

Zhanna glowered at the steward. Her mother nodded approvingly.

'Perhaps any family willing for their child to go should be assigned the sole services of one of the thralls, to work on their land instead?' Osred continued, and Zhanna grinned. 'In that manner, the families could be of service to the town without inconveniencing themselves.'

'We would need to send at least a couple of Black Keep adults,' Daimon said. 'Someone who could speak on our behalf.' He pursed his lips. 'Menaken, perhaps, of our guards.'

'You truly think this is a good idea?' Zhanna's mother said.

'Yes, your husband does,' Daimon replied, his dark eyes serious. 'Amonhuhe's folk are not truly Naridans, but we have traded with them since before your husband's grandfather's day. What could stop them from coming at all? We have formed a new alliance with your clan: we should not forget our old one. Besides,' he added, 'a joint expedition into the mountains would be another good example to our peoples of how we can work together.'

'Your wife thinks you forget how many of your people complained about their children receiving the Blooded mark,' Zhanna's mother muttered, but she had the manner of someone who knew they'd lost an argument.

'They were complaining about Tjakorshi then,' Daimon said. 'Complaining about a decision made by their lord is something very different. We will see who wishes to go, and choose the party based on that, but if there is to be a mix of people going then Zhanna will have to go also, so they can speak with each other.'

Zhanna grinned again. She was going to the mountains! She'd grown up in the shadow of one, of course – Kainkoruuk, one of Tjakorsha's five Great Peaks – but she'd never climbed it. These Naridan mountains were different; there were so many of them, for one thing! She'd just been able to see them from the room at the top of the Black Keep itself, and there was something about their distant, craggy and snow-capped shapes that called to her in a way the wide, green land in which Black Keep town sat did not.

Besides, she liked Tatiosh. He was a Naridan roughly her age who'd been adopted by his two mothers when he was a baby, and although he didn't share any blood with Amonhuhe he obviously respected her. He was adamant that if she went back to the mountains then he was going with her, but Zhanna would feel better if she was with him, and she thought he'd probably feel the same.

Zhanna's mother sighed. 'If this friendship with these mountain people is a matter of honour for you, then your wife will not try to stop it. Very well. We will send a group.' She clenched her jaw. 'And Zhanna may go, if she wishes.'

'Thank you, Mama,' Zhanna said in Tjakorshi, as genuinely as she could. 'I won't let you down.'

JEYA

JEYA WAS DUBIOUS about the idea of going back to Galem's house in the morning after the attack, since the killers might still be lurking around, but Galem had insisted.

'There was a reason they came at night, Jeya. These things don't get done in the day.'

Jeya, who had seen plenty of unpleasant things happen in broad daylight, had held hér tongue. Galem was a wreck; hìs eyes were still red from sobbing, and hè hadn't slept well. Jeya hadn't either, to be fair, given that shé'd been sitting up against a wall with Galem's head in hér lap, but shé knew shé was far more used to disrupted sleep than Galem was. Hè'd had hìs own bed in hìs own room, for the Hundred's sake! Which was no more than you'd expect for the Splinter Prince, exiled heir to the kingdom of Narida, even if hè and hìs family had been living as anonymously as they could manage. Jeya was lucky if shé managed to find a bit of dry floor where no one would step on hér.

'Fine,' shé'd said, 'we'll go back. But we don't go rushing in. We should be able to get an idea of what happened without getting too close.'

And they had. They trekked back up to the Second Level, dodging the more distrustful looks from people who clearly thought they were too scruffy to be there, but they were not the only ones who looked out of place. A whole cross-section of East Harbour had converged upon the street where Galem's house stood, and as Jeya and Galem got closer the pall of smoke rising into Grand Mahewa's morning sky made it obvious why.

'I'm sorry,' Jeya muttered uselessly, once they were close enough for it to be unmistakable that it was Galem's house at the heart of the blaze. It would normally be just visible from the road – since what was the purpose of an impressive house if those passing by couldn't get at least a glimpse of your wealth? – but today the raging flames and crackle of burning wood made it easy to pick out, even through the throng of people who had gathered in ghoulish fascination.

'Please don't go running in there,' Jeya murmured to Galem. The look hè shot hér wasn't tear-stained but dry-eyed and furious, although shé was sure that hìs anger wasn't actually directed at hér.

'I am not a fool,' hè replied in a low voice. 'But why is no one *helping*?'

Jeya shrugged uneasily. 'What are they going to do? Have yòu ever been near a fire like that? Yòu wouldn't even be able to get close enough to throw water on it. And besides,' shé added uncomfortably, 'it's a long way from other buildings. No one else's house is going to catch, not before the rain comes. If that was in the markets, everyone would be forming a bucket chain so their own place didn't go up next.'

Galem stared at the burning shell of hìs home, fast on its way to becoming a ruin. Hìs nostrils flared as hè took a deep breath. 'I need to find out if my family is still alive.'

'All right.' Jeya eyed the people in front of them, looking for a likely candidate. There was a wide selection, ranging from labourers who'd paused to gawp, to a couple of people Jeya thought were likely to be neighbours, judging by the richness of their clothing and the sheer fanciness of the cloths they held over their faces against the smoke. Shé nudged Galem and nodded to the possible neighbours. 'Do yòu know them?'

'Ì've seen them before,' Galem said quietly, turning hìs head a little farther away from them, although their concentration was still fully on the blaze. 'Ì can't let them see mè now, even dressed like this. They might have been involved.'

'Fine, not them.' Jeya sized the crowd up again, then sidled forwards to tap someone on the arm. Shé thought they might be a servant from a nearby house: their clothing was of decent quality, but old and largely plain, and had the look of something that might have been worn before by someone of a slightly different size and shape.

'Hey,' Jeya said, when they turned to look at hér. 'Anyone get out?'

The possible-servant shook their head, sending their chin-length locks swaying. 'Not that I heard.'

'It's strange,' someone else put in, so tall and light-skinned that one of their parents must have been a salt-pale southerner. 'They had guards. You couldn't stop to look at this place without someone coming out and waving a spear at you to tell you to move on. How come it burns down without anyone raising the alarm?'

'Unless it was the guards what did it,' someone else put in. 'Take the valuables, do a runner, set a fire. I've known it happen before.'

'Oh yeah?' the possible-servant said, their tone one more of curiosity than challenge. 'Where?'

'My cousin Sarama told me about a place on the south shore—'

'Your cousin Sarama's a liar, Ngana—'

Jeya backed away again as the bubble of conversation swelled, and what had been a group of separate people all watching someone else's house burn down began to morph into a discussion about exactly how untrustworthy people who guarded others for money might or might not be, and notable examples of them allegedly betraying their employers. Shé shook hér head at Galem.

'If yòur family made it out, they haven't made themselves obvious.' Shé sighed. 'Í'm sorry.'

Galem's breathing was quick, but hìs face was a mask: not exactly an emotionless mask, but hè wasn't breaking down into sobs like hè had last night. Naridans were often mocked – usually behind their backs – for their stiffness and reserve, but Jeya had to admit that Galem was drawing less attention to hìmself than hè would have been if hè'd started crying openly.

'Do yòu want to leave?' shé suggested, looking back over hér shoulder at the house. Shé could not see much further purpose to them being here, in any case: Galem's family did not seem likely to appear and clasp hìm into their arms, and all shé and hè were doing now was risking hìm being recognised by someone.

'Yes,' Galem replied after a moment, hìs voice thick with grief. 'Yes, that is a good idea.' Hè dragged hìs eyes away from the fire and put hìs arm around Jeya's shoulders. Shé still felt a slight thrill at hìs touch, even under the circumstances, but locked that feeling away as they walked off together. Right now, hè just needed hér support.

THEY RETURNED TO the Old Palace, the crumbling, plant-choked ruin of Grand Mahewa's former monarchs from before the Hierarchs had risen to power, where they had spent the previous night. Jeya didn't feel as comfortable there during the day. The spirits that were supposed to haunt its grounds wouldn't be abroad, but they were more likely to run into ordinary trouble, since shé was far from the only one in East Harbour to know where the holes in the old wall and the wild hedge were. Nonetheless, they needed a place to plan their next move.

'If yòur family . . . aren't around,' shé said, as they sat next to one of the decorative pools, now covered in water lilies, 'what do we do next? How can we make yòu safe?'

'Ì would have to speak to one of the Hierarchs,' Galem said. Hè was sitting cross-legged on the cracked tiles in the simple maijhi and karung shé'd stolen for hìm, hìs hands in hìs lap, and hìs long, dark hair loose down to the middle of hìs back. 'They would know mè.'

'Speak to the Hierarchs?!' Jeya said, choking back a laugh. 'Just . . . just walk up to them? Strike up a conversation?' Hér incredulity increased as shé looked at hìm. 'Wait, could yòu do that?'

'No,' Galem replied, scratching at the palm of one hand with the nail of the other. 'My family did not associate with them unless it was an official occasion, when we would already be in the ceremonial robes by the time we saw them. However, several have seen mè unmasked, and they would all know of our identities. If Ì could speak to one of them, Ì am sure Ì could convince them of who Ì am.'

'And that's the problem,' Jeya pointed out. 'Í can't speak to a Hierarch. Í've never even got close enough to one that Í'd recognise them in a crowd, let alone talk to one, and if Í can't, then yòu can't. Unless yòu want to try talking yòur way into the New Palace past their guards,' she added, hoping hè wasn't going to say yes.

Galem shook hìs head. 'It would be too risky. Ì still do not know how our identities were discovered. Ì cannot believe it was one of the Hierarchs themselves, because they rely too much on the status the Splinter King confers. Perhaps there are servants who could have pieced things together? Regardless, if Ì was not believed immediately, Ì would be exposed.'

'About that,' Jeya said, casting a quick look around to make sure no one was in sight. 'Yòu can hide on the street with mé until we find a way for yòu to talk to a Hierarch, and no one will look twice at yòu, but yòu'll need to blend in better.' Shé looked again at hìs face. Hìs Naridan heritage was clear, but no more so than in any number of other families who had been in Kiburu ce Alaba for generations. It wasn't that which was the problem. 'Yòu'll need to talk differently, for one thing.'

Galem frowned. 'Ì will?'

'Jakahama's paddle, yòu will,' Jeya said with a grin. 'Yòu just sound so *rich*! And that's fine,' shé added, 'and, uh, Í like it, by the way. But if yòu go around talking like yòu do at the moment, yòu're going to stick out like a shark in a shrimp net.'

Galem looked at hér levelly for a moment.

'Í'm not saying it's *bad*!' Jeya clarified. 'It's just . . . not useful. It would be like mé trying to fit in with the Hierarchs.'

'How should Ì talk, then?' Galem asked.

'Well, maybe don't talk much for starters, when we're around other people,' Jeya suggested. 'Not until yòu've listened to them for a bit. But rich people stretch everything out, it's all . . . ' She waggled her fingers. 'All clear and precise, like a bell.'

'Ì sound like a bell?' Galem asked, raising hìs eyebrows.

'Í like bells!' Jeya protested. 'But you really *notice* them, is what Í'm saying.'

'If Ì sound like a bell,' Galem said, with the faintest hint of a smile at the corner of hìs lips, 'then yóu sound like the ocean.'

Jeya's thoughts immediately went to the harbour. 'With a lot of shit in it?'

'Noisy, and chaotic,' Galem said. 'But beautiful.'

It became very hard to breathe.

'Í'll try,' Galem said carefully. 'Í've listened to yóu talking enough to have a go.'

'Í had another idea,' Jeya said, trying to keep hér voice level and, shé thought, failing miserably. 'Although Í'm not sure if yòu'll like this one.'

Galem's eyebrows quirked quizzically. 'Go on.'

'Whoever went after yòur family must have known who they were looking for,' Jeya said seriously, and cursed hérself as the momentary lightness dropped from hìs face. It was necessary, though. 'Yòu're Naridan, so yòur gender's always been public. Í mean, yòu gendered yòurself to mé when . . . when we first met.'

'When yóu were trying to steal from mè,' Galem put in, and Jeya stopped talking in embarrassment. Hè grimaced, and reached out to gently touch hér hand with hìs. 'Ì am sorry, Ì shouldn't tease. It was not yóur fault yóu were hungry.'

'Well,' Jeya continued, 'Ì mean, yòur *guard* gendered yòu to mé, in front of everyone. That's *so* Naridan. Anyone who's looking for yòu will know they're looking for a high masculine youth with Naridan features, of about yòur age. We can't do anything about yòur age, or about yòur face,' *which would be a crime in any case*, 'but maybe we could, Ì mean, yòu could . . . '

'Adopt a different gender?' Galem finished.

'Well, at least use the neutral formal,' Jeya said awkwardly. Everyone knew that Naridans, at least traditional Naridans like Galem's family, were really touchy about gender. They assigned it for their children at birth, broadcast it openly, and virtually no one ever changed it; unlike Alabans, who let their children work it out for themselves. Jeya had settled almost exclusively on low feminine, but there were some days when shé felt different, and some people's gender moved around all throughout their lives.

Galem hadn't replied.

'Or,' Jeya added, hoping that hè wasn't about to get angry or upset, 'perhaps yòu could grow a beard? Ì know Naridans don't generally do that either, so that could help.'

Galem began to laugh.

It started slowly as a breathy snicker, and then began to escalate. Jeya was about to ask what was so funny when hìs laughter took on a different tone, and shé realised with alarm, as hè buried hìs face in hìs hands, that there were sobs in there too.

'What's wrong?' shé asked, concerned. 'What did Ì say?' Shé had been expecting uncomfortable uncertainty, perhaps an awkward refusal, perhaps even an awkward agreement, although that had been an outside chance. Not sobs, or laughter, and especially not a combination thereof. There had to be something else going on here.

'It is . . . ' Galem said between hìs fingers. 'It is nothing yóu said. Not really.' Hè took what sounded like it was going to be a deep breath, but cut off with a grunt of discomfort before hè'd inhaled very far, and dropped hìs hands from hìs face. There were tears on hìs cheeks, but that wasn't anything new. What was new was the expression of morbid humour.

'Do yóu remember what Ì said last night? About it all being lies?'

Jeya nodded. 'Yes.' Not that shé'd understood what hè'd meant, and shé hadn't raised the subject since.

'It is probably easier if Ì just . . . ' Galem muttered, sat up straight, and reached hìs hands up inside hìs maijhi, the overshirt Jeya had stolen for hìm. Jeya felt hér cheeks heat, even though Galem didn't strip the garment off and shé saw nothing more than the skin of hìs lower belly. They'd done a fair bit of kissing since their clandestine romance had started, but the one and only time shé'd ventured to place hér hands inside his maijhi, hè'd withdrawn sharply.

Galem's hands were working on something on hìs chest. Hè finally seemed to achieve hìs goal, and began pulling something out of the bottom of hìs maijhi.

It was a long strand of cotton wrap. Jeya frowned at it, then saw the subtle difference in the shape of Galem's upper body now the binding had been loosened and removed.

'Not even the Hierarchs could know,' Galem said, hìs tone strangely neutral, almost thoughtful. Hè was looking at the cloth in hìs hand rather than at hér. 'The Naridan blood line runs from masculine heir to masculine heir, so my family needed to provide valid heirs for us to retain our status. My older sìbling would have satisfied that, but my parents decided one masculine child was not enough.' Hè shrugged. 'And they were right. The Naridans killed hìm, years ago. So Ì've lived my life pretending to be the Splinter Prince, even when Ì was just being Galem. If the Hierarchs had ever known how Ì was born, my family could have lost everything.'

Jeya was speechless. Shé'd always known that traditional Naridan families were strange, but this was beyond strange. To make a child pretend to be something hè was not, for hìs entire life?

'Ì should not have worn this for as long as Ì have,' Galem muttered, gesturing with the binding cloth. 'Ì usually take it off at night, but . . . ' Hè straightened, and winced as hè took a proper deep breath. Jeya realised it was the first real one shé'd ever heard hìm take.

'Last night was busy,' shé muttered. 'So, um . . . are yòu *actually* "hè", or . . . ?'

'Ì have only ever been "hè",' Galem said. 'Even from my parents and my siblings. Ì have never had the chance to try anything else, but . . . ' Hè hesitated. 'Ì think . . . Ï think, Ï would like to try being "thëy".'

Jeya nodded. '"Thëy" it is.' Traditional Naridans never used neutral pronouns for themselves, not even the neutral formal that most folk used until they knew people well. That, and a slightly different body shape that no one would associate with a masculine Naridan, might actually be enough of a disguise so long as Galem could work on not sounding so damned rich. 'Yöu'll need a new name, though.'

'Ï will think about it,' Galem said, nodding. 'But no, Ï don't think Ï could grow a beard, even if Ï wanted to.' Thëy rubbed thëir naked cheek. 'It is . . . *It's* just lucky Naridans don't tend to.'

Jeya's stomach complained at hér, loudly. 'Well, yöu've got from here until the market to come up with a new name. We can work on how to get yöu to the Hierarchs later. For now, Í need breakfast.'

DAIMON

DAIMON FELT LIKE he had been sleepwalking through everything since he'd killed his father. Even in the battle for Black Keep, he had fought and reacted and spoken as he would normally, but it had been like he was observing everything from somewhere inside his own body. Since then he simply kept going, because that was what he had to do, that was the duty of a sar, but by Nari he had just wanted to lie down and sleep. Yet sleep was hard to find, when the darkness behind his own eyelids morphed into gouts of red as his blade bit into his father's side.

The demands of his duty had not stopped. There were traitors to deal with. Yoon, Shefal, and Kelaharel had been exiled, but Nadar was another matter. He took the life of another Naridan, his own captain, and so his own life was forfeit. Darel had been prepared to do it, as thane, but Daimon had offered to take the responsibility instead. He was surer with a blade than his law-brother, and he felt guilt over Malakel's death, since the man had only been following Daimon's orders in the first place. Daimon had taken Nadar's head off with one blow, and had masked the sudden panic he felt as blood spurted forth.

That night, as he had lain in his bed wracked with sobs, Daimon Blackcreek had never felt more like a failure. A sar was supposed to be hardy. A thane was supposed to be strong. What good was he if he could not enforce the law? Was this the weakness of his peasant blood coming through?

His marriage to Saana remained technically unconsummated. He was unsure if she had as little interest in physical intimacy at present as he did, or if she was just being considerate, but either way he was grateful for the lack of pressure on that front. He had not invited her to stay in his quarters – traditionally a lord would command his wife to attend him, but that was a laughable notion when it came to Saana Sattistutar – and she had not offered.

Today, at least, Daimon's responsibilities did not weigh too heavily on him. The rebuilding of Black Keep was not just a matter of buildings and walls, for Fireheart's raiders had not inflicted a substantial amount of damage in that respect: it was also reorganising the town, and the Blackcreek household.

'Abbatane,' Daimon said to the girl in front of him. 'It is this lord's wish for you to become stable master.'

Abbatane looked up, her eyes wide with disbelief. 'Lord?'

'The decision is yours,' Daimon said gently. 'But this is our wish.' In fact, his usual instinct would have been to go with Faaz, the stable boy. When he voiced this, Saana had challenged him on whether this was just because Faaz was male, or whether Daimon honestly knew which of them was better with the longbrow and frillneck dragons that were their charges. It turned out that Saana had some quite strong views on Abbatane succeeding Tavi, apparently based on a conversation she had with the stable master himself on the night of the Festival of Life, before Tavi's untimely death defending Black Keep. Daimon had known nothing about this, but he trusted his wife, and trusted Tavi to know about dragons.

'Lord, your servant accepts most gratefully!' Abbatane said, bowing low, and that was the matter decided. Faaz would be disappointed, of course, but hopefully he would throw himself into his work. He lost his father Yaro to Fireheart's raiders, just as Abbatane lost her father Rotel, one of the Black Keep guards.

There were a lot of recently dead fathers, just at the moment.

There was one more person Daimon needed to talk to, and it had the potential to be a very awkward conversation. Saana was dealing with recruiting new guards for the castle, and they'd come to an agreement about it: Sagel, as the senior remaining man, would be the captain, with Ita and (once he returned from the mountains) Menaken. Saana was talking to a couple of her experienced warriors, the Scarred who were a chief's elite, and would get others from those of Zhanna's 'crew' that hadn't gone with her. That was keeping her busy, while Daimon went in search of Evram.

He found the man tending to his small plot of land, behind the house – barely more than a hut – in which he lived. Usually the thane of Black Keep would have summoned one of his lowborn to him, but Daimon was trying to behave a little more like a Tjakorshi chief, who would only issue such a command in the most extreme of circumstances. It felt demeaning, but how could Daimon expect his people to be happy about being treated in one manner, when their new neighbours would not be? A commitment to equality had been one of the things Saana and he had agreed to in their marriage vows.

'Evram,' Daimon said softly. The man looked up, and nearly dropped his hoe in shock.

'Lord Daimon!' He bowed, in what looked like equal parts respect and panic. Evram had, after all, been the man who fled north to alert Thane Odem at Darkspur about the Brown Eagle clan's arrival, despite Daimon's warnings of what might befall them all if word got out too soon.

'How can your man be of service, lord?' Evram asked, straightening from his bow but still keeping his eyes lowered. As was right and proper, Daimon reminded himself. He was getting too used to the Tjakorshi's habit of just staring into the face of whoever they were talking to.

'You are a brave man, Evram,' Daimon said, without preamble. Evram's eyes widened in surprise.

'Lord? Your man doesn't understand.'

'On the first night the Tjakorshi arrived, you identified Ristjaan the Cleaver as the man who killed your brother,' Daimon told him. 'You would have fought him.'

'B-but you fought him, lord,' Evram stammered.

'This lord did,' Daimon admitted. He had challenged, and then killed, Saana's best friend on Evram's behalf. That was another reason why Daimon had come here, alone. Ristjaan's death was a dark, unexplored gulf that did not exactly lay between his wife and him, but certainly lurked nearby. He felt it best not to draw attention to it unless necessary. 'But you would have done. You had already drawn your knife. That speaks of great courage.'

'You honour this servant, lord,' Evram said quietly.

'It also took great courage to travel to Darkspur alone,' Daimon said. He noticed how Evram stiffened, perhaps fearful of what would come next. Had the man been waiting for his punishment all this time? Had he seen the fates of the traitors and had been dreading the moment when he would be exiled, or beheaded?

'Your man begs your forgiveness, lord,' Evram said desperately. 'He knows he shouldn't have gone, but Shefal's words seemed so reasonable!'

'Evram,' Daimon said gently. 'No harm was done. Had you not gone north, Thane Darkspur would not have sent word to the Southern Marshal. Had the Southern Marshal not come when he did, Black Keep would have been overrun by Fireheart's raiders, and we would likely all have died.' The fact that Odem Darkspur had clearly wanted the Southern Marshal to declare the Blackcreek family traitors, execute them and probably award their lands to Darkspur was another matter entirely, and not one that Daimon felt like getting into right now.

'What you have demonstrated, Evram,' he continued, 'is that you have a strong sense of what is right. You will do what you believe should be done, regardless of the cost to yourself. That is admirable.'

It was more than admirable. It was something that Daimon himself felt he was clinging on to by his fingernails.

'You are too kind, lord,' Evram muttered. He clearly had no idea where this was going.

'This lord has spoken to people of the town,' Daimon told him. 'The town needs a new reeve. Kelaharel saw our people living in harmony, and still freed this lord's father with the hope of causing harm. In doing so, he assisted in taking the life of one of this lord's guards. You carried word north on the day the Tjakorshi landed, fearing what might come, and ended up saving the town. The town considers, and this lord agrees, that you should be the new reeve.'

Now Evram did look up at him, in utter astonishment. 'Lord, this servant is honoured, but he wouldn't know where to begin! And what of the Tjakorshi? Won't they hold the man Ristjaan's death against this servant?'

Daimon shook his head. 'The Tjakorshi know a blood debt. Those who remember you will have seen you willing to fight, and they'll respect that. Besides, Ristjaan accepted this lord's challenge as a warrior. He accepted the consequences, and so did his fellows.'

And then he died for it, another victim of Daimon's blade. Daimon had managed to rationalise that death, at first. It was only afterwards, as the pressure began to mount on him, that he felt the shell of who he was supposed to be begin to crack, and the deaths had begun to bleed into one in his head.

A sar was not meant to enjoy combat, or death, but he was certainly not supposed to be shaken by it.

'That's good to know,' Evram said, in response to Daimon's last words. 'But lord, this man doesn't have their speech. If he's to be reeve, is he to be reeve only for Naridans?'

'Their man Nalon the smith will help,' Daimon told him. Saana had promised him that Nalon would, although how she persuaded him was anyone's guess. As a Naridan who had lived with the Brown Eagle clan for many years, Nalon was irritatingly indispensable, and also just plain irritating. 'Will you take on this role for your town, Evram?'

Evram looked down at his hoe, as though considering. It wouldn't have been much of a choice, for most people. Evram was poor, with only a small amount of land to his name. The reeve earned a salary paid by the thane, and could live considerably more comfortably. Still, Daimon was glad to see the man thinking it over, rather than jumping at the opportunity that would afford him more money.

'Yes, lord, your man will,' Evram said after a few more moments, looking up with a smile. 'It would be a great honour.'

'Then let this lord give you some advice on where he'd like you to begin,' Daimon said, moving a step closer and beckoning Evram to him. The man approached with trepidation, clearly wondering what he'd got himself into. It was not an unjust concern.

'This lord does not think it is the Tjakorshi who will require your immediate attention, in any case. What do you know of witches?' Daimon asked quietly, once he judged Evram was close enough. He did not wish to be overheard, even though there was no one else near them.

'Witches, lord?' Evram said, alarmed. 'Precious little, and your man's glad of it.'

'While you were away, a Tjakorshi woman died in great pain,' Daimon told him. 'Aftak the priest found a stone buried on the south side of her house. He said it was a curse stone, such as a witch might use. The texts in the Black Keep library that warn thanes of what to watch for agreed. This lord set Kelaharel to search out the witch quietly, so that no one would suspect, but the reeve did not seem eager to do so, and he made no progress. Looking back, this lord wonders if this might not have been because Kelaharel never wished to find the witch at all: that he would rather a servant of the Unmaker was loose in our town and cursing our new neighbours.'

Evram's eyes had gone wide again. 'A witch, lord? In the town, and cursing people?'

'We believe so,' Daimon confirmed.

Evram's brows lowered, and his face took on the same determined expression that Daimon remembered from that fateful night when he got up off his bench and advanced towards Ristjaan the Cleaver, dagger in his hand.

'Your man won't stand for that, lord. The Divine One didn't drive the Unmaker out of this land for us to suffer witches.' He took a deep breath, and nodded. 'Your reeve will speak to Aftak. And he'll find this witch for you.'

TILA

Tila watched them file into the council chamber, one after another. Resentfully. Ungratefully. Scowling and shuffling, because they were men of power and authority, and like most such men, their opinion of their own worth ran rather higher than any objective analysis.

'You do not have the right to convene the God-King's Inner Council,' muttered Kaled Greenbrook, Narida's Lord Admiral.

'And yet you are here,' Tila replied softly, and Kaled's scowl deepened, because he knew the truth of her words. Each of these men were as much the slaves to their power as their power served them. It was true that the Princess of Narida theoretically had no authority to call an Inner Council meeting on behalf of her brother the Divine God-King, but each member feared that if they did not come, their colleagues would meet without them and make decisions in their absence. And so they came, unwillingly and yet voluntarily, to try to ensure the world did not change beneath their feet.

Tila did not sit in her brother's seat, of course. That would have pushed things too far. She sat in her usual position on its right instead, as the rest of them arrayed themselves around the oval table.

Kaled Greenbrook, the Lord Admiral. An impressive title for

a man in his early forties who was not even the thane of his own lands, but the power the title conferred was considerably less than it might appear. The crown had few ships under its own control, and those that could be called upon by the coastal thanes would be ultimately commanded by the High Marshals. Kaled's voice on the council was a small one, and his appointment had little to do with any understanding of seacraft.

Adan Greenbrook was the Lord of the Treasury, and that certainly *was* a position of power. Adan was a few years younger than his cousin, and they shared a slightly bulbous tip to their noses and a thinning of their hair at the temples, but otherwise the casual observer might not conclude that they were related. Adan was the eldest son of a thane whose health was not good and whose mind wandered. Needless to say, he could count on Kaled's full support, since Kaled knew better than to antagonise the man who would become his liege-lord before many more years were out.

Meshul Whittingmoor was the Law Lord. Tila wasn't sure exactly how old he was, but his hair was almost entirely silver and he walked with the aid of a cane. His mind was still as sharp as a pin, however, and he could work his way through even complex and apparently contradictory interpretations of Narida's laws with little or no recourse to the texts. Tila loathed him, although that was more for his office than his person. Whittingmoor was of the opinion that the law was sacrosanct and immutable, and would strenuously resist any attempts to change or modernise it in ways he saw unfit, which generally concerned the granting of more power to Naridan women.

Sebiah Wousewold was the Lord of Scribes, a man who presented himself in even recent memories as little more than a grey outline, despite being of larger than average size and possessed of a face that was at least passingly comely. He interpreted the rulings and decisions of the council into words, and controlled exactly what was proclaimed to the kingdom at large through the network of crown messengers. That was responsibility enough, for while a God-King would never draft such a document himself, many a Lord of Scribes through Narida's history had found himself briefly but quite thoroughly unpopular as a result of his final wording not being to his monarch's liking. Wousewold had held on to the position for longer than many due to his scrupulous exactness, and also thanks to turning his network of scribes and proclaimers into informers. News came to Lord Wousewold more quickly than it did to most of his colleagues, and Tila had no illusions that he shared everything he learned. Still, he shared enough that even Natan had realised the man was undeniably useful.

Then there were Master Temach, the elected representative of the Royal Universities, and Omrel of Godspire, the high priest. Omrel was an earnest young man who performed for the priesthood a role equivalent to that which Lord Wousewold did for the kingdom as a whole, although how he managed to garner much substance from the words and deeds of Natan Narida was something Tila had never been certain. Temach was primarily an advisor, present to update the Council on advances and discoveries that had come from Narida's institutes of learning, many of which received some form of funding from the Crown.

Finally, there was the Eastern Marshal, a Hand of Heaven, Lord Einan Coldbeck. He was approaching his sixtieth year, and was as hard and sharp as the longblade on his hip. He was the overall military commander of Narida, superior even to the Northern, Western and Southern High Marshals. Only the God-King could overrule him in matters of war, but it was his duty to ensure the God-King never needed to. Exactly what came under the Eastern Marshal's authority was something that had varied over the centuries, according to the ambitions and strength of will of all involved. Some had been glorified sword-bearers, others God-King in all but name. Coldbeck had been appointed young, and had trodden a middle road for as much of Tila's life as she could remember. She did not like him much, but she respected him.

'And so the Divine Princess deigns to grace us with her presence once more,' Lord Whittingmoor drawled, settling into his seat with a click of his cane on the stone floor and an audible, accompanying crack from his right knee. 'Back from whatever leisure has attracted her interest for the past months.'

'Moderate your tongue, Whittingmoor,' Adan Greenbrook said, a touch too blandly. 'We all know how Princess Tila's dark moods swallow her mind. It is no wonder she cannot join this council on a more regular basis.'

Tila eyed them both from behind her veil, and cursed herself again for ever using that as an excuse for her disappearances. She still could not think of a better option, but it left the council free to portray her as weak-willed and easily overwhelmed.

No matter. She had cut crosswise across tradition and forged her authority in the Sun Palace through fear, intellect, and force of will, not any respect that these men held for the sister of their monarch. A Divine Princess could have been the equal of them all in terms of knowledge and experience, and the Inner Council would still not be under any obligation to pay her the slightest bit of attention. Nari's teeth, but she hated this country sometimes.

'This princess thanks you all for your enquiries into her well-being while she was indisposed,' she said, and at least Adan Greenbrook had the decency to look very slightly ashamed. Tila knew well that the Inner Council would have revelled in her absence rather than questioned it, let alone sent their good wishes. 'She also thanks you for the work you have done while this princess's brother has been ill.'

'It is, of course, this council's duty to see to the rule of the realm when the God-King is unable to do so,' Lord Wousewold said, and everyone nodded. The fact that Natan rarely had the patience for council meetings even when he was in good health was something that no one present was going to comment on openly, but everyone knew to be true.

'Lord Wousewold,' Tila said, directing her attention to him. 'You hear of many things. Do we yet have any corroboration that the prophecies have come true? That this princess's divine ancestor has been reborn?'

The table went very still, and very quiet. It was one thing, Tila was sure, to speak of such things in hushed tones behind closed doors, and quite another to be asked directly about it by the person whom such an event would see replaced.

Lord Wousewold poured himself a goblet of wine from the flagon on the table, and took a sip before he answered. Tila might have fumed at his delay, but instead took the opportunity to watch the faces of the others.

Coldbeck was as impassive as a sar's war-mask. Master Temach was looking determinedly at the table, while Omrel of Godspire's eyes were fixed on Wousewold with almost unseemly eagerness. Whittingmoor was fiddling with the head of his cane, which he only did when on edge, and Adan Greenbrook's stare was so intense that Tila was almost surprised Wousewold's cheek did not dent under its force, but Kaled was looking at his cousin instead. Interesting.

'This lord has not heard anything definite,' Lord Wousewold said, setting his goblet back down. It was a nothing answer, but his pause had allowed her a quick glimpse at the council's reactions, and the glance he threw in the direction of her veil made her wonder if he performed that little piece of showmanship for her benefit. 'It is a great shame, of course,' Wousewold continued. 'It would be best for all the nation to have confirmation, one way or the other.'

'Omrel,' Tila said, turning her attention to the high priest. 'This princess assumes that you have nothing to add on this matter?'

'This priest doesn't,' Omrel replied with a duck of his head. He was from common stock, and quietly took the view that his office made him the equal of everyone on the council save for Tila and her brother, which Tila found hilarious to watch.

'It is surely a strange turn of events when our priesthood holds no opinion on whether or not our god has been reborn,' Whittingmoor said, rubbing his thumb over his cane's head.

'It isn't strange at all,' Omrel countered, fixing the Law Lord with a direct stare that Whittingmoor met sullenly. 'The prophecy regarding Nari's rebirth is unclear in many ways, but one of the things on which all scholars agree is that the Divine One will present Himself to the monastery at Godspire, the site of His greatest triumph where he drove the Unmaker from this land—'

'This lord is well aware of his history, high priest,' Whittingmoor interrupted him testily.

'And yet you seem unaware that the Divine One's rebirth can only be accepted as such once the Godspire monks have proclaimed it to be true!' Omrel said forcefully. 'Nari will present Himself to His followers, as we once presented ourselves to Him. They'll determine the truthfulness of His claim and, should He be who He claims to be, they'll then go forth and proclaim His return. That's unarguable. Until that happens, this priest can give no insight.'

'So it seems reasonable to conclude that since whoever is claiming to be Nari has yet to present himself at the monastery, he must be in some doubt as to the monks' opinion of the veracity of his identity,' Lord Whittingmoor said. 'These rumours have been persisting for some time, after all.'

Tila did not turn her head, but eyed Whittingmoor sideways through her veil. That was a welcome sentiment to her ears, and it made her immediately suspicious. On the other hand, the Law Lord distrusted change. What would be more likely to bring about change than a reborn god with the authority to tear up the laws and the Code of Honour, all of which had been written since the death of that god's first fleshly body?

'That does not seem a wholly logical conclusion to draw,' Master Temach murmured, not looking up from the table.

'The good master is correct: we can't question the Divine One in such a manner,' Omrel said flatly. 'It's not for us to make such assumptions. He'll present Himself when He's ready.'

'What is the country to do in the meantime?' Marshal Coldbeck asked. 'Narida cannot exist in a state of uncertainty for ever, high priest.'

Omrel shrugged. 'Until such time as a prophecy's fulfilled, it's not fulfilled. Until the rebirth of Nari has been confirmed, it hasn't happened.'

Tila leaned forward slightly. 'So the official opinion of the priesthood is that . . . this princess's divine ancestor has *not* been reborn?'

Omrel spread his hands. 'The Divine One can't reveal Himself at the wrong time. He can't be *late*. When He needs us to know, we will know.' He glanced at Whittingmoor, and added in a somewhat quieter voice, 'This priest didn't think it was that hard a concept to grasp.'

'We are left with the same three possibilities we had before,' Adan Greenbrook said. 'Either these rumours are baseless and no one is claiming to be Nari reborn; or someone is claiming to be Nari reborn and, if he presents himself to the monks at Godspire he will be denounced as a fraud; or Nari has actually been reborn, and we await the official confirmation of that fact.' He tapped his pipe irritably on the table and then clamped it unlit between his teeth. 'It is all well and good that we here understand the nuances of the theological principles,' he added around the stem, 'but this does not help us bring order to a country that is increasingly divided. The lowborn are starting to question what authority the Sun Palace holds. Even some thanes are wavering. These are people for whom "wait and see" is not a satisfactory position.'

Tila eyed him as he spoke, trying to gauge where he stood. Was he alarmed? Did he see the prospect of personal gain? Tila knew well enough that a person could achieve power either by exploiting existing structures – as she had done in the Sun Palace

– or by imposing their own will on chaos, which was how Livnya the Knife had risen to prominence in the Idramese underworld. If the country slipped into confusion and disorder, there could be scope for an unscrupulous man to rise even farther than a place on the Inner Council.

'This uncertainty cannot be borne,' Lord Whittingmoor declared sharply.

'The Divine One can't be hurried!' Omrel almost snapped.

'Why not?' Tila heard herself say, and every face around the table turned to look at her. She instantly regretted speaking, but she could feel the edges of a new, exciting idea under the restless fingers of her mind, and she would just have to discover the shape of it with an audience.

'You said yourself, Omrel, that the Divine Nari can't reveal Himself at the wrong time,' Tila addressed the high priest, who nodded uncertainly. 'Therefore, if we were to step up the search for Him, with the intention of assisting Him to Godspire, we cannot be acting inappropriately.'

'Marshal Taladhar is already searching for—' Kaled Greenbrook began, but Tila cut him off.

'Marshal Taladhar is an old man who would give his life defending the Torgallen Pass against the filth of the Morlithian Empire,' she said, 'but when it comes to matters of religion he is overcautious to the point of foolishness.'

'This priest hardly thinks that one can be foolish about such things!' Omrel protested, and Tila wished that her veil would not mask the eyebrow she was going to cock at him.

'The last time this princess was face to face with Taladhar Torgallen, he requested to wash her feet. In front of his thanes, sars and armsmen. It was quite mortifying.'

It was almost entertaining to watch the thoughts spiral around inside Omrel's head, as he tried to reconcile what he might consider to be appropriate devotion to the Divine Nari's blood descendant with what that actual blood descendant thought was appropriate. Not for the first time, Tila got the distinct feeling the priesthood might prefer it, in some respects, if she and her brother were not actually around at all. After all, the sun did not come down from the sky to tell the Morlithians that they were worshipping it incorrectly.

'That might have been excessive,' Omrel muttered, after a moment.

'The Divine Princess is correct about the Western Marshal's piety,' Einan Coldbeck said, every word as guarded as his defence in an honour duel, 'but this marshal fails to see the relevance of it in this discussion.'

'Marshal Taladhar would lack the conviction to act in any way regarding the Divine One's rebirth until it was confirmed by Godspire,' Tila said. 'His searches will be cursory. We must act instead, and give our people the clarity they need. We must bring anyone claiming the Divine One's name to Godspire.'

'By force?' Kaled Greenbrook protested, the loudest and clearest of the various utterances that greeted her statement.

'And why not?' Tila demanded. 'The high priest has already stated that this princess's divine ancestor cannot reveal Himself at the wrong time! Perhaps we can bring this time forward; and if we can, then we should. What would you do, Lord Greenbrook,' she continued, when he opened his mouth to respond, 'if this princess's brother, the God-King, finally succumbed to his sickness tomorrow?'

Kaled's mouth clamped shut. Tila looked around the table.

'Anyone? Does anyone have a plan, should such a tragedy befall us?'

No one spoke. Everyone's eyes darted around the table, searching out those of their colleagues: everyone's except for Master Temach, who was resolutely staring at his thumbs and quite clearly wishing he had never come to this meeting.

'No plan,' Tila said quietly. 'The God-King of Narida lies abed sick, as he has done for weeks now, and his Inner Council has no plan for what should occur if the illness claims him? Will none of you stand forward to take the reins of leadership?'

She was laying a bald-faced trap. To declare that you believed yourself suitable to step into the role of the God-King . . . At the very least, it would set you up to be torn down by your colleagues, with a side note of being the most prominent suspect should Natan actually pass away. At worst, it smacked of heresy.

None of them took the bait, of course.

'This princess suggests that we immediately dispatch search parties under trusted commanders to find the truth of these rumours,' Tila said, as though the thick, awkward atmosphere did not exist. 'Should this princess's brother succumb to his illness then it is vital that Nari, should He have been reborn, take on the rule of Narida as soon as possible. Even if Natan recovers, as this princess prays that he will, we must provide answers. High Marshal,' she continued, turning to Einan Coldbeck. 'Will you make the appropriate arrangements?'

Coldbeck stared at her for a long moment before answering, and Tila tried to read him. Was his hesitation due to disliking acceding to a request from the Divine Princess? Had the man made his own schemes that relied on increased discord? Had she wrong-footed him by pushing for Nari's discovery?

'This marshal will,' Coldbeck said with a stiff nod, and raised one hand to silence the mutters of surprise or disapproval. 'The dispatch and use of Naridan troops are this marshal's prerogative, and he agrees with the Divine Princess's line of reasoning. If it is not the time for the Divine One to reveal Himself then so be it, but in the interests of bringing harmony back to these lands, we must make the effort.'

'You do not think that sending soldiers to hunt down our god might be inappropriate?' Kaled Greenbrook asked acidly.

'They will be sent to ensure His safety,' Coldbeck replied. 'They will not be hunting Him; they will be searching.'

'That is a fine distinction of words,' Kaled sneered.

'Our kingdom operates on a fine distinction of words,' Lord Whittingmoor said. 'Thus do we shape and use the laws that govern us. This lord has already stated his opinions on this ongoing uncertainty, and he applauds the Eastern Marshal's decision.'

He did not applaud the idea of the Divine Princess, Tila noted, but she was not overly concerned about that. With the Eastern Marshal and the Law Lord in favour, the wheels would start to turn.

Adan Greenbrook sighed. 'The Treasury will, of course, make the appropriate arrangements for this venture, but depending on the numbers of men that are sent, it will take a short while to procure the necessary supplies.'

'This marshal thanks you for your assistance,' Coldbeck said with a shallow nod. They had clashed before over costs, many times, but it seemed that Greenbrook was not going to try to flex his golden muscles on this occasion.

'To other matters, then,' Lord Wousewold said, having avoided offering an opinion one way or the other. 'What of the Splinter King? Marshal Coldbeck?'

'We are still in the planning stages,' Coldbeck said, with some reluctance. 'A direct military operation against the Splinter King, and by extension Grand Mahewa is, of course, out of the question . . .'

Tila only half-listened, but didn't speak. Coldbeck would try, but no one on the council truly expected him to succeed. When they passed the resolution to make another attempt on the life of her exiled relatives, it had not been for Coldbeck's benefit. They suspected, even though none of them liked the knowledge, that Tila had knives at her command, and they expected her to somehow solve this problem for them, without ever openly requesting it or acknowledging her involvement. She had never worked out if it was because they were uncomfortable with a member of the divine bloodline being actively involved in such matters, or because she was a woman who had some sort of power and influence they did not understand. She suspected it was probably both.

The question was when news of the murders would reach Idramar. Assuming Kurumaya's killers had done what they were supposed to, the Hierarchs of Kiburu ce Alaba would be unable to cover up the fact their pet royal exiles had been slaughtered. However, that might not become public knowledge until the Hierarchs were unable to produce the family for their next appearance, and Tila was not familiar enough with Alaban festivals and celebrations to know when that would be. It would be good to have confirmation that at least one of the threats to her bloodline had been eliminated.

As for this supposed Nari . . . Well, Omrel had the truth of it. If Tila's divine ancestor truly had been reborn, His return to power was prophesied and unstoppable. Which meant that anyone she sent to kill 'Nari', slipped into Coldbeck's men, wouldn't succeed. Any deaths they might cause would, by definition, only be of false pretenders, not the Divine One.

Coldbeck would not send all his own troops away from Idramar on this hunt. He would send a mix of men he could trust, and fresh recruits. All Tila had to do was make sure that some of the recruits held strong opinions about pretenders, and knew how to use a weapon.

Luckily, Livnya the Knife had just the right sort of contacts.

ZHANNA

ZHANNA HONESTLY HADN'T realised exactly how many Naridans there were. She understood, of course, that Narida was larger than Tjakorsha, even all of the islands put together, and that suggested there would be more people. Even so, as she and her group had followed the Blackcreek River over its flood plain towards the mountains, they encountered village after village, and the sheer number of people was starting to add up in her head. This town was called Ironhead and was near as big as Black Keep, although it lacked the surrounding wall.

And, it seemed to her as they approached, most of the occupants. 'Where are people?' she asked. The land here was higher and rougher than on the coast, for they were starting to climb up towards the mountains proper. There was not the space for as many fields, but she would have still expected to see more locals working the land than the few she had laid eyes on so far.

'Under the ground,' Amonhuhe replied, gesturing to the odd, conical buildings scattered here and there. 'Digging up metal.'

Amonhuhe of the Mountains was not a tall woman, especially not by Zhanna's standards, but she had a presence that lent her a definite authority. Amonhuhe walked with a bow stave, the strings for which were in a pouch on her belt that sat next to a long, sheathed metal knife, and although she'd been wearing

Naridan clothes in Black Keep, now they were heading higher she'd brought out her old mountain furs. She still wore the strings of intricate wooden beads around her neck, but her change of clothing made her look a lot more Tjakorshi.

They were a strange group, in fairness. The nominal leader was Menaken, nicknamed 'the Handsome' by some of the Brown Eagle women (although no one had told him that). He was one of Daimon's guards, and wore his Black Keep livery so that everyone they met complied with what he asked. However, Menaken had never been more than a couple of days' travel inland from Black Keep and had little experience in life away from his town, so Amonhuhe had swiftly taken charge.

Besides Zhanna, there were five other Tjakorshi. The most prominent was Tsennan Longjaw, probably the biggest clansman since Ristjaan the Cleaver had died, and coming into his eighteenth summer. Zhanna had been friends with him for years, to the point that her mother had once threatened to beat him bloody when she thought he was being over-familiar, but Zhanna had never got any indication that the Longjaw was interested in her in that way. He was probably what an older brother would be like: sometimes annoying, sometimes amusing, often looking out for her even when she didn't want him to.

Tsennan had already been Blooded before the battle against Rikkut Fireheart. So had Tamadh Avljaszhin, son of Nalon, the Naridan man who'd been snatched off a ship by Avjla Ambastutar, and later married her. Tamadh's younger brother Ingorzhak, however, hadn't lifted a weapon in earnest until he'd been part of Zhanna's counterattack against Fireheart's raiders. They were both here, looking to live up to their mother's reputation as an adventurer, although so far Zhanna thought they were only living up to their father's reputation for being an arse. Somewhat frustratingly, their Naridan was even worse than hers, since it seemed Nalon rarely spoke it at home.

Other than Amonhuhe, the rest of their expedition were

youngsters who had fallen in behind Zhanna on the bloody day of Fireheart's attack. She had started calling them her crew, like she was a ship's captain, and they followed her lead. So far as Zhanna was concerned, that meant they *were* her crew, and shockingly it seemed her mother agreed.

'A captain finds their own crew, those who are willing to sail with them,' she said, when Zhanna's party had been preparing to leave. 'A chief doesn't get involved in that. You'll be a strange captain with no ship, but you'd have no use for one where you're going in any case.' She shrugged. 'You just have to make sure you don't steer them wrong. Set your sail for their benefit, not yours.'

Zhanna intended to do just that. Being the first Tjakorshi to climb the Naridan mountains would be something to sing about, and all her crew had wanted to come once they heard where she was going, so the party had been filled out without Daimon or Zhanna's mother needing to order anyone to go. Besides, Zhanna thought, having a group of Naridans *and* Tjakorshi who all got on had to look good for the villages they stopped at along the way.

Now, though, they were coming into a larger place, and on the edge of Blackcreek lands. Zhanna was well aware that, underground or not, there were enough people in Ironhead to swallow her party up if those who lived here decided they didn't want visitors, and didn't fancy respecting Menaken's livery. She noticed that, as they'd got farther from the sea, the expressions of fear on Naridan faces at the sight of Tjakorshi had lessened, presumably because they were less likely to have seen one of her people before. She'd have been amazed if anyone in Ironhead looked at her and thought 'Raider', but that didn't mean they would be friendly. She could not have walked for the length of a summer's day from her home back on Kainkoruuk without crossing into another clan's lands, where she'd have been thoroughly unwelcome. Zhanna was astonished, and frankly quite dubious, that all the inhabitants of this land were supposed to be one people.

There were a few locals working the land immediately around the main cluster of houses, and they straightened up from their labour as Zhanna approached, casually shifting tools on to their shoulders and eyeing the newcomers warily. In fact, Zhanna noticed, a few began to drift in around and behind them, as she and her companions followed the worn wagon ruts of the main track into Ironhead.

'They want fight?' she asked in Naridan.

'Maybe they've seen your dragons,' suggested Avisha, the granddaughter of Osred the steward. Thorn was trotting along within the group, while Talon was taking his turn riding in Zhanna's deep hood. The two little rattletails – the Naridan name for this sort of dragon – were growing fast, and Thorn would soon be too big to hitch a lift from her. The Naridans used them as hunting animals, but the adults at Black Keep were still half-wild. Zhanna had raised Thorn like he was an orphaned crow chick, which had made him much more affectionate.

It had also nearly got her killed for witchcraft, but that was Naridans for you. Daimon and Tavi had tried the same tricks with rattletail hatchlings from later clutches, to prove it was not some sort of Raider magic.

'They're just being cautious,' Amonhuhe said to her. 'You Tjakorshi look a bit like this woman's folk in your furs, but the furs are wrong, and you're too tall, and we're coming from the wrong direction.' She pointed to the north-west, where the Blackcreek River wound up into the mountains between two of the first peaks that rose so high their heads were no longer swathed in trees. 'The Smoking Valley lies that way.'

'There is no road beyond here,' Zhanna noted.

'This woman's people don't need roads,' Amonhuhe snorted, and Zhanna nodded. All the same, she felt that the Naridans' habit of deliberately making and clearing a route for others to follow when travelling any distance overland was quite useful. Trees and bushes got in the way more than waves, and were virtually as featureless, which made navigation very hard. They even had a similar risk of killing people during high winds.

'We need to find the home of Sar Benarin,' Menaken said. 'He answers to the Thane of Black Keep, and will help us.'

'Follow,' Amonhuhe said, veering off to the right as they passed the first house. Zhanna trailed behind, eyeing one of the high, conical buildings and wondering at their purpose. She had never seen their like before and, unlike the other buildings in the town, they did not have their own fenced-off patch of garden. Then, as she rounded the nearest one and saw an opening in the side, a filthy Naridan man appeared from the shadowed interior bearing a wooden crate full of dark rock, which glinted in the light. His eyes widened as he saw her, and he dropped the crate with a crash that caused everyone's heads to snap around. Apparently even more unnerved by this scrutiny, the man disappeared back into the darkness.

'Come on,' Menaken said uneasily. 'Before we terrify half the town.'

SAR BENARIN'S HOUSE was almost the Black Keep in miniature, being a sturdy two-storey building that sat atop a raised platform of mortared stone. There was nothing miniature about Sar Benarin himself, however, who was both tall, and built as solidly as his home. He stood a few steps up on the narrow stair that led to his house's single door, while the inhabitants of Ironhead shadowing Zhanna's party closed in curiously.

Sar Benarin peered down at the parchment in his hand, delivered to him with a respectful bow by Menaken, and snorted. 'This sar has not seen Lord Asrel in years. Now you bring him news that not only has Lord Asrel died, but Lord Darel has travelled to Idramar and you come here on the authority of young Lord Daimon, who is not even thane? And that Raiders, Nari save us, *Raiders*, have settled at Black Keep?' He crumpled the parchment in his fist and looked down at them, his eyes flashing. 'You ask a lot of credulity from an old man.'

'You will notice, Sar Benarin, that s'man wears the livery of Black Keep,' Menaken said stiffly.

'Aye, and the parchment carries the seal of the Thane of Black Keep,' Benarin said. 'But this sar doesn't know you, man, nor any of these others with you. These pale giants: these are Raiders, hey? We may be too far from the sea here to have fallen foul of their depredations, but we know them as no friends to Narida.'

Zhanna did not know what 'depredations' meant, but she had the gist of the sar's words. Then Sar Benarin's eyes narrowed as they came to rest on Amonhuhe.

'You.'

Amonhuhe raised her chin in response, and Sar Benarin spoke again. For a moment Zhanna thought that her ears had suddenly stopped working properly, as she tried to place the sounds into the Naridan that she'd learned, and failed. Then she realised that Sar Benarin was not speaking Naridan, although it was something close enough that it sounded like she *should* be able to work it out if she concentrated.

Amonhuhe replied in the same tongue, and Sar Benarin's face was split by a smile that showed a lot of teeth. The two of them conversed, and as they did so Zhanna looked about her and realised that several of Ironhead's people wore carved wooden beads, and had features that looked closer to Amonhuhe's than to any of the Black Keep Naridans.

'Well,' Sar Benarin said, raising his voice for the benefit of those in the town, and Zhanna brought her attention back to him. 'The woman Amonhuhe has the speech of Smoking Valley, she claims kinship with some of those known to this sar, and she says the news her party bears is true.'

'Have you seen the Smoking Valley people this spring?' Menaken asked, and Benarin's expression darkened.

'No, and it troubles us. More than one family in this town

shares blood with the mountain folk. They always stop here, both on the way down to the plains and back again. We hoped they'd merely passed us by for some reason, although we knew not what that would be, but to learn they never made it to Black Keep either . . . ' He grimaced. 'It speaks well for the new lords of Black Keep that they would send you. What assistance would you have from us?'

NABANDA

Nabanda and hîs crew had searched all night, but they'd found no sign of their quarry. Now the morning had come and hîs eyes felt sandy and sore, hîs feet ached, and the anger and frustration in hîs belly was starting to curdle into fear. Kurumaya wanted this family dead, and had trusted Nabanda to get it done. You didn't fail a Shark: not if you wanted to keep all your limbs attached.

The problem was, no one seemed to know that much about who it was Nabanda had set out to kill. They'd tracked the family crest to a rich house on Second Level, but they'd had no names, only descriptions: two parents, an adult masculine child, and a younger feminine one, all of Naridan heritage. Nabanda and hîs crew had gone at night, but the adult child had not been in the house. Now hê was left to hunt a nameless, faceless fugitive through the streets of East Harbour, a city that could have a hundred hundreds of people worshipping a god in the Court of the Deities and still be bustling with life and activity everywhere else.

Nabanda had considered lying, going back to Kurumaya and reporting a success. Three out of the four family members were dead, and the house was burned down. They left Guelan's body in there, after hê took a mortal wound from a guard, so there would even be the correct number of bodies if someone decided to go trawling through the ruins. The missing target would have to be a fool to stand up and publicly declare hìmself. What were the chances Nabanda's lie would ever be discovered?

The chances were low, but still too high. Hê would be placing hîs life in the hands of hîs crew, for one thing. That was fine in the moments when the blades were out, when you relied on each other not to die, but relationships could change and loyalties could shift over time. All it would take was one person deciding they didn't want to cross Kurumaya, or seeking to gain favour, and the secret would be out.

Nabanda would just have to keep hîs eyes and ears open. Gossip moved fast in East Harbour, and the fire would have attracted attention. If anyone heard of a survivor being taken in by another rich family, the news would soon be all over: then Nabanda would just have to find hîs quarry and kill hìm before Kurumaya pulled hîm up on it. Similarly, a rich Naridan youth showing up on the street would be immediately obvious, and just as worthy of comment. Nabanda probably wouldn't even need to wet hîs blade for hìm to die, but hê'd do it anyway, just to be sure.

Hê had gravitated to the docks this morning, mainly out of habit. Hê needed to take fewer and fewer labouring jobs as hîs standing in Kurumaya's ranks rose, but this was where hê had grown up, and where hê still felt the most comfortable. Besides, the docks were always a good place for gossip, both about East Harbour and the world beyond. No one talked like sailors trying to impress, but the work gangs gave them stiff competition.

Anyway, Nabanda felt hê should have something to hîs life that wasn't hired knife work for one of Grand Mahewa's most notorious Sharks. Hê still had some friends who didn't know about the jobs hê did for Kurumaya, and hê wanted to keep it that way. Hê couldn't imagine explaining hîmself to Jeya, for one; hê'd find it hard to put into words how very different their lives had become. But Nabanda was older than Jeya, old enough that hê'd been starting on the docks when shê'd first come to Ngaiyu's place as a crying orphan child looking for somewhere to sleep. Jeya might still be living hér life from dawn to dusk, not thinking about anything more than where the next meal came from, but Nabanda had quickly decided hê didn't intend to break hîs back for others until hê died with nothing when hê could no longer lift the loads. For someone with hîs size and strength, the simplest way up was working for a Shark.

Hê made hîs way along the dock front, past the open doors of taverns and over the small stone bridges that spanned where Grand Mahewa's streams flowed down to meet the water of the harbour. It was still early, with the sky turning a vivid pink in anticipation of the sun rising over Lesser Mahewa in the east. Hê would get a few hours of work in: solid, mindless labour that didn't involve knifing anyone, or hunting for a youth who had, for whatever reason, ended up on the wrong side of Kurumaya. Then hê would go back to hîs home and rest.

At least, that was hîs plan. It lasted until hê walked up to Maradzh and the gang master turned to face hîm with an expression that rapidly soured.

'You look like shit,' they said, without preamble. Maradzh was somewhere in their middle years, and stout, with the pale skin and facial tattoos of the far south.

'I didn't sleep well,' hê replied, which was true enough.

'Not well?' Maradzh demanded. 'Or not at all?' They tilted their head as they looked at hîm, and their long, red-blond hair swayed when they shook their head. 'I'm sorry, Nabanda. I've got nothing for you today.'

Hê stared at them in confusion. 'What?' Hê gestured at the ships moored all along the dock front. 'You can't tell me there's not work!'

'Oh, there's work,' Maradzh said, almost sadly. 'But not for you. Not today, Nabanda. Not when you're like this.'

Hê couldn't hide hîs frustration. 'I can still lift! I can still carry!'

87

'Yes, and when you put things in the wrong place, or lose your balance and fall off the plank into the harbour because you're so tired?' Maradzh demanded.

'Then I pull myself out, and you take it out of my wages,' Nabanda snapped.

Maradzh stared at hîm, unblinking. 'Do you think I don't know who you work for at night?'

Nabanda felt hîs face shut down, without even intending it to. Hê said nothing, because hîs mind couldn't come up with anything to say.

'Exactly,' Maradzh said, as though hê had spoken to confirm it. They shook their head again. 'I'm not disciplining one of Kurumaya's, and if I don't when I should, then the rest of the gang will take issue with it. I can't have favourites.'

'I work for you; you pay me,' Nabanda argued. 'Kurumaya has nothing to do with it. Kurumaya won't hear of it.'

'Maybe not from your mouth,' Maradzh snorted. 'Word travels on the docks, remember? I don't want a visit from a Shark's people, telling me how I shouldn't be disrespecting one of theirs! No, Nabanda, not today,' they continued, when hê opened hîs mouth to protest again. 'Go home and rest. Maybe come back for the evening shift, when this lot are tiring.' They drew themselves up to their full height. 'But I won't be taking you on this morning.'

Nabanda stared at them, but hê was still trying to form a response when Maradzh turned away and marched off down the dock barking orders, leaving hîm standing.

MARIN

THE UNIVERSITY OF Idramar was the finest seat of learning in all of Narida, and also a thoroughly haphazard collection of buildings. Most impressive of all was the God-King's Hall, the huge central building constructed entirely of stone, with its soaring ceilings and carved archways. This was where the university's records and treasures were kept, and where its great events were held. Other buildings radiated out from it as they had been added: the River College; the High Marshal's College; the North College; the New College, which was further north than the North College; the spiralling, leaning shape of the Drunkard's Tower; the mill, the bakery, and so on. However, the one Marin was most interested in was the inn known as the Gatehouse, which sat just beyond the actual gatehouse and served ale brewed on the university grounds.

The general mix of customers had not changed much since Marin had studied here; a handful of university masters, a few handfuls of students, and a scattering of other locals who gravitated to the place. There was at least one thief and pickpocket in the crowd, which was him; which was also the reason he'd had to leave the university's sheltered environment behind and make a living for himself in the hard world beyond, from which he only originally escaped by landing a scholarship. However, not all his old relationships had slipped when he retreated from his rooms in the River College. There were still those who valued intellect, learning and friendship over slavish adherence to the niceties of property law.

'You're certain of this?' Master Daltan asked. He had been Marin's master some twenty-five years ago, and was sharp even then. Now he was a vinegary old man with a liver-spotted scalp easily visible through the thinning strands of his grey hair, and nails that he'd let grow long.

'As certain as this man sees you,' Master Temach replied, fiddling uncomfortably with his mug. 'Coldbeck will announce it any day. Idramar will be sending troops west. The Inner Council claims it's to assist the Divine Nari, should He have truly been reborn, but their purpose seems clear enough. They intend to flush Him out: that, and kill any pretenders.' He kept his voice low, and glanced uneasily at Marin as he spoke. Temach was a few years older, but they'd become friends when they'd both wound up studying Narida's oldest religious texts. Now Temach was the Master of Learning on the God-King's Inner Council, and Marin . . . Well, Marin had his own talents, he reminded himself firmly. He'd like to see any of these others survive, living as he'd done.

'Or kill the Divine One?' Master Genyel asked, with his customary lack of tact. Temach glowered at him. Daltan actually hissed.

'There's no point pretending the thought hadn't crossed your minds,' Genyel continued on blithely, taking a swig of his own ale. 'At least, this man hopes it had, else he's not sure how you can justify calling yourselves Cupbearers.'

'It is not this man's habit to consider blasphemy,' Daltan spat.

'This man always did consider your approaches somewhat limited,' Genyel replied blandly. Marin leaned forwards before Daltan could make an ever more venomous response.

'Regardless of the truth of your words, Master,' he said,

addressing Genyel, 'the Cupbearers were founded on the basis of promoting and protecting knowledge and wisdom, and might s'man suggest that it is not the wisest course of action to accuse the Inner Council of blasphemy in the middle of an Idramese ale house?'

Genyel looked around lazily. 'This man sees no Keepers present.'

'If you think Princess Tila needs Keepers to know what occurs in this city, you're an even greater fool than this man gave you credit for, Genyel,' Temach said bluntly. 'This man has sat on that council for the best part of five years, and she *knows* things. She knows things no princess of Narida has any business knowing, and she's usually proven correct.'

'You're saying the Divine Princess has a little spy network?' Genyel smirked, then abruptly stopped smirking when he realised that none of the rest of them had cracked a smile. 'You're *actually* saying that?'

'It's the only logical explanation,' Temach said. 'This man doesn't know how, or who, but Princess Tila has contacts in the city, and not just the nobles. He'd stake his position on it.'

Genyel blinked a couple of times, then sniffed, leaned forwards, and lowered his voice. 'Very well. That doesn't invalidate this man's words, you realise? We have to consider the possibilities.' He looked directly at Temach. 'As you say, you've sat on the council for five years. You know the . . . ' He glanced around. 'You know *that woman* better than the rest of us. She's clearly not the type to just let events unfold as they will. Do you think her capable of what this man suggested?'

Temach did not reply immediately. He inhaled and exhaled, and stared into his mug.

'Yes. Yes, this man does.'

'This is outrageous!' Daltan protested, although to Marin's relief he did so quietly. 'What you're suggesting is blasphemy!'

'And yet it may be true!' Temach said firmly. 'This man takes no pleasure in it either, Daltan, but we have to face facts. If the rumours of the rebirth are accurate, they change everything. *Everything*. Who's to say a family so used to privilege wouldn't try to cling to that privilege in any way they could?'

'S'man has read the prophecies,' Marin added. 'When they mention the Divine One returning to take His throne again, there is no mention of His bloodline in anything other than the vaguest hints, if that. If the prophecies are true—'

'Which is an entirely separate conversation,' Temach cut in.

'*If the prophecies are true*,' Marin repeated, 'then the influence of Nari's bloodline disappears once He has come into His power once again. Everything we've heard of Princess Tila, at least, suggests she would not welcome that.'

It was fair to say Marin had heard other accounts of Princess Tila Narida than those brought by Temach. Marin's husband Alazar had been the lover of Natan III, many years ago, before that business with the death of the old God-King, Natan II, for which Alazar had been blamed. Alazar had not known Princess Tila well, but when he spoke of the divine family at all – which was rare – he painted her as a sharp-tongued witch who turned her brother against him in the aftermath of the tragedy.

Marin supposed that, in some sense, he should be grateful to the Divine Princess. If Alazar hadn't become a blacksword and been cast out from the Sun Palace, Marin would never have met the love of his life. All the same, it was hard to take much pleasure in the event that had caused his beloved so much pain, for all that it was so long ago and had, as Laz himself strenuously maintained, worked out for the best.

'What are you suggesting?' Daltan asked, drumming his long nails on the table. 'Regardless of what the princess wishes, this man can't believe Marshal Coldbeck will be sending out his men with express instructions to execute.'

'All it would need is one knife in the right place,' Temach said gloomily. 'There was talk of how the rebirth, if it has happened, cannot be interfered with; that the Divine One's return to power is inexorable, no matter what men may do. Even Morel seemed to be of this opinion. That manner of thinking feels complacent, at best.'

Daltan grunted. 'That's the problem with priests. They'll hold anything up as a sign of what they want it to mean, no matter how tenuous. Ask them if they've actually *studied* the texts, and they'll look at you like you've grown a second head.'

'The prophecies are a map for the faithful,' Genyel said, 'and maps are meant to be used and followed. If the Divine One's return was inexorable, what purpose would there be in a prophecy? Quite clearly, they are for learned men to study and to act upon, to help bring them to pass.'

Daltan looked at him in some surprise. 'That's the most intelligent thing you've said in years.'

'So we're in agreement that we don't fully trust the motives of the Inner Council?' Marin said, before Genyel could respond. 'The rest of the Inner Council,' he amended, seeing Temach's annoyed expression. 'We need to find the Divine One first. We need to keep Him safe, and get Him to Godspire without any harm coming to Him.'

Slowly, heads nodded.

'Well volunteered, Marin,' Master Daltan said, draining his mug and setting it back down again. 'Your husband is a member of the Brotherhood, is he not? Just the sort of dependable mercenary the Eastern Marshal will be hiring to head west.'

HEADING BACK FROM the inn through Idramar's dark streets, Marin tried to work out whether Laz would be furious with him or not.

He had never volunteered to head west and find the Divine Nari. Not as such. It had not been why he'd insisted they come back to Idramar even though he had to leave in a hurry five years before after a particularly tenacious Keeper had managed to track a few thefts back to him, and Laz hated coming here anyway due to the occupants of the Sun Palace. Marin had just wanted to make sure the other members of the Idramar Cupbearers had heard the rumours, and find out what they were intending to do about them. It wasn't like he had a desperate yearning to be the first of his order to meet their resurrected god. Not *really*.

Fine.

So what if he did? Marin of Idramar, the boy from the docks who'd had the guts to present himself at the university on pauper's day, and had proved his mind was quick and nimble enough to be granted one of only three annual scholarships? Who had endured the sneers and mockeries of his contemporaries, the third and fourth sons of sars and minor thanes? And was it any wonder, in that sort of environment, surrounded by those richer than him, if certain small, valuable items that the original owners didn't care to pay close enough attention to had ended up in his possession? It was just a matter of levelling the playing field between them. But of course, when the situation was discovered, the university had taken the side of the rich kids, not the scholarship boy.

Should anyone be surprised if he still felt the need to prove himself, after all that? Besides, he would be doing his country a service. And Laz could hardly object, either. Marin's husband had nursed his smouldering resentment of the God-King for twenty years. If the Divine One's rebirth was real, Natan III's world would come crashing down around his ears. It wasn't that Laz didn't honour Nari, he just took particular issue with His current spoiled, conniving descendants, so really, he should jump at this opportunity. Taking the crown's money to help bring it down? That was almost poetic.

They had taken lodgings down by the docks, since Marin still knew folk there and could rent a cot in a corner for less than most people, but that was some way downstream from the university. Marin walked the route almost absent-mindedly, for even after many years away, he still knew the city. As he walked, he pondered how to approach Laz about his fellow Cupbearers' suggestion. His husband had not been best pleased when Marin had come back two days previously with a carved jade brooch that he might possibly have acquired from a drunken lady who'd practically collapsed on him in the street, so it was fair to say Laz was already feeling put upon. He might react badly when otherwise he'd have been open to the notion, and that was Marin's own fault, he accepted that. Laz didn't like it when Marin stole. On the other hand, Marin wasn't too fond of the fact his husband's main recourse for earning money was to put himself at risk of harm. Over the years, they'd mostly worked it through.

He was just coming on to the docks when he heard the shouting from ahead. There were still plenty of people, for ships needed to be loaded ready to leave with the tide, even if that tide was at first light, so Marin couldn't see the source of the noise at first. He recognised the cadence after a couple of moments, though: he'd run from it often enough, in his younger days.

Keepers. Keepers, chasing someone. Someone foolish enough to flee along the docks, through the stevedores and sailors and over the mooring ropes, rather than cutting away inland. Crowds could be the thief's friend, but not when the Keepers had you in sight. Then it was best to find an empty street, put your head down, and run like the wind.

The thief squirmed between two startled sailors and bore down on Marin. He had a momentary glimpse of wide, panicked eyes in a young face, and then the luckless – or careless – unfortunate was past him, breath coming in gasps.

The Keepers came next, three of them in their boiled leather and steel caps, with the determined expressions of men who might not be as fleet as their quarry but reckoned they could outlast him. Marin had a momentary pang of sympathy for the young fool they were chasing, and it might have been this that caused him to dither and then, purely accidentally of course, step into their path instead of out of it.

They collided with him and over they all went, sprawling on to the hard cobbles with a force that made Marin instantly regret his decision as at least two of the Keepers landed on him. He began burbling apologies, aware even as he did so that he'd probably done something quite stupid for no personal gain whatsoever, but his words were cut off when a leather-gloved fist connected with his jaw and snapped his head sideways.

'Nari-damned shitheel!' someone raged above him. He grabbed at the exploding pain in his jaw and waited for the next blow, but it never came. They were none too gentle in pushing themselves up off him, but it seemed that had been a punch born of momentary frustration, and he was not about to be laid into with fist, boot and cudgel. All the same, he'd been a fool.

'We'll never catch him now,' someone growled, and spat. The spittle landed on Marin's shoulder, and he suspected it had not been an accident. He rolled over with a groan and began to push himself back to his feet, murmuring apologies as he did so.

'Wait.'

A hand reached out and grabbed the shoulder that had just been spat upon, then hauled him around. Marin winced, and shielded his face from the anticipated punch, but his hand was pulled aside.

'S'man *knows* this rat-faced little fuck!' a voice exclaimed triumphantly. 'Get him into the light!'

Marin's bowels turned to water, and now he tried to wriggle loose and get away, but he'd committed the cardinal sin of any thief: he'd let the Keepers get close enough to lay hands on him. He was dragged across the dock front into the light of a torch burning on a wall, and found himself staring into a face washed with triumphant glee. It looked vaguely familiar, but Marin didn't have a name to put to it. This was a shame, because the other man appeared to have no such problem.

'Hello, Marin,' he leered. 'Long time, no see. Missed the cells, did you?'

DAREL

THE PORT OF Tainmar was five days behind them when Darel saw the sail to the east.

He had not spotted it, in fairness: that had been the man at the top of the mast, who'd sung out a 'Sail ho!', but Darel, having nothing to do on the ship, made his way to the rail and peered out. The sea was calmer here – they were in the lee of the mighty Crown Island, which broke up the ocean rollers even though it was well over the horizon – and he could make out the dark spot despite the rising and falling of the *Silver Tide* beneath his feet.

'Anything for us to be concerned about?' he asked the man who moved up to the rail next to him.

'We shall have to see,' replied Kaldur Brightwater.

Kaldur Brightwater, the Southern Marshal and Hand of Heaven, was one of the four most powerful men in Narida, beneath the God-King. He was Darel's liege lord, and was a lean, handsome man somewhere beyond his thirtieth year. Darel was only a minor thane, and a new one at that, but Brightwater had paid little attention to their different ranks so far on the journey, conversing with Darel largely as an equal. The two of them had enjoyed several in-depth conversations about the merits of different Naridan philosophers, and even delved into a couple of the better-known minds from the Morlithian Empire. Brightwater had shown a keen interest in the minutiae of Black Keep, claiming he rarely had a chance to see the direct relationship between a minor thane and his people. He was also a poet, and although Darel might have slightly exaggerated his approval, it was clear the Southern Marshal was not without talent in that area.

However, Darel was keenly aware that no matter how friendly, no matter how informal Kaldur Brightwater was, he was still taking Darel to Idramar to seek the God-King's approval of letting the Tjakorshi settle in Black Keep. If the God-King disapproved, there was no question of Brightwater ignoring their monarch's wishes. Anything could happen at that point, from the Blackcreek family being stripped of their lands and it being awarded to another – almost certainly the odious Thane Odem of Darkspur – to the entire town being put to the sword.

'Your servant has heard of pirates sailing these waters,' Darel said. The crew of the *Silver Tide* were not panicking, by any means, but the watchful tension in the air had not been present before.

'They do,' Brightwater acknowledged. 'Mainly from Crown Island. It is a mountainous place, according to the records, with little soil suitable for tilling, otherwise one of the coastal thanes would have tried to claim it in times past. As it is, it has always been viewed as too much trouble to be worth settling,' he continued grimly, 'and so pirates, the lawless and the exiled skulk there instead.'

Darel nodded noncommittally. He felt like saying that perhaps the island should have been taken simply to expand the rule of Naridan law, but these were still the lands where the Southern Marshal held authority, and such a suggestion could easily be taken as critical of the man on whom Black Keep's future depended. He held his tongue, and watched the sail as though it could provide further answers to a man who had never previously left the shore in anything larger than a rowboat.

'It is not one of the Raider ships that fled Blackcreek lands, is it?' Brightwater asked a few moments later. Darel shook his head.

'No, lord, the sail shape is wrong. Besides,' he chuckled, 'we would have seen it gain on us by now, if it were. And if they intended to.'

Brightwater looked at him in surprise. 'Their ships are truly that swift, that the difference in speed would be noticeable so soon after sighting one? This marshal had heard tales, but Brightwater is far from the coast, and he had never seen Raiders in person until he came to your town.'

'Your servant is no expert,' Darel admitted, 'but from what he has seen, they significantly outpace our vessels.'

'Perhaps we should have commandeered one for this journey,' Brightwater mused. Darel bit his tongue.

The other sail appeared content to shadow them for the next two bells, remaining at a distance that was no immediate threat, yet also far enough that the *Silver Tide* could not easily identify it. That changed as the sun reached its zenith.

Another cry of 'Sail ho!', and a new dark spot on the horizon, not far from the first. For Darel, novice sailor though he was, this seemed an ill omen. The two ships began to swell in size as they started to gain on the *Silver Tide*, and Darel could think of no benign reason why one ship should have waited for company before it began to overhaul them.

The *Silver Tide* put out all the sail it could, but it was far from being even the fastest of Naridan ships. Tainmar was not a large port, and Marshal Brightwater had taken passage on the swiftest vessel there of sufficient size to transport him and his immediate household, but it was a wide-bodied merchantman that wallowed through the waves. It was still far quicker than making the long journey to Idramar by road, but there were clearly fleeter ships on these seas.

'Blackcreek!' Marshal Brightwater barked. He was emerging from belowdecks, and was now armed for battle, with his helm under one arm. 'Make yourself ready! If these are pirates, as the captain suspects, then we will be seeing combat soon.'

'They would attack a ship bearing the banner of the Southern Marshal?' Darel asked in astonishment, looking up at the tip of the mast, from whence flew the crossed golden spears on blue of Brightwater.

'If these vermin recognise it, it may only serve to convince them that there are riches aboard,' Brightwater replied grimly. 'The sight of sars dressed for war will give them pause as they close, however.'

'As you command, high marshal,' Darel replied with a bow, and hastened past Brightwater and down the ladder to the first mate's cabin, allocated to him by the Southern Marshal's command. It was dark down here, with only the dim light filtering through the thick, flawed, diamond-shaped pieces of glass set into the hull. However, it was more than enough for Darel to open his chest and ready himself.

Other thanes, even some of the richer sars, might rely on pages to assist them in dressing for war. Lord Asrel, by contrast, had believed that a warrior who needed another's help to prepare for battle was no warrior at all, and so Darel had become well-practised in garbing himself in a time frame to his father's liking.

First he pulled on his coat-of-nails; the twin layers of fabric, embroidered with the green and black of Blackcreek, between which lay a concealed shirt of maille anchored in place by the 'nails' themselves, the only metal externally visible save for the twin breastplates. He fastened the central clasps, then tied on his greaves. His sword belt went on next, on a looser notch than before, to accommodate the bulk of his armour, with his longblade and shortblade hung from it. Finally, he slid his hands into his gauntlets, the outsides of which also had metal plates sewn into place through the thick leather beneath.

Darel's armour was considerably less ornate than the Southern Marshal's, whose coat-of-nails was embroidered with golden thread and whose armour plates were artfully engraved, but it was smart and serviceable just the same. He picked up his plumed helmet and made his way back up on to the deck, his rising heart rate not just due to the exertion of climbing the ladder while dressed for battle.

When Sattistutar's people had landed at Black Keep and Lord Asrel had tried to kill her under her flag of parley, Darel had – very briefly – ended up fighting the monstrous Ristjaan the Cleaver, which was the first time he had drawn his blade against an enemy. He ended up on his back with a splitting headache from where the giant man's huge axe had struck his helmet, and if it had not been for his father's intervention, Ristjaan would surely have killed him. Then Darel had stepped in to protect Sattistutar from Lord Asrel's treacherous attack during his and Daimon's honour duel, after which Darel had been immediately disarmed. When Fireheart's raiders had attacked, Darel had guarded the River Gate; an entirely viable target for the Tjakorshi, but one they had avoided. He had fought when the attackers had made it well into the town, but the Southern Marshal's forces had arrived at around the same time, and besides, Darel's steed Quill had done most of the damage.

If the pirates came, Darel Blackcreek would finally have a chance to prove himself. He had trained and sparred with his father and with Daimon, but rarely had the beating of either of them. The question was, how did he measure up against the rest of the world? The Divine Nari knew that martial skill was not the only attribute a thane was supposed to possess, but a hale, healthy young thane who showed little skill with a blade was a target for mockery and disdain.

It also made him a target for death, of course, but Darel was trying not to think about that.

The Southern Marshal's four other sars were with him on the deck, each one armed and armoured in his heraldry. They were his household warriors, sars with no land to their names who lived at Brightwater and might be granted a minor title, should they provide suitable service. Technically Darel outranked them all, but in practice they would take orders from no one except Kaldur Brightwater. Darel felt out of place as he approached them in his green-and-black, pulling his helm down over his head.

'Blackcreek,' the Southern Marshal greeted him, then shifted to address all of them. 'These are not the fields we know. Sea combat is outside of this marshal's experience and, he believes, all of yours as well.'

The assembled sars nodded, and Darel joined in. He did not want any of them assuming that he might know what he was doing, simply because his home lay on the coast. Around them, sailors were running and shouting, doing incomprehensible things with ropes, sails and rigging, and making far more recognisable preparations involving handing out blades. The two pursuing ships were looming large now, and Darel could clearly see their crews swarming across their own decks.

'We shall give ourselves to the instruction of Captain Akav,' Marshal Brightwater said, and Darel blinked in surprise. The Hand of Heaven, allowing his men – and himself – to be commanded by a ship's captain, a lowborn? 'He will know where we may best lend our blades to repel attackers,' Brightwater continued, and Darel had to admit that the Southern Marshal had a point.

'Now,' Brightwater said, drawing his longblade, 'let us see if these whelps still have stomach for battle when they see what awaits them!'

His men drew their own weapons with a shout, and Darel joined them half a heartbeat later. Together, they moved towards the stern of the ship, seeking to place themselves where their pursuers could not help but see them.

'Ye're wearing a lot of steel there, goodsar,' a sailor with deep lines burned into his face by the sun and wind said to Darel, as he stepped up alongside him at the starboard rail. 'Mind ye don't go over, wearing that.'

'A fisherman from this lord's town nearly drowned, until he

was pulled out and revived by his fellows,' Darel replied absently. 'He said it was remarkably peaceful. This lord suspects that taking a sword through the chest would not be, so it is a trade he is prepared to make.'

'Aye,' the sailor muttered, with a glance at the crew of the nearest ship. 'Might be something t'what ye say.'

'Have you fought pirates before, man?' Darel asked, doing his best to count their foes. Neither of their pursuers was as large as the *Silver Tide*, being somewhat narrower across the beam, but between the two of them they would have considerably more men available.

'S'man can't say as he has,' the sailor said. Darel looked around at him now, and saw the ship-issue cutlass in his hand, and how it trembled. The man was surely old enough to be Darel's father.

'What is your name, sailor?' Darel asked him.

'Gershel, lord.'

'Stay behind this lord, Gershel,' Darel told him quietly. 'Watch his back, and he will watch yours.'

'Ware archers!' came the shout, and Darel saw that a few of the pirates did indeed have bows. They were small things, more like hunting bows than the true longbow of war, which in any case required a man to practise with them from youth. The deck of a ship was not the most stable shooting platform either, and the *Silver Tide*'s pitching and yawing made it impossible for them to pick out an individual target, but as the first ragged volley arced across the gap between the ships, Darel realised that marksmanship was hardly their intention. They simply wished to inflict whatever injury they could, to make their boarding easier.

An arrow flashed towards him, on a downwards curve rather than a flat trajectory. He lashed out at it on instinct and, to his surprise, made contact. The arrow clattered across the deck behind him, sheared in half by the famous edge of a Naridan longblade, and a great cheer of defiance rang out from the watching crew of the *Silver Tide*.

'You see that?' Gershel yelled at their pursuers, scrambling across the deck to find one half of the arrow, and holding it up to brandish at the pirates. 'That's what's waiting for you, you sea-shits!'

More arrows looped towards them, slow and weak compared to those from a warbow, but still with enough force to skewer an unarmoured man. Darel lunged to his left, batting another one out of the air before it could strike Gershel. 'This lord said to stay behind him!' he shouted at the sailor.

Another arrow struck Darel in the shoulder, knocking him sideways a step. It failed to pierce his maille, and he pulled it out of where it had snagged in the fabric of his coat-of-nails, then dropped it to the deck. His breathing was already coming quickly, and he could feel it reflecting back at him off the inside of his war mask. A nervous energy gripped his limbs, and he wanted the pirates to be here, now, so he could engage them, rather than wait a moment longer. Was this the battle-fever he'd heard of, that could grip warriors? Was it not a desire for combat so much as a desperate wish to end this uncertainty that bubbled within him?

The *Silver Tide*'s sails were slackening as one of the pirates' ships began to pull alongside, taking the wind for itself. Even Darel could tell their pace was slowing.

'Ware hooks!' someone shouted, and a few moments later curved, triple-pointed spikes of iron were hurled through the air across the rapidly narrowing gaps between the ships, trailing ropes behind them. Most snared the *Silver Tide*'s rigging above head height, but some landed on the deck, and were pulled back towards their throwers to snag upon the rails. The *Silver Tide*'s crew threw these overboard as swiftly as they could, before they could be drawn taut, but the ones in the rigging were already doing their work as the pirate crews hauled on them, seeking to bring their vessels alongside.

'Cut them loose!' Captain Akav bellowed, pointing at the

grappling lines, and Darel leaped to obey, clambering up on to the rail. He steadied himself with one hand, suddenly all too well aware of the waves beneath that would swallow him in his armour without trace, and slashed at the nearest line. His longblade severed one strand of the rope, and two more blows cut it through completely, but there were many more lines than could be reached even by all of the sars on the *Silver Tide*, and the steel carried by the crew lacked the edge to cut with the same speed.

'Get yourself back to the deck, lord!' Gershel called from behind him. 'They'll be coming in moments!'

Sure enough, the pirate ship to the *Silver Tide*'s starboard was being hauled closer, and was now mere yards away. Darel dropped off the rail and took up the guard position of a sar, his blade raised in a two-handed grip. This was a different setting, but it was what he had trained for. Now the moment was almost on him, he was finding a rhythm in his heartbeats and his breaths, fast though they were.

With a colossal, communal grunt, the pirates gave one more heave on the ropes of their boarding hooks, and the distance between the two ships narrowed to the distance a person could jump. Pirates, men and women clad in an odd mix of sailor's clothing, rags of high-quality cloth taken as plunder and even some salt-stained liveries of sars or nobles, climbed up on to the rail of their own vessel, yelling threats, curses and promises, and brandishing their weapons.

The first pirates made the jump.

Darel swung.

JEYA

GALEM HAD CHOSEN to be known as Bulang for the time being. It was an unremarkable Alaban name that no one would think twice about when they heard it, and that combined with thëir stolen clothes – considerably less ornate than the ones thëy'd worn before – and thëir unbound chest meant thëy could far more easily pass for a poor Alaban with Naridan blood, rather than a rich masculine Naridan youth with some Alaban blood.

What was far more difficult was getting thëm to pass for someone from the streets. Jeya had come to the life early, and was used to it, but Galem had no experience of living like this and didn't know where to start. For Galem, food had always just *happened*, and was provided by other people. You didn't have to steal it, or beg for it, or even buy it, unless it was a treat you bought spur-of-the-moment like rich people did from Abbaz, the merchant from whose barge Jeya had first seen Galem's house. You didn't have to *think* about food, because it would be there whenever you wanted it.

Jeya dimly remembered the first days after hér môther had died, when hér fàther had already been lost at sea. Shé could recall the awful, aching feeling in hér belly when shé had not eaten, worse than it had ever been before. Shé couldn't remember how shé'd found Ngaiyu's place, whether shé'd stumbled across it hérself or whether some kindly neighbour had told hér where to go, but Ngaiyu had taken hér in and did what thëy always did with newcomers: provide a hot meal, a place to sleep and advice of where to go in the morning.

The easiest place to get free food was the Temple of the Rays. The Morlithians worshipped the sun, which they said provided everything a person needed, and their priests tried to emulate it so far as they could. Jeya had never quite understood how anyone could get anything from the sun other than sunburn, but shé'd never questioned it too strenuously given the temple gave out food to the poor and needy. You had to listen to a sermon first, but hungry people would put up with a lot in the interests of getting less hungry.

Jeya bought food from the market for them both on the first day, but that couldn't last. Shé had limited money, and it had been hard enough to feed hérself, let alone another person. Shé debated the merits of introducing Galem to the arts of thievery, but decided that was a bad plan, and unfair. Galem would probably try it if shé asked, but they weren't yet that desperate; although, it had to be said, they might make a good double act. Quite a few of the market stallholders knew Jeya as a thief and would watch hér closely, but would still sell hér goods if shé had the money. Shé could walk up, bold as you like, with hér money in hand, and while they were watching hér, Galem could have something away from the other end . . . but that sort of thing took practice, and timing, and instincts that Galem did not yet have.

Best to stick to the Morlithians, for now. They had a reputation as magicians, but Jeya had never met a person with Morlithian blood who was any more magical than hérself; and besides, shé was prepared to put up with possible magic in the interests of free food.

It had been a week since Galem's house had burned down, and the third time they'd gone to the Temple of the Rays to break their fast. Jeya had not come here regularly for several years: shé felt it was greedy to do so, now shé was able to feed hérself by other means. The food had not come out yet: the priest still was waving their arms and proclaiming the power and wisdom of their god, as they stood beneath the burnished golden sun on the wall behind them that glinted in the light from the windows. Jeya took the opportunity to look around at the other faces present, more out of curiosity than anything else. Was it the same people as yesterday? Were they sitting in the same places? Was there anyone shé remembered from when shé came here more regularly?

It seemed like the same crowd, more or less, which wasn't particularly surprising, and no one shé knew personally. There was the beggar with no legs who spent most of their time in a sheltered nook near the Court of the Deities, whose name Jeya had never learned, and Whitebeard the singer, whose real name no one knew. Otherwise the assembly was an unremarkable mix of hungry-eyed children, hollow-cheeked adults and frail elders who could no longer work to support themselves and, presumably, had no family on whose aid they could rely.

The priest wound up their sermon, calling upon the sun to bless everyone present with its bounty and power, and that was the signal for the door to the right of them to open, and the temple's servants to come out with great cauldrons of stew on wheeled wooden bases. Conversation broke out again, and the assembled hungry waited patiently on the hard wooden benches lined up at bare wooden tables, with rough wooden bowls and wooden spoons arrayed in front of them. The Morlithian priesthood would feed all those who presented themselves, but they wouldn't tolerate disruption. Try to push in front of your neighbour or take their portion and you'd find yourself escorted outside by some of their larger initiates, and not welcome to return.

It wasn't until the cauldron had started down the bench at which shé and Galem were sitting that Jeya noticed the person doling out the stew, ladleful by ladleful, with an expression of ferocious concentration.

'Shit,' shé muttered to herself, then nudged Galem as surreptitiously as shé could manage and spoke without looking at thëm. 'Until we leave here, we don't know each other, and don't show yöur face too much to the person with the ladle.'

'Fine,' Galem murmured back. Thëy seemed to be getting used to thëir new self – although thëy'd been skittish as a spooked wind drake for the first couple of days without thëir binder, and using formal neutral pronouns – but thëy were still keeping a low profile in any case.

Jeya waited until the cauldron was three or four people away, then raised hér voice enough to be heard over the babble of voices and the scrape of wood on wood around them. 'Hey, Damau!'

Damau looked up and around at the sound of their name, and their face lit up in a smile when they caught sight of hér. 'Jeya! How are you?'

'I'm good,' Jeya replied, as casually as shé could. 'What are you doing here? I didn't know you worshipped the sun.' Damau had seen hér and Galem's first meeting, and had followed Galem back to thëir house. It was Damau who had shown Jeya where it was, by means of persuading Abbaz, the barge merchant, to let Jeya help Damau punt the barge for the day.

Of course, Damau had only been thinking of the house as somewhere Jeya might want to rob, since the occupant of it was clearly rich. That had been Jeya's original intention as well, at least until shé'd been honest with hérself and admitted that the real reason was because the stranger shé'd tried to pickpocket had been one of the most beautiful people shé'd ever seen. Regardless, Damau knew of a connection between Jeya and the rich house that had burned down a week ago, and had seen Galem before, albeit only once. Shé was going to have to play this very carefully.

'Oh, I don't,' Damau answered hér question cheerfully, pouring a brimming ladle of stew into someone else's bowl. 'But I ate here when I was poor, so now I can afford my own food I thought I'd come back to help them when I can.'

Jeya smiled back at them. On the face of it, Damau seemed slightly simple, perhaps a bit naive, and not always the best at reading others. On the other hand, Jeya had seen Damau play on that before to make others underestimate them, and shé'd resolved never to do the same. Shé and Damau were friends to an extent, but Galem's safety wasn't something shé wanted to entrust to anyone.

'That's good of you,' shé said, as Damau filled another person's bowl. It was hér turn next, and then Galem's, who had let thëir hair fall over thëir face between thëm and Damau. 'Are you still working for Abbaz, then?'

'Most days, yes,' Damau said happily. They dipped their ladle into the cauldron again, and Jeya brought hér bowl close, to minimise the loss of stew on to the floor. 'You haven't seen Lihambo, have you? They were due to be helping this morning, too.'

Jeya frowned. Lihambo was another of Ngaiyu's street rescues, like hér and Damau, an Adranian youth with a sunny smile and one milky eye. 'No, not for a few days.'

'Oh.' Damau looked thoughtful for a second, then their face brightened with intrigue. 'Jeya, did you hear about that house? You know the one?'

Jeya's throat tightened, but Damau might not be surprised at that reaction. After all, so far as Damau knew, shé'd gone to case the house for burglary. That wasn't something you wanted to have a conversation about in the middle of a large group of people, and in a temple, to boot. Jeya didn't worship the Morlithian god, but shé knew it wasn't supposed to look kindly on stealing, and shé saw no point in aggravating a god needlessly.

'I heard, yes,' shé said shortly, and gave Damau a meaningful look to suggest they drop the subject.

'Most of the family died in the fire,' Damau continued

obliviously, taking another step to keep pace with their companion who was wheeling the cauldron along. Galem held thëir bowl out, just as thëy'd be expected to, and Jeya could see thëir hands shaking. 'But they think one of them might have got out.'

Please don't give yöurself away. Please don't give yöurself away . . .

'They do?'

'Apparently,' Damau said, ladling stew into Galem's bowl, 'a reward's been offered for anyone who helps them get back to the Hierarchs.'

Jeya didn't have to fake the shocked expression that overtook her face. That wasn't news you heard every day, even if the person concerned wasn't sitting next to you. 'A reward? From the Hierarchs?'

'It might have been the Hierarchs,' Damau said uncertainly. 'It must have been, I guess. Maybe the family was really important?'

'Who told you this?' Jeya asked, very deliberately not looking at Galem, who wasn't spooning thëir stew eagerly into thëir mouth but was sitting motionless, with thëir back still to Damau.

'Er . . . Nabanda!' Damau said, with a nod. 'Yes, it was Nabanda.'

Jeya frowned. 'And where did Nabanda hear it from?'

Damau shrugged. 'They didn't say.'

Jeya forced a laugh. 'Well, if I see a rich person walking around looking lost, I'll be sure to claim that reward! And I'll give you some of it, for telling me,' shé added.

'That would be nice of you,' Damau said with a smile of their own. The cauldron-pusher nudged them, and they turned to ladle stew into the bowl of Galem's neighbour. 'I'll see you later, Jeya!'

'See you later, Damau,' Jeya said, as casually as shé could manage, and swivelled in hér seat to give hér bowl hér full attention. 'I'll have yours if you don't fancy it, friend,' shé added in a lower, deliberately casual voice, and Galem's spoon began to move. That was good: the last thing they wanted was for Galem to draw attention to thëmselves by not eating thëir food, in a place where everyone was hungry.

A reward, though, and from the Hierarchs to boot. That potentially solved some of the obstacles to getting Galem and the Hierarchs in the same place. It admittedly threw up some potential new ones, but Jeya was used to obstacles.

Spoon by spoon of fish stew, carefully not looking at the person on hér left, shé began to formulate a plan.

TILA

TILA WAS ALWAYS amused to hear how Narida's nobility thought criminals met. The Inner Council and, to be fair, popular tales and plays, had fanciful ideas of masked men meeting in smoke-filled backrooms or dank cellars, each with a hand on the hilt of a blade, ready to knife their rivals at a moment's notice.

The serving girl poured another cup of yeng for them all, moving around the table to the right as tradition dictated. It wasn't a Naridan tradition – yeng came from the lands beyond Kiburu ce Alaba, and the City of Islands' stranglehold on shipping and commerce was one of the reasons for its great wealth – but the appeal of a yeng house lay as much in the exotic experience as it did in the fragrant drink that such a place served. Even if it had been a Naridan tradition, it certainly wouldn't have been tradition for Tila to be served first, but no one in the room was going to object. Certainly not the serving girl: Tila owned the Three Storks yeng house, after all.

She sipped her drink, and inhaled its fragrant steam. She hoped it would help clear her head. She was tired, and this was not company in which she wanted to slip up. It would have been bad enough coming back to the life of either Tila or Livnya after being away for so long. Trying to catch up with the private affairs of both women was almost more than she could manage.

'How have we fared with the coastal patrols?' she asked, as soon as the serving girl had left the room again.

'Fair,' Captain Avrel said cautiously. 'Their ships rarely sail at night, and the shore parties can't hope to cover all the coastline. They still haven't realised we're using Stoney Bay to the north, and the tavern in Highwake Cross stores the goods until they get moved into the city.'

Tila nodded. The coastal patrols to prevent smuggling came under the jurisdiction of the Lord Admiral, and it was not a great surprise that Kaled Greenbrook was not up to the job. 'And the gatekeepers?'

'Still as amenable to bribes as they ever were,' Draff chuckled. His father ran the Blue Shark tavern on the docks and appeared as unconcerned by his advancing years as the weathered oak tree he resembled, which was just as well given Draff had greater ambitions than taking over from him. The Blue Shark was a small piece in the criminal empire of Idramar, merely a meeting place and safe house for certain deals, but Draff had thrown his support behind Livnya when she made her first moves in the power play that had eventually seen her overthrow the crime lord Yakov. She rewarded loyalty, and Draff now had a large role in the storage and dissemination of smuggled and illegal goods.

'It's good to know some things never change,' Tila said with a smile. It wasn't, of course, but that was why she had pursued this double life, after all. *Thefts and smuggling and knives in the dark*, her father had raged to her mother in front of her and Natan, many years ago. *How much is chance, and how much is arranged by those who wish to see us brought low? Your husband would kill to have a loyal eye on those streets, aye, he would!*

Tila *had* killed for it. She killed Yakov, for starters.

The meeting moved uneasily on, as each man around the table set out how he and his associates had conducted themselves while Livnya had been away. Each one wanted to show they had been active and enterprising, solving problems as they arose, but

Tila was listening more to what they did not say. They would dwell on their successes and hastily skate over their failures, and it was these gaps that she was looking for; the things they should have been proud of, but did not mention, or spoke of in vague platitudes. None of them knew how much she knew, but all suspected she might know more than they wanted her to, and that kept them on their toes.

All this, of course, only worked for so long as they either feared or respected her. That was the nature of power everywhere, as soon as it was no longer about the ability of one person to physically harm a second if they wished, and instead was about influencing others to do or threaten the harm. If all the men around the table joined forces, and all their associates remained loyal to them, Livnya would be overthrown. If each man thought that voicing such a plan to any of his peers would result in him being betrayed, he would keep such thoughts to himself.

Tila sometimes thought that running the underworld was like the shell games that took place on Idramar's streets, except the people searching for the correct shell were using knives. She just had to make sure the knives always landed somewhere else.

And so she pried. She asked awkward questions, as they sipped their gradually cooling yeng. She tried to make each of them appear weak at least once in front of their fellows, to remind them of her authority and dissuade them from placing too much trust in each other.

' . . . but, of course, we'll likely be losing some men shortly,' Kradan was saying. He was a plump man with a scar down one cheek and eyes of surprisingly clear hazel, and had a lot of influence over those elements of the city that could be persuaded to engage in targeted violence. Tila considered him rather attractive, and had a nasty suspicion he knew it. She had already resolved to double-check any decisions she made regarding him, or any advice he might give her.

'Why is that?' she asked.

'This recruitment to go westwards, courtesy of the Lord Marshal. The criers are saying that if more men don't come forward to volunteer on regular pay, they'll start conscripting on half pay.' Kraden grimaced. 'They're trying to frighten folk into joining now, but s'man wouldn't be surprised if they went through with it. If they do, the Keepers'll likely direct 'em towards some of ours, names what they think make trouble but can't pin anything on. They'll see sending our men west as a way of cleaning the city out.'

And it would not be a bad plan at that, from the Keepers' perspective, Tila conceded to herself. She drummed her fingers on the table a couple of times, mulling it over, but this gave her exactly the opportunity she'd been looking for. 'Very well, then we lean into it. Put the word out. A man of ours who puts himself forward for the Lord Marshal's recruitment will have his family taken care of while he's gone.'

'High lady?' Kradan asked, the surprise writ clear across his features. The rest of them seemed equally taken aback. Now Tila just had to make her explanation work.

'If it'll happen anyway, we make it happen on our terms,' she said bluntly. 'You've all heard the rumours of the Divine Nari's rebirth.'

'Aye,' Captain Avrel said, something akin to awe filling his face. 'To think we should live to see it!'

'These rumours have come before, and they've never been true,' Tila pointed out. 'But the country's gone into turmoil every time, and Idramar with it. This lady's studied her history, remember! Desperate times don't make for good business for the likes of us. Right now, the Keepers are lazy. If trouble truly starts, they'll be paying a lot more attention to what comes in and goes out of our gates, and there'll be curfews in the streets.'

'All the more reason to have our men here, surely?' Draff said.

'The Lord Marshal's looking for Nari reborn,' Tila told him. 'We should be too. If he's not who he's supposed to be – if he's just a fraud, milking the gullible country folk and stirring up trouble that might come back to us – then we've got our men in the right place to do something about it.'

Elkan, who ran most of Idramar's gambling dens, blinked at her. 'You mean . . . '

Tila nodded. 'This lady means exactly that.'

'What if,' Draff began shakily, then cleared his throat and continued. 'What if one of them . . . ?' He tailed off and gestured vaguely with one hand.

Tila raised her eyebrows. 'Kills the Divine Nari?'

Draff nodded mutely.

'Then this lady suspects he wasn't that divine to begin with,' Tila said dryly. 'Kradan, don't send anyone you suspect capable of killing a god.' She looked back at Draff. 'Satisfied?'

'High lady, would the troops not be doing this anyway?' Kradan asked. 'Executing imposters?'

'We might think that, and we might hope that, but who is to say what the Sun Palace is thinking?' Tila said darkly. 'The God-King is ill, but he has not yet succumbed. Perhaps some of the courtiers think a fake Nari will distract the people. Perhaps some of them even wish to use a fake Nari to assume power themselves, from behind the Sun Throne.'

The assembled men of standing in Idramar's underworld looked at each other. Tila had rarely found such piety as she had in the murky waters of crime. It was as though these men knew they were adrift, and thought that if they kept the light of Nari in their view everything would still be fine, and their misdeeds would count for naught.

'S'man can't see the Divine Princess allowing that,' Elkan said, more to the others than to her. 'They're all scared of her, from what s'man hears.'

Tila cursed inwardly. The last thing she needed was for any of the lowborn to associate Tila Narida with fearsome ruthlessness, just in case they began putting pieces together. It would surely be unthinkable for these men, common criminals of Idramar, to be sharing yeng with the Divine Princess of Narida . . . but they weren't fools.

'Lady Livnya has the right of it, though,' Kradan conceded. 'We can't trust the nobles to do what's right. Only interested in themselves, they are.'

Tila had a momentary vision of swapping the Inner Council with this group of thieves, extortionists, and murderers, and wondered whether her nation would be that much worse off. Alarmingly, it might fare slightly better.

'Well, s'man supposes that it's true what you say,' Draff admitted, looking at her. 'If the Divine One is reborn, His triumph is foretold. A knife from Idramar won't change that, and any imposters deserve to die.'

Avrel looked uncertain, but Elkan nodded. 'Agreed. S'man won't stand for those in the palace having final say over what happens out west. We put a few of our men in the ranks, to make sure things fall out as we want.'

Avrel sighed. 'S'man's not comfortable with it, but the captains won't set ourselves against it if you've all made your minds up. But may Nari Himself forgive you, if you're wrong.'

'This lady is certain that won't be necessary,' Tila said with a smile. She drained her cup, and looked out of the window at the lowering sun. 'Now, she thinks we've spent enough time here. Unless any of you have anything further you wish to discuss . . . ?'

TILA RETURNED TO her chambers to find a letter had been pushed under her door, with the seal of Greenbrook. She stared at it distrustfully for several long moments before she opened it, since neither councillor of that family, Kaled nor Adan, had ever communicated with her in such a manner before. In fact, both preferred to pretend she did not exist, unless they could not avoid her.

It appeared this had changed, which was why she was now

standing alone on the very top of the Sun Palace, on the roof of the Eight Winds Tower, and waiting for Kaled Greenbrook as the sunset turned the waters of the Idra red.

Kaled. It was interesting that it was the Lord Admiral who requested this meeting with her, not his cousin. It was also interesting that he wanted it to take place here, rather than somewhere in the depths of the palace. Eavesdropping would be virtually impossible, so what did Kaled Greenbrook fear was going to be overheard? He surely would not have chosen this location simply for the view, stunning although it was.

Unless he intended to woo her. Tila snorted with laughter at the thought. Lord Kaled's wife had died several years before, and he had yet to remarry, but Tila would have expected him to court even one of the scullery maids before her. If she intended to marry, she would have found a spouse by now. It was bad enough that she was supposed to obey her brother, let alone be beholden to anyone else. Besides which, she was living two lives already: she simply did not have the time for a husband.

Footsteps alerted her to the fact that she was no longer alone. She turned to see Kaled Greenbrook emerging from the stone staircase that spiralled down into the body of the tower.

'Divine Princess,' he greeted her with a respectful bow, but his face gave her pause. He looked far too satisfied with himself for a man who had just climbed a lot of stairs.

'Lord Admiral.' She made a slight bow in return. 'Given that you wished to speak to this princess alone, and at such short notice, she assumes that the matter is particularly urgent, sensitive or both?'

'This lord apologises for requesting your presence so quickly,' Kaled said, with a smile as smooth as oil. 'Were you otherwise occupied?'

Tila narrowed her eyes. 'If you simply wished to have a conversation about this princess's daily routine, she will be leaving now.' She took a step towards the stairs, but Kaled moved to block her way.

He did not touch her, but even impeding the path of the Divine Princess was a gross breach of etiquette. A servant who got in her way could legally be flogged, if Tila so chose. The penalty for a nobleman would be less severe, but it was still an unthinkable act.

'Explain yourself, Greenbrook,' Tila said, watching him closely. She was not going to try to dance around him. He had made a play, and it was a bold one. Whatever this was about, he clearly had a lot invested in it.

Now his smile turned nasty. 'Did you know what tremendous gossips sailors are, princess?'

Yes, actually. 'It is not in this princess's nature to consort with sailors,' Tila replied, as scornfully as she could manage.

'As Lord Admiral, this lord does,' Greenbrook said. 'And the rumour travelling around the docks is a ship called the *Light of Fortune* travelled to the City of Islands and back with a woman known as Livnya on board.'

Not for the first time, Tila was glad of her veil, which masked shock or surprise on her face, so long as she remembered to breathe and act normally.

'And who is that, and why is she important?' she demanded, but she could feel her entire body quivering like a taut bowstring.

'Livnya is rumoured to be a very prominent criminal,' Greenbrook said smugly. 'Her trip to and from the City of Islands also appears to correspond with your absence from court, shortly after the Inner Council agreed to move against the Splinter King. Call this lord suspicious if you will, but unlikely though a connection might seem, he is unable to avoid one.'

Shit.

Tila had underestimated Kaled: underestimated his intelligence, underestimated how involved he was in his role as Lord Admiral, and underestimated exactly how prepared he was to look at what was in front of him and draw a conclusion that most would immediately dismiss as impossible. Those were all potentially useful traits under normal circumstances, but as of this moment it made him a serious threat.

'And who have you told about these absurd fancies of yours?' Tila asked, keeping her voice light and mocking. 'Your cousin? This princess imagines he laughed you out of his halls.'

'Only this lord has pieced this information together,' Kaled said, 'and you can keep it that way, princess. This lord will not ask anything too demanding from you.'

Oh, Kaled. You fool.

'This princess does not see why she should listen to your baseless threats,' Tila snapped, placing her hands into her long sleeves. 'You would do what? Produce ale-soaked sailors before the Inner Council and claim their testimony outweighed that of the Divine Princess, and all reason?'

'How many allies on the Inner Council do you suppose you have, *Tila*?' Kaled sneered. 'With his Divine Majesty still bedridden? Should Whittingmoor or Wousewold have placed something like this before us, this lord would have supported them in a heartbeat in order to rid us of your feminine meddling. The Veiled Shadow holds little fear when we learn her spies are mere common cut-throats!'

'So you propose to bring this princess into disgrace in front of the Inner Council,' Tila said. 'Is that it?'

'This lord could do that tomorrow morning,' Kaled said. 'Then we could commence investigations into this "Livnya" and see what ties she has to you. This lord is certain they will emerge, once we start digging.' He shrugged. 'But of course, this is mere conjecture. The most sensible course of action would be to retain your status and standing, and avoid heaping further distress on your mother and brother by acquiescing to this lord's requests.'

Tila sighed, but she might as well play this farce out to its conclusion. 'And they would be?'

Kaled Greenbrook's face was swallowed by naked greed and

ambition. 'This lord intends to become Eastern Marshal.'

Tila couldn't help it. Despite the tension, despite her anger, she burst into laughter. 'Eastern Marshal! Would you also like this princess to make Godspire march to the capital, and bow before you?' She shook her head in wonder at his folly.

'The God-King could set Coldbeck aside,' Greenbrook said, his tone dangerous. He clearly had not appreciated her reaction.

'The God-King is sick,' Tila reminded him.

'All the easier to influence, then,' Greenbrook said. 'We know he obeys your wishes.'

'If this princess's brother obeyed her wishes, he would attend more Inner Council meetings!' Tila snapped. *Not to mention marry a woman, and father a child.*

Greenbrook snorted derisively. 'That is your concern. This lord suggests you find a way to do as he has asked, but do not think that you can stall him overlong. Removing you from your position of influence would be both satisfactory and beneficial in its own way, so if this lord feels that you are unduly delaying, he will settle for the lesser of two pleasures.'

Tila nodded. 'Then you leave this princess with no alternative.' She turned away from him and took two measured steps towards the far rampart of the tower.

'What are you—?'

Tila drew a knife from her concealed vambrace and turned with her arm raised. Greenbrook was still exactly where he had been, three paces away. The blade left her hand and buried itself in his throat before he even realised what was happening.

She had underestimated him, but he had underestimated her. Of the two of them, she was by far the more dangerous.

'Did you honestly think this princess would be able to maintain influence over *criminals* without being able to dispose of minor annoyances?' she sneered at him as he staggered backwards, reflexively pulled the knife out, then stared stupidly at the blood gouting out over his hands. 'The first lesson in intrigue is to never confront someone and admit you are the only person who knows the information you are holding over them.'

Greenbrook lurched towards her, scrabbling to draw his longblade with blood-slicked hands, making an ugly bubbling noise. Tila tutted and shook her head as she stepped backwards.

'Cease this foolishness, and die quietly.'

She drew another knife, and put that one into Greenwood's thigh. He let out a wet, agonised moan, and fell sideways as his leg suddenly refused to obey him. When he tried to push himself back up, his arms lacked the strength to do more than tremble.

Tila stepped past him and cocked her head to listen to the stairs over the pounding of her own heart, but there was no sudden thunder of boots; no indication that Greenwood had concealed allies waiting out of sight. He had truly thought that he could browbeat her into ensuring his rise to power, and, since she was a woman, had never considered she might be dangerous in her own right.

'Congratulations, Lord Greenbrook,' she muttered, turning back towards him. 'You are, without doubt, the perfect example of a Naridan man.'

Her mind was already whirling as she worked out her next move. She could not have let him go and pretended to play along with him for now. There was too much risk of him letting something slip, even by accident. She had to kill him here. The question was, how would she get away with it? This wasn't an Idramese back street. This was the Sun Palace, and Kaled Greenbrook was Lord Admiral, not some alley muscle who would only be missed by his own family.

She could reclaim her knives and leave. Just walk away, and pretend it had never happened. Let someone else find him, and raise the alarm about an assassin. The problem was that the spiral stair was the only way down from the roof of the Eight Winds Tower, and it was entirely possible she would encounter someone else before she could disappear. Then she would be undone. Even meeting a servant would be disastrous, and she could not just kill everyone she met.

No. She would have to attempt to pass this off as a desperate act of self-defence, and trust that everyone else would have as inaccurate an idea of her abilities and character as Kaled Greenwood.

The life was draining from him now. Tila approached him cautiously and drew his shortblade from his belt, then slashed it across his throat. He jerked, and she knelt down to bloody her hands, which she then grimly wiped on the front of her dress. Had she been close enough to snatch the shortblade from him and inflict these wounds, she wouldn't have remained clean. She had to make this look realistic.

What of her knives? She couldn't leave them here, but nor could she throw them off the roof to dispose of them. The Eight Winds Tower was high enough that nowhere else on the palace roofs would easily be able to see what had occurred up here, but something being thrown off might definitely draw attention if anyone else happened to be looking.

She would have to take another considered risk. She retrieved her knives, wiped them off on Greenbrook's robes as close to the existing blood stains as was possible, then sheathed them in her vambrace. The notion of anyone searching the Divine Princess's person was laughable, and that would be enough to see her clear until she could get back to her chambers, or at least find some less incriminating place to dispose of them.

She plunged Greenbrook's shortblade into his now unresponsive leg to occlude the wound her knife had caused, just in case anyone should compare it. Then she took a deep breath, and ran for the stairs with the bloody blade still clutched in her hand.

'Help! Help!' she wailed, as she began to clatter downwards.

ZHANNA

They were into the mountains now, and Zhanna felt more at home than she had in a long time, and yet simultaneously adrift in an unfamiliar world.

As they climbed higher, following the Blackcreek River as it flowed downhill, the trees had changed. The strange, bare-branched ones that had been starting to put out green buds had thinned, and the dark boughs of the conifers she knew from Tjakorsha began to dominate once more. Every now and then, she could almost convince herself she was back in her homeland, walking through a piece of woodland she had never seen before.

Then, however, she would catch a glimpse through the trees of the mountains that rose up on either side of the valley; not just the one mighty summit of Kainkoruuk, but ridge after ridge. Every time they walked far enough to see around one peak, there was another beyond it. In its own way, it was as awe-inspiring as her first sight of a dragon.

The air was different, too. Walking was fine, but when the river had tumbled over a sill of rock in a waterfall twice Zhanna's height they needed to scramble up a steep slope of boulders and tree roots, and that had strangely left her gasping for breath.

'Lowlanders,' Danid of Ironhead chuckled to Amonhuhe, while Zhanna stood and wheezed. Danid was a hunter, sent with them by Sar Benarin, and he spent much of his time in the hills and valleys above Ironhead. Zhanna was glad he was with them, because while she thought it was unlikely Amonhuhe would have forgotten the way back to her tribe's lands, it sounded like a good idea to have someone who'd been this way at some point since Zhanna herself had been born. Danid wasn't of the Smoking Valley tribe himself, but his wife's father was, and Danid wore a string of carved beads around his left wrist that seemed to signify his marriage.

'We are still in the lowlands,' Amonhuhe told him blandly, pushing on ahead, and Zhanna smirked at the look of chagrin that crossed Danid's face. Then she turned around and reached out a hand to Ravel, hauling him up the last part of the climb.

'S'man could have made it on his own,' Ravel muttered, dusting off his hands. He seemed to have decided that he was definitely an adult man now that he had the stripe of the Blooded tattooed down his forehead, and was using that identifier at every opportunity. He was Naridan, the son of Achin the fisherman and Inba the alewife, and Zhanna knew that both of them had disapproved of him marking himself like a Tjakorshi. His sisters, on the other hand, had simply mocked him for it in the manner of siblings everywhere.

'Of course,' Zhanna replied, smiling at him. Ravel took a moment to try to work out if she was joking with him – or possibly just to get his breath back – then headed off after Amonhuhe.

Other than Amonhuhe and Danid, the Naridans didn't seem to be enjoying the journey that much. They were used to walls around them and roofs over their heads, with a fire pit nearby to keep them warm at night. Zhanna had to admit that the roots and rocks on the ground were less than comfortable, but she and the other Brown Eagles had lasted the long voyage from Kainkoruuk to Black Keep with no warmth other than that provided by the sun, or other warm bodies inside the deckhouse. The warmth of their small cookfire, and the food that came from it, was a luxury compared to weeks of being chilled to the bone with stale sailing rations supplemented by raw fish.

The trees eventually began to thin out, and they collected sticks for firewood from the ground before they continued on. As the sun began to sink towards the peaks in the west, Zhanna's party were walking through brown grass that would have been knee-high had it not clearly been flattened by now-melted snow, and through which the green shoots of spring were starting to show. The trees still clung to the edges of the valley, but the central part through which the river ran was open ground, stretching away on either side with only the occasional hillock or large boulder to break it up.

'Look,' Danid said, pointing away to the left, across the Blackcreek. Zhanna followed his gesture and narrowed her eyes, to make out a group of light brown lumps some way in the distance.

'What are they?' Tatiosh asked. Zhanna realised that a couple of them were moving, and she could just make out the suggestion of head and tail.

'Spinebacks,' Danid replied. 'They'll be moving up into the mountains to feed for the summer. Good eating on them.'

'Are you going to catch one?' Avisha asked eagerly, but Danid just snorted.

'S'man won't be trying to cross the river here, it's too fast and too deep. Besides,' he added, 'there's already a hunt under way.' He pointed again, at a slightly different angle. Zhanna couldn't see what he was referring to for several long moments, and was about to open her mouth to ask when something shifted in her perception and she realised that what she'd taken for a rock had moved as well, keeping low in the grass.

'Is that . . . ?' she asked, reaching up one hand to scratch at Talon's neck. The little dragon was perched on her shoulder, and watching attentively.

'Rattletails, aye,' Danid said, glancing at her passenger. Her pet dragons had been the source of considerable consternation and discussion in Ironhead – as had her sword, come to that – but the townsfolk had stopped short of decrying her as a witch. She was the subject of many snatched looks and much whispering, but so were the rest of the Tjakorshi. In Ironhead, it seemed, they were far enough from the sea to not have fought the Tjakorshi themselves, and, thanks to Amonhuhe's kin, were familiar enough with the notion of different peoples with different languages living together. In Ironhead, the Tjakorshi were just different, not Raiders to be treated as enemies.

More rocks moved, and Zhanna realised there was a whole pack of them: half a dozen at least. 'In Black Keep, there a man was,' she said to Danid. 'He called huntmaster, used rattletails.'

'Aye, you can use them as hunting beasts,' Danid said. 'If you're fierce enough to drive them from the prey once they've brought it down, that is, and fast enough to keep up with them. If you've got a longbrow or a frillneck to ride, that might do it. S'man wouldn't use them himself; he'd be more likely to end up as their meal.' He cast another look at Talon. 'Yours seem uncommon tame, mind, even for that small.'

Zhanna grinned, pleased with the compliment, and was about to ask something else when the adult rattletails in the distance sprang into action.

She couldn't tell if there was a signal – she was too far away to hear a call, let alone the rattle that gave them their name – but the entire pack went from slinking almost imperceptibly forwards to running full pelt within the space of a couple of heartbeats. The spinebacks took a few moments more to realise the danger, but then they wheeled and began to run, their motion strangely juddering and jerky compared to the fluid bounds of the predators behind them, but eating up the ground nonetheless. Zhanna watched transfixed as the pursuit sped away, until the shapes dwindled and became impossible to make out against the grass, the rocks and the dark line of conifers hugging the valley's far edge.

'We'll have a fire tonight, for sure,' Danid said, as he started walking again. 'Rattletails don't normally trouble a party of men, but if they haven't made a kill and they're still hungry there's always the chance they'll try their luck.'

ZHANNA HAD FALLEN asleep after a meal of strips of dried mutton and fish, some of the bread and cheese they'd got in Ironhead, and a small slab of the strange cake Black Keep made from sticky, sugar-laden tree sap and goat's milk. She'd soaked two strips of her own mutton jerky in water to soften them a little and given them to her dragons, who proceeded to tear at them with every sign of enjoyment. They had already begun chasing insects as they walked along with her. Soon, Zhanna hoped, they might start hunting for themselves.

She woke again with a start, as something scratched at her face.

'What . . . ?' she muttered, brushing a hand up and encountering a small body that bounced away. She opened her eyes and saw Thorn, his feathers dully lit by the remaining flames of the fire, for it was still dark. The little dragon was staring around, sharp jerks of his head taking in all angles.

'What are your beasts doing?' Menaken said, curiously. Daimon's guard was clearly on this watch, since he was sitting up and warming his hands.

'I don't know,' Zhanna admitted, then realised that was Tjakorshi instead of Naridan. She was trawling through her sleep-addled brain to find the correct words when a rattling erupted from behind her.

She rolled over, her hand clawing for either her blackstone axe or her longblade, whichever she could grab first, but instead of a full-sized predator bounding out of the darkness it was only Talon, shaking his little tail a foot from her head. She scowled at him, but then Thorn echoed him, and another warning rattle went up into the night.

'They've scented something,' Menaken said, rising to his feet and picking up his spear from off the ground. He was trying to sound calm, Zhanna could tell, but his hands were shaking. Menaken was a town dweller, with little idea of what lived in the mountains, and he knew it.

'Up!' Zhanna shouted in Tjakorshi. 'Up!' she repeated in Naridan, slipping her forearm through the loops of her alder roundshield. Her blackstone axe was next to it, and she snatched that off the ground as well. The steel of her longblade was more durable, and near as sharp, but she'd been using the axe for longer, and it had more weight to it. Against an adult rattletail, that might come in handy.

The rest of the sleepers were coming alive, calling out questions as they struggled out from under their blankets and grabbed their weapons. Zhanna faced outwards, blinking furiously and trying to get the after-image of the fire out of her vision. She could barely see a thing—

The rattling stopped. She looked around, and saw both Thorn and Talon streaking away from her, past the fire and out into the darkness.

'No!' Zhanna shouted after them. 'Come! Come!'

Menaken screamed.

There was a sound like the night ripping in half, and a nightmare landed in a stinking gust of wind.

It was huge, so huge that it took Zhanna a moment to properly register it. She'd thought Bastion, the old thane of Black Keep's mount that had been killed by Rikkut Fireheart, had been big, but this dragon was something else entirely. It stood on four limbs, but whereas Bastion's back had been the height of Saana's head, this creature's neck reared up as tall as the mast of a tsek, the fishing vessels her clan used. Its front two limbs were massive wings, folded in on themselves to support it, but as it thundered forwards it became immediately clear that it could move at least as fast as Zhanna could herself.

'Kingdrake!' Danid yelled in terror. 'Scatter!'

Scatter? Zhanna's feet wouldn't move. The monstrous creature bore down on her, and then a pointed beak as long as she was tall flashed towards her.

She managed to get her shield up, but the force of the impact sent her sprawling on to the grass and knocked the wind from her. She tried to raise her shield, her left arm screaming at her, but the dragon's beak clamped down on it and wrenched it from her grasp, then sent it sailing away into the night as the monster realised it wasn't food.

'Move!' a voice shouted, and Zhanna desperately rolled to one side. The beak lashed out again, snapping at the ground where she had just been, and she tried to swipe at it with her axe but was too slow; it had already withdrawn, ready for its next strike.

A bowstring thrummed, and the kingdrake hissed and jerked in pain as an arrow buried itself into its pale breast feathers. Zhanna scrambled back to her feet and retreated hastily, trying to get out of its range. Another bowstring sounded, and a second arrow struck home. Zhanna snatched a glance sideways and saw Amonhuhe on the far side of the fire, drawing back her bow for a second shot while Danid, next to her, plucked another arrow from his quiver.

Zhanna looked back at the kingdrake, and saw what was about to happen a moment too late.

'Ingor, no!' she yelled, but Ingorzhak Avljaszhin was already too close. The newly Blooded Brown Eagle warrior, one of Zhanna's crew, charged in to land a blow with his blackstone axe on the kingdrake's left wing.

It was a preposterous act, like a small brown shore shark trying to make a meal of a full-grown krayk. The strike hit home, but the kingdrake's resulting hiss of pain was accompanied by a sweep of its wing that knocked Ingorzhak sprawling with a scream. Then the beast's beak snapped down, and this time it found a leg instead of a shield.

Amonhuhe's bow sang once more, but the arrow sailed over the kingdrake's shoulders as it hoisted Ingorzhak up, then whiplashed its neck to pummel him against the ground with bone-breaking force. His weapons dropped from his hands, and the kingdrake tossed him up again, almost delicately, to catch his limp body and begin to swallow him headfirst.

'Ingor!' Zhanna screamed. 'No!' She tried to charge the monster, blind rage and horror overwhelming any sense she still had, but Longjaw loomed up out of the night on her right and grabbed her, pinning her in place. She heard Tamadh wailing as his brother was eaten in front of him, but Tatiosh and Sakka Bridastutar had a hold of him, too.

Danid loosed again, and the arrow struck the kingdrake just as Ingorzhak's feet disappeared out of sight down its throat. It lurched into motion, lumbering away from the light of the fire even as the body of Zhanna's crew member passed down its neck as an obscene bulge, then leaped into the air and spread its wings with a noise like a sail snapping taut with a sudden gust of wind. Zhanna heard the first few beats of its wings as it powered away into the darkness, then everything went quiet once more, other than Tamadh's grief-stricken wailing.

'Shit!' Danid barked. He kicked at the remnants of the fire in rage and frustration, sending up a spray of sparks. 'When s'man tells you to scatter, you *scatter*, do you understand him? You don't stand around, or try to kill a Nari-damned kingdrake by yourself!'

'You never told us there were things like that up here!' Ravel yelled back, his eyes wide and white with fear.

'There shouldn't be,' Amonhuhe cut in, before Danid could reply. 'Not here, not now. S'woman's never heard of a kingdrake taking prey from around a fire at night before.' She suddenly sounded old, and it might have just been the low light of the fire highlighting the lines on her face, but Zhanna thought that she looked it, as well.

'It's not the first thing s'man's heard of, where dragons are bolder than they were,' Danid said darkly. 'The rumours say the Divine One's been born again, and may s'man be forgiven for saying it, but if He could see Himself to taking His throne back as quick as may be, that would be best for us all. We don't need the beasts getting worse than they are, but that's what the prophecies say, supposedly.' He turned towards where Tamadh was weeping. 'For the love of Nari, will someone shut the boy up?!'

'That was his brother!' Zhanna yelled, breaking free of Longjaw. It felt good to shout at someone. It was a good job Tsennan couldn't understand Danid, or he'd likely have swung for him.

'Brother or not, if he keeps wailing like that he'll have every rattletail within a league down on us!' Danid snarled at her. 'They come for the sound of animals in pain, girl, and he doesn't sound too far different!' The hunter grabbed his pack, and began to shove his belongings into it. 'We move! There's no telling if that beast will be back, or others like it! We move away from the fire, and tomorrow night we go to the valley's edge and camp in the trees. The kingdrakes can't follow us in there, at least.'

'But it dark is,' Zhanna argued. 'What if we fall, hurt leg?'

'Then walk carefully,' Danid snapped. 'Unless you want to see an adult rattletail up close.'

SAANA

BEING A LADY of Black Keep was something Saana was struggling to get used to.

For one thing, although she was the only person the Naridans viewed as a lady within Black Keep, she was not *the* lady of Black Keep. That title would be reserved for the wife of the thane. Since Darel seemed very unlikely to take a wife – Saana still wasn't fully comfortable with the Naridan notions of partnering men with men and women with women, but she'd given her word that she and her clan would raise no objection to it, and by the Dark Father she was going to hold to her word – it seemed there would be no other lady of Black Keep, and yet it still wouldn't be her. It wasn't that she *wanted* to be the lady of Black Keep, since the title and concept both seemed ridiculous when she was already a chief, but it surely didn't make sense.

There was also the strange Naridan habit of passing on rank to their children. Darel, again, seemed unlikely to have children, although he could adopt one. If he did not, then should he die before Daimon – and Saana dearly hoped that both of those days were a long way off – then Daimon would become thane. At that point Saana *would* become the lady of Black Keep, and should she have no other children – which she certainly intended not to – then Zhanna, *Zhanna*, would become heir to Black Keep . . . but not heir to being the chief of the Brown Eagle clan.

They were going to have to do something about that. Saana didn't intend to die for some time, but it simply wouldn't work for Blackcreek to have one chief for Naridans and one chief for Tjakorshi, when those chiefs weren't part of the same family by marriage. However, she couldn't see her clan agreeing to accept the rule of someone simply on the basis of who their parents had been, and nor could she see the Naridans unbending far enough to accept their thane being chosen by a council of witches. The Naridans *hated* witches, even if their definition was rather different to the Tjakorshi one.

All that besides, the main thing Saana was struggling with was what she was meant to *do*. She'd given up the empty house she'd taken for her own in order to live with Daimon in the castle, and her sheep, goats and chickens had been added to the Blackcreek animals, but she didn't care for them any longer; there was a servant for that. She had gone to work the ground around her old house, for she had already planted seed, only to find it being tended to by one of the Naridans, apparently on her behalf. Servants provided her meals. She still went out into the town and walked among the people – well, limped among them, given the wound she'd taken from Rikkut Fireheart – trying to do the things a chief should do, but it was almost like she was looking for problems in order to feel useful.

She felt she could understand a little of how it had been for Zhanna, living as a hostage in the stronghouse when tensions between Black Keep and Brown Eagle had still been high. Ironically enough, Saana had ended up doing roughly the same thing in order to keep busy as her daughter had.

Daimon came at her, his wooden practice blade whirling and feinting. They were showy moves, intended to distract the eye and mask her husband's true intentions. Saana knew she was no great warrior, but she had sparred against the best in her clan, and gained a certain intuition for the link between footwork and bladework. She backed and circled, keeping her shield up and waiting for the moment when the pattern of his steps changed.

There. Daimon stepped in, looking to send his blade up and over her shield, down towards her neck, where she still had a bruise from his strike two days before. This time Saana stepped into him behind her shield, putting her weight on to her good leg: his stab overshot her and flashed down harmlessly behind her back, and her shield barge knocked him staggering backwards. She took a swipe at his ribs with her axe – shaped like a blackstone axe, but without the viciously sharp dark, glossy teeth – and he narrowly twisted aside from it, then stepped hurriedly away from her backswing and flowed back into his ready stance, his sword in both hands and his weight perfectly balanced, just out of her reach.

Saana grunted irritably. Daimon had practised fighting against his father and brother, one-on-one duels with room to move. It had served him well enough, but when Tjakorshi warbands met on open ground, it was shield wall against shield wall, where you had no space to duck backwards because there was already someone behind you. Similarly, she would have liked to see him pull his fancy moves on the deck of a yolgu in the grip of the ocean's swell, as it was boarded by enemies.

On the other hand, no fight was won by pondering how much better you would do under different circumstances. She flexed her fingers on the handle of her axe and prepared to make the first move, rather than waiting for him.

A horn rang out: not the throbbing shell horn of her people, but the brassy call of Narida. Daimon turned his head, frowning.

Saana lunged forwards and swung her axe into the meat of his left thigh, then clattered him to the ground with her shield.

'Ow!' her husband bellowed, clutching his leg and glowering at her. 'What in—'

'You did not say to stop,' Saana chided him.

'There was a horn!' Daimon protested.

'And since your wife was not distracted by it, and so killed her enemy, she can now go and see what it means,' Saana said. She shifted her axe to her shield hand and offered her empty palm to him. Daimon's expression did not improve much, but he took her grip and allowed himself to be pulled to his feet.

'You hardly killed—' He winced as soon as he put weight on his leg, and staggered sideways. 'Nari's teeth!'

'If this had been blackstone, you might not still have a leg,' Saana told him. 'If you did, you would be bleeding badly. You would certainly not be getting up to continue!'

'Fine,' Daimon muttered. 'But if whoever this is wants a fight, your husband will expect you to deal with them, now he only has one leg.'

Saana laughed. 'A fair exchange.' Then she sobered. 'You do not think that is likely, do you?'

'Your husband cannot hear screaming,' Daimon said bluntly, 'so we can hope not. Still, anything is possible.' He discarded his practice sword and took up the belt holding his longblade and shortblade, which he wrapped around his waist with a quick, practised motion. He then glanced over his shoulder and grimaced at the wet, dirty stain on the back of his robes. 'Your husband is hardly in a fit condition to receive visitors.'

'Naridans are strange,' Saana said, laying down her own weapons to pick up her fur jacket. It had been discarded for their sparring, and she weighed it in her hands, trying to decide whether she would need it now. She decided against it: spring had arrived in Black Keep, and the day was only continuing to warm. 'Why should you be ashamed to have been sparring?'

'Getting dirty is for the lowborn,' Daimon replied absently.

Saana frowned. 'You are expected to fight without getting dirty?'

'In an ideal world,' Daimon said, nodding. 'Although the blood of your husband's enemies would be acceptable, so long as the robes were not worn for any longer than they had to be.' He finished tightening his belt. 'Come, let us go and see who has arrived.'

Saana eyed his swords. 'Should your wife bring her weapons?'

Daimon hesitated. 'Would you normally, as a chief?'

'Not unless your wife distrusted whoever had arrived, and did not mind them knowing that.' She waved a hand at his belt. 'It is strange to her, that you should wear these at all times.'

'According to the Code of Honour, a sar should wear his blades to focus his mind on the harm he can do, and the dangers of harsh words and swift actions,' Daimon said.

'Do you find that to be true?' Saana asked him.

Daimon was quiet for a few moments. 'When your husband considers the various tales and songs he has heard, he must admit that is not always the outcome.'

The sound of running footsteps on gravel made them both look around, and Ita the guard appeared. He came to a halt in front of them, and bowed somewhat hastily.

'We heard the horn,' Daimon said. 'What news?'

'Lord, lady,' Ita said, straightening. He looked uncomfortable, Saana thought, and not just from running. 'It's a party from Darkspur.'

'Darkspur?' Daimon repeated, perplexed. He looked at Saana, and she saw uncertainty there. 'He can barely have got home before coming back again. What does he want?'

'Begging your pardon, lord, but it's not the thane,' Ita said. 'There are sars there, it's true, but . . . Well, it's the Lady Yarmina.'

Saana looked from him to Daimon, waiting for someone to explain. 'Who is that?'

'Lady Yarmina is the thane's daughter,' Daimon said. His expression had fallen back into the studious blankness she still struggled to read, even after having known him for weeks, and spending much of that time in close proximity. 'She is . . . she *was . . .* '

'Yes?' Saana prompted.

Daimon glanced at Ita, then sighed. 'It is no great secret. Several years ago, Thane Odem suggested – quite strongly – to your husband's father that when she came of age the Lady Yarmina should become either your husband's wife, or Darel's.'

Saana stared at him in shock. An uneasy sensation was creeping over her, as when you were cleaning your catch on the deck of your fishing tsek and realised that what you'd taken for the shadows of waves in the water around you were sharks.

'Your wife thought that your father and Thane Odem had a great disagreement,' she managed.

'They did,' Daimon agreed. 'Because Lord Asrel refused.' He took a deep breath, then exhaled. 'How many are with her, Ita?'

'Four sars, lord, and perhaps twenty men-at-arms.'

Daimon set his jaw, and looked at Saana.

'Bring your axe.'

JEYA

THEY'D GOT UP well before the sun, and Jeya had prayed especially long and hard to Jakahama of the Crossing, the god shé favoured the most out of all the Hundred. Shé would normally have left an offering at the god's shrine, but there was no time for that: it was open court day, which meant petitioners could present themselves directly to whichever of the Hierarchs were holding court, and *that* meant the longest lines that East Harbour ever saw. Even having risen so early, and having hurried through the shadowy, grey-drenched streets to the New Palace, Jeya and Galem had still been many, many bodies back from the gold-inlaid doors that would open come sunrise.

Sunrise had come, the first petitioners had been granted entry, and the line had shuffled forwards, painfully slowly.

'Í still think we should try at the Feast of Ash,' Galem muttered from beside hér. 'My family would be there.'

'That's two weeks away,' Jeya told thëm firmly. 'If this doesn't work, we can always try at the festival. But yöu might actually get to speak to a Hierarch face-to-face like this: how likely do yöu think that is, on a festival day?' She chuckled to hérself. 'Do yöu know, Í once had a plan to steal one of the fancy masks yöu wore?'

Galem gaped at hér, stunned. 'Í . . . what . . . *why?*'

143

It was Jeya's turned to be stunned. 'What do yöu mean, "why"? It was silver, with jewels on it! Ï'd have been rich!'

'Yóu'd have been dead,' Galem muttered. Ahead of them, the line moved up a few paces as the next group of petitioners were admitted, and they shuffled up accordingly. 'The guards would have got yóu before yóu got close to any of us.'

'Well, yes,' Jeya admitted. 'That was one of the reasons Í decided against it.'

It might have been a risk, talking like this in public, but they were keeping their voices so low that no one could have overheard without being so close it was obvious; and besides, both of them were nervous. For Jeya, this was the first time shé'd ever tried to approach a Hierarch directly, and that would have been nerve-wracking enough even without standing next to the exiled heir of Narida. For Galem, it was the first time thëy would have come before a Hierarch with thëir identity in doubt.

'How are yöu doing?' Jeya asked. Galem had bound thëir chest once more, to bring thëir appearance back into line with what the Hierarchs would expect, and thëy would be using high masculine pronouns in front of anyone else. Jeya felt that was a shame, but it was probably necessary under the circumstances, and it had been Galem's suggestion.

'Oh, yóu know,' Galem said, with a rueful chuckle. 'It's familiar, at any rate. It's not më, but Ï'm more used to not being më than Ï am being më, if that makes sense.'

Jeya smiled, but the other problem was that it negated a large part of Galem's disguise. They would just have to hope that the line gave them enough concealment, if hostile eyes happened to be nearby.

The line crawled on, as the sun rose higher into the sky. The heat began to creep up again, too, for the wet season was well and truly under way now, and the sun was growing ever more ferocious. Storm clouds would probably gather by the afternoon to drench the assembled petitioners, while lightning tore the sky apart above them. However, even with how slowly the line was moving, Jeya hoped they would have been seen by then.

The line crawled on. A hawker moved down it, attempting sell pickled fish, but few took them up on the offer. The rich and influential had other means of accessing the justice they desired: the people queueing around Jeya were largely like hér, with little coin to spare simply to quell a pang of morning hunger.

The line crawled on, and now the main entrance of the New Palace was in plain sight, a dark portal leading to the shade within. The Old Palace had been surrounded by its own grounds, a buffer between the monarchs and the people over whom they ruled, and which perhaps had insulated them from the reality of life in East Harbour, and in Grand Mahewa as a whole. The New Palace had been intended to be accessible, and so there were no grounds, no gardens, no long drives winding through stands of trees. It sat not far from the Court of the Deities, bordered on all sides by the streets of the capital, and in it the Hierarchs conducted the business not only of Grand Mahewa, but the entire City of Islands.

Galem was getting more and more tense, the closer they got to the entrance. Jeya had taken thëir hand, but thëy weren't even gripping hér hard: it was as though thëy hadn't even registered the contact.

'Be calm,' Jeya murmured. 'We'll be inside soon.'

'And what if this doesn't work?' Galem whispered back.

Jeya shrugged. 'We'll think of something else.'

'Something else?'

'Most of my life has consisted of having to think of something else,' Jeya assured thëm. 'Í'm used to it.'

Now they were at the doors, standing on the wide stone steps leading up to them, and Galem kept the straw hat shé'd procured for thëm low over thëir eyes. It reminded Jeya of the first time shé'd laid eyes on thëm, which was a pleasant memory, but it was mainly so there was less chance of thëm being recognised until thëy wanted to be. Still the line snaked ahead into the Petitioner's Hall, where palace servants would come and conduct members of the public to the Hierarchs.

The line moved, and Jeya stepped over the threshold into the building of hér rulers for the first time.

As they moved forwards, she gasped in awe. The building around them was stone, but this place had clearly been intended to look much more like a traditional Mahewan house: certainly far more so than the interior of the Old Palace, although admittedly that had been looted.

The walls were wooden panelling, which had to have been attached to the stone somehow, and delicately carved in a manner similar to the walls of the temple at the northern end of the Court of the Deities. However, Jeya saw other events interspersed with scenes of religious, such as what looked like a whole series of panels dedicated to the overthrowing of the monarchs. The pillars holding up the arched roof were probably stone, but were wrapped in bright, gauzy cloth of orange and green that caught the light coming in through the windows and almost glowed, like the sun rising over the forest. The overall effect was of something that felt far more Alaban than the stark lines of, say, the Morlithian temple, but still far grander than any normal person's home, should they even have one.

Jeya got the distinct impression it was trying to intimidate hér while pretending to be familiar and welcoming. Shé glowered at it accordingly.

A small gaggle of people appeared, probably a family, being ushered through the room by someone in the white-trimmed grey clothes of a New Palace servant. The family moved on towards the main door, their query or claim clearly resolved – at least in the eyes of the Palace – and the servant jerked their head at the person directly in front of Jeya.

'You. Come.'

The person started forwards, following the servant as they were led off to an antechamber, and Jeya and Galem shuffled forwards another couple of steps. Behind them, the line kept pace, keeping the Petitioner's Chamber constantly full of people awaiting their turn for justice.

Jeya, as was hér habit, was already noting the possible exits – not many – and the guards present – quite a few, although not the most alert-looking. Shé was hardly going to steal anything here, but shé'd had too many unpleasant, unexpected run-ins with members of the Watch to be particularly comfortable around armed people in uniform.

Another servant materialised in front of hér, and looked at the pair of them. 'You two. You are together?'

Jeya nodded, and the servant jerked their head. 'Come, then.' They eyed Galem briefly, and frowned. 'And take your hat off, you're inside now.'

Galem reluctantly removed thëir hat, but no one appeared to look twice at thëm. Jeya couldn't understand it: if shé was seeing Galem for the first time, shé'd look more than twice. Or possibly just once, but for a really long time.

They followed the servant across the wooden floor, its shining polish beginning to suffer under the back-and-forth tread of muddy feet, down a short corridor, and to the doors of an antechamber. These were closed, and the servant knocked three times with the air of a ritual before opening them without waiting for any response.

'The Hierarch Chamuru,' the servant announced, somehow sounding both bored and respectful at the same time. They stood aside, and Jeya and Galem stepped inside.

This room was far smaller, although it was still nearly the size of Ngaiyu's place where Jeya often slept, on a floor that could host at least twenty sleepers, with Ngaiyu's rocking chair in the corner and thëir cook fire in the middle. The light here came not from the sun, but from candles that burned with the sweet smell of beeswax, and the walls were white with a painted mural of twisting creepers. In front of them was another servant sitting behind a simple wooden desk – a scribe, judging by their pen and the sheets of paper in front of them – flanked by two more guards. Sitting beyond and above them all, behind a far more ornate desk on a raised platform, was Hierarch Chamuru.

They weren't in full festival finery, which was the only time Jeya normally saw the Hierarchs, but this was also far nearer than she'd ever been to one of them before, and at this distance the quality of their clothing was evident. Their maijhi and karung were of the same orange and green as the cloth in the Petitioner's Hall, and made them stand out starkly against both the white wall behind them and the grey of the servants. They were old; their hair contained more grey than any other colour, their brow was furrowed, and their smile – a study in empty politeness – drew a series of stark lines across their face. Nonetheless, they wore an aura of comfortable and careless authority, enhanced by the rings on their fingers and the headpiece of sparkling metal in which rested what looked like tiny sapphires. Clearly, serving the people of Kiburu ce Alaba was profitable.

'What brings you before Hierarch Chamuru?' the scribe asked. They didn't look up from their paper, and they sounded just as bored as the servant who had ushered Jeya and Galem in.

Galem cleared thëir throat. 'Two weeks—'

'Kneel before you address the Hierarch!' the door servant snapped, outraged, and Jeya tugged on Galem's sleeve. They both sank to one knee, Galem somewhat more hesitantly. Jeya realised thëy'd probably never knelt before someone before, which was a concept shé found hard to wrap hér head around. What must it be like, to go through your life without the fear of someone else taking everything from you if you displeased them?

Shé waited for a heartbeat or two, which was generally considered long enough, then nudged Galem again and they both rose back to their feet. Jeya looked up at Chamuru. The Hierarch had folded their fingers together and was looking at them slightly more intently now.

'Proceed,' Chamuru invited.

'My home was attacked,' Galem said, and paused. Chamuru's lips pursed slightly.

'That is most regretful. Are you aware of the culprits?'

'Ì am not,' Galem replied. Jeya could hear the slight catch in thëir voice as thëy shifted back into the high masculine tone for the first time in days. 'But Ì have heard that the Hierarchs are seeking the survivor.'

Chamuru frowned. 'I am not aware of any such thing.' They looked over the front of their desk, down at their scribe. 'Ongowe, have you—?'

They paused, then looked back up at Galem, and now their eyes were as hard as the stones in their headpiece. Jeya's heart began to speed up. Shé didn't know if Galem would recognise it, but shé knew the look of a rich person who'd just heard something they didn't like, and was wondering how to deal with it.

'Which house was this?' Chamuru asked carefully. Jeya might as well not have existed, so fixed was their gaze on Galem.

'It was on Second Level,' Galem said carefully, watching the Hierarch's face. Thëy and Jeya had planned how Galem would make thëir identity known to a Hierarch without shouting it out to any scribes, servants, or guards who might be in the vicinity. That might be the cause of Chamuru's unease: wondering how to determine if what they thought was being said was in fact being said, before anyone else realised it.

Or then again . . .

Chamuru's eyes narrowed. 'The fire?'

Galem nodded. 'Yes. My family—'

'There were no survivors of that fire,' Chamuru cut thëm off. 'Guards—'

They were too slow. Jeya had already seen their eyes flicker away, and you didn't survive on the streets without picking up when a rich person was going to shout for the guards before they even knew it themselves.

'Run!' shé shouted, grabbing Galem's hand and turning for the

149

doors. The hows and whys of Chamuru's reaction could wait: the most important thing was to get clear. At least the guards were placed between petitioners and the Hierarch, rather than between them and the door.

The servant who had shown them in made a clumsy grab for hér, but Galem threw thëir hat at their face and they flinched backwards instinctively, and then shé was past them and back into the corridor. Galem was behind hér, but the clatter of feet suggested the guards were already on their tail.

Of course, there were quite a few more guards in the Petitioner's Hall, some of them directly between Jeya and Galem and the main doors out into the street, but Jeya already had a plan to deal with that.

'*Fire!*' shé yelled at the top of hér lungs as they burst back into the Petitioner's Hall. 'Fire! Get out, get out!'

Panic. Instant, mass panic. Most of East Harbour's buildings were wood, especially where the poor folk lived, and fire was their greatest enemy. The New Palace might be huge and rich, built by the rich, and used by the rich, but every person in the Petitioner's Hall was poor. As soon as the concept entered their heads, they knew exactly how flammable the polished wooden walls, polished wooden floor, and the beautiful cloth wrapped around the pillars was, and none of them wanted to be trapped inside it while it burned.

The petitioners turned and ran, piling into a massive crush of people fighting to get through the doorway all at once. Jeya and Galem were already moving, and were into the main body of the queue before it had fully reacted. Those at what had been the front of the line closed in behind hér, screaming and pushing, and the entire mass began to fight its way out into the sun. Jeya saw guards moving from their positions, but shé couldn't tell if they were attempting to apprehend hér, close the doors, or just get out themselves. You didn't get many guards from rich families, no matter how much better than the average person they ended up thinking they were, and the fear of fire would probably ring loud in their heads, too.

'Stop them!' someone shouted from behind hér, but it was one lone voice, and it got lost in the panicked skirl. Jeya pushed and shoved, simply trying to make sure that shé kept hér feet, as the furious scrum edged closer and closer to the doors.

Closer . . .

Closer . . .

A hand latched on to hér left shoulder. Shé didn't look around to see if it was a guard, a fellow petitioner trying to haul their way past hér, or even the Hierarch themselves. Shé reached back with her right hand and dug in with hér nails as hard as shé could, then managed to twist away from it despite the press of the bodies around hér. Shé heard someone swear loudly, but then shé was out and clattering down the New Palace's steps: nearly falling over hér own feet as hér forward momentum threatened to trip hér and send hér sprawling on to hér face, but free and clear. Shé risked one glance back, when shé had the street surface beneath hér feet, and Galem nearly collided with hér.

'Don't stop!' thëy shouted, tearing past hér, and shé broke into a run once more. The rest of the petitioners were spilling everywhere, some still running out of fear of the fire, others pausing and looking back up at the New Palace as though expecting to see gouts of flame emerging from its windows at any moment. Most importantly, however, the two guards she could see were battling against the flow of humanity and not making anywhere near enough headway to have a hope of catching them.

'What now?' Galem asked breathlessly, as they ran. Thëy'd have to slow down soon: the binding on thëir chest made deep breathing difficult.

'Now,' Jeya told thëm, hér mind whirling, 'we think of something else.'

And also, shé added to hérself, *find out where Nabanda heard about that reward . . .*

ZHANNA

THEY HAD SEEN no more kingdrakes, but the damage to the party's morale was unmistakable.

They had all seen death, of course, when Rikkut Fireheart and his warriors had come. Zhanna had expected that; had known since she was a child that to be an adult of the Brown Eagle clan, she would have to be Blooded. That meant fighting, and of course that carried the risk of not surviving. She had been scared, but managed to squash her fear down into something she could cope with, picked up a weapon and fought. She had trained for that.

You couldn't train for a dragon dropping out of the sky and eating your friend.

It wasn't even as though Ingorzhak had been eaten by a krayk. Saana knew krayk, understood them as well as anyone reasonably could. They were huge, implacable monsters that wrecked ships and swallowed people whole, but the Tjakorshi knew the signs to watch for, and knew how to avoid them. Father Krayk's true born children were a danger of the sea, like storms or unexpected rocks. If you went to sea, you accepted the risk of krayk. But what could you do about dragons that could fly, that could swoop down and attack whether you were on the sea *or* on the land?

You could stay in the trees, and that was what the party had done since the loss of Ingorzhak. They'd skirted the open grassland of the valley floor and stuck to the edges of the conifers that clung to the sides, keeping a wary eye on the sky when they'd cut across between clumps of woodland instead of taking the longer, more difficult route where the trees clung to slopes of scree and boulders. When they stopped at dusk to light a fire and cook food, Tamadh had spoken, haltingly at first and then with greater confidence, about his brother. Zhanna had done her best to translate for the Naridans, but he was good with words, and she didn't know enough Naridan.

'Is this what you do for your dead?' Avisha asked Zhanna, staring into the fire. She looked very young, although Zhanna thought they were probably of an age. 'Talk about their lives?'

'They usually sail out to sea with them,' Ravel put in. He looked over at Zhanna. 'Isn't that right?'

'We do,' Zhanna said, feeling the ache in the pit of her stomach grow a little larger. 'Chara the soul marks makes, and we to the sea return them. We all came from the sea,' she elaborated. 'Father Krayk waits to take us back.'

'What about if someone doesn't die near the sea?' Tatiosh asked.

'We always die near the sea,' Zhanna said shortly. 'Until today.' She took a deep breath, and heaved it out again. 'That is why Tamadh sad is. Ingor's soul cannot to sea return. Trapped here in mountains.' She poked the fire with a stick, and sent up a cloud of sparks. This was her fault: her idea to accompany Amonhuhe, her idea to persuade members of her crew to come with her. She had liked the idea of being in charge; of being the captain, like her mother was a chief. All she had done was get one of her clan killed, and his soul doomed.

Something nudged at her elbow, and she looked down to see Talon pressing close into her side. She tickled the little dragon, ruffling its feathers as her finger scratched at the base of its neck, and it chirruped in what sounded like happiness. To her great relief, her two rattletails had come back when the party had been grabbing their things in the immediate aftermath of the kingdrake's attack.

She supposed perhaps that had helped. Without her rattletails' warnings, their camp would have been caught completely unawares, and more lives than just Ingor's might have been lost. At least he had died like a warrior, trying to strike the beast down, no matter how foolish an act it had been. Perhaps his bravery meant his soul would still find a way to Father Krayk.

Amonhuhe began to sing.

It was a low, melancholy sound in the language of her people, that sounded close enough to Naridan that Zhanna still thought she should be able to understand it if she concentrated hard enough. Amonhuhe had taught all of them some words of her tongue – such as yes and no, a greeting and a goodbye, and their different words for 'we' that meant variously 'you and I', 'you and I and them', and 'all of us except you' – but that was no help now. Zhanna just sat and let the sounds wash over her.

She was almost certain it was a mourning song from the sound alone, but Tatiosh and Danid had bowed their heads. They must have heard it before, or something like it. Zhanna wondered if Amonhuhe had sung this song in the aftermath of Rikkut's attack, when Zhanna herself had been busy helping to prepare the bodies of her own clan for Chara's administrations.

Then she wondered if Amonhuhe had sung this song in years past, when Black Kal had been chief and the Brown Eagle clan had come to Narida not to settle and live, but to raid and pillage. That made Zhanna's breath catch in her throat. It was one thing to know what the elders of your clan had done, back when you were a child. It was another to watch someone singing a death song for your friend, and wonder if they'd done the same for their own friends because of your elders' actions.

Amonhuhe's song went on, rising and falling like the

mountainsides around them until it finally faded away. Then there was no sound except for the gentle pop and crackle of the fire as it ate its way through the resiny wood stacked on it, and the slight rustle of wind through the branches above.

And, from behind Zhanna, a warning rattle.

They moved as one, each person grabbing a weapon. Zhanna drew her longblade and peered through the trees, cursing the after-image of flames in her vision. 'Thorn?'

Her other rattletail bounded out of the darkness to wind around her legs, but he was clearly spooked by something, for he stared back out and rattled again. Talon joined in, adding a second hollow alarm. Zhanna stole a glance upwards, but the dark boughs of the trees were laced thickly overhead: there was no way a kingdrake could land on them here, and such a beast was far too large to pick its way through the wood towards them.

'Adults?' she asked warily. 'Adult rattletails?'

'Perhaps,' Danid replied. He had picked up his long hunting spear, and held it ready in both hands. 'Who's out there?' he shouted. 'Our dragons can smell you, so you might as well show yourselves!'

The night remained silent, but there was a tension in the air. Zhanna knew it was probably her imagination, but it was as though the woods were holding their breath. She became abruptly certain there *was* someone out there, although she was unsure how many, or where. Thorn seemed to know: he was still staring in the same direction, his big hunter's eyes trying to pierce the darkness.

Amonhuhe called out in her own language, her voice stern but not aggressive. She pulled back her hood and drew out her necklace of beads, holding them in one hand and showing them to the darkness.

A voice answered her from the direction in which Thorn was looking. It was trembling, and high, and it spoke the language of the Smoking Valley.

Amonhuhe inhaled sharply, as though in shock or surprise, and called out again. Danid grounded the butt of his spear, although he did not put it down. Then, picking their way hesitantly through the trees, a figure emerged from the shadows.

Zhanna raised her blade, sudden fear gripping her. The halting steps, the stumbling gait that looked like permanently delayed falling: these were things that came straight out of a Long Night tale, when the clan told stories of how draugs took the bodies of the sick, or those who had died and not been marked by a corpse painter. The draugs would cause their hosts to rise and fall upon the living, clumsily but implacably, and ignoring all but the most grievous wounds inflicted on them.

The figure reached the circle of light from their fire, and Zhanna was able to see them properly. She lowered her weapon, for what had staggered out of the night was not a draug that had crept up out of Kainkoruuk's crater, but a living girl perhaps a couple of years younger than Zhanna herself. She had black hair to her waist, clothes that looked nowhere near warm enough for being this high in the mountains at this time of year, and the glazed eyes of someone at the end of their strength. She passed between Tsennan and Menaken without looking at them and almost collided with Amonhuhe, to whom she clung as though her life depended on it.

Amonhuhe looked shocked: she clearly hadn't expected this, even after receiving the reply to her shouts. She folded her arms cautiously around the girl and spoke in low, soothing tones, then angled her towards the warmth of the fire.

'Do you know her?' Zhanna asked uncertainly.

'No,' Amonhuhe said, her tone gentle, as though she did not want to scare the exhausted person in her arms. 'But she's from the Smoking Valley.'

'Where are her beads?' Tatiosh asked, frowning at the girl, whose neck and wrists were indeed bare.

'Your mother doesn't know,' Amonhuhe said, and Zhanna could see the concern on her face. Up until this point, Zhanna had assumed the beads were simple jewellery worn for decoration, like the fishbone shards some of her clan wore through their ears. It seemed they held a deeper meaning, since their absence was clearly noteworthy.

'You'll talk to her, see what she has to say?' Danid asked Amonhuhe, who nodded. 'Very well then,' the hunter continued. 'Everyone else, backs to the fire and eyes on the night. The children of the Smoking Valley don't go wandering in these parts, and not dressed like that: she was running from something, or s'man's a Morlithian.'

Zhanna picked up her roundshield and settled it on her left arm, readied her longblade in her right hand, and stared out at the darkness. She knew little about these high places, but Danid's words made sense.

This girl would not have staggered into the campfire circle of a group of armed strangers had that not been the least worst option available to her, and that begged the question what her other options had been.

AMONHUHE'S QUESTIONING OF the new arrival was thorough, despite the fact that her voice rose in incredulity at times, and also that the girl was crying for a lot of it. Whatever had happened clearly wasn't good, although the rest of them had to wait some time before they found out exactly how bad it was.

It was bad.

'This is Kakaiduna. She tells this woman that our people,' Amonhuhe said, her voice quivering with tightly controlled fury, 'have been enslaved.'

Danid's eyes bulged. '*What*? Who by?'

'Naridans,' Amonhuhe told him grimly, 'and some of the Two Peaks people, from the next valley north. We had disputes with them when this woman was young, before she left to live in Black Keep, but there's been peace for years.'

'What is "enslaved"?' Zhanna said. She could tell from the Naridans' reactions that it was bad.

Menaken bit his lip in thought for a moment. 'You know the thralls in Black Keep? They serve for a year and a day, yes?'

Zhanna nodded. 'Yes. Warrior yield in combat, can become thrall.'

'Slaves are like thralls, but for ever.' Menaken grimaced in distaste. 'We don't do it in the south. Some of the northern thanes do, or so rumour has it, and those decadents in the City of Islands.'

Zhanna just stared at him for a moment. Thralls *for ever?* How could anyone think that was right? 'The Naridans?' Zhanna asked Amonhuhe. 'You know who they are?'

Amonhuhe shook her head. 'She doesn't know. She's never even been as far as Ironhead.'

'They're not from Ironhead,' Danid said immediately.

'This woman knows that!' Amonhuhe snapped at him, then exhaled ferociously. 'Sorry. We know Ironhead are friends to us. We don't know who these slaver Naridans are, *but,*' she continued, pointing at the darkness in the direction Kakaiduna had come from, 'there are some of them out there.'

'Out there? Now?' Menaken asked nervously.

'She managed to get away, but a couple of men came after her,' Amonhuhe said. A grim smile crossed her face. 'She may only be a girl, but these are our mountains, not theirs. She saw them behind her. They could not catch her, but she thinks they're still hunting her. She was hoping to reach Ironhead, but she didn't know how far it was.'

Zhanna looked at the girl, who was now huddled in a blanket by the fire and staring into the flames with tears still glistening on her cheeks, chewing methodically on a piece of mutton jerky. She would not have made it to Ironhead. The days were bright and even warm up here when the sun broke through the clouds, but the nights were still bitter.

'How did she find us?' she asked.

'She heard this woman's song,' Amonhuhe said, with a sad smile. 'She heard her own language and came towards it, then saw our fire through the trees.'

'So others may have heard the song too,' Zhanna said, her stomach starting to jump. She turned to the other Tjakorshi and gave them a quick rundown of what Amonhuhe had said. They looked at each other.

'Please thank her for singing her song for Ingor,' Tamadh said. His lip was trembling, and he was clearly trying not to show it. 'I'm glad she did, especially if it helped bring this girl to us. Ingor would have liked that.'

'I think,' Tsennan Longjaw said, spinning his blackstone axe in his hand, 'we should try to find these men who were hunting her. Only a couple of them, she said?'

'That's what she said,' Zhanna confirmed. 'She could be wrong.'

Longjaw shrugged. 'Life is never certain. Our Naridans can stay here, around the fire. We'll spread out, see if we can catch these others coming in.' He grinned at her. 'What do you say, Zhanna Longblade?'

Zhanna looked again at Kakaiduna, sitting by the fire. Stumbling through the woods without the right clothes, lacking her beads – whatever that meant – and running from grown men who had enslaved her people. Zhanna could barely imagine what that would be like. The desire to do something about it was strong.

But was it right?

'What does she want us to do?' she asked Amonhuhe. 'If she reached Ironhead, what was she ask going to?'

'For help,' Amonhuhe said simply. 'Help to free her people. This woman's people,' she added, standing up.

'That means killing these Naridans, and these other mountain folk,' Zhanna said. 'Yes?'

'We should—' Menaken began.

'Yes,' Amonhuhe said fiercely. 'It does.'

Zhanna nodded, trying not to show how her heart had sped up. 'Then we should make sure they do not know coming we are.' She turned back to the other Tjakorshi, each one with the dark strip of a Blooded warrior running down their foreheads. Sakka was her crew, as was Olagora, the daughter of renowned captain Inkeru. Tamadh and Longjaw were not, but they seemed content enough to listen to her, for now at least.

'Tamadh, you go with Sakka,' she said. 'Olagora, you come with me. Longjaw . . . ' She looked up at him, towering over everyone else around the fire. 'You're on your own.'

'Fine by me,' he grinned.

'Spread out, watch each other's backs and don't do anything foolish,' Zhanna told them, hoping that this was something like what her mother would have said in a similar situation. 'We need to make sure that if they get close enough to see the fire they don't get away, but if we can keep one alive then we might be able to find out how many of them there are.'

The others nodded agreement, and she turned back to the Naridans around the fire. 'Stay here. We will be back.'

'Where are you going?' Menaken protested. Zhanna smiled at him.

'Raiding.'

NABANDA

NABANDA KNELT ON the warehouse floor, with each arm held firmly by one of Kurumaya's thugs. Of course, hê was one of Kurumaya's thugs hîmself, but that was a mere technicality at the moment.

'I gave you a job to do, did I not?' Kurumaya said, pacing slowly back and forth in front of hîm. The Shark was a small person of Fishing Islands blood, shorter than most full-grown adults and slim with it, but they ruled the Narrows of East Harbour with a grip of steel. If you needed muscle, or blades, you came to Kurumaya. If you could afford their price, the job got done. That was their reputation.

That was why Nabanda was in so much trouble.

'You did,' hê muttered, looking down at the dirt floor. That dirt had absorbed the blood of many in the past. It might absorb hîs today.

'And you haven't completed it,' Kurumaya continued.

'No,' Nabanda acknowledged. 'The older child wasn't in the house, and we've been unable to find hìm. But we're still looking,' hê added, trying to sound determined and confident.

'One Naridan youth in all of East Harbour?' Kurumaya scoffed. 'We may as well call hìm lost, mightn't we? By all the Hundred, hè could have taken a boat to any of the islands! Hè could have fled to the mainland by now!'

'I've spread a rumour that the Hierarchs have offered a reward for information on hìs whereabouts,' Nabanda offered, as the thugs holding hîs arms twisted a little more, in line with their boss's displeasure. 'It was vague. I'm hoping if anyone hears about it, they'll come asking me questions. Or at least that we'll hear about someone making a fool of themselves trying to see the Hierarchs. I figured that a rich family like that, the Hierarchs might do such a thing, or at least that people would believe they would.'

Kurumaya stopped pacing. 'I'll admit, it's not the worst idea in the world. Rich families think everything revolves around them. It will only work if this fugitive is now moving in our circles, though.'

'I know people who serve those sorts of families,' Nabanda said. 'The rich love gossip, but I've not heard anything about the only survivor of the fire being taken in somewhere else. If hè's not fallen in with hìs own society, hè's somewhere in ours. Or already dead,' hê added hopefully.

'Or already fled the island,' Kurumaya reminded hîm.

'In which case, I can do nothing,' Nabanda replied honestly. Hê felt surprisingly calm. Hê'd always known that working for Kurumaya was going to be dangerous, both from the jobs hê would do, and the price of failure. Perhaps hê'd already accepted this moment, years ago, without really realising it. 'I've served you as best I can, and I'll continue to. I recognise I haven't succeeded in this yet. If that's not enough for you, I understand.'

Kurumaya sighed. 'You've been a good servant, Nabanda. It would be a shame to waste your talents. But I have a reputation to maintain, and those whose failures damage that reputation . . . ' They looked around. 'Does anyone have something to say?'

Kurumaya's deputies looked at each other. Dalachanya, plump, beautiful and shaven-headed; Menduba, young and intelligent, with eyes that could pick your pocket; and Turakandu, a mess of busted knuckles and scars, past their prime as a street fighter but still a figure of fear in East Harbour's back alleys.

'Revered One,' Menduba said carefully after a moment. 'Most

of the family is dead. The last survivor, if hè has indeed survived, is in hiding. Will the person who paid you even know that not all of their contract has been fulfilled?'

'This was the feminine Naridan?' Turakandu asked, their voice like rusted nails. 'The one who was there when the Watch raided the warehouse on Fourth Channel?'

'The same,' Kurumaya agreed. 'And that is what concerns me.'

'What's concerning about a Naridan noble, far from home?' Dalachanya asked. 'Has shé even been seen since?'

'No,' Kurumaya admitted. 'But when the warehouse was raided, I've been told that shé and hér bodyguard joined with Sar Blacksword and hìs spouse to fight their way clear.'

'Naridans helping each other isn't that remarkable, is it?' Turakandu asked. 'They speak the same language; it would make sense if they were running from the Watch.'

'Sar Blacksword hasn't been seen since, either,' Menduba said. 'Nor has his spouse, Marin of Idramar. I asked around, and the Naridan noble arrived on a ship called *Light of Fortune*, out of Idramar. That ship left shortly after the incident at the warehouse, without taking on cargo.'

'We all know that Naridans have strange ideas about things,' Kurumaya said. 'A feminine noble, so far from home, without a masculine spouse? Practically unheard of.'

'Could the bodyguard have been hér spouse?' Turakandu asked, but Kurumaya shook their head.

'No. A Naridan noble would never disgrace themselves so.' They looked around at their deputies, then at Nabanda. Hê met their eyes, and noticed with some shock the hint of an expression hê didn't think hê'd seen on Kurumaya's face before.

The Shark was worried.

'A rich feminine Naridan, accustomed to being obeyed, with no masculine spouse, is a long way from home on a ship out of Idramar. That ship leaves East Harbour at hér command, we have to assume, without even taking on cargo, and might also have been carrying a Naridan sar and hìs spouse, who hails from Idramar, whom that noble supposedly only met that night?' Kurumaya shook their head again. 'I can't help but think we were paid a visit by the Knife of Idramar hérself.'

There was a moment of stunned silence.

'Revered One,' Menduba said, sounding like they were choking. 'You're telling us that you think *Livnya the Knife* walked into the warehouse on Fourth Channel, and bought these deaths from you?'

'Looking at it now?' Kurumaya replied. 'Yes. I asked a high fee, which shé paid without problem. Shé spoke casually of death, as though such arrangements were nothing new for hér. Since then, we've learned these other details. So now I wonder, how does the Knife of Idramar dare to walk into East Harbour and buy deaths from me? How far-reaching is hér influence? Who on this island actually answers to hér? Were Sar Blacksword and Marin of Idramar always hér agents?' Kurumaya tapped their lips with one finger. 'Does shé have an alliance with one of the other Sharks?'

Nabanda went cold. Livnya the Knife was a name hê'd heard, and hê knew that shé supposedly ran the underworld of the Naridan capital, despite the Naridans' odd views on gender. Apart from that, shé hadn't featured in hîs life at all. The idea that hér web might extend farther than anyone had expected, and that shē might lend hér support to one of Kurumaya's bitter rivals in East Harbour . . . that was concerning. That could change a lot of things.

'So to answer your question, Menduba, I think we need to honour this contract,' Kurumaya said. 'We don't know what The Knife might do, otherwise. We don't know what information shé might give to others about how we are not flawless. And in the meantime, we need to start asking questions. Is anyone richer than they were before? Has anyone been changing Naridan gold?'

The Shark's deputies nodded uneasily. They all knew what that meant. A purge was coming.

'Nabanda, you've served me well in the past,' Kurumaya said, finally turning their attention properly back to hîm. 'You shall have one more opportunity to prove your usefulness. But your failure to this point cannot be ignored.' They turned and raised their voice. 'Bring them in!'

The warehouse door opened, and four figures were dragged unceremoniously inside. Nabanda gritted hîs teeth as hê recognised hîs crew, those who'd been with hîm when they'd attacked the house and left it aflame. Tungkung, Kedenta, Perlishu and Badir: hê'd left them outside, to take Kurumaya's displeasure upon hîmself, but it seemed the Shark had other ideas.

'Four deaths were bought,' Kurumaya declared. 'Three have been achieved, leaving one to go.' They knelt down in front of Nabanda and pulled hîs chin up to lock eyes with hîm. 'You have four people here. Which one of them dies, as penalty for your failure?'

Nabanda stared at them in horror. This was not what hê'd expected.

'Four of you should be able to find this one remaining Naridan,' Kurumaya continued. 'You don't need a fifth. Who dies, Nabanda?'

Nabanda forced hîs voice to work. 'I do.'

Kurumaya shook their head.

'I do!' Nabanda repeated, louder, but the Shark slapped hîm across the face.

'You don't die yet. I've told you: you get another chance. But one of these four pays the price for your failure. Pick one, or I kill them all and leave you to find the last Naridan on your own.'

Nabanda shook hîs head, hîs guts churning. Kurumaya exhaled in annoyance.

'Very well.'

They stood, and raised their hand. Their people who'd dragged Nabanda's crew inside drew blades.

'Wait!' Nabanda shouted. 'Wait!'

Kurumaya drew their own blade, a short knife. They looked down at Nabanda. 'If I've had no name out of you by the time this hits the floor, they all die.'

They threw the knife in the air. It spun, the blade glinting dully in the light, and began to fall towards the dirt that had, Nabanda knew well, absorbed blood before this day, and would do so today as well.

It was up to hîm how much blood that was.

'Badir!' hê shouted, the name forcing itself out of hîs lips before hê could clamp them shut again. Hê was not even quite sure why that was the name that had come to hîm. Perhaps it was as simple as Badir being the one hê'd known for the shortest time.

Kurumaya's knife hit the floor.

The three people who had hold of Badir reacted immediately. The Morlithian cried out as three blades pierced hìm, in the throat, stomach and groin. Hè fell backwards and was followed down to the ground by hìs killers, who stabbed hìm again, and again, and again.

It was brutal, but it was quick. Badir had stopped moving by the time the first of Nabanda's tears hit the ground.

'Now get out of here,' Kurumaya said, their voice coming from a hundred leagues away. 'Kill the person you were supposed to kill. Otherwise, I will have to do this again.'

TILA

THE HALL OF HEAVEN was the greatest and grandest chamber of the Sun Palace, the throne room from whence the God-King's rule emanated forth across Narida. From here, generations of monarchs had exerted their will across the land to the Catseye Mountains in the west, the Hudanar mangroves and the Sundai River in the north, on the border with the mainland territory of the City of Islands, and south to the lands of Blackcreek. It was draped with banners of war, long paper scrolls upon which were written accounts of great triumphs, and the decorated longblade scabbards of sars who had fallen while performing great deeds in service to their divine ruler. Here, the sandstone used for so much else of the palace had given way to marble, and it gleamed in the sunlight pouring in through the high windows.

Most of all, the sunlight filtered down on to the golden throne that sat on the dais at the far end. The Sun Throne, the literal seat of power of the kingdom of Narida, was not exactly a subtle affair. It had a cushioned seat, back and arms, all upholstered in blue, but the main body of it was uncovered, unhidden gold. Tila well knew the value of appearances, and the fact that the God-King of Narida routinely sat on something worth more than some of his thanes' entire estates did a lot to remind everyone exactly who was divine, and who was not.

The Sun Throne was empty. Standing in front of it, one step down on the dais, his back as straight as a blade and looking roughly as unyielding as one, was the Eastern Marshal, Einan Coldbeck.

Tila stepped forwards, well aware of the palace guards standing on either side of her, and all the eyes on her. She had let Coldbeck take charge of matters once her 'confession' had become common knowledge, and Kaled Greenbrook's body had been found. Coldbeck had ordered her confined to her quarters, and for those quarters to be placed under constant guard. The old soldier had not been able to mask his unease at what was happening, or how he was supposed to deal with it, but Tila had accepted that she would have to give account of herself. Not even the Divine Princess could go around killing members of the nobility as she pleased.

However, she had not expected the Hall of Heaven to be so crowded. It looked like every member of the Divine Court had crawled out of the woodwork to be here, down to the lowest nobility with sufficient blood to enter, and who had been able to make it in time.

Nor had she expected the Sun Throne to be empty.

'Where is the God-King?' she demanded. She chose neither to name her brother nor refer to their relationship. Tila, at least, believed in being subtle when she could.

'His Divine Majesty is still ill, as you are well aware,' Coldbeck declared severely.

'His health is improving,' Tila countered. Her brother had been making the appropriate noises, and indeed, Lord Wousewold had put out the word that the God-King had beaten the illness that had threatened his life. Natan was trying to avoid suspicion by pacing his 'recovery', but the fact that it was occurring was common knowledge.

'It is,' Coldbeck agreed, 'but He is not well enough to be here, particularly for a matter concerning his own sister, one that would surely tax his heart so greatly.'

Whirling, nebulous suspicion abruptly crystallised in Tila's mind. 'Does he know?'

'His Divine Majesty remains unable to deal with matters of state at this time,' Coldbeck replied. 'It falls to the Eastern Marshal to conduct affairs in his absence.'

Tila weighed him up. She had understood the intention of keeping her isolated; her deed was a severe one, after all, even given how she had framed it. Coldbeck had to make it look like he was taking it seriously. However, there was no doubt that Natan would declare her actions justified as soon as he learned of them, although he would make a show of considering the arguments put to him. So what was Coldbeck's play?

'We are gathered here to consider the matter of the Divine Princess, Tila Narida, who slew the Lord Admiral Kaled Greenbrook on the Tower of the Eight Winds four days ago,' the Eastern Marshal declared loudly. 'The Divine Princess has admitted the killing, and was discovered holding the Lord Admiral's shortblade and with his blood on her clothes. She claims that she performed this action in self-defence, when the Lord Admiral attempted to throw her off the tower. Do any here dispute this?'

'This lord does so dispute it!' a voice thundered immediately. Tila did not need to turn her head to see who had spoken, for she was expecting it, even if she had not recognised the voice. It was that of Adan Greenbrook, Kaled's cousin.

Now she would learn whether Kaled's claim to have told no one of his discoveries had been true.

'The Lord Treasurer is given leave to approach the Sun Throne,' Coldbeck declared loudly. 'Lord Greenbrook, on what grounds do you dispute the Divine Princess's statements?'

'This lord's cousin, Kaled Greenbrook, was a man of honour,' Adan Greenbrook declared, sweeping into Tila's view. The Lord Treasurer's arms were thick with mourning ribbons, which Tila had expected since it was the custom in the west, and he wore a veil similar to Tila's own, which she had not. The veil was generally only used when mourning a relative of one's immediate line, rather than a cousin, but Tila supposed that if Adan was looking to press some sort of case, it was in his interests to play up the relationship.

'Kaled honoured the Divine Nari, and was a loyal servant to His descendant, the God-King,' Adan declared. 'He would not have threatened the person of the God-King's sister, let alone laid hands upon her.'

'The God-King's sister', not 'the Divine Princess', Tila noted. Adan was doing his best to frame her in relation to her brother, rather than according to her own title.

'Princess Tila has stated that no others were present on the tower save for herself and Lord Kaled,' Coldbeck said. 'Do you claim that you were there?'

'This lord does not,' Adan Greenbrook acknowledged.

'Were you aware of the meeting before it occurred?' Coldbeck asked him, and Adan shook his head.

'This lord was not.'

Coldbeck held up the letter that had awaited Tila in her chambers. 'The princess has provided this, with Lord Kaled's seal and written in what this marshal recognises as his hand, asking her to meet Lord Kaled atop the Tower of the Eight Winds at sundown. It appears clear this meeting was requested by your cousin, but you are not aware of its purpose?'

'This lord is not,' Adan Greenbrook admitted.

It was a weak argument, Tila was sure. Even in front of the Divine Court, by whom she was disliked and feared in roughly equal measure, it would struggle to gain traction. She had proved that Kaled had wanted her there, and Adan had nothing of substance to counter her assertion that Kaled had intended her harm. She had deliberately stated that Kaled had said nothing of why he was intending to kill her, or indeed anything of any moment at all: it was simpler that way, and lies should be as simple as possible.

'This marshal considers the arguments of the Lord Treasurer,' Coldbeck declared. 'The Lord Treasurer states that Lord Kaled Greenbrook was a devout man, who honoured the God-King. This marshal can confirm, from many meetings of the Inner Council, that this was true.'

It was in fact a downright lie, but Tila knew that Coldbeck would never admit to it. For him to say so would be to invite question as to why no one else on the Inner Council had done something about it. Besides which, none of the councillors, Kaled included, had ever voiced contempt for their monarch outright. It was in the things they did not say, in the pregnant pauses before they uttered the praise that should have flown from their lips unhindered, in the carefully chosen wordings that reflected the truth in a manner that fell just short of actual disrespect. In many respects Tila had actually been more scathing than the rest of them, over the years, although she too moderated her tongue.

'To cause harm to the God-King's sister would undoubtedly further impact on our monarch's health, when he came to learn of it,' Coldbeck continued. 'This is, again, almost unthinkable for the sort of man we knew Lord Kaled to be. He knew that the well-being of our kingdom hinges on the well-being of the God-King, who still lies weak and delusional.'

Tila frowned. Delusional? That was the first time she had heard that description given to Natan's illness. Besides, had the announcement not been made that he was improving?

'And yet,' Coldbeck said, 'Lord Kaled requested this meeting with the princess, and in a singular place where they could not be overlooked, nor overheard. These could be the actions of an honourable man, but they raise more questions than answers.' He turned to Tila. 'Do you have anything to add to the statement you gave to this marshal upon that night, two days ago, when you said that Lord Kaled Greenbrook, having sent a letter arranging to meet you, attempted to force you over the top of the Eight Winds Tower without any word as to why he was doing so?'

'This princess does not,' Tila replied simply.

'And you maintain that, as Lord Greenbrook laid his hands upon you, you seized his shortblade, drew it, and cut his throat?'

'This princess does,' Tila said, as neutrally as she could.

'This, too, raises more questions than answers,' Coldbeck declared. 'Why should Lord Greenbrook do such a thing? How is it that Princess Tila, a woman, managed to draw Lord Greenbrook's blade before he could stop her? We have no other witnesses, and there is no obvious interpretation of these events that makes sense.'

Tila held her tongue, despite her anger. None of the Divine Court would expect her to be a sobbing wreck, now that the moment was past: that simply was not the person they knew her as. Besides, she had concluded that attempting to appear shaken – halting, stumbling over her words, appearing uncertain – might be taken as evidence of falsehood when she spoke. By the same token, though, she needed not to appear too confident.

'In summary,' Coldbeck said, 'Princess Tila admits to killing the Lord Admiral of Narida, but her reasons for doing so remain unproven. This marshal cedes the floor to Lord Meshul Whittingmoor.'

Lord Whittingmoor stalked forwards, his cane clicking on the marble floor, and Tila narrowed her eyes. The Law Lord was hardly an ally.

'In cases where the evidence is unclear, we must of course look to the divine for guidance,' Lord Whittingmoor said without preamble, and Tila felt herself relax a little. It would be odd for them to call on Natan so soon after declaring him delusional, but he would end this farce.

'If a lowborn man should kill a noble, with no witnesses around to determine the truth of the matter, we conclude that since the noble was appointed to that station by the will of the divine, his right is the greater,' Whittingmoor droned. 'In that circumstance, the lowborn man would be punished. Should a noble kill a lowborn man with no witnesses, the law dictates that as he was appointed by the will of the divine, his intention is the more likely to be justified.'

The Divine Court nodded. This was how things were done.

'In this case, we appear to be at an impasse,' Lord Whittingmoor declared. 'Lord Kaled Greenbrook was of lesser blood than the Divine Princess.'

Tila frowned. The intonation in the old man's voice suggested a follow-up sentence which she was going to like less.

'However, we must consider the *will* of the divine,' Lord Whittingmoor continued. 'Lord Greenbrook was appointed to the position of Lord Admiral, a post on the Inner Council, by the instruction of His Divine Majesty.'

By the instruction of his sister, Tila thought viciously, *even though it was Natan's seal on the decree.*

'The Divine Princess, however, is of divine blood through no will of His Divine Majesty,' Whittingmoor said, looking at her directly with nothing but cold challenge in his eyes. 'Her children, had she had any, would not be divine, and would not be heirs to the Sun Throne. In these circumstances, we may conclude that His Divine Majesty intended Lord Kaled Greenbrook to be his close adviser, whereas he had no choice in the proximity to him of his sister.'

Tila stared at him, utterly astounded, as a low murmur ran around the Divine Court. Whittingmoor had drawn his legal knives and thrust for Tila's heart, and she realised bleakly that she had too few allies to challenge him. Her power here was a tenuous thing, built on shadows and intimidation, and Whittingmoor had decided to step up. Natan was not here to nod through her words and deeds. Naridan law was always going to favour a man over a woman, even if Whittingmoor had not been capable of making it dance to his tune.

'This princess suggests that you put your line of reasoning to the God-King, and see what he says!' she shouted.

'The God-King is not to be disturbed by this or other matters of state, until such time as the Grand Physician dictates that he is well enough!' Marshal Coldbeck cut in. Tila looked around for the Grand Physician, and saw him shrink away behind a pillar from her glare. Something cold gripped her heart.

'Is this your intention, then?' she demanded of Coldbeck, rounding on him. 'To keep your monarch confined to his chamber until such time as you see fit, hiding behind the words of a Grand Physician who now answers to you? To rule in all but name?'

'And how would that be any different to what you have done these past years?' Adan Greenbrook shouted at her. 'Bending the God-King's ear, swaying his decisions, ruling—'

'*Enough!*' thundered Einan Coldbeck, drawing his longblade, and the scandalised hubbub of the assembled nobles immediately ceased in shock. 'This marshal will not be accused of treason, either directly,' he levelled his blade at Tila, 'or by comparison!' he continued, turning it towards Adan Greenbrook, who took a step backwards and lowered his head.

The Hall of Heaven was silent for a few moments, as everyone present took stock of the new situation. The metaphorical ground had shifted under their feet. Tila waited for the first outcry, the first voice of dissent, the first noble to step forward and declare that the Eastern Marshal had overstepped his authority, or to demand to see the God-King so they could judge his health for themselves.

'Sheath your blade, High Marshal,' Lord Whittingmoor said, his voice quiet and not a little strained. 'It is a grave breach of tradition to bare steel in this hall.'

Einan Coldbeck looked at the Law Lord for long enough to make it clear that he was not obeying an instruction, but acting in agreement with advice, then sheathed his longblade.

'The God-King's health remains fragile,' Marshal Coldbeck said loudly, the challenge clear in his tone. 'All here are aware that we are even now equipping an expedition to find the truth in rumours of Nari Himself being reborn and, if they are indeed true, to bring

Him to this city to assume His rightful place. The situation with Natan III only encourages our haste in this regard.'

'This is a coup,' Tila hissed at him.

'And you would have us instead hand control of the kingdom over to a woman?' Coldbeck scoffed. 'This marshal is the highest-ranking noble, acting in the interests of a monarch too sick to discharge his duty. In the absence of direct instruction from the divine, mortals must do their best.' He turned his back on her, an act so callously dismissive that it drew a couple of gasps from the assembled nobility. 'Lord Whittingmoor, your final judgement on the matter of the princess's killing of Kaled Greenbrook?'

Whittingmoor seemed hesitant, but if anything, Coldbeck's claim to power was more legally sound than what the Law Lord himself just trotted out about Tila's claim to divinity. He swallowed, then spoke quietly but clearly.

'Since the prevalence of blood is weighted equally between descent from the divine and the intent of the divine, the princess is neither cleared of responsibility, nor guilty of it. In these circumstances, she will continue to be held in the same manner she has been over the last two days: afforded the comforts appropriate to her rank, but confined to her quarters, and under guard.'

Tila clenched her fists so hard that her nails dug into her palms. To be held prisoner in such a way would ruin everything. Not only would it give Coldbeck free rein in the Sun Palace while he held Natan prisoner and searched for Nari – or more likely, for a convenient puppet he could claim was Nari – it would prevent her from being Livnya. Her privacy would be gone, should Coldbeck choose it. If she were found not to be in her quarters when she should be, all hell would break loose. She stood to lose control over everything she had built in the last twenty years: everything she had tried so hard to hold together for the sake of her father.

'Does this judgement satisfy the complainant?' the Eastern Marshal asked, turning to Adan Greenbrook.

'It does not,' the Lord Treasurer ground out.

Coldbeck raised an eyebrow. 'Then you know the recourse left to you.'

Adan Greenbrook turned to Tila.

'Divine Princess,' he spat, the venom audible in his words. 'This lord names you murderer, and calls upon the High Marshal, acting in the name of the God-King, to disown you.'

The Divine Court gasped again, but Tila had expected nothing less. Greenbrook had overstepped himself by claiming that her accusation of the Eastern Marshal was no worse than what she had done, since that risked legitimising her words, but he was on safer ground now. Einan Coldbeck and Meshul Whittingmoor together had cut Tila's power out from under her, and now the razorclaws would begin to circle, scenting blood. Greenbrook intended to have her status revoked, and see her ousted from the palace. Once that was done, it would be an easy matter for him to arrange her death.

Or so he thought. It was almost tempting to call his bluff. Adan Greenbrook assumed she would have no one to rely on, nowhere to go. He knew nothing of Livnya the Knife, and that Tila had another life into which she could drop if needed. In fact, the Lord Treasurer had no idea how difficult Livnya could make things for him, if she decided to work against the Sun Palace instead of surreptitiously to its overall advantage.

But that would mean leaving her brother to the tender mercies of those claiming to rule in his name, and Tila would not do that if she had any options left.

'This princess denies your words,' she responded, as she had to.

'Then this lord calls for trial by combat,' Adan Greenbrook declared, looking at Einan Coldbeck. 'He calls upon the crown to recognise his claim.'

The Eastern Marshal took a long, cool look at Tila, then nodded.

'The crown, through this marshal, does so. The Divine Princess must present a champion within three days, or be found guilty.'

PART TWO

'TO GAIN A TRUE *understanding into the character of the Naridans, it is instructive for us to consider not only how they think of themselves, but how they think of others in comparison.*

'One of the most striking examples is how they call us an empire, while referring to their own land as a kingdom. In Naridan eyes, these things are very different, and yet it is hard for us to see why this may be. They view Morlith as a disparate group of peoples, each answering to their own ruler, who have been brought under the auspices of the single Imperial Throne (occupied at time of writing by the Most Glorious Empress Kadina az Tifet), and this is, by some standards at least, true. However, is Narida not similar?

'Scholars who have travelled through Narida speak of great differences in building styles, in food, in dress, in mourning and marriage customs; and even in use of language, despite there being a nominally common tongue. How then is this different to the lands of the Empress? Moreover, Narida is divided into lands ruled by thanes, who in turn answer to four marshals, each responsible for a larger area of land, who are themselves commanded by their God-King. In what way is this not an empire, in the same way as the Naridans themselves define us? The marshals have all the powers of a ruler, save that there is one figure above them.

Here we come to the Naridan character, which is insular and distrustful. Much of their land was brought under one rule in the lifetime of just one man: Nari, after whom their kingdom is named, and whom the Naridans venerate as a deity. Such is their belief in his infallibility that, I would suggest, they cannot comprehend doing anything that he did not. As a result, no one who is not already a Naridan can become a Naridan, and no one who is a Naridan can stop being one. In this manner, their use of the term "kingdom" implies a single, homogenous, indivisible and unchanging structure, in contrast to the "empire" of Morlith which they view as inherently unstable and loosely connected . . .'

Extract from *A World Away Across the Mountains*, by Ghaba Nimaz

DAREL

IMPACT.

Shouts.

Blood.

Darel's blade shuddered as it bit into bodies, tearing screams from the pirates as easily as it tore their clothes and flesh, drawing lines of glistening red across torsos like an artist wielding a pigment-laden brush. This wasn't the dance of combat Darel had read about, or heard given voice to in the songs, where warriors clashed against each other in an elegant interplay of move and counter-move. This was instinct and reaction, where he parried and cut and ducked and flinched without thought, without fear, without warlike joy or righteous fury, without even thought of consequence. Nigh-on twenty years of training with a blade guided his hands and set his feet.

The edge of a true Naridan longblade was the keenest in the known world, and Lord Asrel had commissioned Darel's ten years ago, from the finest swordsmith in Brightwater. Darel's slashes took off hands, left arms hanging by shreds of flesh, bit deep into legs and necks, opened great wounds in stomachs and sides. He had no time to pick his targets; he simply swung at anyone standing within reach of his blade, and against such poorly armoured foes his blade wreaked havoc.

Something flashed at him from the left, too fast for him to dodge, and struck his helm. He staggered and fell, the unsteady deck of the *Silver Tide* throwing off his balance. His attacker, a man wielding a boathook on a long pole, howled in triumph and raised his weapon again to bring it down, and Gershel plunged his cutlass into the man's side.

The pirate let out a bone-deep moan of agony and stumbled sideways, borne towards the ship's rail by Gershel's momentum. Darel rolled on to his front and lashed out with his blade at the legs of another pirate moving to attack the *Silver Tide* crewman, and that pirate cried out, stumbled and fell. A woman cut down at Darel with her own sword, but although the blow knocked the breath from his lungs as it landed across his shoulders, it could not penetrate his coat-of-nails. He reared up to his knees and cut wildly at her thighs, and she back-stepped hurriedly, only to be brought down from behind by Sar Hanan, of Marshal Brightwater's household.

'Blackcreek!' Hanan bellowed. 'Get to the other rail! Did you not hear the captain?'

Darel staggered up, just in time to see a pirate reach around from behind Hanan and knife him in the throat. The sar staggered forwards as blood began to sheet out, and when he turned to cut at his killer he staggered and fell without his blade striking home.

Darel swung for the pirate's knife hand, and although he missed taking the man's hand off, he struck the blade and sent it spinning away. The pirate wielded a cudgel in his left hand, though, and his desperate counterblow with it caught Darel's right forearm.

Darel's longblade fell from suddenly nerveless fingers.

Instinct and training came to his rescue again. As the pirate whooped and stepped forwards, Darel was already closing with him, trusting in the protection of his armour. Now inside the cudgel's reach, he swung his gauntleted left fist at the pirate's face and struck the man on the cheekbone, then managed to trap the pirate's cudgel arm beneath his right, despite the furious ache below his elbow.

The pirate reached up, trying to grab at Darel's helmet and twist it so he could not see. Darel pulled the man's right hand away with his left, then drove his helm forward into the pirate's face. The impact staggered him, but the crack of bone and howl of pain from the pirate strongly suggested the other man had come off worse. With his opponent's cudgel arm still trapped, Darel reached to his belt with his left hand and drew his shortblade. Then, still holding it blade-downwards like an ice pick, he slashed it diagonally across the pirate's throat, then drove his knee into the other man's gut to send him slumping down to the deck.

No new attack came, and Darel took the opportunity to take hurried stock of the situation, as well as several deep breaths into his burning chest. Pirates had stopped boarding from the nearest ship, and although struggles were still going on, the *Silver Tide*'s crew appeared to be holding their own. At the other rail, though, a vicious knot of combat still raged, and he could see the Southern Marshal and two more of his sars, Modorin and Kyrel, laying about themselves.

Darel snatched up the cudgel from the rapidly weakening grip of the pirate he'd just cut down, and hurled it at a woman clambering over the rail on the far side of the ship. It struck her as she was off-balance, and sent her tumbling backwards with a despairing cry into the waves that swelled beneath. Then he scrambled for his longblade, taking it up before the movement of the ship's deck could tip it any further towards one of the sluice-holes cut into the rail to allow water to drain away.

'Gershel!' Darel shouted, and the sailor looked around from where he was hacking at one of the lines binding the *Silver Tide* to the pirate ship on their starboard beam. He had a wound on his left arm, although it didn't look deep, and blood slicked the blade of his cutlass.

'Come!' Darel ordered, and turned away from him to charge across the deck.

It was not, in truth, the noble charge of a mighty warrior, because even when recounting combats that took place on the firm soil of Narida, the songs and tales tended to skip over the details of uneven ground, hidden roots and unexpected dragon burrows. They certainly made no allowances for a ship's deck tipping with the ocean swell, and cluttered with abandoned ropes, dropped weapons and more than one prone body. As it was, Darel's advance was more of a controlled stagger than anything else, but he made it far enough in the right direction to land a cut across the back of a pirate doing his best to grab Modorin's sword arm with his left hand and drive a dagger through the sar's armour with his right.

There was a flash of red flesh and white bone as Darel's blow cut into the attacker's spine, and the man fell limply to the deck. Modorin, now free of the pirate's interference, took down another. Darel moved to his side, still swinging despite the pain in his shoulders and the aches starting to build up in his arms, and together they moved in on the rest.

The pirates' attack fell apart. Prevented from advancing by determined resistance from the crew of the *Silver Tide*, the Southern Marshal and his sars, they had nowhere to go as one end of their line was rolled up, save back over the side. Some made it. Most turned to flee, and were brought down from behind as they did so.

'Cut them loose!' bellowed the voice of Captain Akav, and the man himself fell upon one of the grappling lines, hacking at it with his cutlass. With the last pirates diving desperately into the waves, the *Silver Tide*'s crew turned their attention to the ropes still attaching them to their would-be attackers, and they came away one after another. The *Silver Tide* began to drift free, and the captain grabbed the tiller.

'To your stations!' he bellowed at his crew. 'Get the surgeon up here! Those who can, tend to the lines and the canvas! This filth may have friends nearby, so let's put some distance between us and them! High Marshal,' he continued, in a lower and far more respectful tone. 'Your servant humbly begs that your men turn your blades to dealing with the pirates' wounded, for your servant hasn't the crew to spare.'

Kaldur Brightwater was spattered with blood, but none of it seemed to be his. His polished helmet nodded wearily. 'As you say, captain. We will ensure none of these wretches rise up to trouble us again.'

'Gershel!' Darel called, and was relieved to see the sailor still stood. He was but one man out of the crew, and not one Darel had spoken with before the pirates had been sighted, but for some reason Darel felt responsible for him. 'Show us who needs to go over the side!'

'Aye, lord,' Gershel nodded. He was trembling in the aftermath of his exertions, and Darel realised that he was as well, although the bulk of his armour probably hid it better.

Then it hit him that he had just survived his first battle.

Not a skirmish with the Raiders where he had taken a blow to the head and been incapacitated, until he had been overwhelmed and held captive. Not riding invaders down from Quill's back. An actual battle, in which he fought and, Nari's teeth, he *killed* . . .

'Blackcreek?' Brightwater said, catching Darel's shoulder as he swayed on suddenly unsteady legs. 'Are you well?'

'Y-yes,' Darel managed, although his breathing was coming fast, and his helm and war mask suddenly felt very claustrophobic. 'Your servant just . . . it was his first battle like this, face-to-face and on foot,' he concluded, somewhat more quietly. Why could he not have his brother's nerves? Daimon would never have been so unmanned in the aftermath of combat.

To Darel's surprise, and great relief, no shaming words spilled forth from Brightwater's helm. The Southern Marshal merely nodded, and leaned closer.

'It takes many men like that, the first time. Not necessarily just the first, either.' He lowered his voice. 'Perhaps the business of cutting throats is not for you, today.'

'Aye, lord,' Darel said gratefully. He had not flinched from the fight when it came for him, but that was a very different matter to taking his blade to a helpless man, even one for whom death would be welcome release. Judging by the wails heard across the ship, there were several such souls nearby.

'Kyrel! Modorin! Tenan!' Brightwater barked. He looked about himself. 'Where is Hanan?'

'He fell, lord,' Darel managed, pointing to where Sar Hanan's armoured body lay, a pool of blood leaking from his neck.

'Ach! May the Divine One welcome him,' Brightwater said sadly. 'He was a good and noble man.' He squared his shoulders. 'But mourning comes later. For now, we must deal with the remaining pirates. It is a wretched job, but the captain speaks true: it would be good for us to be gone from here, and if he cannot spare the crew, then those of us more familiar with blades than they are with sails will have to do it.'

'Foul wretches,' Sar Modorin growled. 'Growing fat off the plunder taken from honest men!'

Darel cast a glance down at the bodies at his feet. Pirates, for sure. Some he remembered bringing down, others had been slain by his companions, and some he honestly could not say how their end had come. Clad in rags or the faded finery of other lives, or taken from others. Armed with, it seemed, whatever weapons they had to hand.

Not a one of them, so far as he could see, looked to have had the luxurious life Sar Modorin was alluding to.

DAIMON

DAIMON HAD NOT laid eyes on Yarmina Darkspur in perhaps ten years and she was, if he recalled correctly, two years younger than him. He remembered her as a demure child, wary of straying away from her father, but insistent on being a proper host to him and Darel when they visited Darkspur with Lord Asrel. That had inevitably led to Daimon dragging both his bookish brother and their reluctant, self-appointed chaperone around as he explored, and occasionally getting them all into trouble by sneaking into the chambers of the thane of Darkspur – Yarmina's grandfather, at that point – or stealing sweetmeats from the kitchens. Looking back, Daimon was unsure why Lord Odem had ever wanted him as a son-in-law.

The attractive young woman in front of him in Black Keep's reception hall, her hands clasped together in the sleeves of her riding robes and her face downturned, looked to have a similar demeanour to the girl he remembered. She had always been self-conscious about her teeth, he recalled suddenly. They had all been losing their first teeth when first they met, but Yarmina had mumbled and covered her mouth rather than let the gaps be seen. He had a sudden memory of pulling down his lip so she could see the bloody socket where one of his had recently fallen out, and making her squeal in disgust. It had seemed like excellent fun at the time. Now, looking at this composed – and, Nari damn him, beautiful – Yarmina, Daimon felt suddenly embarrassed.

Saana shifted at his side, and Daimon remembered himself. Here he was, acting in his brother's stead as thane of Black Keep, and he had left noble visitors standing while he thought back to his childhood.

He hoped no one present thought that he had been rendered speechless by Yarmina's appearance. That would never do, with his wife next to him.

'Lady Yarmina, this lord bids you welcome,' he said formally, and as honestly as he could manage. In truth, he had no quarrel with Yarmina. The sars who were with her, on the other hand . . .

'We thank you for your welcome,' Sar Omet Darkspur replied. He was Thane Odem's cousin, and Daimon disliked him intensely. The man had been in Black Keep when Darkspur had ridden as part of Marshal Brightwater's force, and Daimon distinctly remembered Omet's look of displeasure when the Southern Marshal had declared that he would not be executing Daimon after all. Given that, Daimon felt he was quite justified in harbouring some resentment.

Yarmina nodded her head slightly, but remained silent. As the heir to Darkspur, and a woman of age, she would theoretically have the rank in their party; unless Sar Omet's status as Darkspur's steward somehow combined with his blood tie to the thane to outrank her? Daimon wished Darel was here. His brother would know whether Omet was acting within propriety, or was technically overstepping his bounds, and therefore who Daimon should address. It was definitely one of those two, though: the other three sars hadn't even entered the hall with them, and had instead remained with the escort of twenty armoured men who were now, against Daimon's better judgement, waiting inside the walls of the castle.

'It has not been long since your presence graced our halls, Sar Omet,' Daimon said, letting Omet choose whether or not to take his words as sarcastic. 'This lord did not expect you to return so soon.'

'And we were expecting to be received by the thane of Blackcreek,' Sar Omet replied smoothly, 'rather than yourself. This sar presumes that you have not incarcerated him once more?'

'Cousin,' Lady Yarmina said uncomfortably, her eyes widening slightly. Daimon leaned forward in his chair without thinking, gripping the arms, outraged at the man's temerity.

'Hah!' Saana laughed from beside Daimon, startling him. She nudged him, and pointed at Omet with a smile. 'He is funny!'

If anything, Omet looked somewhat chagrined at having made Saana laugh, but he smiled nonetheless. 'A jest of course, Lord Blackcreek. The bonds of fidelity between your law-brother and yourself are well known. After all, did he not restore you to the family?'

'He did,' Daimon agreed, settling back into his chair. So, Omet intended to rile him. That suggested he was better off not rising to the bait, at least until he had a better idea of the man's intentions. 'As a result, this lord serves as the thane of Blackcreek in his brother's stead. You were not aware that Lord Darel was travelling to Idramar with Marshal Brightwater?'

Sar Omet's cheek twitched. 'Indeed we were not. You may recall, Thane Odem took his leave before the Southern Marshal did. We gather that their party took the coast road, and therefore did not pass Darkspur.'

'Since this lord is acting in his brother's stead, he asks your business with his brother,' Daimon said, as patiently as he could manage.

'Some years ago, this lord's cousin suggested to your father, Lord Asrel, that his house and yours should be joined in marriage,' Sar Omet said, and Daimon felt his heart sinking. 'Your father refused to consider the proposition, on the basis of the Lady Yarmina's parentage.'

Daimon saw Yarmina wince. Beside him, Saana leaned closer.

'What does he mean?' she asked quietly.

'Lady Yarmina's mother is a Morlithian,' Daimon said, covering his mouth with his hand. 'They live beyond the mountains. At about the time she was born, Morlithians killed the old God-King.'

Saana's eyebrows raised. 'So Naridans hated them after that?'

'We had not been on the best of terms anyway,' Daimon admitted, 'else they'd have hardly done what they did. But yes, that news meant death for many Morlithians in Narida, especially when the God-King's death meant that the plague came. Your husband's father . . . ' He paused, trying to work out how to best describe Lord Asrel's disdain for the notion of a mixed-blood child being married to either of his sons.

'Your father tried to kill your wife twice for being Tjakorshi,' Saana said grimly. 'She can imagine his thoughts on this.'

Daimon nodded. His memories of his father were a confusing, painful tangle. The many good years of care and love, albeit expressed through stern discipline, had been distorted by the last few weeks of bitterness, rage and, ultimately, murderous intent. Saana had only ever known Lord Asrel as a man intent on killing her and her people, in defiance of good sense or indeed, in the end, the wishes of his sons and his lowborn. It was pointless trying to defend his father to her. In fairness, Daimon was not sure he wanted to, or even that he should. The fact remained that Yarmina had always been a nice girl, and undoubtedly innocent of the atrocity committed by people she was nominally related to.

'Lord?' Sar Omet said, and Daimon realised that he and his wife had been whispering to each other in a way that would look very rude. He straightened in his seat and inclined his head in a slight apology; his opinions of Darkspur aside, he owed them at least that much. He directed it more towards Yarmina than Omet, however.

'Your pardon,' he said politely.

'We are in your hall, Lord Daimon,' Sar Omet replied. 'The

norms of behaviour are as you set them.' Which was an utterly underhanded way of saying that he damned well felt Daimon had been rude, but was not going to call him on it openly.

'This man may not understand enough Naridan,' Saana said loudly, looking directly at Sar Omet, 'but she still does not think you have said why you are here.'

That *did* startle the steward of Darkspur, who eyed Saana as though his mount had just spoken to him. He regained his composure after a moment, but Daimon could tell that Saana's bluntness, and the manner in which she referred to herself, had rattled him. Yarmina jumped as well, and her eyes flickered to Daimon for the first time since she entered the hall, before she studiously resumed examining the floor a pace or so in front of where she stood.

'Lord Asrel is . . . no longer here,' Sar Omet said, and Daimon could have sworn that the man's eyes lingered for a moment on the grip of Daimon's longblade. 'His objection to any such unification no longer exists. The thane of Darkspur would, once again, like to offer his daughter's hand in marriage, to unite two of the southernmost noble houses in Narida. Since you have so readily accepted your . . . new neighbours,' Omet continued, nodding in Saana's direction, 'the thane of Darkspur presumes his counterpart of Blackcreek would not share his father's objection to Morlithian blood.'

There it was. Daimon had been half-expecting this from the moment he heard that Yarmina was here; he had known for certain it was coming as soon as Omet mentioned Odem's previous attempt at betrothal. To put an added twist on it, they had made explicit reference to the Tjakorshi. How unreasonable would it be to refuse such a marriage offer, under these circumstances, from Blackcreek's larger, richer neighbour?

'This lord cannot, of course, speak for his brother in this matter,' Daimon admitted. 'However, he can say with certainty that so far in his life, Lord Darel has never expressed attraction to a woman. It is of course possible that Lady Yarmina may be the exception, but,' he smiled politely, 'he does not consider it to be likely.'

'The offer of marriage applies to yourself as well, Lord Daimon,' Sar Omet said quietly.

Daimon heard Saana breathe in beside him, and leaned forwards in his chair before his wife could erupt. 'This lord thanks the steward of Darkspur for reminding him of that fact, but as both you and Lord Odem are aware, this lord is already married to Chief Saana of the Brown Eagle clan.'

'Of course, lord,' Omet replied, his eyes not leaving Daimon's. 'However, we were of the understanding that this marriage was more of a political affair, conducted to give some legitimacy to the settling by the Raiders. As such, with the Southern Marshal now convinced of their right to be here, we were not sure if you would consider the marriage to still be necessary. We would never, of course, propose the dissolution of a marriage that was genuine in the sight of Nari.'

Daimon tried not to shift uncomfortably. The honest truth of it was, his marriage was *not* genuine in the sight of Nari, although there was no way Omet could know that; that last remark had to have been a gamble on the steward's behalf. But the fact remained, he and Saana had still not consummated their union. Should he choose to, he could speak to Aftak the priest, make a declaration, and the marriage would be annulled.

'You are taking a great interest in this man's marriage,' Saana said, addressing Sar Omet. 'Are you certain you are not seeking her husband for yourself?'

That might have served as a cutting remark or even a grave insult in Tjakorshi society; Saana had promised to prevent her clan from acting on their beliefs, but such attitudes still slipped through. Sar Omet merely smirked, however.

'Lord Daimon is undoubtedly handsome, but this sar is already married, and to someone closer to his own age.'

Omet was only a few years older than Saana. The judgement was clear in his words, and judging by the way Saana's face fell, she had picked up on it.

'This lord's marriage is not up for discussion, by you nor by the thane of Darkspur,' Daimon told Sar Omet sharply. 'Lord Darel will be gone for some time, and this lord will pass on your suggestion regarding a betrothal to him when he returns. In the meantime, this lord offers accommodation at Black Keep while you prepare for your journey back to Darkspur. It would not do for us to keep Thane Odem without his steward,' he added, somewhat pointedly.

'We accept your gracious offer,' Sar Omet replied, bowing. He straightened, then hesitated. 'Lord Daimon, another matter, but . . . our dragons?'

Daimon frowned, irritated and somewhat confused. 'What of them? They will be stabled with our own.'

'Indeed, lord,' Sar Omet said, nodding, 'but upon our arrival, a serving girl informed us that she is your stable master?'

His incredulity was not hard to pick up on. Daimon sighed.

'Tavi, Black Keep's former stable master, was killed in the battle. Abbatane was one of his apprentices, and she has indeed taken on his role. This lord assures you that your mounts will be well cared for.'

Sar Omet's mouth tightened, but he did nothing other than nod again. 'As you say, lord. By your leave.' He turned to depart. Yarmina made a light bow of her own, as befitted one thane's heir to another in his hall, and followed him without meeting Daimon's eyes.

'That man,' Saana said dangerously, as soon as the hall's doors had closed behind the Darkspur delegation, 'can go fishing with the Dark Father.'

It was not a phrase Daimon had heard her use before, but he was familiar enough with the menacing nature of the Tjakorshi god to pick up on the sentiment. 'Agreed.'

'And the girl barely spoke!' Saana continued, waving a hand angrily. 'Is this how Narida marries? A girl's father sends his cousin to trade, like a fisher with a prize catch?'

'Sometimes,' Daimon muttered uncomfortably. He was used to the notion of parents – usually fathers – arranging marriages for their children, especially among the nobility. He also had no experience of seeing it himself, since the previous offer from Odem Darkspur had been put to Lord Asrel without either him or Darel being present. However, he was sure that what he just sat through was unusual, even by those standards.

'Did you think she was pretty?' Saana asked him, and Daimon had to work very hard to keep his expression calm as his heartbeat accelerated. That was a worrying question to be asked by his wife.

But he had knelt next to Saana while Aftak had implored the Divine Nari to give both of them the strength to be honest, among other things.

'Yes,' he said. 'Your husband did.'

Saana nodded, eyeing him, and Daimon found himself studying her in turn. She was a stark contrast to Yarmina in so many ways – her pale skin, her blonde hair, not to mention her sheer size – but the contrast that caught him at this moment was the faint lines at the corners of her eyes, and across her brow, where Yarmina's skin had been smooth and unmarked. Omet's words about age seemed to hang in the air.

'If we were not married,' Saana said slowly, 'would you consider this offer?'

Daimon's first instinct was to deny it; but again, was he being honest? He forced himself to pause, and think, no matter how uncomfortable it made him feel under Saana's gaze.

'Your husband is not sure,' he said slowly. 'A marriage with Darkspur could be beneficial, but your husband distrusts Thane Odem, and his motives. The man has no fondness for us, so it seems strange that he should offer his daughter's hand. But perhaps her mother's blood means that she will struggle to find a match elsewhere, and we truly are the best prospect for her? It could be Odem is doing what he thinks is best for his daughter, despite his own feelings, and there is no malice or secret purpose in it that could harm Blackcreek.'

'And the girl herself?' Saana pressed.

'Your husband remembers her from when we were children,' Daimon admitted. 'She was a shy girl, and he and his brother were not, perhaps, the kindest to her. It is . . . odd, to see her now. She is comely, but your husband still thinks of her as . . . It is hard to see her as she is. Does that make sense?'

'Your wife believes so,' Saana said, nodding. She did not seem angry, merely thoughtful. 'The sar mentioned our marriage. We spoke before about how your god watches your marriage bed.'

That was perhaps more literal than Daimon had phrased it, but only slightly. Saana had been utterly appalled by the notion that gods could or would watch you when you lay with another, although bearing in mind the bestial visage and callous nature of Father Krayk, that was hardly surprising.

'We did,' he agreed. He felt he could see where this was going.

'Nothing has happened in it,' Saana said bluntly. She inclined her head towards the door through which Yarmina and Omet had left. 'If you wished to . . . '

Daimon gaped at her. 'Is that what you wish?'

Saana snorted. 'Your wife agreed to marry you to save her clan, and your people. She did not take that decision lightly, and having made it, she does not seek to cast it aside. But she knows you made your decision for the same reasons, under the same pressures. You even said it would not have been your choice.'

Daimon tried to suppress a grimace. He had said that, and he could have been more diplomatic about it, but he had been trying to drive home the political necessity, and not that he had taken leave of his senses.

'Your wife's clan know why we married,' Saana continued.

'She thinks they would understand if the situation changed.'

Daimon shook his head. He had accepted his decision as a necessary one, and had resolved to see it through. Yet oddly, now confronted with not only the ability to cancel it, but with another – younger, and somewhat attractive – option, he found his position unchanged.

'No,' he said firmly. 'This man has no regrets. If you do not wish for things to change, then nor does he.'

Saana smiled at him. 'Good. Your wife is glad.' She paused for a moment, then raised her eyebrows. 'Well, there is *one* thing she might like to change, if her husband was agreeable to it.'

Daimon's heartbeat began to quicken again.

'Your wife is not saying that you have to,' Saana added hastily. 'You do not need to prove anything. But if you wished to, then that would be welcome.'

Daimon nodded. It wasn't that he hadn't wanted to in abstract, as such, it was just that his emotions had been in too much of a whirl to really contemplate such a thing. Then, as the days had passed, it had become more and more difficult to think about broaching the subject. But now his wife was broaching it, and seemed keen, and . . . well, Saana might not look like any Naridan woman Daimon had seen, but he would be a liar if he said that she did not stir his blood.

'Then your husband invites you to call upon him tonight,' he said, trying to keep his voice steady. 'He trusts you know where to find him?'

Saana grinned at him. 'We shall have to find out, shall we not?'

MARIN

IDRAMAR'S CELLS HAD not improved since Marin had last been resident in them. They were still dark, still stank of piss, still housed spiders that were far larger than he was comfortable with, and were still damp enough to have moss growing on the walls and give a man a troubling cough, if he stayed too long. Marin already considered that he had spent too much of his life in them, and yet here he was, back again.

He had been an utter, utter fool. He had decided to intervene on behalf of some young incompetent who did not even know how best to run away from the Keepers, and as a result he had landed himself right into trouble: and, more importantly, rendered himself unable to head west in search of the reborn Nari. It was foul luck that he happened to trip a Keeper that knew him from the old days, but thieving was all about luck, and knowing when not to push it.

That was not something that Marin had been good at, historically.

Laz came to see him, once. There were no hard-and-fast rules about who was allowed down to see the prisoners, and it depended on which Keepers were on duty and what sort of mood they were in. They tended to be respectful around Laz, though; most people were with a sar, even a blacksword. Marin felt like a damned fool telling his husband how he had ended up here, but at least it wasn't because he'd stolen anything this time. The Keepers did not know about the brooch; this was just an old grudge. Laz had shaken his head sadly, but at least he had not said, 'Your husband told you so.' He could have done, because he had indeed told Marin so, but he did not mention it. Just one of the many reasons Marin loved him.

The real question was what was going to happen now. At some point, presumably, Marin would be hauled before one of Old Man Whittingmoor's reeve-courts. Exactly what they were going to try to do him for remained a mystery: yes, that bastard Yamrel had been certain Marin had committed several thefts, but Marin had no idea how they were planning to link him to them now, five years later. But any time he asked what was happening, the Keepers just laughed and walked away.

The main door creaked open, and Marin looked up automatically as light spilled in. The cells were simply cages of iron bars, with no walls save the one at the back. You had to stand or lie in the middle of your cell to be out of reach of those on either side of you, although putting your hands into another person's cell was a risky move. It did mean that everyone had a very good view of who was coming and going, and who was doing what. The Keepers encouraged it: ratting on the other inmates could see them slip you the occasional treat, although you had to do it quiet-like, to avoid making enemies that might come find you when you were out again.

Marin never got involved in that sort of thing. Never make the Keepers' lives easier: that was his motto. It meant they didn't like you, but there were rules about how Keepers behaved, at least nominally. There were no such rules in Idramar's underworld to protect those who went against their own.

'Who goes there?' a grey-haired old man nearest the door shouted, then cackled at his own wit. The Keepers ignored him, pulling in the newest arrival between them.

It was a young woman, wearing a rough peasant dress of brown wool, in a style from some way further north. Not a city girl, Marin was instantly certain of that. She was not struggling against the Keepers, but she was far from calm: he could see that much in her face. If she had been in these cells before, then Marin was a left-handed Morlithian.

'You can't leave her here!' Big Taman protested from across the way, in his booming voice. 'A young girl like that? She won't last a day in here!' He wasn't trying to be helpful: Big Taman liked to intimidate people. The trouble was that others seemed to have picked up on his manner, and from what Marin had seen in his short time here so far, imitated him. The result was quite the most noxious cell environment Marin had ever been in, with a couple of the less robust-minded inmates swiftly reduced to tears after their arrival.

Marin had paid the threats and whispers no mind, but they had died away anyway after Laz had come and spoken to him. The rest had seen the Brotherhood tattoo on the back of Laz's hand, and no one in here was foolish enough to threaten the husband of a blacksword who made his living as a mercenary.

'Pipe down, Taman,' one of the Keepers growled at him. 'She's none of your concern.'

There were three empty cells, one of which was on Marin's right, boundaried on its far side by the rear wall. The Keepers walked the young woman down between the doors, glowering at anyone who approached the front of their cell, all the way down to Marin's.

'There we are,' the second Keeper said with false cheerfulness, unlocking the door to the empty cell. 'Only one neighbour for you, and that's Marin. He won't hurt you.' He looked at Marin and laughed. 'He'll steal the smile from off your face if you give him half a chance, but he won't hurt you.'

'S'man'll steal your heart, and get you to let him out,' Marin bantered, and the Keeper laughed again and tapped his chest.

'Not today, king of thieves. S'man's wife still has it locked up.' He and his companion ushered the young woman into the cell, then locked it again and set off back down the row. Marin watched them go, then edged slightly nearer to the bars that separated him from the new arrival.

'Decent enough, those two, as Keepers go,' he said quietly. 'Give 'em a laugh and a joke, and they'll be reasonable with you. S'man can tip you off which ones aren't to be trifled with, if you want the advice.'

The young woman was looking at him side-on, as though she did not trust him enough to face him outright. Or possibly she did not trust her new surroundings enough to give anything her full attention.

'Thanks,' she muttered, just when Marin was about to decide that she was either deaf or choosing to ignore him for her own reasons. She stood lightly on her feet, as though ready to move at any moment: a sure sign of nerves, in a place where there was nowhere to move. Marin leaned back against the wall of his cell.

'S'man is Marin of Idramar. And you are?'

'Ravi,' the young woman replied, after another moment or two of weighing Marin up with her eyes, as though to decide whether her name was something she should give him. She folded her arms against the slight chill of the place. 'You're a thief?'

'Never listen to what the Keepers say,' Marin chided her. 'S'man's in here due to a misunderstanding from a good five years ago, would you believe? He came back to the city with his husband, and may Nari have mercy on him, he only runs into a Keeper who has bad memories of him. Literally ran into,' he added ruefully, for his jaw still ached.

'They do seem quite . . . determined,' Ravi said. She was looking at the floor when she spoke, so it was almost as though she were talking to herself rather than to him. 'You must've annoyed someone important, for them to still be after you after five years.'

'Tracked you down, did they?' Marin asked, nodding knowingly.

'Aye, they'll do that.'

'For something s'woman never did!' Ravi protested indignantly.

'Ah,' Marin said encouragingly. 'Often the way.'

Ravi squatted down, still just out of arm's reach from the bars between them. She was looking straight at him now, and her face was clouding in anger. Clearly, her desire to be heard out had overcome her uncertainty.

'S'woman does some work for this merchant and his wife, gets paid and is on her way, thank you very much. Then a few days later, the Keepers come knocking up s'woman's lodgings and haul her out into the street, because she's supposedly stolen a brooch from their house!'

'A brooch?' Marin asked, unease creeping through him.

'Aye, some jade thing, supposedly,' Ravi snorted. 'Keepers didn't find it, of course, because s'woman never had it, but they're saying she must've already sold it on! As though s'woman would know what to do with a jade brooch!' She hissed in irritation. 'S'woman almost wishes she *had* stolen something from them, rich, ungrateful shits that they are. At least she'd have had better money for her work!'

'What work is that?' Marin asked, eager to move the conversation away from jade brooches that had been removed from their rightful owners.

'S'woman's a healer,' Ravi said, resorting back to shorter sentences and even looking a little shamefaced at her outburst, now her ire had run its course. 'Their son had a coughing sickness. Nice lad. He should be better now.'

'The coughing sickness?' Marin nodded, impressed. 'That takes some shifting.' He chuckled. 'Bit of country magic, was it? They do say that the old ways are still—'

He'd not been mindful of his distances, now there was someone new in the cell next to him. Ravi got to the bars between them and reached through them faster than Marin could react, grabbed him and hauled him right up to the metal.

'What—?' he yelped, trying to twist his legs under him to get some sort of purchase.

'Let s'woman make something very clear,' Ravi spat, her face a mere bar's-width from his own. 'She. Is *not*. A *witch*.'

'S'man never said witch!' Marin protested, as a couple of the other inmates began hooting and laughing at the spectacle. He grabbed at her hands, seeking to pry them loose from his clothes. 'He just said magic—'

Ravi released her grip with her right hand and caught his wrist, digging her thumb into a point that was suddenly the gateway to a whole new world of needle-tipped pain.

'No magic!' she snarled, as he yelped, momentarily paralysed by this unexpected new agony. 'Just herbs and poultices!'

'No magic! No magic!' Marin agreed desperately, and as swiftly as she'd grabbed him, Ravi let him go again. He scrambled back from the bars, but remembered himself in time before he got within reach of the rangy fellow on the other side of him, whose name Marin hadn't learned and whose acquaintance he was not eager to make, judging by the smell of him.

Ravi was breathing hard, and her eyes were hard in her face as she studied him from her side of the bars, her hair hanging loose and reaching near to the floor, for she hadn't left her squat yet.

'Have you travelled far, Marin of Idramar?' she said softly.

'Farther than you, s'man dares to say,' he replied, somewhat shakily.

'Do you know what they do to witches, out in the hills?' Ravi asked him. 'Have you ever seen it?'

Marin shook his head. Ravi sniffed, exhaled, and seemed to relax a little.

'Pray you never do.'

She rose to her feet, took the two steps to the pile of straw her cell came with and sat down on it, then adjusted the neckline of her dress, which had shifted during their brief grapple. Marin caught sight of the thick, dark line of what looked like a tattoo before it was hidden away again under the rough brown wool.

'Made a new friend then, Marin?' Big Taman called, from the far side. Marin threw the sign of the Unmaker's Eye at him, drawing a hiss of anger, then sat back down on his own straw pile.

After he had shifted it far enough to no longer be reachable from either side of his cell.

TILA

THE MAID POURED the yeng, her concentration absolute and her execution perfect, then set the pot down. 'Will there be anything else, Your Highness?'

'No, thank you,' Tila said. 'This princess will ring for you if she has need of anything.'

The maid bowed, and exited through the door of Tila's reception room. She was almost soundless, even managing to keep the door's noise down to the faintest click of the latch.

'These girls are very good at not drawing attention to themselves, are they not?' said Hada Narida, the Queen Mother, raising her cup to her lips.

'If that is intended as an oblique criticism of your daughter, then at least say it outright,' Tila replied, adding a drizzle of honey to her yeng and stirring it in.

Tila's mother sighed. She was past her sixtieth year, and grey had chased out all but a few threads of black from her hair, but her face still held strong echoes of the famous beauty that she'd once possessed; beauty enough to attract the attention of the Crown Prince of Narida, the man who would become Natan II.

'Tila, you *killed a man*.' She shook her head and studied Tila's face sadly. Tila did not wear her mourning attire in her chambers, so she had no veil behind which to hide from her mother's scrutiny. 'Your mother always knew you were more like your father than your brother is, but this . . . ' She set her cup down again and frowned at the contents, although Tila did not think it was the quality of the yeng that was bothering her mother. 'And the Lord Admiral, at that? You have kicked the hornets' nest.'

'He was threatening your daughter,' Tila replied, trying not to let her anger bleed through into her voice, and took a sip of her own drink. The yeng, at least, was perfect.

'And why was he doing that?' Hada asked softly. 'You have involved yourself in the affairs of men, time and time again, and then you wonder why they grow frustrated with you?'

'These are not the affairs of *men*,' Tila snapped. 'These are affairs of *state*! The entire country of Narida: men and women and children and all besides! If these men were able to run our land properly, your daughter would not feel the need to get involved.'

'And look what happens when you do!' her mother said. 'Tila, do you not understand what will happen? You have been challenged to trial by combat! You should be petitioning the Eastern Marshal to select you a champion, else you will be disowned.'

'You daughter will be disowned by the crown, by the instruction of the Eastern Marshal acting on its behalf,' Tila said bitterly. 'This is despite the fact the God-King himself is recovering from his illness—'

'Tila, the guards won't even let your mother in to see him, his condition is so poor!' Hada protested. 'Those instructions come from the Grand Physician himself!'

'The Grand Physician is in Coldbeck's pocket,' Tila said dismissively. How like her mother it was, to let herself be prevented from seeing her own son by a pair of guardsmen! 'Your son is being held prisoner, Mother! And your reaction to your daughter being threatened badly enough to kill a man is to say that it is your daughter's fault, for interfering in men's business!' She took another sip of her yeng before her tongue ran away any further. She had not invited her mother here to start a fight, but her frustration was boiling over.

'And what would you have your mother do?' Hada asked softly. 'She thinks you forget the difference between her and you. You are divine, daughter: you have the blood of Nari Himself in your veins. Your mother is not, and does not.'

A denial reached Tila's lips, but she held it there while she considered her mother's words. For certain, she had only ever heard of the Queen Mother being spoken of in terms of reverence and love, blessed by the spirits and Nari Himself, the beloved of Natan II. Of course, no one would speak ill of Queen Hada around her daughter, but Tila had not heard an unkind word said about her, even as Livnya. It was a stark contrast to Tila's own reputation, but she made peace with that long ago as the price for actually having and voicing an opinion, the lack of which – in larger affairs, at least – was something for which she had long judged her mother, although she rarely said so.

It had truly not occurred to Tila that even among their family there were differences. Everyone honoured and paid respect to Queen Hada, even now, but perhaps there was something to what she said. Perhaps that honour and respect was indeed wholly contingent on Tila's mother's behaviour. Perhaps, if Queen Hada had tried to influence matters in the same way as her daughter did, she would have received considerably shorter shrift.

'Your daughter does not feel especially divine,' she muttered.

'Perhaps that is because you have never been anything else,' her mother suggested. 'You cannot imagine what it is like to be one of us, just as we cannot imagine what it is to be like you.' She took another sip of her yeng. 'But now you face losing it all. They cannot strip you of your divinity, but they can take its trappings from you. What will you do then, when you are cast out? You must either petition Marshal Coldbeck to put forward a champion for you, or you must acknowledge your wrongdoing.'

'You have not been listening, Mother,' Tila sighed. 'Einan Coldbeck *wants* your daughter disowned! He is not a neutral arbiter in this! Any fighter he would put forward on your daughter's behalf will not be worthy of the name. And since he is acting in the name of the crown,' she added bitterly, 'your daughter cannot command any of the crown's sars whose prowess she would trust to stand for her: Coldbeck could overrule it.'

'So what do you propose?' her mother asked. 'To seek aid from another thane? Request they stand a sar for you, in exchange for an alliance?'

'Your daughter could not trust a one of them,' Tila said. 'To stand against the Eastern Marshal and the Lord Treasurer? They would be more likely to betray her in the hope of seeking favour.'

'You are still unmarried,' her mother suggested, and Tila's temper flashed.

'*If* your daughter ever chooses to marry, she will do so because she wishes to, not because she has been forced into it out of desperation!'

'You say you cannot trust anyone, and cannot find a champion,' her mother said despairingly, 'so what option do you have left? To take up arms yourself? You might provide the Divine Court with some amusement, at least.'

'Your daughter did not say that she could not find a champion,' Tila retorted. 'Merely that she could not find one within the Divine Court.'

Queen Hada looked at her for a few long moments, then set her yeng cup down and leaned back in her chair. There was an expression in her eyes that Tila didn't think she'd seen before: not one of judgement and disappointment mixed with frustrated love, but of pure consideration.

'And what contacts do you have outside of the Divine Court?'

This was it.

'Follow your daughter, if it pleases you,' Tila said. She finished her yeng in one swig, which was not a particularly mannered thing to do, but it would have gone cold long before she returned. Her mother's mouth quirked in disapproval, but she still followed when Tila got up and headed for her bedchamber.

'Please tell your mother you do not have someone smuggled in here,' Queen Hada said uncomfortably, as they entered.

'That would be more convenient,' Tila replied absently. She crossed to the far wall, opened her wardrobe and removed a metal bar as long as her arm.

'What is that?' her mother gasped in shock.

'This is a pry bar, mother,' Tila told her matter-of-factly. She pushed aside her dressing table and kicked back the woven reed mat to reveal the sandstone flags beneath, then slotted the thin end of the bar in a gap between one flag and the next. She heaved downwards and levered the slab of stone up far enough to bend down and get hold of it, then dragged it to one side.

Beneath it was a wooden trapdoor, which she pulled up to reveal a hole in the floor, into which descended a narrow metal ladder.

'Tila, what is this?' Queen Hada said, clapping her hands over her mouth in utter horror.

'Do you remember that when your daughter was younger, she would complain how cold her bedchamber was?' Tila asked, undoing the belting cord of her gown. 'Some years ago, she realised the floor over here seemed cooler than the rest of the room, and she noticed a small gap in the flagstones. She has always been inquisitive, and . . . ' She gestured at the floor.

'You did not make it?' her mother asked, increasing agitated. 'Where does it lead? Who else knows? You could . . . Someone could . . . '

'Calm yourself, Mother,' Tila said, slipping out of her robe and opening her wardrobe again. 'Anyone who tried to come up would be attempting to open a trapdoor under a flagstone, which would itself be under your daughter's dressing table, and they would be working from a position in which they could not brace themselves well. It would be practically impossible to get into this room without the consent of the occupant. Which is what seems to have happened,' she added. 'You are familiar with the rumours concerning Queen Sarra?'

'Your great-grandmother?' Queen Hada said, in a small voice.

'You remember how she was persistently rumoured to have been courted by a certain nobleman in the years after King Nahel died, even though there was never any evidence that such a thing occurred?' Tila asked.

'Those were lies and slander,' her mother replied instantly, and automatically. 'They were invented to sully her name, and that of—'

'Your daughter looked into it,' Tila cut her off, as she pulled one of Livnya's dresses out of her wardrobe. 'These were Queen Sarra's chambers, at that time.' She nodded at the hole in the floor. 'Personally, your daughter considers a suitor who would tunnel through rock to get to her more off-putting than appealing, but to each their own.'

'These were her chambers?' her mother repeated, her eyes drawn to the hole in the floor. 'Oh. Oh, by the Mountain.' She looked up at Tila, who was now pulling the dress on. 'Tila, what are you *doing*? Where does this lead?'

'You will forgive your daughter for keeping some secrets, she hopes?' Tila replied with a smile. The sandstone was soft enough that one man with a pickaxe, enough determination and a decent sense of direction could have made the tunnel by himself in a not unreasonable timescale, and the other end of it was hidden by panelling in the walls of one of the houses built up against the base of the sandstone rock on which the Sun Palace stood. Tila had found that it was still technically owned, although disused and in a state of disarray, by the estate of the very same noble rumoured to have seduced Queen Sarra, and had set about buying it as Livnya.

She shrugged her shoulders to get her dress to settle. Livnya's clothes were of a fine quality, but considerably less complex than those belonging to the Divine Princess. They only took one person to get in and out of, for one thing.

'Tila, please tell you mother that you are not intending to go down that damnable hole and leave the palace!' her mother begged her. 'It cannot be safe!'

'Your daughter has been using this for nearly twenty years,' Tila told her. She opened a drawer and pulled out her vambraces. 'Before your inevitable next question: these are knives. Yes, your daughter knows how to use them.'

'Why did you bring your mother here?' Queen Hada demanded. 'Why show her all this, that you have kept secret from her for so long? Do you intend simply to worry her to death?'

'Privacy in these chambers is no longer certain, with Marshal Coldbeck playing his games,' Tila said, buckling her vambraces on. 'However, even he would not be so impolite as to have his men intrude upon the Queen Mother visiting her daughter. Your daughter will be as quick as she can, but this is something she must do, and do now, and she must rely on your assistance.'

'And what is your mother supposed to do while you are gone?' Queen Hada demanded.

'There is still at least half a pot of yeng, and your daughter's zither is in the reception room,' Tila replied. 'If you played it, then anyone listening would think your daughter was playing it for you. And you would certainly do a better job,' she added, throwing a shawl around her shoulders.

'Tila, this is folly,' her mother tried again. 'This is worse than your mother had feared! You are already mired in these men's games at court, and now you throw yourself even deeper!'

'Mother,' Tila said, taking her by the shoulders and looking her in the eyes. 'You misunderstand. Your daughter is not playing their games. They are playing hers, and she is about to change the rules.'

*　*　*

IT WAS A DESPERATE balancing act, despite Tila's bold words to her mother. She had to rely on her servants to send messages, and had risked compromising herself by, for the first time, allowing Tila's world and Livnya's to cross paths. Still, high stakes required high risks.

She was not using the Three Storks today; she dared not. Instead she had gone to the Rose Tree, and slipped her veil on as soon as she was in one of their small, private back rooms. It was nearly the third bell of the afternoon, and she would soon find out if her gamble had paid off.

She heard the distant sound of the hour being sounded just as the door to the back room opened. He was punctual, then: that, at least, had always been true.

Alazar Blade, blacksword and one-time lover of her brother the God-King, stepped into the room and took one look at her veil.

'What the *fuck*?'

'Come in, close the door, and sit down,' Tila said, as calmly as she could. She was speaking in the cleanest, most courtly tone she could manage without slipping into a parody of it. Her childhood elocution tutor would have wept tears of joy if he could have heard her at this moment, because Tila Narida really, *really* needed Alazar Blade not to connect the woman sitting in front of him with the speaking habits of Livnya the Knife. It was a poky back room, and she had her veil: she had to hope it would be enough.

Alazar hesitated, his jaw working beneath that ugly beard of his.

'You lose nothing by hearing a proposition out,' Tila said. Why could the man not just do as he was bid for once?

Alazar grunted and shut the door behind him, but he did not move to sit. Instead he folded his arms and glowered at her, dark eyes beneath dark brows. 'What in the name of Heaven are *you* doing here? Nari's teeth, have you fled the palace? This sar had heard of a scandal there, but—'

'This princess has fled nothing,' Tila cut him off icily. 'It will take more than a few men with spears to keep her from going where she chooses. Now, she assumes you were interested in her proposal, else you would not be here.'

'This sar did not know it was *your* proposal,' Alazar snorted. 'How did you know he was married, or in Idramar at all, let alone that his husband is in the Keepers' cells?'

'They do not call this princess the "Veiled Shadow" for nothing,' Tila replied. 'She knows much of what occurs in her city. Her message to you was an honest one. She proposes to use her influence to free your husband, on condition of you performing a service for her.'

'You have no influence,' Alazar replied. 'The scandal, remember?'

'This princess has been challenged to trial by combat,' Tila said. 'Once her champion triumphs, her status will be restored.'

Alazar snorted again. The man seemed to have a veritable language of his own, made entirely of forceful exhalations through his nose. 'And who is your—?'

He stopped, blinked a few times, and stared at her.

'That would be the service you would perform for this princess,' Tila said levelly.

Alazar appeared to be genuinely at a loss for words. Tila took the opportunity to pour two cups of yeng, and pushed one towards the edge of the table closest to where he stood. 'Come. Sit. Let us discuss this.'

'What is there to discuss?' Alazar said. He walked to the seat and sat, but did not pick up his cup. 'This is a laughable proposal.'

'What other options do you have for freeing your husband?' Tila asked him. 'The Keepers seem certain he has stolen quite a few items of value from prominent people.'

'This sar will have to work something out,' Alazar replied, but he didn't sound as sure of himself as he probably hoped he did.

'This princess requires a champion,' she said, carefully manoeuvring her cup under her veil. 'He must be a sar, to satisfy the requirements of the honour challenge. He cannot be sworn directly to the crown, for that would place him under the control of the Eastern Marshal. A blacksword mercenary is the perfect solution.'

'It's not a perfect solution when he's only a blacksword because of your damned family!' Alazar growled, and Tila's jaw clenched.

'As this princess recalls, her family did not instruct you to retreat from the Morlithian patrol and leave her father, the *God-King*, to be shot dead by a Morlithian arrow in the Torgallen Pass!' she snarled. 'Yet you have built a reputation as a swordsman since, so presumably you grew into your courage late in life!'

Alazar's face darkened, and for a moment Tila genuinely thought he was going to strike her. Then, for a wonder, he took up his cup in hands that shook with rage, and took a sip of yeng.

'You never got the full account of what happened that day.'

'This princess heard your words in the Hall of Heaven,' Tila told him. 'She heard you admitting to your own cowardice.'

Alazar tilted his head to the side. 'You heard lies, made up by a lovesick fool to ease the pain of the man he loved, whose father had just died.'

'What?' Tila felt like she had been punched in the chest. She had got very used to telling when someone was lying over the years, in both her lives, and every instinct was screaming at her that Alazar had just been truthful. Yet that could not be. She had heard him!

You heard him when you were seventeen, her own voice cautioned her. *You heard him when you were seventeen, and distraught, and desperately looking for someone to blame.*

'We encountered the Morlithian patrol, as this sar described,' Alazar said. There was a weariness in his voice. 'They attacked, and we fought them back, but they regrouped and were coming again. We shouldn't have pushed that far into the pass in the first place, but we were all young fools who wanted to prove our bravery to the God-King, that part is true enough. He never told us to turn back, but why should he? He didn't know the terrain; didn't know how far the Morlithians were likely to approach. We ignored the local guide. That was our first mistake.'

'They regrouped, and came again,' Tila said, fighting the hollowness in her chest. 'And you ran.'

'No,' Alazar said. He shook his head, but held her eyes. 'We held. 'Your *father* ran.'

Tila couldn't breathe. 'No.'

'Yes,' Alazar said, almost gently. 'This sar yelled at him to stay with us – he yelled an order to the God-King! – but your father fled. He didn't trust we could hold the pass. Had he stayed with us, we could have protected him behind the shields of the men; once he broke cover, that was it. They only had a pair of archers, higher up the slope, but that was enough. This sar doesn't know if they recognised your father for who he was, but they couldn't have mistaken him for anything other than a high-ranking noble. They shot for him, and they were either skilled or lucky.'

He was telling the truth. Tila dealt with liars. Alazar was either the most brilliant liar she had yet met, or he was telling the truth.

'Why did you not retreat with him?' she whispered. 'Why did you not fall back when he did?'

'We already held the best position!' Alazar snapped. 'The pass was narrow! Besides, have you tried a fighting retreat in combat, princess? It's far harder, far more dangerous, than holding your ground. Had we retreated, it would have turned into a rout, and you father would have died in any case!' He shook his head angrily. 'Your father gave this sar command of his detail, and then turned and ran rather than listen to him—'

'This princess's father did not give you command because of your skill or experience, you witless oaf!' Tila hissed. 'You were twenty-one years old, barely three years a sar! You were given that command because Natan *begged* our father to honour the man he loved!'

Alazar started as though she had slapped him. 'He . . . He did what?'

Tila rolled her eyes behind her veil. 'Tolkar's arse, were you honestly so self-absorbed that you thought you would be given such an honour simply on merit? Perhaps, *perhaps* you might have been assigned to our father's side and instructed to guard him with your life, you were a competent enough fighter for that. But given command of his detail? That should have gone to a far more experienced warrior. However, our father cared too much for the feelings of his son, and gave not enough thought to his own safety.'

Alazar set his cup down, very carefully. 'This drink is somewhat bitter.'

'It is,' Tila agreed. She could taste bile at the back of her throat. 'This has been an . . . instructive conversation.'

'Indeed.'

'But it concerns matters from long ago,' Tila continued, 'and that is not the concern for either of us, as it stands.'

Alazar nodded, once. 'Also true.'

'You wish your husband to be released,' Tila said. 'This princess needs a skilled fighter to stand for her as her champion. Once her innocence is proven by the trial, she will have your husband freed. On this matter, she gives you her word.'

Alazar tapped the tabletop with his right index finger, as though in thought. 'When is the trial?'

'Tomorrow, at noon,' Tila said. She had used up nearly all her time arranging this meeting, but she was confident in her gamble. Alazar loved his husband, and Marin was in trouble. In the City of Islands, she had seen Alazar take on three men at once, kill two of them and send the third fleeing. A skilled opponent would be a different matter, of course, but there would only be one of him.

Besides, if there was one thing that Tila had worked out about Alazar Blade in the time they'd spent on the *Light of Fortune*, it was that he had a chip on his shoulder the size of a mountain when it came to Narida's nobility. Despite his personal dislike of her, and her brother, she was willing to bet that he would like nothing more than to walk into the Sun Palace as a blacksword, a despised, shamed outsider, and utterly thrash a champion of the Inner Council.

'This sar will speak to his husband,' Alazar said. 'If he is fighting for Marin's freedom, Marin should have his say. He often frets when this sar fights.'

'This princess—' *Remembers*, Tila was about to say, and caught herself at the last moment. 'Understands,' she finished instead. It had been Livnya the Knife who had met Marin by chance in a warehouse in East Harbour, when he approached the only other Naridans there to make anxious small talk while he waited for his husband to fight. Tila Narida had, of course, been nowhere nearby.

Alazar did not seem to notice her momentary hesitation. 'If Marin agrees, this sar will present himself at the Sun Palace gates before noon tomorrow.'

'And if he does not agree?' Tila asked, as he rose to leave.

'Then you may be out of luck,' Alazar replied. He bowed with a mocking smile, and left, leaving Tila staring at the cup of yeng in front of her.

JEYA

THE COURT OF the Deities was packed from side to side with bodies, as the people of Grand Mahewa gathered for the Feast of Ash to venerate Mushuru. The god had burned on the fires of knowledge so the peoples of the world could gain understanding and become more than mindless beasts, and offerings would be given to fires all across Kiburu ce Alaba in the evening, in memory of that sacrifice.

Jeya had said a whole handful of prayers to Mushuru, in the hope of working out whether what shé and Galem were planning was wise or not, but the god had remained silent. Nor had shé seen any sign of Sa, god of thieves and tricksters (amongst other things), since the night they had guided hér to the hole in the Old Palace's wall so shé and Galem could sleep in relative safety. Then again, shé supposed that Sa would have less interest in what shé was up to now: the trickster god approved of subterfuge and deceit, so a thief who was trying to hide would attract their attention. A thief attempting to reveal the truth was far less likely to be of interest.

'We need to be as close to the front as possible,' Galem muttered in hér ear. 'That's the only way the Hierarchs will have a hope of seeing my face.'

'That's a lot easier said than done,' Jeya told thëm. 'That's where the rich people go.'

'Ï thought the worship of the gods was equal for all,' Galem said, surprised.

'Supposedly, yes,' Jeya said, 'but when did yöu see anyone looking like mé down at the front, when yöu were up on the temple?'

'Ï could never really see that much out of the mask, to be honest,' Galem admitted. 'The eye holes weren't big enough, and sat in slightly the wrong place. Ï just smiled and waved.'

'Why did yöu smile when yöu had a mask on?' Jeya asked. Galem shrugged.

'It would have seemed rude not to.'

'We'll get as close as we can,' Jeya told thëm. 'But Ï can't guarantee anything.'

Shé led the way through the press of bodies, since Galem had begun to adapt to life on the streets, but still hadn't really got the hang of forcing thëir way through crowds. Shé kept one hand in thëirs at all times, to make sure they didn't get separated, and ducked and wriggled through increasingly rich-looking people. It would have been far easier with Nabanda to lead the way, but shé'd not seen hîm for a couple of weeks now. That wasn't unusual; sometimes the docks were very busy, and sometimes hê had other work which kept hîm occupied. Besides which, Jeya wasn't sure shé wanted to introduce Nabanda to Galem. Nabanda had always had a poor opinion of the Splinter King – 'foreign beggar' was the term hê'd used at the Festival of the Crossing – and wasn't too kindly disposed towards the rich in general. Hê might not be sympathetic to Galem's plight.

Jeya weaved past another couple, and heard a distinct noise of disapproval from one of them as shé did so. Sure enough, the rich of East Harbour weren't pleased about a couple of scruffy paupers wending their way into the area from which they were normally excluded, by tradition if not by law. Jeya decided to ignore the disapproval, and see whether anyone took enough issue with their presence to actually accost them under the eyes of the gods. Jeya didn't think the gods would approve of that, and shé hoped that opinion would be shared by others.

They were close, now: a mere few lines of people away from the dark, carved rock wall of the temple. It had five levels, and the walls of each bore designs of the various deities that had come to rest in Kiburu ce Alaba: those who'd been birthed here and those who'd travelled here with their worshippers. Even Nari was up there somewhere, and although Jeya didn't hold the Naridan god in any particular reverence, it was a strange feeling indeed to know that shé was currently holding hands with hìs descendant.

A blur of colour and movement appeared above them, and the crowd began to cheer as the Priest of the Hundred made their way out, swirling and dancing in their sky-cape of brilliant feathers taken from the birds of the forests. Following the priest, as always, came the Hierarchs, resplendent in their vivid maijhi and karung. Jeya searched through the faces and found Chamuru, who didn't look quite as at ease as the rest of them. Perhaps they were concerned about what might be about to happen; and with good reason.

'Are yöu ready?' shé asked Galem, standing on tiptoe to speak into thëir ear and make hérself heard above the noise of the crowd. The plan was simple: try to attract the attention of the Hierarchs Galem knew best, so they could see thëm standing in the crowd and realise thëy were still alive. Chamuru might have their own agenda, and disapprove of the Hierarchs sheltering the Splinter King's family, but even if that were true, they surely had to be in the minority.

'Yes,' Galem said, nodding. 'Ï will—'

Thëy broke off, an expression of utter shock crossing thëir face, and Jeya looked up at the temple to see why.

There, walking imperiously out at a respectful distance behind the Hierarchs, was the Splinter King. Behind hìm came the Splinter Queen, the adult Splinter Prince, and the younger Splinter Princess. All were robed in the Naridan style, with long, trailing robes held up by children. Their faces were obscured by the spectacular jewel-encrusted silver masks Jeya had seen so many times before, and which Galem had just described to hér as being hard to see out of.

They were there, and yet that was impossible, because Galem was *here* . . .

Jeya's words failed hér. Shé found hérself simply gaping, looking from Galem to the temple, and back again.

'We need to leave,' Galem said. Thëir tone was flat and expressionless, but the eyes looking up at the temple were wide and horrified.

Jeya grabbed for thëir arm. 'No, wait—'

Galem didn't wait. Thëy cut off to thëir right and plunged through the crowd, who were already preparing for the priest to lead them in the songs to Mushuru. Thëir arm slipped out of Jeya's grip, and for a moment shé stood there transfixed. Should shé just let thëm go? What did this mean? Had Galem lied? Were thëy not the Splinter Prince at all?

No. No, that couldn't be it. Why would thëy come here with hér if thëy'd known there was no reason for the Splinter King not to appear? Besides, Galem's reaction had been genuine. Thëy'd barely believed what thëy'd seen. Something here was very wrong, but it wasn't Galem.

Jeya set off after thëm. Shé was a couple of heartbeats behind, but it wasn't hard to track Galem's progress; shé just had to follow the trail of angry, ruffled rich people who were outraged at being jostled when the worship was about to begin. Jeya offered up some more prayers to Mushuru, begging the god's forgiveness for not participating in the songs, but surely Mushuru, of all the gods, would know what shé was doing, and why?

Then again, Mushuru was simply ash now. Who could say what a god like that would think of hér?

Galem was making a beeline for the edge of the Court of the Deities, as direct a route as thëy could manage through the crowd. Jeya caught sight of the back of thëir head and redoubled hér efforts. Shé was slightly smaller, and slightly more nimble, and just that bit more experienced at getting through a press of bodies. Shé caught up with Galem about halfway to the edge.

'Bulang!' shé called. 'Wait!'

Galem at least recognised the name thëy'd adopted, and slowed. Jeya managed to latch on to thëm, and pulled thëm close as everyone around them began to raise their voices in song.

'What's going on?' shé demanded, which shé felt was a reasonable question. Galem looked up over her shoulder, back at the temple, licking thëir lips nervously.

'Do yóu think they can see us here?'

'Not a hope!' Jeya said. 'If yöu want to get off the Court, we can, but follow mé! Yöu'll only draw attention otherwise!' Shé pushed past Galem and took the lead again, weaving hér way through the most obvious gaps and timing their advances to the movements of the crowd.

The press of bodies thinned out towards the edges, where the carved pillars stood, and Jeya slowed to a more normal pace as they descended the steps that raised the Court above the level of the streets. As soon as they reached the bottom, shé turned and took both of Galem's wrists in hér hands.

'What was that?' shé asked, without preamble.

'Ï don't know,' Galem said baldly. Thëy still seemed to be in a state of shock, and thëir eyes were darting around as though thëy could find the answer somewhere just by looking. 'Sorry, Jeya, Ï panicked. When Ï saw they had a new family up there . . . '

'Yöu don't know who they were?' Jeya asked.

'No!' Galem wheeled around, even though the column behind thëm now hid the front of the temple from view. 'It must be . . . the Hierarchs can't have wanted to lose face by not having the Splinter King on hand for a festival. They must have got impersonators in, perhaps told them that we were ill, or, or . . . '

Something ugly was clawing at Jeya's stomach. 'Galem. What if the Hierarchs all want the Splinter King in Kiburu ce Alaba, but they're not that bothered about it being the *real* Splinter King?'

Galem's eyes went wide. 'But . . . but . . . '

'The whole idea was that no one knew who yöu were the rest of the time, right?' Jeya asked. 'So if they grab another family, a poor family, and say, "Hey, we'll give you a nice house and guards and money. All you have to do is wear a mask and wave at festivals, and never tell anyone", who's going to know?'

'No one,' Galem said, in a small voice. 'No one, really.'

'So they don't need yöu,' Jeya said urgently. 'Which means yöu're actually *dangerous* to them now. Maybe that's why Chamuru tried to have the guards grab us: they were worried yöu were going to put a hole in the Hierarchs' plan for covering up what had happened!'

Galem's eyes went wide again. 'What if it was the Hierarchs who sent the killers? What if they found out that Ï'm . . . that Ï'm not . . . '

'If they did then it's their fault, not yöurs!' Jeya snapped. She wouldn't let Galem blame thëmselves for this mess again! 'And why would they? Why not just have a word and suggest your parents had another go at it? But if the killers were sent by the Naridans to kill the Splinter King and his family, they're going to see that family up there, or hear about them, and think they got it wrong, right? Which means maybe they won't still be after yöu. Maybe they'll go after *them*.'

'Not if they care about getting rid of the actual bloodline,' Galem said miserably. 'They've tried so many times, Ï . . . '

Thëy tailed off, blinking.

'Jeya, what if they succeeded? All the stories say the Splinter King and his family survived, or enough of them did, but what if the Hierarchs have done this before, to cover up an assassination? And the Naridans never realised their killers had actually succeeded? What if . . . What if my family . . . ?'

Galem grabbed Jeya by hér arms, thëir face a picture of terror and uncertainty.

'Jeya, *who am Ï*?'

ZHANNA

IT WAS DARK and cold away from the fire, but Zhanna wasn't overly concerned. Back in Tjakorsha, Father Krayk swallowed the sun for days at a time during Long Night, when the winds raged and the inlets froze and twisting spirit lights lit up the sky, assuming your view of them wasn't blocked out by thick cloud vomiting snow down at you. For sure, it was colder up here in the mountains than down in Black Keep, and the scudding clouds kept obscuring the imperfect discs of the moons, but it wasn't anything Zhanna hadn't experienced before.

She wondered if these Naridans, whoever they were, could say the same.

The light of her party's fire was just visible behind her, but the trunks of the trees combined to block out most of it. The ground was easy enough to move over; not much grew between the pine trunks, and the floor was spongy with shed needles. Zhanna and Olagora could hunt quietly, without needing to crash through undergrowth and announce their presence to anyone listening. Talon and Thorn were at her heels, but they moved silently, and were neither rattling nor squabbling.

A whistle came from their left, towards the valley floor. It was a fairly poor imitation of a white-headed diver, but it was recognisable as a Tjakorshi bird, if you didn't question why a white-headed diver was up in the mountains and calling at night. A chill ran across Zhanna's skin, wrapped in her furs though she was, and she touched Olagora's arm. There was someone here who should not be, or else the call wouldn't have gone up. They cut to their left, moving as quickly and quietly as they could in the darkness.

They were upon Tsennan before Zhanna realised, as a deeper patch of darkness abruptly detached itself from a tree trunk and turned into a towering shape with blackstone axe in hand. She clamped down on a squeak of surprise.

'Did you call?' she murmured, keeping her voice low and avoiding 's' sounds. They could hiss through the air and alert hostile ears; she remembered that much from listening to older raiders talking about how to sneak up on enemies.

'Not me,' Tsennan replied softly. He jerked his head, an almost imperceptible motion in the dark, indicating down the slope. 'Over there.'

Zhanna's heart was speeding up, and she took a deep breath to try to calm her nerves. Tamadh and Sakka had seen something, then. Tamadh had raided before, and was no more likely to go jumping at shadows than Tsennan.

She needed to get closer.

'Come on,' she said. She tried to angle her shield so it was covering the pale wood of her longblade's scabbard as much as possible. Her sea bear furs were dark, her hair was covered by her hood and they had all rubbed dirt into their faces, so the Naridan scabbard was the thing most likely to give her away. She had considered rubbing dirt into that too, but she remembered what she'd been told about how the scabbards of shamed sars were stained black. Zhanna wasn't shamed, and she felt that if Daimon and Darel were willing to give her their own father's weapon and a new scabbard then she should treat it like a Naridan would.

The slope was not too steep, but it was hard to pick their way down it in the dark. Zhanna lost her footing more than once as the soil or a rock shifted beneath her, and it was only through the proximity of a tree trunk that she managed to avoid either falling over or careering downhill in a stumble that would likely have ended in her twisting an ankle.

It was just after she thudded into a tree shoulder-first, to muffle the impact as much as possible by hitting it with her furs instead of her shield, that she heard voices. They were low and indistinct, but they were male. Unless Tamadh was having a conversation with himself, or Sakka's voice had dropped considerably since they left the fire . . .

'Call back,' she whispered to Tsennan. He pursed his lips and whistled in what could, if you were being very kind, be interpreted as the call of a white-headed diver, if the bird was either drunk or ill.

'That was awful,' Olagora murmured from behind him.

'If you think you can do better—' Tsennan began, but Zhanna clicked her tongue for quiet. It was something she had picked up from her mother, and Longjaw stopped speaking, to Zhanna's partial surprise. It did not matter how bad it had been: what was important was that Tamadh and Sakka now knew that someone else had seen, or at least heard, the people about whom they'd raised the alarm.

But who were these night walkers?

'Thtay here,' she lisped, to prevent the sibilant sounds from carrying to unfriendly ears, and slipped out from behind her tree.

The voices were still talking, and sounded more urgent than before. She picked her way towards them as well as she could, one hand on the grip of her longblade. All she needed to do was hear one word she recognised and it would confirm they were Naridans, which meant they were almost certain to be the same ones who had been chasing Kakaiduna. However, the last thing she wanted was to start a fight in the dark with Smoking Valley men who had somehow got free from the slavers.

Suddenly, the voices resolved.

' . . . 's not a bird.'

'What d'you know about birds?'

'What do *you* know about birds? S'man's telling you, there's something out there, and it's no bird!'

Naridans. Two Naridans, one of whom was suspicious about the whistles he'd heard, for which Zhanna couldn't fault him.

'Does anyone live in this valley?' That was a third voice. Three of them, then. Zhanna cursed inwardly.

'Well, there's Ironhead,' said the first, after a pause. 'But that's almost out of the mountains.'

'So no one lives here?'

'S'man doesn't know! How should he know?'

'It's not like we saw a damned town when the sun was still up,' the second voice put in, somewhat scathingly. 'There could be shepherds or some such. Why?'

'Because there's a fire up there,' the third voice said. 'Shepherds?'

Zhanna held her breath.

'Nari's teeth, there is and all,' the second said. 'Good eyes.'

'We'd best see who it is,' the first voice said. 'Perhaps the girl saw it too.'

'Nice and quiet, then,' the third voice said. 'Let's take a look who else is out here.'

Naridans, trying to find a girl. The possibilities of this trio being anyone other than those chasing Kakaiduna had basically disappeared, which meant they were enemies. Zhanna had known what it would mean if she'd encountered them, but they'd doomed themselves beyond question now they intended to approach the fire, so she edged further down the slope, hoping their movements would mask the sound of hers as she slipped behind them. Then, once she could dimly make out their shadowy shapes trudging away from her, she cupped her hands to her mouth and let out the loudest, harshest crow's *caw* she could.

The Naridans jerked around, but other *caws* rang out from

either side of them. They didn't know it, but the sound of Father Krayk's sacred birds was their death-knell. The rest of Zhanna's crew would be advancing on them now, ready to attack when they saw an opening.

'Who are you?' Zhanna shouted in Naridan. She might get an answer now, or she might not, but it was worth a try.

'Show yourselves!' one of them snapped back.

'We want one alive if possible!' she shouted to her crew in her own tongue. She drew her longblade and stepped out from behind a tree, holding her shield ready, her heart hammering in her chest. This would be near-blind fighting, where luck grabbed skill by the throat and choked it. It was hard to even tell exactly how far away from her the three Naridans were, let alone what they might be armed with.

One of them started towards her, and she caught the faint glint of metal from what looked to be a spear tip. He'd have reach on her, then, but if she could get inside that he was as good as hers. She held her sword up, hoping they'd see its shape and that would perhaps make them think they were facing a sar of their own land. That might give them pause.

Talon and Thorn sounded their tails, the hollow noise shockingly loud in the night, and she saw the Naridan stiffen.

'Shit, ratt—!'

She heard Tsennan Longjaw's bellow a moment before there was a loud thump and panicked cries from the Naridans. A sprawl of shadow suggested Longjaw had simply barrelled into one of them at full tilt, shield first, and knocked him to the ground. It looked like the second had been flattened by the tangle as well, and then two other shapes appeared: Sakka and Tamadh, who fell upon the Naridans with their blackstone weapons.

The Naridan facing Zhanna whirled, then brought his weapon up as Olagora charged him from Zhanna's left. Zhanna didn't wait; she broke into a run, and as the Naridan yelled his own war cry and thrust at Olagora, his spear point smacking into her shield and staggering her, Zhanna slashed her longblade into the back of his thigh.

He howled and fell backwards, and she darted back a couple of steps to try to get out of range of his spear. He gave a screaming grunt and rolled over on to his front, and she saw something flash out at her legs. Zhanna danced back further, and then Olagora brought her axe down on the arm that held the spear. The Naridan screamed again and dropped his weapon, and Zhanna heard the thump as Olagora threw herself knee-first on to his back, then raised her axe.

'Wait!' Zhanna snapped at her, trying to see what was happening only a few ells away up the slope. 'Who lives?'

'Me,' Tamadh replied, his breathing coming fast. 'This one's dead.' Judging by the amount of blows Zhanna had heard land, he and Sakka must have virtually hacked their Naridan apart.

'I'm alive,' Sakka added, sounding not a little shaky.

'This one's alive, but he may not be for long,' Longjaw replied. 'I've got my dagger at his thr-*arrgh!* Bite me would you, you fucker?' Zhanna heard the sound of a fist meeting flesh and bone.

'This one's alive too, though he won't be walking well,' she said. She could hear the Naridan's breath coming fast, but he didn't seem to have it in him to try to throw Olagora off him.

'Well, we only need one,' Longjaw said, and Zhanna heard a wet puncture sound that her mind immediately filled in as a spearfish-bill dagger being driven into a neck. She suppressed a shudder. Had the man yielded? Every warrior knew you shouldn't kill an enemy who had yielded, but Tsennan wouldn't have understood anything the man had said.

She pushed the thought from her mind. Longjaw had said the man probably wouldn't have lived for long anyway. Zhanna would consider it a mercy blow, and couldn't see to know otherwise.

She walked up to the last one, still weighed down by Olagora on his back, and put the edge of her sword against his neck.

'Your friends are dead,' she said in his language. 'Who are you?'

'Go fuck yourselves, mountain devils!'

Zhanna snorted a laugh despite herself. 'He thinks we're the mountain people!' she called to the others, and they chuckled in turn. She knelt down next to him, keeping her blade in place.

'We are not mountain devils,' she told him, slowly and clearly. 'We are Raiders.'

She used the Naridan word deliberately, and heard his intake of breath in response to it.

'What did you say to him?' Olagora asked. 'He just went stiff as a board.'

'I told him who we are,' Zhanna replied. 'I don't think he was expecting us.' She raised her voice. 'Longjaw! Tamadh! Are you hurt?'

'Not me.'

'Nor me.'

'Get over here then, see if he's got any other weapons hidden on him, and get him up,' Zhanna told them. 'We'll take him back to the fire and see who he is.' She changed back to Naridan and spoke to the captive. 'Listen to me. Fight more, and you die. Do not fight, do not die.' She wasn't sure how true that was, exactly, since she couldn't see how badly he was bleeding, but she wouldn't take a blade to him again.

The Naridan yelped and groaned as he was hauled upright, with his wounded left leg and right arm, and it didn't help much that both Tamadh, and Tsennan in particular, were taller than him. Longjaw grumbled irritably as he stopped to take the Naridan's arm over his shoulders, but he did as Zhanna had commanded, and they set off back up the slope to their fire.

All in all, it had gone as well as she could have hoped. Her crew had taken on enemies and had achieved their aim without taking a wound. Granted, they outnumbered those enemies, and the darkness meant they'd been able to surprise them, but even so, it was a triumph. Zhanna found herself grinning as she trailed behind their prisoner, her longblade wiped off and back in its scabbard, her own shield on her left arm and the Longjaw's on her right, and her rattletails skittering around her feet.

'Who's there?' came a shout from ahead of them, as they got closer to the flickering light.

'We have one!' Zhanna shouted back, and hurried ahead. The others were where she'd left them, and they began to relax when they saw her. Menaken shook his head at her, looking for all the world as though he thought he was her father.

'Are you hurt?'

'We are good,' Zhanna grinned at him. 'Three men, two now dead. One, we have.'

Longjaw and Tamadh hauled their captive into the light of the fire, flanked by Olagora and Sakka, and Zhanna got her first proper look at the Naridan.

The man wore furs and skins rather than Naridan robes, but then again, so did the Naridans with her: it would be far harder to stay warm up here without them. He didn't look like one of the mountain people though, at least not judging by what Zhanna had seen so far, even with a growth of beard. Whoever he was, he hadn't kept up the usual Naridan practice of keeping his face free from hair.

'Where are you from?' Danid asked, striding forward. Zhanna felt a moment's irritation at the hunter taking over, but it made sense for the interrogation to be done by someone who spoke the language fully. Besides, Danid was more likely to understand the answers.

'Go kiss the Mountain,' the captive spat at him. Well, that was easy enough to understand, although Zhanna wasn't sure if he was talking about a particular mountain, or just whichever one was closest.

'Get his furs off,' Danid instructed Tsennan and Tamadh, and Zhanna translated. 'Maybe he has something that will tell us what we need to know.'

The captive was forced down to his knees, not without another strangled yell from him as he took pressure on to his injured left leg, and questing fingers wrenched open his fur jacket. What was revealed made Zhanna draw her breath in sharply in shock.

He wore a dark green tunic beneath, and embroidered upon it was the image of a flying white kingdrake, the animal that had eaten Ingorzhak. Surely such an omen could not bode well?

Menaken pushed forward, his face thunderous, although for a different reason. 'Darkspur? You serve Darkspur?'

The captive, his face now hanging down towards the ground, simply spat at Menaken's feet.

Zhanna remembered Darkspur. Their chief had come with the Marshal, and had not been pleased to find the Brown Eagle clan living in Black Keep. In fact, from what she'd gathered, their chief had argued against the Marshal when he had decided he didn't need to kill Daimon after all.

'Why is Darkspur in the Smoking Valley?' Menaken demanded, sounding as angry as Zhanna had ever heard him. He was usually cheerful, but there was nothing friendly about his expression now. The man didn't answer.

Danid kicked him in the stomach.

The breath exploded out of him, and he doubled over as far as he could with Tamadh and Tsennan still holding on to his arms. Danid folded his arms and glowered down at him.

'S'man's friend here asked you a question. You might want to answer it.'

The captive was gasping, trying to get air back into his lungs. Zhanna shifted uncomfortably. She didn't like the way this was going, but then she looked over at the Kakaiduna, now curled up on the far side of the fire with Amonhuhe of the Mountains stood over her like some protecting god, and remembered that this man had been hunting her.

'*Gold*,' the Darkspur man wheezed.

Danid and Menaken looked at each other, then down at the captive.

'What?' Danid said.

'Gold,' the Darkspur man repeated, with slightly more strength in his voice. 'There's gold in the river.' He hissed out a laugh between his teeth. 'The savages don't know what they've got!'

Menaken made a sucking noise with his teeth. 'How many of you are there? How many of the clan you're working with, the . . . ' He looked back at Amonhuhe, whose expression could split stone. 'The Two Peaks people?'

'A hundred,' laughed the captive. 'No, wait, a score. No, wait, two hundred!' He grinned up at Menaken and Danid, the grimace of a man fighting off pain with blistering contempt. 'If you want to see, you'll have to go and look.'

'We will,' another voice announced, and Amonhuhe pushed between Menaken and Danid. She reached out and grabbed the captive's hair, pulling his head back as though to stare into his eyes. Zhanna didn't see the knife in her hand until she drew it across his throat, opening a high tide wound out of which his red life began to flow.

Menaken recoiled and Danid grimaced. Tsennan and Tamadh each let go of the arm they were holding, in apparent surprise more than anything else, and the captive slumped forwards making a wet gurgling noise. Zhanna looked over at Tatiosh, who was staring at his mother as though he'd never seen her before.

Amonhuhe exhaled, wiped her knife clean on the back of the captive's furs, and sheathed it on her belt.

'Why you do that?' Zhanna demanded, stepping up to her. She was taller than the Smoking Valley woman, but Amonhuhe looked back at her without a trace of fear in her eyes. 'That man yield did! He this warrior's! This warrior say to him, no kill!'

'He did not yield to *this* woman,' Amonhuhe growled back, 'and this is *her* ground. *He has enslaved this woman's people.* She doesn't give a storm's mercy what promises you made to him!' She kicked the captive in the ribs, and he rolled over to expose the red ruin of his throat. Zhanna looked away.

'We should go back to Ironhead,' Danid said. 'We should get help.'

'You do as you please,' Amonhuhe said coldly. 'This woman will not leave her people to suffer while you run back to the lowlands. She will be going on in the morning, and she will bring death to these . . . ' She spat a word in her own tongue, one Zhanna didn't know, and didn't want to. Amonhuhe turned to her.

'What about you, Raider? Have you lost your taste for battle now?'

Zhanna ground her teeth. The woman questioned her courage, which was enough to start an argument among Tjakorshi, but Amonhuhe wasn't Tjakorshi. Besides which, Zhanna was here to represent Black Keep, and Black Keep was friends to the Smoking Valley.

'We go on,' she said, speaking for all her crew, and hoping they would agree when she told them what she'd decided. 'We come with you. And we bring death.'

SAANA

SAANA JERKED AWAKE. It was still dark outside, with only the dim light of the shuttered oil lamp illuminating the chamber, and everything was quiet. She had not woken naturally, with the morning light and the harsh chorus of the little wind drakes shouting their territorial claims at each other. Something else was responsible.

It wasn't her husband, that was for certain. She could hear only the faintest of sighs next to her as Daimon's breaths came and went in the smooth patterns of sleep, and the mound he made under the blankets wasn't moving. Saana smiled to herself. Well yes, *that* had happened. Daimon had proved to be as mannered when it came to lovemaking as he was with everything else, which perhaps shouldn't have taken her by surprise. He'd been far from skilled – unsurprising, since these had apparently been his first attempts – but he'd readily taken gentle correction, and had been gratifyingly enthusiastic—

Chok.

Something hit the window shutter: not that hard, and not that loud, but enough for Saana to be abruptly certain that this was what had woken her. She stiffened instinctively, and her thoughts went to her axe, which was still in her bedchamber in the so-called women's quarters. Daimon's longblade was in here somewhere, if it came to it . . .

'*Daimon!*'

It was a hoarse whisper from outside, and it did nothing to ease Saana's nerves. On the other hand, someone trying to attract her husband's attention probably was not going to be attempting to break in and kill anyone. But who would be doing such a thing? She wondered about elbowing Daimon awake, but Father Krayk take her, why should she? She was no Naridan woman, forced to let her husband deal with everything. If someone wanted to talk to her husband in the middle of the night, they could damned well explain to his wife why they were throwing things at his window.

She rolled off the bed, wincing as her bare feet met the cold boards of the floor. The charcoal fire pit was still giving off a little warmth, and the nights were certainly warmer than they had been, but sometimes she missed the packed earth floor of her old longhouse. She'd discarded her fur jacket earlier, and she picked it up and threw it over her woollen shift, since the night air was likely to have a bite to it, then strode to the shutters and opened them.

All the dwellings in Black Keep were raised off the ground on stilts of wood, and the living quarters of the Blackcreek family were no exception, so Saana was looking down at the shadowy, hooded figure on the grass as they drew their arm back to throw something, then abruptly stopped once they registered that the shutters had opened.

'...Lady Saana?' the figure said, sounding unsure of themselves.

Saana crossed her arms and scowled. 'Who are you?'

'This . . . ' The figure stood still for a moment, then reached up and threw its hood back with a violence that suggested someone doing it before they lost their nerve. 'Um.'

Saana peered down at them, but the night was not a bright one; neither moon was full, and clouds littered the sky. About all she could tell was that the speaker was female, and that only really because of the voice. 'That does not help,' she said flatly. Behind her, she heard the bed creak as Daimon shifted position, perhaps disturbed by the sound of voices, but not yet awake.

The figure below turned her head this way and that, as though checking to see that no one else could see, then turned her face up to Saana again.

'Yarmina Darkspur.'

Suspicion flooded up in Saana like a high tide at a double moon. What was she doing here, trying to attract Daimon's attention in the middle of the night? What had her husband said to this girl, to make her think she could do such a thing?!

Saana forced herself to think sensibly. Daimon had invited her to join him tonight, so he would have been a fool to try to arrange anything with this noble girl from Darkspur, and Saana's husband was no fool. He was also painfully concerned with honour: she couldn't believe that he would go outside normal Naridan marriage practices.

Also, Yarmina did not have to announce herself. She could have fled as soon as she realised Saana was here. Saana's suspicions did not empty away completely, but they died back down to a level where her immediate instinct was not to jump out of the window and punch the girl in her face.

'What do you want?' she asked, not letting up on her scowl.

'To speak with Daimon,' Yarmina replied. 'And with you. Inside,' she added, hopefully.

Saana's immediate reaction was that the girl could have done that in the hall earlier that evening, rather than keeping her mouth shut and letting her cousin do all the talking, but she realised before she said anything that this was surely the point. For whatever reason, Yarmina Darkspur wanted to have a conversation without her minders. Saana had no loyalty to the girl – after all, her father had tried to get Daimon executed – but had no loyalty to her relatives, either. Besides which, Lord Asrel had hated Yarmina based on her mother's blood, which was automatically a point in her favour so far as Saana was concerned.

'Wait there,' she said, and turned back towards her husband's bed. Daimon was stirring now, whether through the low voices or the wash of colder air from the window, and in the room's dim light Sanaa saw his face turn towards her and blink sleepily.

'Saana? What is . . . ?'

'The girl Yarmina is outside, she says she wants to talk to us, she is whispering,' Saana told him. Daimon's face screwed up in the universal language of a person roused from sleep and immediately presented with a confusing situation.

'But it is still . . . She is here alone?'

'She was throwing stones and calling your name, but quietly,' Saana said. 'She knows your wife is here now, and she still wishes to speak to both of us. What do you want to do?'

Daimon stared blankly for a couple of moments, as though working things through in his head, then nodded. 'We had best speak to her. Your husband cannot imagine what would bring her here in this manner.' He clambered off the bed and pulled on his robe, then headed to the window and leaned out. 'Yarmina! Come to the main door!'

Saana found his sword belt and drew his shortblade. Daimon turned around and pulled up short when he saw her with steel in her hand. 'What are you doing?'

'Being careful,' Saana told him. He might trust Yarmina, having known her as a child, but Saana did not. Naridan men might well underestimate Naridan women, and Saana had no intention of falling into that trap. 'Are you not armed when you meet guests?'

'That is different,' Daimon said uncomfortably. 'To invite a guest in privately, but meet them with a drawn blade . . . that is not polite.'

'Your wife is a Raider,' Saana told him. 'No one expects her to be polite.'

Daimon said nothing for a moment, then shrugged. 'True enough. Let us see what Yarmina has to say, then.'

The Blackcreek men's quarters, much like the women's,

consisted of a series of personal bedrooms and studies surrounding a communal room, which was also the location of the door. That opened on to stairs down to the gravel garden, on the other side of which were small quarters for servants. Only Tirtza the serving girl and Osred the steward lived there at the moment, so far as Saana understood it; the other servants, such as the cooks, dragon grooms and so on, lived in the second yard, next to their places of work.

Daimon unlocked the main door and pulled it inwards, and Yarmina hastened in immediately. She'd put her hood back up, and didn't drop it until Daimon quietly closed the door, at which point Saana raised the lamp she was carrying. The girl looked worried but determined, at least up until the moment she saw the naked steel of the shortblade in Saana's hand, when worry became by far the dominant emotion.

'Daimon?' she squeaked, her eyes widening.

'Saana does not know you, and does not trust you,' Daimon said flatly. Saana was quite impressed he didn't pass her behaviour off by appealing to notions Yarmina might hold about Raiders and their savage ways.

'Do you?' Yarmina asked, looking at him, and away from Saana with what Saana thought to be a considerable effort of will.

Daimon hesitated. 'As a child, this man trusted you, but we were children. Many years have passed. Why are you here, and why now, in this manner?'

Yarmina sighed, and looked from him to Saana, and back again. 'It is good you are both here. This woman wishes to tell you something, but she must also ask you to keep it secret, and she must beg a favour of you.'

Saana grimaced, her patience already starting to be tested. 'Why do Naridans always tell you what they are going to say before they say it?' Daimon looked over at her with an expression of reproach, and she felt herself bristling. 'Your wife should be asleep!' She turned to Yarmina. 'Either speak, or do not.'

Yarmina seemed somewhat in awe of her, as the Naridan girl cleared her throat, nodded, then spoke in such a hurry that the words almost tripped over each other on their way out of her mouth.

'This woman's father sent her here with instructions to seduce you.'

Had Saana not seen Daimon in the throes of passion before they slept, she would have thought her husband's reaction to this statement was the least controlled she'd ever seen him. All pretence of calm fled from his face, leaving utter astonishment mixed with horror.

'*What?*'

'It wasn't this woman's idea!' Yarmina hissed back at him. 'Nari's teeth, Daimon, this woman hasn't seen you for ten years, you think she wants to jump into bed with you?! You used to get her into trouble by stealing things, you're hardly her idea of a perfect match!' She seemed to remember herself and stiffened in alarm, then turned to Saana and made a quick bow. 'Your pardon, of course, Lady Saana.'

Daimon was standing open-mouthed. Saana had her own question, although she made conscious effort not to move her hand that held the shortblade when she asked it.

'Seduce who?'

'Either of you,' Yarmina said dismissively. 'No offence, Lady Saana, but you are not any more to this woman's taste than your husband is.'

'You have no need to apologise to this man for that,' Saana told her, her voice a little faint even to her own ears. She'd had a hard enough time getting her head around the Naridan nobility's notions of arranging marriages for their children; this was something else entirely.

'But *why?*' Daimon asked Yarmina incredulously. 'What is the purpose of this foolishness?'

Yarmina sighed. 'To benefit our family, of course. Ideally, this woman was supposed to seduce Darel to "unify our houses" and become the Lady of Blackcreek. Father didn't listen to his daughter when she told him Darel prefers men, despite that being obvious even when we were younger. But if that didn't work, she was to try to seduce one of you, to damage your marriage and the alliance, so Father could point the Southern Marshal at you again and perhaps this time take Blackcreek as his own.'

'That utterly venal, self-centred—' Daimon began.

'Why tell us this?' Saana demanded, taking a step closer to Yarmina.

'Father married Mother for love, but his daughter is supposed to use herself to further his ambition?' Yarmina said. 'No. This woman's mother answered to no one, and nor shall this woman. Father is too greedy; he should be glad Narida has made peace with the Raiders, not seek to disrupt it. Nari knows, he has enough trouble in the foothills with the mountain people raiding his farms. He could do well to learn about diplomacy, instead of sending his men after them, and you should be made aware of what he intends here.'

'So what is the favour you wish?' Daimon asked. 'If you would seek to stay here, away from your father, that would surely bring him down upon us. This man cannot subject his people to that.'

'That is not what this woman asks,' Yarmina replied firmly. 'She merely wishes you to not send her away immediately. Let her and her escort remain here for a short while; perhaps say that you would like us to renew our friendship. This woman swears to Nari Himself that she has no dishonourable intentions, but at least she can then return to her father and Cousin Omet will tell him that she tried her best.'

Daimon's expression darkened. 'You would have this man give the impression that you have caught his eye?'

'Only to those that are looking for it,' Yarmina said, with a nervous glance at Saana. 'Daimon, if you send this woman away immediately, Father will take *that* as an insult. He was in a foul mood when he returned to Darkspur, and he will be looking for any excuse. Let this woman stay a short while, and when she returns she can say that you were courteous and friendly, but nothing more, despite her efforts.'

Daimon looked at Saana as well. 'What do you think?'

Saana rubbed her forehead. She was growing increasingly tired with the games of Naridan nobles. 'Your wife thinks Yarmina should sort these problems with her father without asking us to help her lie.'

'A fair point,' Daimon conceded. Yarmina's face fell, and Saana sighed. The girl was only a few years older than Zhanna – which was an uncomfortable reminder that Daimon was only a couple of years older than Yarmina – and it was difficult not to feel for her. Saana could remember her own arguments with her mother about when she could go raiding; not because she wanted to fight and kill, but because that was how she would become an adult. She could barely imagine the rows they would have had if her parents had told her she had to go and marry someone.

'But your wife thinks the thane of Darkspur is an arse,' Saana added, 'so perhaps there is no harm in it.'

Yarmina actually snickered, then composed herself rapidly and bowed again. 'You have this woman's thanks, Lady Saana.'

'It is good that this man knows her husband will hold to his marriage,' Saana told her calmly. 'That means she does not need to threaten to punch you in the face if you try to fuck him.'

Yarmina's eyes went very wide again, and she visibly swallowed.

'This man thinks we are done here,' Daimon said carefully. 'He only spoke to you and Sar Omet yesterday, about when you should leave. He can announce tomorrow that we will host you for a week. That should suffice.'

'You have this woman's gratitude, both of you,' Yarmina said. 'Now, with your permission, she will take her leave.'

Saana didn't say anything until after Daimon had opened the door for Yarmina and then locked it again behind her.

'Your wife wonders how your people get anything done. They want to tell you what they are going to say before they speak, and what they are doing to do before they do it.'

Daimon raised his eyebrows. 'Your husband is going back to bed. Will you join him, or did you wish to discuss idiosyncrasies of language?'

Saana wasn't certain what an idiosyncrasy was, but she glowered at him. 'You just did it too.'

Daimon grunted in exasperation, then leaned forward and kissed her. Her assessment of their first kiss when they married was that he might well get better with practice, and it seemed like that was being borne out. She withdrew after a long, hot moment, and laughed.

'See? *Much* easier.'

TILA

TILA COULD PRACTICALLY taste the tension in the Sun Palace.

Accused of a heinous crime, she had denied it, and her accuser had demanded trial by combat. All of this was perfectly within the remit of the laws of Narida, and yet it was a farce. Marshall Coldbeck had known what was happening, and he surely intended to provide her with a false champion, one who would be easily bested by whoever Adan Greenbrook put forward. The only honest part of the whole affair was that she had indeed committed the crime she had been accused of. Granted, that might be a fairly important point, but Adan had absolutely no evidence that Tila had killed his cousin for any other reason than to defend herself. Besides, she *had* been defending herself. Just not against a strictly physical attack.

When all was said and done Tila Narida was the Divine Princess, daughter and sister of God-Kings. If anyone expected her to play by someone else's rules then they had not been paying attention.

Everyone was on edge, because no one knew what was going to happen. Even those who despised her – and there were enough of them – did not dare gloat or make their plans too openly, not yet. They were all aware, from Eastern Marshal down to the lowest of servants, that after today there might be a dramatic shift in power in the Sun Palace, one that could have a huge impact on everyone's standing. But by the same token, there might not be, and at this point that in itself would feel like a dramatic change. If Tila came through this, if she were exonerated, that would be a slap in the face for Einan Coldbeck, and especially for Adan Greenbrook. A lot of those cautiously backing themselves away from Tila, or who studiously avoided voicing an opinion, might well decide the wind was favouring her.

One way or another, things were going to change after today.

She had dressed in her finest robes, and applied paints and powders to her face even though she would be wearing her customary veil. This was going to be a show, and she intended to play her part. Let everyone see the full majesty of the Divine Princess, and set that against Coldbeck, Greenbrook and their ilk. She was her iciest, most regal self when the guards had come to fetch her for the trial. She was technically the accused and in theory a prisoner, albeit in her own quarters, but she refused to be escorted like a criminal. She strode at her own pace, and let the guards arrange themselves around her as they pleased.

At least, until she went to take a turning towards the Hall of Heaven, and the guard captain coughed, embarrassed. 'Uh, this way, if it please Your Highness.'

Tila stopped, turned and looked at him, gesturing uncertainly to his right. 'Where is our destination, then?'

'The . . . ' He couldn't bring himself to say 'trial': to do so would be to indicate that the Divine Princess had been accused of a crime, and this guard captain did not want that hanging over his head if she was found innocent. 'It's taking place in the Sun Gardens, Your Highness.'

Tila considered this. It was a fine day, certainly, but the Hall of Heaven had been used for trials by combat before, when nobles had been involved. The Sun Gardens were more spacious, but how much space was needed? Unless . . .

'The High Marshal has not opened the gates to the public, has he?' she asked carefully. The captain did not flinch, but the man next to him did. 'He has?'

'Begging your pardon, Your Highness, but he has,' the captain said, nodding. He looked decidedly uncertain of himself. Tila could hardly exact a punishment on him in her current situation – and nor would she, she was not the sort of person to punish a servant for giving her bad news – but he was clearly uncomfortable with how the conversation was going.

Tila smiled widely at him, wide enough that it would be visible even from beneath her veil. 'This is no concern at all, captain. Please, lead on.'

The Sun Gardens were the lowest level of the Sun Palace, immediately within the main gates and separated from the rest of the grounds by a raised wall. The gates had been opened to allow admittance to the city on certain special occasions previously, although not within Tila's lifetime: the most recent had been upon the wedding of her parents. The Sun Gardens were an area where the Divine Court could stroll and take their ease in the beautiful surroundings, but were also designed so that if the main gate was compromised or the western wall breached, the palace's defenders could retreat to the next tier and abandon nothing of importance.

It was packed with people.

Coldbeck was not a fool: he had not let the place fill up to its capacity. That would have been dangerous. Nonetheless, a lot of the lowborn had been allowed inside, and they milled around like lumbering longbrows, trampling over the beautifully maintained grass. As Tila and her escort reached the second wall, along which guards had been stationed in case any of Idramar's population decided they wanted to take a closer look at the more private areas of the God-King's residence, Tila saw a smaller group of far more richly dressed individuals directly beneath her: the Divine Court itself.

'So the Lord Marshal wishes the public to see this trial, and its outcome,' she said to the guard captain.

'This captain couldn't say, Your Highness,' he replied, taking refuge in a soldier's greatest friend: a refusal to comment upon potentially dangerous speculation by someone far more important.

'Very well,' Tila said. 'Let us get this farce over with.'

They passed through the first gate, went down a steep flight of stone steps, and then through the second gate at the bottom of the wall. From there, it was a short walk to join the Divine Court, most of whom were looking decidedly ill-at-ease without a wall between them and the God-King's subjects, no matter how many guards were stationed around.

'Lord Marshal,' Tila called, pushing ahead of her escort through the assembled dignitaries. She took a great delight in the fact that each one of them knelt on one knee to her, as was appropriate, which given they were outside was going to do nothing for their fine clothes. It also meant they were even less likely to move aside for her escort, who found themselves trailing behind her. 'To what do the citizens of Idramar owe this privilege?'

'Your Highness,' Einan Coldbeck replied, turning to her and bowing to an exactly appropriate level: the Hands of Heaven knelt to no one except the God-King himself. 'This Marshal thought it would be instructive for the people of the city to see what occurs today, so that there can be no doubt. After all, we all know that you are beloved of the lowborn.'

That was no more than a half-truth at best, and both of them knew it, but Tila smiled at him. 'It is very considerate of you. This Princess hopes the Lord of Treasury's champion is not one to get overawed by big occasions.' She looked around, taking in the Divine Court as they got to their collective feet once more, while her guards milled uncertainly and somewhat uncomfortably in their midst. 'Is Adan not here?'

'Lord Greenbrook is with his champion as we speak,' the Eastern Marshal told her. 'Your Highness, you have not spoken to this marshal about your own champion.'

'No, the princess has not,' Tila replied airily, looking out across the crowd and trying not to show her sudden uncertainty. It was not certain that Alazar would have come, of course, but she had been sure he would. So where was he? The man was a mercenary, through and through: everything she saw of him in Kiburu ce Alaba and on the voyage back had suggested he would draw his blade to protect himself, his husband, or to earn money, and for those things only.

She hoped her assessment of him was correct, in more ways than one.

'And where is the God-King?' she asked, since she could not see her brother anywhere. 'Is he not present to see the fate of his only sister?'

'Unfortunately, His Divine Majesty is still indisposed with illness,' Coldbeck said gravely.

'You are full of shit, Coldbeck,' Tila declared, loudly and clearly enough that several of the Divine Court abandoned all pretence of not eavesdropping. No matter what happened here today, Tila intended to make sure that everyone realised that the Eastern Marshal was as crooked as a hustled street dice game.

For his part, Einan Coldbeck simply smiled disdainfully, as though tolerating a child that was not his to discipline. 'You have more pressing concerns than filling your mouth with such docker's language, Your Highness.'

'Indeed,' Tila agreed. 'How goes the muster to find this princess's supposed reborn ancestor?'

Coldbeck exhaled in a manner halfway between a sigh and a snort. 'It proceeds, and should be ready to depart within the next day or so. Certain *other* matters distracted the Lord of Treasury for a time, as you may imagine. Speaking of which,' and now his manner became one of an exasperated father trying to reason with a wayward youth, 'Your Highness, do you not wish to know who your champion will be?'

'You have undoubtedly selected an appropriate candidate,' Tila told him sweetly. 'However, he may not be necessary.'

Coldbeck's eyes narrowed. He was an astute enough tactician, even in matters of courtly intrigue, to realise when something was playing out unexpectedly. 'What do you mean?'

'We shall have to see,' Tila replied. She looked towards the sky: the sun was at its zenith, and the late spring heat was considerable. 'Is it time?'

Coldbeck cocked his head. As if on cue, the gongs of the city began to sound, tolling out the hour. 'It is time.'

The lowest area of the gardens was cordoned off by rope stretched between posts hammered into the turf, and it was towards this that they now proceeded. Seeing the Divine Court on the move attracted the attention of the lowborn, and they too began to congregate, with the slight slopes leading down to the separated area affording many more a view than would have been possible otherwise. It felt somewhat alien for Tila to be standing below other people rather than above them, but it would serve well for her purposes.

She hoped.

Meshul Whittingmoor and Sebiah Wousewold awaited them. The Law Lord bowed creakily; no one expected him to kneel. The Lord of Scribes, by contrast, knelt fluidly, held his position, then rose just as smoothly as he had descended. Tila nodded in acknowledgement. The other lords of the Inner Council were hedging their bets, as was wise. She expected nothing less.

'Begin,' Einan Coldbeck instructed Whittingmoor. The Law Lord cleared his throat, centred his cane in front of him and raised his voice.

'We are gathered here to witness justice!' he thundered. Although his body might be aged, his voice still had power when he needed it. 'The Divine Princess has been accused of the most foul murder of the Lord Admiral Kaled Greenbrook. She does not deny that she killed him, but she claims she was acting in defence of her own life. Since she was the only witness to the death, she has been challenged to trial by combat by Lord Kaled's cousin, Adan Greenbrook, to determine the truth before Nari!'

A general muttering went up from all around, interspersed with the occasional shout. It didn't sound to Tila like there was a particular consensus of whether she was innocent or not: most people were probably just here for the show. It was not every day the lowborn got to see a member of the Divine Family tried for murder.

'Let the accuser, Adan Greenbrook, come forth!' Whittingmoor bellowed, and the Lord of Treasury emerged from the crowd. Beside him strode a sar, dressed in the Greenbrook livery, but unarmoured save for his gauntlets. Tila did not recognise him, but there was no reason why she should: up until this point, he would have been of no importance to her.

'He must be very confident,' she remarked to Coldbeck.

'The combat is to first blood,' the Eastern Marshal replied. 'Armour would only prolong matters. We can't have the man losing his fingers, though.'

'First blood?' Tila had lived as Livnya long enough to recognise a stitch-up when she saw one. At first blood, whoever Coldbeck had set up as her champion would only need to take a minor wound to lose on her behalf, meaning there was not even the chance of an unskilled man fighting for his life getting lucky. Her 'champion' could be well rewarded for his injury, and her sentence assured.

'Indeed,' Coldbeck replied. He looked sideways at her, and she saw the glint of triumph in his eyes. 'If you had spoken with this marshal about your champion, we would have been able to discuss the details of the trial.'

Not that it would have changed anything, other than to weary Tila's temper. She declined to answer. Adan Greenbrook shot her a vicious glance, and gestured to indicate his champion.

'Sar Amrul, of this lord's own household!'

A general round of applause went up, accompanied by a few jeers from the lowborn who thought they were well enough hidden in the crowd to get away with it. Amrul was a long-limbed young man, probably not yet at his thirtieth year, and while appearance was no indication of competence, he certainly carried himself like a fighter.

'Let the accused, Princess Tila Narida, come forth!' Whittingmoor intoned, and all eyes turned to Tila. She stepped forwards, despite the immediate resentment she felt at being summoned as though she were no more than one of the crowd. She squashed the feeling down. This was either going to work, or it was not. Whether or not it did, she would be best served by a calm exterior.

Einan Coldbeck followed her a moment later. 'The Divine Princess's champion: Sar Ravel, of the Sun Palace!'

That was a name Tila did know, at least vaguely. She looked around to see Ravel, somewhat closer to her own age than Amrul, step out in his turn. He was heavier set, with the hint of a gut beneath his clothes, and he looked to have a little less reach than his opponent. He was no greenling – he was an experienced fighter – but nor was he a greyhead: Coldbeck was not leaving himself open to allegations that he deliberately picked a man to lose. Still, Amrul looked formidable, and Tila was certain Ravel had been instructed to let himself be cut.

The crowd cheered on general principle. Tila walked over to where Sar Ravel stood, and he dropped to one knee.

'Rise, my champion,' Tila murmured, and Ravel returned to his feet. Any doubts she might have harboured about his intentions withered when he looked anywhere except her eyes. She leaned in, close enough for her veil to brush his cheek, close enough for him to smell her perfume. He was actually a very handsome man, in a slightly weathered way, and obviously utterly terrified of her.

'This princess knows what is going on here,' she whispered to him. 'Consider that.'

Sar Ravel did not answer, but his neck jerked in something approaching a nod. Tila backed away from him and turned. Meshul Whittingmoor drew in breath once more, and Tila raised her hand. The Law Lord was so surprised that he paused, his lungs still full of air.

'People of Idramar!' Tila shouted, turning on the spot. 'This princess has now seen her champion, selected for her by the Eastern Marshal.'

She paused to let that sink in for a moment. Plenty of them would not realise the significance of what she had just said, but there would be a few who put the pieces together.

'Sar Ravel is known to be a good fighter,' Tila continued, ignoring Coldbeck's furious gaze as she deviated from his planned script, 'but this princess feels that he will be representing her out of duty, not because he believes in her innocence.' She spread her hands. 'This princess's champion must be a sar, to satisfy the requirements of the honour duel. Are any such men present amongst you, who would represent her?'

'Aye!'

A shout went up immediately, followed by a gale of laughter, because the hair of the man who pushed forward out of the crowd was not even grey, but white. He moved somewhat stiffly, but he bore a longblade on his belt, and he knelt to her with only a slight intake of breath. 'Sar Nahel, named for your great-grandfather, Your Highness.'

Tila bit her lip. Unless she had shamed Ravel into fighting for her instead of for the Eastern Marshal – which was not a bet she wanted to take – this elderly sar might actually be a better prospect. At least he would be trying to win . . .

'Aye.'

She looked up from where her grandfather's namesake knelt, and her knees briefly weakened in relief. It was not a sensation she would have expected at laying eyes on Alazar Blade, but there he was, pushing his way through the crowd.

He was, she had to admit, an imposing figure, even with his ridiculous beard. Alazar was at least of an age with Sar Ravel, but was possessed of a certain rough-edged swagger that the palace sar lacked. He moved like a fighter, a trait that Tila knew well enough, and exuded an easy lack of concern that was thoroughly at odds with the poker-faced solemnity of the other men present.

He walked to her and, for a miracle, went down to one knee by Sar Nahel. It would hardly do for a man allegedly fighting for her out of loyalty to refuse to kneel, after all.

'And who are you, goodsar?' she enquired. Alazar looked up at her, clearly annoyed, but he had a role to play, just as she did.

'He's a blacksword, is who he is!' someone from the crowd yelled, and suddenly everyone seemed to be shouting at once.

'Quiet!' Whittingmoor boomed over them, or tried to. 'Quiet!' But he was not making a great deal of headway. Tila motioned to the two sars kneeling in front of her and both rose. Sar Nahel turned to face the new arrival, and displeasure was plain on his face, but it was as nothing compared to the thunderous countenance of Marshal Coldbeck when he arrived at Tila's elbow.

'What is the meaning of this?' he practically spat. 'This is a farce!'

'If farce it is, it is of your own making,' Tila retorted, pitching her voice low and venomous, for his ears only. 'This princess may choose her own champion, so long as he is a sar.'

'Who is your choice, then?' Coldbeck sneered, no longer even pretending to offer her civility. 'The greyhead, or the blacksword?'

Tila turned back to them. 'Sar Nahel, your offer is gratefully received, but this princess declines it. May you have many more years of health and happiness.'

'Your Highness. . . ' The old man looked as though he was going to protest further, but a mere sar made no protests to the Divine Princess. He bowed, murmured an 'As you wish, Highness,' and withdrew.

'Well?' Coldbeck demanded, looking Alazar up and down. 'Who is this?'

'This sar is surprised you don't remember him, Lord Marshal,' Alazar replied neutrally.

Coldbeck frowned at him for a few long moments, his eyes searching the bearded face in front of him for clues. Then he actually started backwards in shock and recognition. 'Alazar of White Hill!?'

'The same,' Alazar said. 'Now, if it please the High Marshal, this sar would have a private word with the Divine Princess.'

'*This man* is your champion?' Coldbeck demanded of Tila, turning to her and ignoring Alazar completely. 'The man you loathe?'

'Sar Alazar was the cause of a lot of pain for this princess's family,' Tila told him blandly. 'How fortuitous it is that he should return now, and pledge his sword to her defence. Almost poetic, one might say.'

Coldbeck's nostrils flared, but he bit down on whatever response he might have made as Meshul Whittingmoor arrived.

'Princess, can you confirm that you are choosing this man as your champion?' he said briskly. 'The trial must continue, regardless of showmanship.'

'This princess so confirms it,' Tila informed the Law Lord. 'Sar Alazar of White Hill is her champion.'

'Alazar of . . . ' Whittingmoor's reaction was similar to Coldbeck's, in that he looked as though he had seen a spirit of the dead, but he raised no objection. Tila saw his eyes flicker between Alazar, Coldbeck and herself. Whittingmoor may or may not have been involved in Coldbeck's plan, but he looked to be reassessing the situation regardless. 'He meets the criteria. As such, he may represent you.'

Einan Coldbeck was not prepared to let things go so easily, however. 'You expect this marshal to believe that this man came here by chance today, seeking to defend you, after all that happened between you?'

'You may believe what you wish,' Tila told him. 'He is here, he is a suitable candidate to be this princess's champion, and she chooses him over the noble Sar Ravel.'

'Very well.' Coldbeck bit out. 'May he serve you as well as he—'

Served your father, Tila finished in her head.

'—can,' Coldbeck said, after only the slightest pause. To say otherwise would be an admission that he hoped she lost the trial, and he was supposed to be neutral. Angry though he was, Coldbeck was too intelligent to utter something that damning. He finally deigned to acknowledge Alazar's presence once again, with the briefest of nods. 'Sar Alazar.'

'Lord Marshal,' Alazar replied, and Coldbeck strode away. Meshul Whittingmoor moved away as well, and raised his voice.

'The Divine Princess has chosen her champion: Sar Alazar of White Hill!'

That created a new stir, for there were not a few in the crowd who knew that name and what it meant. Shouts and jeers – more than a few jeers, this time – went up again, and as they did so Alazar stepped closer to Tila.

'This sar has an additional condition for him to represent you.'

Tila's stomach clenched. 'If you think—'

'There is a woman in the cell next to Marin,' Alazar said, speaking quickly and quietly. 'Her name is Ravi; she's a healer of some sort. Marin insists that she be released also.'

This was ridiculous. 'What? Why?'

'Damned if this sar knows, but Marin was adamant that if he is to be freed, she is too. He seems to feel responsible for her in some manner.'

Tila hissed in exasperation. 'Why is she there? At least tell this princess that!'

Alazar shrugged. 'Stole from the wrong family, as this sar understands it. You'd not be putting a murderer back on the streets.'

No, but you're keeping one in the Sun Palace. 'Fine,' Tila said, flapping her hand irritably. 'You have this princess's word: the woman Ravi will be released also.'

'Then we're good,' Alazar said, nodding. He began to turn away from her, then paused. 'By the way, this sar thinks the Lord Marshal doesn't like you much.'

'You noticed,' Tila said between her teeth. 'How nice.'

'Champions!' Whittingmoor bellowed. 'To this lord!'

Alazar rolled his shoulders and walked towards the Law Lord. From the opposite direction, Sar Amrul began to advance as well. Tila made her way back to where the Divine Court was clustered, but kept her distance from Einan Coldbeck. He did not seem to object.

'This sar hopes you weren't expecting an easy victory, boy!' Alazar called out to Amrul as they approached each other. 'If you're having second thoughts about dying, feel free to turn around!'

'Sar Alazar,' Meshul Whittingmoor said, making sure his voice was loud enough to be heard by the crowd, 'this contest is to first blood, not to the death!'

Alazar rolled his neck. 'The two are much the same when this sar fights.'

The crowd hooted their bloodthirsty approval at his bravado, and Tila looked over at Coldbeck. The Eastern Marshal's jaw was furiously clenched. Beyond him, Adan Greenbrook was unmoving and apparently emotionless, all save for the intensity of his stare, which could have set the ground on fire.

'Sar Alazar,' Whittingmoor said. 'As the champion of the challenged, you may decree whether you will begin with blades drawn or sheathed.'

'Sheathed,' Alazar replied, and Tila felt her heart speed up a little. If there was one thing Amrul was likely to be, it was fast. Honour duels began in close proximity; it would be easy enough to make a lunging draw cut and wound your opponent, if you were the faster man. She had reasonable confidence in Alazar's ability with a blade, but why risk giving your advantage away?

What was done was done, however. Whittingmoor removed a strip of red silk from his pocket and held it up.

'No blade may be drawn until the silk touches the ground. An early draw results in forfeit. Champions, ready yourselves!'

Sar Amrul seized his longblade's grip in his right hand, his scabbard in his left, and leaned forward slightly with his right foot advanced. It was the classic pose for a sar preparing to make a draw-cut.

Alazar raised his palms outwards at chest height, like a young sar showing off how he was controlling his dragon with only his knees. 'Look. No hands.'

The crowd laughed. Tila wanted to scream at the man. Had this been his plan? He was willing to make himself look like a fool in order to gain his ultimate revenge on her, and damn his own husband? She dared not look at Coldbeck, for fear of the gloating she would see on his face.

'Sar Alazar, ready yourself,' Whittingmoor said, warning in his tone.

'Concern yourself with your role, Law Lord,' Alazar replied. 'Let this sar worry about his.'

Whittingmoor's mouth twisted, but he clearly had no patience with recalcitrant sars. 'As you wish. Let the trial commence!'

JEYA

GALEM WAS SHAKEN, worse than Jeya had ever seen, worse even than when thëir family had been killed. Thëy'd been prepared for that, or at least had known that it was a possibility: after all, Galem had lived through one previous assassination attempt. Thëy'd grown up knowing that who thëy were put thëm at risk.

Now, it was no longer certain thëy were even who thëy'd always thought thëy were.

Jeya had little comfort to offer. What could shé say? Galem had been abandoned by the Hierarchs, the only people other than hér thëy'd thought might help thëm. Thëir whole life had been built on staying secret and therefore staying safe, and now that might all have been a lie. Thëy had no one to turn to.

Jeya had one place to go when shé needed help, and that was Ngaiyu's. Shé didn't know what Ngaiyu could do for Galem, but anything was better than nothing. Jeya could help Galem live on the streets, get money, get food, and make a living, although it would be sorely different to what thëy were used to. Perhaps more important than that, though, was taking care of thëir spirit, and here Jeya felt out of hér depth. Shé loved Galem, fiercely and dearly, but shé struggled to find any words shé thought might help thëm. This needed older and wiser heads, and Ngaiyu was both.

Ngaiyu's place was in one of the oldest parts of East Harbour, where the houses had fallen and burned and rotted and blown down and then been rebuilt so many times they probably had nothing of the original building about them any longer. Jeya had steered clear of it since the attack on Galem's house, for fear of thëm being noticed, but Ngaiyu's place was generally crowded at night, when people piled in to find a place to sleep. It should be quieter during the day.

'How much are yóu going to tell them about më?' Galem asked as they walked down the narrow dirt streets, overhung by the broad-leaved yangyang trees that sprouted everywhere.

'That's up to yöu,' Jeya said. A splay-legged lizard scuttled across in front of hér, and disappeared into the shadows beneath someone's porch. 'Ngaiyu won't push for details if yöu don't want to give them.'

'Do yóu trust them?'

Jeya didn't even have to think. 'Yes, as much as Í trust anyone. Ngaiyu will kick you out if you break their rules, but they've never done mé wrong. Í probably wouldn't be here without them.'

'Good enough for më,' Galem nodded. 'Which one is—?'

Thëy were cut off by a rasping, tearing noise that made Jeya grab for Galem's arm in alarm. Shé had hold of the handle of her belt knife before shé realised that it was the alarm call of a gold-maned monkey, screaming down at them from a yangyang branch some twenty feet up. The little animal was making a tremendous noise, despite being no larger than an infant, and Jeya could see its large, sharp teeth.

'Yöu can see it, right?' shé asked Galem, a little shakily.

'See it and hear it,' Galem replied, not sounding the calmest thëmselves. 'Why?'

'It doesn't matter,' Jeya murmured. Galem hadn't seen Sa when they'd taken the form of a gold-maned monkey to guide hér into the Old Palace that night, but shé'd not been sure if that was because Galem had been looking the other way when the god

264

appeared, or because Sa had only appeared to hér. This monkey, however, was abroad in the daytime and clearly visible and audible to all; it was probably just a regular gold-maned monkey, angry about two people being too close to it.

They moved off down the street, leaving the screaming monkey behind them, until they got to Ngaiyu's place, another four houses further on. Jeya ascended the steps to the rough wooden door and knocked, careful as always not to get splinters in hér knuckles.

There was no reply.

Jeya frowned. It was the Feast of Ash, and Mushuru was one of Ngaiyu's gods. Thëy wouldn't have gone to the Court of the Deities – thëy claimed to be too old for such a crush of bodies – so would likely be honouring the god in thëir home instead. That would be a perfectly good reason to ignore a knock at the door, but Jeya could hear nothing inside that might suggest Ngaiyu was engaged in worship; no shuffling or humming or singing.

'I'm just going to check around the back,' shé told Galem, hopping back down to the ground and skirting around the outside of the building. Galem followed hér, picking thëir way across the puddles that the most recent rainstorm had left.

Ngaiyu's vegetable garden was as neat and tidy as ever, but what immediately caught Jeya's attention was the washline. Clothes were hung out, but the basket in which Ngaiyu hauled thëir washing down to the creek to scrub and swear at it – or sometimes get one of thëir guests to do it for thëm – was still half-full. Ngaiyu didn't leave tasks half-finished; that was one of thëir particular dislikes.

The back door to the house was slightly ajar. Jeya drew hér belt knife.

'Trouble?' Galem asked quietly, from behind hér. Jeya hadn't found thëm a knife yet, and now wished shé had. Shé far preferred running from trouble than fighting it, but sometimes you needed to give trouble a moment's pause while it considered if you were worth its time after all, and two knives would be better than one.

The sensible thing to do would be to turn around and leave, and perhaps come back later. If there was trouble inside, there was no need for Jeya to walk into it. 'Sensible means safe' was one of Ngaiyu's favourite sayings, although thëy did have certain caveats for it.

But this was Ngaiyu. Jeya hadn't been exaggerating when shé'd told Galem that shé likely wouldn't be here without thëm. If there *was* trouble inside, then Jeya owed Ngaiyu enough to walk into it.

'Stay close behind mé,' shé told Galem, 'but not so close that yöu'll be in my way if we have to run. Step where Í step.'

Galem nodded.

Jeya advanced cautiously up the rear steps, shifting hér weight from one side of them to the other, avoiding where shé knew the particularly creaky parts were. Galem followed behind, matching thëir footsteps to hérs, like a spirit tracking hér every move.

Jeya really wished shé hadn't thought of it like that.

Shé reached the rear door and peered through it into the shadowed interior. The shutters were still across Ngaiyu's windows, so the sun cast thick stripes of shade interspersed with brilliant narrow bars of light, which illuminated whatever they touched without giving context to the room as a whole. The fire wasn't lit: that much was immediately obvious. Jeya cautiously pushed the door open wider, leaning to one side to let as much light in as possible.

When shé realised the bundle of clothes slumped in the rocking chair was a body, shé just about managed to stifle the scream that welled up inside hér. Only a small hiccup of terror emerged, but even that set hér nerves jangling in case it brought the same fate down on hér.

'What is it?' Galem hissed, pushing forward until thëy were at hér shoulder, all instructions about not getting in hér way forgotten. Jeya didn't trust hérself to answer. Shé stumbled into the house, waving her knife vaguely at the corners, at the front door, but hér feet took hér straight to the crumpled figure on the far side, disturbing a small collection of flies that took off, buzzing indignantly.

It was Ngaiyu.

Thëir throat had been cut, and thëy'd bled out over thëir own chest, and yet thëy were sitting in thëir rocking chair as though thëy'd just fallen asleep. The blood on thëir throat had dried, but thëy didn't look to have been dead for long, not for days, and there was only a faint bad smell in the air around thëm. Jeya had seen dead bodies here and there, on the streets and in the harbour, and shé had an idea how they changed colour, and got stiff, and how the insects got to them. If you removed the brown crusted down thëir throat, Ngaiyu could sit up and open thëir eyes and thëy'd look no different to how thëy always had. Shé took hold of thëir hand and squeezed it, but the fingers felt oddly waxy beneath hérs, and the stark difference between that unresisting limpness and the hands that had shown Jeya how to comb hér own hair was what finally brought tears to hér eyes.

'Oh, by the Mountain,' Galem breathed in horror. 'Is this them?'

Jeya nodded, hér throat too tight with grief to speak.

'I'm so sorry, Jeya,' Galem said. 'I'm so sorry.'

Jeya was sorry too. Shé was extremely sorry, but shé was also terrified. Ngaiyu had been there for hér for most of hér life. Losing thëm was like being orphaned again, but this was a much harder, much sharper pain than the dimly remembered tears from hér youth. A world without Ngaiyu was a far darker and more difficult place than the one shé'd woken up to this morning.

More importantly, though, someone had walked into Ngaiyu's house and killed thëm. Ngaiyu's place had always been safe; that was why the street kids congregated here. For someone to do this was as though they'd reached into Jeya's head and run their fingers through hér mind. Shé couldn't think of anything more invasive.

'Jeya? Jeya!'

Galem was gripping hér shoulder. Shé started, realised that shé'd gone stiff and hér chest was heaving. Shé tried to calm hérself, tried to think.

'Jeya, has anything been taken?' Galem asked, slowly turning hér away from Ngaiyu's body.

'What?' Jeya asked. Shé'd heard and understood the meaning of every individual word, but working out what they meant all together was more than hér mind could manage.

'Has anything been stolen?' Galem asked, gesturing around at the house. 'Did someone kill to steal from them?'

'Why?' shé demanded, angrily. 'Thëy're dead! Isn't that enough?' Shé could gender Ngaiyu to Galem now thëy were dead, and the change in intonation nearly tripped hér voice and sent it stumbling into tears.

'Jeya,' Galem said quietly, 'if someone killed thëm to steal from thëm, that's awful. If someone killed thëm but didn't steal from thëm . . .'

Jeya picked up thëir meaning now. Did Ngaiyu have old enemies who held grudges? Possible, although Jeya had never heard thëm mention them. If that wasn't the case, what might have driven someone to murder this old person in thëir house?

The only murders Jeya knew of recently were those of Galem's family. Perhaps the killers were hunting for thëm, demanding information, and had then killed Ngaiyu to cover their tracks. Which would mean they knew the sorts of places people who lived on the streets might go to take shelter . . .

'Just think like a thief,' Galem said, thëir voice soft. 'Yóu know the house. Is anything missing? Is anything still here that shouldn't be?'

Jeya took a deep breath and looked at this house – the nearest thing shé'd had to a home, over the years since hér môther died – with fresh eyes.

There was precious little here, and little that was precious.

Jeya didn't know where Ngaiyu hid thëir money – Ngaiyu had been too canny to let that slip to any of thëir guests, even those thëy'd known for years, like Jeya or Nabanda – but there were a few other items that would have been worth taking. There was a beautifully carved piece of crystal that Ngaiyu kept in an alcove on one wall, which captured and refracted even the faintest glimmerings of light. The stone from which it was formed was worth very little, and Ngaiyu had always said the only value it had to thëm was as a memory of an old admirer, but it was an attractive piece. Jeya could have traded it for a few coins, or perhaps a meal. It was still there.

Ngaiyu's cooking pans. The big cauldron in which thëy would simmer a stew for thëir sleepers in exchange for a copper was too big and bulky to take, and blackened with fire and dribbles of food besides, but Ngaiyu had other, smaller pans in which thëy'd cook thëir own meals. Decent metal, clean and shining, and small and light enough to carry in a sack. Again, worth a few coins, and still here.

Thëir needles, thëir thread, other odds and ends that weren't valuable as most people would think of it, but which could make the difference between having a coin or not: all still here. There was nothing in this house Jeya knew of that was worth making the effort to steal, and certainly nothing worth killing someone over, so if you were desperate enough to steal from here then you would steal any or all of these things.

'No,' shé whispered. 'Nothing's missing.'

Galem nodded slowly. 'So it was personal. Or . . . '

'Or . . . business,' Jeya agreed, swallowing against the lump in hér throat. A wave of revulsion washed over hér, and shé suddenly had to be outside, away from the still, blood-soaked corpse on which the flies were already clustering again. Shé bolted for the back door and clattered down the steps into the garden. A creak behind hér told hér than Galem had followed, albeit at a less frantic pace.

'What do we do now?' thëy asked. Thëy sounded weary, so bone-achingly weary. Thëy'd seen all their hopes turn to ash twice today, and Jeya knew well enough that Galem would be blaming thëmselves for Ngaiyu's death. Thëy'd assume that Ngaiyu had been killed because people had been looking for thëm. Perhaps thëy were right.

Jeya didn't care.

It wasn't Galem's fault. Thëy were just trying to stay alive. It was the fault of whoever had done the deed, whoever had drawn their blade across Ngaiyu's throat. That might be one of the same people who'd murdered Galem's family and set thëir house ablaze, or it might not. Jeya wanted to see them dead, whoever they were.

'Í have to tell people about this,' shé said, surprised at how steady hér voice was. 'People need to know. We need to tell the neighbours, then someone will go and get the Watch. But there are people Í need to tell myself.' She turned to Galem and took thëir hands. 'Í know we've been staying away from other people, at least the ones Í know, in case they know they haven't seen yöu with mé before, and wonder who yöu are. But this is . . . ' She swallowed again, thinking about how shé was going to tell Damau, and what sort of impact it would have on them. 'This is something Í have to do. Do yöu understand?'

'Í understand,' Galem whispered.

ZHANNA

THE WIDE VALLEY had continued to climb, but the mountains around them had risen accordingly, so Zhanna almost felt like they'd climbed no distance at all. Or at least, she would have done had she not still occasionally felt light-headed when she'd exerted herself particularly hard. There was something different about the mountain air; it didn't seem to fill her lungs in quite the same way.

When they finally reached the Smoking Valley itself, her breath was taken away for an entirely different reason.

She'd expected a continuation of the river valley they'd been following, perhaps a different branch of it, or simply a new section that Amonhuhe's people viewed to be theirs. She had not expected to emerge from the trees to find herself on the edge of rolling grassland that stretched away from her across a huge distance, interspersed with darker clusters of pine forest. The surrounding peaks had retreated until they were barely visible.

The Smoking Valley was a gigantic bowl, hidden in the mountains.

'S'man had no idea,' Menaken managed, staring about him in awe.

Amonhuhe took a deep breath and smiled. 'It's good to be here again.' She turned to Tatiosh. 'Well? What do you think?'

'It's beautiful,' Tatiosh replied, and Zhanna got the impression he wasn't just saying it to make his mother happy. He wasn't wrong, either. She could imagine that in winter this place was just as cold as Tjakorsha, if not colder – there was still snow on even the lower slopes of some of the surrounding mountains – but at the moment it looked like a place springing into vibrant life.

Movement caught her eye, and Zhanna frowned at it, trying to make sense of what her eyes were seeing. Then the scale of things snapped into place, and she gasped aloud. All eyes turned to her, but all she could do was point at the impossibilities in the distance.

'Ah,' Amonhuhe said knowingly, 'yes. The . . . well, Naridan doesn't have a word for them. Not that this woman knows.'

'What do you call them?' Menaken asked shakily. Amonhuhe was silent for a few moments while she thought.

'The closest this woman can get is "head-touches-the-clouds", but that's not really . . . ' She sighed. 'Naridan needs better words.'

Zhanna supposed that they were dragons, but like nothing she had seen before. It was hard to tell, because of the distance, but she suspected their shoulders were somewhere around three times her height. A massive neck supported a huge head, topped with curved horns that looked small in relation to the dragon itself, but couldn't have been shorter than her arm, and a ridge of bony plates ran down their backs to where their tails terminated in a solid lump of bone, like a club. There were at least two dozen of them, moving ponderously along the edge of a piece of woodland and biting off chunks of branch to chew. The kingdrake had perhaps been nearly as tall, but that had been a gangly thing for its size, mainly wings and neck and beak; and besides, it had been a nightmare from the dark that barely seemed real. These dragons were massive, and solid, and as clear as day.

'Are they dangerous?' Ravel asked in a tiny voice.

'If you disturb them,' Amonhuhe said. 'Then they'll squash you flat with one foot.' She slammed one fist into her other hand. 'Or hit you with that tail. When she was young, this woman saw a thundertooth take a hit from a tail. Killed it stone dead.'

'There are thundertooths up here?' Menaken asked in some alarm, and Amonhuhe laughed.

'Of course there are! Did you think dragons only lived in the lowlands?' She pointed. 'You don't have a word for them, either. It would probably be "brownbacks" in Naridan.'

Milling around the enormous dragons were other creatures, nowhere near as large, but still clearly big animals. Zhanna frowned: they had horns as well, but these were strange, many-pointed things. That wasn't the only reason they didn't look like dragons, either.

'They are what we get our furs from,' Amonhuhe said, fingering her clothes. She looked at Zhanna. 'Where do the Tjakorshi get theirs?'

'Sea bears,' Zhanna replied. 'Big. Swim in the sea.'

Amonhuhe looked puzzled. 'They have fur, but swim in the sea? That doesn't seem right.'

Zhanna pointed at the head-touches-the-clouds. 'You show us them, then say an animal cannot be right?'

Amonhuhe shrugged, conceding the point. 'Is there such a thing as a land bear?'

'If there is, they are not on Tjakorsha,' Zhanna replied. She moved aside slightly as Kakaiduna came to stand beside her. The girl was gazing across the grasslands too, but her face still held the haunted look she'd worn ever since arriving at their fire. At least she looked warmer, ever since they'd dressed her in hastily cut-down furs taken from the man Amonhuhe had killed.

'We need to move on,' Amonhuhe said, sobering. 'This woman's people live farther north. We might reach there by sundown.'

'And what do we do then?' Danid asked her. None of the Naridans questioned that Amonhuhe was leading them now, despite the fact that Menaken was theoretically representing Black Keep. However, in her turn, Amonhuhe was treating Zhanna as the leader of the Tjakorshi.

'We shall have to see what is what,' Amonhuhe said uneasily. 'Kakaiduna says Darkspur and Two Peaks are living in our people's cliff houses now, while our people are in store huts in the open, and she doesn't know exactly how many of the enemy there are. We'll go through the trees where we can, to save being seen.'

She turned to head in the direction she'd indicated, ducking back under the canopy of branches. Zhanna moved up alongside Ravel as the party began to follow.

'What is a thundertooth?' she asked the Naridan.

Ravel looked at her in consternation. 'You've never seen a thundertooth?'

Zhanna shook her head. Obviously she hadn't, or she wouldn't have needed to ask the question.

'They're big dragons,' Danid said from her other side. 'Not as big as those . . . things . . . but big enough, and they eat meat, not branches. They can swallow a man in one bite.'

Zhanna huffed out a breath. It was amazing there were so many Naridans left, given all the dangerous animals they had. 'Then it is a good thing this warrior is a woman.'

ZHANNA HAD WONDERED why it was called the Smoking Valley, but that became clear when the ground exploded.

They had reached the edge of an area of dead forest, perhaps a stone's throw wide, where for some reason the trees stood bare. Zhanna could see a series of pools between the trunks, where a wide stream had spread out to fill several depressions, and she thought she could see smoke rising from the water. Amonhuhe paused, rubbing her chin thoughtfully.

'This is a spirit ground. This woman does not remember one here, although that was many years ago.'

'Is that what killed the trees?' Zhanna asked, looking around.

Amonhuhe nodded. 'They boil the water, and kill plants.' She looked to her left and right, but the strip of dead forest seemed to follow the line of the stream. 'We'll have to cross it; there may not be an easy way around.'

'What will the spirit do?' Menaken asked uneasily.

'This woman doesn't know this spirit, or its nature,' Amonhuhe said. 'She cannot say. If it grows angry, kneel and press your head to the ground.'

'How will we know if it grows angry?' Ravel asked.

'You'll know,' was all Amonhuhe said. 'Come, let's go.'

Zhanna, following behind her and Kakaiduna, had got perhaps ten steps towards the stream when a rumbling, hissing noise reached her ears.

Talon and Thorn began rattling in alarm, and the rest of the party stopped in their tracks. Zhanna looked around, wondering what was happening, and whether it was a threat. Was this the spirit? Was this the approach of the cloud-headed dragons they saw earlier?

A column of hissing white shot up out of the ground ahead of them, startling her so badly that she backed away, tripped and fell. Up and up it billowed, roaring as it did so, and she heard shouts and cries of alarm from her companions.

All except Amonhuhe and Kakaiduna.

'Do as we do!' the Smoking Valley woman snapped, kneeling down. Kakaiduna joined her, and they leaned forwards to press their heads to the ground. Tatiosh followed suit, and the other Naridans began to do the same.

'Copy them!' Zhanna told the other Tjakorshi. She had no real idea what was going on, but she wasn't about to argue with Amonhuhe in this place. She got up to her knees and bent forwards too, hoping against hope that the ground beneath her face wasn't going to erupt in the same manner. Ahead of her, she could hear Amonhuhe and Kakaiduna chanting something lilting and calming.

It seemed to work, even though most of them had no real idea what was happening. Zhanna heard the roar of the plume begin to die away, and when she looked up cautiously she saw it subsiding back into the ground from which it had risen so abruptly. Amonhuhe and Kakaiduna kept their heads down for a few moments more, until it had gone completely, then both leaned back up on to their haunches.

'We should move on now,' Amonhuhe said, getting back up to her feet. She seemed troubled. 'The spirit is calmed for now, but this woman doesn't want to linger.'

That seemed sound advice. Zhanna hoisted up her pack, which had come loose when she'd fallen and then knelt, and they pushed on, over the smoking stream and away from the tree-killing spirit.

It wasn't the only one they saw. They were skirting the woodland's edge just as the sun passed its zenith, and Zhanna saw a herd of ridgebacks grazing, until their heads came up at the same time and they all looked in the same direction, towards an area of pale ground around which the grass didn't grow. Then they began to run, just as a white plume began to boil up out of the ground and a spirit showed itself.

'Do we need to do what we did before?' Zhanna asked Amonhuhe, pointing. The mountain woman shook her head.

'No, we're too far away. It wouldn't hear us from here.'

'What do they want?' Zhanna asked, awestruck by the sight of the thing. It was less terrifying than when one had been rearing over her, close by, but it was still a sight that made her skin crawl. It was as though there was a leviathan beneath the ground, and this was its breath-plume. Could there actually be some sort of ocean underneath the ground on which they stood, with such monsters moving about in it?

'They are spirits,' Amonhuhe said with a shrug. 'This woman was never a spirit-talker, and she hasn't been here in many years. She can't say. The only spirits she knows well are the ones near our homes.'

The sun was sinking towards the distant mountains by the time their party reached land that bore the marks of people. Instead of grassland, the ground at the edges of the forest had been turned for crops; although, Zhanna thought, it did not look to have been turned recently.

'They haven't planted this year,' Amonhuhe said, her voice tight and angry. 'Kakaiduna said the Darkspur men came early, led into the valley by Two Peaks people before the snow had left. Our people didn't get a chance to sow crops, and now it may be too late for them to grow.'

Zhanna grimaced. It didn't sound good for the Smoking Valley people, no matter what happened. She didn't like to think about what might happen in a winter up here with no food.

'How much farther is it?' Menaken asked. In answer, Amonhuhe pointed north, to a spur of rock that jutted out at the foot of a mountain.

'That's where the cliff houses are, where our enemies are living.'

Zhanna took another look at the sun. Amonhuhe had been right: they probably could get there by dusk, or thereabouts.

'Tonight will be a cold one,' Danid said grimly. 'We'll not be able to have a fire, in case it's seen and we bring Nari knows how many Darkspur wretches down on us.'

Amonhuhe spoke with Kakaiduna, then pointed again, more north-east than before. 'There are some caves there. South-facing, so we don't use them, but one of them would give us more shelter than the trees will, and we could build a fire with little risk of being discovered. Then this woman will rise early tomorrow and go to see what our enemy is doing.'

'This warrior will come with you,' Zhanna said, in a tone that she hoped brooked no argument. Amonhuhe was an essential guide, but she – understandably – had only one thing on her mind, which was freeing her people. Zhanna didn't want to entrust the lives of her crew to Amonhuhe's word alone, if they were going into battle.

She just had to hope that her own judgement would be any better.

EVRAM

EVRAM HADN'T KNOWN how to be a reeve, and was wary of getting it wrong. Happily, it seemed as though that was one of the main qualities the role required.

He had three reevesmen at his theoretical command; Azer, Keimar and Shemel, all of whom had served under Kelaharel. Each of them had expected Evram to discharge them and pick his own men to replace them, which would have seen them lose the extra coin they were paid for their service, and each of them was grateful to him that he did not.

'It's a weight off s'man's mind, and no mistake,' Azer had said with some relief, when he'd called the three of them together.

'Key to being a reeve, it seems to us,' Shemel had said conspiratorially, 'is to let people sort themselves out where you can. Everyone knows what they owe to the thane, and when it's due payment. Likewise, no one wants us and our sticks poking our noses in. So long as the reeve's visible, that just helps people remember what they should be doing.'

'That's not s'man's memory of Kelaharel,' Evram had said. The former reeve had thrown his weight about at times, and hadn't been shy of wading into any sort of disturbance with the reevesmen's staffs waving.

'Well, that was him,' Keimar had said with a shrug. 'We did

as he bade, because he'd picked us, after all, and the old Lord Blackcreek gave him his blessing as reeve. But he might've trod a bit more lightly.'

Evram had nodded thoughtfully at that. 'And what are your opinions on the Rai— the Tjakorshi?' he corrected himself. They had a name for themselves, and it was hard to say, but Evram supposed he'd best use it given Lord Daimon had married one of them.

The three reevesmen had looked at each other uncertainly.

'Well, they're here,' Shemel had said, after a pause in which it became clear that no one else was going to speak. 'And they're not going away again. In fact we've got more of the bastards than before, now there are those prisoners. Might as well make the best of it, s'man supposes.'

'And that drink of theirs isn't bad,' Aver had added. 'Shorat, s'man thinks it's called. 'S'got a kick to it, and no mistake!'

'They seem to know what they're about in the fields,' Keimar had said, as though that were the only thing that mattered, and perhaps it was, to him.

'Would help they if they spoke our tongue,' Shemel had said. 'But there's nowt to be done about that.'

He had not been entirely correct.

Nalon the smith, who came to Black Keep as part of the Brown Eagle clan and had a Tjakorshi wife, had begun teaching the two peoples the basics of each other's languages, in the main square at sundown. Evram was told by Lord Daimon himself that Nalon was only doing it because Chief Saana told him to, but do it he did. Lord Daimon had also told Evram to keep count of those of the town, Naridan and Tjakorshi, who turned up, since those who came every day for one week were assigned one of the thralls to help with their tasks for a day the following week. In being there and watching who attended, Evram and his reevesmen had found themselves picking up words of the Tjakorshi language: nothing complicated, but it was a start. Evram didn't think he'd ever have much cause to engage in a long conversation with one of them anyway, but at least he might manage something more than the blank staring he'd seen around the town.

However, although he'd learned some Tjakorshi, and come to know a few of them to nod at, and got a welcome boost to his income for a man with only a small plot of land to call his own, Evram had little luck with tracking down witches.

He'd viewed the texts Lord Daimon had mentioned, and although his reading was hardly the best, he'd seen the odd scratch-lines of runes that someone had recorded at some point in the past, for the benefit of watchful thanes. Evram didn't think of himself as a wise man, but he'd looked at them and couldn't see how such things could bring harm. But wasn't that the thing about witches? No one really knew how they worked their magic, just as no one really knew how Tolkar the Last Sorcerer had wielded his. Perhaps there were other things that had to be done as well: cantrips, or dances, and suchlike. But he had been keeping his eyes and ears open, and he'd not witnessed any woman doing anything out of the ordinary.

It was approaching sundown and the fishers were returning from the ocean, chased from it by the dark clouds of a rainstorm sweeping in from the south-east. Evram could see both the little fishing boats of Black Keep and the faster, two-hulled vessels crewed by the Tjakorshi. There'd been some mixing of crews – as in some Naridans had joined with the Tjakorshi on their ships, for no Tjakorshi seemed to want to sail in a Black Keep boat – but there was still a divide. Evram walked down to the River Gate as they started to land their catch, the staff of his office in his hand still not yet feeling much more familiar than the day he'd taken it up at Lord Daimon's request.

When he heard angry shouting, he sighed and stepped through the River Gate, past the line of old people, Tjakorshi and Naridan alike, mending nets in exchange for some of the catch.

It was Old Elio, who'd been plying the seas for as long as Evram could remember, getting older and greyer and more wrinkled as the years had passed, but still with the strength in his wiry frame to bring in a net or haul on a line. He was gesticulating and raising his voice in the general direction of a Tjakorshi who Evram thought might be called Otim, who was tying his little vessel up while remaining turned away from Old Elio, and looking in no hurry to turn around and engage. Young Elio had his hand on his father's shoulder and was speaking to him urgently, but the old man was having none of it.

'What's the problem?' Evram called out, stepping onto the wooden jetty. The other fishers were hauling their nets up onto it, and doing their best to ignore an argument in which only one side was taking part.

'Took our bloody fish, so he did!' Old Elio snarled, turning his attention to Evram. 'Sailed right up, bold as you like, cut the wind out of us, and netted what was ours!'

Beyond him, Young Elio was shaking his head.

'S'man's not a fisher,' Evram said, trying to sound reasonable as he walked past where Otim was tied up, 'but he's not sure how fish that aren't yet in a net is one man's and not another's.'

'Otim just had better luck than us, Da,' Young Elio tried to say, but his father shook his hand off.

'S'man's had enough of it, so he has! You there! You overgrown milk-faced bastard!'

Evram stiffened, waiting for the corresponding shout of outrage from behind him, but if Otim heard and understood the words, he was making no reply. Unfortunately, Evram realised, Otim was not the one who was supposed to.

'Now then,' he said, putting a little more force into his voice. 'That's no way to talk, Elio! That man fought for this town, same as you did.'

'Thieves and murderers is what they are,' Old Elio grumbled, and his son rolled his eyes.

'Murderers?' Evram snapped, and now the edge came to his

voice unbidden. 'Aye, s'man remembers! Or had you forgotten about s'man's brother Tan?'

Elio shut his mouth then, and his eyes focused on Evram properly for the first time, instead of looking past him at the Tjakorshi.

'Aye, well . . . '

'Aye, well nothing,' Evram said. 'S'man has reason enough to hate them, but what's done is done. Lord Daimon saw to that, and Lord Darel agreed with him when it came to it, and then the Southern Marshal did as well.' Evram still couldn't believe that he'd ridden with Kaldur Brightwater, High Marshal of the South: ridden with, dined with, given advice to about Black Keep and its surroundings. He had been, for a short and glorious time, almost a close confidant of a Hand of Heaven! Those would be memories to take to his dying day. 'If the Southern Marshal has no quarrel with them being here, Elio, you surely can't.'

'A fish thief is a fish thief, and no man can tell s'man different,' Elio said stubbornly. 'That's something that don't change, no matter who it is! Raider or no, s'man's been fishing that bank since before his lad was born, and no other's got a right to—'

'Da, *give over*,' Young Elio blurted in utter exasperation. He was not so young, in truth, only a few years Evram's junior, but he'd be known as Young Elio so long as his father still lived. 'You never gave a peep about Yaro taking a catch there when his nets were bare!'

'You leave Yaro out of this!' his father said, rounding on his son and shaking his finger. 'He died fighting the Raiders, and he'd not have wanted—'

'That's enough,' Evram broke in loudly. He had liked Yaro, and missed him dearly, and didn't want Old Elio using his name to make a point Yaro would likely not have agreed with. Evram had heard that Yaro had been a team captain for the Great Game at the Festival of Life, and had picked Tjakorshi for his team, even if Gador the smith had been the first to do so. If Yaro had done that, it seemed unlikely he'd begrudge them a few fish, for all that fisherfolk had their own ways and their own rules. 'That's enough.' He looked over his shoulder and saw that Otim was still there, sorting out his nets with two of his countrymen. 'Come on. S'man thinks you'd best get back to your house, before you manage to start a fight Lord Daimon would be none too pleased with.'

'Aye, go on, Da,' Young Elio said, eyeing his father. 'This son'll sort the fish.'

Old Elio looked none too happy, but after a couple of huffing breaths he gathered up the things he needed and stepped up onto the jetty, while his son began tidying the boat. Evram walked alongside Elio, making sure he kept himself between his fellow Naridan and the Tjakorshi as they passed where Otim was tied up.

'Lousy fish thief,' Elio growled, but he said no more than that, and did nothing foolish. Evram, looking back, saw Otim raise his head, and he gave the man what he hoped was an encouraging nod. Nari knew, the Tjakorshi needed to think the reeve was on their side, after Reeve Kelaharel had been revealed as a traitor who'd freed Lord Asrel.

'You can't be happy with these savages living here,' Elio muttered as they passed through the River Gate and walked up the street towards the town square, with the bulk of the castle on their right.

'S'man would prefer if they'd never come here, that's true enough,' Evram agreed honestly.

'Ah, s'man thought as much!' Elio cackled triumphantly. 'See, there's a true Naridan heart in that chest of yours! It's not right, having to share our town with 'em.'

Evram wanted to disagree, but also found it hard to. He had received his justice with the death of Ristjaan the Cleaver, and counted himself lucky for it, but that didn't mean he could easily accept the Tjakorshi as his neighbours. Not for himself, at least, but Lord Daimon and the town had made him reeve, and the reeve couldn't play favourites. Besides, he kept coming back to the fact that the High Marshal had proclaimed the Tjakorshi as citizens of Black Keep. How could the Hand of Heaven have erred?

'S'man doesn't trust these others, either,' Elio added, casting a long look at a pair of the thralls, traipsing back towards the house where they slept with several of their fellows. 'How can we be certain they'll keep this peace of theirs? We've only got the savages' word for it, after all.'

'They've held to it so far,' Evram replied. He didn't understand how it was that so many men and women would agree to serve their enemies, and cause no trouble even when walking free in the town, but he couldn't deny that it was what was happening. 'Why would they do all this work if they were only going to rise up? They'd have done it straight away, surely, or else they'll not do it at all.'

'You can't trust 'em,' Elio said darkly.

'It seems to be an honour matter,' Evram suggested.

'Honour!' Elio laughed harshly. 'They're no sar or lords, Evram! What do they know of honour?'

And to that, Evram had little answer. He didn't like the Tjakorshi, didn't see why he should like them, but he'd got a sense that they weren't false. Not as a people, anyway; certainly, there'd be men or women among them who were liars of the worst sort, but as a general rule it seemed that if they had a problem, they spoke of it to your face. He could respect someone for being honest and open, even if he didn't like them, but he found that hard to put into words.

'You knew they weren't to be trusted,' Elio continued. 'That's why you went to Darkspur when Freeman Shefal spoke to you, after all.'

Evram grunted. Let the man take that as agreement if he wished. Evram increasingly wanted to simply get Elio back to his house so he started no further arguments, not exchange any more opinions with him, and then leave him be. Evram had his duty to fulfil at the square, after all, keeping count of who was at Nalon's lesson.

'And now Darkspur's here again,' Elio said. The Darkspur delegation had been in Black Keep for several days now, which had set Evram's nerves on edge a little. He'd not been mistreated by Thane Odem's men as such, but he'd been a virtual prisoner until Marshal Brightwater had arrived.

'So what would you have us do?' he asked. He was tired of Elio's grumblings, but one of the jobs of the reeve was to listen to the people of the town. Evram would do his job, if nothing else, so he made his question sound as genuine as he could.

Elio looked at him for a moment, as though sizing him up. They were coming up to Elio's house now, where he'd lived on his own ever since his son had moved out, many years before. 'Why don't you come in, and we can have a talk?'

Evram groaned inwardly, but something in Elio's face made him reconsider the polite refusal he'd been about to give. The man was looking at him expectantly.

He'd mentioned Shefal. The freeman had come to Evram on the night the Tjakorshi had arrived and asked him to go to Darkspur, that was true enough. However, Evram realised he didn't know how many people were aware of it. The lords Blackcreek did, and Chief Saana, perhaps that daughter of hers, and Aftak. Oh, most everyone knew that Evram had gone to Darkspur, but how many knew Shefal had spoken to him first?

There'd been a small group of conspirators, it had been revealed: men who'd not just disliked the Tjakorshi's presence, but had organised themselves to do something about it. Ganalel the guard, who'd died in the Raider attack, and Duranen the former huntmaster, had apparently acted against the Tjakorshi solely from their own malice. However, Nadar and Yoon the guards, Shefal and Kelaharel the reeve had been in cahoots, and had come up with the scheme to free Lord Asrel.

If Old Elio knew that Shefal had been the one to send Evram north, had he been involved in the conspiracy as well? Were there still Naridans in Black Keep who were plotting against the newcomers, and therefore against not only their liege lords, but the will of the Hand of Heaven himself?

'Aye,' Evram said. 'S'man will hear what you've got to say, Elio.' His reevesmen would just have to watch Nalon's session without him; this might turn out to be more important.

Elio nodded in satisfaction, and they walked the few more paces to his house in silence.

Evram had never been inside Old Elio's home before. It smelled, unsurprisingly, strongly of fish, and the tang of the sea. The old fisher dropped kindling into his fire pit, along with a hunk of dried moss, and took up his flint and steel to strike the sparks that would light it. 'Take a seat, while s'man gets this going.'

'So what's on your mind?' Evram asked, resting his staff against the doorframe and sinking on to a stool.

'Milk-faced bastards, that's what,' Elio grumbled, with his back to Evram. 'It's not just our fish they're taking! We'll be lucky if the stores last us until harvest, and where's that harvest going to go, s'man would like to know? Won't be food enough for us all.'

Evram grunted. He knew the Brown Eagle clan had brought their own seed, grain and animals with them, and he'd not heard that they'd needed to take food from others. They'd also cleared land to plant more crops, and such was the number of hands the town now had to do the work, everything looked to have been put into the ground in good time. As for the fish, the seas were not running out yet.

'So that's the problem,' he said, looking around the house as a small flame blossomed in front of Elio and cast long, flickering shadows. 'What would you suggest as a solution?'

'You and s'man both know Shefal had the right idea,' Elio said, arranging his kindling over the burning moss. 'You know these Darkspur sorts, Evram. You went there before.'

Evram tried to keep his voice level. 'You're suggesting s'man should speak to the Darkspur sars and persuade them to get Thane Odem to attack Black Keep?'

'Not attack Black Keep!' Elio said. 'Attack the *Raiders*. The people here are cowards, but they just need a push.' He let out a laugh, as the flames began to rise higher. 'Get some Darkspur soldiers coming at night and let someone open the gates for 'em, let 'em make a start on dealing with these bastards, and Black Keep'll find its courage, you'll see!'

Nari's blood. Evram found himself struggling for words. Elio was actually calling for a massacre, for bringing Darkspur soldiers in secretly and then killing the Tjakorshi as they slept: which was, Evram remembered vividly, what the townsfolk had been worried might happen to them when the Brown Eagle clan first arrived.

Perhaps Evram would have been receptive to this scheme once upon a time, but now . . . It was a matter of honour. He might not be a sar or a thane, any more than the Tjakorshi were, but he could not countenance such treachery. How could anyone see themselves as being in the right, to do such a thing when the Brown Eagle clan could have done the same, but had chosen not to?

'Who else thinks like this?' he managed, his stomach churning. Part of him wanted to take up his stave and beat the answer out of Elio, but the man clearly thought of him as another of Shefal's confidants for now. He would get what information he could, then go straight to Lord Daimon with it. He waited, ready to hear names of those he knew and liked, dreading that he'd hear the names of his own reevesmen.

He'd not mastered his voice well enough. Elio rose from his crouch and turned, backlit by the flames he'd called. 'You sound like you're not of a mind with s'man, Evram.'

Evram rose to his feet too, wary of still being seated. 'Not seeing as how it's the safest plan. There's a lot of these Raiders, and no telling they'd all stay in their beds long enough for it to be done.'

'That's craven's talk,' Elio hissed. 'You want this handed to you on a platter? "Safe" be damned man, this is a matter of *honour*!'

'Aye, it is,' Evram replied, reaching for his stave, ready to take his leave. 'And—'

His fingers brushed the doorframe, and he felt carvings. He moved the stave aside, and there they were: small, stark lines, angular and old, marked into the wood. He might not have even noticed them in daylight, but with the sky darkening outside and the shutters closed, and the deep shadows thrown by the flickering fire, they stood out against the background.

'S'man's seen these before,' he said without thinking, horror rising in his gut. 'They're—'

Elio spat a word Evram didn't know, and was suddenly on him, his shape growing and blocking out the light of the fire. Evram tried to turn, but he wasn't fast enough, and an unseen force struck the side of his head.

Pain blossomed, and the room swam. He flailed, then realised he was on the floor. He heard fleeing footsteps clattering down the steps outside. His limbs felt weak and sluggish. He touched his head and his fingers came away bloody.

The door was open. Elio was gone, but the evidence of his crimes was plain to see now, for those whose eyes knew what they were looking for.

Witch runes, carved into the lintel, now marked with a dark smear of blood where Evram's head had struck it.

Evram staggered upright, fighting against the nausea and leaning on his stave. He stumbled towards the door. He had to get help.

He had to warn everyone.

TILA

THE LAW LORD threw his scrap of silk up between Alazar Blade and Sar Amrul, and took several hasty steps backwards. No one wanted to be in the immediate vicinity of battling sars.

The silk floated down, with what seemed to Tila like agonising slowness. Finally, the first edge of it kissed the green grass.

Sar Amrul began to draw.

Alazar Blade was already moving.

He did not reach for his own blade. Nor did he step back, allow Amrul's draw-cut to slice the air in front of him, then make his own counter-cut to catch the other sar off-balance. Instead he stepped *in*, grabbed Amrul's arm with his right hand to block the draw-cut while the blade was still half-sheathed, and smashed his left elbow into the other sar's face.

Amrul staggered backwards and fell, caught completely off-balance and by surprise, reflexively clutching at his face with his left hand while his right still struggled belatedly with his longblade.

'He's bleeding,' Tila heard Alazar say to Whittingmoor, stepping back and pointing at his opponent. On the ground, Sar Amrul removed his hand from his face to reveal a bloody nose, and his gauntleted fingers smeared with red.

Tila clapped her hands to her mouth in astonished glee, and did not even bother to stifle the slightly hysterical laugher that spilled forth. By Nari, the Mountain and all the spirits, the man had actually done it!

Needless to say, others were not so impressed.

'This is outrageous!' Lord Greenbrook ranted, stalking forwards. 'The blow was not made with a blade!'

Alazar drew his longblade with deadly swiftness and placed it under the throat of the groggy Sar Amrul, who froze.

'You want this sar to cut him with a blade?' Alazar demanded of the Lord of Treasury. 'Say the word.'

Greenbrook halted in his advance, as though getting closer would cause Alazar to open his liegeman's throat, but pointed his finger accusingly. 'You were moving before the silk hit the ground!'

'The Law Lord said no blades were to be drawn before the silk hit the ground,' Alazar drawled. 'He gave no other restrictions.' He raised an eyebrow. 'Do you think this is this sar's first honour duel, Lord Greenbrook? He knows how to listen to instructions.'

Greenbrook, quivering with rage, turned his attention to the Law Lord. 'Whittingmoor?'

The Lord of Treasury's voice was quiet and calm, but it forged those qualities into a knife. There could be no doubt of his wishes. Had the trial been conducted in the Hall of Heaven, in front of the Divine Court, it was just possible Meshul Whittingmoor might have folded.

But they were not in the Hall of Heaven, and the Divine Court were not the only ones in attendance. A crowd of lowborn folk from Idramar were present, folk who had little notion of Tila as anything other than the descendant of their god, rather than as a hostile, politicking force within the corridors of the Sun Palace. They had just seen the Divine Princess's champion prove her innocence in trial by combat without even drawing a blade: a champion who was none other than the man those of them who knew their history believed to be responsible for her father's death. It was, as Tila had told Einan Coldbeck, almost poetic.

Meshul Whittingmoor was no fool. He knew what the likely outcome would be if he declared the combat null and void, or attempted to disqualify Alazar: public outrage, possibly even a riot from those lowborn who were now so inconveniently packed into the Sun Gardens. More importantly than that, Tila realised, the man was a servant of the law. And the law, it seemed, was clear.

'Sar Alazar speaks truly,' the Law Lord declared, facing down Adan Greenbrook without flinching. 'He drew first blood, and he did not draw his blade before the silk hit the grass. He is the victor. By our laws, and in the eyes of Nari Himself, Princess Tila is cleared of the murder of Lord Kaled Greenbrook.'

A roar went up from the crowd, who if nothing else appreciated a spectacle when they saw one. Tila took a moment to breathe and compose herself, then bore down on Einan Coldbeck.

The Eastern Marshal saw her coming. He looked unwell, which surprised Tila not one bit. The treacherous worm had tried to play with loaded dice, and only discovered too late that she had switched them when he had been looking the other way.

'This princess will give you one chance,' she told him, without waiting for him to speak. 'Order the guards to accompany her to her brother's chambers, and for the door to be opened.'

'You have been found innocent of murder,' Coldbeck growled. 'You have not been made God-King yourself.'

'You would prefer this princess to appeal directly to the people you brought inside the Sun Palace, then?' Tila demanded. The guards were already beginning to usher the lowborn out, but that would take long enough that her threat would remain a real one for some time. 'You wish her to inform them how the Eastern Marshal is keeping the God-King trapped inside his chambers, despite the fact that he is recovering from his illness, and ask them for their assistance?'

Coldbeck's eyes went wide with shock and sudden fear. 'You would not dare goad this rabble into storming the palace!'

'Einan,' Tila scoffed, 'you should have learned by now that your opinions of what this princess is capable of are hilariously inaccurate. Give the order, and then this princess advises you to flee the city. This princess's brother may lack focus at times, but by the Mountain, she can guarantee that your attempted coup will have cured him of that so far as you are concerned.' She tilted her head. 'Or this princess can call on the rabble, as you call them, and tell them of your meddling. In which case, given they have just seen her absolved in the eyes of Nari, she rather suspects you won't make it to the gates.'

She would do it, too. Tila did not like to make threats she would not follow through on. Greenbrook could wait; his anger at her was genuine, and understandable, and would need careful handling. Coldbeck, however, had to be removed, and this was Tila's best chance. She could hope her acquittal would sway the Divine Court behind her, and give her the leverage she needed, but she was still a woman. There was every chance the court would cling to Coldbeck's lies, and her brother would remain imprisoned. In that case, Tila suspected it would not be long before her own body was found. After all, Adan Greenbrook would make a convenient and convincing scapegoat.

If it came to it, she would harness this mass of lowborn, free her brother by force, and take the risk of what would happen when they were unleashed in the Sun Palace itself. Better that than have the God-King subservient to the whims of this man purporting to act on his behalf.

For a moment, Tila thought Coldbeck was going to test her. The anger in his eyes rose, and she braced herself for his defiant reply, calling what he thought to be her bluff. Then his lip twitched, and he exhaled deliberately.

'Captain!'

The guard captain who had escorted Tila to the Sun Gardens approached respectfully. 'Yes, High Marshal?'

'Accompany the Divine Princess to the God-King's chambers,'

Einan Coldbeck said, his voice clipped and emotionless, his eyes not leaving Tila's. 'The doors are to be unlocked. The Divine Princess assures us that her brother is recovering from his illness.'

The guard captain must have been able to feel the tension, even though he was likely unaware of the Eastern Marshal's chicanery, so he did what any sensible soldier would in such circumstances: he bowed obediently low and began to fulfil his orders without question or comment. 'Of course, High Marshal. Your Highness?'

'One moment, captain.' Tila turned away from him and walked to where Alazar had sheathed his blade, and stood waiting for her. 'Nicely done,' she complimented him, when she could speak and still have him hear her without raising her voice. 'Somewhat unorthodox, but efficient enough.'

'If there's one thing you learn as a blacksword,' Alazar replied, 'it's that too many people heed how they think things should be, rather than how they are.'

If only this princess had that luxury. Tila would have dearly loved to live in a world where she could forget that an accident of her birth meant she could never hold power through anything other than intrigue.

'Come,' she said. 'This princess goes to ensure her brother is freed.'

Alazar's face dropped into a scowl. 'This sar will leave you to that.'

'He still thinks you were responsible for our father's death,' Tila said.

'All the more reason for this sar not to see him.'

'Tell him what you told this princess!' Tila said, trying not to sound like she was pleading. 'It will be hard for him to hear, but better that he knows the truth. Besides,' she added, when Alazar opened his mouth to refuse again, 'your husband's freedom will be most easily procured if Natan signs the order. Come with this princess to ensure there are no further surprises awaiting her, and nothing else that may threaten her brother's freedom or well-being, and therefore your husband's release.'

Alazar sighed and closed his eyes. 'You are as manipulative as ever.'

'This princess would hardly have survived otherwise,' Tila told him bluntly.

'Lead on, then.' Alazar's voice was resigned. 'This sar suspects that neither he nor your brother are going to enjoy this reunion, however.'

It was a strange procession that Tila led through first the grounds and then the corridors and stairwells of the Sun Palace: a group of guards, none of whom were quite sure from where their orders now came; a few hangers-on from the Divine Court, who had either overheard or surmised where she was going and had no intention of missing it; and Alazar Blade, her brother's ex-lover, and formerly one of the men she detested most in the entire world.

It was a different pair of guards standing in front of the God-King's chambers to when she returned from Kiburu ce Alaba and came to see him in the night, but they had equally alarmed expressions on their faces when they saw the party approaching them.

'Stand aside,' Tila commanded.

'Orders of the High Marshal, Your High . . . ' one of them began, then tailed off as the guard captain made a hasty hand signal coupled with a shake of his head. 'As you say, Your Highness.'

They stood aside. Tila produced her key – one way or another, she intended to either come here herself after the trial, or slip it to someone she thought she might be able to trust – and inserted it into the lock, then twisted it and threw the doors inwards.

The smell hit her immediately.

It was not overpowering, but it was certainly unpleasant. Some of it was caused by the trays of old, mouldy food left just inside the door, but there was also the distinct odour of an unwashed body.

For a moment Tila wondered how this could be, but of course, Natan had been declared delusional. He would undoubtedly have been trying to get out, but the servants and guards would be keeping him imprisoned under the impression that they were doing the right thing. They would open his door, push in food, and shut it again as soon as they could, to minimise the risk of having to lay their hands on their monarch. Nor would they risk removing the old trays or bringing bath water.

Tila's anger rose up inside her, but she held it down. Those who deserved it were Einan Coldbeck, who if he had any sense was already fleeing, and the Grand Physician, not the guards carrying out the instructions of their supposed betters.

'Natan!' she shouted. The last thing she needed was for him to come lunging out of a side chamber and making a rush for the door; that would hardly help her claim that he was in his right mind. 'Natan, it is Tila! This foolishness is over!'

A shuffle of feet sounded from the bedroom. Tila braced herself, waiting for her brother's appearance, praying to their divine ancestor that he would not appear as deluded as Coldbeck had claimed; and for that matter, that the Eastern Marshal had not been telling the truth, and her brother in fact *had* lost his mind at some point over the last few days.

'Tila?'

Natan Narida, the third of his name, walked through the doorway of his bedchamber, and Tila breathed a sigh of relief. He looked thinner than before, he was unkempt and unshaven, and as he approached she could tell that he smelled none too good, but there seemed nothing more amiss with him than tiredness. He was the image of a man recovering from sickness, but certainly not of one who was not in his right mind.

Natan stopped, noticing the people with her, who fell to their knees. 'What is this? What has happened? Why have they been keeping your brother in here?'

'Coldbeck and the Grand Physician told the guards you were

delusional,' Tila said briskly. 'Your sister has been held and tried for murder, and exonerated this very hour, or she would have been here sooner.'

'Murder?' Natan gaped at her, then his expression closed down into something far more threatening. 'Where are Coldbeck and the Grand Physician?'

'Your sister left the Eastern Marshal in the Sun Gardens,' Tila told him. 'She does not know where the Grand Physician may currently be found.'

'Well, then someone should *bring them to this king*!' Natan roared at the guards behind her. 'As soon as may be!'

The guard captain, Tila thought, was not having a good day. He bowed his head to the floor in acknowledgment, then rose and hastened back out Natan's chambers, with his men on his heels. Natan looked over the rest of the Divine Court, all of whom were still on their knees. 'And what are you all doing here?'

'We wished to see the truth of Marshal Coldbeck's words for ourselves, Your Divine Majesty,' someone piped up.

'It would have been better had you thought to do that *before* the Divine Princess had to free your king from captivity brought about by traitors,' Natan said acidly. 'Yes, your king is recovered, and is thinking very clearly. Leave him.'

The handful of nobles and courtiers rose and backed away out of the door with assorted murmurings and apologies. Natan's eyes fell on Alazar, who had not moved, and he looked at Tila.

'Who is this?'

'It has been some time since this sar was on his knees in front of you, Your Majesty,' Alazar said, rocking back on to his haunches. 'He understands if you have forgotten him.'

Emotions flashed over Natan's face too quickly for Tila to get a proper read of them all, but she saw shock, fury and grief. She hastily closed the doors behind her, then turned back to Natan just as he was drawing in breath for she dared not think what sort of utterance.

'Natan, we both owe Alazar our freedom,' she said quickly. The words were sour on her tongue, but they were true enough, and they stayed her brother's outburst. 'He was your sister's champion in the trial by combat that Coldbeck arranged, and it was only through his triumph that she was able to overrule the orders that kept you trapped here.'

Natan swallowed. Tila could see words bubbling beneath his surface, and the fingers of his right hand were almost spasming as he tried to formulate a sentence, but when he spoke it was far more controlled that she expected.

'Fine,' the God-King of Narida said, his voice somewhat tremulous. 'But *why* is he in your brother's chambers?'

'The Divine Princess promised this sar your assistance in freeing his husband,' Alazar said, before Tila could reply. She could have kicked him in the back of the head.

'Your *husband*?' Natan repeated, and if Tila wasn't very much mistaken, her brother was strongly considering kicking Alazar in the front of his head. 'You . . . You have . . . '

'Alazar, get up, and stop being so obnoxious,' Tila instructed him crisply. 'You're not helping. Natan, Alazar has something to tell you: something he told your sister yesterday, and which she sorely wishes he had told us twenty years ago.' She sighed. 'But she can understand why he did not. It is fair to say we were all young and foolish, in our different ways.'

Natan looked at her, and she saw genuine consideration in his eyes. He pursed his lips and looked at the kneeling sar in front of him, quite possibly the only man he had ever truly loved, and who had caused him the most grief in all the world.

'You heard her,' Natan said, more calmly. 'Get up.'

Alazar rose back to his feet. He was a couple of fingers'-breadths taller than Natan, as he always had been, but the weathered, dark-bearded man he had become bore little other resemblance to the arrogant young sar who accompanied their father on his final trip to the Torgallen Pass, two decades before.

'You have your king's thanks for serving his sister,' Natan said, 'and in doing so, serving your king. Whatever promise she made to you will be honoured. Now, if you have something further to say then your king suggests you start speaking, because otherwise he has a lot of matters to address.'

Tila raised her eyebrows. That did not sound like her brother. Alazar, however, sighed, and seemed to deflate a little. Tila suddenly became aware exactly how much of his presentation to her so far had been a facade, even when he had known her as Livnya. Faced with the man he had loved many years ago, and speaking of that time, he was as vulnerable as she had ever seen him.

'You have to understand, Natan, that this sar never wished to hurt you . . .'

STONEJAW

ZHELDU STONEJAW HAD never captained a ship before, let alone led a whole raiding party, but the key seemed to lie in being sure of yourself and giving your followers direction. Thankfully, Korsada the Dry had given her the perfect thing to dangle temptingly in front of them. The City of Islands, Korsada had explained, lay far to the north, where the sun was even fiercer than during Long Day on Tjakorsha, and the rain was warm as blood.

'And what's there for us?' Zheldu had demanded. 'More monsters?'

'Riches,' Korsada had said, with a sly grin.

Now here they were, ten yolgus spread out across the waves in a wide passage between two huge islands, sailing into this strange place where the air was so thick Zheldu felt like she was suffocating. She had stripped down to her woollen undershirt and was considering removing that, and the Dark Father take her decency. The rest of her crew were in much the same situation, displaying more naked flesh than Zheldu had seen in one place at any time in her life. Even Korsada seemed subdued in the heat and moisture, and her mother came from the Drylands. Then again, Zheldu had been to the Drylands, and while it was punishingly hot there, the air lacked this strength-sapping humidity.

'There's a bay coming up, towards the setting sun,' Korsada said, pointing ahead. Zheldu peered in the direction of the extended finger. They were indeed approaching a gap in the shoreline of the island on their left, and she could see stonework topped by guard towers.

'And they won't think we're coming to attack?' she asked dubiously.

'They'd not be concerned with the likes of us,' Korsada said casually, which did nothing to improve Zheldu's mood. She had well over a hundred warriors with her, which was no small amount, and disliked the idea that any place would easily dismiss such a force. Where exactly was Korsada leading them?

'Sound a horn as we haul through,' Korsada advised her. 'When I've come here before, that's how we announced we were here to trade.'

'A horn is to sound the attack,' Zheldu told her, but Korsada shrugged.

'To them, it means we're here to trade.'

Zheldu blew the shell-horn herself, incongruous though it was in these circumstances, and she looked up uncertainly at the towers watching over the artificially-narrowed entrance into the bay. There were strange contraptions atop them that resembled terrifyingly oversized versions of a Drylander bow, which made her nervous. Then they were through, past a tall-masted ship of a style she didn't recognise, and into the bay itself.

'By the Dark Father . . . ' someone said in awe.

Zheldu had no idea that there were this many people in the world. The bay was enormous, full of ships, and built up all around with buildings of stone and wood, many of which were far larger than the longhouses she knew from Tjakorsha. At the far side of the bay the land began to rise gradually away from the shore, and she could see more buildings perched higher up, looking over the harbour.

'Reef the sails!' Korsada called, pointing towards a small boat heading towards them, propelled by several oars. 'That one will need to come aboard to see our cargo.'

Zheldu grunted, looking over her shoulder at the cargo. 'To do what?'

'To tell us where to moor, so we can sell,' Korsada told her.

That seemed fair enough; the shoreline was so long, and Zheldu had no idea where she should go. When she sailed to the Drylands to trade there would be a handful of jetties at a port, and it made little difference where you tied up. Here, you could clearly be a long way from where you needed to be, due to the sheer size of the place.

They reefed sails, and slowed to a coast across the calm waters of the harbour as the local boat approached. Korsada let out a piercing whistle and waved as the craft approached. Someone in light, loose clothes – much better suited to the temperature than Zheldu's wools, she noted with some envy – stood up in the bow and called over in a language Zheldu didn't recognise. Korsada shouted back, and Zheldu caught a word here and there: the woman was talking in her mother's language.

The boat drew up alongside. There were six rowers, and the one who they'd been transporting, who stepped onto the deck of the *Storm's Breath* as though they'd done such a thing a hundred times before. Perhaps they had. Zheldu had no idea how common it was for Tjakorshi ships to come here, since it was clearly a Sorlamanga destination, and she was an easterner from Vorgalkoruuk.

The newcomer, who seemed not at all concerned about being among Tjakorshi warriors considerably bigger than them, exchanged another few words with Korsada, who beckoned them forwards to the deck house. The local followed her, and Zheldu shadowed them. This was her ship, after all, and she felt she needed to see what was going on, even if she could not understand the conversation. Korsada pointed into the deck house, and the local peered in at the cargo.

Slaves.

The City of Islands had an appetite for a lot of things, according to Korsada, but a particular liking for slaves taken from a cluster of low, flat islands several days' sailing to the south. She had been able to navigate Zheldu's raiding party there, despite approaching it from the south west instead of the south east, as she would have if coming from Tjakorsha. The people themselves had been easy to find and subdue. They lived in small villages, and the raiders had picked off a few, one after another, then headed north with their captives tied up using rope-like plants they found nearby.

Zheldu didn't think much to slaves, if she was honest about it, but her options were limited. Faced with a choice between trying to make a living by predating the Flatland coast and dodging their monsters, braving the long voyage back to Tjakorsha with The Golden waiting at the far end, or capturing some people she'd never met before and selling them on to someone else for the riches Korsada had promised, Zheldu hadn't hesitated.

The local certainly didn't seem to think it anything unusual. They nodded in approval, then spoke to Korsada again. Korsada's face fell, and she turned to Zheldu somewhat uncomfortably.

'We need to pay, otherwise we won't get told where to go.'

'Pay what?' Zheldu demanded. 'What do these people think is valuable? One of the slaves?'

'Fire gems might do it,' Korsada suggested, and Zheldu laughed.

'Fire gems! Oh yes, I brought a pouch just in case I was going to do a spot of trading in the Flatlands!' She shook her head, then paused as a thought struck her. 'What about Fireheart's axe?'

Rikkut Fireheart had dropped his blackstone axe when he was busy killing one of the Flatlanders' monsters, and someone had snatched it up when the battle had become a hasty retreat. It had hung from its leather belt loop on the wall of the *Storm's Breath*'s deck house ever since, an uncomfortable reminder of the man who'd led them so close to glory, but who'd ultimately made one voyage too many in pursuit of his own song.

There were fire gems embedded in it. Fire gems for the Fireheart, as he had loved to say. Zheldu wouldn't mind being rid of it, but it hadn't seemed right to just throw it overboard, she hadn't wanted it herself, and nor had she wanted to gift such a renowned warrior's weapon to anyone else, lest they get too full of themselves. This seemed like the ideal opportunity. She reached in and seized it, then offered it to the local, handle first, taking care not to cut herself on its vicious teeth. They accepted it, after a moment's hesitation, and ran their fingers appreciatively over the fire gems.

They nodded, and spoke again to Korsada, pointing towards an area of the shore. Then they turned and departed, back to their boat, which pushed off from the *Storm's Breath* and began to row back whence it had come.

'That did the trick,' Korsada said. If she had any qualms about disposing of Fireheart's weapon, she kept them to herself.

'You know where we're to go?' Zheldu asked her.

'More or less,' Korsada said, and grinned. 'Riches await.'

THEIR DESTINATION PROVED to be a series of narrow stone jetties extending out into the harbour, leading to a stone quay behind which rose a selection of mismatched yet still impressive buildings. Zheldu had never seen so much worked stone in one place, nor so well crafted. There was a definite art to building a good stone longhouse – selecting the right pieces, knocking them down to size and shape, mortaring them together and so forth – but the stones and slabs used here were almost uniform, with smooth, clean lines. She could not imagine the amount of time and people it would have taken to make such a place, but then again, the City of Islands didn't seem to be short of people.

'Ho, the yolgus!'

One of those people was approaching now, as she roped the *Storm's Breath* to a mooring post and clambered up onto the quay. The other ships in the harbour rose higher out of the water, with raised decks that were more on a level with the docks; the yolgus' decks sat not a great distance above the waves, which meant a slightly undignified climb to get ashore.

The man who had hailed her was, she realised with some surprise, Tjakorshi: or at least, he looked and spoke the part, despite his speech being oddly accented. His clothes were unfamiliar, being the same sort of loose, light tunic and leggings as those worn by the port guide, but she could hardly fault him for that. His skin was tanned, a deeper and darker shade than her own had gone in her relatively short time being exposed to this ferocious sun, but his hair and beard was a red-blond, he wore bone shards in his ears and even one through his nose, and his brow bore tattoos Zheldu recognised as belonging to one of the Sorlamanga clans, although she couldn't recall which one.

'I didn't expect to see one of our own here,' she said. 'Sorlamanga, yes?'

'My mother,' the dock hand said agreeably, looking down at her ships with what seemed to be a mixture of admiration and curiosity. 'Came here on a trading voyage once and didn't leave. My father was born here, as was I.' He looked back up at her and smiled. 'So what's the news from the Great Peaks?'

That was an odd way of referring to Tjakorsha, but Zheldu had never before met someone whose tattoos proclaimed than as Tjakorshi but who'd never set foot on its soil. Besides, the answer to his question was far more disturbing than his wording of it.

'The draug rules all,' she said shortly, and she might as well have slapped him, judging by the way his eyes widened and eyebrows rose.

'Draug?' He laughed, slightly uncomfortably, and gave her the look she might give someone whom she suspected was touched by the Dark Father. 'What draug?'

Now it was Zheldu's turn to stare in surprise. 'The Golden?'

'We've . . . not had many ships from the Great Peaks recently,' the man said as explanation, although he still looked a little confused. 'I've not heard of this . . . Golden.'

It felt to Zheldu as though someone had cut a cord that had been holding her shoulders in permanent tension. She took a deep breath of air, tinged though the sea salt was with dock weed and associated filth. A land that had never heard of The Golden! And, judging by the amount of people here, one that might have the strength to throw it back, should the draug ever decide to cross the ocean.

'And with luck, you never will,' she told the man instead. 'I'm Zheldu Stonejaw, of the Stone Eaters.' It was a strange feeling to give her clan name again; the one they'd been given by others as a pejorative in times long past to mock their barren, rocky home, and which they'd adopted as a mark of their own hardiness. She was used to not voicing it, after The Golden had taken their chief's belt and declared them broken, along with all the others. Perhaps her clan was broken now, but she could still carry its memory.

'Maradzh,' he replied. 'My mother is a Sea Bear, my father a Broken Rock.' He looked down at the ships again. 'So what brings so many Stone Eaters to the City of Islands?'

'We're not all Stone Eaters,' Zheldu told him. Truth to tell, she thought there were only about three or four of her former clansfolk in her fleet; her clan had been small, and only a few had been the sort of proven warrior The Golden had sent with Rikkut Fireheart.

Maradzh frowned. 'I thought the clans didn't travel together.'

'The Golden changed a great many things,' Zheldu told him dryly, and he pursed his lips.

'Seems to be the way of the world, at the moment. Did you hear the news from Narida?'

Zheldu gave him a level look. 'I don't even know where that is.'

'No?' Maradzh waved one hand vaguely behind him. 'It's a big land, towards the setting sun.'

Zheldu's throat tightened. 'Do they have warriors that ride . . . monsters?'

'The dragons? Yes, so I hear. I've never seen one myself, though.' Maradzh laughed. 'Well, we have dragons, obviously, but the sailors say theirs are huge beasts. I'd love to see one, one day.'

'Take it from me,' Zheldu told him. 'You wouldn't.'

Maradzh said nothing for a moment, seemingly unsure quite how to take her words, then shrugged. 'Well, anyway, news is that their God-King is ill, and close to death. He has no heir, so the gods only know what will happen. Utter chaos, I expect. And of course, we have the Splinter King here, so—'

'I don't mean to be rude,' Zheldu interrupted him, 'but it's been a long voyage, and the crews will want to find some decent food. One of us said there were buyers for slaves here.'

'Oh, buyers aplenty,' Maradzh said. 'How many do you have?'

Zheldu gestured at the yolgus around them, and Maradzh's jaw dropped a little as he understood her meaning.

'They *all* have cargo?'

Zheldu nodded. Maradzh's face lit up, and he clapped her on the shoulder.

'My friend, you and I are about to become very popular . . . '

ZHANNA

THE NIGHT HAD indeed been cold, but their party found one of the caves Amonhuhe had spoken of, and its rock walls reflecting the heat from the fire meant that Zhanna had been warmer than at any point during their journey from Ironhead. The morning was bitter, though, with a gentle drizzle of sleet from the gradually lightening sky as Zhanna, Danid and Amonhuhe crept out of the cave and across the ground that was glazed with white frost. Spring had reached the Smoking Valley, but winter crept back in every night.

They reached a low rise in the ground, and peered out from between the trunks of the pines to look down over the land of Amonhuhe's people. Zhanna's breath caught in her throat.

The rocky outcrop Amonhuhe had pointed out yesterday was the spur of one of the mountains rising up in the east, and a small lake ran up almost to its base. There was enough light that Zhanna could make out steam rising here and there from its surface, as though the water was being heated by a giant fire beneath it, and the river that ran away northwards had a similar haze above. However, unusual although this sight was, it wasn't what had surprised Zhanna so. From this position she could see the cliff houses Amonhuhe had mentioned.

An entire section of the cliff face, from the ground upwards, had been carved and shaped, working with the existing curves of the rock. Zhanna could see narrow stone stairways switchbacking up the outside, balconies within natural overhangs, and small openings in the rock face that served as windows for chambers within. It was magnificent.

'Winterhome,' Amonhuhe said softly, 'or so it would be named in Naridan. Where we shelter from the worst of the snows and the frosts, and the hungry predators. In summer we go our separate ways through the valley, ranging out to gather wild fruit and hunt game, while others stay to tend the crops here.' Her voice turned bitter. 'But not this year.'

'How could it have been taken?' Zhanna asked, for while Winterhome had several entrances she could see, she would not have liked to fight her way up those stairways in the snow. Thorn shoved his snout into her hand, and she idly scratched his head.

'Treachery, perhaps?' Amonhuhe said. 'Kakaiduna didn't know exactly how it happened.' She hissed between her teeth. 'They must have been determined, to walk through the winter snows.'

'Men will do a great deal for gold,' Danid said darkly. 'Or the men who give the orders will make others do a great deal for it, on their behalf. S'man doubts the thane of Darkspur is here, but it's his coffers the gold will go into.'

'How did they know there would be gold here?' Zhanna asked. The Tjakorshi had little use for gold; it was pretty, but steel served far better. The small golden discs on the chief's belt belonging to Zhanna's mother signified that the chief had all the steel they needed, and had the luxury of possessing other metals as well.

'The Spirit River runs north into the Two Peaks lands, and from there down into Narida,' Amonhuhe said. 'If they found gold in their waters, they might think there was more higher up.'

'The Spirit River?' Zhanna asked, and Amonhuhe nodded grimly.

'You see how the water smokes? The spirits keep this water free of ice so that we may fish even in the worst winters, and we honour them. This woman has seen flecks of gold here and there along the banks, but we don't take them; the gold belongs to the spirits.'

'Here they come,' Danid muttered, pointing at Winterhome, and Zhanna looked back. One of the heavy pelts that covered an entrance was being pushed aside, and a small group of people clad in furs emerged, carrying spears.

'Naridans?' she asked, trying to see. However, the figures were some way off and had their hoods up, and the sleet made it harder to see in any case.

'Yes,' Amonhuhe said, with no doubt in her voice. Zhanna wasn't sure what the Smoking Valley woman could see to make her certain these weren't people of the Two Peaks, but she wasn't going to argue.

'S'man counts five,' Danid said. 'So how many others are there?'

'And where are they going?' Zhanna asked. Her question was soon answered.

There were a series of long, low buildings not far from Winterhome: she hadn't noticed them immediately because compared to the smoking lake and river, and the grand spectacle of the cliff houses, they were somewhat drab. They looked almost like the longhouses she knew from Koszal, except built from turf rather than rocks.

'The storehouses,' Amonhuhe said, as the Naridans approached them. 'There isn't room in Winterhome for all the winter stores, not with everyone there too.' She was fiddling with the knife on her belt, clearly wishing she could exact some revenge on these people.

'So we need to work out how many we're dealing with,' Danid said uneasily. Five Darkspur men was good odds, but Zhanna would have been very surprised if that was all that was here. Where were the Two Peaks people, who'd led them here in the first place? 'Perhaps we can take some by surprise if they're out foraging, or—'

A sharp intake of breath from Amonhuhe cut him off, and Zhanna could see why. The Naridans had opened a stout wooden door built into the front of one of the storehouses, and had gone inside shouting. Which, Zhanna had to admit, was odd behaviour if they were simply going in to where food was stored.

'Kakaiduna said your people were being held in there?' she asked Amonhuhe.

'Yes,' Amonhuhe said, her voice tight with anticipation and dread. 'Some are clearly still alive, but . . . '

The Naridans began to emerge again, and following after them came a chain of Smoking Valley men. They were all men, Zhanna realised, and they were indeed in a literal chain; she could see the glint of metal linking their ankles together. They were also thin, and she could see that because they had none of the warming furs their Naridan captors wore, merely tunics and leggings. She supposed that they might just about be warm enough if they all huddled up together at night, in that storehouse with its sod walls and turf roof, but there was a reason she, Amonhuhe and Danid had donned their furs before leaving the cave.

Amonhuhe spat something in her own tongue, harsh and snarling, and Talon hissed as though in sympathetic response.

'Calm and quiet,' Danid murmured, laying one hand on Amonhuhe's shoulder. 'Let's not let them know we're here.'

'Those are this woman's people,' Amonhuhe replied, and her voice was hard enough to shatter rocks. 'Enslaved by lowlanders!'

'S'man can see that,' Danid said, 'but we can't help from here, and if we go down there, the three of us are as good as dead. We've no clue how many are still in your Winterhome.'

'This woman knows that!' Amomhuhe hissed at him. 'Which is why she is still here, and not down there!' Her fingers curled against the bark of the trunk next to her, as though she wished to rip it off and inflict damage on the tree in lieu of the Naridans in the distance. 'Ack! Look at that!'

One of the chained-up men had stumbled to the ground and

was struggling to rise. His fellows on either side of him in the chain rallied and began to hoist him up, but not before one of the Naridans had hurried up and landed a kick into his ribs.

'This warrior sees around thirty men of your people there,' Zhanna said, trying to distract her. 'Are there more?'

'There were,' Amonhuhe said grimly. 'When this woman's people came to trade last year, they made no mention of many deaths. But they would have fought; it is likely that many died.'

'Look there,' Danid said, pointing. 'They came from inside the building.'

Sure enough, two more Naridans – or at least, people wearing furs – were now walking from the storehouse the men had emerged from, and heading towards Winterhome.

'Guards for overnight,' Zhanna said, frowning. 'But thirty men could beat two, even tied at ankles. Why did they not?'

'The children,' Amonhuhe said heavily. 'The children must be in another one of the storehouses; maybe even kept in Winterhome. If the adults fight back, the children die. That would hold them, perhaps.'

'Here come some more,' Danid said, pointing at Winterhome, as another group of fur-clad Naridans emerged, greeting the two who were returning as they passed each other. This second group of Naridans to emerge from Winterhome brought out a group of women from a different storehouse, similarly thin, who were also harried and herded down to the Spirit River and set to work on its eastern bank, while the men worked one of the streams which ran down to join it. Meanwhile, a third storehouse produced no one other than two more overnight guards, who were replaced.

'There's something worth guarding in there, then,' Danid observed.

'The children?' Zhanna asked Amonhuhe.

'Most likely,' Amonhuhe replied, her face a mask of controlled fury. 'It could be our elders, or the sick, but who's to say that those who cannot work would not have already been killed?'

The three of them sat and watched until the sun was high in the sky, Smoking Valley and Naridan and Tjakorshi, counting their enemies and attempting to puzzle out who was where, and how many. The conclusions were not encouraging.

'Thirty of them, near enough,' Danid said heavily. 'Naridans, but no Two Peaks folk; they must have returned to their own valley. Assuming we've seen all of them that are here, of course.'

'Too many to fight face to face,' Zhanna said. Of those with her, only Tsennan and Tamadh were experienced fighters. Were the Naridans they were looking at warriors, or cowards who'd fallen upon unsuspecting victims to slaughter and enslave them? It was safer to assume the former. 'Not at first. We must pick them off.'

'That can be done,' Amonhuhe said grimly, fingering her bow stave and eyeing the distant Naridans on the bank of the Spirit River as though she'd like nothing more than to send some shafts their way, improbable though the distance was.

'It can, but must be carefully,' Zhanna told her. 'Killing two will not help us if all rest find us.' She tapped her lips with one gloved finger, thinking. 'There are hunting dragons here, yes?'

'Yes,' Amonhuhe said. Zhanna smiled.

'So if a man goes missing, it not need be enemy. If we kill a man quietly, and others do not see, then hide body . . . Could be dragon.'

'That could work, if we can catch one alone,' Danid said. 'But only until they learn to go everywhere in groups.'

'It is a start,' Zhanna said with a shrug. 'Better than eleven against thirty.'

Amonhuhe's face had lost some of its impotent anger, now they had at least the start of a plan. 'This woman swears: if any of them come within range of this woman's bow, they will die.'

MARIN

KEEPER YAMREL ENTERED the jail to be greeted by the usual hoots and hollers from the inmates. Those same hoots and hollers died down when he was followed in by three of his companions, and ceased abruptly when – Marin's heart leaped in joy and relief – the imposing, bearded form of his husband brought up the rear. The Keepers trudged down the central strip of floor, looking neither right nor left, then came to a halt in front of Marin's cell.

'Marin of Idramar,' Yamrel declared, his voice and face carefully neutral in the manner of someone who was nevertheless somehow able to project his disapproval to all those around him, perhaps through the very pores of his skin. 'Due to divine pardon, you are free to leave.'

Marin could have said something clever. He could have said something insulting. He could have revelled in this moment, and rubbed it in the Keepers' faces as he danced out of the cell. He did none of those things, because he was trying hard not to be a total fool. He was stuck here through his own poor decisions, and his husband had risked his life to get him back out. He would not jeopardise that for the chance to sneer at an Idramese Keeper.

'Thank you,' he said earnestly, as his door was unlocked. Yamrel's words – particularly the 'divine pardon' part – had sent whispers running around the rest of the jail. Marin had just been elevated in their minds from 'man with a deadly husband' to 'man with a deadly husband and the favour of the Divine Family'.

'Ravi of . . . ' Yamrel trailed off, but Marin's neighbour just looked up at the Keeper with disinterest.

'Of here, for the moment.'

'Due to divine pardon, you are also free to leave,' Yamrel said. Marin slipped out of his own door, before anyone could change their mind and lock it again, and into Laz's arms.

'Thank you,' he whispered, hugging his husband tightly. 'And sorry. Again.'

'It was an old mistake, Mar,' Laz said, kissing his forehead. 'And your husband has had enough of talking about those for today.'

Marin's attention was drawn to Ravi who, in defiance of all common sense, seemed to be questioning her freedom.

'What do you mean, "by divine pardon"?' she demanded. She was on her feet with her hands on her hips, positively glaring at Yamrel. 'This woman doesn't know the Divine Family! She's never seen them, let alone spoken to them!'

'Most important lesson of jail?' Marin piped up. 'Take freedom when it's offered!'

Ravi's eyes flickered to him, dark and distrustful. 'There's no such thing as freedom.'

'The royal order says you're to be freed,' Yamrel growled at her. 'That means you leave this cell. Now, if you want to go back in there again then you can walk out of this door, walk over there, kick Marin in the shins, and then this keeper will put you right back in that cell if that's truly your heart's desire, but right at this moment you are taking up the city's cell, to which you no longer have any entitlement.' He folded his arms. 'On the very small but not impossible chance the Divine Princess herself drops by to ensure this order has been carried out, this keeper's not going to still have you sitting in a cell unless he has good reason for it.'

Ravi looked at him for a few moments longer, seemingly still trying to find the deceit in his words, then shrugged and picked her shawl up off the floor. 'Very well.'

'Piece of advice,' Yamrel said, as she walked past him. 'Don't waste second chances like this.'

'Piece of advice,' Ravi replied, turning to face him. 'Buy some brightsage leaves; you'll find some at the market. Crush one between your fingers and wipe it over your face every morning. It'll help your skin. Also, it smells nice.'

Yamrel, whose face bore several red, angry-looking spots, blinked at her. His expression was warring between gratitude, suspicion, embarrassment and anger, but anger was starting to take control.

'You see how your husband didn't do something like that?' Marin said to Laz.

'Very restrained,' Laz murmured.

'We'll be going now!' Marin said, raising his voice and hoping to Nari that Ravi took the hint. 'Thanks for the food, Yamrel. A fine, clean jail you run here, surely the finest s'man's been in.'

'Get out, Marin,' Yamrel said in a tone of utter weariness. 'You'll be back. This keeper would wager a week's pay on it.'

'Take that bet,' Marin instructed the Keeper standing next to Yamrel, who just snorted.

'No chance.'

'Bye then!' Marin called cheerily, waving at the four of them, and turned his face towards the jail door, and freedom. Ravi, he was happy to see, followed behind Laz and him without exchanging any further words of dubious wisdom with Yamrel or his companions.

Once they were outside on the street, and Yamrel had shut the jail's outer door behind them, Ravi turned to him. 'What in the name of the Mountain is this all about?'

'S'man's husband Alazar did a favour for the Divine Princess today,' Marin told her, enjoying the look of consternation that crossed her face as she registered his words. 'As a result . . . ' He spread his hands to encompass their newfound freedom.

'So that's what you two were whispering about yesterday,' Ravi said, her eyes wide as she looked from him to Alazar. Then they narrowed again, back into the expression of distrust that Marin had come to associate with her in the short time they had been neighbours. 'Right, fine, that . . . happened, which is extremely unlikely, but the evidence suggests that it did. Your husband does the Divine Family a favour, and as a reward, you're pardoned.' She gestured to herself with both hands. 'Why is s'woman free?'

'This sar is wondering the same thing, as it happens,' Alazar commented to her. 'Mar didn't give an explanation for why he wanted to barter for your freedom along with his own.'

'Let's, ah, move away,' Marin said, glancing back at the jail, and beckoning the other two across the street. They followed, although Laz's brow now had the slight furrow between his eyebrows that formed when he was expecting bad news.

'S'man didn't think you really belonged in there,' Marin told Ravi when they were far enough away that he thought there was no chance of them being overheard through a window. 'Also, it's possible he might have been the reason why you were in there in the first place.'

Both Laz's and Ravi's brows shot up at the exact same moment, and in almost the exact same manner.

'What?' they both asked at once.

'It's possible that the item you were arrested for stealing . . . Well, it sounds similar to an item that found its way into s'man's possession, without the knowledge of its owner.'

Laz closed his eyes and groaned. 'Oh, Tolkar's *arse*, Mar!'

'That's not why your husband was arrested!' Marin quickly pointed out. 'They knew nothing about it! That's not why you had to do what you did; that was for an old mistake, like you said—'

'*You* stole that . . . brooch, whatever it was?' Ravi exclaimed, rather louder than Marin would have liked. They were standing at the side of one of Idramar's busiest streets, which meant there was a lot of other noise, but conversely there were also a lot of people around to potentially overhear incautious exclamations.

'The description sounded similar, yes,' Marin said, keeping his voice down and hoping she would do the same.

'All you had to do was tell them!' Ravi hissed, advancing on him with menace in her eyes. 'You could have just said you did it!'

'S'man's really not sure they'd have taken his word as good enough to let you out,' Marin said hastily. 'It's not the Keepers' jobs to make decisions like that. They'd have likely held you until trial anyway, but now you're free again and don't have to worry about it, right?'

Ravi didn't reply, but her expression suggested that was not because she'd forgiven him.

'S'man made a poor decision,' Marin said. 'He never intended it to impact you; when he realised it had, he tried to make up for it.'

'Mar,' Laz said, sounding tired. 'You said you were going to stop.'

'Your husband said he would *try* to stop,' Marin replied, which was true, although guilt was eating at his stomach anyway. 'And he did try, and he'll keep trying. It's just that he's a lot better at stealing than he is at making himself not do it.'

Laz sighed. 'But you'll keep trying.'

Marin nodded. 'Your husband will.' And that was true, as well, for all that he'd make no guarantees. Sometimes he just couldn't help himself. Or rather, he *could* help himself, all too easily, and that was the point.

Laz nodded. 'Well, that's all your husband can ask. He loves you Mar, and he really doesn't want you to end up in a cell again. There won't always be princesses who need favours so he can easily get you out.'

'What was the favour?' Ravi asked, her curiosity apparently overtaking her anger towards Marin, at least briefly. Laz shrugged.

'She needed someone beaten in an honour duel to clear her name of murder.'

Ravi's mouth dropped open. 'That's what you count as "easy"?!'

'Well,' Laz muttered, 'the other guy wasn't very good.'

'Is he dead?' Marin asked, somewhat apprehensive about the answer.

'No, your husband didn't even have to draw his blade, as it turned out,' Laz said, as though winning an honour duel against the champion of Narida's Lord Treasurer without unsheathing your sword was a matter of mild interest, rather than the sort of feat that would be turned into songs sung in taverns across the land. 'But Adan Greenbrook's a powerful man, and he might not take the slight too well, even though his sar's still breathing. Your husband's thinking it could be a good idea to leave Idramar.'

'It's certainly done nothing to endear itself to your husband this time around,' Marin admitted.

'This city,' Ravi said with feeling, 'can be swallowed by the ocean.' She turned to Laz. 'Goodsar, thank you for your help, even if you didn't know why you were doing so.'

'This sar was doing it because his husband asked him to,' Laz said, in what might have been an attempt at mollification, but Ravi was already rounding on Marin.

'You,' she said, waving a finger under his nose. 'You haven't even broken even with this woman. Now she's going to have to return to her lodging, and pray to the Divine Nari that her bag of remedies hasn't been thrown away!' She backed off, still wielding her finger like a weapon, then turned on her heel and stalked away down the street, giving off such an aura of foul temper that Marin was surprised people didn't scatter from her path.

'She seems nice,' Laz remarked, with forced joviality.

'Another triumph for your husband's winning personality,' Marin said miserably. He sighed, then tried to put the healer out of his mind. She was free again; that was all he could reasonably have done for her. 'So, about leaving town. Your husband was on his way back from meeting with his friends when the Keepers seized him—'

'Your secret society, yes,' Laz said, with an amused snort.

'We're not a—' Marin stopped, before the old argument started again. 'You make it sound very dramatic,' he said instead, reproachfully.

'You're a society, with members,' Laz said, with irritating patience and accuracy, 'who don't advertise your existence to anyone except those whom you want to recruit. You're a secret society.'

'We are a group of *scholars* who seek to do what's best for the country!' Marin protested. It looked like the old argument was going to happen anyway. 'It's not like we lurk in dens plotting assassinations, or, or, spreading rumours that the Divine Family have lain with dragons, or—'

'Wait, that's actually a rumour?'

'Probably.' Marin flapped his hands, irritated at how easily he'd become sidetracked. 'Argh, this doesn't matter! They said, and your husband agrees, that it would be a good idea to enrol in the forces heading west in search of the Divine Nari's rebirth, if it exists.'

Laz tilted his head to one side. 'By "enrol in the forces", you mean your husband enrolling, don't you?'

'You are the warrior out of the two of us, yes,' Marin admitted. 'But the term "camp followers" exists for a reason. And perhaps your husband can find work as a quartermaster or some such.' He sighed. 'Don't look at him like that, what's he going to steal from army rations? Biscuit and beans?'

'Your husband is sure we'll be able to work something out,' Laz said. 'He's a Brotherhood mercenary and a sar, after all: he must be able to get some sort of concessions.' He scratched his jaw. 'So what's the reasoning?'

Marin lowered his voice. 'The Cupbearers—'

'Secret society.'

'For the love of . . . !' Marin glared at his husband, but Laz just smiled at him to show he was joking, and Marin's anger faded away again. By the Mountain, but he was a lucky man! 'Fine. Anyway, we have concerns about the Sun Palace's reasoning for ordering this expedition, or whatever it's being termed as. We're not sure their intentions towards the Divine Nari, assuming he has actually been reborn, are all they should be.'

Alazar's face sobered, and he glanced around, then leaned closer. 'You're saying you think Princess Tila will send assassins to kill the Divine Nari reborn, in order to keep her family's grip on the throne secure?'

Marin winced. 'Well . . . '

Laz pondered it for a second, then shrugged. 'Yeah, I can see it. So what's the plan, that your husband fights off all the Lord Marshal's soldiers? He's flattered by your faith in him, Mar, but he's not sure that's realistic.'

'There's no way that can be the general order,' Marin said. 'There'd be a mutiny. But there could be, you know. Assassins. Hidden in the ranks.'

'Your husband thought your secret society *didn't* sit in dens talking about assassinations?'

'We were in a tavern!' Marin protested. 'And your husband said we didn't *plan* them! We were talking about foiling someone else's, that's entirely different!'

Laz took a deep breath and looked about him. Marin saw that, whether by accident or design, his husband's gaze alighted on the roof of the Sun Palace, towering over the city.

'We need to leave Idramar,' Laz said, nodding slowly. 'Marching with the army will pay, which helps.' He sighed. 'And if the Divine Nari has been reborn then he needs to take his place on that throne, without any of Tila's schemes getting in his way. All right, we'll do it.'

THEY RETURNED TO their lodgings and collected their possessions, meagre though those were given that back in Kiburu ce Alaba they'd hastily boarded the *Light of Idramar* with nothing except wet clothes and the coin in their purses. Then they presented themselves at the recruiting station in one of Idramar's main squares, where Laz had talked very seriously about the sort of monies he would be expecting, as a sar who was a member of the only officially recognised order of mercenaries in Narida. Blacksword or no, a Brotherhood sar could expect to receive well above the standard soldier's pay, even if he was bringing his husband with him, and the recruiter wasn't inclined to argue: he would more than likely receive a bonus himself for signing on such a recognised warrior. Laz was just making his mark on the roll when a voice behind Marin nearly made him jump out of his skin.

'Are you *fucking kidding*?'

He whirled around to find Ravi staring at him in a mixture of disbelief and anger. She had a bulky satchel slung from one shoulder now, and – Marin noticed with unease – was dressed in the sort of sturdy clothing and boots one might wear if one was anticipating a long journey, such as that which the Lord Marshal's forces would shortly be undertaking.

'You found your bag, then,' he said, smiling. Ravi rolled her eyes at him.

'Luckily, the owner of the tavern where s'woman was staying made sure her things were stored away, him being a decent man. Unlike some she could mention,' she added pointedly.

Laz stepped away from the recruiting station, and the man behind it eyed Ravi up and down. 'We've got three women with us as swear they can use a weapon, and you look like none of 'em. If it's a spouse or a father you're running from, girl, s'man suggests you take your chances with them, not us.'

'This woman is a healer,' Ravi said, patting her satchel. She'd moderated her tone, at least, which was more than Marin had expected. 'Armies sometimes have a use for those.'

'This is the Sun Palace's own forces,' the recruiter said, sounding bored. 'We've our own healers.'

'Bonesaws,' Ravi sniffed. 'Fine for taking off a wounded limb before it goes rotten, so far as these things go, but are they going to stop the camp going down with the coughing sickness? Or the bloody flux? By the time your tent mate's crying in the latrine trench as he shits his life away, it's too late for you to go running to the nearest village and hope there's someone there with some herblore.'

The recruiter was speechless for a moment. Marin could see the man's uncertainty, and before he quite realised himself what he was doing, he'd stepped forward.

'She knows her work, this one,' he said confidently. 'S'man was abed for three days with a fever before she gave him a cure for it.'

Ravi looked at him in disbelief. The recruiter was nearly as surprised.

'You've met him before, then?' he asked Ravi.

'Yes,' the healer replied, still looking at Marin as though he were a pet dragon who'd just performed an unexpected trick. 'S'woman can't say she took to him.'

'Goodsar?' the recruiter said, turning to Alazar. 'Is this true?'

Marin tried not to grimace. Laz didn't like telling lies.

'She's a healer,' Laz said after a moment. 'This sar's not been treated by her, but his husband's up and walking about the city, when he wasn't for the last few days.' All of which was entirely true, and yet phrased in a manner which suggested conclusions that were completely false.

The recruiter bought it. 'Well,' he said, writing something on his roll, 'it won't be soldier pay. Truth to tell, you'll get food, and that's about it: the men themselves'll have to cough up whatever you fancy charging 'em.' He cackled at his own pun, then proffered his quill to her. 'Mark your name here, then.'

Ravi stepped forwards with all the confidence of someone who'd never doubted this outcome would occur, and scratched her name down, which was interesting: far from everyone had their letters, and she'd seemed to suggest she'd come from a small place that hadn't been blessed with a great deal of learning. Still, Marin reflected, a determined person could sometimes do a lot to change the circumstances of their birth.

'We leave tomorrow,' the recruiter told them, handing all three of them a small square of marked cloth. 'There's beds and a meal in the new barracks that's been converted down the way, if you've nowhere else for the night. That way you won't be late, at least.'

'Are we even now?' Marin asked Ravi, as the three of them walked away from the recruiting station and towards where the soldiers of the Eastern Army had turfed out a warehouse's goods in the name of the crown, to the considerable consternation of the owner, and had set up rows of pallets for those who'd signed up to head out west in search of the Divine Nari.

'Yes, Marin of Idramar,' Ravi replied, nodding. 'We're even now.'

PART THREE

'WHEN DAWN BREAKS, *we go into battle against the Unmaker. If we are to die, then this sorcerer would have you know one thing.*'
'*And what is that?*'
'*He cannot stand the sight of you.*'

Exchange between the characters of The Last Sorcerer and The General, as portrayed in *The Band of Seven* by playwright Andegel of Low Lees, first performed in the three hundred and forty-third year of the God-King (Andegel of Low Lees was later publicly flogged, and his work banned)

DAREL

THE WAVES WERE running high as the *Silver Tide* sailed into the estuary of the River Idra, and Darel Blackcreek caught his first sight of Idramar, Narida's capital city and the seat of the God-King.

It was immense, so much larger than Black Keep that he was unable to even guess at how many times bigger. The northern shore was clustered with docks and buildings, and lined with ships, and rising above it all was a magnificent edifice which had to be the Sun Palace. It sat on a sandstone bluff, and was formed of stone of such a similar colour, and worked so cunningly and so beautifully it was as though the rock itself had risen up and taken shape to form the home of Narida's ruler. Of course, various accounts suggested that Tolkar, the Last Sorcerer, had played a part in the raising of the Sun Palace, so perhaps there was a grain of truth in the notion.

'Impressive, is it not?' Kaldur Brightwater said from beside him. The Southern Marshal was dressed in one of his finest robes, ready to disembark, and he sighed as he looked at their destination. 'There is not a time this marshal has come here and has not been struck again by the majesty of this place. He has only arrived by road before; in truth, the sight is even more marvellous when approaching by sea.'

'Thank you, lord,' Darel said with wonder, 'for bringing your servant here.'

'Do not thank him yet,' Brightwater replied seriously. 'We have business to attend to, and you may not find the Divine Court a welcoming place, Lord Blackcreek. There are good men here, and true, but just as many sycophants, if not more. You are a thane from the far south, with little influence; they will not tread carefully around you, and will not hesitate to involve you in their petty games for power, if they feel they can use you.'

Darel digested this. It sounded like the Sun Palace was full of Shefals, which was hardly an enticing proposition. 'Your servant is surprised that the God-King tolerates such behaviour in his court.'

'The God-King . . . ' Brightwater sighed once more, although this time he sounded more resigned than contented. 'Many of these people are necessary; they hold important roles, perform important functions, or are from powerful and influential families. Those families would never turn against the throne, of course, but Narida functions more smoothly when the nobles are content with their lot. Or as content as they ever get,' he added, somewhat darkly.

Darel nodded. That sounded like sensible diplomacy, and the sort of approach he would expect a noble and just ruler like the God-King to take.

'Darel.'

He looked sideways at the High Marshal in surprise. Their relationship on the voyage had been cordial, but Brightwater had never yet addressed him by his first name in isolation.

'Do not . . . ' Brightwater drummed his fingers on the ship's rail for a moment before continuing. 'Do not seek to judge the God-King by the standards you might ascribe to any other man. His blood is of the Divine Nari, and so he does not see the world as we do. He guides the nation; lesser men concern themselves with the minutiae and details.'

'Your servant understands,' Darel replied, although it would remain to be seen whether he actually did.

'Warmer than the south, is it not?' Brightwater said after a few more moments, and Darel realised that his own brow was damp.

'Oh no, lord,' he replied, dabbing at it with his sleeve. 'It gets warm enough in the long days of summer at Black Keep. This, your servant must confess, is nervousness at the thought of meeting the God-King.'

'Understandable,' Brightwater said, with a slight smile. 'This marshal could not address him with a steady voice, when first he met him.'

Darel tried to picture that meeting for himself, and realised that he had not, until this moment, given much attention to what Natan III might look like. Black Keep possessed no likenesses of the current monarch, and Darel's mental image of him consisted mainly of a golden glow. He wondered if he was handsome.

The *Silver Tide* coasted into a berth on the docks with the easy confidence of a ship that knew it was flying the banner of a Hand of Heaven. It was immediately attended by port officials and dockhands eager to serve a High Marshal of Narida, and runners were dispatched to alert the palace of his arrival, and to procure a carriage. This, when it arrived, was drawn by two dragons of a species Darel had never seen on Blackcreek lands. They stood near as high as a frillneck, but were far slimmer, although clearly strong. They hooted softly through the twin hollow, spiralling horns atop their heads as they waited while Darel's travel chest was loaded into the carriage along with Marshal Brightwater's.

Only Darel, the High Marshal, and Brightwater's manservant Elishel rode in the carriage; Sar Kyrel sat up front with the driver, while Modorin and Tenan would be following on behind with the rest of the High Marshal's belongings. Darel used one finger to pull the curtain slightly away from the viewing grille set in the door, and looked out as they rattled through the streets.

Bakers and butchers, blacksmiths and swordsmiths; silversmiths and jewellers, an armourer; a market where he saw stalls of what had to be the year's first vegetables, having grown quickly and early in this northern clime where snow rarely fell. He saw several shrines to Nari, some richly decorated and others plain and humble, all with offerings and candles. He saw taverns, but also several buildings which appeared to serve a different drink, and a different clientele.

'What are these places?' he asked, gesturing outside. Brightwater leaned over and peered out, then made a neutral noise in his throat which, while hardly approval, was not exactly disapproval either.

'Yeng houses,' the Southern Marshal said. Darel's querying expression must have been obvious, as he frowned. 'Yeng has not reached Black Keep?'

'Your servant has not heard of it,' Darel admitted.

'It is a drink, made from plants grown in the far north, beyond the City of Islands,' Brightwater said, leaning back into his seat again. 'It is palatable enough, although this marshal prefers his mixed with honey. The yeng houses are a place where people with money, if little nobility, will go to socialise and be seen drinking something that costs a lot.' He snorted. 'It is a harmless enough frippery, this marshal supposes.'

'You must think your servant a witless country imbecile to be gaping so,' Darel admitted sheepishly, as the carriage rattled on and the shape of the Sun Palace on its rocky foundation loomed larger. 'But he swears, in the course of this carriage ride he has seen more different people than in all of his life before this day.'

'This marshal hardly thinks you witless, Lord Blackcreek,' Brightwater said, 'but take a care that you do not give that impression to others. Unless you wish to do so,' he added, after a moment. 'In the machinations of court, it can be beneficial to pretend to be less than you are.'

Darel nodded in what he hoped was a suitably sagacious fashion. In truth, he liked the sound of the Divine Court less and less, the more the High Marshal spoke of it.

The carriage rounded the final bend, and approached the main gates of the Sun Palace. They were huge things of dark, iron-studded wood, at least fifteen feet high, and they were also well and truly shut.

'What is the meaning of this?' Brightwater asked angrily as the carriage rolled to a halt. 'This marshal sent on ahead; they should be expecting us.'

'Who comes?'

Darel heard the challenge shouted down from the palace's walls, and hooked the curtain back once more to peer up at the towers of the gatehouse. There were a pair of guards visible, who seemed in no hurry to open the gates.

'The carriage of the Southern Marshal!' Sar Kyrel called up, not bothering to keep his irritation out of his voice. 'Open these gates!'

'We'll need to see the Southern Marshal himself,' one of the guards called back. Darel looked over at Brightwater; the Marshal's eyes narrowed, but he made no move to leave the carriage.

'Do you have no respect?' Sar Kyrel demanded. 'Open the gates with no further delay, and perhaps the Hand of Heaven will say no more about this!'

'This man's orders come direct from the God-King, goodsar,' the guard said. 'No carriage may pass these gates until we see the occupants.'

Darel saw Brightwater's expression shift from anger to surprise. He still looked displeased, but he arranged his robes, and reached for the carriage door.

'Lord—' Elishel began, but Brightwater waved him to silence.

'No, Elishel. If this is the God-King's will, then so be it.' He pursed his lips. 'This marshal has never known him take such an interest in the business of the gates before.' He pushed the door open and stepped down on to the cobbles outside, then turned his face up to the walls. 'There! Are you satisfied now?'

'Thank you, High Marshal,' the guard replied. To Darel's amazement, the man did not sound apologetic at inconveniencing the Hand of Heaven. 'Please be welcome into the Sun Palace.'

'This marshal will expect an explanation for this, when his carriage has entered,' Brightwater said dangerously.

'You shall have one, lord,' came the reply, and one of the two guards disappeared. Brightwater got back into the carriage, muttering about guards and their insolence, and the huge gates began to crack open.

Despite the strange nature of his arrival, Darel still felt a thrill as the carriage passed between the gates. He was inside the Sun Palace! His father had never come here; nor indeed had his grandfather or, to his knowledge, any of his line before this day. He went to look out again, but no sooner had the carriage entered than it drew to a halt again as the gates shut behind it, and Darel saw a guard approaching them.

It was clearly the man who had called down to them from the top of the wall. He knocked politely on the door, and Elishel leaned over and opened it.

'Well?' Brightwater demanded, without preamble. 'What is the meaning of this?'

'Treason, High Marshal,' the guard said bluntly. 'Marshal Coldbeck has been declared a traitor to the crown, and has fled the city. The God-King has commanded that no one may enter the palace without their faces being seen.'

Darel gaped at the man in utter astonishment. He realised after a few moments that he was doing a fair job of portraying himself as exactly the witless country fool he had feared he would be marked as, and it was only a moment after that that he realised the Southern Marshal was just as stunned.

'Coldbeck?' Brightwater managed, after starting the first syllable of a couple of sentences and giving up on each one. 'Einan Coldbeck. The Eastern Marshal. A *traitor*?'

'It was hard to believe for us as well, lord,' the guard said honestly, shaking his head. 'Word is that he conspired to keep the God-King imprisoned in his chambers when he was recovering from his illness, and sought to seize the throne for himself. He had the Divine Princess tried for the murder of Lord Kaled Greenbrook, too, although her champion won her innocence.'

'Lord Kaled is dead?' Brightwater said, the astonishment and horror in his tone matching the feelings squirming in Darel's chest. What had he walked into?

'Aye, lord, killed by the Divine Princess, true enough, although she was defending herself from him,' the guard reported. He leaned a little closer into the doorway. 'Truth to tell, High Marshal, we're glad to see you here. These are strange days, and no mistake. Perhaps a military man can make sense of what's occurring.'

Brightwater nodded soberly. 'Very well. Thank you for the information, man.'

'You said the God-King was recovering from an illness,' Darel put in, before the guard closed the door again. 'Is he well? Has he fully recovered?'

'Aye, lord,' the guard said, eyeing Darel's robes and quickly coming to a conclusion of rank. 'He's well, praise be to Nari, and holding court once more.'

'Thank you,' Darel said, and allowed the guard to shut the door. The driver whistled up the dragons, and the carriage set off again, crunching along the gravel drive that led away from the gates through the Sun Gardens, and towards the secondary wall.

'Strange days indeed,' Kaldur Brightwater muttered. He looked at Darel. 'Coldbeck a traitor? The Lord Admiral dead? Be on your guard, Blackcreek. The court's fangs have clearly grown sharper since this marshal was last here.'

'As you say, high marshal,' Darel replied. He looked out at the Sun Palace. What had looked like a masterpiece of the builder's art now seemed to squat menacingly, hiding dangers he might not see until it was too late. 'As you say.'

DAIMON

It had been an awkward few days.

Yarmina had been true to her word, behaving in all the proper manners towards him. In fact, Daimon felt they had regained a little of the friendship they had when they were children, despite the different circumstances. Then again, perhaps it was not that different: as children, they were brought together by the whims of their parents, had no option but to spend time around each other, and developed a loose friendship in the manner children had in such circumstances. Now, Daimon was in his position at Black Keep due to his duty in his brother's absence, and Yarmina was here because of her father's instructions.

It was also true that Yarmina was engaging company. She was intelligent and had a quick humour, seeming genuinely interested in how Naridans and Tjakorshi were living together. She would offer observations, comparing things to how they were at Darkspur; not in a manner intended to disparage Black Keep, but to discuss differences and similarities. She even wrote a poem for Saana and him, using paper and ink and quill she apparently kept on her at all times, for just such an eventuality.

And yet . . .

Daimon found her easy to talk to, mainly due to the half-faded memories of their times as children, which broke down some of the walls he would have felt when interacting with a noblewoman, especially an unmarried one. She was, in some ways, easier to talk to than his own wife, simply due to the fact that there was so much shared context between them. Saana was learning about Narida in the same way as Daimon was learning about the Brown Eagle clan, but there were some things he doubted he would ever be able to make her truly understand. With Darel gone again, so soon after their only communication for weeks had been conducted in a stilted manner through a wooden door, conversation with Yarmina was . . . nice.

Was that the point? Faced with his blunt rebuff of her visit, was this Yarmina's next tactic; not to save face with her own father, but to continue her attempt to drive a wedge between Daimon and Saana, by highlighting how better suited she was to him? Was Daimon being overly paranoid, exceptionally arrogant, a mixture of the two, or neither? The rest of the Darkspur contingent certainly took fewer steps to preserve their lady's honour than might have been expected, since often neither Yarmina's maidservant nor her cousin Sar Omet were present when Daimon spent time with her, in defiance of propriety. Daimon had seen Sar Omet casting considering glances at him when he thought Daimon was not looking.

Saana, meanwhile, seemed thoroughly unconcerned by the whole thing. 'Your wife trusts you,' she said to Daimon bluntly. 'If you would spend time with the girl, do so. Just do not leave your wife to deal with all the issues of the town.' And that had been that.

It had been a warm day, but a wet one, and a storm was sweeping in off the ocean from the south-east. Daimon could hear the grumbles of thunder as it approached, even from inside Black Keep's hall where the evening meal was being served. He tried to block them out as he listened to what a Darkspur sar was saying regarding rattletails, because Black Keep still had no huntmaster since Duranen had been dismissed for his duplicity.

'—not complicated beasts, lord,' the sar, a slightly portly man in his late middle years, was saying over his soup. His name was Lahel, and he was the oldest of those with Yarmina. 'Dominance is key, and that can only be asserted through force.'

'For adults, perhaps,' Daimon agreed, 'but this lord has found a different method can be used with the young. He hand-reared a rattletail hatchling, rather than leaving it in the nest with its mother, and the beast is comparatively docile and biddable.'

'"Docile and biddable" are not words usually associated with rattletails, lord!' Lahel said with a laugh. 'Are you quite sure you've not got a ridgeback instead?' That garnered a laugh from his companions, and Daimon raised his eyebrows.

'This lord hopes you are not suggesting that he is really so foolish as that, goodsar.'

Lahel's smile faded somewhat. 'Your pardon, lord, this sar meant no disrespect, but it must be an unusually peaceful beast. Such a method would not work on any other rattletail.'

'Have you tried it yourself?' Daimon asked him. 'The stablemaster Tavi did as this lord has done, as did this lord's law-daughter Zhanna, and—'

'A Raider girl raised a rattletail by hand?' Sar Omet broke in incredulously. 'Lord, you truly are stretching the bounds of our credulity now!'

'This lord gave her a runt, and she raised it!' Daimon said, perhaps snapping at the man a little. 'Tavi and this lord followed *her* methods with hatchlings we selected for ourselves, and produced the same results: animals far more amenable than those raised in the nest by the parent.'

If Sar Omet was trying to hide his scepticism, he was not doing a good job of it. Sar Lahel, however, appeared genuinely astonished.

'Truly, lord? Three animals, all behaving the same? Were they from the same clutch?'

Daimon shook his head. 'Three different clutches.'

'This sar must admit, he would dearly like to see these biddable rattletails,' Sar Lahel said. 'Do they still live?'

'This lord's does,' Daimon said, 'and you may see it on the morrow. However, as Tavi was killed in the most recent battle here, Zhanna took his hatchling to continue to raise herself, and she is in the mountains.'

'The mountains?' Sar Omet said, taking an interest again. 'Why so, if you will forgive this sar for asking?'

'The people of the Smoking Valley did not come to trade this spring,' Daimon told him. 'They have been here for the Festival of Life every year since long before this lord was born, and one of their women lived in our town. We sent a small party to their lands, to see if any misfortune has befallen them.'

'A noble gesture,' Sar Omet said. 'Have you had any word?'

'They have only been gone a little over two weeks,' Daimon said. 'We think they might have reached the Smoking Valley by now, but it will be a while yet before we know the truth of what, if anything, has occurred there. You look concerned, Sar Omet,' he added. 'Does Darkspur have many dealings with the people of the mountains?'

'We have had some trouble in the valleys at the edges of the Catseyes,' the steward of Darkspur replied, and Daimon thought he saw the man's eyes flicker briefly to Yarmina, who appeared to be paying far more attention to her food than to the conversation going on around her. 'Attacks on farms: that manner of thing.'

'Well, this lord is sorry to hear that you do not have the same relationship with your neighbours as we do with ours,' Daimon said, keeping his voice neutral. 'We are lucky that—'

The hall's main door crashed open, letting in the last of the day's light and the first spattering of the storm's rain. Along with it came a staggering man being supported under one arm by Ita, and bracing himself with the other on the carved staff of Black Keep's reeve.

Evram.

'Lord!' Evram shouted, wobbling as he did so. 'Witchcraft!'

Daimon was on his feet with his fingers on the grip of his longblade before he realised that he had done either. The shout brought everything in the hall to a stop.

'Who?' he demanded. 'Where?'

'Elio!' Evram said, swaying. 'Old Elio! His door . . . the marks . . .'

'Lord Blackcreek, is your reeve drunk?' Sar Omet demanded, pointing at Evram.

'This lord suspects not,' Daimon rounded the high table and made for Evram. 'Bewitched, perhaps.' The man's eyes were glazed, and he was unsteady on his feet. 'Evram, where is Elio?'

'He ran for his boat,' Evram managed, although his words were slurred. 'Sorry, lord, your reeve . . . Elio struck so fast . . .'

'To his boat?' Saana demanded, arriving at Daimon's side. She looked up and around as thunder sounded again outside, even louder. 'He cannot run to the sea! This is a storm from the Dark Father!'

'Or the Unmaker,' Daimon said uneasily. The Unmaker had fled to the south when she was banished from her lair under Godspire by the Divine Nari, and it was from the south that she still sent her storms. If Old Elio really was one of her servants . . . 'To the walls!'

He sprinted out of the door, leaving the rest behind him, and into the teeth of the rain that was now sweeping down on Black Keep. The drops were hard and heavy, and while they lacked the biting chill of winter, they seemed driven by a malign purpose, blinding him as he ran for the steps that would take him up onto the stronghouse walls. When he reached the top the growing tempest attempted to slap him back down, and it was only by grabbing on to the stonework that he avoided losing his balance. To his left, townsfolk were scurrying to their homes to seek shelter from the rain, but out where the River Blackcreek met the sea, Daimon could just make out a small, dark shape: a fishing boat, buffeted by the wind and the growing waves, but still somehow upright. Even as he watched, the boat began to tip, but righted itself despite looking certain to capsize.

Daimon swallowed back the taste of bile in his throat, as the boat rode through another wave that should have swamped it. The fact the man had fled rather than argue his case was almost evidence enough of his crimes, but such seamanship in the face of a storm like this was surely enough to damn him.

A huff of breath announced the arrival of his wife.

'He is a fool,' Saana said from beside him. 'The storm still grows; this is not something that can be ridden out!'

'There is no hope of putting to sea to catch him?' Daimon asked her, spluttering his words through the rain being thrown into his face.

Saana shook her head, raising her voice to make herself heard over the wind. 'Your wife cannot ask a captain to do such a thing, not in weather such as this! It is to be endured, not entered into willingly!'

Daimon nodded. He was starting to lose sight of Old Elio's boat now, but he could still see its dark shape bobbing among the waves. It looked to have turned north, running before the storm up the coast. 'Then if we cannot question the witch himself, let us see his house.'

Ita, may Nari bless him, had sent someone for Aftak, and the priest arrived at Old Elio's house just as Daimon and Saana did. Sar Omet and the Darkspur sars had come as well, and rumour had clearly run through the town as well, since a small group of both Naridan and Tjakorshi were braving the weather to cluster around the building.

'Get back!' Aftak roared at them, waving his arms and his staff, and they grudgingly obliged. He turned to Daimon, his face thunderous above his bristling beard. 'Lord, this priest hears that Evram is bewitched, his senses and speech fouled. It may not be safe to enter.'

'We must know the truth,' Daimon told him firmly. 'Evram said that Elio struck at him somehow, perhaps through some unnatural means. It may be that the house itself is not cursed; many people have entered it in the past, this lord knows. Besides, he does not intend to linger.'

'Very well,' Aftak replied. He closed his eyes and muttered a prayer to Nari, then took a deep breath. 'Let us see what we may find.'

Aftak was first up the steps, with Daimon behind him with his hand on his longblade, and Saana behind him. She had found her blackstone axe from somewhere, and looked as grim as he had ever seen her. Daimon knew she was remembering her woman Brida, who sickened and died shortly after arriving in Black Keep.

'The door, Evram said?' Aftak asked, peering at it. 'This priest can see nothing, although . . . ' He looked up at the sky, then wiped his eyes. 'The light is not the best.'

'It surely cannot be on the outside, where all could see it,' Daimon said. 'Perhaps inside?'

Aftak cautiously pushed the door open. 'The fire still burns, although it is low.' He sniffed. 'It does not smell foul. Witches may use powders or herbs to poison the mind and ensnare the senses of their victims, but this priest can detect nothing like that.'

'Then either go in, or stand aside,' Saana called. 'This man is getting wet!'

Aftak huffed in irritation, but advanced into the house with his staff ready, although Daimon was not quite sure what he was expecting. Witches were rumoured to have familiars – the tameness of Zhanna's rattletail had caused a brief panic among the servants of Black Keep and, he had to admit, himself – but Old Elio was not known to have kept any bird or beast as a pet, and if he had, surely he would have taken it with him when he fled?

Nothing flew out of the shadows to attack the priest, so Daimon entered as well, and Saana pushed in behind him with a noise of mild disgust as she shook the rainwater from her hair. Aftak moved around to the rear of the door, and grunted as he examined it.

'This priest can see nothing here, either.'

'What are these?' Saana asked, and Daimon turned to see his wife examining the wood of the frame itself. He looked closer, where her fingers were tracing over its surface, and his stomach clenched.

Marks. Marks like those in the books Darel had directed him to previously. None of them looked exactly the same as on the curse stone Aftak had shown him, but why would a witch place a curse on their own house? Perhaps these were intended to protect Elio, to conceal his foul practices from others, or to dispel suspicion.

'Aftak?' he said, and the priest was at his shoulder.

'By the Mountain,' Aftak growled. 'This priest hoped it would not be true . . . ' He made a noise of disgust. 'We must burn the house, lord. The house, and all his possessions. It's the only way.'

Daimon deliberately avoided looking at Saana. They had a conversation which involved burning houses shortly after the Brown Eagle clan had arrived, and it had led to a raging argument: although, in fairness, the main cause of the row had been over Tjakorshi attitudes to men who loved men, and women who loved women.

'This lord doubts flames will catch in this storm,' he said. 'Besides,' he added, as he caught sight of a face in the gradually growing crowd below, 'we will need to question his son.'

'Lord?' Young Elio shouted over the noise of the rain, pushing his way to the front of the people gathered around. 'Your man's father! Is he unwell?'

'Your father's house bears the marks of witchcraft!' Daimon called down. The townsfolk gasped in horror, and several made the sign of the Mountain. 'What do you know of this?'

Elio gaped, clearly stunned by Daimon's pronouncement. Those nearest him backed away, although it was unclear whether this was due to fear of any taint, or if they thought Daimon was about to lunge for Elio with his longblade.

'Witchcraft?' Sar Omet said, staring up at Daimon. 'You are certain, lord?'

'As certain as we who do not follow such foul practices can be,' Daimon replied grimly. Sar Omet's face dropped into a scowl.

'This sar cannot allow his noble cousin to remain here a moment longer. We shall take our leave immediately!'

Daimon stared at him in confusion. 'But the storm, man! The night!'

'This sar cares not for the weather, or for the night!' Sar Omet roared. 'Better to brave them both than to linger another moment in this cursed town!'

He turned on his heel, flanked by his fellows, and they marched off in the direction of the castle, leaving Daimon with an ugly knot of apprehension in his gut.

JEYA

NGAIYU'S NEIGHBOURS HAD been horrified at the news of thëir death, and someone's child had been sent running to get the Watch. Jeya had planned to be well away from Ngaiyu's place before they arrived, since shé and the Watch were rarely on good terms, but a pair of them had been only a couple of streets away. They hurried up while shé was still trying to console one of the old people who'd lived in the next house down, but luck was with hér, for one was Mahatir, with whom shé was on reasonable terms. Rumour had it they'd been one of Ngaiyu's orphans, although it was before Jeya's time if so, and Nabanda said hê didn't remember them. Either way, Mahatir was more understanding than most.

'Ugh, that's ugly,' the watchperson said, re-emerging from the house only a few moments after they walked in, their hand over their mouth and their eyes haunted. 'You didn't see anyone leaving the house before you arrived, Jeya?'

'No,' Jeya replied. 'But the blood was dry when I got here, so it must have been done a little while ago.'

'And you don't know anyone who had a grudge against thëm?' Mahatir asked. Jeya shook hér head.

'No one.'

Mahatir huffed out a breath, and Jeya could almost see the deliberate effort they made to move themselves from being a person who had just seen the body of someone they knew, to a watchperson dealing with a gruesome crime. 'It's an evil thing, and a senseless one. And on a feast day, as well!' They waved a hand. 'Go on, Jeya, if you want to. You might have found . . . thëm . . . but we know you didn't do this.'

'Do we?' asked Mahatir's companion, who was still in Ngaiyu's doorway, and glowering down at hér distrustfully from under lowered brows.

'Yes,' Mahatir said firmly. 'Jeya was one of Ngaiyu's kids. None of them would have hurt thëm.'

'Thank you,' Jeya said softly. Shé turned her back on the house that had saved hér life, and the person who had ensured it had done so. 'Come on, Bulang.'

Galem had been hanging back from things, having exchanged only a few words with neighbours and avoided talking to the Watch, but thëy fell in by hér side as shé began to walk away. Thëy slipped thëir hand into hérs and Jeya squeezed, taking comfort in the warmth and pressure of thëir grip, so different to Ngaiyu's dead fingers.

'Í'm sorry, Jeya,' Galem whispered again.

'Í'm not sorry,' Jeya said, trying to keep control of the tide of emotions roiling inside hér. 'Not anymore. Í'm *angry*.'

'Í understand,' Galem said softly, and thëy would, by all the gods, thëy really would.

'Whoever did this . . . they didn't just take Ngaiyu from mé,' Jeya said. 'Í'd hate them for that anyway, but it's not just mé. It's everyone who ever needed that house. It's everyone who won't have a safe place to sleep tonight, or tomorrow, or maybe ever again. The kids who don't know enough to find their own way yet. Maybe some of them will die, and then *that's* on whoever killed Ngaiyu, too. And even if Í could find whoever had done this, and kill them, it wouldn't bring Ngaiyu back, or give those kids a safe place to stay, but it would mean that person would never kill someone like Ngaiyu again.'

'Are there many other people like Ngaiyu?' Galem asked.

'No,' Jeya said. 'I don't think so. If there are, there aren't enough.' Shé breathed out, long and slow, and realised shé'd probably been squeezing thëir fingers too hard. 'Is this how yöu felt? Did yöu wish you could kill the people who'd killed yöur family?'

'Yes,' Galem said quietly. 'But Ï know it would barely make any difference. My family's true enemies are in Idramar, not walking the streets of East Harbour. Those people we saw . . . they would just be hired knives, assassins. Even if they were killed somehow, more would be sent, sooner or later.' Thëy made a noise of disgusted grief. 'More probably will be sent now, just after that new family instead of më. It's strange: Ï find myself thinking it would almost have been better for my family to have been killed . . . if there was a *point* to it? But instead the Hierarchs change things to suit themselves, and my family's death goes unremarked. We truly were nothing more than useful props for them, as much a mask as the ones we wore at public events.'

'And after all that, after all the danger they put yöu in, they wouldn't even help yöu when yöu needed it the most,' Jeya added bitterly. Shé'd never given too much thought to the Hierarchs before. They were just there, ruling over the City of Islands and its mainland territories, their existence as far removed from hérs as those of the birds in the high forests, or the long-necked sea dragons in the bay: shé'd see them, now and again, but with no thought that their lives and hérs would ever coexist. Shé'd supposed they did a good enough job, since although shé'd gone hungry many a time, East Harbour was a thriving place where there was food and goods and trade. Rich people had those things, and people like Jeya stole from them: that was how the world worked. Shé'd always expected rich people would look after other rich people: that was just how the world worked, too. To find out that rich people wouldn't even do that made hér question things in a way shé'd never done before.

'Ï'm lucky Ï have yóu,' Galem said. 'Lucky in so many ways.' Thëy snorted a laugh tinged with melancholy. 'If Ï hadn't met yóu, Ï'd probably have been in my house that night, and then Ï'd be . . . ' Thëy trailed off, and thëir breathing stuttered a little. 'Gods, Ï miss them, Jeya. Ï don't even know which gods to pray to, now. Ï used to think Ï had divine blood. Ï used to look out at everyone in the Court of Deities and think that was mine by right. When Ï was a child, Ï used to dream about what it might feel like to look out of a window in the Sun Palace in Idramar and know that everyone Ï could see paid më honour as the descendant of their god.' Thëy sighed. 'Ï no longer know if they should. It could all have been another lie of the Hierarchs.'

'Í used to dream of marrying a rich person,' Jeya said slowly, thinking back to hér childhood. 'Not because Í wanted to marry anyone. Just because then Í knew Í'd never be hungry.' They walked a few more steps without Galem saying anything before Jeya realised how that might have sounded. 'That is, Í didn't—'

'Yóu didn't come and find më at my house because Ï was rich?' Galem asked, and there was a faint note of mirth in thëir voice again.

'No,' Jeya said. 'Well, sort of. But that was only when Í was thinking of stealing from yöu.'

'That doesn't make it sound a lot better,' Galem chuckled.

'It wasn't because yöu were rich,' Jeya said firmly. 'It was because yöu're beautiful.' Shé shrugged. 'Í don't know if that sounds better or not.'

'Ï'm not going to complain about hearing it,' Galem replied. Thëy squeezed hér hand, and leaned in to gently kiss the side of hér head. 'It's a strange thing, that our dreams used to be so different, and now we're walking down the same road together. And Ï wouldn't change that. There are a lot of other things Ï would change, if Ï could, but not this.'

'A god and a thief in love,' Jeya laughed. 'That's got to be worthy of a poem, someday.'

They avoided the New Palace, just in case any of the guards would recognise them, and cut through East Harbour's back streets instead. It was quieter than usual due to so many people being in the Court of the Deities, and that made it easier to move: certainly easier than if they'd hugged the harbour front, since trade and tide waited for no god.

'We'll call by the Morlithian temple,' Jeya told Galem. 'Í can leave a message there for Damau; they need to hear what's happened. It might be an idea for yöu to stay there while Í try to find another friend of mine, Nabanda.'

'Do Ï have to?' Galem asked wearily. 'They're nice enough at the temple, but they talk about their sun-god a *lot*. Ï might not know which gods to pray to now, but Ï don't think it's theirs.'

'Yöu don't have to stay there,' Jeya acknowledged, 'but Nabanda works on the docks, and there's nowhere that rumours and gossip fly faster. We can't keep yöu out of sight for ever, but it's probably a good idea to keep yöu away from the docks for a while longer, at least.'

'We're going to need to come up with a story for who Ï am at some point,' Galem pointed out. They were approaching the Court of the Deities now, and the streets were beginning to fill with people: it looked like the worship of Mushuru had finished, and people were spilling back out. Jeya cursed their luck. Not only would this slow them down, but shé wasn't even going to get much of a chance to pick some pockets. The coin would be most welcome, but Nabanda needed to hear what had happened. That was the most important thing; hê'd have come straight to hér if hê'd been the first to hear the same news.

'Yöur story is no one's business except yöurs,' she told Galem firmly. 'If people ask mé about my life, Í just tell them Í can't remember why Í live on the streets. But maybe we should have something, since no one will have seen yöu before,' she acknowledged. 'Have you ever been to any of the other islands? Could we say you've come here from one of them?'

'We went to Lesser Mahewa a few times,' Galem said. 'Any number of sailors would know it better than më and could pick holes in anything Ï said, though.' Thëy tutted through thëir teeth, thinking. 'What about if we keep it simple? We could say Ï was a servant in the house of a rich family somewhere else on the island, maybe in West Harbour, and they fired më.'

'That could work,' Jeya said, nodding. 'Why did they fire yöu?'

'Perhaps one of my employers took a fancy to më, and their spouse didn't like it,' Galem suggested, with a hint of mischief in thëir tone, as thëy pressed up close to hér to avoid them being swept apart by the wave of babbling, sweating people coming the other way.

'Completely plausible,' Jeya agreed with delight. Having Galem pressed up so close against hér was a far from unpleasant sensation. 'Ï would certainly throw over my spouse for yöu, if yöu were my servant!'

'Well, that's a starting point,' Galem said, giving hér hand another squeeze. 'Ï'm sure Ï can even remember one or two of the rich families in West Harbour, if Ï try hard. Ï can do that when Ï'm pretending to pray to the sun—'

'Jeya!'

The shout came from Jeya's left, and shé looked around past Galem to see who'd called. It became harder to keep hér place on the street as soon as shé wasn't looking at the jostling mass of people to find the gaps to steer into, and shé was buffeted twice before the person who'd hailed hér appeared between two passers-by. They waved happily, even though they were now barely two paces away.

'Damau!' Jeya exclaimed, immediately dropping Galem's hand. Shé wasn't sure exactly why, just that shé still felt it wasn't safe to draw attention to thëm in any way, including demonstrating affection. That applied doubly where Damau was concerned: shé just had to hope that 'Bulang' looked different enough from the richly dressed, definitely masculine Naridan youth Damau had seen in the market that time.

'Jeya, what's wrong?' Damau asked, frowning in concern. Their clothes were patched with sweat; they must have been worshipping Mushuru as well, and not working for Abbaz as Jeya had supposed.

'I . . . ' Jeya hesitated, then remembered that yes, there *was* something wrong, something that was completely unconnected to hér fears about Galem being recognised. Tears welled up again, unbidden and unexpected, as shé began to speak. 'Oh, Damau, I'm so sorry! It's Ngaiyu. Thëy've been killed.'

Damau's face crumpled instantly, their good mood instantly subsumed by horror, and Jeya felt a little extra kick at hér heart at the misery shé'd just inflicted. It was unavoidable, and necessary, but that didn't make it any easier to bear. Shé dreaded to think how Nabanda would take it.

'Mushuru's ashes!' Damau breathed. 'Not thëm as well!'

Jeya blinked. 'Wait, "as well"?'

'You remember I said Lihambo had been missing?' Damau asked. Jeya nodded; shé vaguely remembered Damau mentioning them when they'd been handing out the fish soup, but shé hadn't paid much more mind to it. Shé'd never known Lihambo that well, and people came and went from time to time in any case.

'They were found dead in the street two days ago,' Damau said. 'We wouldn't have known it was them, the birds had made a mess of their face, but they had that fish tattoo on their shoulder. It was near where Abbaz moors their barge, by the canal lock. I was one of the first people there, so I was able to tell them who it was.' Damau's face looked wretched now. 'I always liked Lihambo. And now Ngaiyu as well?'

'Yes,' Jeya said. Hér stomach was churning. 'Bulang, you head off to the temple. I'll find you there later.' Shé didn't say which temple, and Galem simply nodded and then disappeared into the throng. Damau didn't appear to be paying much attention in any case, to Galem or to anyone else. Jeya moved a bit closer, since two people standing together were slightly more noticeable for those who would take the care to avoid bumping into them. 'Damau, you said Ngaiyu "as well". Was Lihambo killed? Was it a knife? Was their throat cut?'

Damau's eyes focused on hér properly again, and they nodded silently. Jeya hissed between hér teeth. 'That's how Ngaiyu was killed. We— I just found thëm, at thëir house. No one else was there. The neighbours hadn't seen anyone. We told the Watch, but what will they do?'

'Jeya, it might not just be Lihambo and Ngaiyu,' Damau said quietly, barely audible above the chatter around them. 'Suduru was found hanging by their neck in the Narrows last week.'

Jeya grimaced. Suduru had been a bully, and Jeya had steered clear of them whenever shé could, but that was an unpleasant death nonetheless. 'Suduru swam with the Sharks, though,' shé pointed out, 'and if you swim with the Sharks then you become bait.'

'But there are others missing!' Damau said urgently. 'I wouldn't have thought much of it; you know how it is, sometimes you bump into someone every day, more or less, and then you don't see them for a short moon or more. But given everything else, and Ngaiyu being murdered in thëir own home . . . '

Jeya nodded grimly. 'Someone's killing us.' It seemed the most likely explanation, and shé didn't think that was just hér jumping at shadows.

'But *why*?' Damau said, the words almost pleading. 'Why are we important enough to kill, Jeya? We're just street kids! And people who used to be street kids. We don't matter, except to each other!'

'I don't know,' Jeya said. It wasn't a lie; shé didn't know for sure. It was, however, a strange coincidence that these deaths had started just after Galem had escaped thëir family's murder. 'I need to tell Nabanda, about Ngaiyu, at least. Does hê know about Lihambo, and Suduru?'

'I don't know,' Damau said. 'I haven't told hîm, certainly. I haven't seen hîm much recently.'

'Nor have I,' Jeya said, but then, shé'd been generally trying to avoid the people and places shé knew best. Shé laid a hand on Damau's shoulder. 'I need to go and find hîm and tell hîm about Ngaiyu. I'll tell hîm about the others, too.'

'I'll come with you,' Damau said immediately. 'Do you mind? I . . . It's foolish, but I'd like to make sure Nabanda's still here.' They chuckled weakly, but it was forced.

Jeya swallowed. Sa have mercy on hér, but the thought of Nabanda with hîs throat cut in an alley somewhere, or washing up in the harbour, was one shé truly didn't want to entertain. Shé didn't think Damau knew Nabanda as well as shé did, but they still were clearly concerned about hîs welfare. It wouldn't be fair to tell them not to come. Besides, Damau had set Jeya on the route to falling in love with Galem, and although that had not been their purpose, Jeya still felt shé owed them.

'Of course,' shé said, and did hér best to smile encouragingly. 'We'll go and find hîm together.'

ZHANNA

ZHANNA WOULD HAVE preferred to wait for a little longer before they'd made their move against the Darkspur men, but she didn't have that luxury. For one thing, Amonhuhe was impatient, and making it very clear she would begin hunting their enemy without the help of the rest of them, a point of view that Zhanna could understand.

For another and more pressing thing, they were running out of food.

The trail rations they brought from Black Keep and restocked at Ironhead served well enough to keep a belly full and keep them moving, but they weren't inexhaustible. Danid had set snares and gone hunting, and come back with some meat, but the valley was unfamiliar to him, and he could not feed them all. Amonhuhe might have had better luck, but she had no interest in doing so.

'There will be food inside Winterhome,' she said. 'The invaders could not live here otherwise.'

'But we can't get inside Winterhome,' Menaken pointed out.

'Then we need to kill the invaders.'

So it was that Zhanna, Amonhuhe and Tsennan Longjaw were hunkered down on the same ridge as before, two days after they had first seen the truth of what was happening at Winterhome, when one of the Darkspur men set off around the edge of the lake, moving in their general direction.

'Is that a bow?' Tsennan asked. He used the Naridan word, since the Tjakorshi didn't have one; their people had always used slings, which Zhanna personally thought were a lot easier.

'Yes,' she replied. 'He must be going hunting.'

'If they've run out of food as well . . . ' Tsennan muttered. He tapped Amonhuhe on her shoulder, pointed at the gradually approaching man, and switched to his clumsy Naridan. 'Wait, and kill?'

Amonhuhe nodded and reached into her belt pouch for her bow strings.

'We must wait,' Zhanna said urgently. 'Wait until he is out of sight of the rest.'

'This woman intends to wait until he's not just out of sight, but out of earshot as well,' Amonhuhe said, not looking at Zhanna as she selected a string and tested it for weakness. 'That would be best.'

Zhanna nodded, relieved.

'But this woman told you,' Amonhuhe continued. 'If one of these men comes within range of her bow, they'll die. If the choice is between risking his companions hearing his death cry, or he walks away alive, we must hope he doesn't scream too loud.'

Zhanna cast a glance at Tsennan, but he, of course, hadn't understood what Amonhuhe had said. Zhanna contented herself with rolling her eyes. 'She might wait; she might not.'

Tsennan grunted. 'I hope you're still good at running, Longblade. If she looses and misses, we'll need to catch him.'

'I don't know how you can be so slow, when your legs are that long,' Zhanna retorted. Tsennan opened his mouth to reply, but she held up a hand and surveyed the ground. 'We need to kill him before he gets to the bridge.'

The Longjaw frowned, clearly making the same calculations that she had. 'That's going to be hard. If he gets away from us and runs back the way he's coming or over the bridge then his friends will see him, and then it all goes to the depths.'

'So don't let him get away,' Zhanna told him. 'Amonhuhe's going to take a shot at him anyway, so we need to make sure this works.'

'Fine,' Tsennan said. He strapped his shield on his arm and unhooked his blackstone axe. 'I'll cut off his retreat. You be ready to get between him and the bridge. Given you're so fast,' he added with a wink. He got up and began moving cautiously towards where the ridge they were on dipped down towards the lake shore.

'If he's seen . . . ' Amonhuhe began darkly.

'Let him worry about that,' Zhanna told her. Tsennan was big, but that didn't mean he blundered around everywhere. 'You shoot. This warrior will run for the bridge if you miss.'

'Just make sure your beasts don't scare him away,' Amonhuhe said, with a dubious glance at Talon and Thorn. The two rattletails rose to their feet when Zhanna clicked her tongue at them. She had been training them to respond to commands using bits of jerky as bribes, but she was hoping they were going to start hunting for themselves soon, not least because the jerky was running low.

She set off down the slope, trying to keep her eyes on the far end of the ridge around which their quarry would appear, while at the same time watching where she was putting her feet. Talon and Thorn trotted and bounded around her with no concerns for their footing at all.

'Show-offs,' Zhanna muttered at them.

She got most of the way down to the river, less than the length of a large yolgu away from the bridge, when she saw the first hint of movement. She ducked down behind a pine sapling, barely as tall as her but with enough spread of branches to hide behind – she hoped – and gave a soft whistle. Her rattletails hunkered down once more, and with any luck their grey and brown plumage would help them blend in.

The Darkspur man had an arrow to the string, and was looking around and up the slope as he followed the faint path towards the bridge worn into the grass by generations of feet. Was he searching for game, or had some instinct told him he was being watched?

He was probably as close to the bridge as Zhanna was, now. She peered through the branches of her sapling, trying to see if Tsennan was cutting in behind him, but there was no sign of the Longjaw. Either he'd found some cover and was sticking to it, or he was too stealthy for her eyes to make out from this distance, looking through pine needles. They were pressed up against her nose, and filled her nostrils with the scent of fragrant resin. To her left, the river chattered quietly as it rode over rocks down towards the lake. The grip of her longblade was rough under her fingers, and her right ankle was getting uncomfortable, but she didn't dare shift to ease it in case he saw the movement. Everything seemed caught in a moment of balance, a tranquillity that belied what was about to happen.

Amonhuhe needed to do something soon, or he'd be able to reach the bridge before Zhanna, no matter how fast she was . . .

The thrum of a bowstring, the hiss of a shaft through the air. The Naridan jerked backwards, but not because he'd been hit. He'd seen something flashing towards him at the last moment, perhaps, or had caught sight of movement to his left and had begun to turn towards it, thinking to bring his bow to bear on whatever game animal it was. Regardless, Amonhuhe had missed.

It didn't matter. Zhanna was running, breaking out from behind her tree, with her rattletails on her heels and her longblade in her hand. She didn't yell a war cry, but ran as hard and as fast and as quietly as she ever had. If he ran, she had to beat him to the bridge. If he drew for her . . .

Well, then she'd just have to trust to her shield, and hope that the Dark Father wasn't calling her name today.

Glory to all the heroes, the man was looking up the slope! He'd ducked behind a trunk to shelter from any more arrows, and was now drawing his bow to aim up at Amonhuhe. Zhanna willed him to loose the arrow, let it clatter away between the trunks, and then let him fumble his next shaft while she bore down on him—

He didn't.

Her running footsteps must have reached his ears, because he looked towards her, then pivoted and aimed his bow. She heard the thrum of a bowstring again, and saw the arrow heading for her in time to jink to one side and let it pass her by, but in doing so she lost her footing.

She tripped and fell, swearing as she did so, and hit the ground hard, shield-first. She rolled over and pushed herself back up, panting in fear as she tried to get her shield between her and him again, worrying that he'd have notched and drawn already, that at any moment her chest was going to sprout an arrow.

But her dragons ran on, accelerating past her, leaping over dead branches and ducking under fallen tree trunks, heading towards the Naridan with the bow.

Zhanna set off after them, but there was no way she was going to catch up with them. She was a person, laden down with a shield and furs, and they were predators: young predators, perhaps, and nowhere near full-grown, but still well able to outpace her.

The Naridan was already reaching for another arrow, but something about onrushing rattletails, even small ones, must have shaken something instinctive in his brain. He turned to flee, but a large figure bearing an alder roundshield and a blackstone axe emerged from the underbrush behind him: Tsennan Longjaw, wearing his murder face and moving just as silently as Zhanna.

The Naridan could have perhaps made it past Tsennan if he ran as fast as he could and stuck to the very edge of the lake, but he didn't take the chance. He turned back again, and Zhanna saw his eyes focus on the bridge.

She tried to run faster. The Naridan still hadn't shouted, for reasons she couldn't guess at: perhaps he feared drawing more attackers down on him; perhaps he was too concerned with escape to have considered it; perhaps he simply didn't want to waste his breath. Whatever the reason, she had to get to him before he decided to do so.

Talon leaped for him. The Naridan swung his bow desperately and swatted her dragon out of the air, sending it flying to land on his side a yard or so away. Thorn managed to close his jaws on the man's thigh, and he yelped in pain and lashed out with his bow again, catching Thorn on the head and making itwhimper and release its hold. Then he was running again, away from Tsennan, away from her dragons, towards the bridge.

And towards her.

Zhanna's palms were sweating, and her stomach was churning. This was not the desperate, self-preserving fight at Black Keep, where she'd been fighting for her life, and had run Rikkut Fireheart through from behind to save her mother. Neither was it the night-time encounter in the valley up from Ironhead, where she had been looking to capture her man alive. Here, she was intending to kill someone who clearly wanted nothing other than to run away. Father Krayk did not look kindly on cowards, but he was none too fond of warriors who killed those who yielded, either. This man hadn't yielded, but he was running.

Zhanna forced herself to remember the tired-looking Smoking Valley men and women in their chains, and the storage hut where the children were kept under guard, ready to be killed if the adults misbehaved. This man had been willing to threaten others with death when he thought there was no risk to himself. That was cowardice twice over.

They were both coming up on the bridge now. They would reach it at the same time.

The man slowed, notched an arrow and aimed it at her face. Zhanna ducked as much as she could of herself behind her shield, and kept running blindly, unable to see beyond her own feet.

The bowstring sang, but instead of an impact on her shield, something hot tore along the outside of her right thigh. She staggered, but managed to keep her feet this time, and looked up over the upper rim of her shield just before she collided with him.

She took a swing with her longblade, seeking to open him up, but he parried desperately with his bow stave held in both hands, and the edge of her sword bit into it. She swung her shield at him, expecting him to try to wrestle her blade out of her grip, but he had already abandoned his bow and darted past her, heading for the bridge. Zhanna swore and went after him, trying to pull the bow off her longblade with her free hand, but he had a start on her, and her right leg was not responding quite as it should.

Another bowstring thrummed, and this time Amonhuhe hit her mark. The arrow hit the Naridan to the left of his spine, driving diagonally into his body. The breath huffed out of him in one agonised exhalation and he staggered sideways. Then, perhaps realising he would not make the bridge, he stumbled towards the river. Zhanna wrenched his bow loose and dropped it, and went after him.

He waded knee deep, then threw himself headlong. He was already weakening, and he'd never reach the far shore, but his body might float out into the lake, and no Naridan would believe one of their fellows had been killed by a hunting dragon if he washed up with an arrow through him. Zhanna followed him in, the water sloshing around her boots, raised her longblade with the grip reversed, and stabbed it downwards.

The blade punched into his body, driving him under the surface and pinning him against the riverbed. She gritted her teeth and drew it out, then stabbed him again, and again, and again.

'I think he's dead,' Tsennan offered from the shore behind her, having arrived too late to do anything other than give useless observations.

'Then drag him out before he washes away!' she snarled at him, leaning on her sword. She could still feel the man shuddering faintly on the far end of her blade, as blood left his body and water flooded into his lungs, and it was the most unpleasant sensation she had ever experienced.

As least Tsennan did not argue with her, but waded in and grabbed the Naridan's feet, then hauled him out as soon as she withdrew her longblade. Thorn and Talon, neither of whom seemed particularly the worse for wear, came and sniffed at the body curiously. It was only after Zhanna had dried off her longblade – at least the water had washed the blood off – and sheathed it that Amonhuhe reached them. Zhanna was expecting the Smoking Valley woman to be happy that they had killed one of the men who'd enslaved her people, but instead she looked horrified.

'What is wrong?' Zhanna asked, her gut twisting sickeningly. She looked down at the man, but he was definitely Naridan, so far as she could tell, not one of the Smoking Valley people. 'You knew this man?'

'You spilled blood in the Sacred River!' Amonhuhe hissed, looking at the water as though she expected it to rise up and attack them. Given what Zhanna had seen so far, that might not be entirely unlikely.

'He would have floated away!' Zhanna protested. 'And he already bleeding was, from your arrow!'

Amonhuhe did not seem at all comforted by those points; in fact, she looked even more worried. Zhanna had seen the Smoking Valley woman look confident, happy, angry, downright murderous, and on some occasions contemptuous, but she'd never witnessed this level of fear on her face before.

'You may have cursed us all,' was all Amonhuhe said. Then she turned and walked away from them and the banks of the river, back up towards the higher ground.

'What's her problem?' Tsennan asked, confused.

'It seems I killed him in the wrong place,' Zhanna said bitterly. She shooed her rattletails away from the body before they took a bite. It was one thing to want the Darkspur men to think one of their own had been predated by hunting dragons, and quite another to let her dragons get a taste for human flesh. 'Come on. We need to do something with him so he's not found.' She shivered, as the sensation of him wriggling on the end of her blade ran through her mind again.

'"Let's go and see the mountains", you said,' Tsennan grumbled. '"It'll be an adventure!" you said. There wasn't anything about carrying corpses and letting them bleed on me . . . '

Zhanna glared at him and clucked her tongue. Immediately, Talon and Thorn went rigid, their muzzles pointing in his direction.

Tsennan froze. 'Did you do that on purpose?'

Zhanna paused. That was supposed to have been the command for 'follow', but it was possible she got it wrong. And in truth, she probably actually *wanted* her dragons to menace Tsennan, just a bit.

'Not on purpose,' she admitted slowly. Tsennan looked at her, then at the dragons, then back at her.

'Fine,' he muttered, 'I'll carry him.'

DAREL

THEY HAD BEEN at the Divine Court for four days, and Darel had not yet been summoned to see the God-King.

He should not have been surprised. He had thought about the audience, about how it might play out, about how he could justify his brother's – and later his own – acceptance of their ancestral enemies, welcoming them as neighbours and, perhaps, friends. He had thought it might be a matter of some note, for a whole different people to be joining Narida. Certainly, the various occupants of the Catseyes had integrated to some extent with the Naridan lands nearest them, and there were Morlithians and Alabans here and there across the kingdom, but he was not aware of anything that had happened previously like the Brown Eagle clan's migration. He had entertained images of him holding forth to the Divine Court about the differences in their cultures, and the steps they took to overcome them.

However, such a delay was hardly surprising. The God-King was, after all, the ruler of the greatest country in the known world. He had many things to be paying attention to, even though Marshal Brightwater had suggested that Natan III left much of the detail to others.

Deep down, though, Darel knew it was not that his news and presence was not notable, or interesting. It was not, he doubted, even that the God-King was consumed with the usual affairs of state. Rather, it was because of the news he had heard as soon as he entered the Sun Palace's gates in Kaldur Brightwater's carriage.

The Eastern Marshal had been named traitor.

Four High Marshals, the North, South, East and West – or the Sun, Ice, Sea and Mountain Marshals, as they were also somewhat reductively known – commanded Narida's armies. Each had a force of fighting men they could call upon; in times of war or great need, they would instruct the thanes under them to raise more armies through levies, and then they would command the thanes who would in turn command their men. They were the Hands of Heaven, the highest of the high, save for the God-King himself. Their word was law, their conduct an example to every corner of the country.

And yet, one of them had been named traitor.

Not just 'one of them', either, but the Eastern Marshal: the man who sat in the Sun Palace alongside his monarch, and held overall command. The lineage of the post ran back to Gemar Far Garadh, who stood and fought alongside the Divine Nari against the forces of the Unmaker and the petty kings before Narida was even a country. Darel could only think of one other time when any of the High Marshals had been named as traitor, and that was during the Splintering, when the lineage and succession of Narida's very throne had been in doubt.

Back in Black Keep, Marshal Brightwater had spoken of Narida's need to stand as one. He had spoken of his fears of another Splintering, as rumours rose of how Nari Himself had been reborn. Darel could barely bring himself to believe that another such event could happen, but he prided himself on being a man of learning, who could look at facts and draw conclusions with little regard for his own preferences or preconceptions. An event such as the Eastern Marshal being named traitor could not easily be waved away. Narida was not splintering, not yet, but it had just taken a step closer to that terrifying prospect.

For most of his nearly twenty-five years, Darel had regretted not living in an age of great deeds. Daimon had felt the same, he knew, although the specifics differed. Daimon had always dreamed of being a warrior of high renown, riding into battle against a dishonourable foe at the head of a gleaming wave of soldiers, and breaking the enemy in the name of the God-King. Darel, by contrast, wished he could be there for when a nation was being forged, when lines were drawn and alliances made.

'Those things are boring and pointless,' Daimon had told him once, when they were children. 'That is all just paper. It is just what happens after the battles have been fought, with the men who did not fight them.'

'It is not pointless!' Darel had replied. 'Without the paper, the men who fight are not fighting for anything!'

Darel had an inkling, now, that the age he was living in was not what he had thought it was. It might not be one of great deeds, perhaps, but it might be one of great change. He felt the metaphorical ground shift beneath his feet: it had not given way, and maybe it never would, but the firmness of his footing could no longer be taken for granted. A wrong step by the wrong person could change things catastrophically.

He spent the first two days waiting in the chambers that had been assigned to him. However, when no immediate summons had come, he took to walking in the Sun Gardens. These had been tended to with great care by the palace gardeners in the aftermath of the public being let in to witness the Divine Princess's trial, and were now somewhat healing. Darel had seen lawns rolled and new grass seed sown, and wayward, broken stems sheared off to leave plants looking neater and tidier, if slightly sparser. How much of that, he mused, was a reflection of the Divine Court itself in the aftermath of Marshal Coldbeck's treachery? No matter how things were tidied and neatened, some things had been damaged and lost. While they might grow back, they would not be the same as they were before.

On the other hand, nothing remained the same for ever. People came and went, plants aged and died. Would it be better to think of the Divine Court, or indeed Narida itself, as a garden? The individual items that made it up might change, indeed the garden might be redesigned as it came under new hands, but the garden *itself* would continue, still bearing the same name . . .

'Good morning, cousin!'

Darel looked up, breaking out of his reverie to find himself being hailed by a man in a deep red robe with black trim. He was perhaps a few years older than Darel, but only a few; his dark hair was as yet untouched by grey, and his eyes – dark blue, unusual among Naridans – carried only the faintest of lines alongside them. He was remarkably handsome, with the traditional bone structure of the northern nobility, and he was complementing it with a warm smile. A woman was on his arm, of a height with him and her robes a mirror of his, and she too smiled at Darel.

'Good morning,' Darel replied politely, smiling back. It seemed that the Divine Court – or at least, the more minor nobles among them – addressed each other as 'cousin' regardless of any blood relationship. It was supposedly a reference to the fact that the noble families of Narida were all part of a union beneath the God-King, and were separate from those whom they ruled. Darel wondered whether this was the natural result of putting a lot of people who thought they were important into a space where a lot of people around them were just as important as them, if not more so. You would never have caught his father calling Odem Darkspur 'cousin', even though their family records suggested there was in fact some kinship, many generations ago. In Blackcreek, and indeed most of the southern thanelands, it was easy to work out who was nobility: they were the only one for miles around who lived in a castle.

'You must be Lord Blackcreek,' the man said, strolling closer. Unlike Darel, his hair hung loose rather than in a sar's braids, and he wore no blades on his belt. He was clearly not a man to whom combat called, and yet he was obviously welcome in the God-King's court. Darel felt a surge of envy, since he had been forced into martial pursuits by his father, despite his wishes. On the other hand, that training had saved his life when the pirates had boarded the *Silver Tide*. Had they lived in Idramar, where Raider ships were seen but rarely and made landfall even less often, perhaps Darel's childhood would have been different.

'You are correct,' Darel replied with a neutral bow, since he did not yet know this man's rank in relation to his own. 'However, this thane confesses that you have him at a disadvantage.'

'That cannot be a common occurrence!' the man replied with a chuckle. 'The Lord Marshal's accounts suggest that you are both a scholar and a warrior!'

Darel felt his cheeks heat with embarrassment, but he kept a tight grip on the somewhat foolish smile he felt about to break out over his face. This man knew more about Darel than Darel did about him, and was flattering him. These things could be benign, or they could be the sort of manipulation about which the Southern Marshal had warned him.

'This man apologises,' the newcomer said, with a cough that sounded slightly embarrassed himself, when Darel did not immediately respond. 'He is Hiran Threestone, second son of Thane Mattit.'

A second son. Hiran's elder brother would inherit the land and the title and then, assuming he had children, it would pass to those. Hiran might get a stipend to live on, but nothing more. A second son would usually leave home to 'seek his fortune' in the world, as it was somewhat romantically referred to. For a young noble whose family's lands were reasonably close to Idramar, it would make sense for him to come here and seek favour in the Divine Court.

'This thane is honoured to meet you,' Darel said politely. Here was one of the thorny problems of etiquette Darel was likely to run into: as a thane, he theoretically outranked Hiran. However, he was an outsider, and hailed from a small, rural thaneland very far away. Hiran might be the second son of a thane who still lived, but he was probably far more comfortable here at court than Darel was, and likely had his own circle of cronies; possibly even the ear of someone truly powerful. 'And your . . . companion?'

He hesitated as soon as he started speaking, because he realised he wasn't sure if it was good manners to ask after the lady if she had not been introduced, and nor was it clear to him what the relationship between the two of them was. The similarity in their robes suggested husband and wife, and yet . . .

'This woman is Yae, sister to Hiran,' the woman replied, bowing smoothly, and Darel gave himself an imaginary pat on the back for not jumping to embarrassing conclusions. Yae's hair was a fantastically complex arrangement of braids and plaits, interspersed with artful loose strands, and set with tiny bells that tinkled slightly as she moved.

'A pleasure,' Darel replied, although in truth, her law-brother was the far more pleasurable sight so far as Darel's eyes were concerned. 'What brings you both here?'

'Hiran is neglecting his studies,' Yae replied, before her brother could open his mouth to respond. 'Since neglecting them at the university would be too obvious, he prefers to neglect them elsewhere and claim that he is going in search of fresh air.'

Darel was not quite sure how to respond to that. It seemed that Hiran was not either, as he struggled to prevent his face from showing the mortification within, with only limited success.

'As introductions go,' Hiran said tightly, 'that is among the worst you have ever given your brother.'

'Only among the worst?' Yae replied, a mischievous smile quirking her lips. 'Clearly your sister must try harder.'

'And what is it that you study, when you are not, ah, neglecting them?' Darel asked curiously.

'Languages,' Hiran said. 'The structure and function of them, and how they compare and are related to each other.'

'Related?' Darel said, smiling. 'Languages have . . . families?'

He intended it as a mild joke, but to his surprise Hiran's face lit up eagerly. 'Yes! As different groups split away from each other, their languages change and start to develop independently. We can see this best in Tamrahel's studies of the Catseye peoples, who have not been subject to the same sort of mass conquering and homogenisation of language as either Morlith or Narida, where the language of the ruler became official and—'

'This woman apologises, Lord Darel,' Yae interrupted him. 'She should have warned you. Once her brother gets started on subjects of interest to him, getting him to stop is akin to attempting to dam the Idra.'

'No apology is necessary,' Darel assured her, waving it away. 'New learning is always welcome! So, Lord Hiran—'

'Please, just Hiran,' Hiran said, with another frustrated glance at his sister. 'This man is neither thane nor heir.'

'Hiran,' Darel corrected himself. 'You suggest that Naridans did not always all speak . . . Naridan?'

'Indeed not!' Hiran replied, his face lighting up again. 'Many records were destroyed in the wars against the petty kings, or immediately thereafter, since the Divine One and his advisers saw little need for their preservation. However, from those that survived we can see that the dialects spoken across what we now know as a single country were greatly varied, with some being quite close to the Naridan of the time, and others being so far removed that we would have to class them as entirely different languages.'

'That's fascinating,' Darel said, genuinely. He had barely had time to get any sort of handle on the Tjakorshi language, but it seemed as different from Naridan as a dragon was from a sheep. 'And there are texts that show this, at the university?'

'There certainly are,' Hiran replied. 'Many are copies of copies, of course, as the originals have degraded over time, but they have been copied character for character by scholars. It is one of the greatest treasure vaults of our country's history, and this man believes that we are only now starting to understand exactly how much it can tell us.'

'Forgive this woman, Lord Darel,' Yae said, detaching her arm from that of Hiran, 'but she has heard these words so many times before that she has no wish to hear them again. It was a pleasure to make your acquaintance, but she will leave you with her brother.'

'This thane would not wish this conversation to drive you away,' Darel said hastily, but Yae simply smiled.

'Lord Darel, this woman is glad to see her brother taking an interest in his studies once more, even if it is simply to enthuse about them at someone else. Perhaps he might even set foot into the university again, if he has someone new to show off to!'

Darel looked at Hiran. 'Those who do not study at the university are allowed to enter its grounds?'

'If accompanied by a student or teacher, yes,' Hiran said. 'Yae somewhat overstates this man's neglect of his studies in the interests of comedic effect at his expense, as she is wont to do—'

Yae stuck her tongue out at him.

'—but it is true that he has not been there since Marshal Coldbeck was denounced.' He shook his head. 'It is hard to stay focused in such times. However, if you would be interested in seeing some of the items in the library, this man would be happy to accompany you.'

Darel hesitated. The notion of getting to enter Idramar's university, the greatest centre of learning in the world, was one that greatly appealed. However, he had his own reasons for being in Idramar, and they were far more bound up in duty.

'This thane would love to accept your offer,' he said, as politely and genuinely as he could. 'But he came to Idramar to be brought before the God-King for an audience, and he really feels that he should be on hand.'

'The God-King is still busy with the Inner Council,' Yae said.

'They had to do a lot of organising very quickly when they sent the troops out. They were supposed to be going to find the Divine Nari, assuming He has been reborn, and taking Him to Godspire for the monks to pass their judgement. When Coldbeck was denounced, the task was changed to also finding the traitor and bringing him back to the capital, and they had to change officers whose loyalties might be suspect.' She shrugged. 'Now they're tidying up afterwards, sending out additional orders, that sort of thing.'

'Why not resolve everything while the troops were still here?' Darel asked, frowning. 'Why rush them out?'

'Consider it, Lord Darel,' Hiran said gently. 'You are the God-King, and you have just experienced an attempt to seize the throne by your highest-ranking commander, who has fled the city rather than face justice after he's assembled a considerable force of men under arms within it. Do you keep the men there while you work through the changes that need to be made? Or do you get them outside of the walls as soon as possible, preferably before they find out that their commander is now a traitor, just in case any of them turn out to be harbouring similar thoughts?'

Darel grimaced. 'There is logic to that, of course. This thane . . . The notion that men, that soldiers of Narida could rebel against the God-King in numbers is simply something that would not have occurred to him.'

'Would that it need not occur to anyone!' Hiran said. 'The thought of the bloodshed that would lead to in our streets is enough to worry anyone. But still,' he continued, 'thanks to the wisdom of the Inner Council, that potential problem, if problem it was, has been averted.' He smiled, then bit his lip. 'So . . . would you like to see the university?'

'This thane still feels it will hardly help his cause if he is nowhere to be found, should the God-King find time to grant the audience,' Darel said awkwardly. 'In any other circumstance, he would be delighted to.'

'This woman will gladly tell the seneschal that you can be found at the university,' Yae offered. She glanced around theatrically and hoarsened her voice in a stage whisper. 'Besides, it is tradition at the Sun Palace to blame the servants for a noble's delays.'

That didn't make Darel feel much better, since he had no quarrel with the servants of the Sun Palace, but it seemed unlikely to him that the first thing the God-King would do upon resolving whatever urgent matters were occupying the Inner Council would be to summon the thane of Blackcreek. Darel would surely have some warning of when he would be expected to attend his monarch.

Besides, if the audience went very wrong then he could possibly be imprisoned or sentenced to death, and if he had neglected the opportunity to see the University of Idramar before either of those things happened – and in the company of a very attractive and interesting man, no less – then he was not sure he would forgive himself.

'Very well,' he said, and a small, pleasant warmth spread in his chest at Hiran's answering smile. 'Lead on!'

JEYA

Jeya and Damau found Nabanda at hîs usual dock, but hê was not hauling and carrying like usual. Instead hê sat over to one side on an upturned half barrel, watching a flurry of activity which involved a lot of people and, so far as Jeya could see, very little cargo.

Hê also looked utterly drained, shé noticed with dismay. Although hîs frame was still large, hîs neck looked thinner than usual, there were noticeable bags under hîs eyes, and those eyes seemed dull and lifeless compared to the familiar spark shé knew so well. Shé'd be amazed if hê'd been sleeping properly, and shé instantly felt a stab of guilt. Shé'd been so wrapped up in helping Galem that shé'd almost taken Nabanda's absence from hér life as a blessing: it meant shé hadn't had to work so hard to hide Galem, or come up with a hastily constructed story about who thëy were and where thëy'd come from. Now shé chided hérself for not being more perceptive. Clearly, hér friend was experiencing hîs own problems, and shé'd been too busy to notice. What sort of a friend was shé?

The sort about to deliver bad news. That was possibly the worst sort of friend there was, but it needed to be done. Better Nabanda hear it from hér than from anyone else. After all, hê'd do the same for hér.

Hê looked up when shé called hîs name, but blearily, as though recognising that the syllables held some meaning but not immediately connecting that meaning to hîmself. Nor did hîs face brighten upon seeing hér and Damau, either: instead, hê almost seemed to close in on hîmself a little more for a moment, before hê put on a smile that Jeya could tell was forced, and tried to sit up straighter. It was a poor act, but at least it showed that hê knew hê wasn't quite right.

'No work today?' Damau asked, casting their eyes over the dock. It seemed they were just as reluctant to broach the unpleasant subject as Jeya was.

'Not for mê,' Nabanda said wearily. 'A whole fleet of Southerner ships came in with a cargo of slaves from the Fishing Islands. Slaves don't need lifting and carrying, the poor bastards, so there's nothing for mê to do.' Hê sighed. 'Truth to tell, Î'm not complaining today. Î've not been getting much sleep.'

'Do they normally come here in such numbers?' Jeya asked, looking at the collection of large, strangely flat ships bobbing gently at rest next to the jetties. 'I don't think I've ever seen this many in one place before.' Nor had shé seen so many slaves arrive at once. They looked thoroughly miserable, being led off in chains by those wealthy Alabans who had bought them, and Jeya couldn't blame them. Shé might at times have struggled to find a meal, or a safe place to sleep, but at least shé could make hér own choices. It didn't seem fair, but what was? It wasn't like Jeya could do anything about it.

'Nor mê,' Nabanda replied. 'Maradzh says the Southerners are fleeing some sort of evil spirit that's taken over their homeland, so maybe more will show up: who knows?' Hê sighed. 'What brings the pair of you here?'

Jeya swallowed, the hollow space in hér chest growing a little larger. 'Nabanda, I'm so sorry. It's Ngaiyu.'

One of Nabanda's eyes twitched, and hîs eyes bored into hér face. 'What about thëm?' Hê was trying to sound calm, but Jeya could see the sudden tension in hîs shoulders and the grip of hîs fingers on the rim of the barrel where hê was sitting.

'Thëy've been murdered,' shé said, the last word fluttering as a sob constricted it. 'We found thëm earlier. Thëy were killed, in thëir house. Nothing was taken; it wasn't thievery. Someone walked into that house and cut thëir throat.'

'Mushuru's ashes.' Nabanda squeezed hîs eyes tight shut for a few moments, and breathed deeply. When hê opened them again, wetness sparkled at their edges. 'Î'm so sorry, both of you. No one should have to see that.'

'I didn't see it,' Damau piped up. 'Jeya told me about it just now. I'm really glad I didn't see it. I don't want to see it.'

Nabanda frowned at Jeya. 'I thought you said "we" found thëm?'

Jeya's throat tightened, and shé inwardly cursed herself. All this time being careful, and now grief made hér let something slip on the docks! 'Yes, there was someone else there too.'

'Was it the Naridan you were with earlier?' Damau asked hér, and Jeya could have pushed them into the harbour right there and then.

'Bulang's Alaban,' shé said, perhaps a little more sharply than shé should have, but then again, it wasn't polite for Damau to comment on the ancestry of someone they didn't know. 'And yes, they were with me at the time.' Shé turned back to Nabanda. 'Do yôu—?'

'Do Î know Bulang?' Nabanda asked, frowning as if trying to recall a face to go with the name.

'No.' Jeya cursed hérself again. 'At least, I don't think so. They came here from West Harbour fairly recently, I think.' Well, that was the story they were going to have to run with now. Shé just had to hope Galem could come up with a believable name for a family to whom thëy'd been a servant.

Nabanda nodded, as though that made sense. 'Sorry. You were saying?'

'I . . .' Jeya tried to remember what shé *had* been saying, before shé'd had to improvise. 'I was just going to ask if yôu knew anyone who had any sort of grudge against Ngaiyu? Anyone who might have wanted thëm dead?'

Nabanda exhaled, and a little bit more life seemed to leave hîm with the breath. 'No. No one wanted Ngaiyu dead. Not that Î know of.'

'It's so strange,' Damau said miserably. 'You'd have thought that if anyone would know, it would be us.'

'Ngaiyu was old,' Nabanda said heavily. 'Thëy'd had a long life before any of us met thëm; even mê, and Î'm older than either of you. Thëy might have had any number of enemies we didn't know about, from whatever life thëy had before thëy ran that house. Sometimes people can take years over vengeance.' Hê shrugged listlessly. 'Or it could have been someone thëy'd pissed off in the street that morning, who followed thëm back home. People are strange and vicious, sometimes.'

Jeya found that hard to believe. Not that people could be strange and vicious – shé knew that well enough – but that Ngaiyu might have offended someone badly enough they decided to kill thëm. Ngaiyu had always been the one urging caution, telling thëir nominal charges to be careful, plan ahead, know your escape routes, not to trust too easily or too cheaply. Ngaiyu knew thëy were old, and getting frail. Thëy'd not have given someone cause to harm thëm, not without very good reason indeed.

Still, Jeya could not blame Nabanda for trying to come up with an explanation that might make this horrific thing make some sort of sense to hîm. *Most people don't want the truth*, Ngaiyu had told Jeya once. *Most people just want things to make sense. And those two things don't always go hand in hand.*

'Ngaiyu's not the only one,' Damau said, into the brief, miserable silence that followed Nabanda's words. 'Lihambo and Suduru are both dead as well.'

Nabanda scrubbed one hand over hîs face, but it was as though hê was already so numb hê couldn't feel this new pain. 'By all the Hundred. How? When?'

'Lihambo was in the street, over by where the canal meets the dock,' Damau said. 'Their throat had been cut, like how Ngaiyu's was, according to Jeya. Suduru was hanged, in the Narrows.'

Nabanda sighed. 'Suduru was mixed up with the Sharks, and when you swim with the Sharks—'

'—you become bait,' Jeya finished for hîm. Hê'd warned hér about that often enough, using those words.

'That's a shame about Lihambo,' Nabanda said. 'You're sure it was them?'

'There's a tattoo on their shoulder,' Damau said. 'Or, well, there was. I knew it was them.'

Nabanda nodded glumly. 'The streets aren't safe. Where are you two off to next?'

'The market. I need to find some food,' Jeya said. She glanced at Damau, daring them to contradict hér and tell Nabanda that shé'd said shé would be going to the temple to meet 'Bulang'. For once, however, Damau decided not to be irritatingly accurate. They just sighed, wrapped their arms around themselves, and looked down miserably at the stones of the harbour.

'I don't know. I was worshipping earlier so I suppose I should be hungry, but I'm not, not really.'

Nabanda eased off hîs barrel. 'Since there's nothing for mê to do here, Î'm going to go to Ngaiyu's. Do you want to come, Damau?'

'Oh.' Damau looked uncertain. 'I don't know. I don't want to see thëm like that.'

'You might think that you don't now,' Nabanda said gently, 'but you might change your mind when it's too late, and then you'd regret not seeing thëm one last time.'

'Won't there be a funeral?' Damau asked, looking between Nabanda and Jeya.

'Maybe,' Jeya said uncomfortably. 'I guess it depends. I don't know if thëy had any family. I don't know who'd organise it, or who'd pay for it, or . . . '

'We'll have to see if we can sort something out,' Nabanda said. Hê grunted. 'Ngaiyu set enough of us on our way that we might be able to get something together between us. Jakahama knows, thëy deserve that much.' Hê placed hîs hand on Damau's shoulder, gently but firmly. Jeya recognised that touch from hîm. 'Come on, Damau. If we get there and you decide you don't want to see thëm, you don't have to. But walk with mê anyway, just in case you do.'

'All right,' Damau nodded. They still didn't look particularly sure about it, but Nabanda's suggestion seemed a reasonable one. 'I'll walk with you, and I'll see what I feel like when we get there.'

'Take care of yourself, Jeya,' Nabanda said to hér, as hê and Damau began to walk away. 'And don't stay away for so long. You had mê worried!'

'Yôu too!' Jeya called after hîm, although shé knew the fault here was hérs, not hîs. Shé watched them move away down the docks, Nabanda's big arm and hand laid across Damau's small shoulders. Then shé turned and began to make hér way back towards the Morlithian temple, trying to block out the little voice inside which said that, slowly but surely, shé was turning her back on all hér friends in favour of one single person.

STONEJAW

OH, THE RICHES they'd made.

Maradzh was as good as his word. Stonejaw's cargo of slaves was of great interest to the flesh-merchants of the City of Islands, and what a strange and varied bunch of people *they* were. Most were broadly of the folk she had already come to think of as Alaban, but even that contained multitudes. They wore the same sort of flowing robes, but that looked to be more of a practical consideration given the heat and humidity, rather than anything cultural. Most had skin that was a dark brown, but one merchant in particular was far darker, had dusted their face with bright powder of red and green which stood out sharply, and wore tiny bells in their hair that tinkled when they moved. There was also someone who looked like at least one parent had Tjakorshi blood, but they didn't try to speak her tongue to her.

'Is that a man or a woman?' she muttered to Maradzh, as the next Alaban approached. There wasn't a huge difference between male and female clothing in Tjakorsha, especially in the winter when furs were furs, but so far as she could tell everyone here dressed more or less the same, and there were far fewer beards than at home. Then again, she wouldn't have liked to have her face covered by a beard in this heat.

'No,' Maradzh replied simply. He looked at her when she

opened her mouth to protest about the foolishness of his reply, and laughed. 'Things work differently here.'

'How can you tell what they've got under their robes, then?' Zheldu demanded.

'Are you interested in fucking any of them?' Maradzh asked.

'Not right now, certainly.'

'Then it's not important.'

Stonejaw considered that for a moment, then shrugged. 'Fair enough.' This place was far enough from Tjakorsha that she'd have been amazed if it didn't have its own strangeness, and at least they didn't ride on monsters here. The fine details of exactly who did and did not have a cock could wait until it was a pressing concern.

Maradzh was rapidly proving to be very useful indeed. Apart from being their representative and translator to the buyers, and giving Stonejaw a very quick rundown on how to avoid mortally offending someone so they wouldn't do business with her at all, he could also tell her exactly what was being offered in terms of what it would buy her, in this strange land. The Alabans used coins of metal to denote the value of things, like the Drylands to the north-east of Tjakorsha. It didn't mean much to her – Tjakorsha worked on barter and promise, and the only metal of real value was steel – but she understood the mindset well enough to know that these coins had value to the people all around her, and that was good enough.

'Why are you so interested in us getting a good price, anyway?' Zhazhken Aralaszhin asked Maradzh suspiciously, after he'd recounted the most recent offer.

'This is my dock,' Maradzh replied with a smile. 'They pay me a fee for trading with you, based on the price of the goods. The more they pay you, the more they pay me.'

'So we could make more out of them if we dealt with them directly?' Zhazhken asked, which was a reasonable point to Stonejaw's mind.

'Theoretically,' Maradzh said, his smile widening. 'But then I could get them arrested for not paying the commission, and have your ships banned from entering East Harbour ever again. And that doesn't sound like a good deal for anyone, does it?'

It certainly didn't to Zheldu, and so the trading ground on. Individuals were poked, prodded and assessed, but when the final price had been agreed, the final misery-faced slave led away and the final pouch of the coins had been passed over, she looked at what they'd amassed and had to consider it a worthwhile endeavour.

They split the take evenly, with a double portion for Korsada the Dry, since it had been her scheme. Then Maradzh led them to a small, nearby section of the city which actually looked very slightly like home, and where taverns sold shorat – shorat, by the Dark Father! – and the people around them looked familiar and spoke a language that was at least recognisable.

It was the first moment since leaving Tjakorsha moons ago that Stonejaw felt she could actually rest for a moment, and the tension leaving her shoulders was as though she'd been carrying a rock around that she'd only just managed to release.

'The Tjakorshi Quarter,' Korsada said, sipping her shorat, and looking around them. 'I've been here a time or two. There aren't many of us here, but enough to have a few places of our own.'

'What about your mother's folk?' Stonejaw asked. The shorat wasn't quite right, but it was worth it to taste something that wasn't as odd as the rest of this huge, humid, sweltering place. By all the spirits, the sun was long below the horizon and she was still sweating! How did people live here and not lose their minds?

Korsada shrugged. 'There are places for them, too. Most people come to the City of Islands, sooner or later, since it's the only way through the Throat of the World. I haven't spent much time in that quarter, though.'

'Why not?' Stonejaw asked, genuinely curious.

Korsada sighed, threw back her shorat, and set the tumbler

down again. 'My mother might have taught me her birth-tongue, but I lived all my life in Tjakorsha.' She shrugged. 'What am I going to get from them? They would be near as strange to me as they are to you.'

'Well, none of us live in Tjakorsha now,' Zhazhken pointed out. 'So what *are* we going to do? Sail back over the ocean to find The Golden and present it with these riches, try to buy our way back into its favour?'

'Fuck that,' Stonejaw said baldly, and a little more loudly than she intended. She realised the shorat was having more of an effect on her than usual. Did they make it stronger here? Or was she sweating so much there was only alcohol left inside? 'Fuck that,' she repeated, in a slightly more measured tone. 'I'm not going near that bloody draug again. It sent us across the damned ocean under Fireheart's command, and he nearly got us all killed.'

'You know,' Enga Zhargistutar said slowly, from further down the table, 'there are a lot of people here. I reckon we could find someone to mock up a chief's belt. A leather worker, a bronze worker . . . ' She extended one hand towards Stonejaw, an invitation to consider her suggestion. 'It's an option.'

'Why?' Stonejaw asked her. 'Why would we do that? Spend what we've just earned on making a fake, to take back to something that will skin us or burn us once it realises we've lied to it?' She shook her head. 'You can if you want. I'm thinking I'm going to buy some thinner clothes, and stay here.'

Zhazhken tapped his fingers on the table, then looked over at Korsada. 'You said something about the Throat of the World. What's that?'

'It's what the Alabans call . . . this,' Korsada said, gesturing vaguely around her. 'This bit of ocean that their islands sit in, all the narrow channels between them. It's the only way through from the southern ocean to the northern ocean.'

Stonejaw looked at her. 'The *northern* ocean?'

Korsada muttered something in what might have been her

mother's tongue, then sighed. 'I swear you southerners know nothing. Yes, the northern ocean. There's a whole other sea north of here, bordered by other lands.'

'And you've been there?' Enga asked her.

'No,' Korsada replied. 'And I don't know anyone who has. The Alabans charge a toll just to pass through their waters from one ocean to another, and no one I know of has ever had reason to. They came here, sold their cargo, then went back home.'

Stonejaw looked around at the rest of them. There were twenty or so around the table, those who'd gravitated to her and the *Storm's Breath* after she'd knocked Kulmar Ailikaszhin on his arse in the mud of that Flatlander village. She'd grown to know them all, those she hadn't already been familiar with, and they were a decent crew, so far as she could tell. Zheldu Stonejaw was not a particularly gifted sailor, but there were those who sailed with her who had that truly innate understanding of wind and waves, sail and paddle. If they trusted her to steer their course, she could trust them to steer the ship.

'That sounds like an adventure worth pursuing,' she said slowly. 'Who's in?'

One by one, her crew knocked their knuckles on the table to signal their agreement. Some of them – most of them – had left friends and family back in Tjakorsha, but what could be done about that? To return would only bring misery to all, for The Golden would assuredly wreak punishment on them for failing it. New horizons and new adventures would help save them from dwelling on what they'd lost, at the least. And who knew? Perhaps tales would be told and songs would be sung about their adventures.

'If we're going to do that, I want us properly provisioned,' she said. Slightly addled by shorat she might be, but she still had a handle on the important points. 'We're going to need plenty of food, water—'

'Should we take a cargo?' someone piped up. 'Something to trade?'

'We don't know what they want to buy,' someone else argued.

'We can talk to Maradzh,' Stonejaw pointed out. 'He'll have an idea about what goods move where.' She looked over at where the wharfmaster had his arms over the shoulders of two of Kulmar's crew, and all three were singing a raucous, ribald and somewhat drunken song about the daughter of Kozhan Lightbearer. 'But not right now.'

'What about one more run south?' Zhazhken suggested. 'Pick up a few more slaves, then either sell them here for supplies, or take them north and see if there's a market there.'

Stonejaw considered it. They'd done well today, but she now had an idea how much it would cost to buy food that would last for a substantial sea voyage, when her ship wasn't being provisioned by the order of a body-stealing draug that would kill anyone disobeying its wishes. Another trip to the Fishing Islands wouldn't take long, and if today was any indication, what they could make from it would greatly overtop the cost of doing it. One more run might set the *Storm's Breath* up nicely to be able to set off on a new adventure, one that would take them a long way from anyone who'd ever heard of Tjakorsha, let alone The Golden.

'That sounds a sensible plan to me,' she agreed. 'We'll go trading tomorrow, get the provisions in. Maybe see if we can find someone who speaks the slaves' language, too: that would be helpful.'

'You think they'll just walk onto the yolgu if we ask them nicely?' Zhazhken laughed.

'I think it's easier to threaten someone that they can do as you say and live, or disobey you and die, when they can actually understand what you're fucking saying,' Stonejaw shot back, and the rest of her crew laughed along with her. Zhazhken's face twisted, but he waved a hand to indicate that he conceded the point.

'Right, then.' Stonejaw reached for the shorat cask and began refilling everyone's tumblers. 'It's decided.' She filled hers last, and raised it to salute the others. 'To the crew of the *Storm's Breath*!'

'*The Storm's Breath!*'

ZHANNA

THEY HAD HIDDEN the man Zhanna killed as best they could, under branches and dead shrubs in woodland some way from Winterhome. Anyone looking for it would see it fairly easily, but they'd have to be looking in the right place first. Zhanna simply hoped that with so much space in this land, the odds of anyone stumbling upon the site were small.

The Darkspur men had not simply accepted the loss of one of their own. Two of them set out the next morning, calling for him. They were ambushed in the Smoking Valley people's overgrown fields by Danid, Olagora, Sakka and Kakaiduna, who'd shown she could use Ravel's bow more accurately than him, and who could talk with Danid well enough for them to understand each other. She and Danid scored hits with arrows, and the other two closed in to finish the enemy off before they could get back to Winterhome. Those bodies were hidden as well, and without spilling any more blood into the Sacred River, about which Amonhuhe was still muttering.

It was the day after, and Zhanna, Amonhuhe, Tatiosh and Tsennan were on the ridge again, looking down at Winterhome. Once more, the Darkspur men relieved the guard on their prisoners, and goaded them out to begin their labour. This morning, however, something was different.

This morning, when the Smoking Valley men emerged from the building in which they spent the night, one of them was clearly unable to move by himself. His companions on either side were trying to help him, but weak as they were, when he collapsed, they went down with him.

The Darkspur men laid into them with kicks, but only two managed to struggle up to their feet. The first man lay unmoving on the ground.

'Animals,' Amonhuhe hissed through her teeth. Her knuckles were white on her bow stave. Beside her, Tatiosh looked like he wanted to cry. Zhanna felt for him – he had come on this journey to see his mother's homeland and meet her people, and all he'd found was them being brutalised by his countrymen.

'Look,' Tsennan said, pointing at the men. He spoke in Tjakorshi, but Amonhuhe clearly grasped his meaning.

'This woman *is* looking,' she said acidly, but if Tsennan understood her, he ignored her.

'They're taking the iron ropes off,' he said to Zhanna. Sure enough, one of the Darkspur men was busying himself around the legs of the fallen captive, while the other Naridans menaced the rest with their spears. It made a grim sense: with the Smoking Valley men all chained together, none of them would be able to move easily if they had to drag their companion with them. Zhanna suspected she knew what was going to happen to the fallen man, and the fact she was going to be able to do nothing about it made the sickness in her stomach even worse.

'It's too late for him,' she said to Tsennan, but the big man just tutted at her.

'I know that! But if the ones who watch them in the day can get the iron ropes off, then we can too!'

'There's a key with the guards,' Zhanna said, as understanding dawned. 'So if we kill the guards, we can get the key!'

'Exactly!' Tsennan grinned at her. 'The captives might be weak, but if we can do that for the men and women both, we've got numbers on our side!'

Zhanna chewed her lip as she looked down at Winterhome again, working it through in her head and trying to visualise warriors moving back and forth. 'We'd need to free the children at the same time, or at least kill the guards watching them. Otherwise they'll be killed, and the adults might not fight if they think their children will die.'

'It's got to be a bluff,' Tsennan snorted. 'If they actually killed the children, they'd be giving up the only thing keeping them safe.'

'We can't trust to that,' Zhanna told him. 'And we can't trust Amonhuhe's people would see it that way, either. We need to know they're going to act with us if we try to free them, otherwise we'll *all* be killed.'

'That's going to be a big job,' Tsennan said grimly. 'Taking out both teams of guards at the same time . . . '

'You didn't think this was going to be easy, did you?' Zhanna muttered.

'What are you two talking about?' Amonhuhe demanded, from the other side of Tatiosh.

'We were planning how to—' Zhanna began, but Tatiosh cut her off.

'Mama, look,' he said, pointing at Winterhome, and they all followed his gesture.

Emerging from Winterhome were not one or two men of Darkspur, but a dozen or more, and they were armed with bows and spears, with short swords on their belts.

'This man doesn't think they're all going hunting,' Tatiosh said.

'Your mother thinks you're right,' Amonhuhe agreed. 'It seems we have their attention now.'

'This warrior does not think that is good,' Zhanna said uneasily. 'They may be searching for their friends, or for those who killed them, or both, but if they find any of us—'

'This woman is not going to be hunted down on her home ground by a group of lowlanders,' Amonhuhe snorted.

'Then we should move,' Zhanna said, 'because they are coming this way.' She looked pointedly at Amonhuhe. 'You are not going to try to shoot all of them, this warrior hopes.'

'This woman is not,' Amonhuhe said, although the way she was fingering her bowstave suggested she strongly wished she could.

Zhanna looked over her shoulder at the river behind them. 'We cannot get across the bridge without being seen. We should move that way.' She pointed off to their right, following the line of the river that snaked back across the floor of the valley.

'Perhaps we should be seen,' Amonhuhe said.

Zhanna looked at her, wondering if the woman had taken leave of her senses. 'What?'

'If one of us were to cross the bridge, it could draw them away,' Amonhuhe said eagerly. 'That is a lot of their number. Then the rest of us could go down there and free this woman's people!'

Zhanna considered it for a moment. It wasn't a bad idea – at least, it wasn't as bad an idea as trying to take on all the Darkspur men at the same time – but she was wary of rushing into something this dangerous without a proper plan.

'One from us leaves three,' she said. 'Not enough, even with these men away.'

'It's enough if the others come to help,' Amonhuhe hissed. She was coiled like a predator ready to pounce, and Zhanna could practically feel the need to act washing off her like waves of heat.

'They may not see us go!' Zhanna protested. The rest of their party were in two groups, with Danid, Kakaiduna, Olagora and Sakka covering the fields once more, and ready to deal with anyone who swung around the back of the rocky outcrop in which Winterhome was built and got too close to the caves they were still using to shelter in at night. Meanwhile, Menaken, Tamadh, Avisha and Ravel were somewhere to the south, and would deal with any isolated Darkspur men who went that way, between the areas covered by the rest. Zhanna wasn't sure if either of them could see the shore of the lake, which Zhanna's group would have to skirt in order to get to Winterhome. 'And the guards would see us coming!'

'Why aren't they moving?' Tsennan demanded from beside her, gesturing at Amonhuhe and Tatiosh. 'We should leave!'

'I'm trying to stop them from getting us all killed!' Zhanna said, exasperated.

'What did he say about us?' Amonhuhe said, glaring at Tsennan.

'Mama, they're spreading out,' Tatiosh interjected. Zhanna shot a glance towards the Darkspur men, who were rather closer now. Sure enough, they were spaced out into a long line as they approached over the open ground towards the trees that began at the base of the ridge on which she and her companions were lurking. There was no indication that the Darkspur men knew they were there, but it looked like they were planning to comb the area thoroughly. A short, sharp cry went up from one of them and she stiffened, but then it echoed down the line. A hunting party call then, to keep in touch and make sure none of them were taken without the others being aware of it.

Zhanna eyed the line. Getting around it, from where they were now, would be all but impossible. If the Darkspur men kept up this steady advance, and with only one of them needing to sight an enemy for them to all to converge, it was going to be hard to even stay ahead of them.

'We run,' she said urgently. 'Now.' Amonhuhe hissed in frustration, but she did not argue further.

And so they ran, as hard as they dared and as quietly as they could, along the eastern side of the ridge and down towards the river. As they ran, they were pursued by the constant yipping cries of the Darkspur men, calling back and forth to keep in touch.

'They're pivoting round,' Tatiosh said, his head cocked as they paused for a moment to catch their breath. 'The ones over there,' he pointed roughly towards Winterhome, 'haven't moved much. The ones that way,' now he pointed back up the river, 'are coming closer.'

'How can you tell?' Zhanna demanded. Tatiosh shrugged.

'You can't hear it?'

'If this warrior could, she wouldn't have asked,' Zhanna huffed. She thought she had good hearing, but Tatiosh was either much better than her at judging distance and direction, or he was deluding himself and the rest of them with equal ease.

'If they're pivoting, they're forming a line coming south,' Amonhuhe said grimly. 'They'll sweep between the river and the mountains.'

'That will give us enough space to avoid them?' Zhanna asked her.

'There's space,' Amonhuhe replied uneasily. 'The river flows from the other side of the valley, so there's more and more land between it and the mountains as we go south.' She grimaced. 'The problem is the grassland. In the trees, we can hear them before they can see us. If they see us crossing grassland, it'll become a hunt in truth.'

'So we stay in trees,' Zhanna said, nodding. She looked at Amonhuhe. '*Can* we stay in trees?'

'Twenty years ago, this woman could have told you yes or no,' Amonhuhe said. 'Now . . . ' She hissed in frustration. 'She doesn't know what may have happened since she left, and she can't remember where all the woods and the grasslands were, in any case. The farther from Winterhome we get, the less she knows.'

'They're getting closer again,' Tatiosh said, as a new line of calls rang out from behind them.

'We keep moving,' Zhanna said firmly. She cast a glance to the east, towards where their companions would be hidden. 'And we hope the others do the same.'

MARIN

THE MUSTERED FORCES of the Eastern Army had been borne up the lower stretches of the River Idra by hastily commandeered ships, seized in harbour and instructed that they were now under the command of Lord Goldtree, who was serving as general. There had followed a period of what had seemed to Marin to be utter drudgery, with nothing to do except watch the farmland of the Idra's wide valley slip by on either side. He was a man who liked walls, and clearly delineated streets, and the ability to find a loaf of fresh bread should he feel the desire to do so – and theoretically have the coin, although that wasn't necessarily an obstacle for him. He liked taverns, too, and places that had things worth reading. He certainly liked the opportunity for some intimate moments with his husband. The ship on which they sailed provided none of those things, and so soon after a far longer voyage back from the City of Islands, with the two punctuated mainly by being in a cell, he was miserable as a result.

'Is this the curse of being so clever?' Laz asked him. 'That you get bored so easily when there's nothing to occupy your mind?' He'd taken to whittling a piece of wood with a small knife, and appeared quite happy to do nothing else for long periods of time. Marin envied him, and attempted to imitate him, but only succeeded in stabbing his own palm.

'You should be more careful,' was all Ravi said. She dressed the gash with a couple of crushed fireroot leaves that would apparently ensure it didn't go bad, which Marin took note of just in case he ever needed to do the same in the future. Ravi was on the same ship as them primarily down to having enrolled at the same time, and did not seem thrilled by the prospect.

When they arrived at the city of Northbank, where the east and west of Narida were considered to meet, Marin expected things to be more to his liking. In many ways they were: it was a city, after all, and while not as large as Idramar it was still sizeable, for this was about as far west as the Idra was easily navigable by ocean-going ships, and so Northbank was a thriving commerce hub as goods moved on to Narida's interior. However, the news they brought with them was not well received.

'This city feels like a hangover,' Laz said, taking a pull from his mug of ale. The two of them were sitting downstairs in a tavern called The Jolly Riverman, in which Laz had managed to procure lodging thanks to his status as a sar. Most of the lowborn soldiers had been forced to set up camp outside the walls, in what had rapidly become a canvas city all of its own, and which had already garnered its share of thieves, sex workers and hawkers from Northbank's more established streets.

Marin looked at his husband quizzically, and Laz sighed. 'You know? Pressure?' He mimed rubbing at his temples. 'When your head feels like it's going to come apart, or drop off, and you might throw up at any moment if you move in the wrong way?'

When he explained it like that, Marin had to concede he was right. Northbank was the family seat of Einan Coldbeck, who had been Eastern Marshal. People here had a strong allegiance to their thane, even though he had spent most of the last few decades in Idramar and left the business of his land to his son. The news he had been declared traitor . . . Well, the locals were not going to defy the decree of the God-King, but the old adage about not stabbing the messenger came to mind. Marin got the impression it might have occurred, too, had the messenger not consisted of an awful lot of soldiers.

'Your husband doesn't think Lord Goldtree handled negotiations at the castle with a great deal of diplomacy,' Marin said quietly. 'That probably hasn't helped.'

'Who could have thought that demanding a noble family vacate their ancestral home because their patriarch is a traitor would have been poorly received?' Laz muttered. 'So far as your husband understands it, Goldtree has a good mind for organisation and coordination, which makes him a suitable general for something like this. That doesn't necessarily translate to being able to talk to other people without making them want to hit him.'

'Any idea what the plan will be from here?' Marin asked. Riding with the army had been convenient so far, but now their goals might diverge. It did not matter to the Eastern Army as a whole who found the Divine One: it mattered very much to Marin. He had a duty to the Cupbearers, but more importantly, he had a duty to Nari. Some might feel that it was arrogant to assume their actions could help the reborn God-King; Marin thought it was indecent not to try.

Laz grunted. 'Most likely, Goldtree will use Northbank as his base camp, and send the rest of us out from here to scour the countryside. He's already dispatched a couple of groups back down the river to find Lord Einan, since he's most likely fleeing this way from the capital.'

'That'll be an interesting meeting, depending on where their loyalties lie,' Marin said, and Laz nodded.

'Tila played this wrong. She wanted to frighten Coldbeck into fleeing to prove his guilt and make sure she was unopposed in the palace, and that worked well enough, but he's been the Eastern Marshal since we were all children. These men have never known another commander. She should have played nice, talked Natan down from his rage, and not taken any action against Coldbeck until after the forces were gone. Word would have got out eventually, but it wouldn't have seen this sort of situation, where no one's quite sure what's going on, or who they should be listening to.'

Marin took a pull of his own ale. 'It's still strange, hearing you talk about the Divine Family as though they're . . . normal people.'

'Oh, they're not normal,' Laz said, staring into his drink. 'That's part of the problem.'

He looked up suddenly, his eyes fixed on the tavern's door. A moment later Marin heard it too: shouting, getting closer. Laz shifted in his seat, easing the longblade on his belt around to be ready to draw.

The tavern door clattered open, propelled by the body of a woman who stormed through it with her dark hair streaming behind her like a cloud, and her face just as thunderous. Marin recognised Ravi, who'd taken lodging in another of the tavern's rooms in exchange for a service to the owner, the nature of which she had not disclosed, a moment before she was pursued in by a man with wings of white at his temples and an expression of rage suffusing his features.

'You can't run any farther!' the man yelled triumphantly, coming to a halt in the middle of the floor and pointing at Ravi as she made for the stairs. 'This man now knows where you lurk, witch!'

'Uh oh,' Marin murmured as Ravi drew level with their table, and he saw her expression shift past furious into something that somehow transcended anger altogether and moved into the realms of elemental wrath. She snatched up a metal tankard from their table before Marin could grab it.

'This woman,' Ravi shouted, whirling on the spot, 'is not a *witch*!'

The tankard left her hand and flew across the room, cracking the newcomer in the face before he could duck or dodge, and sending him staggering backwards with a curse on his lips. The taproom was a mix of Goldtree's soldiers and locals, and about half of it whooped with general approval at the theatre, while others began shouting angrily. The man Ravi had struck shook his head, blinking, then lunged across the room towards her.

'That's enough!' Laz shouted, rising to his feet and intercepting the man with a brawny arm across his chest, as more generalised shouting rose around them. Marin fingered the knife on his belt and looked around, trying to get a read on the room. Drink had been flowing, and he didn't think it would take a great deal for something bad to kick off.

'Did you not see what she just did!' the man raged. He was struggling with Laz, but he was significantly smaller, and unable to get past him.

'You called her a witch,' Laz pointed out. 'Most people don't take kindly to that.'

'She has marks of witchcraft on her body!' the man screamed, pointing past Laz at where Ravi was still glowering at him as though she could kill him with her stare alone.

'Uh, those are tattoos,' Marin piped up. 'Lots of people have tattoos.' To his surprise, Ravi shot him a glare that was barely less venomous than the one she'd been aiming at her accuser. 'And she's a healer, that doesn't make her a witch.'

'This man is Binamin, physician of Northbank,' the man spat at Marin. 'He knows the arts of healing, you rat-faced cur, he was trained at the University of Idramar!'

Laz's restraining arm suddenly switched into a full handful of the front of Binamin's robe. 'That's this sar's husband you're talking to,' he growled, when the physician looked at him in surprise. A couple of other men in the tavern began to rise to their feet.

'University trained, eh?' Marin said to Binamin, getting up himself. 'Under which master? Daltan or Genyel?'

Binamin stared daggers at him. 'Genyel.'

'Hah!' Marin barked a laugh. 'University trained, s'man's arse!

Neither of those two teach medicine!'

'A fraud, is he?' Laz said to the room at large, and an ugly muttering started up.

'What do you know about it, Easterner?' someone shouted from the other side of the taproom floor. 'Binamin's a good man! You let him go!'

'Easterner?' Laz repeated incredulously, turning in the general direction of the speaker. 'Don't you know a White Hill accent when you hear one, you cloth-eared—?'

Binamin, apparently alarmed by being dragged around by an increasingly angry sar, stamped as hard as he could on Laz's right foot in an apparent attempt to get him to let go.

This was precisely the worst thing he could have done.

Laz yelled in pain, but rather than releasing Binamin he hurled him bodily away, colliding with a table of three drinkers. Two of them rose to their feet, bellowing their outrage at Laz, while the third one clearly decided that this was Binamin's fault, and took the opportunity to punch the physician in the face as he sprawled across the table. Someone else grabbed that man from behind to haul him off, and then that entire side of the room exploded into violence.

One of the two drinkers came at Laz, who kicked him in the balls, since Laz had long ago given up on any notions of honour in combat unless under strictly proscribed circumstances. Marin picked up a stool and swatted the man in the head with it as he doubled over in agony, on the basis that most bar fights he'd been in had ended up with weapons used sooner or later, and for a man of his limited physical strength it was best to escalate first. Laz floored the other with a punch, then backed towards the stairs with one hand on his longblade.

'Get the stuff!' he yelled. Marin took the rest of the pub in at a glance – a rapidly expanding brawl, with those few not caught up in it clawing their way out of the door, and the furious and scared face of the tavern owner, who was clearly regretting not stepping in sooner – and ran past his husband for the stairs, dropping the stool as he did so. Their custom was unlikely to still be welcome here, no matter how things panned out.

As he began to climb, he realised Ravi was ahead of him. The healer looked over her shoulder to check who was following her, and he heard her hiss in frustration.

'Nari damn you, Marin, why must you ruin *everything*?'

'No one asked you to throw a tankard at his head!' Marin replied indignantly. 'If you weren't looking for some sort of help, why weren't you having it out with him in the street?'

Ravi's only reply was a guttural noise of utter frustration, and she disappeared through the door into the small room in which she had been planning to sleep. Marin opened his own door and fumbled about to find his and Laz's packs. There was a single, flickering candle on one wall, with a tin plate behind it that was supposed to reflect the light, but it was so blackened by years of smoke it barely helped at all. He managed to get everything together, then winced as a crash from downstairs suggested that a table had been broken, or possibly the door.

'Who'd have thought we'd end up in a fight if we enrolled in the army?' Marin muttered to himself. He shouldered his way back out of the door, since his hands were now full, and nearly collided with Ravi. He gestured to the stairs with his head. 'No, please, after you.'

Ravi began to move that way, then halted as something else crashed, and a scream rang out above the general shouting. She stepped back again and waved Marin forward instead. 'Go on.'

'If you insist,' Marin said reluctantly, and began to pick his way downwards, trying not to overbalance under the weight of their possessions. Thankfully, he not only managed to get to the bottom without tripping, but Laz was still there. He had even attracted half a dozen friendly soldiers, who'd either broken free of the general brawl or had managed to escape it, and who were now standing shoulder-to-shoulder with Marin's husband.

'Got it!' Marin shouted into Laz's ear. 'Let's go!'

'All right, lads!' Laz said to the others, raising his voice to be heard. 'Nice and easy, out the back door, and don't turn your back on 'em!'

They withdrew as one, past the bar behind which the tavern's owner was cowering, down the narrow passage past the kitchen, and outside into the cool air of the early summer evening. There was still the faintest hint of light in the sky to the west, visible between a couple of roofs, but the deep dark of true night had swept in from the east and only the flickering yellow of candles or lanterns escaping through shutters lit up the yard in which they found themselves.

'Back to the camp?' one of the soldiers said. He was a young man, with the cheekbones and jawline of someone unlikely to ever be short of amorous advances.

'Y'hear that?' another, older man said, cocking an ear. Marin listened, and heard shouts. 'That's not inside. Spilled out into the street, it has.'

'Back to the camp, for sure,' said a third.

They moved cautiously to the yard's entrance and peered out into the street. Marin grimaced when he saw a rolling ruck of a brawl outside the tavern's front door: as he watched, a few more onlookers spilled out of nearby houses and, presumably seeing people they knew involved in the fight, piled in to assist or to try to break it up, although the latter only became embroiled themselves.

'There's some of our lot in that, isn't there?' the young man with the cheekbones said uneasily. *Our lot*, Marin noticed. Never mind that they were all Naridans, in service to the same monarch and worshipping the same god: the frosty welcome the Eastern Army had received from Northbank had already drawn lines in the heads of some of his current companions.

'Pfft,' someone else huffed dismissively. 'Daft fools want to get in a punch-up with the locals, that's their lookout.' Marin realised with surprise that the speaker was a woman. She wasn't the smallest in their group, and her nose had been broken at some point in the past, so she certainly looked like someone able to take care of herself.

'Don't look now,' the older man said, 'but here come some more of us.'

Lord Goldtree had set groups of his soldiers to patrol the streets of Northbank, allegedly to ensure none of the rank-and-file caused problems, but more likely because of his distrust of the locals' allegiances. A patrol had apparently heard the commotion and had rounded a corner farther up the street, led by a man wearing the armband of a flagman, and advanced towards the fight at a swift jog. Marin thought they were about to see him and his companions crowded in the entrance to the tavern's rear yard, and was preparing to be bawled at, when the flagman noticed that some of the fight's participants wore the same colours as he did.

Had Marin been that flagman, he might have stopped to consider whether this was some sort of isolated incident that had got out of hand. He might also have thought about his surroundings, and reflected that although he was at the head of a group of armed men he was also in the middle of a city that, if considered collectively, far outnumbered the entire Eastern Army contingent present here. Which was why Marin, had he been that flagman, would not have drawn his blade, yelled 'Treason!' at the top of his lungs, and led his companions into an actual full-on charge into the side of the fight.

'Oh shit,' Laz said, aghast. 'That fucking fool. That's torn it.'

Screams and shouts rang out. A few more locals piled out of the tavern and straight into what was increasingly looking like a pitched battle. Some onlookers from the surrounding houses, who'd so far been hanging back and shouting futile pleas for the fighting to stop, realised that things had just escalated and went in themselves in an attempt to save their neighbours. Marin saw more than one knife drawn.

'Camp?' Cheekbones said urgently.

'Sod the camp,' Laz replied, his voice thick with disgust. 'This is going to get worse, and Goldtree will see it as a rebellion. Come morning, we'll be set to cutting the throats of anyone in this city who steps out of line, you mark this sar's words.'

'S'man didn't sign up for that,' Cheekbones said adamantly. 'He came west to help find the Divine One.'

'Aye,' the older man said, with feeling, and the rest added murmured agreements or nods.

'So that's what we'll do,' Marin spoke up, sharing a glance with Laz. 'We leave the city now, lie low, then get as far away as we can in the morning. All of us.'

'That's desertion,' the woman with the broken nose pointed out.

'You see that?' Laz pointed at the fight. There were several unmoving bodies on the ground now. 'That's your duty. Duty or desertion: take your pick.'

Broken-Nose looked meaningfully at Laz's scabbard. 'You know a lot about desertion, blacksword?'

'Enough to still be alive,' Laz growled. 'Who's in?'

One by one, they all nodded, even Broken-Nose. Even, to Marin's amazement, Ravi.

'Let's get to it, then,' Laz said. 'Out of the north gate. Those of you who need to get things from the camp, do it as quick and quiet as you can. There's a big whitebark a way down the north road: this sar saw it earlier. We'll wait for you there, but we won't wait for ever. We've got a job to do, and this sar's not risking it. Now move, before anyone else turns up and expects us to help them!'

They broke into a shambling run, getting away from the fight as quickly as they could down dark streets. Marin puffed along under the weight of his pack, and found himself running alongside Ravi.

'You're coming with us, then?' he asked breathlessly. 'Thought there'd be more business for you with the rest of them, especially after something like this. The city will need all the healers it can get!'

'This woman didn't come out here just to make money by putting poultices on wounds,' Ravi snapped. 'She could have done that anywhere.'

'Why *are* you here, then?' Marin asked.

'The same reason as you, Marin of Idramar,' Ravi said, not looking at him. 'To find the Divine Nari.'

DAIMON

THE DARKSPUR DELEGATION had not, in fact, departed in the evening of the discovery of Old Elio's witchcraft, as Sar Omet had intended. Yarmina Darkspur had flatly refused to leave at that time and in that weather, drawing Sar Omet into an argument concerning which of them truly had the greater authority, and how far he would be transgressing against the Code of Honour to drag a noblewoman out into the wilderness against her will, even if it was away from a town of witches. The fact the argument itself took place in the pouring rain seemed, to Daimon at least, to somewhat undercut Yarmina's argument about her objections to the weather, but she managed to drag it on enough for Sar Omet to give up in disgust and concede that they would instead leave at first light.

The next morning, as the last sighs of the storm that had howled at them overnight were still tugging at shutters, and the main body of it had rumbled off to the north-west – towards Darkspur, in fact – Daimon stood alongside Saana in the second yard of Black Keep as the huffing, snorting mounts of Omet and his fellow sars were led out of the stables. Rattler lurked around Daimon's legs; he was far too small for the longbrows to be bothered by his presence, but Sar Lahel looked rather perturbed to see the tame rattletail Daimon had described to him the previous evening.

'Have your animals been kept to your satisfaction?' Daimon asked mildly, with a glance at Abbatane. Sar Omet's lips thinned as he inspected his longbrow, but in the end he did nothing more than slightly adjust the saddle.

'This steward has no complaints about your treatment of his dragons, Lord Blackcreek,' Omet said, turning to face Daimon. 'Your toleration of witches, however—'

'We do not tolerate witches in Black Keep!' Daimon barked, surprising himself with his own anger. At his feet, Rattler hissed in echo. 'The witch has fled, and his son has been held to be questioned today, by the reeve, the priest and this lord himself!'

Omet pursed his lips and glanced downwards at Rattler. 'To be questioned, indeed. Not executed.'

'Not yet,' Daimon said bleakly, his stomach twisting. 'If we find evidence he knew of his father's practices, or practised them himself, then he will not be spared.'

Omet opened his mouth as if to answer, but Yarmina laid her hand on his shoulder. 'Come, cousin. It is time for us to be gone, and,' she added, with a long glance at him, 'for us to leave Lord Blackcreek to enforce the law of his land.'

For a moment, Daimon thought Omet was going to answer her back as well, perhaps to comment on how she'd prevented them from leaving the previous night, but the man bit his tongue and instead barked an instruction to his sars to mount up. Yarmina stepped forwards to stand in front of Daimon and Saana, equidistant between them as befitted a noble addressing husband and wife, and bowed.

'Lord and Lady Blackcreek, this woman thanks you for your hospitality and company while she has been your visitor.'

'You are very welcome,' Daimon said, bowing in return. 'It was good to renew a friendship.'

'This man likes you,' Saana said bluntly, with a faint smile. 'You may visit again.'

Yarmina seemed slightly surprised at Saana's words – in truth,

Daimon was a little surprised himself – and hesitated for a moment, then took another step forwards to reach out and place her arms around both of their necks. Daimon stiffened instinctively, for such close contact was simply not done among Naridan nobility except between spouses, or close family members, but Saana barked a laugh and hugged Yarmina in return. Yarmina turned her face towards Daimon's, and her lips brushed his ear.

'Be careful of this woman's father.'

Then she released them and stepped back, looking slightly shamefaced, as well she might. Daimon, blinking in surprise at her actions as much as her words, didn't manage to come up with any sort of response before Yarmina, under Sar Omet's disapproving glower, mounted her own longbrow and turned its head towards the gate.

'Darkspur!' Omet snapped. 'We ride!' They goaded their steeds forward at a gentle trot through the gate to the first yard, and then over the drawbridge to where their retinue of foot soldiers would be waiting for them in the town's square.

'What did she mean by that?' Saana asked quietly, as she and Daimon watched them go.

'Your husband does not know,' Daimon admitted. 'He suspects she does not fully know herself, but he feels it would be wise to heed her warning.' He shrugged, putting it to the back of his mind. 'It is nothing new. We in Black Keep have not trusted Odem Darkspur since your husband was young, so to be warned of him now by his own daughter makes little difference. Besides, we have more pressing concerns.'

With the Darkspur contingent gone, Daimon and Saana made their way to the town square, to where the great chairs of the lord and lady of Black Keep had been moved next to the shrine of Nari. When Daimon sat down, Rattler settled by the side of his chair and was rewarded with a small piece of meat. Some of the townsfolk were working in the fields, or in their homes, or had gone out fishing as usual, but a fair number had come to see the trial. Looking at their faces, a mixture of concerned, fearful and angry, Daimon hoped that Aftak and the reevesmen would be able to keep order.

Aftak bowed to Daimon and Saana, and, at Daimon's nod, thumped his staff on the stone of the square three times. 'The trial for witchcraft of Elio of Black Keep and his son, known as Young Elio, will now begin!'

The muttering in the crowd died down, and Daimon raised his voice. 'Has the house of Old Elio been examined?'

Aftak nodded. 'It has, lord, against the texts you so kindly lent us from your lordship's library. The marks on the frame of Old Elio's door correspond to those the texts identify as being linked to witchcraft, although we do not know their purpose, since the authors of those texts did not either. Other items were found within, the purposes of which we also did not know: twisted and knotted lengths of cord, and an old knife with a thin blade.'

Daimon frowned. 'A knife in a house is hardly evidence of witchcraft.'

'Indeed, lord,' Aftak replied. 'However, it was kept hidden, along with a bowl that looked equally old, and which also bore witch marks.'

Daimon sighed sadly. 'And how fares our reeve?'

'Evram has taken to his bed,' Aftak replied, 'else he would be here. He felt sick in the aftermath of being attacked. This priest has prayed over him, in case his ailment is linked to some dark curse placed upon him.'

'The evidence seems clear,' Daimon said heavily. 'This lord had hoped that Old Elio had lived in his house having given no thought to marks on his door which had perhaps been there before he was born. It is even possible that he struck our reeve and fled out of simple fear, not guilt. However, with no knowledge of witchcraft, he would not know what it was Evram had found, or why it would damn him, and to keep other witch-marked items hidden indicates that he knew their purpose and knew that their existence would put him at risk. There can be little doubt in this lord's mind that Old Elio of Black Keep was, indeed, a witch in the service of the Unmaker. This lord proclaims him as such, and he is to be executed should he be found on Blackcreek land.'

The assembled townsfolk muttered and whispered, and Daimon let them do so. Let them have a few moments to process his judgement and come to terms with it.

'Will you send word out?' Saana asked him quietly, and he nodded.

'Up the coast, in particular. This lord suspect Elio will have more sense than to remain on Blackcreek land, but it needs to be done. With any luck,' he added grimly, 'he will have been pulled under by the waves last night, but we know such storms come from the Unmaker herself, so perhaps her servant would be spared her wrath.'

'Your wife's people know storms,' Saana said. 'They spare no one. If he sailed through those waves and came to no harm, then truly your land's witches are to be feared.'

'Let us hope we do not have another waiting in the cells,' Daimon said. He was not looking forward to this, but he caught Aftak's eye and raised his voice once more. 'Bring forth Young Elio!'

The instruction was passed on, through to where the reevesmen Keimar and Shemel stood guard over the cells where Young Elio had been placed. The muttering of the crowd grew as the two men passed through them, bringing Young Elio between them, but no one shouted out, or threw anything or, thank Nari, made to attack him. The town had been shocked to its core by the revelations about Old Elio, but he had fled, and damned himself in their eyes in the process: and quite rightly so, from what Daimon could see. Young Elio was as much a fixture of the town's life as his father, but, as yet, the only evidence against him was that blood relationship.

Daimon dearly hoped it was all that they would have.

'Elio of Black Keep,' he began. There was no point calling the man 'Young Elio', since with his father gone he was the only man to bear that name, and besides which, he must have been near the age of Daimon's own father. 'Your father has been found guilty of witchcraft and unnatural practices.'

Elio closed his eyes and hung his head.

'You are his only living child,' Daimon continued. 'You lived with him until you reached adulthood. You too now live alone, as he did. Do you follow the same cursed path as him, a traitor to your country and to the Divine Nari?'

'Lord,' Elio said softly, 'your man does not, and never has.'

'This lord will ask you once more, Elio,' Daimon said sternly. 'If you confess to this crime, then he will strike off your head here and now and your body will be burned. If you deny it, but evidence is then presented that condemns you, then we must burn you alive, as Nari Himself decreed.'

'Lord, your man did not misspeak,' Elio replied, more firmly this time, and he raised his head to meet Daimon's eyes. 'He is a follower of Nari, as true as any man here—'

'There are many men here who do not follow Nari at all,' Aftak pointed out, gesturing at some of the Brown Eagle clan, who had clustered over to one side. Daimon caught sight of Nalon in their ranks, who was presumably trying to appraise them of what was happening.

'A figure of speech,' Daimon said to the priest, 'and one which this lord is sure we can allow. The meaning of Elio's words was clear enough.' Aftak nodded his understanding, and Daimon returned his attention to Elio. 'What about your father's practices? Did you know of them?'

Elio shook his head helplessly. 'Your man heard talk of the marks of witchcraft, when you were inspecting his father's house. He does not know what they might be.'

Daimon drummed his fingers on the arm of his – or technically his brother's – chair, but he could see no way in which giving

Elio the information could help the man. 'There were marks carved into the doorframe.' He made no mention of the bowl that Aftak had reported finding.

Elio's eyes grew wide. 'Those, lord? Da once told this servant he'd simply scratched them in when he was a child.'

'And you never asked him again?' Aftak demanded.

Elio flinched away from the priest slightly. 'Truthfully, no. This was when s'man was young, and Da didn't take kindly to being asked about it. He certainly didn't like it when s'man scratched at the doorframe himself as a child. Fair belted s'man, he did, and s'man never mentioned the doorframe to him again. S'man had forgotten those marks were even there, until just now.'

'So you have nothing marked in the same manner?' Daimon asked him. 'You have carved no marks into your own doorframe, or any other part of your house? You have no other items with those marks on? Nothing that your father gave you, perhaps?'

'No, lord,' Elio said. He sighed, and his shoulders slumped. 'Truth to tell, your man and his father are not ones to exchange gifts. We go out and fish together, for the boat is his and it's far easier to handle with two than one in any case, but we have not been close since Ma died in the plague. She always smoothed the waters between us.'

The plague that had been sent by the Unmaker in her triumph at the untimely death of the old God-King. It made no sense that one of her followers would have been claimed by it. What if, Daimon mused, Old Elio had been afraid of showing his blasphemous beliefs too openly in front of his wife, if she did not share them, and thus their son had never been exposed to them?

'Aftak,' Daimon said. 'Is he telling the truth about his house?'

'So far as this priest can tell, lord,' Aftak replied gruffly. 'He went through it with the reevesmen after we'd finished searching Old Elio's place, and there was nothing we could see. No marks on the wood, no similar items—'

'You searched s'man's *house*?' Elio demanded incredulously, rounding on him.

'Aye, to see if we needed to burn you!' Aftak growled back, and the sheer ferocity in the priest's bearded face clearly quelled whatever aggressive thoughts Elio held, for his subsided again without needing to be restrained by the reevesmen. 'But,' Aftak continued, his expression softening, 'as this priest said, we found nothing of the sort.'

Daimon nodded, trying to hide his relief. A thane was supposed to be impartial in such matters, dispensing judgement as required by the evidence, but he couldn't pretend he wasn't glad at Aftak's words. Finding one witch in the town had been bad enough: finding another would be liable to spark panic. Not to mention he would have had a hard enough time executing Elio quickly and cleanly, let alone ordering him to be burned alive. However, that was the fate ordained by Nari Himself for witches who hid their crimes, and it was far beyond Daimon's authority to ignore that.

'Is there anyone of this town,' he said, raising his voice once more to address the whole crowd, 'who has evidence that they wish to present regarding this matter? Bearing in mind,' he added, sweeping them with his gaze, 'that you will be asked why you did not bring it to the attention of the reeve before now.' He doubted anyone would fabricate a story in order to actually get Elio burned alive over the sake of some old grudge, but it was a suitable reminder to them all of their own responsibilities.

There was quiet for a few moments, other than Nalon muttering his translations to those of the Brown Eagle clan who were present.

Then one of the Tjakorshi stepped out of their ranks, raising his hand.

'Otim Ambaszhin!' Saana called out, her concern audible in her voice. She followed up with a sharp-sounding question in Tjakorshi, which Otim waved away.

'You have something to say?' Daimon asked the clansman, wondering if the man could even understand him properly. To his amazement, Otim nodded.

'Him,' Otim said, pointing at Elio. 'Him father. Angry sman.' He tapped his own chest. 'Shout sman. Say steal fish.'

His words were heavily accented, but understandable. A couple of snickers ran through the Naridans present, but Daimon didn't think it was at Otim's speech. He got the feeling it was more that they could imagine Old Elio accusing someone of stealing his fish.

'Him,' Otim said, pointing at Elio again. 'Him no shout sman. Him say, father no shout sman. Him good man.' He stepped back again, and folded his arms with the air of a man who had said all he intended to say.

Daimon leaned closer to Saana as conversation bubbled up around them. 'Did we just see one of your people stand up for one of your husband's people?'

'No,' Saana murmured back. 'We just saw one of *our* people stand up for another one of our people.'

Daimon nodded. 'Your husband takes the correction.' He straightened up in the chair again and raised his voice. 'Does anyone else have anything to say? With specific regard to evidence of Elio of Black Keep committing witchcraft,' he added. Touching and indeed potentially momentous though Otim's testimony was, the point of this was not to get character references for or against the accused.

No one else stepped forward or spoke up. Daimon nodded.

'There is no evidence of crimes of witchcraft being committed by this man, Elio of Black Keep,' he declared. 'The only connection appears to be that his father was guilty of such things, and this lord knows well enough that the thoughts and actions of a father are not necessarily reflected in those of the son.' He raised his hand. 'Elio, you are free to go.'

The tension visibly drained out of Elio's body as the reevesmen moved forward to remove the manacles from his wrists, but he looked up at Daimon immediately afterwards, his face a picture of confliction. 'Lord, s'man's father . . . Is he . . . Has he been . . . sentenced? Already?'

Daimon shot a glance at Aftak, who shook his head, then looked back at Elio. 'Elio, your father struck down Evram the reeve and fled on his boat, into the storm. We last saw him fighting the waves, beyond the river's mouth.'

'The storm last night?' Elio gasped. 'But he'll have drowned!'

'Aye, and good riddance!' someone shouted, and Elio's face broke, but Aftak turned in the general direction of the speaker and thumped his staff on the ground once more.

'Old Elio lied to us all!' the priest boomed. 'Including, it seems, his son! Have the good grace to let his son grieve for the father he thought he knew, before you celebrate too loudly the death of the witch who lived in our midst!'

Various heads nodded at Aftak's words, and Daimon clapped his hands together. 'Right, then! The trial is over, and the storm has passed! Back to your fields and your hearths!'

The crowd began to disperse. Daimon was glad to see that one or two of them even went to Elio and put a hand on his shoulder. He had feared that even if cleared of the charges, Elio would still be regarded with suspicion. Perhaps that would not be the case.

'Would they be so quick to be friends again,' Saana said quietly, 'if he was a woman?'

Daimon paused. 'Your husband does not know. It is true that witchcraft is more common among women. Perhaps it would be harder for the town to believe he was truly innocent.'

'That is what your wife thought,' Saana said grimly.

'But things have changed,' Daimon said softly. Elio clasped hands with those who had come to him, bowed appreciatively to them, then walked across the square to where Otim stood, along with the others of the Brown Eagle clan. 'And things are changing still.'

Elio paused before Otim and then, wordlessly, bowed deeply to him. For his part, Otim seemed puzzled and a little amused by Elio's gesture, judging by the uncertain smile on his face. However, when Elio rose from his bow, Otim attempted to mimic him.

His form was appalling, and under any other circumstance it would have been considered a gross insult. Even Nalon, standing next to him, winced. However, when Otim rose again, Elio made no word or motion of complaint.

At least, until Otim laughed and pulled him into a brief but energetic backslapping hug, then released him and turned to go on his way as though he'd done nothing out of the ordinary. Elio stood where he was, apparently stunned.

Saana snorted a laugh, but she was smiling. 'Perhaps so, husband. Perhaps so.'

ZHANNA

THEY WERE HUNTED through the day, but the men of Darkspur neither found them nor saw them, although it was a close thing at times. Twice, Zhanna, Amonhuhe, Tatiosh and Tsennan had found themselves pressed to the edge of woodland with the yips of their enemies sounding behind them, and had to make a quick decision on whether to push on or to double back and hope to somehow evade notice. They'd made a run for it both times, and had just managed to get into the next patch of cover, chests heaving and legs shaking, before the line of Darkspur had appeared.

Finally, as the sun dipped towards the mountains in the north-west, the calls began to recede back towards Winterhome, and Amonhuhe looked at the rest of them.

'This woman will not be hunted like that again,' she declared firmly. 'We attack tomorrow.'

'No,' Zhanna said, and held her hand up to prevent the outburst she could see forming behind the other woman's eyes. 'We attack tonight.'

She outlined her plan, the plan that she'd been mulling over in her head even while they'd been running and hiding. Amonhuhe agreed with it, although Zhanna was unsurprised by that: the Smoking Valley woman had been agitating for action so much it was a miracle she hadn't gone off and attempted to free the captives by herself. Tatiosh raised no objections either, although Zhanna wasn't sure if he would have anyway, given how strongly his mother was in favour of it. He might have been an adult by Tjakorshi standards now, but Zhanna wasn't sure exactly where he stood in either of his parents' cultures. In any case, even an adult might find themselves loath to contradict their parent.

More surprising to her was Tsennan's agreement, when she laid it out to him. He stroked his long chin thoughtfully as she spoke, and didn't reply immediately, but then nodded.

'It's a bold plan,' he said, eyeing her appraisingly, 'but I shouldn't expect anything different from the daughter of the chief who took us all right across the ocean.'

Zhanna folded her arms. 'Never mind my mother, Tsennan, and "bold" be damned. Do you think it'll work?'

Tsennan grimaced. 'Plans never work once axes are drawn; it's just a case of how badly they fail. I think this is probably our best chance. We'll have to hope for luck, but that's no different to usual.' He eyed her again. 'If you're still sure you want to do this, that is.'

Zhanna frowned at him. 'What do you mean?'

'It's not our valley, not our people,' Tsennan said simply. 'If we want to, we can leave.'

Zhanna opened her mouth to shout at him, then paused. He wasn't telling her they should go, he was just giving her an option. Laying it out in case she'd missed it, so she could set her heading knowing full well what all her possible courses were. It might have been a test, or it might have been a warrior giving genuine advice to his captain. It didn't matter, because she knew what her answer was in either case.

'We're not just Brown Eagle clan any longer,' she told him calmly. 'We're Blackcreek, too. These are their allies, which means they're our allies. We do this.'

'All right then,' Tsennan said. He cast a glance at the sinking sun, and then through the trees in the direction of the mountainside that rose above Winterhome. 'We'd best get a move on.'

They made their way back towards the cave, but Zhanna insisted on swinging by the place where they concealed the body of the man she killed, to see if the men of Darkspur had found their companion. That proved easier said than done.

'Are you sure it was here?' she asked Amonhuhe, squinting distrustfully at the sloping ground in front of her. Thorn and Talon were sniffing at it, and seemed very on edge, but there was quite obviously no body there.

'As sure as this woman sees you now,' Amonhuhe replied testily. She pointed up at a large pine trunk to her left. 'She remembers that tree in particular.'

Zhanna looked at it. 'That tree looks like every other tree in this wood.'

'This woman will leave the sailing to you,' Amonhuhe told her. 'You leave the trees to her. This is the place.'

'In that case, they found the body,' Zhanna said, gesturing. 'And decided to throw the branches covering it a long way away.' Certainly, there was a space where the body could have laid, but whoever had recovered it hadn't just moved them to one side to retrieve it; looking around, Zhanna now couldn't tell which of the ones on the ground they might have used.

'They must know we are here,' Amonhuhe said heavily.

'Mama!' Tatiosh called, from the lowest point of the shallow dell in which they stood. 'Look here!'

Amonhuhe turned, frowning, and Zhanna followed her down to where Tatiosh was kneeling at the edge of the small stream, barely more than a trickle, which ran there. Tsennan came over and stood by them as well, although Zhanna could sense his impatience and desire to be off.

'Look, Mama,' Tatiosh said, and traced his hand across the ground. Zhanna frowned as she followed the lines he marked out, linked them to the depression in the mud . . .

'Oh, by the Dark Father,' she said in a small voice, as she realised what he was showing them.

'Fuck,' was Tsennan's only, and heartfelt response.

Tatiosh's hand had outlined a shape that was blurred and incomplete but, now it was pointed out to her, was clearly that of a gigantic three-toed foot, of a length and width easily that of Saana's upper body. Only a dragon could have left such a print, and a very large one at that.

'A head-in-the-cloud?' she asked Amonhuhe weakly, but the Smoking Valley woman shook her head.

'No. Thundertooth.' She looked back up the slope. 'That could have eaten the body.'

'The whole thing?' Zhanna asked, awed and not a little alarmed.

'Easily,' Amonhuhe said. She cast a look around them, at the lengthening shadows between the trunks and under the branches.

'Then this means Darkspur may not have found the body!' Zhanna said, relieved. 'They still might not know we are here: they may still think their friends taken by dragons were! We could be lucky!'

Amonhuhe turned a withering glance on her. 'Thundertooths aren't "lucky", girl. It will be the spilling of blood in the Sacred River that's drawn it here, you mark s'woman's words.' She sucked her teeth. 'The spirits are angry. Now we have something else to worry about.'

THEY MADE IT back to the cave without encountering any Darkspur men, or indeed any predatory dragons, and Zhanna found to her relief that their companions were all still with them. Danid's group had hidden in the cave when they realised what was happening. Meanwhile, Menaken's group had also retreated before the Darkspur advance, but had managed to get around the far eastern end of it by concealing themselves in and among a large rock pile on the lower slopes, further up on the mountainside than the final Darkspur man in the line had ventured.

Neither Menaken nor Danid were as enthusiastic about Zhanna's plan as Amonhuhe had been, but neither downright refused to participate, either. The rest of Zhanna's crew, Tamadh included, simply nodded without complaint, content to do as she instructed. It was gratifying and terrifying in equal proportion.

They made a good meal from their remaining stores, using a lot of them up. That was the point of this, after all: either they would succeed, in which case they'd be able to get access to the Smoking Valley people's stores – assuming there were any left, and if there weren't then what little Zhanna's party had wasn't going to be of much use anyway – or they would fail, in which case eating would likely not be high on their list of priorities.

'Better to die on a full stomach,' Tsennan said, methodically chewing his jerky. 'Inkeru told me that, years ago.' He grinned at Olagora, Inkeru's daughter, but she did not return his smile.

Zhanna snorted. 'Years ago? You've not been raiding for that long, Longjaw. Stop pretending you're a greybeard.'

'Better not to die at all,' Tamadh retorted. He bit off and swallowed a lump of the Naridans' strange sweetsap cake. 'That's what Khanda said.'

'We're all going to die,' Tsennan said blandly. 'There's nothing we can do about that. Some of us will die old, and some of us will die young, and there's little we can do about that, either. But I *can* make sure I don't die hungry.' He swallowed his jerky, and ripped another chunk off with his teeth. 'Can you imagine being a hungry soul when Father Krayk takes you? That's probably enough to make you a draug.'

'Don't talk about draugs,' Sakka said shortly. Tsennan opened his mouth to mock her, then caught Zhanna's eye and shut it again.

'We're a long way from Tjakorsha now,' he said instead. 'Even if one of them claws its way up from the underworld, it would struggle to find us here.'

'How do you know these mountains don't lead to the underworld too?' Tamadh demanded. 'If it's only the Great Peaks that lead to the underworld, why didn't we leave Tjakorsha a long time ago?'

'Don't look at me, I'm no witch and no chief,' Tsennan protested. He looked at Sakka again. 'Tell you what, when we get back, we'll all go and ask the witches about it.'

'But what if we die?' Olagora asked. She was looking at her boots, and wasn't eating.

'We'll have to make sure we don't,' Zhanna said firmly. 'Otherwise we won't be able to ask.' She cast Tsennan a meaningful look, trying to suggest through her expression alone that he should stop talking about draugs and dying. 'Now you'd better eat up, otherwise I think Tsennan's going to steal your food.'

'I'm not hungry,' Olagora muttered.

'You're not hungry now,' Tsennan said, his joking tone gone. 'But if your stomach starts rumbling later, you'll wish you'd taken this chance to eat. Trust me on that. Besides, we're going to be sneaking around, not charging up a beach. If your stomach starts grumbling too loudly, you'll give us all away!'

'He's right,' Tamadh put in. 'Best to eat now, while you can. It'll keep your strength up.'

Olagora didn't look like she believed them, but she did start chewing, and that was all Zhanna had hoped for. The Naridans were having similar conversations in their own language, trivial banter laced with serious advice and discussion, but Kakaiduna wasn't talking to anyone, not even Amonhuhe. She was sitting in the cave entrance, staring wordlessly out at the darkening sky.

Zhanna was tempted, for a moment, to go over and sit with her. It seemed wrong for the girl who had suffered most to be quiet and alone before they all embarked on this venture. But if Kakaiduna wanted to talk, she could talk to Amonhuhe or Danid, who would at least be able to understand her. Perhaps this was how she wanted to spend this time, as they all prepared to free her people. Zhanna left her to her thoughts.

When everyone had finished eating, they laid down to try to get some sleep: all save Danid, who insisted that as a hunter he was used to long hours of wakefulness, and would rouse them when the short moon showed its face over the mountains. However, sleep never came for Zhanna. She simply laid awake, watching the flickering remnants of the fire paint ever-moving pictures of shadow on the cave roof, and ran over the events to come again and again and again in her mind, until the sky outside took on a slightly more silvery hue, and Danid began moving among them and rousing them.

This was it. There were no more options, no more delays. Everything now came down to Zhanna's plan.

Either they would succeed, or they would die.

DAREL

THE UNIVERSITY OF Idramar was all that Darel had dreamed it might be, and more.

Some people, Hiran had told him, were disappointed by the piecemeal nature of its buildings, having expected a campus that was far more unified in terms of design and style. To Darel, however, the variety was glorious. He found himself delighted at the realisation that year on year, generation after generation, learning had been valued to the point that new buildings had been required, and old ones repaired or extended. This was not someone's vanity project: a decree for something to be built in order to demonstrate a great man's wealth and influence. This was a living, breathing, working place. What did it matter to him if that building was built of stone blocks, and this one hardened clay bricks, and that one mainly timber and thick plaster?

Hiran was an excellent guide, as well. He managed to convey his knowledge of the place – how old the buildings were, their histories, the names of the various notaries immortalised in the statues scattered here and there in the grounds – without going into levels of detail that would provoke boredom. Although, Darel had reflected as he chuckled at one of Hiran's stories about a trick being played upon one of the masters, it would take quite a lot to make him bored of looking at Hiran.

Most delightful of all, however, had been the library. It was several large rooms, each containing shelf after shelf filled with books and scrolls: some originals, and some copies; many from Narida, some from far further afield; some with beautiful illustrations and calligraphy; some barely legible even if you could read the language in which they were written.

For Darel, fascinated by reading ever since he had been old enough to do it, it was like a dream come true.

'And you can just take any of these books to study them?' he asked incredulously. He and Hiran were sitting on a bench at the edge of one of the halls, in the afternoon light streaming in from a high window. Hiran had a text which he said was related to his research, but in truth he waspaying attention to Darel rather than to the book; a fact about which Darel felt vaguely guilty, but not guilty enough to excuse himself.

'Not all of them,' Hiran replied. 'Some are particularly fragile. For those ones, you have to get permission from one of the masters. If you are seen with one without the correct permission, the warders will have your hide. Literally, in some cases.' Hiran nodded to one a sombrely robed man walking through the shelves with his hands behind his back, eyeing the shelves. His gaze fell on Hiran and Darel and he gave them a nod that Darel felt was more an acknowledgement that they were in his domain and that he would permit this, at least for the moment, than it was an actual greeting.

'They would actually strike you?' Darel asked in shock, as the warder moved on, out of sight. 'A nobleman?'

'To use the library, you must forfeit all privileges of rank,' Hiran said with a chuckle. 'The university enforces its own laws, and that includes punishing those who do not take sufficient care with its valuable possessions. After all, "We are all servants to the pursuit of knowledge".'

'Yaro of Idramar,' Darel said immediately, and Hiran actually laughed out loud.

'You are an educated man indeed!'

'We do not have many books at Black Keep,' Darel admitted. 'Certainly nowhere near as many as are here. But this thane has read those that are there many times, and he remembers that line well. He always strongly agreed with it.'

'If only everyone shared such views.'

'So, have you ever fallen foul of the library warders?' Darel asked curiously, and Hiran's smile took on a mischievous edge.

'Not for mistreating the texts, or for taking restricted ones without permission. There might have been one incident, however, where the warder you just saw caught this man doing something the warder did not feel was appropriate for the library.'

Darel laughed. 'And what was that?'

Hiran twisted around to face Darel more fully, and as he did so, his left hand landed on Darel's right. Darel felt his face heat immediately.

'This man can show you,' Hiran said softly. 'But he would have to be quite close to you.'

'You are quite close already,' Darel said, then instantly cursed himself for being the most awkward, wooden-headed fool under both the moons.

'He would have to be closer still,' Hiran said, leaning in just a little bit more, then stopping. Darel could feel the warmth of the edges of Hiran's breath on his cheeks. The other man's face hung there in front of him, drawing Darel in as surely as a light at night drew moths.

'Well, we are all servants to the pursuit of knowledge,' he managed to utter.

Hiran kissed him.

The contact was soft at first, delicate and tentative, then harder and more insistent as the moments passed and their initial awkwardness melted away. Darel slowly twined the fingers of his right hand through those of Hiran's left, and gently took hold of Hiran's arm with his other. Passion and joy warred with incredulity within him, but was it that unlikely that a man Darel had thought attractive the moment he laid eyes on him would reciprocate that desire, and wish to act upon it?

Apparently not.

The moments stretched on and their breaths mingled, hot and heady, until the scuff of a footstep broke the spell and the memory of Hiran's tale made Darel hastily and instinctively break off their contact. Hiran immediately resumed his position poring over the text in front of him as though he had been doing that all along. Darel looked down at the text as well, just as the same warder as before came back into view and glanced over at them. Darel met his eyes for a moment, in an attempt to not look guilty, but the warder seemed satisfied that nothing untoward was occurring in his demesne, since he paced onwards in the same unhurried manner.

'It seems you like to live dangerously, Hiran,' Darel said quietly, and his barely suppressed excitement and mirth made his voice shake.

'What is life without a little excitement?' Hiran replied, flashing him a mischievous grin.

'All the same,' Darel said, 'this man is in Idramar awaiting an audience with the God-King. It would perhaps not help his cause if he were thrown out of the university grounds for inappropriate conduct.'

Hiran stiffened, and the life seemed to drain from his face, but he nodded. 'This man understands, of course.'

'Is there anywhere to which you have access where such conduct would *not* be inappropriate?' Darel asked him gently.

Hope flowed back into Hiran's expression. 'Practically anywhere other than the library, to be honest.'

'Then we should leave,' Darel suggested. 'This is a fascinating place, and this man is grateful to you for showing it to him, but he is sure it will still be here tomorrow.'

'Indeed,' Hiran said eagerly. He closed the book. 'Perhaps that is enough study for one day.'

DAREL HAD NOT spent a more pleasurable day in his life.

They wandered the grounds of the university, chatting easily and kissing frequently, laughing at the occasional exasperated glances they got from others going about their business, at a pair of wind drakes tussling on a tree branch, and in Darel's case, once for no obvious reason at all.

'What amuses you?' Hiran asked. They were walking along by the river's bank, hand in hand, and Darel had to think for a moment of how to verbalise the sheer joy that filled his chest like warm sunlight.

'This is, perhaps, the freest this man has ever felt,' he said slowly, discovering the answer for himself even as he spoke it. 'Here and now, he has no demands on him, other than to keep holding the attention of his attractive new acquaintance.'

'You do not need to try hard to do that,' Hiran said with a laugh. 'But it sounds like your life has not been an easy one, if a walk in the university can spark such delight.'

'Until recently, this man's daily life was overseen by his father,' Darel admitted. 'Both this man and his law-brother failed to meet his expectations, albeit in different ways. Then the Raiders arrived, and that brought its own challenges.'

'What are they like, these Raiders?' Hiran asked, sounding genuinely fascinated. 'They have never attacked our family's lands, since we are too far from the coast. Are they truly as savage as the stories say?'

Darel paused for a moment to consider his answer. It was odd to speak to a Naridan for whom the Raiders were nothing more than a tale. Even before the Brown Eagle clan had landed at Black Keep, Darel had known of Raiders. The last time they had attacked, he and Daimon had watched from the windows of the Black Keep itself. They were a fact of life along the southern coast, just as much as storms, razorclaws and rogue thundertooths.

'They can certainly be savage,' he replied, thinking of Ristjaan the Cleaver striking him down, and the vicious fighting for Black Keep when Rikkut Fireheart had attacked. 'And they have many ways that are strange and barbaric. The way they mark their faces, their heeding of witches . . . '

'Witches?' Hiran exclaimed in alarm, and Darel hurriedly waved his concern away.

'This man has been informed that the word does not translate well: think of them as wise people that claim to read omens and portents in the world around them.' He became uncomfortably aware that he was in Idramar to convince the God-King to allow the Tjakorshi to settle, and yet here he was talking of their barbaric ways to a member of the Divine Court. He hurried on with his explanation. 'When this man's father died he became thane, and responsible for his land. Then he embarked upon the journey here with Marshal Brightwater, and so long in the company of a Hand of Heaven was not without its own stresses.'

'This man heard that you were set upon by pirates during your voyage,' Hiran put in, and Darel nodded.

'Indeed we were, and this man had never before experienced the twin terrors of death by violence and by drowning. It is not an experience that he would care to repeat.'

'Marshal Brightwater has spoken of your courage and ability in that combat,' Hiran said admiringly. 'To know that you were scared while it was taking place merely makes it more admirable.'

'The Marshal is too kind,' Darel said honestly. 'This man must give thanks to his father's training for that.' He sighed. 'And now that is done, this man waits for an audience with the God-King, to find out his fate and that of his land and people. Set against all that, a day walking in the sunshine with a handsome man is a blessing.'

'This man cannot speak of becoming a thane, or fighting pirates or Raiders,' Hiran admitted. 'He knows something of disappointed fathers, however, and he agrees that it is like a constant weight around your neck.'

Darel looked at him. Hiran was looking at the river, and seemed pensive for the first time since they'd met. 'Your father does not approve of your studies?' he guessed.

'This man could have found an occupation that would please him better,' Hiran admitted. 'But no, it is . . . ' He waved a hand vaguely. 'It is complicated. In truth, Yae bears his displeasure more than this man does, but this man's support of her means that he falls under that cloud as well.' He sighed. 'Neither of us are likely to receive a warm welcome should we return home, as it stands. Still, that is our father's choice, and this man does not regret the decisions he has made.'

Darel nodded. 'It is a strange thing, how talking about why this man feels so happy here and now has caused us both to reflect on the things that have caused us worry.'

'And in doing so, lowered our moods,' Hiran agreed. 'This man apologises: he should have known better than to seek an explanation of happiness.'

'Clearly, the secret of happiness is not to think about it,' Darel said with a smile.

'Wise words,' Hiran agreed. He took a deep breath and exhaled, as though trying to clear his mind of melancholy. 'Have you ever tried yeng, Darel?'

'This man has not,' Darel confessed.

'Then it is time we rectified that,' Hiran said. 'Come. This man will introduce you to his favourite yeng house, and from there, we can see where the day takes us.'

Darel hesitated for a moment, then nodded. Why not? Why not make the most of these moments? Nari alone knew if he would have such carefree times again.

He smiled. 'Lead on, friend.'

JEYA

'Ï'VE MADE A decision,' Galem said, as they ate shellfish broth out of wooden bowls, sitting at the street's edge near the Court of the Deities. It was the first meal thëy'd bought for them since thëir family had been killed, but it hadn't been earned with stolen coin. The day after Ngaiyu's death, Galem had approached a dock front scribe – a fellow Naridan by the name of Skhetul – about becoming hìs assistant, citing thëir ability with letters and numbers thëy purported to have learned as a servant in West Harbour. Skhetul had put thëm to work and had apparently been pleased by what hè saw, since hè'd hired Galem at the end of the first day.

'A decision about what?' Jeya asked, then took another spoonful and savoured the next warm mouthful. It was a relief not to be wholly responsible for feeding them both, or to be wound tight with anxiety, as shé had been when Galem had helped with thievery.

'About my name,' Galem said. Jeya put hér spoon down in hér bowl, swallowed, and looked at thëm.

'Oh?'

'Ï had to give Skhetul a name,' Galem said, 'so Ï told hìm it was Bulang. And . . . Ï like it. Ï think it fits më.' Thëy took another mouthful of broth. 'Ï think Ï'm going to actually be Bulang.'

Jeya smiled. 'Í'm glad yöu've found a name that suits yöu better.' Shé raised hér bowl of broth and held it out, like shé'd seen rich people do with wine, at least when portrayed by actors in plays in front of a sheet on one of East Harbour's squares. 'To Bulang!'

Bulang laughed at hér gesture, but mirrored it with thëir own. 'To Bulang!'

They clacked their wooden bowls together and drank straight from them, as though they really were nobles at a banquet, before laughing at each other and coming to a spluttering halt. Jeya licked hér top lip: the broth was tasty, and too good to waste.

'Hey, Jeya!' someone shouted, and shé looked up to see M'bana, who worked on the markets. They were another one of Ngaiyu's former charges, and on a couple of occasions they'd made the walk to Ngaiyu's place with a basket of nearly off fruit that wasn't going to sell at market the next day, but which was still good enough to be eaten hungrily by street orphans that evening.

'M'bana,' shé called in greeting, trying to look relaxed. Bulang had a name and a job now, as well as a backstory, so it was probably about time for thëm to be seen with hér in as natural a manner as possible. 'How's life?'

'Harder work than yours, by the looks of it!' M'bana replied jovially. They had an empty basket slung over each shoulder, and their voice was slightly hoarse, probably from shouting their wares all day. M'bana didn't own the stall they worked on, but they claimed to be easily the hardest working of its hired hands. Their expression sobered. 'I heard you were the one to find Ngaiyu.' They shook their head. 'I still can't believe it. Makes my blood boil.'

'Yeah,' Jeya agreed awkwardly. It had been two days now, and shé still hadn't really got hér head around the fact that Ngaiyu simply wasn't there any longer. Shé'd not dreamed about finding the body, thank Jakahama: the goddess had clearly taken Ngaiyu onwards to the Garden swiftly and cleanly, leaving nothing of thëir spirit behind to trouble thëir friends and loved ones.

M'bana seemed to realise they'd darkened the happy mood of their greeting, because they shifted their baskets and cleared their throat, as though seeking to put the subject definitely behind them. 'Ah, yeah. Um, Nabanda came by the market yesterday, said they were looking for you. You seen them since?'

Jeya looked up, frowning against the sun. Shé hadn't seen Nabanda since the day shé and Bulang had found Ngaiyu: shé hadn't seen Damau either, for that matter. 'No. Did they say why?'

M'bana shook their head. 'Not to me, but I didn't ask. Hard at work, as always.' They winked and grinned, their teeth white against the darkness of their face, and Jeya smiled. It was almost impossible to be miserable around M'bana for very long. 'But yeah, if you haven't seen them, I guess they're still looking for you. Just thought you should know.'

'Thanks, I'll see if I can find them,' Jeya replied. Nabanda was probably on the docks again, so it shouldn't be that hard: even if hê wasn't there, someone like Maradzh would probably know where hê was. 'Take care of yourself M'bana, and keep working hard!'

'As if I'd do anything else!' M'bana replied with a grin, then turned their smile on Bulang. 'Hi, I'm M'bana. I'm guessing Jeya's told you all about me, since they haven't introduced us, but I'm afraid to say they've not mentioned you to me.'

Jeya's cheeks heated a little in embarrassment, but the glare shé shot M'bana was only half-real. 'M'bana, this is my friend Bulang. Bulang, this is M'bana. Be careful of them; they're a charmer.'

'Guilty,' M'bana said, pressing one hand to their chest and giving Jeya a hurt look.

'Pleased to meet you,' Bulang said politely.

'So what's your story, Bulang?' M'bana said, squatting down on to their haunches and flicking a stray bit of hair back out of their eye. 'Haven't seen you around here before, and I'm sure I'd remember.'

Jeya curbed hér immediate instinct to kick out at M'bana's leg, knocking them off-balance and sprawling on to the ground, but only just. Shé hadn't been kidding when shé'd said that M'bana was a charmer, and that was fine, but that didn't mean shé was happy to see them attempting to work their charms on the person with whom shé was in love.

Bulang seemed to have realised the direction of M'bana's intentions as well. Thëy glanced at hér, then back at M'bana.

'My story is this.'

Thëy turned to hér and, before Jeya quite realised what was happening, planted a kiss on hér lips. It wasn't a deep kiss, or a long one, but it was sufficient to make the intention behind it very clear, as well as causing Jeya's heart to speed up noticeably. Bulang withdrew, with a smile that was slightly ashamed yet also slightly proud, as though thëy were feeling guilty for such a demonstration but could also tell the effect it had had on hér, and enjoyed it.

'Well, that's a good story, and eloquently told,' M'bana said, without missing a beat. 'The drama, the suspense . . . I was enthralled. Clear message too, I like it. It should be performed on feast days.' They rose back to their feet. 'And as such, it's only fair for me to leave you to rehearse. I wouldn't want to impose on you with an unwanted audience.'

Jeya burst out laughing, hér brief irritation with them completely evaporating. 'You should be a player yourself, you scoundrel! You're better with words than half of them!'

M'bana spread their hands in a self-effacing manner and shrugged, the motion of which caused their two baskets to slide off their shoulders and land in their grip with a smoothness and cleanness of motion that a juggler or acrobat would have envied. 'I've got to have some way of selling the fruit, Jeya.' They winked. 'See you around.'

They watched M'bana walk off, and Bulang chuckled. 'I like them.'

Jeya shot thëm a look of faked shock and worry. 'Not too much, Í hope.'

'Oh,' Bulang said, turning to hér. 'Are yóu feeling slighted? Or threatened? Do Ï have to prove my affection for yóu?'

Jeya grinned at thëm. 'Maybe yöu do. But first, we should probably finish our meals.'

'That's a fair point,' Bulang conceded. 'It won't be as nice when it's cold.'

'And second,' Jeya added, slightly reluctantly, 'Í should probably go and find Nabanda. It might be important. It could even be about Ngaiyu.'

Bulang nodded. 'Ï understand. Do yóu want me to stay away, or . . . ?'

'No,' Jeya said firmly. 'We can't do that for ever, and we have a name and a story for yöu now. Besides, Í'd like yöu to meet Nabanda. They're probably my oldest friend.'

'Ï'd like to meet them, too,' Bulang said, smiling.

THEY MADE THEIR way down to the docks, where the tide was coming in and was nearly at its highest, judging by the merest smudge of seaweed visible on the jetties above the water. Bulang looked about with interest as they made their way along, making sure to keep out of the way of the work gangs hauling cargo to and fro, and not tripping over the mooring lines that kept the wide variety of trading ships in their berths.

'Do yóu know, Ï'd never been to the harbour front before the last couple of days?' Bulang said. Jeya turned and looked at thëm in amazement.

'Never?'

'No!' Bulang stepped aside from three people carrying what looked like a small tree trunk over their shoulders: some form of valuable foreign wood, Jeya guessed, although in all honesty she had no real idea what it was, or why anyone would transport it

here. 'Obviously, yóu said it wasn't a good idea to come here when
. . . Well, before we knew who Ï was. But my family never came
here, either. It's not really the sort of place rich people come.'

Jeya frowned. 'There are rich people here! Ï've seen merchants
and all sorts.'

'Ah, well they're not rich people like my family,' Bulang said.
'They're rich people who buy and sell things; they're not *noble*.'

'Before Ï met yöu,' Jeya told thëm honestly, 'Ï had no idea that
there were even different sorts of rich people.'

'Ï suppose Ï'm not sure there are,' Bulang admitted. 'Ï think a lot
of it is just what people like my family want to believe. Wanted to
believe. That even though other people might have made money
somehow, they're still not as good.' Thëy sighed. 'It doesn't really
make sense when you say it out loud. Even if everything Ï thought
was true about my family really *is* true, it still doesn't make sense.
If that was true then Ï should feel that Ï'm better than yóu, because
of my blood, and Ï don't think that. Ï really, really don't.'

Jeya thought back again to Ngaiyu's words about truth and
things making sense, and sighed. 'Well, isn't what we feel more
important than what other people might think the truth is?'

'Ï spent eighteen years pretending to be someone Ï wasn't to fit
someone else's idea of what the truth was,' Bulang laughed, 'so Ï'm
definitely agreeing with yóu there.' Thëir laughter died away as
thëy pointed farther down the docks. 'What's happening?'

Jeya frowned. 'Ï don't know.' A group of dock workers were
clustering around the water's edge, and a couple of them were
reaching down to pull something out. Hér gut lurched as they
lifted, helped by others pulling on them from behind to prevent the
weight pulling them in too. 'By the Hundred, it's another body!'

It wasn't a large body, certainly not as big as some of the people
pulling it out. It was definitely dead, though: that much was
obvious from the loose splay of arms and legs, and the fact that
one of the limbs ended in a red, bloody mess halfway down, where
one or more of the harbour's underwater denizens had bitten it off.

Other people on the dock were gravitating towards the grisly find, morbid curiosity mixed with revulsion, and Jeya found hérself pulled in as well. Shé didn't want to see another dead body, not so soon after finding Ngaiyu, but shé couldn't make hérself just walk past and ignore it. So shé slipped between a couple of the dock workers who'd gathered around and stole a look over someone's shoulder, praying to all the gods that at least this time it wouldn't be someone shé knew.

The face of the body lying limply on the stones of the dock had also lost chunks of flesh to the teeth of the harbour's scavengers, but not enough to occlude its identity. Not from Jeya.

Nausea struck hér and bile rose up in hér throat, and shé just made it to the edge of the harbour before the fish broth shé'd eaten came back up as hér gut heaved in protest at what shé'd just seen. A hand took hér shoulder – not Bulang, shé realised dimly as hér stomach heaved again – and gripped hér in what was clearly meant to be a steadying, comforting manner.

'Easy, there,' someone murmured as shé threw up again. 'Easy. You know this poor soul?'

'Yes,' Jeya managed, hér throat suddenly sore from her own stomach acid. Shé wiped hér mouth and looked back, just to be sure, but there was no mistaking what shé'd just seen. 'Their name is Damau. They're one of Ngaiyu's orphans, they work for a barge merchant called Abbaz.'

'Ah shit, they're right,' someone else said in the small crowd, making the sign of Jakahama's Paddle in front of their chest. 'That is Damau.'

It was somehow worse to see Damau than it had been to see Ngaiyu, for all that Ngaiyu had been in Jeya's life for longer, and had arguably done more for hér. Ngaiyu had died in thëir own house, and had been sitting almost peacefully in thëir own chair. It had been horrific, but not grotesque: and, as Jeya had tried to remind hérself in the time between, Ngaiyu had been old. Thëy'd had a good life. It was the smallest crumb of comfort to cling to, and it felt like a false one, but Jeya had been looking for anything that could lessen the weight of grief on hér shoulders, even slightly. There was no such morsel of reassurance with Damau, fished unceremoniously out of the harbour and part-eaten by scavengers, with the rest of their life ahead of them.

'Ï've got yóu,' Bulang whispered in hér ear, wrapping thëir arms around hér. 'Ï've got yóu.' Thëy drew hér away from the huddle around Damau's body. 'Do we need to find yóur friend Nabanda? To tell them?'

'Yes,' Jeya said, nodding, ready to throw hérself into some sort of action, anything to avoid dwelling on what shé'd just seen. Shé'd be taking Nabanda yet more news of horror and death, but it was what had to be done. Shé couldn't believe that only two days ago, shé and Damau had done the same thing. 'We should—'

She stopped, something ugly clawing at hér mind.

'No,' shé said slowly. 'No. We need to find M'bana.'

'M'bana?' Bulang asked, confused. 'But we just—'

'Come on,' Jeya said. Shé slipped out of thëir arms and took thëir hand. 'Ï'll explain on the way, but we need to get off the docks.'

She drew Bulang away from the docks again, running through the streets, heading for the market.

'Where are we going?' Bulang asked as they ran.

'Ï don't think we need to tell Nabanda about Damau's death,' Jeya said numbly. Shé heard a commotion above her and looked up to see a golden-maned monkey, clinging to the end of a thin branch, screaming at a small dragon about the length of Jeya's arm. The dragon had scaled the tree's trunk, and was hissing hungrily at the monkey, but could not pursue it farther for fear of the branch breaking.

'Why not?' Bulang asked.

Jeya swallowed, and felt hér throat burn once more. 'Ï think they already know.'

ZHANNA

ZHANNA HAD NEVER really climbed a mountain before, and hadn't expected her first attempt at doing so to be in the dark, even if that darkness was lit up by the short moon. The skies were virtually cloudless, which was a blessing for their progress, but a curse for the temperature since the dark emptiness above them sucked away any heat the Smoking Valley had managed to accumulate during the day.

What was even worse was the realisation that this had been her idea.

'We're not going to get anywhere unless you can pick up the pace a bit,' Amonhuhe said quietly from behind her, as Zhanna struggled up and over a boulder. 'This is an easy path! We used to climb this at night as children!'

'Good for you,' Zhanna muttered back, gripping as hard as she could through her fur-lined gloves. They slipped more than she'd have liked, but she wasn't prepared to trust her unprotected fingers on the ice-cold rock, given how quickly they'd surely become numb.

To reach the buildings where the captives were held, Zhanna's crew would have to pass Winterhome one way or another. Going around the lower edge of it, where it nearly met the lake, would see them pass far too close to the entrances. Circumnavigating

Winterhome and the lake entirely and approaching from the north would involve swimming across the Sacred River, since there were no bridges in that direction. Amonhuhe had been strongly opposed to that idea, given the blood that had tainted its waters so recently, and also everyone realised that attempting to swim and then fight in soaked furs was a good recipe for being slow, quickly tired, easily chilled, and probably dead.

That left one route: up the side of the mountain and over where the spur of rock that turned into Winterhome joined its flank. Assuming they made it without incident – such as slipping, falling and breaking their necks, Zhanna reflected grimly – they would be able to approach the outbuildings from behind.

They paused at the top, getting their breath and massaging some life back into fingers that had been gripping desperately. In truth, Zhanna conceded, it probably wouldn't have been that challenging a climb in the sunshine, and had she not been so concerned about giving away their presence. In the moonlight, with the fear of discovery looming large over every tiny noise, it felt like the hardest thing she had ever done.

'You're sure this is the best way?' Menaken asked, as they peered down at the outbuildings below.

'Yes,' Zhanna said, trying to sound certain. If she was wrong, they'd likely all die. The important thing was for everyone to believe this was the best plan, so they would commit to it. A captain's course could be correct, but if a crew began pulling in different directions, they were all doomed anyway.

She sketched out their routes in the air with her finger and kept her voice low. 'When we get to bottom, Kakaiduna, Tsennan, Menaken, Olagora and Avisha go that building.' She pointed at the one where they believed the children were being held, nearest to Winterhome. 'Ravel, Danid and Tamadh, that one.' She pointed to the farthest, where the Smoking Valley women were. 'Amonhuhe, Tatiosh, Sakka and this warrior go that one.' She pointed to the middle building.

She had thought it through carefully. Kakaiduna and Amonhuhe could both speak to the captives and make them understand what was going on, so they had to take a building each; Danid's grasp of the language was poorer, but probably sufficient, but he was assigned to the one farthest from Winterhome in case it took him the longest. She sent Tsennan to the children's building since he was the largest, and arguably the best fighter of them all, and that group would be the first in line for any reinforcements from Winterhome. It would have made sense to assign Tamadh, their other experienced warrior, to the next closest building, but Zhanna wanted one of him, Tsennan and her at each building, and she couldn't bring herself to take the farthest one in case it looked like cowardice. So Tamadh got the job of keeping Darkspur men away from the women's building, and she would have to be enough to anchor any defence where the Smoking Valley men were being held.

'Remember,' she added, 'keep buildings between you and Winterhome as long as you can, and no one start fight before signal.' Everyone nodded, no one raised objections and, even more mercifully, there was no indication that anyone from Winterhome had noticed them here, squatting on the lower edge of the mountain. 'On, then.'

The way down was harder. Kakaiduna coped well enough, but the rest of them lagged behind. Even the rattletails seemed more cautious than before, whickering uncertainly in their throats now and again when pebbles shifted beneath their feet. Zhanna had to turn around several times and descend carefully, grabbing at whatever she could find with her hands to steady herself, and hoping that it wouldn't come away in her grasp.

Something moved beneath her right boot; not just a pebble, but a rock the size of her own foot. She desperately tried to take her weight back off it, but it was too late. She didn't slip, but the rock went clacking and clattering away down the mountainside for several long, heart-stopping moments until it came to rest.

Everyone froze in place, and Zhanna's heart began beating so fast and so hard she almost thought it would give them away of its own accord.

One breath. Two breaths. Three breaths. Four breaths . . .

Nothing. No movement, no shout of alarm, no flare of light as someone pushed aside a skin covering an entrance to Winterhome and peered out into the night, backlit by a fire.

'Keep going,' Zhanna murmured. She had to get them moving again, before fear of discovery kept them here for good. 'Keep going!'

They began moving again, cautiously at first but then picking up a little more speed once more – although it was still torturously slow progress. Still, they were a little further away from Winterhome itself now, which could only help them.

The path began to level out. Zhanna no longer had to turn around to steady herself, but could pick her way downwards with comparative ease. She breathed a sigh of utter relief when her boots met the silver-washed stems of grass, and the path disappeared to be replaced by the relatively level land of the Smoking Valley floor. She shrugged her shield off her back and settled it into place on her arm, and the other Tjakorshi and Menaken did likewise. Amonhuhe, Kakaiduna, Danid and Avisha strung their bows. Good shooting would likely be impossible in the dark, but there was always the chance of a lucky shot.

The first obstacle was out of the way. Now for the real challenge: the guards.

Zhanna didn't need to issue any further instructions. Her crew split wordlessly into three groups, and began to advance towards their targets. In her mind's eye, Zhanna had envisaged it as a swift, rushing advance under the light of the moons, a three-pronged move as smooth and coordinated as sharks lunging at a school of fish. In reality, the ground underfoot seemed more uneven in the dark than it did in the daytime, and no one managed to get much above a hurried, careful walk as they sought to avoid rolling an ankle. She cast a worried glance over at Winterhome, convinced that someone looking out would see dark shapes flowing towards the outbuildings, but everything was still and quiet. Kydozhar Fell-Axe, the First Warrior, seemed to be with them for the moment.

They reached the rear of the building in which the men were held. It was long and low, made of turf and thatched with sheaf after sheaf of long, dry grass. It had no window openings – hardly necessary if its original purpose was as a storehouse, as Amonhuhe had said – and so the only risk of discovery from inside would come if they made too much noise as they crept alongside it. Zhanna advanced carefully to the far end, where the door was, and looked to her left and right.

To her right, Tamadh raised his blackstone axe from beyond the building's far corner to signal that they were ready. To her left, she could see Tsennan's group in position. Everyone was waiting on her.

She took a quick look at the door, a few paces away in the centre of the building's front wall. There was a faint glow oozing out from under it. Someone had a light in there.

Zhanna looked around at Tatiosh, who nodded. His eyes were wide, and he looked scared, but Zhanna was prepared to give him the benefit of the doubt and say he was just trying to see in the poor light. She was scared, though, and she wasn't going to try to convince herself otherwise. She was right to be scared. She had more lives depending on her than ever before.

Or perhaps not. She ran her finger over her longblade's whitewood scabbard, where her slaying of Rikkut Fireheart was recorded for posterity. Had she not convinced the Unblooded of Brown Eagle and Black Keep to follow her into the fight against his raiders; had she not saved her own mother – her clan's chief – by killing him, the entire town might have fallen.

She sidled up to the door, keeping her profile as flat as possible against the building's front in case someone from Winterhome looked out, then drew her longblade. She raised it, and lowered it again. That was the signal.

Tatiosh slipped past her and knocked on the door. After all, there was no point in breaking it down if you didn't have to.

'Who's that?' a voice said from inside.

'Got some drink out here, if you want it,' Tatiosh said, speaking quietly, and a little lower in pitch than was natural for him. On either side of them, Menaken and Danid were trying the same thing. Male Naridan voices, ready to answer the male Naridan voices that would likely come from within. What other Naridans would be up here and knocking on doors, save for friends?

'Drink?' The voice sounded confused, but Zhanna heard a scuffle of movement. 'What sort of—?'

A hand pushed the door open. Tatiosh stepped backwards, and Zhanna lunged in.

She didn't see the Naridan inside until her longblade had already made contact, cutting down diagonally across his chest, its superbly sharp edge shearing through the furs and wools the man wore all the way to the flesh beneath. He fell backwards with a cry that was more surprise than pain. Zhanna caught a glimpse of his companion, rising to his feet from a stool in the light of a lantern swinging from a hook, and reaching for the axe at his belt: she lunged, punching her blade through his chest, and he gave a startled cough as he staggered backwards, impaled.

'Help! He—!'

That shout was from outside, but the origin didn't matter: the alarm had been raised, assuming anyone in Winterhome was awake to hear it. Zhanna withdrew her longblade, leaving the man she stabbed staggering, then swung for his neck. Not a clean connection, but the steel blade bit in deep enough to bring blood gushing out, and he collapsed sideways against the wall with a bubbling gasp.

'Aurgh!'

Zhanna whirled around to find Sakka between her and the

man she originally stabbed, but neither the axe nor the shield of Inkeru's daughter was needed. The Darkspur man had been trying to rise, but he was being pulled back down by the grasping hands of some of the Smoking Valley men, who'd risen in a clattering of chains from the shadows at the far end of the building and had swarmed forward in a mass to grab him. Zhanna saw him struggle against their weakened bodies and for a moment it looked like he might fight his way clear – the wound she'd dealt him had clearly not been a deep one – but then a hand found the knife at his belt, and he shuddered again and again as one of the men drove it repeatedly into his chest.

Amonhuhe appeared in the doorway, and said something, her voice loud and clear. The Smoking Valley prisoners looked at her, and Zhanna saw astonishment replaced quickly by hope, and then just as quickly by grim determination. Two of them scrambled for the man she'd just struck down, who weakly raised a hand to try to ward them off, but they weren't looking to confirm the kill. Instead one of them held him and plucked the axe from his belt while the other ransacked his pouches, swiftly pulling out a small metal object.

Of course. The captives knew full well where the key was; they just had not been able to get at it.

'What did you say to them?' she asked Amonhuhe.

'This woman told them that their children and women are being freed just as they are,' Amonhuhe said tightly. She had her bow in one hand and an arrow in the other, and was looking back out into the night. 'She hopes she did not lie, but she can't see . . . '

'What matters is that they fight without fearing,' Zhanna replied. The key was being fitted to the locks on the ankles of the man who recovered it, who looked quite young, and relatively hale so far as it went among the captives. He twisted it and one shackle popped loose, freeing one ankle, then went to work on the other. When that came away, he didn't do what Zhanna had expected and laugh, weep in joy or celebrate. Instead, he attacked the other end of that shackle with the key as well, freeing one leg of the next man in line, then tossed the key to someone else, instead of either of his neighbours.

The newly freed man of the Smoking Valley picked up the loose shackle, the one that had been removed from both men to whom it had once been attached, and approached them with it hanging from his hands. He eyed Zhanna with confusion, but only for a moment before he spoke urgently to Amonhuhe.

There was more shouting from outside. Zhanna looked around at the door, where Tatiosh was keeping an eye out, but it wasn't Tatiosh whose voice boomed out across the night.

'*Zhanna!*' Tsennan Longjaw bellowed, his mighty lungs near as loud as old Tsolga's shell horn. '*Here they come!*'

Zhanna pushed past Tatiosh and took the scene in. Lights were bobbing and waving around Winterhome now, and yes, she could see men starting to stream out of it holding weapons. Now they would learn for sure exactly how many men of Darkspur were here, and whether any of the Two Peaks people had stayed after helping them commit their treachery. She just hoped that however many there were, there weren't more than her small crew and a group of weak, exhausted captives could handle.

'Back inside!' she yelled in Tjakorshi, mainly for Tsennan's and Tamadh's benefit, trying not to think about how shrill and high-pitched her voice sounded to her own ears, how much like a child to whom no one in their right mind should be listening. 'As we planned! Hold the doors!' She pushed Tatiosh towards his mother and switched to Naridan. 'In! In!'

The plan had been simple. The doorways to the buildings were narrow, which made them the perfect place to be held by a couple of warriors with shields, since weight of numbers would have less effect there. Tsennan, Olagora and Menaken would hold the children's building, Tamadh and Danid the women's, and Zhanna and Sakka the men's. Meanwhile, if all went to plan, the people of the Smoking Valley would be freeing themselves. Once enough of Amonhuhe's people were free to turn the tables, they would push out and let superior numbers benefit them, not the enemy.

'Are they willing to fight?' Zhanna asked Amonhuhe. She whistled at Sakka, and the young warrior nodded and made her way to the doorway, her shield at the ready. Two more Smoking Valley men were free now, and one of them held his own shackle ready to use as a weapon, while the other had taken the axe from the Darkspur man who'd had the key.

'They are,' Amonhuhe said, and Zhanna heard pride in her voice as she gestured at the first man to free himself. 'This is Amonani. They had already decided who should be freed first if they could get the key. Amonani is one of our best fighters. He is also this woman's nephew,' she added, and the lantern caught the faintest sparkle of wetness in the lower lashes of her eyes.

'Did he recognise you?' Zhanna asked. It was the first time she'd had a chance to look properly at a man of the Smoking Valley. Amonani's dark beard was divided into short strands that were hung with wooden beads, similar to those that Amonhuhe wore, but the hair nearest to his chin and jaw was loose and unplaited: clearly he'd not had the chance to maintain it while in chains. He looked older than Zhanna, but not by that much, so she wasn't surprised when Amonhuhe shook her head.

'He was but a babe the last time this woman was in these mountains.' She snorted, and gave Zhanna a smile that seemed forced, even under the circumstances. 'She is apparently known to them now as "Amonhuhe of the Lowlands".'

Zhanna grimaced: she could only imagine how that would feel. 'Well, you chose good time to come back. You can be hero to them now.'

She looked back at Winterhome, and cursed under her breath. She couldn't easily count how many enemies there were, not in the darkness, but there were more than she'd want. There was already a crowd clustered around the door to the children's building, and she could hear the clatter of weapons as they tried to break down the resistance of Menaken and Tsennan. There would be no help from inside there, not unless any of the children were of an age to be more help than hindrance in a fight. That part of her crew would just have to hold out until aid came from another source.

The defenders had noticed that all was not right with the other outbuildings either. Zhanna swallowed as a group of them broke off and headed for her, lit up as she was by the lantern light from within. She counted five, ten, more . . .

'Shit!' She ducked back inside and pulled the door to, for all the good it would do, then raised her shield. Her longblade's handle felt slick in her palm. 'Sakka, ready!' She switched to Naridan, and shouted back over her shoulder. 'How is go?'

A cry went up behind her from several throats, but not one of triumph or impending revenge. Instead it was one of grief, of heartbreak, of hope that had been snatched away.

'The key has broken,' Amonhuhe said, and her voice was as dry and dead as a lightning-struck tree.

'*Shit!*' Zhanna forced herself to breathe. 'How many free?'

'Four.'

Not enough. Not nearly enough, four weakened, exhausted men with chains and one axe as weapons, against angry Darkspur men who'd been eating their captives' food for the last few months.

She rolled her neck from side to side, felt and heard it crack, and looked at Sakka.

'Time to meet the Dark Father.'

Sakka's expression shifted from one of barely controlled fear to utter horror. Zhanna just had time to realise that the girl hadn't understood the conversation, and so hadn't realised until Zhanna had spoken just how utterly fucked they were, when the door was hauled open and death came for them.

456

MARIN

It HAD TURNED out that Northbank was not the only place that was less than welcoming to soldiers of the Eastern Army.

They'd all managed to get away, slipping out while the camp was in the first stages of confusion as word of a major disturbance in the city filtered back. Marin had watched from beneath the boughs of the big whitebark as a double line of troops had hurried into the city, weapons in hand.

'We're well out of that,' Aranel had muttered. He was the oldest of the half-dozen soldiers with them.

'And into . . . what?' Channa the Nose had asked. That was how Aranel referred to her, as well as Gershan and Kenan, two brothers. They'd all been in the Eastern Army together before the muster, and Channa seemed to have borne the sobriquet for long enough that she either didn't mind it, or had become resigned to it. The other two with them – Elifel, a hard-faced, scarred man of early middle years, and Adal, the young and handsome fellow whose cheekbones had swiftly earned him the nickname 'Bones' – were as new to the ranks as Alazar, Ravi and Marin himself.

'Into finding Nari Reborn, and helping Him come into his rightful throne,' Marin had reassured her. 'You'd not be getting much searching done when you're too busy putting down a rebellion in a city. Now we're free to do as we need to.'

If only it had been that easy.

It was simple enough for the first few days. They all had their first chunk of pay, which had been doled out when they got to Northbank, and swiped some rations on the way out, so food wasn't an issue. Shelter was somewhat more problematic, especially for Bones and Elifel, who were clearly city men but, unlike Marin, had no real experience of living outside. For two days they headed north along the great crown road that wound from Northbank up to Wousewold Haste and beyond, and split the kingdom into West and East. Then they turned westward down smaller lanes and tracks, but even so, finding their way had been comparatively easy. The real problem was in getting news.

'S'man can't help but feel that the locals have not exactly been warm towards us, so far,' Marin commented, as they approached another village nestled in the fertile farmland and gentle, rolling valleys of Narida's midlands. It was the fifth they'd encountered, and so far they'd had no luck at all.

'What gives you that idea?' Elifel muttered. 'The complete silence when we ask them questions, or the fact they water down the ale they sell us?'

'Farmers always distrust soldiers,' Gershan said, matter-of-factly. 'It's just the way of it. Never mind that we keep them safe.'

'Keep them safe from what?' Ravi asked. She held her hand up to forestall Gershan's irritated response. 'This woman means, these people in particular. We're still leagues from the Torgallen Pass, so far from the sea that Raiders are just a rumour, and it's not like a border skirmish with the Alabans is going to worry them. Barring someone thinking he's Two-Knives the Bandit King come again, they've probably never seen a threat they've needed the army to save them from.'

'Perhaps we're going about this the wrong way,' Marin suggested. 'For whatever reason, they don't trust soldiers.' He thought about adding his suspicions about the Palace's motives, caught Laz's eye, and decided not to. There was no point courting trouble when some of their new companions had been in Natan Narida's army for years, even if their former commander had just been accused of treason against the God-King. 'So perhaps we need to stop coming across as soldiers.'

Channa the Nose put her hands on her hips and looked at him. 'But we *are* soldiers. Except for you and the healer.'

Kenan plucked at his tabard, which was embroidered with the crowned sunburst of the God-King and the flag of Idramar, marking him as a member of the Eastern Army. 'We can pack these away, but . . . ' He tapped the leather cuirass beneath. 'S'man's still going to look like a soldier, even if it's not clear whose he is.'

'You're only a soldier if you're still taking pay from the crown,' Marin pointed out. 'You're deserters.'

'Aye, don't remind us,' Channa the Nose snorted. 'That's not a thing you go singing out to the world, though. Deserters are even less popular than soldiers.'

'Unless they've deserted for a reason the people agree with,' Marin pointed out. 'You left the army because you didn't fancy being ordered to kill a bunch of folk who got into a fight with your colleagues, and you think that finding the Divine Nari is more important than who obeys who in the city of Northbank.' He shrugged. 'Maybe the locals don't want to send a bunch of the crown's soldiers after the Divine One, but will share His location with a group of deserters who wish to follow Him.'

'We're supposed to be taking the Divine One to Godspire, so the monks can make their pronouncement,' Gershan said uneasily.

'And that's a problem we can deal with as and when we find Him,' Marin said smoothly. 'Perhaps He needs a few more reliable fighters around Him before He feels it's safe to announce Himself. Regardless, we can't do anything until we find Him, and it seems no one wants to talk to soldiers of the Eastern Army. Perhaps we try something new.'

'What difference is it going to make?' Bones asked. 'Soldiers, deserters; we're still outsiders looking for the Divine One. What's to make these farmers think we're any more trustworthy?'

Marin smiled at him. 'We start taking our lead from the healer.'

All eyes turned to Ravi, who scowled at him. 'What new foolishness is this?'

'As Channa so accurately pointed out, neither you nor s'man are soldiers,' Marin said, hoping she would agree to what he had in mind. 'Now, s'man is married to the sar in our group, but you have no connection to the soldiers at all, and s'man knows you want to find the Divine One. A group of soldiers taking their orders from a healer instead of a sar sounds a lot more . . . ' He waved his hands vaguely. 'Divine.'

'If healers are so much more divine than sars, then how come it's not healers that rule us?' Elifel demanded.

'This woman has wondered that herself,' Ravi put in, and Kenan laughed.

Aranel scratched his cheek and looked at Ravi thoughtfully. 'Rumours s'man heard did say that the Divine One was supposed to have healed some folk with His power.'

'The Foretellings of the Last Sorcerer say that the Divine Nari will return when the country has strayed too far from His light,' Marin said. It was technically true, for a certain reading of the prophecies, but there were other interpretations. Still, Elifel did not need to know about those. 'And remember, Nari was more than just a warrior; He created this country, moulded it into one. You could certainly say that he healed it. Perhaps what He's bringing us now is change. He's come back to heal Narida once again.'

Elifel did not look entirely convinced, but he looked less skeptical than he had. Gershan and Kenan were nodding, though.

'S'woman knows nothing about commanding soldiers, though,' Ravi said. 'She's going to make herself look like a fool if we go into that village with this story.'

'You don't need to command anyone!' Marin told her. 'You're just looking for the Divine One. Which is true, right?'

'Yes,' Ravi said, nodding.

'And we're following you,' Marin continued, taking in the rest of the party with a gesture. 'That's all. You, a healer, are trying to find the Divine Nari, and these soldiers, who deserted when they didn't want to end up killing fellow Naridans, are doing the same thing. None of that is untrue, but it might play better to the ears of these locals than when a sar at the head of a group of soldiers is the one asking questions.' He flashed a smile at Laz. 'No offence intended, love.'

Laz shrugged. 'It sounds reasonable to your husband. He's had no luck so far; let Ravi try. Besides, healers are more welcome than soldiers, most of the time.'

All eyes turned back to Ravi again, with Alazar having so easily relinquished his authority. The healer grunted in frustration, but nodded reluctantly.

'Fine. S'woman will ask the questions, but she'll need you not to loom behind her when she's doing so, or we'll look no different to how we have so far.'

The village was a small one, and it had no stronghouse where a thane might live, or even a sar. Marin was unsure on whose lands they now were, but they were definitely in Narida's West, and so in the overall domain of Marshal Torgallen. The West held its position as the holiest part of Narida close to its heart, and Marin could easily imagine how folk here would cleave closer to a rumour of the Divine One's rebirth than they would to decrees from distant Idramar, which some viewed as a decadent cesspit by the sea.

In fairness, Marin wasn't sure that description was entirely inaccurate, but he still felt some resentment at it. He grew up in that decadent cesspit, and so had every right to consider it as such, unlike these yokels who probably never set foot beyond their own thane's boundaries.

The afternoon was wearing on, but the sun was not at its strongest today, and the walk was a pleasant one. Still, Marin did not fancy the idea of sleeping outside, for the wind was brisk, and he thought the distant clouds held a hint of rain about them.

'If there's no other village we can reach before sundown, s'man suggests we look for lodging here,' he said.

'Agreed,' Bones said instantly. Of course, the young city man had no wish to sleep outside again.

'Let's see how welcoming they are first,' Aranel said quietly. 'S'man would prefer a night under a hedge to a knife in the throat for the contents of his purse.'

'S'man's sure it wouldn't come to that,' Marin said confidently.

'You ever been this far west before?' Aranel scoffed.

'This sar is from farther west than here,' Laz put in mildly, and Aranel shut his mouth again.

The road through the village wasn't a crown highway, which were surfaced and maintained by the crown's own labourers – in the midlands, at least, although things apparently got somewhat less well-maintained in the far north and south – but it was still a well-worn route between settlements. As a result, to catch the trade of travellers as well as thirsty locals, the village had a tavern, constructed in the western style with a thatched roof that angled down sharply nearly to the ground on two sides, and marked by an old ale barrel hung at the front of it. The tavern sat on one side of what looked to be the central green, across which it faced an open-fronted shrine to Nari, heaped with flowers and piled high with the remnants of tallow candles.

'Looks like a devout place,' Marin commented.

'Why wouldn't it be?' Kenan asked.

'No reason at all,' Marin agreed. 'S'man's just saying that perhaps the Divine One is more on their minds than usual.' He shrugged. 'It could be a good sign.'

'We'll start here,' Ravi said, heading for the tavern. Off to his left, Marin heard a shutter bang, but when he looked around he couldn't see which house the noise would have come from. It could have just been the wind.

Inside the tavern the afternoon sunlight bled in through the open shutters at the front and underneath the low eaves to illuminate a small taproom, perhaps half the length of the building. Marin immediately caught the scent of stew, mixed with the pungent tang of pipe smoke, and blinked to accustom his eyes to the relative dimness outside of the shafts of sunlight.

The woman behind the bar regarded them with the mix of apprehension and cautious optimism found on the faces of hostellers when a sizeable party of armed strangers walks into their establishment. In one corner of the bar, two old men and an old woman, each one grey-haired and with lines on their faces as deep as the furrows in a newly ploughed field, looked up from a game involving marked, polished wooden counters. In the shadows of the other corner was another man; or at least, Marin assumed they were a man, but he couldn't see them properly. They were wrapped in a travel-stained cloak and had their long legs stretched out in front of them, and were the apparent source of the pipe smoke, judging by the faint red glow just visible in the haze of fumes that surrounded them.

'Afternoon,' the woman behind the bar greeted them, putting a cheerful face and voice on, presumably in the hope that it would engender a similarly sunny disposition in her armed guests. 'What can s'woman get you?'

'An ale for us all,' Ravi replied, looking around at the rest of them and finding no arguments there. 'And is that stew s'woman can smell?'

'It is, although there might not be enough for the lot of you,' the barwoman replied, eyeing them dubiously. 'Not as is ready at the moment, anyhow. Are you stopping long? We can cook up more, if it's a meal you're wanting.'

'A meal and a space to sleep for the night would be most welcome, if the price is right,' Ravi replied.

'And, uh, are you speaking for all these men?' the barwoman asked, her eyes lingering on Alazar and his blades. She was clearly reluctant to turn down the offer of coin, but equally uncertain about negotiating with a woman when there was a sar present.

'Excuse you,' Channa the Nose piped up, and Gershan and Kenan laughed.

'Your pardon mistress, s'woman didn't see you there,' the barwoman said hastily, and returned her attention to Ravi. 'Are you speaking for all these . . . ' She paused, clearly wondering about saying 'soldiers', and decided against it. ' . . . people, then?'

'That depends what price she gets,' Aranel said, with a dusty chuckle.

'We're with her,' Laz said firmly, and that seemed to satisfy the barwoman, who began talking with Ravi about costs. It turned out that Ravi was good at haggling – presumably it came with the territory of being a travelling healer – and it wasn't long before she'd arranged a meal, and space to sleep in the tavern's upper floor, for what seemed to Marin to be a very sensible price.

'But you didn't ask about the Divine One,' Bones pointed out quietly, as they all sat down on stools around a couple of rough wooden tables, close to the bar.

'Patience,' Ravi replied, sipping her drink. 'We're here overnight, now. When everyone gets back from the fields, odds are they'll come here, and they'll ask questions of us then, newcomers as we are. If the others don't,' she continued, nodding at where the barwoman had disappeared to scare up more ingredients for the cooking pot, 'Danna the bar certainly will. She was fair bursting with curiosity, but didn't want to say anything in case we took it as her prying, and left again. Now she's got our coin, she'll ask who we are and where we're going.'

'You seem right certain of that,' Channa commented, and Ravi shrugged.

'S'woman's a healer, and she goes from place to place. If you walk into somewhere and announce you're a healer, they'll think you're a fraud there to trick them. If you say nothing of it until you're asked your business, suddenly half the village has a gammy leg, or a cough that just won't go away.' She sipped her drink again. 'No one likes pushiness, and most people are curious, if you give them time to be.'

'S'man's certainly wondering about our friend with the legs in the corner over there,' Marin said quietly. 'He looks like a traveller, and s'man wonders if he's heard any news that might be of interest to us.'

'And the odds are, he's wondering the same of us,' Ravi replied. 'But we've got more weapons than him, so it'll be best to let him make the first move, to save him getting nervous. And if he doesn't, maybe someone else can let you know about him, once we get talking to them.'

'So you're saying we should just wait and see what happens?' Gershan said.

Ravi nodded. 'Unless you have anything better to do?'

Gershan grunted, and took a mouthful of his ale. And so they waited, as the waning light of the afternoon sent the shafts of light from the windows creeping across the tables and up the back wall of the taproom, to see what the evening would bring.

DAREL

THE DIVINE COURT WAS convening.

Darel fussed with the sleeves of his robe, straightening and re-straightening them until Hiran actually tutted at him. Darel looked up sharply at him, but Hiran's face showed only understanding.

'Darel, your presentation is impeccable. You need not be concerned about your appearance.'

'Well, if by that you mean that it will not do any good . . . ' Darel muttered. He was in his finest robes, but he still felt drab and mean compared to the sartorial magnificence he'd seen on other nobles. It wasn't that they were gaudy: they left that to the city's merchants, who as lowborn were unable to wear robes that hung below mid-shin, or which had double-pleated sleeves instead of single-pleated, but made up for it with ludicrous amounts of gold brocade and frogging, about which there was no law other than that of good taste. Nonetheless, Darel felt insecure both about the quality of his clothes' fabric and of the tailoring.

It was better when he was spending time with Hiran – although in fairness, they didn't always have their robes on – or when exchanging day-to-day pleasantries with other low-ranking nobles. For an official audience, however, Darel suspected that everyone would be wearing their finest, and his would not compare.

'Your friend is going to look exactly like the sort of poor, rural afterthought that he is,' he complained. 'It is hardly an appearance that will engender high opinions of him.'

'Do you judge solely on the basis of appearance?' Hiran asked him.

'Well, no, of course not.'

'There is only one person whom you need to impress today,' Hiran said gently, 'and that is the God-King.'

Darel exhaled hard. 'If that is supposed to be reassuring, then your friend has to tell you that it did not work.'

'Darel.' Hiran got up from the bed, walked to where Darel was studying his reflection in the mirror, and placed an arm across his shoulders. 'Some of the Divine Court are posturing feather-drakes, it is true. You will not impress them, but you do not need to. You need only impress the God-King, and King Natan will not be judging the worthiness of your argument based on the lustre of your robes.'

Darel hesitated, looking at his new friend's reflection in the mirror. 'Hiran, have you spoken with the God-King?'

Hiran laughed. 'The second son of Lord Mattit, speak with Natan III? No, your friend's parentage grants him a right to be at court, but His Divine Majesty has no need to talk to the likes of Hiran Threestone.'

'But you have attended court?' Darel asked. 'You have seen the God-King consider matters brought to him, and pass judgement on them?'

'Your friend has,' Hiran agreed.

'Does he seem . . . Did he seem . . . ' Darel sighed, uncertain of how to phrase his worries. 'Does he seem concerned by worldly matters? Is he going to be interested, at all, in events that have occurred far away in the very south of his realm?'

'The God-King's concern is for all of his realm,' Hiran said, sounding slightly confused. 'Why?'

Darel shook his head. 'It is just something Marshal Brightwater said on the journey here, but your friend may well have misunderstood his meaning.'

'Well, your friend will grant you that King Natan has not always been at court audiences,' Hiran said, 'and sometimes matters have been handled by his Inner Council. But your friend has noticed how the God-King has been closeted with the Inner Council for days, in the aftermath of Marshal Coldbeck's disappearance, so it seems to your friend that His Divine Majesty is very much interested in the welfare of his country.'

'You speak the truth, of course,' Darel muttered. 'As usual.'

'Your friend does his best,' Hiran replied. 'Now, come on: one thing that could definitely have a negative impact on His Divine Majesty's opinion of you is if you are late.'

As IT TURNED out, Darel's case was not going to be heard immediately. This was the first day the Divine Court had convened since the God-King had recovered from his illness, and there was going to be a great celebration in honour of his return to health. The Hall of Heaven was packed with courtiers and their hangers-on, and long tables had been set up running the length of it. They were covered with beautifully embroidered cloths, and would shortly be piled high with food, for what was a celebration without a feast?

For Darel, entering the hall, it was a distinctly surreal moment. He had been present at feast days at Black Keep, but there he had sat at the high table, alongside Daimon and his father: or, most recently, alongside Kaldur Brightwater. Here, he was relegated to the farthest end of the tables nearest the side of the hall, the lowest position possible, akin to where a lowborn man with little land to his name would sit at Black Keep. Thus was the way of it, he mused, when the company was so dignified.

'Is His Divine Majesty not here?' he asked Hiran, in puzzlement. The golden throne on the dais was empty, although some of the chairs drawn up next to it had occupants.

'He will be here shortly, so we should take our seats,' Hiran said, at his elbow.

'Can you at least tell your friend who they are?' Darel requested, gesturing at the high table.

'You know the Southern Marshal, of course,' Hiran said, and sure enough Brightwater was there in his blue and gold, deep in conversation with a man in gold-embroidered green. 'That's Adan Greenbrook he's talking to, the Lord Treasurer: it was his cousin that the Divine Princess killed, shortly before you arrived here. Your friend presumes you do not need him to point her out?' Hiran continued, with forced jollity.

Darel eyed the woman on the other side of the throne from Brightwater and Greenbrook. A sparkling tiara rested on what was, he could tell even from the far end of the hall, an impressive construction of artfully coiffed hair, and her robes were a red and gold that boasted of wealth and power, even had he not been able to make out the triple-pleated sleeves that marked her as royalty. He couldn't see her features properly, thanks to her gauzy veil, but as her face turned towards him he nonetheless got the impression that he was being studied intently.

'Then the elderly fellow to her left as we look at them is Whittingmoor, the Law Lord,' Hiran continued hurriedly, nodding to a white-haired man in blue and silver. 'The somewhat reserved chap in the brown is Sebiah Wousewold, the Lord of Scribes, and of course, there's Beloved Hada, the Queen Mother. Now come *on*, Darel. We should not linger in the doorway!'

Darel allowed himself to be guided by his arm over to the right-hand side of the hall, where servants directed them to their seats. Darel found himself between Hiran, on his left, and Yae Threestone, who was already seated, on his right.

'Please,' he said to the siblings, 'if you wish to sit together—'

'Do not trouble yourself,' Yae said with a smile. 'This lady has had many opportunities to speak with her brother before tonight, and will have many more after it.'

'Besides which,' Hiran muttered in Darel's ear, 'we thought you might wish for a friendly face on either side, given that you have been getting visibly more nervous about this for days.'

Darel smiled at him gratefully. 'Your consideration is much appreciated. If your friend could just return to one thing you said, however . . . How is it that Lord Greenbrook's cousin was killed by the Divine Princess, and yet he remains Lord Treasurer?'

Hiran shrugged. 'Princess Tila was found innocent of murder through trial by combat. Lord Adan had no choice but to accept the judgement, and he was not believed to be involved in the conspiracy to keep the God-King imprisoned. He could have left his post of his own accord, of course, but it seems he felt the rank it confers to be more important than the grief he might feel.'

'Hiran,' Yae said, with more than a hint of reproach in her voice.

'It's true!' Hiran protested.

'It might be true. That doesn't mean you need to be shouting it out,' Yae replied primly.

'The Divine Princess is innocent, which means the fault was with Lord Kaled,' Hiran said. 'Your brother is not saying that Lord Adan *should* have given up his post in protest. What reason would he have, given that his cousin was in the wrong? Your brother just meant—'

'What you mean and how you choose to express it are—'

'Lord Blackcreek?' a voice said from behind Darel, and he turned away from the Threestones' bickering that was occurring across his front to find himself being addressed by a man in his middle years, wearing commoner's robes – albeit well-made ones – on which the badge of the university was displayed.

'Yes?' he said, abruptly and unreasonably fearful that he was about to be denounced in front of a hall of his peers for some transgression while on the university grounds.

'Master Temach,' the man said, pressing a hand to his chest. 'Lord of Learning. This man represents the country's scholars to the Inner Council.'

'A pleasure to make your acquaintance,' Darel said, some of his panic subsiding, although it did not drain away completely. He hesitated for a moment, trying to work out how to refer to himself in relation to Temach. The man was lowborn, but he sat on the God-King's Inner Council. There were so many more variables here than at Black Keep! Temach had referred to himself as 'this man', so Darel decided to take the lead from him, and used his title. 'About what did you wish to speak to this thane?'

'This man understands that you have been in contact with the people we know as the Raiders,' Temach began.

Darel nodded. 'That is true, although only for a few days before this thane left his home to come here. His brother spent more time with and around them, prior to that.'

'We know so very little about them,' Temach said, eagerness suffusing his features. 'This man would be indebted to you if he could speak with you at your convenience after your audience: it would greatly increase our understanding of—'

He was cut off by a fanfare of trumpets that could surely mean only one thing: the God-King had arrived. Darel's throat went dry and his gaze was pulled around towards the dais as though on a string. Behind him, he heard Temach utter a swift excusal, and then the man hurried off to find his own seat: not on the dais, Darel suspected, or else he'd surely never have risked being so far from it when the God-King was due to arrive at any moment.

The entire hall rose to its collective feet, and Darel joined them, feeling his heart speed up in a manner far greater than the minor exertion warranted. For the first time in his life, he was about to look upon the living embodiment of his god.

He could not get the best view, since the heads of other nobles were in the way, but his breath still caught in his throat when he saw flashes of the red, gold and green of Narida. And then, *then*, he got a glimpse of the God-King's face.

It was not what he had expected.

Darel had presumed King Natan, the third of his name, would

possess a sort of effortless beauty, that his divinity would shine through and illuminate him from within. Not that he would actually glow – that seemed too far-fetched – but that he would exude an aura of wisdom, and kindness, and calm. In essence, that he would look like the beatific statue of Nari that sat in the Black Keep shrine, only in flesh instead of stone.

Natan Narida looked tired, hollow-cheeked and in a sour mood. He was not ugly, certainly, but neither did he have any sort of divine beauty to him. To Darel's eyes, at least, Hiran Threestone and Kaldur Brightwater were just two examples of men who held an edge on the God-King in terms of sheer physical attractiveness. The crown of Narida sat on Natan III's head, a stylised, jewel-encrusted helmet of steel that was supposed to mimic the simple helm that Nari Himself had worn when fighting the forces of the Unmaker, before Narida's smiths had mastered the art of armour, and before the first true longblade had been forged.

It might have bordered on blasphemy, but Darel thought it looked a little ridiculous. It was supposed to show the God-King's link to his martial ancestor, but it felt out of place when paired with the ostentatious robes. Not that it would have looked any more in keeping with actual armour, he decided. It was neither one thing nor the other, and King Natan seemed almost to shrink under it, as though he felt its weight every time he moved his head.

The God-King sat, and the rest of the court followed his lead. At this signal, servants emerged and brought forth steaming tureens of soup to commence the first course.

Darel had thought that he would be too nervous to eat, but the delicate aromas that curled forth from his bowl quickly put paid to that thought, and he set to with great appreciation. The soup was very different to the sort made by the cooks at Black Keep, and it set both his tongue and his lips atingle.

'Your friend can see why a position at court is so sought after,' he joked to Hiran, as he mopped up the remains with the crust of bread that had found its way to him.

'The food is certainly delicious,' Hiran replied, with a slight smile. 'The company is not always to the same standard, however.'

From across the table, a scar-faced sar looked up at Hiran. 'Do we displease you, Lord Threestone?'

'Your name was not mentioned, goodsar,' Hiran replied to him. 'And please, by rights, "Lord Threestone" is this lord's father.'

The sar looked as though he was going to say something further, but then grunted and went back to finishing his bowl. However, the man next to him, who had been watching the conversation, caught Darel's eye.

'You'd be the Blackcreek sar who came with Marshal Southbank, then.'

Darel set his bowl down. 'This lord is the thane of Blackcreek.' He considered adding 'no mere sar', but decided against it. There was no point in antagonising the man.

'A young thane, with a sar's braids,' the second sar said, eyeing Darel anew. 'Might this sar ask who conferred that honour upon you, lord?'

'This lord's father,' Darel replied, and was sure he didn't imagine the slight quirk at the corner of the first speaker's mouth. 'Are you amused, goodsar?'

'Not at all, lord,' the first man replied. 'After all, we know the Raiders plague the south. You surely performed an act of courage at a young age, and your father raised you to the warriors' ranks accordingly.' He lifted his face and looked Darel square in the eye as he finished speaking.

Darel felt his jaw clench in anger at the unspoken slight, but it was only a slight because it was true. Had he done as the sar had said, he could have replied honestly and without shame. As it was, his father had honoured both Daimon and him more because he felt they had shown sufficient progress in the arts a sar was meant to have mastered, rather than because of any notable achievements on their part.

'Not like here,' the second speaker said, glancing around. 'Why, any number of thanes in the Eastlands will tell their sons to start braiding their hair for no good reason at all, simply because they think it reflects well on them.'

Beside Darel, Hiran tensed. After all, he wore his hair unbraided, for he was no sar, and so these two were clearly baiting him as well. If even unaccomplished sons of Eastland thanes were regularly made sars – or that Darel was, despite not having perhaps done anything to truly deserve it – how did it reflect on Hiran that his hair was still loose?

'Did you have any thanes in mind, in particular?' Yae asked lazily, from Darel's right.

The two sars looked at each other. 'Would not be right for this sar to say,' the first one muttered.

'Hardly an act of courage,' Yae said, with a small smile.

'This sar doesn't need lecturing on proper behaviour from the likes of you!' the first sar said angrily, and Hiran opened his mouth, ready to reply angrily.

'This lord performed no great feats of courage to be named as a sar,' Darel said quickly and loudly, cutting across the potential argument. 'However, goodsar, if you wish to discuss this lord's ability in combat then you can go and ask the pirates of Crown Island: those that still live. Or, if you prefer, you may question the Southern Marshal, alongside whom this lord fought on the voyage here.'

The faint sneer that had crossed the second sar's face at the mention of the pirates – an easy claim to make, and a hard one to verify – disappeared at Darel's mention of the Southern Marshal. It was one thing to know that Darel had come to Idramar in the retinue of Kaldur Brightwater: it was another to realise that Darel was quite confident that a Hand of Heaven held him in high enough esteem to speak to his bravery.

'Ah, the fish,' Yae said pleasantly, as though no harsh words had been exchanged, as servants began to move around clearing the soup bowls and bringing out platters loaded with crisp-skinned trout. 'This lady does so like fish.'

To DAREL'S DISMAY, he was not to get his audience even once the feast had finished. Instead, the performances began. A minstrel strolled through the hall, singing songs of the Divine Nari's ancient and mighty deeds, and receiving a few coins from the nobles as he did so. Darel caught sight of King Natan's face a couple of times during the performance, and he did not look particularly pleased by it. Was he dwelling on the differences between him and his famous ancestor? After all, the current God-King had done virtually nothing of any note since ascending to the throne. And that was of course, Darel knew, because there was little of any note that needed doing in Narida. However, did it nag at King Natan, that he had no great purpose? He had not even fathered an heir to continue the divine lineage.

After the minstrel came jugglers and acrobats, tumbling and flipping in the spaces between the tables. Darel made appropriately appreciative noises, for they were truly very impressive, and he had never seen their like in Black Keep.

'Darel, you seem quite transfixed by the woman in green,' Hiran chuckled from beside him. The performer in question was contorting her body into truly unnatural shapes, and Darel had indeed been staring.

'Your friend just does not understand how she does it,' he replied honestly, as she bent her legs up behind her back, and so far forwards that her heels brushed her ears.

'A purely academic interest, then?' Hiran teased. Darel looked around at him in surprise.

'Does your friend detect a hint of jealousy, Hiran?' He smiled and shook his head. 'Purely academic, indeed.'

'Academia be damned,' Yae murmured from his right, not taking her eyes from the contortionist. 'Do you think she does private performances?'

Diverting though these talented men and women were, Darel still wished that matters would proceed more quickly and that he could, finally, get his audience over and done with. However, to his great dismay, this was not to be: a freestanding backdrop of painted canvas was hastily erected in front of the hall's main doors, facing the dais, and a troupe of mummers began a play.

It was not, in fairness, the best position for Darel to see or understand proceedings, since he – along with the other low-ranking attendees – was at an oblique angle to the performance. However, it quickly became clear that it was intended as some form of farce, set in the City of Islands. In fact, it was not just set there: it was intending to make a mockery of it. Darel was not well versed in the culture of Kiburu ce Alaba, but as other thanes, sars and ladies chortled at men dressing as and thinking they were women, and women doing the reverse, and the supposedly comedic misunderstandings that resulted, he couldn't help but think back to Black Keep. His brother's wife dressed in simple clothes very similar to those worn by her menfolk, referred to herself as 'this man' through a complete refusal to abide by Naridan societal structure, and, he suspected, would take a dim view of this performance.

For most of his life, Darel had thought the Raiders to be little better than animals: that was, after all, the received wisdom in Narida. When he had watched from the window of his improvised cell in his family's stronghouse as they farmed and herded and fished alongside his own folk, he had seen that this was incorrect. When he finally got out, and had spent the scant few days alongside his brother before setting off with Marshal Brightwater for Idramar, he'd seen the Tjakorshi for who they were: strange, certainly, but just people, living in their own manner. They were loud, and coarse, and not always the friendliest, but hadn't he exchanged barbed words with two of his own countrymen earlier that evening? The Tjakorshi had no monopoly on such traits.

If this is how the rulers of this land see the Alabans, then we surely underestimate them, he thought to himself. *And those we underestimate have the greatest potential to harm us, should they so wish.*

Beside him, Yae Threestone was rising to her feet. Darel turned his head to look at her, and saw her jaw clenched as she stepped back over the bench on which they sat.

'Yae—' Hiran began.

'Your sister does not find such *humour* to her liking,' Yae said in a low, tight voice. She turned and walked away, heading for the smaller door set in the wall halfway up the hall, normally used only by servants. Hiran stared after her, grimacing uncomfortably.

'Go see to her, if it will help,' Darel said to him quietly.

'Your friend is not certain that it would,' Hiran replied miserably. 'He will speak with his sister later.'

'Does she have Alaban blood?' Darel asked, realising too late that the question might be a rude one. After all, Yae had been adopted by the thane of Threestone – which was curious in itself, since thanes usually only adopted male children – and so legally her blood was his, in the same way as Daimon was legally Darel's blood.

'No,' Hiran said, looking away from the door as it closed behind his sister. 'No, there is no Alaban blood in our family. But this,' he gestured at the play, 'touches a little on her estrangement from our father. Your friend will say no more. That is Yae's story to tell, if she wishes.'

'Your friend understands,' Darel said, nodding respectfully. An Alaban lover then, perhaps? If a thane's daughter had engaged in an affair with such a foreigner, then that could certainly be a cause of conflict between her and her father, and would explain why she might see the nation in a more positive light than was being portrayed here. He tried to concentrate on the play again, but he'd lost the thread of who was supposed to be who when Yae had left, and could not pick it back up again.

It seemed that he was not the only one who was growing bored of the affair. Just as one mummer was loudly proclaiming that they were in fact neither male nor female, but wished to be addressed as a war chariot, a voice rang out from the far end of the Hall of Heaven.

'*Enough!*' Natan III cried. 'For the love of the Mountain, enough!' All heads turned to the God-King, who drained his goblet and set it down on the table in front of him with a resounding thump. 'Pack up and be gone.'

The mummers knew better than to argue. They knelt and bowed their heads – not an easy feat, given the layers of costume some of them were now swathed in – then hurriedly departed, taking their props and scenery with them.

Darel had been wanting the feast and the entertainment to be over with as soon as possible. Now, as he caught a glimpse of the God-King's sour visage through the heads of his peers, he felt that he could have done with them continuing for a while longer.

'This king has business to attend to,' Natan stated baldly. 'As has been the case for so many of these recent days, thanks to the treachery of our Eastern Marshal.'

It was not that a mutter ran through the hall. If anything, it was the opposite; a spreading, uncomfortable silence as the assembled nobility bit their lips, avoided looking at each other, and definitely avoided looking up at the dais. None of them had realised that the God-King had been being held prisoner in his own quarters under the pretence of ongoing illness, and so none of them had taken steps to free him. As a result, any one of them probably felt they might be singled out at any moment.

In this, at least, Darel did not share their anxiety. The *Silver Tide* had arrived shortly after the God-King had been freed and Marshal Coldbeck had fled, so there was nothing he could have done.

'A new Eastern Marshal is needed,' Natan continued into the awkward quiet of the Hall of Heaven. 'The role requires not just a soldier, but an organiser: a man who can see the individual parts of a thing and understand how they work together to form a whole.' He paused, looking around at them all. 'This king can think of no better candidate for the job than our current Lord Treasurer, Adan Greenbrook.'

Now a mutter did run through the hall, one that amplified and expanded to become shouts of celebration and congratulation, and applause. Adan Greenbrook stood in his seat, bowed low to the God-King, then acknowledged the cheers of the benches with waves of his hand.

'Greenbrook is in the west, is it not?' Darel said quietly to Hiran, as they both applauded.

'It is,' Hiran replied. 'The Eastern Marshal is usually drawn from the eastern thanes, but not always. It is a wily move, though. Northbank is where east meets west, and the old marshal is well-liked in those parts. He could cause a great deal of trouble if he's not located. Greenbrook will need to make sure his home doesn't follow Coldbeck, or else he will be declared a failure and will lose his new position, along with Nari knows what else. It may also mollify him somewhat for the death of his cousin.'

'Politics, then?' Darel said.

'Of course,' Hiran said, as though the notion of it being anything else was laughable. 'But note how it is not one of the other marshals who is being elevated. Torgallen is in the far west, and known for being more pious than a Godspire monk: not the most reliable man for the crown to lean on, when there are rumours of the Divine Nari's rebirth. Marshal Highbridge is in the north, of course, and it would take a goodly while for a messenger to reach him, and for him to get here: time we might not have, if Einan Coldbeck decides to do anything other than go into hiding. But the Southern Marshal is right here in Idramar.'

Darel nodded thoughtfully. Kaldur Brightwater was applauding Adan Greenbrook with the rest, and at this distance at least, seemed genuine in his approval. However, Darel suspected that most people in this room were good at pretending to approve of things that they did not.

'A new Lord Treasurer will be found in due course,' the God-King said, once Greenbrook had sat back down and the applause had died away, and Darel saw several heads perk up among the more senior nobles. That was a job of great authority and a position on the Inner Council, and if it hadn't already been filled then there was, presumably, still time for them to make their case for it. Darel suspected the God-King would be seeing and hearing even more enthusiastic support than usual in the immediate future: probably no bad thing, in the aftermath of such damaging treachery by his mightiest servant.

'As for now,' King Natan continued, 'there is something else that must be dealt with. Darel Blackcreek may approach the Sun Throne.'

Darel swallowed and began to rise. To his surprise, Hiran rose with him.

'Have a care, Darel,' Hiran whispered into his ear as he clasped Darel's shoulder. 'Your friend has not seen His Divine Majesty like this before.'

'What do you mean?' Darel replied. Of all the things Hiran could have said at this point, this was not a helpful one.

'This . . . focused,' was all Hiran said. He squeezed Darel's shoulder once more, and smiled reassuringly. 'You will be fine.'

Darel was unconvinced, but he had no time to further question his friend. The God-King had summoned him, and he could not keep his monarch waiting.

He walked around the lower end of the double line of tables on his side of the hall, through the area in front of the doors where the mummers had until recently been performing, and then up the length of the hall towards the throne. He kept his eyes locked straight ahead, ignoring the curious and downright rude stares that tracked him from either side, until he realised that he did not know exactly how close he should get.

He diverted his gaze slightly to look at Kaldur Brightwater, desperately hoping for some guidance. To his relief, the Southern Marshal made a slight beckoning gesture with the first two fingers of his right hand encouraging Darel forward three more steps . . . five more steps . . . seven more steps . . .

Brightwater extended both his fingers for a moment, and Darel halted. The Southern Marshal gave an almost imperceptible nod, and Darel dropped to his knees, then bent his head to touch the marble floor.

'Your Divine Majesty,' he said, trying to speak loudly enough that he could not be accused of mumbling, but without sounding like he was shouting. His words reflected back to him off the floor and seemed to die in the front of his own robes, so he had little idea if he succeeded.

'Rise,' the God-King said, his tone somewhat peremptory. Darel did as he was bid, and took a chance to glance at the other faces on the dais.

Marshal Brightwater's face was a study in blankness. Adan Greenbrook's was openly curious. The Lord of Scribes' eyes were half-closed as though he were bored, but Darel could tell that those eyes rested on him nonetheless. The Law Lord looked bored in truth. The Queen Mother looked regal and unperturbed, and Darel got the impression that her expression would remain the same regardless of whether she had a lowly petitioner or a rogue dragon in front of her. The God-King's frown did not, on the face of it, appear to bode well. And the Divine Princess . . .

Tila Narida's veil still obscured her face, but Darel could practically *feel* the weight of her eyes on him. It was an unwelcome additional pressure, as he swallowed with a throat that had suddenly become dry.

'Darel Blackcreek,' the God-King said. 'Kaldur Brightwater, the Southern Marshal and one of our Hands of Heaven, has made this king aware of a curious and, it must be said, somewhat unwelcome-sounding event in the far south of Narida. Would you care to explain what has happened?'

Unwelcome-sounding. Darel wetted his lips. 'Your Divine Majesty, two weeks before the Festival of Life, the ships of the people we know as Raiders appeared off our coast. There were more than we had ever seen before, and it transpired that they had brought their entire clan, rather than merely the warriors which we had seen up until that point. Instead of attacking, they flew a flag of parley.'

'Parley?' Adan Greenbrook said. 'Such a thing would not be valid unless they followed the Code of Honour.'

'In fact, Lord Greenbrook,' Meshul Whittingmoor spoke up, 'the Code says that parley can be treated as valid even if the enemy is not known to follow the Code, so long as they are considered an honourable foe. Which obviously, the Raiders are not,' he added.

'Thank you for the correction, Law Lord,' Greenbrook replied, and nervous though he was, Darel did nt think he imagined the edge in the new Eastern Marshal's voice which suggested he was attempting to remind everyone that he now stood below only the God-King himself in terms of power.

'The parley was invalid,' King Natan said, waving his hand irritably. 'That is irrelevant, seeing as this occurred weeks ago, not here and now. What happened?'

'Your servant, his father and his law-brother met the Raiders' chief and her two companions on the marsh to the east of our town,' Darel said.

'"Her" two companions?' Princess Tila cut in.

'Yes, Divine Princess,' Darel said. 'The Raiders' chief is a woman named Saana Sattistutar.'

Lord Wousewold's half-shut eyes glanced sideways towards Princess Tila, but she made no further comment.

'Your servant's father attempted to strike the Raider chief down—' Darel began again.

'He appeared to honour the parley, then broke it?' Wousewold spoke up for the first time.

'It was never valid,' Whittingmoor said dismissively.

'Yes, Whittingmoor, but refusing to honour it in the first place is not the same thing as misleading your foe—'

'*Enough* about the parley,' the God-King growled, and his Inner Council subsided. He gestured impatiently to Darel. 'Continue.'

'Your servant's father sought to kill the Raider chief and die gloriously, along with his two sons, when the rest of the Raiders swept down on us,' Darel said, fighting against the tightness in his throat, and the memory of his fear and confusion in those moments. 'Your servant's law-brother, Daimon, disarmed our father and instead agreed to the Raider chief's request: that her people be allowed to settle on our land, on condition that they would renounce their previous warlike ways.'

That caused a hubbub of shock and anger in the hall, but the God-King raised his hand and it quickly quieted. 'And what were you doing while your law-brother was exchanging words with this Raider, Darel Blackcreek?'

'Your servant was engaged in combat with the Raiders' champion,' Darel replied. It was true enough, and he was not going to admit to having been knocked on his arse in front of the entire Hall of Heaven. 'He sided with his father against Daimon's agreement, but we were disarmed by the Raiders before we could take our own lives, and we were then imprisoned in the stronghouse without blades.'

There was snickering from the benches. It did not sound very brave or glorious to be disarmed by adversaries instead of dying honourably, Darel had to admit.

'So how is it that you stand here now?' King Natan demanded.

'The Raiders, who call themselves Tjakorshi, were true to their word,' Darel said with as much conviction as he could muster. It did not help that he was unsure if he should be looking at the God-King's face, or averting his eyes. How were you supposed to behave in front of the living descendant of a god? Why hadn't he asked Hiran this before? He took a deep breath and continued.

'They did not attack, even when Daimon slew their champion in single combat over a matter of honour. Some men of your servant's household eventually freed your servant and his father with the intent of disrupting matters, but your servant's father challenged your servant's law-brother to an honour duel, then broke the conditions of it, and was killed. Immediately afterwards, the town came under attack from more Raiders, enemies of those who had settled on our lands, and everyone already in the town joined forces to fight them off. We were helped immeasurably by the timely arrival of the High Marshal,' he finished, gesturing to Kaldur Brightwater, 'without whom our victory would have been far costlier, had it been won at all.'

'And now?' the God-King asked, his expression hard for Darel to read.

'The Tjakorshi live in Black Keep, our peoples having fought side by side, bound together by the marriage of Chief Saana to your servant's law-brother Daimon,' Darel said. 'The captured enemies from the battle serve the town of their own will, in accordance with their people's honour. The Southern Marshal was kind enough to confirm your servant as the new thane of the Blackcreek lands.'

The God-King sat back on the Sun Throne and regarded Darel from under low, thick brows. A few low murmurs ran around the Hall of Heaven, but no one spoke up loudly. Natan III's current mood had been communicated to everyone, and no one wished to risk his temper by speaking when he was going to make a pronouncement, or ask further questions.

'These Raiders,' the God-King said softly. 'What god do they follow?'

'They are a seafaring folk, Your Divine Majesty,' Darel replied. 'They worship a sea god, named Father Krayk.' He declined to mention how they depicted him as a black-scaled monster of the ocean depths, and considered themselves to be his children. Such things, Darel thought, might not be well received in northerly Idramar, a long way from where you could look upon the face of a bluff-featured Tjakorshi man and realise that he was no more related to a dragon's ocean-going kin than a Naridan was to a dragon that walked on the land.

Natan sighed. 'The Southern Marshal has spoken to this king of this matter. It was Marshal Brightwater's judgment that this was a good thing. Peace and coexistence between Naridans and newcomers to our land.' The God-King steepled his fingers. 'It certainly sounds harmonious.'

Darel's instincts told him not to celebrate, and they were correct.

'But this king thinks back to the words of Narida's first ever Eastern Marshal, the honourable Gemar Far Garadh,' Natan continued. '"*So too, must our land be guarded against those to whom the Divine One could not bring His wisdom,*" he wrote. It does not sound to this king as though his divine ancestor's wisdom reached these Raiders, and they have not taken it to their hearts since settling in our land.'

Darel wanted to speak up. He wanted to point out that there had barely been any time for the Tjakorshi to do such a thing, and little incentive. He wanted to suggest that as the years passed, they might be brought around to see how Nari and his descendants were tied to this land, and how it was only through that unbroken line of blood that the demons of the Unmaker were kept at bay. However, he held his tongue, because he realised that attempting to contradict the embodiment of divinity was the most foolish thing he could do in this moment. He simply bowed his head, and waited.

'Whose lands border Blackcreek?' King Natan asked, turning to Kaldur Brightwater.

'To the north and west, Darkspur; to the north and east, Tainbridge,' the Southern Marshal answered immediately. His neutral expression remained unchanged, but Darel felt sure that the man disagreed with his monarch's judgement. And yet, how could he? How could either of them? King Natan was the descendent of the Divine Nari!

'And which is the larger?'

'Darkspur, Your Divine Majesty.'

'Send word to the thane of Darkspur,' the God-King declared. 'He is to march on Black Keep. The Raiders there are to be given one day to leave our shores; if they refuse, or if they return, they are to be killed. The Naridans are not to be harmed unless they side with the foreigners, in which case they are given the same choice.'

Breath was not coming easily to Darel. He struggled not to gasp as the enormity of his ruler's casual judgement settled on him.

'The Blackcreek lands will go to the thanes of Darkspur,' King Natan continued, inexorably. 'The Blackcreek line was incapable of guarding the lands entitled to it, and so it shall be no more. Darel of Black Keep; you and your law-brother are both sars, are you not?'

'Yes, Your Divine Majesty,' Darel managed to whisper.

'That rank is not stripped from either of you,' the God-King said. 'Nor is it decreed that either of you must serve the thane of Darkspur; you may find service where you will. Marshal Brightwater appears to think highly of you: perhaps he will grant you a position in his household.'

Darel could muster no words. It was a mercy, perhaps, to not be beholden to Odem Darkspur, but its faint glimmerings were smothered by the mass of darkness that engulfed him.

'These are troubled times,' King Natan was saying. 'The South must be whole, and Blackcreek must be true.' He snapped his fingers. 'Sar Darel, you are dismissed.'

Darel could do nothing else. He dropped to his knees, bowed until his forehead touched marble, then got back to his feet and walked back down the length of the Hall of Heaven, feeling the heat of his superiors' stares on him all the way.

PART FOUR

'THE SINISTER ARTS *known to us as witchcraft are the work of the Unmaker, Queen of Demons, and quite different to the sorcerers of old, whose art has not now been witnessed for some five centuries. The dark boons of witchcraft are bestowed upon those misguided fools who give themselves unto the Unmaker, body and soul, so that they might sow misery and mischief in the lands of good men. However, we should not be afeared, for not only does the Divine Nari protect His true servants from such evil, but the witch can be known to men of learning by the signs that this scholar will here relay . . .*

'* . . . the marks upon a witch's body can be myriad. Most common will be the ravages of the Unmaker's evil, which can be seen in a degradation of the skin, a failing of the teeth, a hunched back or twisting of the limbs, or of a body that seems old before its time. However, a man of learning should not trust to such signs alone, for simplistic thinking is the recourse of knowlessmen and superstitious fools. A witch may also be marked by the presence of a familiar, a beast or bird of unnatural intelligence. The witch of Tamar's Hollow was known to be accompanied by a malign crow that stole valuables for her and secreted them in her house . . .*

'* . . . so too must we look for such markings as are transcribed below, which may be found on objects or, if the witch considers* *it safe, upon the beams or walls of their houses. Some witches, indeed, have marked their own skin with ink or scar to replicate these marks, to devote their very flesh to the Unmaker. These signs on the skin should be marred with a blade before any attempt is made to cast the witch into flames, lest they should ward her from the Divine Nari's punishment . . .*

' . . . of the witchcraft from other countries we know little, but rumour has it that masked figures walk with the armies of Morlith, and that these creatures have their own fell powers not dissimilar to those of the witches of Narida. We do not, however, know whether they serve the Unmaker, or some foul entity unique to their own land . . . '

Extracts from the writings of Telaran Sandhill, Northern Marshal, known as 'The Witchbane', in the five-hundred-and-eighteenth year of the God-King

JEYA

IT WAS GETTING dark. The sun was going down on East Harbour, falling behind the high, thickly forested hills that formed the island's spine, and shadows were lengthening and thickening in the Narrows.

Jeya had not enjoyed much of a childhood, at least not compared to how Bulang had described thëirs. However, if shé'd ever had one, the sun had well and truly set on that, too. It was not hér age – which shé wasn't certain of anyway – that had brought it to a definite end, but grief, and betrayal.

Hér parents had been lost when shé was young, to the sort of misfortune that happened all the time. Hér fàther had died just after shé'd been born, when hìs ship went down, and hér môther had died of sickness. There were any number of people who could tell similar stories, and Jeya had been too young to really understand what had happened until shé'd been old enough to have some distance on it. Shé had vague memories of hér môther, but remembered nothing of hér fàther.

Shé grieved for Ngaiyu, though, and for Damau, and they had been brutally taken from hér.

Shé could smell the salt of the sea here, as you could in all parts of East Harbour that weren't set back from the shore, but the Narrows weren't just near the sea, they were surrounded by it. It bled through them, in small cracks and wider channels, fracturing the island's solid rock into dozens of distinct shards, connected by bridges ranging from great arcs of well-masoned stone to rickety spans of slimy wood, or swaying, salt-soaked rope trusted only by the desperate or the careless. This wasn't Jeya's usual ground, and shé didn't know it as well as the parts of the city where shé spent more time, but well enough for what shé needed tonight.

Shé hoped.

'Jeya?'

The call came from hér left, and the voice that would once have been a source of comfort and joy now sent hér heart into hér mouth. Shé jumped, and turned to face the speaker.

It was Nabanda, sauntering towards hér. They were on Tigren's Isle, one of the larger, more central ones, and Jeya was standing under a palm in a small public garden, maintained by the Hierarchs in an attempt to make the Narrows look a little nicer than the mess of warehouses, workshops and smokehouses that dominated it. It was a little more open than much of the area, and that suited Jeya well, as she eyed Nabanda. Shé'd never before assessed how dangerous hê'd be in a narrow space like one of the cramped streets that surrounded them.

Or in a house.

'M'bana passed a message, said yóu wanted to meet here,' Nabanda continued, walking towards hér. The sun was behind hîm, and so hîs face was in shadow, but hîs voice adequately communicated hîs puzzlement. 'Why here? Yóu could have come and found mê at the docks—'

'Shut your mouth!' Jeya snapped, and Nabanda stopped both walking and talking. It wasn't just the anger in hér voice that had brought hîm to a halt, but the tone. For the first time in many, many years, shé'd used the formal neutral to address hîm in a conversation between the two of them. That said, more efficiently than any words, that shé was no longer hîs friend.

In effect, shé no longer knew hîm at all.

'Jeya?' Nabanda said, cautiously.

'You killed Lihambo,' Jeya said, feeling the fury in hér heart mix with the fear in hér throat and spill through her teeth out into the world. 'You killed Suduru, you killed Damau, *you killed Ngaiyu*! How many others have you killed, Nabanda, whose names I don't know? Whose bodies I haven't found?!'

Nabanda took a deep breath, hîs shoulders rising like the hills behind them.

'Î never killed Suduru. Î told yóu, Jeya: Suduru got mixed up with the Sharks, and when you swim with Sharks, you become bait. A purge was ordered. That wasn't mê.'

The bleak honesty of his admission by omission was a knife in Jeya's heart. Shé'd tumbled to the truth eventually, far too late, but it was one thing to think it was true, to fear it was true: it was quite another to hear hîm fail to deny it when accused. Shé wanted to rage. Shé wanted to scream at hîm until hîs ears bled, but all shé could do was whisper.

'Why?' shé asked, hér voice barely audible over the distant sound of sea water lapping against the isle's edges, and the calls of the birds overheard.

'Because Î'm swimming with the Sharks too,' Nabanda said heavily, 'and if Î don't kill who Î'm supposed to, Î'll be the one becoming bait.' He sighed. 'How did yóu know it was mê?'

'We were being killed,' Jeya said flatly. 'The street people. The orphans. The people I know are the people you know. Ngaiyu was in thëir chair, thëir house was untouched. That wasn't for theft, that was someone who needed thëm dead, but would sit thëm down afterwards instead of leaving thëm to bleed out on thëir own floor, like that shows some sort of respect!' Hér eyes flicked to the long knife on hîs belt. 'And it would have to be someone thëy'd trust, to get into the house in the first place without a struggle. And Damau was easy: you were the last person to see them, and then they showed up dead.'

'The one time Î needed the sharks to take care of a body was the one time the harbour washed it back up again before they could finish their job,' Nabanda said heavily. 'Î'm sorry, Jeya, Î truly am. But it was them, or mê and my crew. Î've already lost one because we didn't do things as quickly as we should. Î won't lose more. Î had to kill Lihambo, and Ngaiyu, and Damau, because Î couldn't trust them not to go talking about the questions Î had to ask them.' Hê sighed again. 'Where's your new friend, Bulang? Hè's the only person Î've ever needed to kill, Jeya. If yóu hadn't helped hìm hide away from mê, all those others would still be alive.'

'You didn't need to kill anyone!' Jeya snapped at hîm. 'And you don't get to address me or Bulang that way!'

'If "Bulang" is from the family Î killed then hè's Naridan, which means hè uses high masculine,' Nabanda said carelessly. Hê began to walk towards hér again. 'Î'm going to ask you again, Jeya: where is hè?'

'Nabanda,' Jeya said desperately, 'you were my oldest friend! I *love* Bulang! Why would you take that from me?'

'Because Î want to live,' Nabanda said simply.

'You trade in lives that easily?'

'We all trade in lives, Jeya,' Nabanda said, spreading hîs arms. Perhaps hê meant it as an expansive, appealing gesture, but it only served to make hîm loom larger and more menacing. 'Every day, on that dock, Î trade a piece of my own life to put coin in Maradzh's pocket. Ships roll up to Maradzh's wharf with slaves on, and the brokers come down to sell the lives of those slaves, and they make coin off that. You take a piece of someone's life and add it to your own every time you steal.'

Hê had nearly reached hêr now. 'Î'm not quick and sneaky like you, to make a living as a thief. Î don't control a wharf. Î don't have the money to buy slaves and sell them on for a profit. Î don't come from a rich family like your friend Bulang. My choices were to break my own back selling my life to someone else a copper at a time, or to use *this*,' hê slapped hîs broad, muscular chest, 'the only thing Î have, and trade in lives in a way that actually gained mê something!'

Hê came to a halt, two steps away from hér. 'Where is hè, Jeya? Î won't hurt you to find out, but my crew will, and Î won't stop them. Î won't watch, but Î won't stop them.'

Jeya drew hér knife.

Nabanda cocked hîs head, and flexed hîs fingers. 'Surely you know that Î'm not going to be threatened by that.'

Jeya nodded. 'I know that. But this isn't a threat. It's a signal.'

The rock came from hér left, and struck Nabanda on the shoulder. Hê gasped in pain and surprise, and pulled the long knife from hîs belt, the knife that had opened Ngaiyu's throat, and ended the lives of Damau, Lihambo and, Jeya realised, who knew how many others.

Now the shapes of hér companions rose up from where they'd been lurking in bushes and behind trees. M'bana, throwing rocks; Mahatir, spear in their hand but not in their Watch uniform, because this was personal; a young Morlithian from the Temple of the Sun, who'd known Lihambo and Damau; and others of Ngaiyu's orphans, young and older alike, those who Jeya knew and who had listened to hér tale of Nabanda's treachery with horror and, increasingly, grim purpose.

Nabanda had turned on hîs own; and now, they turned on hîm.

'Oh, fuck this!' Nabanda snarled, and raised thumb and finger to his mouth to let loose an ear-splitting whistle.

Shouts went up. Jeya looked around, hér brief, vicious triumph wavering, and saw new shapes running in from the surrounding streets. Shé could only see three, but one of them threw a slice of sunset-coloured steel – a wind ring, a vicious, murderous thing – and Mahatir went down immediately, screaming.

Nabanda's crew. Hê hadn't come alone, either.

'Kill any of them that don't run!' Nabanda roared, and suddenly Jeya saw hîm, truly saw hîm, for who hê really was. Hê was a murderer, stone-cold and merciless, and shé'd simply never been on this side of hîm before. Terror swallowed hér rage, and shé turned to run from hîm.

Shé was too slow.

One of hîs massive hands grabbed hér arm and pulled hér back around. Shé lashed out with hér knife, the way hê'd taught her, and buried it into the meat of hîs bicep.

Nabanda howled with pain, and hîs grip slackened. Jeya pulled hérself free, but one of hîs knees came up and buried itself into hér gut before shé could run again. Shé staggered sideways, losing hér grip on her knife that was still jutting out from hîs arm, and fell wheezing to the ground. Shé heaved hér chest, trying to get hér breath back, but there was only a void where air should be, and hér limbs were suddenly weak.

Nabanda shoved hîs knife back into its sheath and reached down for hér with the hand of hîs uninjured arm, hîs face contorted by pain and rage. Jeya tried to scramble out of hîs way but couldn't move quickly enough, and hîs hand clamped around hér throat: not a truly throttling grip, not one intended to choke and kill hér, but hard enough to prevent hér from getting away from hîm.

'Do you know how much you've benefited from being my friend?' hê snarled down at hér. 'Do you have any idea how many people have looked the other way when you've stolen from them, or left you lying when you were sleeping, or failed to rise to a joke that you told, or a comment you passed? Because those people knew who Î am, who Î *really* am, and that Î had put the word out that *you were not to be touched*?'

Even if Jeya had had words to reply, shé wouldn't have been able to get them out. Shé grabbed at hîs hand and tried to pry at hîs fingers, but to no avail.

'Î don't hate this Bulang!' Nabanda hissed, almost sounding desperate hîmself. 'Hê's just a job that needs doing! Î'll make it quick, and clean, and as painless as Î can! But you have to tell mê where hè is *now*, before my friends finish killing yours, because they will not be gentle with you!'

Jeya reached for hér knife, buried in hîs left arm. Hê jerked it out of hér reach, but that had only been a feint on hér part.

Shé grabbed for hîs own blade, back on hîs belt, instead.

Hîs injured arm came down with enough force to knock hér desperate, grasping grip loose before shé could even move it, although hê gave a strangled grunt of pain as the impact jarred through hîm. Hê thrust hér back down to the ground and straightened up, then stamped down on hér chest, knocking loose the little breath shé'd been able to get back.

'Last chance,' hê said, warningly. Hê was no more than a silhouette now, hîs head and shoulders outlined against the deep red of the evening sky. Hê reached around, pulled hér knife loose from hîs arm with a grunt of pain, and threw it away.

'Over here! Î'm over here, just let hér go!'

Nabanda's head jerked up and around, and Jeya followed hîs gaze a moment later.

There, peering out from behind the corner of a building, was Bulang. Not within arm's reach, but close enough to be in real danger.

'Perlishu!' Nabanda yelled, pointing a finger. Jeya tensed, waiting for a wind ring to sail through the air and bury itself in Bulang's body, but nothing happened. Nabanda glanced around, and gave a wordless shout of frustration: Jeya followed hîs gaze and saw one of hîs crew on their back, desperately shielding themselves as M'Bana hacked at them with a butcher's knife.

Nabanda began to shift hîs weight to pursue Bulang hîmself, and in doing so lifted hîs foot off Jeya's chest.

'Bulang!' Jeya screamed, grabbing at Nabanda's leg. 'Run! Run!'

Nabanda cursed and kicked at hér, shaking hér loose, but Bulang had already turned and bolted. Nabanda thundered after thëm, no longer wasting hîs breath on shouts, and a moment later had already passed the corner where Bulang had been sheltering.

Jeya rolled over, forcing hér limbs to obey hér through sheer stubbornness and rage and terror, scrabbled to where hér knife had landed, then set off in pursuit.

Shé cut left, then right, then left again, following the pounding of footsteps even though shé could barely hear them above the noise of hér own heart in hér ears. Bulang was heading for Second Channel which, in a somewhat torturous route, cut right through the Narrows from the ocean on one side to the harbour on the other. It wasn't the widest of the gaps between the islets, but it was known to be one of the deeper ones, and from here, if Bulang didn't intend to be trapped against the shore, there was only one way across: a wooden footbridge, high enough above the seawater for small sailing vessels to pass beneath it, that spanned the gulf between the roofs of two warehouses.

It was towards this that Bulang was climbing, up the ladder on the side of one of the buildings. Thëy were only a third of the way up when Jeya rounded the last corner and brought thëm into view, and by that time Nabanda had already reached the bottom of the ladder, and hê was tall enough anyway that when hê jumped, trying to snag Bulang's ankle, hê nearly made it. Jeya ran forwards, screaming at hîm, but Nabanda had no intention of being delayed or distracted by hér: hê set off upwards as well, and while hê was far bulkier and heavier than Bulang, hê had more than enough muscle to pull hîmself upwards, and hê climbed just as quickly.

Jeya reached the bottom of the ladder and began to climb too, chasing Nabanda's feet upwards. What else could shé do?

Shé heard Bulang reach the top, and the flap of thëir footsteps as thëy fled towards the bridge. Shé heard the huff of Nabanda's breath as hê pulled hîmself over the top of the ladder too, and the thud of hîs steps as hê followed. Shé gritted hér teeth and forced hér arms and legs to keep moving, despite the burning ache in hér chest, and looked only upwards, not down. Shé wasn't *that* high up – the top of the building was perhaps six times hér own height – but a fall from here would leave hér with broken limbs, at least.

But if Nabanda caught Bulang then shé'd be left with a broken heart, and right now, that seemed like the worse option.

Shé reached the top, clamped one hand over the edge of the warehouse's roof, and practically hauled hérself over the edge and onto the narrow piece of flat stone that ran to the bridge. Bulang was hesitating at the near end of it, and Nabanda was advancing on thëm.

'That looks risky,' Nabanda was saying. 'Especially for a rich kid like yòu, who doesn't know these places. It might give out on yòu.'

They were nearly close enough for Nabanda to lunge and grab thëm now.

'Bulang, *run*!' Jeya screamed again, and Bulang did so, turning and pelting across the narrow, old wooden bridge with the confidence that only fear could lend, hopping and leaping to avoid the areas that looked less safe. Nabanda spat a curse, but there was no way hê could abandon hîs pursuit now. If Bulang got to the other side, thëy would be well away before Nabanda could find another route across. With hîs quarry so nearly within hîs grasp, Nabanda gave chase. Hê too ran swiftly and confidently, for Nabanda knew this bridge, and hê knew that, largely unused though it was, it was sturdier than it looked.

Until he reached one of the parts that Bulang had hopped over, a part where Bulang and Jeya had carefully half-sawn through the boards as the sun had begun to sink in the sky, and it gave out beneath hîm.

The wood cracked and parted, and Nabanda's forward momentum carried hîm not into hîs next stride, but chest-first into the splintered opposite edge of the gap. Jeya, following behind hîm, saw hîm flail desperately as hê rebounded . . .

. . . and found a handhold.

The fingers of Nabanda's right hand lodged into a gap between boards: a perilous, tenuous grip, but a grip nonetheless. Hê bellowed with pain and fear as hîs arm took the full, sudden weight of hîs body, but hê held on. And, with an almighty heave and roar, hê reached up and grabbed hold with hîs left hand as well. Injured though that arm was, the fear of falling burned though the pain, and Nabanda began to haul hîmself back up onto the bridge.

Then Bulang was there, stamping at hîs fingers, yelling and screaming and crying all in one. Nabanda howled, Nabanda cursed, and Nabanda screamed right back, but even hîs strength couldn't hold hîmself up when hîs fingers were being broken.

'You!' Bulang screamed.

Stamp

'Killed!'

Stamp

'My!'

Stamp

'Family!'

Bulang grabbed the rail at the edge of the bridge to steady thëmselves, and stamped downwards past Nabanda's clutching fingers, directly into hîs face. Jeya heard the *crunch* of Nabanda's nose breaking.

Nabanda's grip finally slipped, as that last impact jarred hîm loose. Hê fell, screaming and feet-first, into the water beneath, and sank into the shadow-skimmed waves.

Jeya collapsed against the bridge's rail, hér heart hammering so fast that shé almost thought shé was going to lose consciousness. From the other side of the divide that had sent Nabanda plunging into the sea, Bulang looked at hér, tears streaking down thëir cheeks. This had been the backup plan, in case Nabanda had brought hîs crew to the meeting: for Bulang to show thëmselves, and then to flee. By the grace of the gods – and, Jeya thought, one god in particular – the backup plan had worked.

Beneath them, Nabanda surfaced again with a furious, breathy exhalation, blood and seawater running from his nose. Jeya looked down and saw hîm staring up at them, hatred writ large on hîs face.

'Î won't make this easy now!' hê bellowed. 'Î'm going to step on your pathetic little necks and—'

Hê cut off suddenly, and looked down at the water beside hîm. Jeya couldn't be sure, since only twilight was left in the air now, but shé thought shé saw dark shapes congregating around hîm.

Nabanda had always been too big and too strong to kill, even between them both. Even, probably, with help from others who lived on the streets. And, if hê truly had been what shé'd feared hê was, hê wasn't going to stop. Hê had to die, or it would be Bulang's life and, quite probably, hérs as well. Sa, the god of thieves and tricksters – among other things – had shown hér how to drop hîm into the water, when the golden-maned monkey had been screaming from its fragile branch at the dragon trying to eat it, but simple East Harbour know-how had shown Jeya how to deal with hîm once hê was there.

Sharks were attracted to blood. If you were bleeding, you didn't go in the water, or didn't stay in the water. Conversely, if you wanted to attract sharks, you needed to dump in a couple of bucket loads of fish guts or animal waste – anything smelly and bloody, really – and to wait for a while.

Which was exactly what Jeya and Bulang had done, from this bridge, after they'd finished half-sawing through the boards.

Nabanda was from East Harbour as well. Hê knew what the shapes in the water around hîm were, and hê knew hê was already bleeding. Hê knew hê needed to swim to shore swiftly, and with as little splashing and noise as possible. Had the sharks not already been there, or had their attention not been heightened by the chum, hê might have made it.

But they were, and they had been. And hê didn't.

'You swim with sharks,' Jeya whispered softly to hérself as Nabanda gasped and sank out of sight for a second and final time, and a sudden, darker cloud appeared on the surface of the water, 'and you become bait.'

ZHANNA

THE ONE AND only advantage that Zhanna and Sakka had was surprise. Their enemies were not expecting to find two Tjakorshi warriors ready and waiting for them, blocking the doorway with alder roundshields as wide as their arms were long, and armed with blackstone axe and Naridan longblade.

Zhanna lunged as soon as the door opened, stabbing at the fur-swaddled body of the man who had moved it. He staggered backwards, but she had no idea whether she had wounded him or merely surprised him, because no sooner had she made contact than she had to draw her arm back and bring her shield across to catch a spear thrust. She knocked that aside and cut at one of the hands holding it, but the man danced backwards out of reach. Beside her, Sakka screamed and punched outwards with her axe, causing a Darkspur fighter to howl and clutch his face as the sharp rock shards sliced through his cheek.

'I can't swing properly!' Sakka yelled, ducking behind her shield as an arrow *thunked* into it and stuck there, vibrating. 'How are we supposed to fight them like this?'

She was right, Zhanna realised. Her plan to hold the doorway by fighting on a narrow front was all well and good, but the lintel above them prevented the sort of downwards, chopping blows she might employ in a shield wall, and both longblades and blackstone axes were best at slashes that could open an enemy up, not stabs.

Behind them, Amonhuhe let out a piercing whistle. Zhanna shifted to her right at this pre-arranged signal, the other woman's bowstring thrummed, and an arrow sped out to bury itself in a man's chest. Zhanna and Sakka closed the gap between them again, but the Darkspur men piled forwards with shouts of rage, throwing all their weight behind spear thrusts. The blows only landed on shields, but the force was enough to knock them both backwards a step. Zhanna stabbed outwards with her blade again, but could reach nothing.

'Use the dragons!' Sakka screamed at her. Zhanna whistled desperately, and Talon and Thorn bounded forward between them, snarling, but then immediately retreated, their tails rattling furiously before even coming into contact with the enemy. The Darkspur men gave a huge, shuddering grunt in unison, and all pushed as one again. Zhanna stumbled backwards, lost her footing and fell, with her enemies bearing down on top of her. To her left, Sakka was being driven backwards into the building.

The four free men of the Smoking Valley piled into the gap, wielding their chains like flails.

The Darkspur men, intent on butchering Zhanna and Sakka, were unable to bring their spears up in time; their weapons that had proved so useful in driving back a makeshift, two-person shield wall were too long and cumbersome for such close-quarters work. Weak and tired though the Smoking Valley men might have been, the weight of their chains was such that their blows felled the enemies on which they landed. Three Darkspur men went down. The chest of the fourth Smoking Valley man was pierced by a Darkspur spear that came over the shoulder of his intended target, but that target wasn't saved: Zhanna kicked out at his knee, knocking his leg from under him and bringing him down into reach of her blade, then rolled and slashed to open his throat.

He recoiled, grabbing futilely at his neck. The man behind him withdrew his spear from the chest of the Smoking Valley man and raised it to stab downwards at Zhanna, but another arrow from Amonhuhe took him in the stomach. He grunted and doubled over, giving Zhanna enough time to get one knee under her and bite her blade into the side of his neck too, but there was yet another one behind him.

Talon and Thorn rattled again, the sound almost frantic, and from outside came a throbbing, roaring rumble that resonated within Zhanna's bones. It was as though the sky had split open, or the earth had risen up. It sounded like thunder with teeth.

People began screaming.

The press of Darkspur bodies suddenly disappeared. Men turned tail and fled away from the doorway, leaving the two of their number at the front to be clubbed down by chain flails before they could follow their fellows. Sakka, Amonhuhe, Tatiosh and the men of the Smoking Valley fell on them to ensure their demise, but Zhanna stepped forward and, shield raised against any attack, cautiously exited the building to see what was happening.

For a moment, she could make out little in the darkness, the flickering light of wildly waved torches and the jumping shadows cast by them merely adding to the general confusion. Over to her right, a few more Darkspur men were fleeing, and in the light of the doorway of the building where the women had been held she could make out a shape that was probably Danid, and several Smoking Valley women armed, as the men behind her were, with their manacles. At least *their* key had worked . . .

Then a huge chunk of the night in front of Winterhome moved, and turned, and let out a throbbing growl.

Thundertooth.

The name came unbidden into her head, but surely this could be nothing else. It was massive, four-legged and muscular, but not a solid, lumbering beast like a longbrow. Its head was near as long as Zhanna was tall, and packed with curving teeth the size of her hand, while each foot was tipped with claws that were even larger. Its plumage was a mottled dark green and brown that melted into the darkness, and formed a thick ruff around its throat. It dwarfed the war dragons of Black Keep, and while it wasn't the size of a cloudhead, it would surely be able to bring one down.

It was as though the deep wilderness of Narida had been given form, and had come to punish these interlopers into its domain. Zhanna's muscles turned to ice water as terror gripped her chest. Had the beast come for her then, she would have accepted her fate meekly.

The beast didn't come for her. Instead it turned like a flame caught in the wind, as smooth and slick as death itself, and opened its jaws horrifically wide to snatch up a Darkspur man who tried to pierce its feathered side with a spear. He screamed as the dragon tossed him into the air with a heave of its mighty neck muscles, and his screaming stopped as it caught him on the way down and bit nearly clean through his body with a crunch of splintering bone.

Another Darkspur man, driven perhaps by love for the victim – or maybe a vainglorious desire for renown – flew at the beast with a spear of his own, stabbing at its eyes. The thundertooth simply swatted him away with one front foot, and he landed in a broken, bleeding and unmoving heap. Then the gigantic dragon lunged forward after his screaming companions, who scattered and fled.

It must have come around by the lake shore. The shelter of the Smoking Valley rock house was denied to the men of Darkspur by the dragon's arrival, and the buildings in which they'd imprisoned Winterhome's creators and owners were still held against them, and so they ran, casting their torches down and fleeing northwards. Zhanna, her initial bloom of primeval terror now fading a little, counted perhaps a dozen Naridans disappearing into the night: the thundertooth had left several broken bodies on the ground in its initial attack, and their attempts to get past Zhanna's defenders had cost them a high price.

The thundertooth was coming towards her.

Zhanna's instinct was to freeze, hoping against hope that the massive dragon would somehow fail to notice her, but when she heard it inhale sharply and saw its head twitch in her direction, the ice that had encased her spine and held her in place shattered. She ducked back inside, pulling the door to behind her with a bang. She heard a similar banging door from the women's building: clearly, they were no more eager to meet the dragon than she was.

'What's happening out there?' Amonhuhe demanded. She had an arrow to the string, but her bow was not drawn. Behind her, one of the Smoking Valley men was working on the shackle locks with a dagger taken from their fallen captors, although without any sign of success.

'Thundertooth,' Zhanna said shortly, retreating away from the door.

'The curse,' Amonhuhe breathed. 'We should not have—'

The door rattled on its hinges, and several people yelped, Zhanna included. A low, throbbing growl bled through the timber: the sound of a beast whose bloodlust was up. Zhanna eyed the door nervously, but there was no way that the thundertooth could fit through it. Was there?

The door banged again, as something huge and powerful pawed at it from the outside, prompting another chorus of fearful cries, but Zhanna steeled herself and bit down on her reaction. She would not freeze in terror again. She would face this threat bravely, although she wasn't entirely sure why. It wasn't as though the thundertooth would be impressed by her courage.

The door, struck one more time, shattered and burst inwards, and the thundertooth's huge head loomed into view.

It quested forwards, sniffing and snapping. Zhanna set her

feet as the other occupants retreated before it, but her initial assessment had been correct: the thundertooth's head and neck could get in, but its shoulders and body were far too massive. The vast majority of it had to remain outside, and long though its jaws were, it couldn't reach them.

The thundertooth pushed forwards eagerly, and the force of its shoulders against the doorframe caused the entire building to shift slightly. The wooden frame creaked, and dust and soil rained down from the ceiling and the walls. Zhanna had a sudden, terrifyingly clear vision of the thundertooth's eagerness to get to them collapsing the building on top of them all. Amonhuhe loosed, but the arrow glanced off the dragon's hide without appearing to bother it in the slightest.

It shoved again, and the building moved once more. Zhanna coughed as dust swirled around her head, and she screwed up her courage so tightly that it burned inside her like a star. She had not come all this way just to let a dragon bring a building down on her head.

She strode forwards and, screaming loud enough to drown out her fear, brought her longblade down on the thundertooth's muzzle.

She felt the weapon bite, shearing through feather and flesh and jarring on the bone of the dragon's snout, a moment before the thundertooth roared loud enough to set her ears ringing, and snapped at her head. She stumbled backwards, aiming another cut that caught it on the edge of its upper jaw.

The thundertooth bellowed again, but appeared to conclude that there was easier meat than this sort that hid in enclosed spaces, and which bit back. It withdrew past the ruined door, shaking its head as though to try to dislodge the pain Zhanna's blows had caused it. Zhanna followed, cautiously, and watched from the doorway as it picked up and gulped down the man whom it had swatted, then took up into its jaws the mangled corpse which was all that remained of the first man she'd first seen it bite, and prowled off into the darkness back beyond Winterhome.

'It's gone,' she called back softly into the building behind her.

'What of the Darkspur men?' Amonhuhe asked. Zhanna peered northwards, into the night.

'The ones who still lived fled from dragon,' she told the older woman, 'and this warrior cannot see them now.'

Amonhuhe walked out beside her, another arrow set to her bow, and looked towards Winterhome. The gentle light of fires still flickered from within, but there was no sign that any living soul now occupied it. The men of Darkspur had come out to secure their slaves, and they had paid for that gamble.

'Our home is freed,' Amonhuhe said softly, but her face hardened. 'We must take it, now, in case they return.' She looked over at the building where the women had been held, the door of which was now also cautiously opening.

'And,' she added, 'we must see if anyone else has a key . . . '

The people of the Smoking Valley flooded out, their chains clanking where they were still bound together, all of them desperate to see their family and loved ones who had been held in other places. Zhanna found herself overtaken and surrounded by eager bodies, and drew her blade in close to herself avoid anyone accidentally cutting themselves on it. However, she was given a reasonably wide berth by most, perhaps due to Talon and Thorn's presence at her heels. She caught more than one confused and troubled glance at these two apparently tame rattletails, and it seemed no one wanted to get too near them.

'Zhanna!' someone bellowed, and she turned to see Tsennan Longjaw, head and shoulders above pretty much everyone else, and still walking tall, Kydozhar Fell-Axe be praised. Children were clustered around him, which was an odd sight, but they quickly broke away with cries of delight that were echoed by the adults who raced to embrace them, or scoop them up into their arms.

Of course, not all of the Smoking Valley adults could easily do such a thing. Most of the menfolk were still chained together, but, Zhanna saw, Amonhuhe was already hurrying back from a cluster of the women with what looked to be another key. Her suspicion was confirmed when a new cheer went up, and the first half of another pair of manacles dropped away.

'Who lives?' Tsennan asked her urgently, as he reached her side.

'Sakka, Amonhuhe, Tatiosh: they're all fine, although it was close,' Zhanna told him. She looked around again. 'I can see Danid—'

'Menaken is hurt,' Longjaw said, and Zhanna's elation fled, leaving only the taste of bile behind.

'How bad?'

'Spear in the chest,' Tsennan replied. 'Deep.' He shook his head. 'I'm no witch or healer, but I think the Dark Father's eye is on him.'

'Father Krayk won't have his eye on Menaken, he's Naridan,' Zhanna told him, trying to sound encouraging, but her voice sounded flat even to her own ears. Tsennan Longjaw was no grey-bearded raider, but he had seen more fights than her: he probably knew what he was talking about. 'These people must have someone who knows how to treat wounds.'

'If the Flatlanders left them alive,' Longjaw said dubiously.

'Only one way to find out,' Zhanna said, and took a deep breath. 'Amonhuhe! *Amonhuhe*!'

The Smoking Valley woman appeared, weaving her way through her fellows, her expression one of irritation. 'What is it, girl? This woman is—'

'Menaken is hurt,' Zhanna cut her off, choosing to ignore 'girl', for now. 'Do your people have a healer?'

Amonhuhe didn't protest at being interrupted, but sucked her breath in through her teeth and looked around. 'This woman doesn't know, any more . . . Wait.' She began shouting in her own tongue, and heads turned towards her.

Zhanna didn't wait for Amonhuhe's conclusion. 'Is he in the building?' she asked Tsennan, who nodded, and she set off at something just short of a run.

Menaken was an adult, a Naridan, and older than her. He'd been a guard of Black Keep, so he was a warrior; of sorts, anyway. It was he who'd officially been speaking for Black Keep on this journey. He was capable of making his own decisions. If he died, it would not be on her head.

Except that it had been her plan. And even though Menaken had heard her plan, had agreed to play his part in her plan, and hadn't come up with a different plan himself, it was still her plan. If he died, Zhanna knew she would not be able to just let his death go with the tide and forget about it.

She wasn't sure if that was a good thing for a captain, or not. She also wasn't sure that she cared.

She reached the building in which the children and been held and ducked through the doorway, stepping over the bodies of three Darkspur men claimed by the blades and arrows of the defenders. There were no children left inside save for one small, miserable bundle over in the far corner that looked too lumpy to be clothes, and which Zhanna refused to look at. Kakaiduna wasn't there. She'd probably gone to find her parents, and given how long she'd been separated from them, Zhanna could hardly blame her for that. Avisha was still present, though, desperately pressing a bloodstained cloth to Menaken's chest where he sat propped up against one of the walls.

The cloth was inadequate for the job. Menaken's handsome face was already glistening unhealthily, and his breathing was ragged. Zhanna could tell that Tsennan had been correct: this was beyond a healer's art, unless the people of the Smoking Valley had magic more powerful than anything known to either the Brown Eagle clan or to Black Keep.

Zhanna knelt down too, and laid down her sword and shield to wordlessly take Menaken's left hand in both of hers. He looked at her as her skin made contact with his. It was strange, the details she noticed in that moment: the three grey hairs in the stubble that had grown on his face since he'd last been able to shave; the small scar that cut through one eyebrow; the bubble of saliva at one corner of his mouth that expanded and contracted as he breathed in and out, rapidly and raggedly.

'Did we win?' he asked weakly.

'Yes,' Zhanna said, forcing the words through a throat swollen by imminent tears. 'A dragon helped, but we won.'

'That should make s'man feel better,' Menaken said softly. He leaned his head back against the wall, closed his eyes, and spoke again in a voice almost too quiet to hear. 'It doesn't.'

Zhanna's eyes blurred as water filled them. She released his hand with one of hers to reach up and wipe the tears away, but by the time she had done so, Menaken's eyes were shut and his head was starting to loll to one side. He was perhaps still alive, by some measure, but not in any way that counted.

The second one of Zhanna's crew to die. But this wasn't like Ingorzhak, eaten by a monster of the wild in a sudden, unexpected attack on a sleeping camp. Menaken had died carrying out her orders.

'This was my fault,' she muttered to herself. Avisha, who had slowly released her grip on the cloth pressed in place, looked over at her. 'It was this warrior's fault,' Zhanna repeated in Naridan.

'Yes,' Avisha nodded, but then she smiled. It was a brittle thing, but it was a smile, and she pointed one blood-stained hand towards the door, beyond which the sounds of families reuniting could be heard. 'But you helped make that happen, too. Some of us died when we followed you against Rikkut. That doesn't mean what you did was wrong then, just as it wasn't wrong now.' Her expression darkened. 'Those children . . . So thin, so scared. This warrior's never seen anything like it.'

Zhanna blinked at her. 'You say yourself a warrior now?'

'This warrior's been in as many fights as you have,' Avisha replied defiantly. She pointed at one of the Darkspur men on the floor, who had an arrow jutting out of his neck. 'She and Kakaiduna got that one together. She is a warrior.'

'Will Black Keep like that?' Zhanna asked. 'Your parents?' Avisha clicked her tongue.

'This warrior's parents didn't like her tattoo, either.' She pointed to the dark stripe on her brow. 'They can walk into the sea.' She looked back at Menaken, and some of her fire faded. 'He . . . This warrior doesn't know what we should do for him. We need a priest—'

Zhanna jerked around as the door was pulled wide once more, and admitted Amonhuhe with one of her folk in tow. She stopped as soon as she saw Menaken, and her face fell. 'We are too late?'

'Yes,' Zhanna said. She realised her weapons were still lying on the floor, picked her longblade up, and wiped it off on the furs of one of the Darkspur casualties before sheathing it. 'The wound was bad. No healer could help.'

Amonhuhe nodded and said a few words to the person with her, who turned and left again. No doubt there were other people who needed attention, probably many of the Smoking Valley.

'Is anyone else hurt?' Avisha asked. 'From Black Keep, this warrior means.'

'Danid has a cut on his arm, but if it does not go bad, he should be fine,' Amonhuhe replied. Her eyes lingered on Avisha for a moment longer than they perhaps would have done normally, when she heard her calling herself 'this warrior', but she made no mention of it. Instead, she jerked her head at both of them. 'Come. If you want to spend the rest of the night under a roof, we need to make sure Winterhome is free of the enemy.'

Zhanna nodded. Best to simply focus on the next thing to be done, for now. Hopefully all the Darkspur men had come out to fight and had then fled from the thundertooth, but it was better to check with warriors first, rather than risk the people of the

Smoking Valley walking back into their homes and straight on to spear-points.

'This warrior will fetch the Longjaw,' she told Amonhuhe, pushing past the other woman and out into the night again. 'Then we shall go in.'

MARIN

RAVI HAD HAD the right of it, as it turned out. Many of the villagers who had been at work in the fields during the day did indeed stop by the tavern for an ale, and the taproom began to fill up as the light died. The first few through the door gave Marin and his companions cautious glances and a wide berth, but as more bodies came in there became less and less room for them to stand off. Eventually, a young chap with a long nose pulled up a stool and sat down without asking between Channa and Elifel, with the forced casualness of a man already a bit tipsy after one pint of ale and the confidence of someone fairly sure the room would side with him if the strangers proved unfriendly.

'So,' he began. 'What're your stories, hey?'

'Long, and varied, and eight of them,' Ravi replied to him. She was finishing up her stew, which had proved to be as hearty and filling as Marin could have wanted. 'Why the interest?'

The new arrival looked surprised that it was she who had replied to him, but when no one else volunteered an answer to his question, he addressed her. 'Well, not often we see soldiers round these parts.'

'Were you wanting to see soldiers round your parts, lad?' Gershan asked mildly, his deadpan delivery somewhat spoiled by Kenan's inability to fully suppress his snickers at his brother's innuendo.

'Behave,' Channa said, in a weary tone that suggested to Marin it was far from the first time she'd had to listen to such humour from them.

'You've got nothing to worry about from us,' Ravi told the young local, who had raised his eyebrows at Gershan's suggestiveness. 'Well, not apart from soldiers' jokes, anyway.'

'S'man never said he was worried,' the young man retorted. 'Just curious as to what brings you here, is all. Especially since, even out here, we know what the badge of Idramar and the Eastern Army looks like,' he added pointedly, looking at Aranel's tabard.

'Well, it ain't exactly valid no more,' Aranel muttered uncomfortably. He was the oldest soldier among them, and Marin could understand how torn he was to be renouncing his old life.

'What d'you mean by that?'

'You heard about the trouble at Northbank?' Ravi asked him. The youth shook his head, not bothering to hide his frown of concern. Marin cautiously glanced around as the volume of conversation in the immediate vicinity dropped a little. More than one other person had heard the name of the city, and had decided that this was more interesting than their own conversations.

'Bad business,' Ravi continued, wiping her chin. Marin was sure she realised that others were listening to her words now, but she gave no sign of it, and kept addressing the long-nosed youth as though he was her only audience. He internally applauded her for it: it made the whole thing look more genuine.

'Bad business how?' the youth wanted to know. 'What happened?'

'You heard Marshal Coldbeck's been declared traitor?' Ravi asked, and now there was no mistaking the indrawn breaths and shoved-back stools as her words reached others.

'You never said that before!' Danna the Bar exclaimed accusingly, frozen in the middle of drying an ale mug she'd just washed. By the Mountain, but she must have good ears to have heard from there!

'Declared traitor by whom?' someone in the crowd demanded, and all of a sudden the room was filled with incredulous questions that quite overwhelmed Ravi's voice when she tried to answer.

'Let the woman speak!' Laz boomed from beside Marin, so loudly that Marin jumped. He'd never quite got used to how loud Laz could be when he wanted to, since it so rarely happened. 'She'll tell you, if you give her a chance!'

Ravi glanced sideways at him, then turned back to her now very definite and very obvious audience. 'S'woman didn't realise this was news to you all, else she'd have broken it differently, but . . . Yes, the Eastern Marshal was declared a traitor by the God-King, and he fled Idramar, coming west, or so we were told. The Eastern Army was supposed to be marching out in search of Nari Reborn, but then that got changed to finding the High Marshal as well.'

'You're no soldier!' someone shouted.

'No, s'woman's a healer,' Ravi said, as though the fact were of no import. 'Anyhow, we reached Northbank by river, but it seemed folk there weren't entirely convinced that they wanted to take the crown's side over that of the man who'd been their thane. Tempers rose, and . . . '

'And?' the long-nosed youth prompted her.

'And we buggered off when Naridan soldiers started drawing blades on Naridan townsfolk in the name of keeping order,' Channa finished. 'Fuck *that*. S'woman came west to serve Nari, not go stabbing her own over who bows how low to who.'

'There was fighting?' someone asked. 'In the city?'

'Aye,' Laz said, and Marin saw all eyes go to him and linger on the two scabbarded blades on his belt . . . and of course the black stain on them, but that was not to be helped. 'Started by a couple of hotheads, no doubt, but it got bad enough quick enough that those of us who were trying to have a quiet drink decided we wanted nothing to do with it. It's as Channa said,' he continued, nodding in her direction, 'it's not why we came here.'

'So you're deserters, then?' Danna the Bar piped up again, looking a little uncertain of herself. Marin supposed it might not be to her best interest to have served deserters from the Eastern Army, should a punishment detail come to track them down. Marin thought that was unlikely, given the scale of the problems he suspected they'd left behind them in Northbank, but Danna wasn't to know that.

'Depends how you define it,' Channa said with a snort. 'To s'woman's way of thinking, we're just doing what we were told we were going to be doing when the muster was first called. It's those others who got side-tracked.'

There were mutterings in the crowd around them, but Marin was pleased to note that they seemed to be generally well-disposed mutterings. The notion of Marshal Coldbeck being declared traitor was shocking indeed, and the news of the violence in Northbank was understandably uncomfortable – who wanted to hear that their own countrymen had turned on each other? – but at least it seemed the tavern wasn't going to assume that he and his companions were responsible for any of it.

'Just going for a piss,' he muttered to Laz.

'Well, don't get lost,' Laz replied into his ale. 'It's a big place out there. And get your husband another drink, when you get back?'

'You'll be closer to the bar,' Marin protested as he got up.

'Aye, but you'll already be on your feet.'

'Fine,' Marin sighed good-naturedly. 'Another ale it is, then.'

'Get one for yourself as well.'

'Your generosity is astounding, love.' He kissed the top of Laz's head, then made for the tavern's door, picking his way through the crowded taproom with the ease of an experienced pickpocket. He cast a glance over at the corner seat where the hooded, smoking person had been sat, but it was empty, and only a few stronger whiffs of pipe smoke lingered in the air. That was odd, and Marin wondered where they might have gone. Were they a local after all, now returned to their house? Had they been standing and talking with others in the room, and he had simply missed them? He had never seen their face, so if they'd removed their hood they'd almost have been less anonymous to him than if they'd left it up . . .

He was heading for the privy, at the rear of the property, when a shadow detached itself from the tavern's wall and stood in front of him so suddenly that he nearly pissed himself there and then.

'What—?' he stammered, reaching for the knife at his belt, but the hooded shadow brought its own blade up, glimmering in the moonlight, and held it to his neck before he could do much more than twitch.

'Hssh,' the shadow said softly. 'No need for alarm.'

'That's easy for you to say!' Marin squeaked. The figure was taller than him – although that wasn't unusual – and even if it were not, a knife to his throat was not a position from which he wished to try his somewhat limited fighting skills. His panicked breathing caught a whiff of the pipe smoke from earlier, which solved that little mystery, although admittedly not in a manner of which he approved.

'What's your business here?' the hooded man – and it was a man, Marin was sure of it – demanded. 'Five soldiers of the Eastern Army, a woman, a sar and whatever you are? That makes for a strange tale.'

'If you'd care to come back inside, you'll hear s'man's companion Ravi explaining it all!' Marin hissed at him. 'And if you remove your knife now, s'man won't even tell his husband, *the sar*, about that little detail!'

'You won't be mentioning anything if this knife gets pressed a bit harder,' the hooded man growled. 'Sars don't scare everyone, and tales told to taverns rarely ring true.'

'And ones told at knifepoint do?' Marin argued, although on reflection, suggesting that anything he said would be a lie was perhaps not the brightest thing he'd ever done.

'That depends on how good the person holding the knife is at detecting falsehoods uttered under duress,' the hooded man replied. 'Besides, you don't know the agenda of the person with the knife, do you? So you may as well tell the truth and hope it's pleasing, unless you truly have something dark to hide.'

'Don't we all have something to hide?' Marin muttered. He was simply stalling for time now, hoping that someone else would exit the tavern and discover him and his interrogator.

'Some of us have purposes that are pure,' the hooded man said calmly. He pressed the knife a little harder, until Marin worried that the point was about to break his skin. 'No more evasion. The truth.'

Finally, something to go off. In Marin's experience, only three sorts of people worried about purity: alchemists, dragon breeders and the extremely religious. Given the current political circumstances, he was fairly sure only one of those three groups were likely to be lurking around taverns in the Naridan Midlands and holding strangers at knifepoint.

'We seek to serve the Divine Nari,' he said. 'We were with the Eastern Army, but left when they turned on the people of Northbank.'

The pressure on his neck did not decrease, but he heard an inhalation that was slightly sharper than the others, and he knew he'd caught the man's attention.

'Those could be dangerous words,' the man said softly, 'if spoken to the wrong person.'

'How can wishing to serve Nari Reborn be dangerous to anyone except His enemies?' Marin asked, praying he had judged this correctly. If the man was one of Princess Tila's agents – who were theoretical, but highly probable – then Marin had likely just made Laz a widower. Otherwise . . .

'Who's the woman?' the hooded man demanded. 'One of the soldiers' wives?'

'A healer,' Marin replied. 'She signed on with the army in

Idramar, seeking to find and serve the Divine One, like the rest of us.'

To his surprise, the pressure on the knife lessened. It wasn't removed, but he no longer got the feeling he was about to stab himself if he swallowed too hard.

'A healer,' the man said quietly, almost thoughtfully. 'A healer, and a blacksword. "Death and life, standing together".'

'*The Foretellings of Tolkar*,' Marin said, reflexively.

'A scholar!' the hooded man said, with a laugh that was not entirely pleasant. 'Well, now. Answer this, scholar: If you and your companions could do anything, what would it be?'

'We would find the Divine Nari, and accompany Him to Godspire to see Him proclaim his return and take His rightful place on the throne,' Marin said, without hesitation. This was no time for half-measures, and it was the truth, to boot.

For a long moment, the hooded man did not move. Then he stepped away and reached up to draw back his hood, revealing a scalp that gleamed in the moonlight. As the man's cloak opened, Marin saw to his surprise that a sar's longblade was belted at the man's waist, although there was no sign of the accompanying shortblade.

'Sometimes we must let faith guide our steps,' the bald man was saying. 'Very well, stranger. You say you wish to serve the Divine Nari? This priest is named Mordokel. He will take you to Him, and we will see if your hearts are true.'

DAREL

THE SUN HAD long sunk into the west, and the warm light cast by the oil lamp in his quarters was doing little to lift the darkness that spread itself across Darel's soul, and which matched the pouring rain outside. He considered ignoring the knock at his door when it came, but the instincts of behaviour appropriate to a thane still drove him to rise from his chair. His childhood instruction would not be driven out of him as easily as his rank had been removed.

He pulled his door open to reveal Hiran, who held a pair of goblets and a stoppered earthenware jug of what Darel hoped was wine.

'It is not much,' Hiran said apologetically, raising proffering a goblet, 'but it is all your friend can offer at this time.'

Darel sighed, but smiled at him. 'A friend and wine are welcome at any time. Please, come in.'

'You have your friend's deepest sympathies, of course,' Hiran said, stepping inside and nudging the door closed behind him with his foot. 'For all that they are worth.'

'They are better than your contempt,' Darel told him. 'And that is all your friend has received from others.' He gestured to Hiran to take a chair, and slumped back down into the one in which he had been sitting. 'In all honesty, your friend does not know what else he should have expected. Idramar is just so far from Black Keep. How should the people here have any idea what happened there? How can they understand just how momentous an occurrence it is for us to have made peace with the Tjakorshi? But instead of this being seen as a beacon of hope, it is dismissed as a failure of our character.'

'You do not agree with the God-King's quoting of General Garadh's words?' Hiran asked. 'That those to whom Nari's wisdom has not been revealed must not be tolerated, and that Narida must be undivided?' Some of Darel's sudden trepidation must have shown on his face, because Hiran made a dismissive gesture. 'Your friend is not accusing you of blasphemy, Darel! Academics consider such questions all the time, for we must look at things from many angles to understand the truth of them.'

'Your friend would remind you that he has seen shame enough today,' Darel muttered, reaching for the wine jug and uncorking it. 'To openly disagree with the judgement of the God-King would likely see his scabbard blackened, and what remains of his honour would be gone.'

'Your friend was not talking of the God-King's judgement, but of the words he quoted,' Hiran said. 'Your friend has often wondered about those particular beliefs of General Garadh. It suggests that we can never accept those who do not worship Nari into our society, and yet if they are not welcomed, how will they ever learn of His glory? Not to mention the fact Morlithian traders still come through the Torgallen Pass, ever more frequently as the death of Natan II fades in the memory, while our ports welcome sailors from the City of Islands, and sometimes even farther afield. We will trade with these people, for we like what they offer, yet by the words of the man responsible for the ordering of our society, we should view them with great mistrust, and possibly greet them with violence.'

'Viewing merchants with great mistrust is not an unwise decision,' Darel muttered, which provoked a laugh. 'But you are correct. Your friend knows the people of the Catseyes are not always well liked in the lands that border that range, yet those of the Smoking Valley are friendly to Blackcreek, and come to Black Keep to trade every year. One of them even lives in our town, and your friend does not think she is the first to have ever done so.' He poured some wine into his goblet, then did the same for Hiran. 'Our friendship with the Smoking Valley has only brought benefits for both of us, unless they have been engaging in some generations-long deception that has yet to reveal itself. But they do not worship Nari. Amonhuhe respects our beliefs, but she does not share them.'

'Your friend wonders if we trust overmuch in our own wisdom,' Hiran said, taking a sip of wine. 'Narida, that is, rather than us two specifically. We can build on the knowledge of those that came before, of course, but we should not limit ourselves to it. And we are all of us but men. Even General Garadh was but a man, albeit one who stood and fought alongside the Divine One, and guided His infant son after His death.'

'Perhaps the fighting was the problem,' Darel suggested. 'Perhaps if Narida had been at peace for longer before the Divine One died, He would not have seen fit to instruct General Garadh as He did.' He laughed. 'Can you imagine it if Nari had summoned Tolkar to Him instead of Garadh, on His death bed? Would our country have ended up being ruled not by warriors, but by . . . academics, perhaps?'

'Hah!' Hiran laughed in turn. 'And in the capital, there would be a university funded by the crown that taught swordplay to the second and third sons of nobles, or those who showed no aptitude for studying!'

'That would be a strange land indeed,' Darel said. He took a mouthful of wine. He had no intention of getting too drunk: that too was shameful, since a sar should always be ready for combat, and he was very aware of the expectations upon him now his role was so reduced. However, there was no doubt that the alcohol, and the presence of Hiran, was helping take the edge off the sharp-toothed misery that had been pressing down on him. 'Does anyone know what happened to Tolkar, by the way?'

'Not for sure,' Hiran replied. 'He disappears from records very soon after Nari's death. Some contemporary accounts speculate that grief drove him away; others, that he exiled himself rather than see General Garadh take up the position of Eastern Marshal.' He scratched his nose. 'There have been suggestions made since that Garadh had him quietly killed, but they are not from that time. Although of course, if Garadh had done it, and had it done quietly, he would not have wanted anyone speculating in that direction.'

Darel gaped at him. 'People have actually suggested that? That one of the Divine Nari's two greatest followers would have killed the other?'

'Pure speculation, nothing more,' Hiran replied. 'It is easy to draw conclusions that the two men did not like each other, and that once Nari had passed from this world there was no longer the same power to unify them, but you cannot take it further than that. However, the fact remains there are no confirmed reports of Tolkar after he left Idramar for the final time . . . assuming he ever did.'

'THE WINE APPEARS to be gone,' Hiran said, inspecting the jug.

'Well, we have been drinking it,' Darel observed.

'There is more in your friend's chambers,' Hiran said. 'Although he should probably not keep you from your rest any longer.'

'It is fine,' Darel assured him. The oil in his lamp had burned low, and the night was wearing on, but he still felt no urge towards sleep. Illogical though it was, something lurked at the back of his skull which suggested that if he lay down to sleep, then when morning came the truth of his failure would be immovable, whereas if he remained awake it would still be nascent. 'If you do not yet wish for rest yourself, your friend would appreciate your company for a while longer.'

Hiran smiled. 'Well then, if you are up for a trek, we shall go and find it!'

'Lead on,' Darel told him, picking up his sword belt and strapping it around his waist. 'Oh, do not look at your friend like that,' he added, catching the glance Hiran gave the weapons. 'He has already been stripped of his lands and title of thane today; he is not going to give anyone who sees him even at this late hour the notion that he is no longer a sar either.'

'A fair point,' Hiran acknowledged, rising to his feet as well. His negotiation of the table as he moved towards the door suggested to Darel that Hiran was perhaps a little more under the influence of the wine, despite the reasonably sedate pace at which they had consumed it.

Well, at least this sar is not a failure at remaining relatively sober. A small victory, but one he will take today.

The hallways of the Sun Palace were dark and deserted, and Darel's oil lamp cast shadows that slowly shifted and flowed as they walked. The light bled over decorative tapestries, revealing them piece by piece, almost as though they were being created anew, just out of view.

'Your friend hopes you can remember the way back to your quarters,' he said quietly to Hiran. 'He might have managed it in daylight, but he is not yet used to the Sun Palace after dark.'

'Do not concern yourself about that,' Hiran scoffed. 'It is this way.' He took a few more steps before he spoke next. 'Darel, what will you do on the morrow?'

'Your friend had honestly not thought that far ahead,' Darel replied. He grimaced. 'By the Mountain, he has simply been wallowing in self-pity, hasn't he?'

'It has only been one evening, and the God-King's judgement was a great shock,' Hiran replied soothingly. 'Your friend merely meant that he was not sure if you were going to try to get back to

Black Keep before the God-King's message reaches the thane of Darkspur, or at least before Darkspur's forces reach your home.'

Darel could have thrown the lamp down in anger at himself. 'Of course! Daimon must be warned!' He shook his head. 'If anything, this only shows the wisdom of the judgement. Your friend was so concerned about his foolish *honour* that he did not consider what he should be doing.' But to properly consider the ramifications of the God-King's words meant truly accepting what had happened that day, and if he was honest with himself, Darel was not sure he had done so. He still felt as though, at any moment, someone was going to announce that it had all been a mistake, or a test, or . . . Well, perhaps that was the wine.

'In fairness, you should probably not be doing anything of the sort,' Hiran said carefully. 'After all, the God-King's judgement was to send a message to Darkspur, not to Black Keep. However,' he lowered his voice a little more, even though there was no one around, 'if you intend to leave, you will need a mount, or passage on a ship. Your friend has little influence in this city – or anywhere, for that matter – but he might be able to assist.'

'You would do such a thing?' Darel asked him.

'Your friend would prefer you stayed here,' Hiran admitted. 'Perhaps you could even study at the university! But if you wish to go south yourself, rather than entrust such a message to someone else, your friend will do his best to help.'

'That is very kind of you,' Darel said, although the response was a reflexive one. He was already considering what he should do. He was a decent enough rider on Quill, but he had no experience at journeys longer than the few days to some of the outlying Blackcreek villages. The notion of taking an unknown mount and setting off on his own across half of Narida, or near enough, was a daunting one. On the other hand, he had already experienced the dangers of sea travel once, and the next time he would likely not be sailing with other sars. Nor, indeed, would he have the authority of the Southern Marshal to ensure the captain and crew were on their best behaviour. Sailors had a reputation as being dishonest and money-hungry, and although Darel did not like to put stock in such depictions, a man travelling alone would benefit from being suspicious of the motives of others.

'Darel,' Hiran said, breaking into his thoughts.

'Hmm?'

'Are there not usually guards here?'

Darel paused and looked about him. The corridor they had been following now intersected with a larger one that led off to their right, while to their left was a large archway covered by a curtain, in front of which, yes, normally stood two guards.

'Perhaps they are not required at night?' he suggested, but that made little sense. Beyond the archway lay the more private areas of the Sun Palace, such as those given over to the living quarters of the Divine Family.

'Darel,' Hiran said, and this time there was a catch of fear in his voice as he pointed downwards. Darel followed his gesture, and a hand of sickly ice seized his throat as he saw what his friend had spotted.

Poking out from underneath the curtain on one side was a boot, and it was quite clear from the angle of it that the owner of the foot on which it was worn was lying prostrate on the floor beyond.

Darel glanced up at the sconces on either side of the archway, in which tall, fat candles had been burning every time he had come past in the evening. The candles were there, but had been blown out. Not long ago, either; now he was paying attention, he could smell the lingering scent of the smoke.

'Take the lamp,' he instructed Hiran, passing it to him. Then he drew his longblade, trying not to notice how much his hands were shaking. Raiders and pirates had been enough to try his courage, but at least they had been threats in expected places.

This should not be happening in the Sun Palace, the heart of Naridan power.

'Stay behind your friend,' he told Hiran, and drew a curtain back with one hand while holding his sword ready to strike in the other.

Two guards lay on the sandstone floor, both in the livery of the Sun Palace, both with gaping wounds in the side of their necks and a dark pool of blood around them. One was sitting up against the wall, his head lolling over to one side and his right hand drenched in red; it seemed he had futilely tried to staunch the wound. The other, he whose foot had protruded beyond the curtain, was on his front, a drawn dagger next to his limp hand.

'Oh, Nari's teeth!' Hiran exclaimed softly, his hand flying to his mouth. 'Darel, we must get help!'

Darel knelt down, instinctively keeping his robes clear of the blood, and laid his hand on the neck of the guard who had drawn his dagger.

'He is still warm,' he murmured. 'This did not happen long ago!' He rose back to his feet and drew his shortblade, then reversed his grip on it and held it out to Hiran. 'Here. Go and seek aid.'

'What are you going to do?' Hiran asked, his tone laced with suspicion.

'Find whoever did this,' Darel said grimly. 'Something is gravely amiss here, and whatever else your friend may or may not be, he is still a sar of Narida. Go!' he repeated, as Hiran hesitated. 'Or come with your friend, if you wish, but he will seek out this problem himself!'

'At least tell your friend which way you are going, so that he knows where to come to you with aid,' Hiran begged him.

'Towards the God-King's chambers,' Darel said. He took a deep breath, and turned away from his friend and the light of the oil lamp, and towards the unknown darkness of the Sun Palace's interior. 'May the Divine One's blessings go with you, Hiran.'

'And with you,' he heard Hiran reply uncertainly from behind him, and then Darel had turned a corner and was on his own.

YARMINA

THEY WERE THREE days' ride from Black Keep, and after the first day they had left the footmen and Yarmina's maid behind to follow as they would. A dragon's walking pace was not that much quicker than a man's, but Omet had alternated his beast between walking and cantering, and the rest of them had kept up, Yarmina included. When asked why they were hurrying so, Omet had merely muttered something about important business to attend to back at Darkspur. Yarmina had not pushed him on it. She was no Raider chief, fur-clad and with a strange stone-edged axe on her belt, to intimidate men into doing as she pleased. The balance of authority between Darkspur's heir and Darkspur's steward was a delicate one, and one Omet would happily ignore if he thought Yarmina's father would side with him.

That did not mean she had given up on finding out. It just meant she would have to use the traditional methods of Naridan women: to whit, waiting until the men were distracted or drunk, or preferably both, and listening to them when they thought she was somewhere else.

It helped that their baggage animals carried a small tent for her use, since although it was fine for sars and footmen to sleep under the spring sky wrapped in nothing more than their cloaks and with a fire or each other's backs for warmth, such hardship would never do for the female heir of Darkspur. In truth, Yarmina would have dearly welcomed someone else's back – or front, or side, or anything really – but sleeping alone had its benefits. As did the fact she had insisted on bringing her hunting clothes for travelling in, saving the formal robes for her utterly pointless days at Black Keep, parading around the castle and town trying to make Omet think she was flirting with Daimon.

She slipped out of the back of her tent, dressed in close-fitting leathers. Hunting was not a traditional pastime for a young Naridan noblewoman, but neither was it unheard of, and her mother had accompanied her father on enough hunts that Yarmina's interest in it had not been unexpected. In truth, she liked the feel and look of the clothes more than she enjoyed hunting itself, but they were more practical for riding than her normal attire, and certainly better suited to sneaking around after dark.

She had retired early, with her tent pitched far enough from the fire to give her some privacy, and so far as any of her travelling companions knew, she was slumbering within. It was far easier to fool them when they were not expecting to see her actual body sleeping between some tree roots, and sure enough, the four sars were clustered around the fire, speaking in low voices. Yarmina circled around out of the circle of light, relying on the fire's crackles and snaps to occlude any noise she made underfoot, and crept in closer using the great tree trunks to obscure her from view. There she stood, straight and tall in the shadow of the final trunk, mere yards away from Sar Omet's back.

' . . . two more days, and we should be back home by nightfall,' Omet was saying.

'How long to rally the land?' Lahel asked.

'We have been over this before,' Omet replied, somewhat testily. 'A matter of days. It should not take long to be ready again, after the last march.'

'It's the last march that concerns this sar,' said Aharin. He was the youngest of the four sars that Yarmina's father had sent with her, and she had him down as fairly sensible, if perhaps a little more cautious than honour might truly dictate. 'We already marched on Black Keep once, and the Southern Marshal gave them his blessing.'

'That was before we knew they harboured a witch,' Omet said with a snort. 'The Hand of Heaven might see nothing wrong with more backs to labour to put coin in his coffers, even if they are Nari-damned Raiders, but he will not feel the same way about witchcraft, you mark this steward's words.'

Yarmina grimaced. Her father's dislike for his neighbours had not perished along with Lord Asrel, it seemed, and he'd had his eye on Blackcreek for as long as she could remember. She had half-suspected that if his plans to subsume it by marriage failed, he would try a more direct method. She had not thought he would move so blatantly and so quickly, however.

'Besides, where his lordship went wrong last time was waiting for Marshal Kaldur's approval,' Immanel said, and Yarmina winced as she pictured Omet's expression in her mind. Immanel was as skilled in combat as he was unable to guard his tongue, and it was only a matter of time before the latter overtook the former in terms of her father's willingness to keep him around.

'Immanel!' Omet snapped. 'Mind your words!'

'This sar speaks the truth,' Immanel replied pugnaciously. 'Steward or no steward, you can't argue that, Omet! If we'd swept down on Black Keep, butchered the Raiders and declared the Blackcreek nobles as traitors, who would have argued with his lordship? History is written by the victors. You know that as well as this sar does.'

'Mind. Your. Words,' Omet said again, biting his own words off. Yarmina heard a sigh of vexation, but Immanel didn't reply again.

'He's right that we shouldn't wait for the Southern Marshal this time,' Lahel said.

'Of course we will not wait for the Southern Marshal,' Omet

snapped. 'He is in Idramar, if Daimon Blackcreek is to be believed. Even if we wanted to, we do not have the time to wait for a message to get there and back. The Black Keep party to the mountains might have returned by then, and if they bring word of our men up there then Blackcreek will march on *us*.'

Yarmina frowned. What men? Her father had sent some to protect their outlying farms from attacks, as Omet had told Daimon just before the Black Keep reeve had burst in announcing the witch, but they wouldn't be in the lands bordering Blackcreek country.

Aharin laughed. 'You can't mean that, Omet? Blackcreek march on Darkspur? Why?'

'The Blackcreek boys clearly view the mountain savages as their allies, else why send a party into those Nari-forsaken peaks?' Omet said. 'This steward doubts they will take kindly to finding the savages in chains while our men take their gold. Either that party will return with word, or they won't return at all, and Blackcreek will send more. One way or another, they will find the truth before long.'

Yarmina bit her lip. Gold in the mountains? She could see why that would tempt her father into sending men there. And unlike Blackcreek, Darkspur certainly had no alliance with the mountain people on their borders. They had always been aloof at best, and murderous at worst.

Or so she had always been told.

Her father had lied to her: by omission, if by nothing else. Perhaps men had indeed been sent to protect the outlying farms, but it was unfeasible he might have forgotten that either those men, or others, had been sent much farther into the mountains to enslave the mountain folk who traded with the Blackcreek lands. And were the mountain people truly as savage as she'd been led to believe? It seemed unlikely that those from the Smoking Valley would trade happily with Naridans, while those only slightly further north would be rapacious thieves and murderers.

Blackcreek had already made peace with the Raiders from across the sea. Saana had come offering that peace – albeit with the threat of war behind it – and it had won out for long enough that the war had never needed to come. What if, in times past, Blackcreek had approached the mountain folk as allies, whereas Darkspur had behaved like the Raiders of old, taking what they pleased and leaving ruin behind? Could it be *Naridan* attitudes that were key to the difference between friendly, trading neighbours, and ones that would cut your head off as soon as look at you?

Yarmina strongly suspected that even if that were true, her father would not be swayed on it. In any case, things had been too bad for too long for it to be any other way.

That was a worry for another time, however: one for when she was back at Darkspur, at the very least, and perhaps for some day in the future when the rule of the lands had fallen to her. For now, she had a greater concern.

One way or another, war was coming between Blackcreek and Darkspur. Yarmina could not fault Omet's logic: her father would seize on the news of the witch at Black Keep to march on their southern neighbours with all the force he could muster as quickly as he could, both to prevent them from hearing news from their search party and readying themselves for war in turn, and so that no higher authority could call him off. Immanel was correct as well: history was indeed written by the victors.

A proper Naridan noble daughter would pay no mind to this while her father still ruled. Even if she was taking an interest in the affairs of her lands in order to be well-versed in them when the time came to take control of them – assuming she had not been married off first to a young nobleman, whom she would then be expected to obey – she should do nothing other than pay attention. Her father was not only her father, but her thane: in some respects, he wielded twice as much authority over her as he did over anyone else.

However, Yarmina Darkspur had never really been a proper Naridan noble daughter. She had known that from childhood, when the other thanes and ladies would subtly – or not so subtly – turn their noses up at her mother. She had known it when Asrel Blackcreek had refused her father's offer of marriage between their children based on her Morlithian blood. She had seen it in the faces of those sars and servants – not all of them, but enough of them – who, had she not been their thane's daughter, would have happily chased her from the castle thanks to what her mother's people had done in the Torgallen Pass.

Pretty much everyone throughout her life had reminded her that she was not a proper Naridan. Even her father, whom she genuinely believed had affection for her, would thoughtlessly refer to any behaviour of hers he didn't like as stemming from her 'mother's wilfulness'. Oddly, what Thane Odem professed to have admired in his wife, he disliked in his daughter.

Well, if she could not be the proper Naridan daughter of her father, she could certainly be the Morlithian daughter of her mother Izdiyah, who thought for herself, took no shit and paid little attention to the expectations of Naridan nobles.

Least of all, in the latter days before she returned to the land of her birth, those of Odem Darkspur.

ZHANNA

'THAT WAS WHAT the Flatlanders call a thundertooth?' Longjaw said, as they advanced side-by-side into Winterhome with Zhanna's dragons alongside them.

'You saw it?' Zhanna asked. As two able-bodied warriors who hadn't been starved and chained for months, she and Tsennan had volunteered to be the first in to check the Smoking Valley's rock house for stragglers.

'I did,' Tsennan confirmed. 'I tell you, Zhanna, if these mountains *don't* lead to the underworld, then there needs to be a very good explanation for all the shit that lives up here.'

Zhanna snorted with amusement. 'I wonder if it would be possible to ride one.'

'What, are you spirit-touched?' Tsennan exclaimed, looking at her in consternation. 'Never try to ride something that can eat you!'

'Just keep your eyes pointing that way,' Zhanna said, nodding past him. Longjaw sighed, but turned away from her again.

'That just seems like a good rule, in general,' he said.

'Not looking at me?'

'I meant "never try to ride something that can eat you", but that works too.'

Winterhome was like nothing Zhanna had seen before. She had

no idea how long the Smoking Valley people had used it, but the floor was worn down to an almost uniform smoothness – so smooth, in fact, that in places where a passage sloped upwards or downwards the footing wasn't always entirely secure – and the ceiling was stained black with the collected smoke of countless nightfires and cookfires. She tried to imagine how much time it would have taken to carve it all out of the mountain's arm, and her mind simply retreated from the concept.

Generations. It must have taken generations. Unless they had simply been enlarging on caves that had already existed, such as the one her party had sheltered in, but even then . . .

They drew level with an opening that led off the passage and into a room of some sort, and Talon sniffed, stiffened, and rattled at it. Zhanna snapped around and brought her longblade and shield to bear, but the room, illuminated in flickers and starts by the small, dying fire in the centre of it, did nothing to draw her eye.

'What is it?' Tsennan asked from behind her.

'Don't know,' Zhanna replied. She did not want to come across as jumpy, but she'd found that it was worth listening to her dragons.

'Well, if there's someone in there, give them a chance to show themselves,' Tsennan said. 'Your Naridan's better than mine.'

Zhanna nodded, and switched languages. 'Who is there? Come out!'

Nothing. She eyed the room closely. There were several piles of blankets on the floor, and on the other side of it was an animal hide drawn across to obscure an alcove of some sort. This must have been one of the places where the men of Darkspur had been sleeping, prior to being roused by the commotion outside. None of the blanket piles looked to be occupied, but it was better to be safe than sorry . . .

'Find,' she ordered in Tjakorshi. Talon and Thorn bounded forward, and headed unerringly for the animal hide. Zhanna and Tsennan followed them, even though Zhanna for a moment wondered if it was just the hide that they'd scented, but then they gripped it in their teeth and hauled on it until it tumbled down to reveal someone who yelped in fear at the two dragons so revealed. He flinched again as he caught sight of the two Tjakorshi, then froze as Zhanna whipped her longblade up under his jaw.

'That's not a Naridan,' Tsennan said, lowering his blackstone axe, and he was right. The person now staring wide-eyed at Zhanna down the length of her blade bore a greater resemblance to one of the Smoking Valley people than he did to the Naridans like Avisha or Ravel, but there were differences there, too. He also wore wooden beads, but instead of around his neck or in a beard, these were sewn on to his clothing. Zhanna hadn't seen that on anyone else, and she was sure she would have done, even though the ex-captives' clothes were unwashed and ripped.

'I think he's one of the Two Peaks people,' she said slowly to Tsennan, not taking her eyes off the person at the other end of her blade. 'Did you see any others outside?'

'Not that I remember,' the Longjaw admitted. 'I wasn't looking too closely at the ones trying to kill us, though.' He hissed through his teeth. 'So what do we do with him? Kill him?'

'No,' Zhanna said immediately. She eyed her captive and switched back to Naridan. 'You. Any others in here?'

The Two Peaks man – if that was the right term, given that he probably wasn't any older than Tsennan – just looked at her, his eyes as wide and unblinking as those of a dead fish, and with about as much comprehension. Either her accent was awful, or his command of Naridan was non-existent, or possibly both.

'I don't think he understands me,' she told Tsennan.

'You don't say.'

She sighed. 'We'll take him back out to Amonhuhe.'

Tsennan snorted. 'Are you sure you don't want to just kill him here? It would probably save time.'

'No,' Zhanna said again, firmly. There was a difference between killing people trying to kill her or those she'd taken it upon herself to protect, and killing someone who posed no threat. Perhaps that made her soft, or foolish, but she was increasingly certain it was the right way. 'Amonhuhe doesn't rule here, anyway. It might not be her who makes the decision about him, and someone out there can probably talk to him in a language he understands. I'd rather know if he has any friends hiding in any other corners.'

'Fine,' Tsennan said. He took his blackstone axe into his shield hand, then used his empty hand to tap the man on the chest and then point at the door. The captive, with another nervous look at Zhanna, began to edge in that direction as instructed. 'But I'm not standing next to him when we get out there. I've got enough blood on my clothes for one night.'

'HE IS Two Peaks,' Amonhuhe confirmed to them. The captive had been interrogated none-too-gently by a collection of the older Smoking Valley members, but he was still alive. Amonhuhe herself had stood by and listened, although Zhanna had been able to see the other woman's impatience. However, whatever the Smoking Valley's attitude was to a woman who'd been living elsewhere for twenty years, it didn't seem to include granting her authority, and their equivalent of a witches' council still appeared to be in charge. 'His name is Tatan Igan. And he is a fool, and a coward,' she added, scathingly.

'For not fighting with the Darkspur men?' Zhanna asked.

'For not helping this woman's people to fight *against* them,' Amonhuhe countered. 'He claims the lowlanders have been causing his people problems for years; blaming them for raids in the lower hills, and then hunting them down and killing them. He says they fought back sometimes, but there were always more lowlanders to replace the ones they killed.' She sighed and spat. 'This woman supposes that part is true enough. Anyway, his family were found by these men of Darkspur, who'd seen gold in the river running through Two Peaks land and thought there would be more higher up. They were all set to come here and enslave this woman's people – they had the chains, and the numbers – but they needed guides.'

'So his family was to be guide,' Zhanna said heavily.

'They refused to come here for payment,' Amonhuhe said. 'Not because they didn't want to betray us; they were just scared. But then the lowlanders threatened to kill their children if they didn't do as they said, so he and his father and his uncle agreed to show the lowlanders the way to Winterhome, and pretend to us that they were trusted traders known to their family.' She hissed through her teeth. 'They could have crept away once they were in this valley. Or our tongues are close enough: they could have spoken with this woman's people and told the truth. Instead they kept up the pretence out of fear, and that first night the lowlanders struck while everyone slept.'

Zhanna tapped her fingers on the hilt of her longblade. 'Where are his father and uncle?' No one else had been found in the rock house.

Amonhuhe sucked her teeth. 'Killed by the lowlanders for fun, or so he claims. He watched them die, and was too scared to do anything about it.' She shrugged. 'A coward and a fool, as this woman said.'

Or perhaps he feared what would happen to the rest of his family once the lowlanders were done here if he disobeyed them, Zhanna thought to herself. 'What will be done with him?' she asked instead.

'The elders haven't decided,' Amonhuhe said, casting a long, dark look in Tatan Igan's direction. 'They may decide to let him go, and if he can make it back to his family alone, then so be it. Or they may decide to kill him, and be done with.' Her tone of voice clearly indicated which option she would prefer.

'How are your people's supplies?' Zhanna asked. It wasn't just an attempt to steer the topic on to less bloody grounds: if there was no food left then they were all in trouble, not just the people of the Smoking Valley.

'Poor,' Amonhuhe said bitterly. 'The lowlanders ate wastefully, and obviously planned to leave once our food was gone, letting this woman's people starve.' She shook her head. 'There may yet be time for some crops, but not many, and this woman's people are weak. It will be hard work to clear the weeds and break the ground, and they do not have much strength to hunt, or gather the other food we would normally find at this time of year.'

Zhanna nodded gloomily. 'What about us?'

Amonhuhe sighed. 'This woman's people are grateful. They were ready to fight, but the chance never came where they could be sure the children would not be harmed. We gave them that opportunity. They will share what they have with us, but we must leave soon, otherwise we may do more harm than good here.'

That was better than Zhanna might have expected. She could have easily envisaged a scenario where, with food stocks low, the people of the Smoking Valley would prioritise their own over outsiders. Perhaps it helped that Amonhuhe was with them; and Tatiosh as well. Zhanna had seen him greeting people to whom he was apparently related through his mother, and speaking to them somewhat haltingly in their own tongue. Some had seen him before, of course – those who had made the trading trip to Black Keep since his birth – but some had never met their new relative.

There were others to whom Tatiosh was related who had never got the opportunity to meet him. Behind each building were shallow graves that had been dug by the enslaved for their own dead. Zhanna hadn't counted them, but it was many more than just one or two. Menaken would join them in the morning. For now he was in a small antechamber with a couple of the Smoking Valley people who had fallen in the fight, and Avisha and Ravel had said what prayers they knew of their folk over him.

It wasn't enough to have come here and helped these people free themselves. They were better off than they had been, but that didn't mean they were in a good position. The winter up here looked to be as harsh as any on Tjakorsha, despite being further north, and that was not something to be braved without enough food stores.

'What if we stay long enough to break ground?' she suggested. 'We are not weak from hunger. Can make start, do hardest job.'

Amonhuhe raised her eyebrows. 'You would do that?'

'We come here because Black Keep is ally,' Zhanna told her. 'Come here to help. To leave people like this would be to only half help.' She smiled, somewhat wearily, because she was bone-tired herself right at this moment. 'Would not be honourable.'

Amonhuhe nodded slowly. 'That would help. Crops need to go into the ground as soon as possible if this woman's people are to stand any chance, but few would have the strength to use the tools.'

'Then that is what we will do,' Zhanna said. She reckoned she could talk Longjaw into it, and if she could persuade him, then Tamadh would follow, and so would Sakka and Olagora. Avisha and Ravel would surely see the sense of it too, since they were Naridan, and would appreciate the honour involved. And if not, what were they going to do? Head back to Black Keep on their own? 'This warrior is sure her mother and Daimon can cope without us for a while longer.'

'It still may not be enough, though,' Amonhuhe said sadly, looking around her. The Smoking Valley people were making Winterhome their own again, finding their spaces and removing anything left behind by Darkspur: or at least, anything they couldn't use.

Zhanna debated inwardly with herself for a moment, then decided to speak. You'd never catch a fish if you didn't cast your net, after all. 'What about the gold? Did the lowlanders leave it?'

'We can't eat gold,' Amonhuhe sniffed dismissively.

'Obviously,' Zhanna said, trying to hide her own impatience. 'The Tjakorshi do not care much for gold either. But Naridans do.

Maybe could buy food from Ironhead, or near.'

'That gold is from the Sacred River!' Amonhuhe snapped.

'Is it still sacred now it is out?' Zhanna asked. She spread her hands to try to show that she was simply asking a question, not making an argument. 'Will you be putting it back?'

Amonhuhe opened her mouth as though to reply, then paused and looked around again.

'If not,' Zhanna continued cautiously, 'it might make difference. Some could stay to work crops, others come to Narida with us and buy food.'

Amonhuhe sucked her teeth again. It seemed to be a Naridan thing, and Zhanna wondered, with the slightly fuzzy thought processes of the very tired, if it would mark Amonhuhe out among her own.

'This woman will ask. It would be for the elders to decide.' She reached out and took Zhanna's shoulder, gripping it firmly, and looked her in the eyes. For the first time, Zhanna thought she saw true respect there, as of one adult to another. 'Thank you, Zhanna. For everything you did today.'

'It is what we came here to do,' Zhanna replied. 'Once we knew it was needed, anyway.'

'Thank you, nonetheless,' Amonhuhe said. All the tension seemed to drain out of her. Perhaps she was finally realising that making decisions was someone else's problem now, at least for a short time. 'This woman should find the others, thank them too. You've all done so much—'

'Tomorrow,' Zhanna said gently, gripping her arm in return. 'Do that tomorrow. For now, we should sleep.'

Would she be able to find sleep? Zhanna half-expected it to be populated with screaming faces, vicious enemies against whom her weapons found no purchase, and the dark, looming shape of a thundertooth hunting her from the shadows.

As it turned out, the pitch black of sheer exhaustion pulled her under, and kept her there.

DAREL

THERE WERE BASICALLY no circumstances under which Darel should have been doing what he was doing.

He was no longer even a minor noble; he was only a sar, and a moderately disgraced one at that. He had absolutely no business being in this part of the Sun Palace, and certainly not with his longblade drawn. If he was discovered, the punishment would be execution.

The trouble was, someone else had clearly done exactly the same thing before him, which meant that the guards who would have discovered and executed him were already dead. He found two more uniformed corpses, as he got closer to the God-King's chambers, and his heart was pounding so fast he could barely feel the spaces between the beats. Someone was murdering their way towards Natan III, and there could surely be no good reason for doing that.

A shout rang out from ahead of him, followed immediately by a clang of steel, and Darel moved towards it immediately. He raced past ornamental vases presented to the Divine Family by vassals seeking favour or atonement, past a great tapestry depicting a battle, past a suit of armour that had undoubtedly belonged to a former God-King, and turned right to race up a small flight of stone steps.

His ears had not led him wrongly. In front of what could only be the doors of the God-King's personal quarters, judging by the sigil emblazoned above them, was a knot of struggling men, all armoured.

'Help!' one of them was bellowing. 'Treachery! Treach—!'

A blade found its mark, and the guard's desperate cry broke off into a wail of agony as he was driven back into a stone pillar by a sword in his chest. His killer withdrew the longblade, then plunged it into the guard's throat, who slumped down to join his companion who was already bleeding on the floor.

'Get that door open,' the man instructed the others with him. There were three of them, and when the door did not move at their first attempt, they began to throw their weight against it, grunting with the effort.

They had not seen Darel. He could turn and run away from these four men and their murderous intent. He could leave the God-King to his fate: after all, was Natan not the heir of Nari? The rule of the family was divine, and everlasting. There was surely nothing Darel could do to influence that, one way or the other.

Besides which, the God-King had shamed Darel in front of the Divine Court earlier that day. What loyalty did Darel have to a man who had stripped him and his brother of their nobility, and condemned the people with whom they had agreed to share their lands – including his brother's wife! – to exile or death at the hands of the thane of Darkspur?

All those thoughts flashed through Darel's mind in a moment, swift as summer lightning, but when they had passed he was still standing where he had been, longblade drawn.

The God-King was the heir of Nari, and Darel honoured Nari. To turn his back simply because of what seemed like a personal slight was the height of arrogance and hubris. Almost more importantly, he realised, he was a sar now, and *only* a sar. Would a sar turn his back on a group of men trying to unlawfully kill another man, and dismiss it as not being his problem? As being too high a risk to get himself involved in?

Darel did not think so. If being a sar was all that was left to him, he would do his best to be as true to that calling as he could.

He meant to shout something intimidating and bold: something that would halt the attackers in their tracks, give them pause, make them realise that they were dealing with a battle-hardened warrior who had fought Raiders and pirates without flinching. What in fact actually came out of his mouth was:

'*Oi!*'

It certainly halted them. All four men spun around, weapons in hand, but it wasn't the amount of sharp steel being levelled in his direction that made Darel's already overactive heart jump into his mouth. It was the face of the man closest to him: he who had killed the second guard and instructed the others to break down the God-King's door.

'Darel?' Kaldur Brightwater said, frowning. 'What in the name of the Mountain are *you* doing here?'

'This sar could ask you the same thing, High Marshal,' Darel said warily, his mind racing. Could it be that . . . ? No, there was no plausible reason why the Southern Marshal would have crept through the Sun Palace, killing guards, and was now trying to break into the God-King's chambers. Darel had not thoughtlessly intruded on some legitimate activity of the Inner Council. This could only be treason, plain and simple and shocking.

No one was to be trusted in the Sun Palace, it seemed. Not even the man who had given Darel that very same piece of advice.

'This marshal did not tell you to stop,' Brightwater snapped over his shoulder, and after a moment's more hesitation the three men with him – the sars Modorin, Kyrel and Tenan, Darel realised – turned back to putting their shoulders to the door. It was holding for the moment, but who could say for how much longer?

'Blackcreek,' Brightwater said, returning his attention to Darel, 'you should—'

'That is not this sar's name,' Darel snapped at him. 'Not any longer.'

'And is that not the point, Darel of Black Keep?' Brightwater demanded. 'We come here to Idramar, we bring news of a historic, peaceful alliance between our people and the Raiders from across the sea, and it is dismissed out of hand!' He swung his own free hand as if to illustrate his words, and Darel realised that the anger on the Southern Marshal's face was not directed at him, for interrupting proceedings.

Kaldur Brightwater was furious, and he was furious with the God-King.

'Once again, the South is ignored!' Brightwater practically spat. 'Your work, your efforts, and those of your brother, ignored! This marshal's recommendations, ignored! And that fool Greenbrook is raised to Eastern Marshal, for what reason? As a sop to the fact the Divine Princess killed his cousin, and escaped judgement for it?'

'This sar does not disagree with anything you have said,' Darel replied, edging closer. How long could he engage Brightwater in conversation like this? How long until he needed to do . . . *something* about the men trying to break into Natan's chambers? 'But your response to these slights is to assassinate the God-King?!'

'Is he the God-King?' Brightwater demanded, with such venom that Darel froze instinctively. 'Is he really? We have spoken before of the rumours and signs that the Divine One has returned, Darel! This can only lead to the sort of strife that occurred in the time of the Splinter King, but how much worse will it be now the issue of rightful rule is not between half-brothers, but a descendant and the reborn? This marshal spoke to you and your brother about the need to avoid another Splintering; that the South must be whole, and Blackcreek must be true! *It is upon us!*'

Darel bit his lip. 'A new Splintering? You truly think so?'

'Of course!' Brightwater said. 'As every day passes, it becomes clearer and clearer! The Divine One has been reborn, and Natan and Tila will refuse to surrender the throne; they refuse to even consider the possibility. Marshal Coldbeck knew this, but he sought to isolate Natan until the true ruler could arise to replace him. He lacked vision. He lacked commitment. The prophecies say that Nari will return when His people have need of Him, Darel.' Brightwater gestured at the door behind him. 'When we remove the God-King, Narida will need guidance like never before. Nari will make Himself known, and He will return to us.'

'What do you think He will think of the man who killed His lineage?' Darel asked. He kept his eyes fixed on Brightwater to look for signs of an attack, but there was no indication the Southern Marshal was planning on anything other than swaying him with words.

Brightwater shrugged in response to Darel's question. 'This marshal cares not. That He will have returned to us is enough. If He feels that this marshal must be punished for his actions, that is a price this marshal is willing to pay.' He extended his hand. 'Come, Darel. This marshal will become steward of the throne until Nari Himself arrives to claim it. In the meantime we can right certain wrongs, such as the decree for Darkspur to drive the Tjakorshi from Black Keep and subsume the lands that are rightfully yours.'

Hope clutched at Darel's heart. Selfish, greedy hope, that he might once again be a thane. He had never known anything but the status of nobility, and to have it stripped from him had been the greatest shock of his life, even for the duration of one evening in which he had barely interacted with the world. Now the possibility of restoration was being waved in front of him and it glittered in his mind. He could tell himself he would be doing it for Daimon too – to prevent his brother from being disowned for a second time in a matter of months – but that would be a lie. Darel wanted this for himself, and he wanted it desperately.

All he had to do was stand by while these men over whom he had no authority, and who he had no hope of stopping by himself, took power from the man who had so callously dismissed Darel's family into oblivion.

'You say you will "remove" the God-King,' he said to Brightwater. 'You mean "kill", do you not?'

'The God-King, and the Divine Princess,' Brightwater replied shortly. 'Narida has seen what happens when a pretender to the throne is not dealt with appropriately: the exiles in Kiburu ce Alaba, who have mocked us for centuries with their bloodline's continued existence. This marshal will not make that same mistake. This time, there will be no rallying point left for the misguided.' He beckoned once more. 'Come, Darel. You have proved yourself both in wisdom and in combat to this marshal. Join him: for the sake of reclaiming Blackcreek, if nothing else.'

On the marshland east of Black Keep, Darel's brother Daimon had turned his back on honour in the interests of ensuring the survival of his home. He had betrayed his father, and Darel himself, to ally with the Raiders from across the sea and prevent war. Darel, stuck in his ways as he had been, had been unable to see the wisdom of Daimon's actions. He would have clung to loyalty in the face of sense, and doomed himself in the process.

He would not make that mistake a second time.

He lowered his longblade and forced his neck muscles into a nod. 'Aye. This sar is with you, High Marshal.'

What looked to be a genuine smile spread over Kaldur Brightwater's face. 'Truly, this marshal is glad. Now come. We must get this done, and quickly!'

'It's moving, lord!' Sar Modorin said breathlessly and, sure enough, something cracked in the door as they rammed themselves into it one more time. Darel, moving up behind them at Brightwater's side, was abruptly aware of his missing shortblade and the fact he had sent Hiran to get help. He had been so astounded at what he found that he never thought to threaten the High Marshal with the prospect of reinforcements, and it was too late now in any case. There was nothing left to do but to see this through, and deal with the aftermath whenever it arrived.

Darel found himself desperately hoping that, whatever the outcome of this night was, Hiran would not despise him at the end of it.

Brightwater's armsmen made one more charge at the door, and whatever lock or bar had been holding it closed burst out of the frame. The door lurched inwards and Brightwater's men staggered with it, readying their weapons for whatever might be within.

'What is the meaning of this?' a voice thundered, and there in a doorway, silhouetted against the flicking light of a lamp, was Natan III, God-King of Narida, a naked longblade in his hand. 'Brightwater?'

'Your Majesty,' Brightwater said, his voice as tight as a bowstring. 'It is over.'

'Brightwater?' a female voice echoed the God-King, and another figure appeared alongside Natan. It had to be the Divine Princess: even Darel knew that the God-King was not going to have a female lover in his chambers. To his greater surprise, she had a gleaming knife in each hand, one of which she pointed straight at the Southern Marshal. 'You piece of shit-stained harbour filth! Go fuck your mother's corpse!'

This outpouring of profanity from the Divine Princess, more appropriate for a sailor, momentarily stopped everyone in their tracks in utter shock. Brightwater recovered himself first and took a step forward, his longblade in his hand.

Darel's lashed out for Sar Tenan's neck.

Haste and fear made him clumsy, and his blow only caught Tenan's shoulder. None of Brightwater and his men were wearing helmets – that would have been too strange if they'd been seen in the palace – but each was in his coat-of-nails, and the maille within turned Darel's blade, although the force of the blow knocked the other sar a step sideways. Darel parried Tenan's instinctive counter-cut, dodged back from the man's next stroke delivered with killing intent, then lunged along his centre line. A sar's longblade was a weapon more designed for slashing cuts than for thrusts, but the tip of it was still pointed and sharp enough to pierce his enemy's throat. Tenan staggered backwards, all thoughts of fighting gone as he clutched at the wound that was now leaking blood down his neck.

'Blackcreek!' Brightwater snarled, rounding on him. 'What in—?'

'Blackcreek must be true!' Darel shouted at him, trying to keep the Southern Marshal, Sar Kyrel and Sar Modorin in view all at once. They were all armoured, and he was in naught but his robes: there was very little chance of this ending well for him. 'This sar might not bear its name any longer, but he still carries its honour!'

'You would turn on the man next to you without warning, and call it honour?' Brightwater bawled. He rolled his neck and gripped the hilt of his longblade in both hands, then spoke to the remaining two sars. 'See to the God-King. The fool's death belongs to this marshal.'

Kyrel and Modorin turned and made for the God-King and the Divine Princess, but Darel could do no more about that, because the Southern Marshal was coming for him.

Darel could flee, of course. He was closer to the door than Brightwater, so he could escape and run for it, or back off and seek to draw his enemy after him. However, he had made the decision to try to prevent Brightwater's men from killing Natan Narida, and he couldn't very well do that if he was halfway down a corridor, even if he managed to defeat Kaldur Brightwater while he was there.

'You do not wish to sully your own sword with divine blood?' he said, hoping to provoke a rash attack.

'Those deaths are necessary,' Brightwater replied. 'Yours will be this marshal's vengeance for your treachery!'

'Treachery? Where is the honour in breaking into the God-King's chambers at night with armed men and seeking to murder him?' Darel demanded. Brightwater was, annoyingly, not being easily drawn.

'Service to a higher purpose transcends such considerations,' the Southern Marshal snarled, gliding closer.

'Honour is only ever a convenience for us, is it not?' Darel replied, grinning mirthlessly. All his life he had assumed that other nobles, more important nobles, knew without question and embodied without effort the ideals he struggled to enact. Now he had spent a matter of days in the heart of Narida's nobility, and all his illusions had been swept away.

So why risk his life for Natan Narida?

Even a man who had lost his faith in his betters still needed something to hold on to. Until the Divine Nari Himself returned and declared otherwise, Darel was going to presume that His descendants were the rightful rulers of Narida, and behave accordingly. If that meant lying to deceive a traitor, and performing a coward's blow on a fellow sar, so be it.

As the Southern Marshal himself had said, service to a higher purpose transcended such considerations.

Kaldur Brightwater's lip twitched, but he made no further rejoinders. Instead he flowed into the attack, and there was no more time for words.

TILA

THEY BOTH HEARD the shouts and screams from outside, and the shout of 'Treachery!'. To Tila's astonishment, not to mention alarm, Natan approached the door as it began to thump on its hinges.

'What are you doing?' she hissed at him, grabbing his arm. 'Get back here!'

'Get back to where?' he demanded, shaking himself loose. 'Should we try climbing out of a window?'

Tila grimaced. 'As high as we are?' She looked down at herself. She was still in her dress from the feast. 'Not in this. Your sister might as well break her own neck and have done with it.'

'And your brother does not have your experience in climbing walls,' Natan pointed out. He drew their father's sword from its scabbard and put his eye to the peephole in the door. 'At least we can see who we are dealing with.'

Tila expected the door to give way and strike him, but it held long enough for her brother to sneak a look, then back away hurriedly with his weapon raised somewhat inexpertly in front of him. 'There must be a few of them on the door, but it looks like Brightwater is in command, and he's talking to that Blackcreek fellow.'

'Shit!' Tila reached into her sleeves and pulled out two knives, although she had a nasty feeling they would be somewhat less effective against armoured sars and marshals than against dock toughs and overconfident Lord Admirals. 'Your sister warned you that Brightwater would be angry about Greenbrook being elevated past him!'

'If he is the type of man to turn traitor over a snub like that, he is hardly the sort of person your brother wants in command of his armies!' Natan retorted, which was, Tila had to concede, a fair point. 'There are only a few of them out there, though. They cannot have raised the whole palace against us.'

If there was one good thing that had come of Einan Coldbeck's treachery, Tila thought, it was that Natan had finally been jolted out of his blasé attitudes. The notion that someone here in Narida wanted him off the throne, rather than a distant relative in the far-off City of Islands with no military might to accomplish it, had instigated an abrupt shift in his approach. He had never been an unintelligent man, merely disinterested. It was fair to say he was interested now.

'The windows,' Tila said, backing away from the chamber's main door. 'We can't climb out of them, but we can shout for help! If Brightwater is acting alone, then the door might hold long enough for others to get here and bring him down!'

'Go, then!' Natan commanded her, setting himself in a doorway. 'They will be after your brother first, not you. If he can hold them—'

'You are the God-King, not a warrior!' Tila snapped, taking both her knives into one hand and using the other to haul on his arm. 'If they do get in, at least let your sister put knives into a couple of them before you go waving that thing in their faces!' She dragged him back, past the antechamber in which they had been poring over a map of Narida and worrying about what Coldbeck might be up to, and into his bedroom.

Natan hauled open the shutters, and they looked out over a sleeping Idramar. Only a few lights burned here and there, and even the eastern sky showed not a hint of sunrise. Dawn was still some way off, and the light of it would come late in any case, thanks to the rain that was lashing down from the thick clouds above.

'Do you see any guards?' Natan asked, peering this way and that. Patrols walked the grounds and the walls, equipped with lanterns to spy intruders, but no such moving glimmers of light were visible.

'No,' Tila said, her stomach sinking. Was it just chance dictating that no patrols were here at this moment, or was some darker force at work? Had Brightwater in fact seized far more control than they thought? Would no help come, no matter what they did?

There was only one way to find out.

'*Help!*' Tila yelled at the top of her lungs. '*Traitors! Traitors at the God-King's chambers!*'

'*Treachery!*' Natan bellowed beside her. '*Help your king!*'

Nothing. No movement, no kindled light, no answering shout.

'*Will someone fucking wake up?*' Natan yelled in frustration, but that sparked no response either.

'It's the rain,' Tila said grimly, turning away from the window and casting her eye over her brother's bedchamber in case any obvious weapons or escape routes came to mind, which they did not. 'It's drowning out our noise.' She flexed her wrists, readying herself to throw. 'A "murder-sky", we used to call it. No one would hear the victim shout for help, and any that thought they might have heard something wouldn't want to step outside to find out for sure.'

'You are incredibly encouraging,' Natan growled. 'How do you get out into the city when you are living your double life, anyway?'

'Secret passage under the flagstones in your sister's bedchamber,' Tila told him. There was no harm in Natan knowing, especially now.

Natan looked at her. 'There are *secret passages* in the Sun Palace and you never told your brother?'

'Well, there won't be any in here,' Tila snapped. 'You're three storeys up!'

'How do you *know* there aren't? That is the entire point of a secret passage!'

Tila bit her lip. Could it be possible? Her brother's chambers were large, and while she could not imagine lifting up a flagstone and dropping down into the rooms below, was there an especially thick wall somewhere that might have a cramped staircase hidden within? It was clutching at straws, but with no other way out and no help on its way, was it worth discarding out of hand?

'Fine,' she said. 'Look for—'

There was a *crunch* from the direction of the chamber's main door, and Tila cut herself off as bile rose in her throat. 'Never mind. Too late.'

'Your brother will try to intimidate them,' Natan muttered. 'Are you ready to throw?'

'Your sister has been sticking knives into fools for twenty years,' Tila replied, trying to sound more confident than she felt. 'These are just more foolish than most.'

The door crashed again, and this time Tila heard the clatter of men stumbling into the chambers behind it.

'Here we go,' Natan murmured, and stepped out to where he could see the intruders. 'What is the meaning of this?' he cried, putting as much bass into his voice as he could. 'Brightwater?' For just a moment, Tila saw in him the shadow of their father, that imposing regal figure she remembered from her youth.

'Your Majesty,' Kaldur Brightwater's voice replied. 'It is over.'

Even knowing that it was the Southern Marshal who had been outside, hearing his voice fanned the flames of anger in Tila's chest so violently that they consumed the fear that gripped her, and she stepped up beside her brother. Sure enough, there he was, lurking behind three of his sars and alongside that miserable wretch from Blackcreek.

'Brightwater?' she spat at him, holding the knife in her right hand and aiming it at his face. The manners of the Naridan court failed her, and she fell back on Livnya's vocabulary to truly convey her disgust at his treachery. 'You piece of shit-stained harbour filth! Go fuck your mother's corpse!'

Her outburst seemed to shock the traitors into pausing for a moment, but only a moment. Kaldur Brightwater's face was set, and he stepped forwards with the grim determination of a man intent on discharging an unpleasant but necessary duty.

Shit. He genuinely thinks he's doing the right thing. The most dangerous kind of enemy.

Tila's arm had barely begin to twitch backwards when the Blackcreek boy twisted and swung, somewhat clumsily, for the man next to him. There was the briefest clash of blades, and then Blackcreek's sword opened the other sar's throat and he was backing away from the others as they rounded on him.

'Blackcreek!' Brightwater snarled, rounding on the man. 'What in—?'

'Blackcreek must be true!' Blackcreek shouted at him. 'This sar might not bear its name any longer, but he still carries its honour with him!'

Tila hesitated. All three remaining traitors were facing away from her, but they were all armoured, and not the easiest target for a thrown blade. It might be more prudent to see whether Blackcreek could distract them for long enough for other help to arrive.

'You would turn on the man next to you without warning, and call it honour?' Brightwater bawled, which Tila thought was somewhat ludicrous coming from a man who was trying to murder his divine ruler in the middle of the night. 'See to the God-King,' he added to his armsmen. 'The fool's death belongs to this marshal.'

So much for a distraction. Brightwater's two remaining household sars turned back to her and Natan.

'Cease this!' Natan commanded, but they advanced without giving any indication that they even heard him. Tila could see the tension on their faces. These were men who knew that to stop now was simply to invite execution, so they were going to see this through one way or the other.

'Fine,' Tila snapped, drawing her arm back. 'Die, then.'

She threw at the nearest one, but his reflexes were equal to it, and he leaned aside to slap the knife out of the air with the flat of his longblade. It slowed him, though, and so when the man next to him charged the last few steps towards her brother, he was alone.

Natan screamed and swung their father's blade, but that too was knocked aside, and the sar crashed bodily into her brother, sending him stumbling backwards into the bedchamber. Tila lashed out with her other knife as the sar bundled past her, but the point struck high between his shoulder blades instead of in the back of his neck as she intended, and the force of the blow simply added to his forward momentum. Then the other one was coming at her again, and her throw as she backed away simply whipped past his face and clattered against the stone wall beside him. He grinned viciously, and she fled towards Natan's bed.

She had more knives, of course – she pulled another from her left vambrace without thinking – but when faced with an armoured opponent with combat-trained reflexes who was expecting her tricks, the odds were very much stacked against her. Still, she sent her next effort towards his eyes as he followed her through the doorway, and was rewarded with a red gash opened down his cheek and a chunk taken out of his ear when he failed to move his head quite quickly enough. He howled in pain, but kept coming.

Tila's eyes lighted on the oil lamp.

She just had time to grab it and hurl it before the sar reached her. It was a fine ceramic piece, beautifully decorated as befitted the God-King of Narida, and it shattered on one of the sar's gleaming breastplates. His torso was bathed in sticky oil, which immediately caught alight as some of it came into contact with the still-burning wick.

That stopped him. The sar screamed and backed away from her, flailing at himself with his arms, which merely caught fire in turn as the flaming oil was transferred to them. Tila looked over to see Natan, now apparently disarmed, with both hands around the sword wrist of the sar trying to kill him. The sar tried punching him with his free hand, but Natan ducked his head behind his shoulder, took the punch, and held on.

Tila grabbed a chair from next to her brother's bed. It was clumsy and heavy, but it served well enough as a club against a sar who had lost all sense of what was going on around him as fire spread over him. Something cracked as Tila's improvised weapon made contact, although she was not sure if it was the chair or the man's skull. Regardless, he went down and stayed down, allowing her to jump past him – praying that her trailing robes did not catch fire as she did so – and go to the aid of her brother.

At that moment Natan, still with both hands wrapped around his opponent's wrist, fired a knee up into his enemy's groin. The sar buckled with a gasp and a shudder, and Tila grabbed his warrior's braids in her fist and jerked his head back to open his throat with her knife. He slumped backwards to the floor, spraying Natan with blood as he did so.

'Gah!' her brother spat, looking down at himself, but he wasted no time in picking up their father's blade from where it had fallen. 'Thank you,' he added. 'Are you hurt?'

'No, somehow,' Tila replied. She weighed the knife in her hand, then shrugged and wrenched the longblade from the hand of the rapidly dying sar. 'You?'

'A few lumps, but no cuts,' Natan replied. He looked at her, his face marked by deep shadows in the light from the burning sar. 'Brightwater.'

'Brightwater,' Tila replied grimly. She turned and thrust her newly acquired longblade through the neck of the burning man, just in case he'd been about to come around and somehow put himself out, then left him to die. 'Let us finish this.'

Side by side, she and Natan ran from his bedchamber, through the antechamber, and entered the reception room just as Kaldur Brightwater's sword twisted the Blackcreek sar's weapon out of his grip. Blackcreek groped at the empty sheaths on his belt for a shortblade that wasn't there, and the Southern Marshal brought his longblade back for the killing blow.

Tila threw her knife at him, with a yell of both hatred and effort. Kaldur Brightwater swayed back from the throwing knife that flashed in front of his eyes, and for a moment he looked towards Tila and her brother, assessing this new threat.

'Blackcreek!' Natan was already shouting, as he threw their father's longblade underarm across the room.

Blackcreek caught the royal weapon by the hilt, and stepped forward to swing it two-handed at Kaldur Brightwater's neck. His form was good and his hands were swift, but had the Southern Marshal been facing him there was no way the blow would have landed.

However, Tila's throw had bought Blackcreek a moment of the Southern Marshal's inattention, and that was all he needed. The keen edge of the longblade that had belonged to Tila's father, one of the finest weapons ever forged in the kingdom of Narida, sheared through muscle and bone to take Kaldur Brightwater's traitorous head off as cleanly as any executioner's strike.

The Southern Marshal fell with a thump, a muffled clink of the maille in his coat-of-nails, and the clatter of his own longblade on the sandstone floor. Blackcreek, wide-eyed and panting, slowly lowered the borrowed weapon as though he expected Brightwater to spring back up at any moment. Then, apparently remembering in whose presence he stood, he sank to his knees and began to prostrate himself.

'Stop that,' Natan snapped at him, crossing the floor to him. 'Get up, man! We do not know if there will be more of them coming! We need to send for help!'

'This sar sent his friend Hiran Threestone to find aid when we found the first pair of murdered guards, Your Majesty,' Blackcreek replied, hastily obeying Natan's instruction. He seemed very young to Tila, as she came up alongside her brother, although perhaps that was the wide eyes.

'You were not with Brightwater from the beginning?' Tila asked him, surprised.

'No, Divine Princess,' Blackcreek said. 'We found dead guards, and this sar came here in case he was needed. The Southern Marshal tried to persuade this sar to join him, and this sar decided that appearing to do so would give him a better chance than a direct attack on all four of them at once, dishonourable though it might have been.'

'Pssh!' Tila spat. 'He who fights fair, fights stupid. You helped save our lives, goodsar: that is honour enough.' She looked over to the door, where her brother was peering out. 'Natan! Any sign of anyone?'

'There are footsteps approaching at a run,' Natan replied, ducking back inside. He picked Blackcreek's sword up from the floor where it had fallen and snapped his fingers at the man. 'Take this; give your king that one.'

'Of course!' Blackcreek stammered, hastily swapping swords with Natan. 'Your royal blade: this sar did not mean to—'

'Bollocks to that,' Natan cut him off, raising their father's bloodstained weapon and flanking Blackcreek to face the door. 'You might as well have the one you are used to, that is all. Tila?'

'For all the good it will do us,' Tila muttered, but she gripped her own stolen longblade in both hands and took up position on her brother's other side. She had never used a sword, and this seemed like an exceedingly bad time to learn, but she had already seen how ineffective her throwing knives were.

'If we die,' Natan said, as the sound of running footsteps became audible to Tila's ears, 'know that your brother is sorry that he let things get this way.'

Tila opened her mouth to reply, although she was not sure entirely what she was going to say – an acceptance of his apology? A rebuke for how meaningless the sentiment was? Empty reassurance that they would live? – but she was cut off by a shout from beyond the ruined door.

'Your Majesty! Your Majesty?'

A motley collection of armed men piled into view and Tila raised her blade, but they stumbled to a halt and dropped to their knees as they laid eyes on her brother. Not all of them stopped at the same time, of course, and so some genuflections occurred because someone else had collided with them and knocked them forwards, but the main thing was that none of them seemed to be here to kill her.

Tila let out her breath, and sat down suddenly as the tension in her body abruptly drained away.

'Hiran!' Blackcreek cried joyously, and yes indeed, that *was* the son of the thane of Threestone at the front, clutching what had to be Blackcreek's own shortblade. In fact, Tila realised, it was not just armed men who had come to their aid: she could see Threestone's sister Yae further back, with a long knife, and there was even a woman in servant's livery holding a large, heavy-looking candlestick.

'This king is, largely, unharmed,' Natan declared to their would-be saviours. He probably cut an impressive figure to them, with a spray of blood across his chest from the sar whose throat Tila had opened. 'The traitor was the former Southern Marshal, Kaldur Brightwater. If he has any other men under his direct command in the Sun Palace, this king wants them seized and imprisoned immediately. Go!' he snapped, when no one immediately sprang to do his bidding. 'You, you, and you, see to it. You and you, go to the chambers of the Queen Mother and ensure that she is safe!'

'The rest of you, stay here!' Tila added, pushing herself back up to her feet again. The new arrivals hastily got back to their feet and the ones her brother had instructed ran off, while the others milled awkwardly and tried not to gawp at their ruler, and the decapitated body of Kaldur Brightwater.

All except Hiran Threestone, that was, who clasped Blackcreek into a hug. 'Darel! Your friend is so relieved you're well!' He pulled back almost immediately, his face radiating abject embarrassment. 'A-and of course you, Your Majesty.'

'Sar Darel told us he had sent you to get help,' Natan replied, and Tila could tell that he was trying not to smile at the young nobleman's discomfort. 'The fact that you did so is greatly appreciated, even though we managed to overcome the immediate threat.'

'We will make sure your father hears of it,' Tila added, looking from Hiran to Yae, and noting their carefully controlled reactions. She did not know exactly why Lord Threestone's two younger children had found their way into his disfavour, but she suspected the personal gratitude of the Divine Family might go some way to ameliorating it. And if it did not . . . Well, what thane would *not* want his children to be in favour with the God-King? One that might not keep his position for very long, that was who. At least, if Tila had any say in the matter.

'Sar Darel,' Natan was saying. 'Defending your king by drawing your sword on four enemies, even by surprise, is loyalty that deserves reward. There can be no greater demonstration of your faith and commitment to the kingdom, and it is now clear to this king that your character could not be corrupted by the southern Raiders. The Blackcreek family will retain its full title and lands. And you,' he added, 'will be raised to the rank of Southern Marshal.'

Darel Blackcreek's mouth dropped open, but no recognisable words emerged.

'Brother?' Tila asked, managing to hide her own grimace and wondering how in the name of their divine ancestor she was going to question this edict, issued in front of half-a-dozen witnesses.

'All he had to do was turn around and walk away,' Natan said, turning to her. 'At any point, Tila. When he saw the dead guards, when he saw Brightwater's men trying to break down the door . . . Had he done that, we would have faced four instead of two, and we would probably be dead.'

Her brother had the truth of it. Blackcreek might not be experienced either in court or in war, but after half of their High Marshals had turned on them in quick succession, perhaps loyalty *was* the primary consideration at the present time. The man had certainly had little enough reason to think kindly of Natan up until this moment, so his loyalty, at least, could not be in doubt.

Very well, then. She would take this, and work with it, and try to bring it around to favour them. As she always did.

'Congratulations, Marshal Blackcreek,' she said, smiling at Blackcreek, who had more or less got his lower jaw under control again. 'This princess looks forward to many long and loyal years of service from you.'

Blackcreek sank down to one knee, lowered his head and grounded his blade, resting the point on the sandstone floor. Then he looked up at her and met her eyes, and Tila was struck by the determination she saw there.

'Your Divine Majesty. Divine Princess. You will have it.'

And may Nari help her, but Tila believed him.

STONEJAW

THE STORM'S BREATH had set sail two days later, gliding out of East Harbour with the falling tide and setting course for the Fishing Islands to the south. They hadn't been alone.

Kulmar Ailikaszhin clearly had the same idea, since the *Grey Shark* was already gone by the time they'd got under sail, and Stonejaw had seen a speck that could well have been his yolgu on the horizon as they'd headed south. Then, after Grand Mahewa had faded out of sight behind them, another dot keeping pace with them suggested that someone else also had eyes on repeating their last voyage's successes.

'I hope there'll be enough slaves to go around,' she'd remarked dryly to Tajen, a Tjakorshi who'd been recommended to her by Maradzh as someone who spoke most of what he called the 'Southern languages' with a reasonable degree of fluency: Tjakorshi, of course, but also the language of the City of Islands, the Drylands tongue, the Flatlands tongue, the language that apparently came from over the mountains beyond the Flatlands, and even that of the Fishing Islands.

Tajen had just smiled at her. 'If there isn't, that just makes them all the more valuable, doesn't it?'

They skirted the first large island, low and green-swathed, because Stonejaw suspected Kulmar would have put in there:

he'd always lacked patience and would try to seize the first opportunity he got. There was no point in two crews fighting over the same spoils, so she guided the *Storm's Breath* around its shores and over the sharp-edged reefs that flanked it – reefs that would have torn out the bottom of other ships, but over which Tjakorshi yolgus could skate without harm – and struck out for the next one.

'What do you think?' Stonejaw asked Enga. 'Check the west shore first?'

'There are more islands over that way, so it's likely to be more sheltered,' Enga agreed. 'That's where I'd look to settle, if I was living here. Although the Dark Father alone knows why I would,' she added, plucking at the neck of her light shirt. Most of Stonejaw's crew, herself included, had stashed their furs and reclothed themselves from East Harbour's markets in items far more suitable for the temperatures they were now enduring.

'At least we get a breeze when we're on the sea,' Stonejaw said. She eyed the dark ranks of tall trees with leaves as long and as broad as she was, so very different to the conifers of home. 'Can you imagine living in there, where the air's all thick and still? Ugh.' She shuddered at the thought.

The wind was coming from the east, and it dropped away as the *Storm's Breath* passed into the island's lee, so Stonejaw ordered the paddles to come out and her crew stroked their way steadily onwards, looking for any sign of a settlement. However, there were few easy landing sites: instead of gently sloping beaches of sand, much of the shore was raised, jagged rock, much like what lurked beneath the waves.

'If anyone does live here, they'd have a hard job getting to the ocean,' Korsada commented from where she was wielding the steering oar. 'I think this is one of the easternmost islands, too, and our ships would come from the east. Maybe fewer people live here, because they've learned this is where we'll land first.'

'Maybe,' Stonejaw replied. There was already a nagging feeling in her gut that they were wasting their time, and the sun was dipping towards the horizon: something which it seemed to do far more rapidly in these warmer lands, despite how much higher it rose overhead in the middle of the day, threatening to roast them all. She frowned at the shoreline ahead, which curved inwards. 'Is that an inlet coming up, or a channel through?'

Zhazhken, on the far fore corner of the *Storm's Breath*, leaned out a little further. 'Looks like an inlet: it doesn't go far back.'

'Is there anywhere we can land?'

Zhazhken waited for a few more strokes, then nodded. 'Yes, there's a bit of a beach. No sign of any people using it, but it's somewhere we can haul out for the night.'

'Then that's what we'll do,' Stonejaw declared. She took another look at the sun, but it did nothing to change her mind. 'I don't fancy trying these waters in the dark, and there'll still be cargo for us to find tomorrow, unless Kulmar Ailikaszhin tries to overload the *Grey Shark* so much that the damned thing sinks.' Her own crew gave a few laughs at that, because they could all believe that Kulmar would be that greedy, and as they came up on the inlet they turned into it, with Korsada on the steering oar and the paddlers doing the rest of the work.

One of the advantages about these climes, Stonejaw had to admit, was that you weren't likely to freeze to death overnight. Instead of huddling together under furs in the yolgu's deckhouse to keep warm, her crew stretched out on the deck or even on the beach itself. As the light died and they lit a fire, Stonejaw saw a couple of figures disappearing together into the nearby bushes, although she could not quite make out who it was.

'Let us know if you find any monsters!' she called after them, prompting another round of laughter.

'Monsters?' Tajen asked her, raising an eyebrow.

'Have you ever been to the Flatlands?' Stonejaw asked him, poking the fire with a stick.

'A couple of times. I even went to Idramar once, their biggest city, although I stayed on the ship. They don't much like Tjakorshi there, apparently, and the captain didn't think the fact I was born in Kiburu ce Alaba would have mattered much to them.'

'Did you see the monsters?'

Tajen frowned. 'You mean the dragons?'

'If that's the word.' Stonejaw sighed. 'We . . . met them in the south of that land. Great beasts with warriors on their backs.' She shuddered at the memory. 'Ach. If I never see one again, it will be too soon.'

'You know there are dragons on Grand Mahewa, don't you?' Tajen asked, eyeing her uncertainly.

'So I've seen,' Stonejaw replied. 'They're skinny little shits compared to the ones that rode down our raid and trampled my warriors into the dirt.' She spat. 'Give me my axe, and I reckon I could take one of those in a fight. The Flatland ones . . . ' She shuddered again. 'Well, I had my chance at that, and I ran from it, and I don't feel like a coward to say that I did. There's bravery and then there's foolishness, and I know which one that would have been. The Dark Father has even less time for fools than he does for cowards.'

'Well, I've never heard of any dragons here,' Tajen said, settling back with his hands behind his head. 'Not any longer than your arm, anyway.'

'Good enough for me,' Stonejaw replied, shuffling away from the fire a little and imitating him. 'Let's see what tomorrow brings, then.'

TOMORROW BROUGHT JERKING awake into grey twilight, out of dreams of her old village on Vorgalkoruuk burning while The Golden watched from the shadows, to find a dark figure standing over her. She reached instinctively for her axe, only to find a boot planted on it and a different weapon at her throat.

A different weapon, but still a blackstone axe.

'Who the fuck are you?' she demanded. There were people all around her, far too many people, and she could hear shouting. Then there was a quick clatter as of an axe on a shield, and a scream, and the wet *thud* of weapons on flesh, and then the screaming stopped.

'You don't remember me?' the man standing over her asked. 'I'm insulted. I remember *you*, Stonejaw, and I doubt I'll be the only one who does.'

Stonejaw squinted up at him, trying to make out his features properly. She couldn't remember all of the warriors who'd been on Fireheart's raid, but she was fairly sure this man hadn't made it to the City of Islands with her. Could some others have escaped from the rout in the south of the Flatlands and gone their own way?

'You're going to have to help me out,' she snapped.

The man leaned down to pluck her axe out of the sand, while keeping his own weapon at her throat. 'Get up.'

She recognised him now he had bent down far enough, and her throat clenched. A face she had not seen since leaving Tjakorsha. 'Kullojan? Kullojan Sakteszhin?'

Sakteszhin snorted. 'So you do remember. I'm honoured. A shame you didn't remember what you were sent across the ocean to do.' He straightened again, with her axe in his off-hand. 'Get up, Stonejaw. The Golden will want to speak with you, I've no doubt.'

'The . . . ' The comparative cool of the early morning now felt like a deathly chill. 'What do you mean? Why are you here?'

'Tjakorsha sailed,' Sakteszhin said. 'The draug commanded, and we obeyed.'

Stonejaw sat up cautiously and looked around. The beach was full of warriors she didn't recognise, at least not as part of her own crew, or any of the others who'd been with Fireheart. 'How many of you did it send?'

Sakteszhin laughed. 'Send? You misunderstand me, Stonejaw.

Tjakorsha sailed. All of us. And the draug didn't *send* us; it's here with us.'

'The Golden is here?' Stonejaw had reached one knee, but now she froze in place. This couldn't be. They'd got away! They'd left their homes behind and found somewhere new, cursedly hot and moist though it was, and now the damned thing had *followed* them?

She fought her thoughts down. The Golden could see thoughts in its fires: that was known. She had to control her mind and be the good, obedient warrior it had known her as before . . . Except that there wasn't any point. The whole reason they never returned to Tjakorsha was that they'd failed The Golden, and now they weren't just failures, they were traitors as well.

'I'm not going to tell you again, Stonejaw,' Sakteszhin said coldly. 'Get up, or I'll have my warriors tie you up and we'll drag you to The Golden in ropes.'

Father Krayk had no time for cowards, and The Golden had less. For one brief moment Stonejaw considered swinging for Sakteszhin with her bare fists and forcing him to cut her down where she stood, rather than face whatever fate The Golden had in store for her, but that was simply cowardice of its own sort. She had not pressed the attack against the Flatlanders, nor even sailed back across the ocean to report the raid's failure. What she was about to face was the consequence of those choices, and to take the easy way out now would simply be to invite the Dark Father's scorn.

She took a deep, shuddering breath, and stood up. All around her, her crew had been subdued and were being held on their knees, surrounded by the far, far more numerous warriors of Sakteszhin and those with him.

'Fine,' she said, forcing the words past her teeth. 'Let's get this over with.'

She followed Sakteszhin to where his yolgu was beached. His crew pushed off, navigating their way past the others all rammed in tight to the shore, and out into the clearer water farther out.

Or what she'd assumed would be clearer water, at least. In fact, she realised as they cleared the inlet, the sea was filled with ships. Everywhere she looked, there was mast after mast. More ships than she could count, stretching away north, south and east.

Until that moment, she hadn't realised exactly what Sakteszhin had meant when he'd said 'Tjakorsha has sailed'.

'Why?' she whispered to him. 'Why did you all leave? What did The Golden say to make you do this?'

Sakteszhin didn't reply for a moment. Then he sighed before speaking.

'It told us our home was going to die.'

Stonejaw looked at him in shock. 'Going to *die*? How?'

'The mountain spirits,' Sakteszhin replied. 'They were growing more restless. The Golden told us they were going to wake properly and break free of their prisons.'

'That's a tale for children,' Stonejaw muttered, and it was. Still, to hear that it had been repeated from the lips of the draug was terrifying.

'You can tell The Golden that yourself, if you want,' Sakteszhin said, with a snort. 'But it knows, Stonejaw. It saw Fireheart's failure in its flames, and here you are, a broken crew with no chief's belt that I can see.'

The Golden saw our failure? The thought of the draug's ice-green eyes peering at them across weeks of sailing was no less terrifying than the notion of the mountain spirits waking.

They hauled close to another yolgu and the paddlers stopped, and Stonejaw's heart leaped into her throat as a well-remembered figure stepped out of the deckhouse.

The Golden looked like a man, for that was the nature of a draug: they crept into the bodies of the sick, or the recently dead with no soul marks to ward them from further harm, and took them for their own. However, no man could have carried the patchwork of scars that dotted The Golden's body and still lived.

It had been hung by the neck for half a day, the mark of which was an ugly blemish around its throat, and still it had not died.

Zheldu had been scared of the giant Flatlander dragons, but that was understandable; as understandable as being scared of krayks. They were both giant, ferocious beasts, and only a fool would *not* be scared. The fear The Golden instilled into her was of a different sort. It was so close, *so* close to being a man, and yet there was a subtle wrongness to it. It moved too smoothly; when it spoke, it formed the words slightly incorrectly; and its green eyes were as cold and dead as ice.

No one still lived who claimed to know what name the draug's body had originally carried, which meant that even if there had been witches foolish enough to try to banish the spirit, their attempt would have been doomed before it began. Only the second death of its body could stop it, and the scars it wore were testament to how futile an enterprise that would be.

The first rays of light peeked over the island behind her and struck the gold-inlaid steel mask of the draug, setting it ablaze in her sight just as they pulled alongside. The mask hid every feature of The Golden's face above the mouth except for its eyes, and Zheldu could already feel those eyes on her. It was a sensation like ice down the spine.

'Zheldu Stonejaw,' The Golden said, as Sakteszhin nudged her across the gap between the two vessels, and the sound of her name on the draug's lips dried her mouth and nearly buckled her knees. 'The fires told me you had failed.'

There was nothing she could say to that. She could not even look at it properly, thanks to the light reflecting off its mask. Her eyes fell to the Flatlander sword thrust through its belt: the sword it had taken from Ludir Snowhair, the former chief of the Seal Rock clan. It had decapitated Amalk Tyaszhin with that blade when he had displeased it: taken his head off with a one-armed swing, if the stories from the Witch House were to be believed.

'Tjakorsha is dying,' The Golden continued, the words of her tongue still sounding slightly wrong in its mouth, as though it was forming the sounds without properly understanding the meanings behind them. 'Soon it will be no more. My witches read the signs of fire and wave, and told me I would find our true course here. And here I find you. So tell me, Zheldu Stonejaw . . . '

The Golden stepped up close to her, and Stonejaw had to fight the urge to flinch backwards from it.

' . . . do you still have a purpose? Can you still serve your people? Or am I to skin you, and leave your unpainted corpse for the krayk to fight over?'

Stonejaw thought quickly. She could tell The Golden about the City of Islands and send it north. There would surely be many northerners from Sorlamanga among this fleet, who could confirm her tale. But then she thought of this mass of ships trying to fit through the narrow entrance to East Harbour, and the great bolts that would come raining down on them from either side, and held her tongue. That would be a slaughter, and would ruin any hope she might have for a life there. Some of the other islands, perhaps? No, that would hardly be any better: she was willing to bet the combined force of the City of Islands would be enough to see off The Golden's fleet, and it would still sour them for ever against the Tjakorshi.

An idea surfaced in the roiling waves of her mind, and under the intense pressure of that otherworldly stare, she seized on it before she'd truly examined whether or not it was a good one.

'The Flatlands.'

The Golden's head tilted to one side. 'The place where you failed me.'

'Sattistutar had made common cause with the people who live there, and they rode monsters to fight us off,' Stonejaw said. 'Her witches must have told her we were coming.'

'Rode monsters?' Sakteszhin scoffed.

'You don't believe me?' Stonejaw snapped at him. 'You go ask any of my crew! They were all there; they saw it the same as me!

Or do you think we invented a story beforehand, just in case you all appeared from out of nowhere and jumped us while we were sleeping?'

'Let her speak,' The Golden instructed Sakteszhin, who nodded obediently. 'So, Sattistutar still lives. That is of . . . lesser importance to me, now. Why should the Flatlands be our course?'

'Because,' Stonejaw said, desperately trying to remember what Maradzh had said to her, 'their God-King, who rules them, is ill: it's reckoned he's going to die. They're in disarray.' She gestured around them. 'With this many warriors, you could sweep down on them, kill their god and any of his underlings, and we could have as much of their land as we wished.'

'Their god is ill?' The Golden asked. It was the first time Stonejaw could remember the draug seeming surprised about something. 'Their *god*?'

'So I was told, and by someone who had no reason to lie to me,' Stonejaw replied. Maradzh had mentioned it in passing, as news of interest. She had no idea how true it was, but if it distracted the draug, it would serve its purpose so far as she was concerned.

'And do you know where this . . . God-King is?' The Golden asked.

'No,' Stonejaw told it. 'But so long as your warriors haven't killed him,' she continued, casting a sidelong glance at Sakteszhin, 'I've got someone with me who does. And who speaks the Flatlanders' language, to boot.'

The Golden paused. It was not the hesitation of a mortal man. It simply stood motionless for a few heartbeats, with only one slow blink of its ice-green eyes. Then it blinked once more, and suddenly it was moving again, with the same supple fluidity as always.

'Find this man, and bring him to me,' it told Sakteszhin, pointing at him. 'I would like to hear about this sickly god, and his lands.' It looked back at Stonejaw and smiled at her, although its lips held no true warmth or mirth. 'Rejoice, Stonejaw. You still have purpose. At least for the moment.' Then it turned and walked away, back towards the deckhouse, and Sakteszhin had taken her arm and was pulling her towards his own yolgu.

'What's this man's name?' he demanded.

'Tajen,' Stonejaw replied.

'And he's Tjakorshi?'

'Tjakorshi parents, at any rate.' She shrugged. 'I hope for his sake they taught him how to read wind and wave and cloud, so he can guide us back to where he's been before.'

'For his sake, and for yours,' Sakteszhin replied. 'The Dark Father help you if you promise The Golden a god to kill, and then your man can't deliver.'

The Dark Father wouldn't help her, Stonejaw knew that much, but she'd bought herself time. She didn't know how far it was to the Flatlands city Tajen had spoken of, but it had to be at least a couple of weeks' sailing. Plenty of time for the *Storm's Breath* to 'accidentally' get separated from the rest of the fleet, turn about and run northwards. Maybe grab a few captives from the Fishing Islands, or maybe just go straight through the Throat of the World and see what was on the other side of it.

Let The Golden fight it out with the dragons. Zheldu Stonejaw wanted nothing more to do with either of them.

YARMINA

THE VILLAGE WAS called Deepglade, and it sat in a clearing in the Downwoods, alongside a gurgling stream. To the west, the Catseye Mountains were beginning to rise. Yarmina Darkspur looked up at them, just peeking over the tops of the trees, as she buckled the saddle strap around Taisa's impressive bulk. Yarmina's mount was a frillneck; no great war dragon like the longbrows of her father's sars, but she possessed the very desirable traits of docility and great stamina, and she had carried Yarmina a long way westwards over the last two days. Yarmina had spent the previous night in a hay loft, which had actually been a great improvement over the root-filled ground she endured when she first left Black Keep, and she was well refreshed and ready to continue her journey.

The sound of galloping behind her made her turn, and two sars burst out of the near edge of the clearing, coming down the road from the east: the same road Yarmina had arrived on, late the previous night. Yarmina smiled as she recognised Sar Immanel and Sar Aharin.

'Friends of yours, lady?' asked Yiska, the woman in whose hayloft Yarmina had slept, who was holding Taisa while Yarmina worked. She was a Blackcreek woman, for this was still Blackcreek land, but she had been happy enough to take Yarmina's coin for the lodging and some food. She seemed more than a little nervous at the sight of the new arrivals, for which Yarmina could not really blame her. They were approaching rather quickly, after all.

'Sars of this lady's household,' she replied, as reassuringly as she could.

'They seem in a great hurry,' Yiska said.

'Well, this lady did give them the slip two days ago,' Yarmina said calmly. 'It is only to be expected.'

'S'woman's going to leave you to greet them then, begging your pardon,' Yiska said, and hurriedly disappeared inside. Yarmina could not blame her for that, either: it probably was not a good idea for a lowborn to be seen assisting a young noblewoman who had just confessed to having run away from her escort. She tightened Taisa's saddle strap and turned, waiting for the two sars to rein in. When they did, Taisa snorted and moved to rub noses with Galliant, Immanel's mount. The greetings between riders were somewhat less cordial.

'Lady Yarmina,' Sar Aharin said tightly, sliding from his saddle. His bow to her was perfunctory, and his expression could have curdled goat's milk. 'This sar is relieved to find you well.'

Yarmina bit down on her lip to prevent a smile. Aharin had put enough edge into that sentence to make the true meaning of his words abundantly clear. He was absolutely furious with her.

'And you as well, goodsar,' she replied courteously. She looked up at his companion, who had not dismounted. 'You too, Sar Immanel.'

'What in Nari's name do you think you're playing at, girl?' Immanel snapped, his hot tongue getting the better of him once more. 'And what's that you're wearing?'

Yarmina frowned at him. 'This lady does not intend to give an account of her actions to a lout such as yourself, especially when he is addressing her in such an uncouth manner.'

'It is not a cloak appropriate for a lady,' Aharin said disapprovingly, looking at the hooded, dark brown garment that swathed Yarmina's shoulders. 'Where did you get it?'

'One of the pedlars we met on the road,' Yarmina told him. He, at least, was still being polite. 'This lady purchased it from him before she rode off, while you were all still abed.'

'Lady Yarmina,' Aharin said, clearly controlling himself with some difficulty. 'Why would you do such a thing? Why would you leave your escort and risk travelling alone, and away from Darkspur at that?'

'Because, Sar Aharin,' Yarmina said, allowing her own voice to become decidedly chilly, 'the night before we met those pedlars, this lady overheard her escort talking about a number of things of which she was not aware. Not least, the presence of Darkspur men in the Catseye Mountains, enslaving the mountain folk and taking their gold.'

'Keep your voice down!' Aharin hissed at her, shooting Immanel a glance that the other sar returned with considerable unease. 'We are in Blackcreek land still!' Both of them laid a hand on their longblades, but although a few residents of Deepglade were abroad, several of them casting curious glances at the sars on the edge of their village, none of them had approached close enough to be able to overhear conversation. That was a sure way to garner unwelcome attention from armed men, something most lowborn wanted to avoid.

'This lady knows we are in Blackcreek land,' Yarmina told him. 'She intends to find a way up into the mountains so she can see for herself exactly what is transpiring.' She sniffed. 'If Father did not want this lady to investigate such matters for herself, he should not have kept the details of his activities from her.'

'Surely you cannot be serious!' Immanel burst out.

'This lady is serious,' Yarmina told him coldly. 'And do not—'

'Lady Yarmina,' Aharin cut her off, the voice of reason set against Immanel's hot-headedness. 'A hunting trip into the foothills is one thing, but to attempt the high passes dressed as you are, with no suitable equipment or provisions, is . . . Well, it's folly. Besides, do you even know the trails? Any of them, let alone from here?'

'And what about the savages?' Immanel put in. 'They'd kill you as soon as look at you!'

Yarmina gave him a long look, intended to suggest that she held a similar opinion of him. 'Then this lady supposes that you will both have to accompany her, for protection.'

'Out of the question,' Aharin replied immediately. Immanel just laughed.

'We could hire local guides!' Yarmina protested. 'Find more appropriate clothing and equipment as well, if you insist! Then you can accompany this lady and whatever guides we need up into the mountains, so she can see for herself what is happening.'

'Lady Yarmina, this is not going to happen,' Aharin declared firmly. 'You will accompany us back to Darkspur. Once there, you can speak with your father about this and, if he agrees, you can accompany a properly prepared party up into the mountains.' He gave no indication of how likely he thought that outcome would be, and Yarmina did not need him to. If her father had intended her to see what he was doing, he would have already told her about it.

'And if this lady refuses?' she demanded, looking him squarely in the eye.

Aharin swallowed, but Immanel just laughed again. 'You're coming back with us, girl, whether you like it or not. Omet gave us our instructions, just like he did to Lahel.'

'Where are Omet and Lahel, anyway?' Yarmina asked, ignoring his disrespectful manner for the moment. She could deal with that later.

'Sar Omet rode on for Darkspur in case you had gone on ahead,' Aharin told her. 'Lahel rode towards Black Keep, to see if you had doubled back.'

Now they came to it. Yarmina willed herself not to flinch, or give any other tells. 'Why would this lady ride back for Black Keep? She would only have encountered our footmen, in any case.'

'The steward believes in being thorough,' Aharin said. 'The pedlar told us you had set off in this direction, but it was always possible you had bribed him to lie to us.'

Yarmina smiled despite herself. 'You give this lady a lot of credit for duplicity. She simply rode off because she knew Omet would not agree to her going to the mountains, and this lady's mother had a saying that it is easier to seek forgiveness than permission.'

'Well, you didn't get far enough to need either,' Immanel said. 'Now come on. We're to accompany you back to Darkspur, your whims be damned.'

'You still have not said what you will do if this lady refuses to obey you,' Yarmina said to Aharin. 'Will you bind her limbs and sling her over your saddle horn?'

She was staring directly into the young sar's eyes when she said this. She was reasonably certain Aharin's gaze had strayed towards her on more than one occasion, and she also knew that some of her father's sars used the term 'saddle horn' to mean more than just an item of tack, when they thought they were alone with their peers.

In truth, also, Aharin was not unpleasant to look at, and the notion of trying out his saddle for size was not one Yarmina would necessarily have been opposed to. However, she mainly intended to make him feel uncomfortable, and judging by his expression, she succeeded.

'Yes,' he managed, after a moment.

Yarmina raised her eyebrows.

'The steward was clear,' Aharin continued, his voice now slightly more under his control. 'You are to return with us to Darkspur. No other options were given.'

'And you think this lady's father would be pleased with you laying your hands on his daughter?' Yarmina asked him.

'Omet has authority to command us,' Immanel said. 'We would simply be obeying the orders that he will tell your father he gave us.'

Yarmina snorted. 'You think Omet would not hang you out to dry? He will give you the orders, yes: and then deny ever having said such a thing when Father takes him to task for it.'

She could see uncertainty in both their faces, because they suspected she might be telling the truth. In the end, however, her attempts at sowing doubt were to no avail. Sar Aharin shook his head.

'Lady Yarmina, we cannot think of such things. We have been told to bring you to Darkspur as quickly as we may, and so that is what we will do. It would undoubtedly be quickest if you were to accompany us willingly, but if you will not, then we will do what we have to do, and face any consequences as they come. It would be no more than we deserve, for allowing you to elude us in the first place.'

Yarmina sighed. She had pushed it for as long and as hard as she dared, but she did not fancy actually being bound by these men: not least because if she made them do it once, she strongly doubted they would trust her enough to release her until they had returned to Darkspur to present her to her father. If it was Aharin alone, he might not have gone through with it no matter what he said, but she knew Immanel would, if pushed. Better if she consented, however grudgingly.

'Very well,' she said, as haughtily as she could manage. 'If you are so set upon behaving so discourteously, you give this lady no alternative. She will accompany you, and gives you her word that she will not elude you again.'

Now she just had to hope her distraction had worked.

DAIMON

It was usually a time for merriment when the first pedlars appeared in Black Keep. As far south as their town was, it was a welcome reminder that the rest of Narida still existed, and it provided a chance to get news – often somewhat distorted and overblown, perhaps, but news nonetheless. The pedlars' main purpose, of course, was to bring goods from elsewhere in the kingdom, be that a couple of small casks of wine for the thane's cellars, from farther north where grapes grew well, or a different strain of chewleaf for the lowborn who liked it, but news always came too.

This year, however, things were different. Black Keep had already had visitors from farther north, including the Southern Marshal, and he brought Daimon news: not minor gossip about a thane dying and his son succeeding, or how the harvest in the west was suffering from too much or too little rain, but rumours about Nari Himself being reborn. Daimon was all too well aware of the rest of Narida, and he was not sure what, exactly, was going to happen to it. Blackcreek had not long been settled by Naridans when the Splintering had occurred, and so far as Daimon had heard, by the time news had reached them it had more or less finished, but it was still enough to make him uneasy.

When Ita the guard brought news that one of the pedlars

claimed to have a letter for him, Daimon wasted no time in having the man summoned.

'Do they often bring such messages?' Saana asked him. They were in the first yard of the castle, watching their new guards training against each other.

'Sometimes,' Daimon replied. 'Some of the town have relations elsewhere, although not many, and few far enough away that it is worth them entrusting a letter to a pedlar. However, if your husband was to be receiving a message from another thane, or even the Southern Marshal, it would likely be carried by a servant of their household, so he does not know what this may be.'

'It looks like we are about to find out,' Saana commented, as an old man with a beard more grey than brown stepped hesitantly out of the guardhouse after Ita, eyeing the clatter of practice blades wielded by Naridan and Tjakorshi somewhat nervously.

'Over here, man!' Daimon shouted, and Ita nudged the pedlar in his direction. The man hurried over, quite obviously doing his best not to stare at Saana, then bowed low to Daimon.

'Lord Blackcreek, 'tis an honour.'

'This lord's man said you had a letter for him,' Daimon said, without any further preamble. 'Who from?'

'From a noblewoman this servant met on the road here,' the pedlar replied, digging into one of the packs slung at his hips. 'Young, she was, younger than you or so this servant would guess. She didn't give her name, and this servant wasn't going to ask, but since this servant knows your lordship would like to know, he can say that she looked to be travelling with men who wore the colours of Darkspur.'

'Yarmina,' Daimon muttered. 'Why did she give you this letter? Supposing you can find it,' he added, as the man rummaged further.

'Ah! Here we are!' The pedlar pulled out a piece of paper, folded and sealed with a blob of wax. There was no obvious imprint on it, but then again, did Yarmina wear anything with the Darkspur crest with which she could have marked the wax? 'This servant can't say as to why, your lordship, but it was early in the morning when she bought a cloak from him and gave him this letter to bring to you, and then she took off before the sars with her were even awake.'

Daimon blinked in surprise as he took the letter. For her to ride off without her escort was very strange behaviour. 'Which way did she go? Was she heading back here?'

'No,' the pedlar said, looking at him oddly, 'the other way, off towards Darkspur, although this servant can't say if she kept to the South Road; or the North Road, as you'd think of it. Why would she be giving him a letter for your lordship if she was coming back here herself? Begging your lordship's pardon,' he added after a moment, perhaps worrying that he'd been overfamiliar.

'Hmm.' Daimon hesitated, looking at the letter in his hands.

'Are you going to open it?' Saana asked, and to his surprise, Daimon found that he did not want to. It was very odd, Yarmina writing to him like this, and then – if the pedlar could be believed – disappearing away from her own escort. He worried something dark was afoot, and that by opening the letter he would be drawn into it.

That was foolishness, of course, and he would look like a fool himself if he ignored this letter after demanding the pedlar be brought to him.

'Begging your lordship's pardon,' the pedlar said again, somewhat nervously, 'but the young lady did say that your lordship would give this servant a gold piece for bringing the letter to you. She said that she wrote as much in the letter,' he added hurriedly, when Daimon looked at him, startled, 'but if your lordship isn't going to open it here and now then this servant thought he'd better mention it . . . '

A gold piece? Either Yarmina's notions of Black Keep's wealth were wildly inaccurate, or she truly believed her letter would be that valuable to him. Or the man was lying, Daimon reflected, but there was only one way to find out.

He broke the wax seal, unfolded the paper, and began to read.

Daimon,

Please forgive the roughness of this handwriting; it is futile to attempt decent calligraphy when writing in a tent by the light of a solitary candle. And besides, this lady must be both swift and brief.

If the conversation of Omet and his men is to be believed, the failure of your mountain allies to appear is due to Darkspur men enslaving them to take gold which their lands apparently contain. Omet believes that you will learn of this shortly, and will then march on Darkspur to seek revenge. He intends to advise this lady's father to march on you first, and use the news of a witch in Black Keep as an excuse. This lady believes that her father will agree.

This lady will take flight towards the mountains, to distract her escort and delay us reaching Darkspur. She will promise the bearer of this letter that you will pay him a gold piece for delivering it unopened: hopefully that will be enough of a bribe to prevent him from speaking of it to Omet, when Omet asks if he saw in which direction this lady has gone.

Do with this warning what you will,

Y

Daimon rubbed his jaw as he read back over what Yarmina had written. It was her hand; there was no doubt about that, despite the evident haste in which it had been composed. Even the paper was the same as she used for the poem she wrote for Saana and him. Its authenticity of origin could not be denied, but what about the contents?

'You do not look happy,' Saana offered. The Tjakorshi had no history of paper or any real written language as Naridans understood it, and there was no hope of her reading the letter herself. He had to tell her, but not in front of the pedlar.

Regardless of whether Yarmina was telling the truth, the letter itself was certainly valuable one way or the other. 'Ita!' Daimon called, and the tall, thin guard hurried over to him.

'Yes, Lord Daimon?'

'The pedlar is to be paid a gold piece from the strongbox,' Daimon told him. 'Find Osred, and tell him he is to see it done.' He looked at the pedlar, whose face had lit up. 'Do not tell anyone that you brought this letter here, or what payment you received for it, is that clear?'

'No fear, lord,' the pedlar replied with a grin. 'It doesn't do for us lowborn to go flashing gold around! Uh, that said, would it be possible for this servant to take the equivalent in silver, instead of gold? It would cause fewer questions, and be easier for him to use . . .'

'Fine,' Daimon agreed. 'Ita, silver instead of gold. Then Sagel, Osred, Aftak and Evram are to come to the great hall.'

'Aye, lord,' Ita replied with a bow, and turned to the pedlar. 'Go back to your cart. S'man will bring the money to you.'

'As you say,' the pedlar said, sketching a quick bow to Ita, and a deeper one to Daimon. 'A pleasure to be of service, Your Lordship.'

'What is going on?' Saana asked Daimon, as Ita hurried off. 'What does the message say?'

'Darkspur might be coming for us,' Daimon told her in a low voice. 'Yarmina writes to say so, but can we trust her?' He bit his lip thoughtfully. 'We need to decide how we will respond to this warning, and quickly. Who would you take counsel from?'

'The witches,' Saana replied immediately, 'and the Hornsounder. If fighting is to be involved, some of the captains, too.'

'Get whoever you need to the great hall,' Daimon told her. 'And it would be best to bring Nalon, too, to help with translation. We will take this decision as one town, Naridan and Tjakorshi together.'

Saana raised her eyebrows. 'It is hard enough to get the witches to agree on anything, and you would bring more people into this?'

Daimon smiled tightly at her. 'You did not think this would be easy, did you?'

Saana smiled back. Clearly she too remembered their first real conversation, outside of the walls of Black Keep. 'No. No, your wife did not.'

'Good,' Daimon said. He folded up the letter again and shoved it into his belt. 'Because your husband fears that nothing which is about to come will be easy.'

THEY GATHERED AROUND the long table in the great hall: Daimon, Osred, Sagel, Evram and Aftak for the Naridans; Saana, Tsolga Hornsounder, Inkeru Kjanjastutar, and the witches – Ada, Esser, Kerrti and Ekham – for the Tjakorshi. Somewhere between the two, and looking as reluctant as always, was Nalon of Bowmar: Naridan by birth, Tjakorshi first by kidnapping and now by choice, and disagreeable by nature.

Daimon read them the letter and waited for it to be translated to the Tjakorshi by Nalon. The reaction was much as he'd expected.

'This is outrageous!' Aftak fumed. 'It makes this priest wish he'd put his staff down Thane Odem's throat when he spoke out at the victory feast!'

'Only if the girl's telling the truth,' Nalon said wearily. Saana translated his words, and Inkeru said something in response. 'Inkeru wants to know why she wouldn't be telling the truth,' Nalon continued, 'to which my reply would be: because she's a bloody noble. Your presence excepted,' he added, with a nod to Daimon.

'Yarmina Darkspur is the daughter of a man who has no love for Blackcreek,' Daimon said. 'That said, she seemed friendly when she came here: in fact, she claimed to disagree with her father's agenda, which was supposedly to either marry her to this lord's brother, or for her to seduce either this lord or his wife in order to weaken our alliance.'

Both groups made appropriate noises of consternation at that statement, and Daimon held up his hand for quiet.

'The trouble is, we cannot be sure. This lord had not spoken to her for many years, and her words when she visited might have been a trick to make him think that she was opposed to her father, when in fact she was merely trying to win this lord's trust in order to deceive him at some future point.'

'If the Lady Yarmina is lying, what does Darkspur gain if we believe her?' Evram asked. The reeve had completely recovered from the sickness that had gripped him after Old Elio's attack, for which Daimon was grateful. He liked the man, and he seemed both reliable and tenacious.

'If we take it as true that Darkspur has indeed enslaved the people of the Smoking Valley, we cannot let that stand,' Osred said. 'They are our friends, and their people live in our land: including in this town, at least until Amonhuhe left to discover what has befallen her kin. Honour would compel us to march on Darkspur.'

'Which would be foolish,' Daimon added. 'Darkspur is larger than Blackcreek, and not only commands more men, but more sars. They were able to spare four just to accompany Yarmina here, whereas Blackcreek no longer has any household sars. We could send out to Lenby, Ironhead and so on, but we would be hard-pressed to match what Darkspur could assemble easily, let alone if they called in all their strength. Honour would compel us to march to our own doom.'

'So it could be a trap?' Saana asked, and Daimon nodded.

'They could be seeking to draw us to attack them, yes.'

'If you did attack them,' Ada asked, translated through Nalon, 'what would the Southern Marshal think of it?'

Daimon looked at Osred. 'That would depend. The mountain folk are not true Naridans, as it is reckoned, and our friendship with them might not be seen as reason enough to attack another thanedom.'

'So they could also be trying to make you look bad in front of your chief,' Ada pointed out. 'Make you start the fight over a fish you dropped yourself.'

Daimon raised an eyebrow at Nalon, who shrugged. 'What? That's what she said! It's difficult enough to keep up with everyone's actual words, let alone trying to remember which of you use what sayings.'

'She is correct,' Daimon conceded. 'Marshal Brightwater took our side when we could prove to him that we wanted peace, and could coexist with each other. If we make war on another thanedom without good reason, he might not be so understanding.'

'But the suggestion that Darkspur might come for us first could be intended to rush us, and make us take this rash decision,' Inkeru pointed out.

'So let's say they do,' Tsolga Hornsounder said. 'Let's say the bastards come south to kill us because they think we're all witches, or whatever. Is that better for us than us going to them?'

Daimon looked at Osred. 'Probably. If Yarmina's letter is genuine, Darkspur will not know we suspect their coming. We would have more time to prepare than they would expect, and we can send out for help. Odem's best hope would be to wipe us out quickly, before anyone else can arrive to demand answers from him. Even if Gilan Tainbridge comes, our other neighbouring thane, Odem would have to treat him as an equal and explain himself. Gilan could demand to be allowed to speak to this lord, to get our side of events. If Odem refused, Gilan might conclude he was not acting honourably. He might send word to the Southern Marshal: he might even take up arms against Odem himself.'

The Hornsounder spat, to Osred's visible disgust, and crossed her arms. 'Sounds like we're better off waiting here, then.' The other Tjakorshi were looking at her in apparent surprise, and she looked back. 'What? You want to go start a fight with a bunch of dragon-riding sars on their own ground, you go right ahead.'

'That is literally what you did for *years*,' Kerrti pointed out, but Tsolga just shrugged.

'Old age comes to us all.'

'The other thing,' Nalon put in, now clearly speaking for himself, 'is what's going on in the mountains. Hopefully, the party we sent should be coming back before long to let us know what's happening up there. If they don't . . . ' His fists were clenched and his knuckles were pale, and Daimon remembered that both of the man's sons were in that party, along with Inkeru's daughter and Osred's granddaughter. And of course, Zhanna.

'This lord cannot see any benefit to marching on Darkspur,' Daimon said. 'Not now. We would be acting on a letter whose truthfulness is unknown. It seems more sensible to prepare for an attack, and wait for word from the mountains. If our party returns and tells us that Yarmina was telling the truth in this matter, and no force from Darkspur has marched on us by that point, then we can reconsider. If Darkspur arrives before our people return, the point is moot.'

'That would seem wise,' Inkeru agreed, after a quick discussion among the Tjakorshi.

'And if our people don't return from the mountains, and Darkspur hasn't come?' Nalon asked.

Daimon grimaced. 'We are not at that point yet. Nor does this lord think we will be for at least a couple of weeks. We will set a date after which we will consider if we need to send a greater force. We know they reached Ironhead, at least.' The miners' first load of ore of the year had arrived via boat three days before, bringing welcome news about Zhanna's party, and the aid given by Sar Benarin at that settlement.

'So what do we do?' Ekham the witch asked. 'On Tjakorsha, our clan mostly lived all together. Your clan is spread far away.'

'We will send out messengers, calling all the sars that answer to Blackcreek to us, along with any fighters they have,' Daimon said, looking at Osred, and receiving an encouraging nod in return. 'We make ready with weapons: at least we have taken a boatload of ore from Ironhead, so Gador can bolster our armoury without needing to melt down ploughs and scythes. He may need help,' he added, looking at Nalon, who nodded in his turn.

'We should send out scouts,' Sagel offered. 'It's all very well being prepared, but we need to know when Darkspur is actually coming, if they are. The only decent route is the North Road, and it's the quickest as well, so that should be easy to watch.'

'If we hear they are coming, we should consider sending some of our people away,' Daimon said. 'The children, the old, the . . . ' He caught himself before he said 'women'. 'Those who cannot fight. If Odem seeks a quick victory in order to avoid questions, he must take Black Keep first. Those who flee into the rest of our land should be safe, at least unless and until Black Keep falls, at which point they would have perished anyway.'

'If we're going to do that, should we send messages with those people?' asked Esser the witch. 'To keep the biggest number of fighters here?'

'The people we would be sending away would probably not be able to travel fast or far,' Saana replied in Tjakorshi, causing Nalon to glare at her as he had to translate back into Naridan even though she spoke it herself. 'We would need to know our messages stood a good chance of getting where they needed to go fast enough to be of use.'

There was a pause for a few moments.

'So what about that lot who've just turned up with all their things to sell?' Tsolga Hornsounder asked, jerking a thumb over her shoulder in the general direction of the town square. 'They look like they walk for a living.'

Daimon looked at Osred. 'That . . . could work?'

'The pedlars won't necessarily have reason to go where we want them to,' Osred mused. 'They might not be selling their goods there.'

'So promise them money for it,' Saana suggested. 'Just as Yarmina did with the one who brought this letter.'

'If we give them money here, they might not go,' Aftak pointed out.

'This man said to *promise* them money,' Saana said. 'Tell them they will get it when they arrive, and put it in the letter, as Yarmina did.'

'The sars your husband will be writing to might not have the money to spare,' Daimon said uneasily. 'At least, not enough to convince the pedlars that the trip is worth their while.'

'But the message will have got there,' Saana said. 'Is the pedlar going to start a fight with your sar for not getting paid? You can find the men and pay them what you promised afterwards, if you wish, but at the moment the most important thing is to get the messages out, yes?'

There was nothing really to say to such logic, and so Daimon nodded. 'You are correct. Our survival is the most important, and we will have a better chance at that if we collect as many fighters as possible.' He looked up and around at the rest of the table: this odd mix of faces he had known all his life, and the strange, pale, foreign ones who until a few moons ago had featured only as enemies in his dreams. 'Are we agreed? We will prepare for an attack, but we will wait for word from the mountains before deciding if we need to take any such action ourselves?'

All around the table, heads nodded, and Daimon felt himself relax a little. The role of a thane was to command his people, but Daimon was not a thane; the thane, his brother, was far to the north. Besides which, the chief of a Tjakorshi clan did *not* command like a thane did, and a Tjakorshi clan would not accept being dictated to in such a manner.

Most importantly, Daimon realised, this was easier. The responsibility of authority and decision-making was not a pleasant one. It weighed on him, and made him sharp and irritable. Being able to talk matters through with people who felt freely able to give their own opinions, and coming to a conclusion based on that . . . Well, if this was any indication, it was a method he preferred.

'Spread the word, then,' he said. 'Our people need to know what may be coming. And this lord has some letters to write.'

Now he just had to hope they would get there. And if they did, that their recipients would heed them.

ZHANNA

THE GROUND HAD been stubborn, but Zhanna had climbed up into the mountains, fought Naridans, helped a captured people free themselves, and driven off a damned dragon: she wasn't going to be defeated by a bit of dirt with an attitude problem. She and the rest of her crew had thrown themselves into breaking up the soil and clearing the worst of the growth that had flourished in the Smoking Valley people's fields since they'd harvested their last crop. Even Danid had helped, despite only having one good arm at the moment. His cut had been dressed by one of the local healers, and although he said it was still painful, it didn't seem to have become infected.

After a few days of rest, and something more like a reasonable amount of food, the Smoking Valley people had begun to be able to take on the work themselves. Even so, Zhanna could see that there was worry about how much provision they had, and on the fifth evening after the battle, she drew Amonhuhe aside.

'This warrior thinks we should go,' she said, without preamble. 'Some work is done, but we must not eat too much food.'

'You're right,' Amonhuhe said, nodding. She looked around and sighed. They were standing in one of the entrances to Winterhome, and snow-capped tops of the nearest peaks were still catching the very last rays of the westerly sun. 'This woman is glad she came back to the land of her birth, but regrets she found such sadness here. If only she could have seen it in happier times.'

'Happiness can come again,' Zhanna told her. 'Brown Eagle clan had to leave our home. We will probably never go back. But this land is not so bad, even though it is new, and we can be happy here. Your people still have their home, at least.'

'Very true,' Amonhuhe said with a smile. 'And there has been no sign of the Darkspur men returning. Spirits willing, they won't. And preferably, will die soon,' she added.

'Another reason we should leave,' Zhanna said. 'We must tell about Darkspur.' She wasn't sure exactly what that would lead to, but she doubted Daimon would take the news well. 'And must show we are well. Those of us that are,' she added, her mind drawn back to the grave in which Menaken lay, and Ingor's soul, trapped somewhere in these mountains. Zhanna didn't relish the thought of bringing that news to Avjla and Nalon.

'This woman will talk with the elders,' Amonhuhe said. 'And we will see who intends to accompany us back to the Lowlands.'

'Some are coming, then?' Zhanna asked, and Amonhuhe nodded.

'Yes. The elders sought counsel from the spirits, and have decided that the gold already removed from the Sacred River is no longer sacred, since our people were forced to do so under threat of our children's deaths. We can use it to trade with the Lowlanders.' She sucked her teeth. 'The problem is deciding who will be sent. Any who are hale enough for the journey could also be working the fields, or hunting, or could help protect us if Darkspur returns.'

Zhanna made a weighing motion with her hands. 'Is choice. Not having all fish in one net.'

Amonhuhe snorted. 'That is how we are viewing it. Speaking of which, this woman hopes you like fish, because that will be a lot of what we're eating on the way back . . . '

* * *

SHE WAS RIGHT. The Smoking Valley people had not yet been up to the rigours of hunting beasts for meat, but fishing the streams that ran down to the Sacred River was another matter, and slivers of dried, smoked fish formed a large part of the supplies provided the next morning for their return journey. Zhanna looked over her new band of travellers as the Smoking Valley people said their goodbyes to each other, and tried to commit them to memory as they milled about with one of the great, snow-capped peaks looming behind them.

There were the Brown Eagles; Tsennan Longjaw and Tamadh Avjlaszhin, sharing a joke about something, and Olagora Inkerustutar and Sakka Bridastutar, checking each other's packs were fastened securely. The Naridans: Avisha, who'd accepted a gift of a wooden bead on a string to go with her tattoo and probably further annoy her parents; and Ravel, whom Zhanna was sure she'd seen pressed up very close with a Smoking Valley boy in a dark corner the previous evening. Tatiosh counted as Naridan as well, she supposed, and maybe Amonhuhe too. But then again, although Tatiosh's parents had both been Naridan, he wore the beads of the Smoking Valley and spoke the language – not perfectly, but he'd told Zhanna he thought he'd already improved – and although Amonhuhe had lived in Narida for twenty years, she still referred to the Smoking Valley as 'her' people.

And then there were the Smoking Valley people themselves, nine of them. Kakaiduna, now dressed and shod rather more appropriately to travel, had expressed a wish to see Ironhead, and her mother Kakainena was coming too. Amonhuhe's brother Amonomin was with them, and then the rest were people whose names Zhanna hadn't yet learned. Some were Kakaiduna's age, or thereabouts. Others were older folk who might be past their prime as warriors, if Winterhome was attacked once more, but felt hardy enough to manage a trek down into the lowlands and back.

It occurred to Zhanna, as she looked at them all, that the dividing lines between Tjakorshi and Naridan and Smoking Valley would not necessarily be permanent. Amonhuhe was proof enough of that; as was Danid's wife, and some of the other folk from Ironhead. And of course, Zhanna's mother had married Daimon. When it came down to it, Zhanna was sure that she would prefer the company of people like this, with whom she had eaten and drunk and laughed and sang, and fought alongside, than she would any of the Tjakorshi who now honoured The Golden.

All the same, she did not intend to stop speaking Tjakorshi. Naridan was clumsy, and that was an end to it.

'There is a gift for you,' Amonhuhe said, making her way to Zhanna with something in her hands. 'Amonani picked it up off the floor of the store hut that night, and has been working on it since.'

She held it out, and Zhanna looked down at a cord like Avisha's. However, instead of a carved wooden bead, her cord bore a carved tooth as long as her hand.

'This is . . . a thundertooth fang?' she asked in awe.

'Aye,' Amonhuhe said with a smile. 'Your blade wounded it, and cut this from its mouth. Amonani found it and thought you might want proof of it, to show your clan.'

Zhanna could feel her face nearly split with her smile as she threw the cord over her head and let the carved tooth hang free. 'He was right.' She waved and smiled at the Smoking Valley warrior, who raised his hand in return.

'Are we ready then, captain?' Amonhuhe said with a smile, as the Smoking Valley folk finished their goodbyes. Zhanna grinned back. She knew the other woman had only used the word for the sake of it, but that was good enough for her.

'Yes, we are.' She whistled, and Thorn and Talon left where they were sniffing around in some bushes and bolted over to her, to the surprise and startlement of several of the Smoking Valley folk, who still didn't seem to have got used to a Raider who could command rattletails. 'To the Lowlands!'

SAANA

DARKSPUR WAS COMING.

Black Keep had only a day of warning, since the scouts they sent to watch the North Road were not able to outpace the advancing force by much. Daimon had already ordered any ears of spring wheat that looked ripe enough to be gathered in, but left the rest in the fields in the hope that help would arrive to break the siege, and so Black Keep might be able to salvage some of the crop. Saana wasn't sure about that, but her husband knew this country better than she did, so she left him to it. Besides, she had other things to concentrate on.

'They tell me you're in charge,' she said to the crow-haired woman picking at her teeth with a fingernail. They were sitting in a thrall house, where ten of the men and women formerly of Rikkut Fireheart's raid all slept, and the smell of so many bodies in close proximity was quite unpleasant. Saana had come here alone, safe in the knowledge the thrall's vow would keep her from harm, but she had to admit there was something a little intimidating about being in a confined space with so many people who, not so long ago, had been intent on killing her.

'As much as anyone is,' the thrall replied. 'I was captain of the *Storm's Breath*, before . . . ' She waved a hand dismissively. 'Before.'

Saana nodded. 'What's your name?'

The former captain straightened her back a little, and looked Saana in the eye. 'Akuto Merngustutar, known as the Wavechosen.'

Saana raised her eyebrows. 'The Wavechosen?'

Akuto Wavechosen shrugged. 'Come sail with me and tell me it's not true. And I was given the name, I didn't pick it myself.'

Saana nodded. 'I'm Saana Sattistutar, chief of the Brown Eagle clan.'

'We know who you are,' a wiry man with a plaited beard grunted from the far side of the house. 'Why are you here?'

'She's talking to me, Rodhnjan!' Akuto snapped, and the man – Rodhnjan – subsided.

'There's trouble coming our way,' Saana said to Akuto. 'Probably going to be reaching our gates before nightfall.'

'So I've heard,' Akuto agreed. 'It's why we're all in here instead of out in the fields, after all.'

'Everyone The Golden sent after us was a warrior,' Saana said carefully. 'We could use more warriors, about now.'

Akuto snorted and spat. 'By the Dark Father, Sattistutar! Thralls don't bear arms, you know that! I don't give a fuck how much this land and these people have changed you, you should know better! We yielded to you, so we work for you for a year and a day: we don't fight for you!'

There was a murmuring of agreement from around them. The Golden had broken the clans, but it seemed the draug had not shaken out some of the other underpinnings of her people, including adherence to the thrall's vow. Which was just as well, really, or else Black Keep would have been dead as soon as they turned their backs on the enemies they allowed to live in their midst.

'You know that the Flatlanders who are coming hate all of us?' she asked. 'Brown Eagle or Clanless, they won't know or care about the difference. They'll be trying to kill us all.'

Akuto stared at her, unflinching. 'The moment someone comes up to me and swings, that's when I start fighting. Not before. I failed The Golden: I'm not going to fail myself as well.'

Saana looked around at them. 'And you're all of the same opinion?'

'Of course we are,' Rodhnjan growled, and his sentiment was echoed by the others. 'This is child's stuff, Sattistutar.'

Saana nodded. 'Good. I needed to know.' She rested her hands in her lap and fixed Akuto with her gaze once more. 'What about if you were no longer thralls?'

Akuto frowned. 'What?'

'A large group of people who won't fight but still need feeding isn't going to help us,' Saana said bluntly. 'We could kick you out and let you take your chances with the Flatlander army. Maybe you'd take a few of them down for us if you got caught, or at least wear them out a bit. Maybe you'd get away from them altogether, and find a way to build some new ships and sail back across the ocean to The Golden, I don't know.'

'You've never met The Golden,' Akuto snorted. 'You wouldn't suggest that if you had.'

'Or,' Saana said, 'I can release you from your vow. You get your weapons back, you fight alongside us, you become Brown Eagle and Black Keep, both at once.' She shrugged. 'We'd have to sort out houses and land after we've dealt with these Flatlanders from the north, of course, but—'

'Wait,' Akuto cut her off, raising her hand. 'Let me be certain about this. You're offering to release us from our vows?'

'I'm offering to release you from your vows, and I'm offering you a home here,' Saana told her. 'What would you do at the end of your year and a day, if you don't want to go back to The Golden? Thralls sometimes join their captors' clans anyway.'

'After a year and a day!' Rodhnjan protested. 'Once the hot blood has cooled! We killed these people's families and friends! I've seen the looks we get! We wouldn't be welcome here!'

'Oh, and you think we were?' Saana demanded. 'I only got peace because I threatened to kill them all if we didn't get it!'

Akuto blinked in surprise. 'That's . . . an interesting tactic.'

'It worked, didn't it?' Saana pointed out. 'Sort of. Mostly. All I had to do was convince them not to fight us for long enough that they realised we meant no harm so long as they meant us no harm.' She gestured around at them. 'You don't get that luxury, and you probably won't get your year and a day for us all to get used to you. But you know what will make you welcome to us? Picking up weapons, and standing alongside us to defend this place against the people who want to kill us all. And if you won't do that as thralls – which you shouldn't – then I would have to release you from your vow.'

Akuto's face was a picture of distrust. 'If we pick up weapons, you've got a perfect excuse to kill us.'

'The Flatlanders have no custom of thralls,' Saana told her. 'They'd have killed you where you knelt.'

'Savages,' someone muttered.

'If we wanted you dead, you'd already be dead,' Saana elaborated. 'There are enough of you that if I gave you all weapons and you wanted to, *you* could probably kill most of *us*.' She sighed. 'Please don't think I'm doing this because I want to. Some of you killed friends of mine. I'm doing this because we need your help, and because you'll die if you don't and that would be pointless, and because I think I can trust that if you say you'll join the clan and fight alongside us, you won't then turn on us if as soon as I release you from your vow.'

'Can you even release us early?' another woman asked. 'I thought the vow was unbreakable.'

'You can,' a man from the far side of the house said. 'My clan did it a few years ago. We had a thrall, and we let him go because he was pretty useless, and just bloody annoying. We all figured keeping him longer was more trouble than it was worth.'

'We're not in Tjakorsha any more,' Saana said to Akuto, 'but we're still Tjakorshi. I don't know what The Golden is going to do with the rest of us, but I doubt it's anything good. I'd like the Tjakorshi to continue here, in our new home. And to give us the best chance of that, I need your help.'

Akuto took a deep breath and looked around the room, at the faces of her fellow thralls, then back at Saana. 'I can't speak for anyone else. But I'm in.'

'Me too,' called the man whose clan had released their own thrall early.

'Aye,' Rodhnjan grunted, and then the rest all chimed in at once with their agreement.

Saana smiled. It wasn't a decision that had been taken gladly or easily, and there had been some bitter back and forth among the Black Keep council – for so their collection of witches, priest, reeve and all the others had become known – but in the end it had been agreed. Once it became clear that Darkspur was coming, Black Keep needed the thralls to fight, and if they fought, they would be offered a home afterwards.

'Can you go and speak to the others?' she asked Akuto. 'Explain the offer to them, and see what they—'

She broke off as the noise from outside suddenly increased, and a clear, metallic sound rang out above it.

'What's that?' Rodhnjan asked, getting to his feet.

'The bells in the shrine,' Saana said, looking around as though she could see through the walls. 'They're here.' She glanced back at Akuto. 'Anyone who's willing to fight should go to the castle gates and get a weapon. There'll be the blackstone we took from you when you yielded, but there might be some spare steel, if that's more to your liking.'

'And you release us from our vow?' Akuto said. Saana nodded.

'As soon as you take up a weapon to help defend us, you're not a thrall.'

'You heard the chief!' Akuto bellowed, and suddenly she was a ship's captain once more. 'Get the word out, then get your hands on an axe and be ready to lop off anyone's nose if they poke it over that wall!'

Saana's work here was done. She hurried down the steps outside and ran for the walls closest to the Road Gate, while Akuto and her newly formed crew spread out with similar haste, heading for the nearest houses where other thralls resided.

There were already defenders in place, armed and armoured as well as Black Keep could provide with the warning they'd had. Daimon was standing directly over the gate in his full sar's war gear, although he still held his helm in one hand. Saana hurried to his side, and he turned to greet her with a quick kiss on her cheek.

'There they are,' he said, gesturing out at the North Road. 'Less than we feared, but still plenty.'

Saana grimaced as she took in the scene. There were perhaps a dozen sars on dragonback leading the way, and at least a couple of hundred men flooding out of the trees behind them, armed with spears or bows.

'Yes,' she muttered. 'Still plenty.' There were more people in Black Keep than there were attackers, but they had to assume that each of the Darkspur men was a fighter, and trained to at least some extent.

'You are not wearing your armour,' Daimon noted in a quiet voice.

'Not yet,' Saana replied. 'It would not do to visit the thralls wearing sea leather. It would have shown distrust.'

'Are they with us?'

She smiled. 'They are.'

Daimon huffed a sigh of relief. 'That may prove to be its own problem, down the line, but for now it is a blessing.'

'What hope do you think Osred has of convincing this Tainbridge?' Saana asked. The steward was the only person of recognisable authority Black Keep could spare from the defence, so he'd been sent up the coast on a taugh with a Tjakorshi fisher crew led by Otim Ambaszhin as soon as the scouts had confirmed Darkspur was coming. Saana had wanted to send Nalon with them, to make sure that Osred and the crew could understand each other, but Nalon had flatly refused, saying that he wasn't leaving Black Keep until he knew if his sons were coming back from the mountains. Saana couldn't really blame him for that; and besides, as Avlja's brother, Otim was Nalon's brother-by-marriage, and had a better grasp of Naridan than most of her clan.

'Reasonable,' Daimon replied. 'Your husband does not know Gilan Tainbridge well, but he was never our enemy, and your husband does not think he has any great love for Odem Darkspur. As for Idramar . . . ' He shook his head. 'That will likely depend on what manner of success Darel has had.'

'He is a clever man,' Saana said, doing her best to reassure him. 'Your wife is sure he will have argued well.'

'Well, he was always good at arguing,' Daimon muttered.

The attacking force began to fan out, surrounding the town at slightly more than a bowshot from the walls. However, one sar rode up towards the gate.

'Do not shoot,' Daimon instructed the archers with them on the wall. 'One man alone comes to talk. Let us see what they say.'

'You do not intend to walk out to meet him?' Saana joked.

'Your husband got away with that once,' Daimon murmured. 'He suspects this man's intentions are not as good as yours were.'

The sar brought his mount to a halt a few paces from the gate, and removed his helm. Saana found herself looking down on the visage of Sar Omet.

'Sar Omet,' Daimon called. 'Did you forget something when you left in such a hurry?'

The Black Keep folk on the walls with them laughed, but Sar Omet merely glowered.

'This steward would have thought that you recognised the seriousness of your situation, Blackcreek. You consort with witches and foreign demons, and bring shame upon your family name and that of Narida.'

'This lord recognises the seriousness of you being an utter arse,' Daimon retorted. 'Where is your cousin? Does he not have the decency to speak with this lord himself?'

'Thane Odem has no words for you,' Omet sneered, then raised his voice. 'Hear this steward! Any true-born Naridan who grants us entry to this town will be spared! Should we have to breach the walls ourselves, all those within will be burned alive as witches, be they man, woman or child, as decreed by Nari Himself!' With that, he rammed his helm back on his head and turned his mount about, heading back for the Darkspur lines.

Saana heard Daimon growl in his throat. 'Shoot him.'

'Lord?' someone asked, astonished.

'Shoot him!' Daimon hissed. 'They claim we are all witches, and so they free themselves of any duty of honour towards us: we will return the favour! This lord has no more patience for games when his people's lives are in danger!'

All around Saana, wood creaked as bows were drawn, were held for a moment, and then loosed.

Some of the arrows missed. A couple were turned away by Sar Omet's coat-of-nails, and all those that struck his mount appeared to bounce off, but two of the long shafts pierced Omet's armour to lodge into his back. Saana heard his agonised cry, and as his mount sped up in response to the noise and the blows it had been struck, Sar Omet toppled sideways and fell on to the road.

There was a moment of silence, which Saana could tell was the result of a group of lowborn Naridans realising that they had just wounded a noble, possibly mortally. It was broken by Daimon turning to them.

'Mark that!' he snapped, as outraged shouts rang out from the Darkspur lines. 'They seek to burn us alive, and wish to use the fear of that threat to intimidate some of us into treachery! That is because they have no stomach for a true siege, and they know that if they cannot take this town quickly, they will not take it at all! The Tjakorshi ship that left yesterday will soon be at Tainmar, and will send word upriver so Thane Gilan will learn of what is happening here. Then it will sail on for Idramar, and after they reach it Thane Odem will have to explain his actions to the Southern Marshal, and even the God-King himself!'

Saana saw nods and murmurs of agreement in the people around them. Daimon was quite good at this.

'Sagel will come around with the watch details,' Daimon continued. 'Serve your shift on the walls, and stay alert. Send for this lord if it looks like they wish to treat with him again, but,' he cast a glance at where Sar Omet lay, 'he doubts they will have anything to say that we can trust.'

He began to push through them, heading for the steps that led back down to Black Keep's streets, and Saana fell in alongside him. He sighed and looked at her. 'Thank you for being here. Your husband does not know what he would do without you, facing down a threat such as this.'

Saana smiled at him, although she could not dislodge the worries clawing at her belly. 'We will see this through together. First we deal with the night, and then we see what tomorrow brings.'

'Yes,' Daimon said, looking towards where the sun was setting. 'Tomorrow. May Nari grant that it blesses us. We may well need it.'

MARIN

MARIN TOOK AN immediate dislike to Mordokel, and not just because of being held at knifepoint on his way to the privy. The priest had had the eyes and bearing of a fanatic, and the sort of burning sincerity that went right past naivety and became a weapon in its own right. Laz had been quite perturbed simply by the notion of a sar becoming a priest. For Marin, to whom casual falsehoods were as common as eating or drinking, the priest made a worrisome travelling companion, because Mordokel spoke the truth, always, and his eyes said that if he found you hadn't returned the favour then he'd come for you with his blade.

Nor would he tell them where they were going. Instead, all of them – several had joined from the village, once Mordokel had announced his identity and purpose of recruiting followers for Nari Reborn – simply had to follow where he led them, and he was not inclined to dawdle. For Bones and Elifel, city born and bred, Mordokel's pace was punishing, but the priest had no sympathy.

'God awaits,' he simply said through a cloud of pipe smoke, when Bones had complained of blisters. 'If your faith is not sufficient to overcome this discomfort, feel free to stay behind.'

It took four more days of punishing walking, after which time even Marin's travel-hardened feet and legs were feeling a little weary, before they reached their destination.

Marin no longer had any real idea where they were, only that they had been travelling steadily westwards. It wasn't until they'd fought their way up an interminably long road that wound its way back and forth up a steady rise in the land, and finally crested the top, that he saw the peaks of the Catseye Mountains in the distance and, more immediately, the mass of humanity spread out in the river valley below.

'That's the Greenwater, isn't it?' he asked Mordokel, leaning against a fence to get his breath back. The river was nowhere near the size of the Idra, especially near the sea and the capital, but it was still substantial, and on the near shore of it was a great clump of people. Marin could see some tiny specks that could well be tents, and even what looked to be a few crude shelters made of branches, but mainly it looked as though they were just . . . there.

'It is,' Mordokel confirmed. 'The Holy River, that flows down from Godspire.' He pointed, and Marin followed his finger towards a peak towering above its neighbours, nearly lost in the far distance and late afternoon haze. Then Mordokel lowered his finger to point at the camp, and Marin saw what looked like one of the few decent-sized tents, a rectangular affair of brown canvas. 'And there waits our god.'

Marin swallowed. Now he was actually here, part of him was wondering if this had been such a good idea. Who was truly ready to meet their god in the flesh? Marin probably wasn't. Would he not be judged for all the wrongs he had done, all the lies he had told, all the things he had stolen? Then again, if the priests were to be believed, such things were judged after you died in any case. Perhaps it was better to get it over with?

'This sar hopes the Divine One doesn't have any enemies nearby,' Laz observed from behind him. 'Because a dozen mounted sars would go through that camp like a blade through butter.'

'There have been unbelievers.' Mordokel smiled in that unnerving manner he had. 'They were . . . dealt with. We have not been here long, and the local thanes recognise that the glory of the God-King has come again to bless their lands. That tent, for example, was a gift from one of them.'

Marin rubbed his beard. 'And of course, that thane gets his emblem on the tent used by the God-King.'

'He does,' Mordokel conceded. 'But no one should read anything into it. The God-King is above, and we are below, thane and lowborn alike.'

'What does that mean, then?' Channa the Nose demanded.

'The God-King breaks the chains that bind us under the nobility,' Mordokel said, and Nari help Marin, but the priest's eyes grew even more fervent as he spoke. 'The old order will fall, as befits a flawed order in a flawed world. The Divine One will create His new order, and if He sees fit to elevate a man, that man shall be elevated. However, until then, we are all the same.'

Marin looked at Mordokel in shock. 'He intends to dismantle the thanedoms?'

'Thanes, sars, the so-called Divine Family,' Mordokel replied eagerly. 'None of it is fit for this world any longer. And He does not *intend* to do anything,' he added, looking sharply at Marin. 'His decrees have been made. Now the faithful must take them to the world, and the world must listen.' He tutted. 'But we are wasting time.'

'Just one thing, before we move on,' Bones piped up, and if the handsome young man was doing his best to keep a pleading note out of his voice, then he hadn't really succeeded. 'Does the Divine Nari . . . Is that His name? Is He Nari again? It's just that when s'man was a lad, the local priest said that when Nari was reborn, he'd have a different name at first.'

Mordokel looked for a moment as though he was going to walk off without deigning to answer, but then he spoke once more. 'The Divine One goes by the name given to the body he was born into, which is Tyrun. If you get the chance to address Him in person, "Divine One" will suffice.' Then he turned on his heel and strode off down the road that wound down the other side of the ridge and, eventually, towards where the camp lay.

'Address Him in person?' Bones said, the wonder in his voice overriding the pain. 'S'man never thought . . . '

'Don't get your hopes up, lad,' Elifel chided him, throwing a distinctly uneasy glance at Mordokel's departing back. Was it the prospect of coming face to face with a god that was troubling the man, or the nature of the god's priest?

'Come on,' Marin told them, as the villagers began to follow Mordokel. 'There's still a way to go if we want to get there before nightfall.'

'May Nari give s'man strength,' Bones muttered, wincing as he took his first step.

'Get a move on, and He might just,' Marin told him, and headed off after Mordokel.

IT WAS DUSK by the time they made it to the shores of the Greenwater, and fires were being lit in the camp. Marin was increasingly frustrated with Mordokel's behaviour as a guide: the priest would push on ahead, disappearing into the crowd, then reappear and snap at them for losing him. In the end, Marin simply aimed for what looked like the largest tents, and hoped he was moving in roughly the right direction.

'This is more like a market than a camp,' Laz muttered, as they squeezed between bodies.

'No one's really selling anything,' Marin pointed out. 'It's a bit like a festival.'

'That would make sense,' Laz agreed. He slapped at the hand of someone beyond him whom Marin couldn't see. 'Hands off that blade, unless you want to be introduced to it!'

Marin tutted, and turned away – who would be foolish enough to try to steal a sar's blade from its scabbard? – and stopped in his tracks as he found himself faced with an old man, his straggly hair nearly pure white, and a staff clutched in one swollen-knuckled hand. It was his eyes that made Marin blink uncertainly, however: they didn't have the fervour of Mordokel's, but were old, and deep, and not entirely friendly.

'Does s'man know you?' Marin managed, when the old man made no move to get out of his way.

'Heh.' The right side of the old man's mouth crooked into a smile. 'Not yet.'

'What—?'

The old man stepped backwards, and another body immediately took his place. Marin hissed in frustration and squeezed past this new obstacle, but once he'd done so the old man was nowhere in sight.

'Did you see him?' he asked Laz, who was frowning around at the crowd.

'Aye. Can't now, though.'

'He was a strange one,' Marin muttered, more discomfited by the brief interaction than he wanted to let on.

'We're in the camp of Nari Reborn,' Laz pointed out. 'There are bound to be some strange folk here.'

'Well, keep an eye out for him,' Marin said. 'Your husband would like to know what he meant by that "not yet" crack.'

The crowd was even thicker as they moved towards the God-King's tent, since everyone wanted to be close to Him. However, Marin still managed to navigate his way through, until suddenly he was stumbling out into a small area of clear space in front of the tent's entrance, and some serious-looking men with white robes and the same shaved head as Mordokel were pointing spears at him. Mordokel himself was waiting beyond them, with his arms folded.

'Here they are at last!' he snapped, as the others began to emerge from behind Marin. 'Come, then! The Divine One will meet his new followers!'

'He . . . ' Marin looked around at his companions. 'He will?'

'This priest told you we would see if your heart was pure,' Mordokel said with a smile. 'It will just happen a little sooner than he imagined. Come!'

With that, he turned and walked into the tent. Marin hesitated, eyeing the spears warily.

'Oh, for the love of the Mountain!' Channa snapped, brushing past him. 'This is why we came! Hang around out here if you wish!'

She walked past the white-robed men unchallenged. Marin turned around to check that Laz was with him, but what he saw instead was Ravi, wide-eyed and muttering something soundlessly over and over.

'What's wrong?' he muttered, falling in alongside her as they all passed through the entrance flaps. Laz, clearly overhearing, frowned and slowed on Ravi's other side. Ravi looked like she might have been about to answer, but then all worry fled from her face and was replaced by awe.

Marin turned, and as he did so he breathed in.

The air was not exactly sweet within the tent, but it was fresh: fresher than he had ever smelled before. He shivered, not through cold – there was a brazier of glowing ash in the middle of the tent, and the summer's heat had not yet faded from the day – but from something else that seemed to run a finger down his spine. The tent was lit by lanterns, hanging from poles, and sitting between them on a chair that looked to have been carved from a single great stump of wood, was Tyrun, the God-King.

Mordokel was prostrating himself in front of the enthroned figure, but Marin barely needed that detail, or the throne, to make his deduction. Tyrun wore a simple robe of white, much like the spearmen outside his tent and the two more standing one on each side of Him, and a narrow golden circlet rested on His brow, but it was the placid calm of His expression that told the true story. He was young – still some years short of His twentieth summer, if Marin was any judge – but His face was timeless.

Marin looked on that face, and it felt as though a little of its calm flowed into him.

'Your servant brings you new followers, Divine One,' Mordokel was saying.

'Then they had best approach,' Tyrun declared. His voice was smooth, and clear and light as a spring stream. He raised a hand and beckoned. 'Come forward, new friends.'

They approached in a cautious cluster, until they stood just behind where Mordokel still bowed. Then, and Marin could not say which of them moved first, they all knelt and prostrated themselves in the same manner as the priest. It felt . . . right.

'Rise, Mordokel,' Tyrun commanded, and Marin heard the priest getting to his feet. 'Now, new friends, look up. This god would see your faces as He speaks with you.'

Marin sat up, rocking back onto his haunches. Tyrun rose from His throne and moved to the far end of their loose line, where knelt a woman from the village in which they had met Mordokel.

'What is your name?'

'Arraba, Divine One,' she replied, eyes shining.

'Arraba,' Tyrun repeated. He nodded. 'Be welcome here, Arraba.'

He moved along the line, repeating the same exchange with the other village lowborn, then with Gershan, Kenan, Aranel, Channa and Alazar, until He got to Ravi.

'And what is your name?'

Ravi stared up at him, eyes wide and lips tight. Tyrun raised His eyebrows, and when Ravi still didn't speak, the two spearmen stepped forward.

Marin could see nothing else for it, so he nudged Ravi in the ribs. She grunted, but it seemed to jolt her out of whatever reverie she was in, at least enough for her to stutter 'R-Ravi, Divine One.'

'Ravi.' Tyrun nodded and did not hesitate. 'Be welcome here, Ravi.'

The spearmen stepped back, but Ravi bent forwards. Marin was startled to see that she was weeping. He wanted to ask her if she was unwell, but now Tyrun was standing in front of him.

'And what is your name?'

'Marin, Divine One,' Marin said, finding his voice surprisingly raspy in his throat. This was it, a moment he could never have believed would come to pass. His ambitions of being the first Cupbearer to look upon the face of his god dissolved like an arrogant mist, and he knew peace and awe in equal measure.

'Marin.' Tyrun's calm eyes held his gaze for several heartbeats, but Marin got the distinct feeling that behind that calmness lay something else entirely.

'Be welcome here, Marin,' Tyrun said, and moved on.

Marin stared blankly ahead, forgetting about Ravi's silent weeping. How could he hope to direct the course of such a being? Whatever reason Tyrun had for not yet making the pilgrimage to Godspire, it must be correct. Only a person of great hubris would seek to—

Beside him, the rhythm of Tyrun's questioning was broken.

'And what is your name?'

'Elifel, Divine One.'

'Elifel.' Tyrun hummed to Himself, and the tone sounded disapproving. Then He stepped backwards.

'You are not welcome here, Elifel.'

Elifel did not protest. Instead, he lurched to his feet with a snarl and drew the knife at his belt.

Righteous fury seized Marin, and he lunged for Elifel off his knees, wrapping his arms around the other man's thighs and knocking him sideways. They tumbled to the ground together in front of Bones, who yelped in fear and scrambled backwards. Marin reached up, trying to grab Elifel's knife hand, but Elifel dragged the weapon back out of reach with a curse and kicked his legs, striking Marin in the chest and knocking him clear. Marin tried to drag himself up again, but the breath had gone from his lungs, and Elifel was already halfway back to his feet and raising his knife with a snarl—

He never got any farther. Tyrun had retreated towards His throne, and His two spearmen's blades punched into Elifel's chest and drove the would-be assassin back down to the ground, then held him there as he gasped and died. Marin, still trying to get his own breath back, saw the light fade from Elifel's eyes.

'Divine One!' Mordokel cried. He had drawn his longblade, and held it like one who knew how to use it. 'We must get you away—'

'There is no need,' Tyrun interrupted his priest, raising His hand. 'This god's servants ensured that He was in no danger.' His eyes lit on Marin, who swallowed and lowered his gaze as his muscles began to shake. It was only now dawning on him that he had thrown himself, unarmed, at a man wielding a knife with murderous intent.

'Mar!' Laz was at his side now, and wrapping an arm around him. 'Are you hurt?'

'Your husband is fine,' Marin assured him, leaning into the comfort of Laz's side. The commotion had attracted attention from outside the tent, and other spearmen burst in. Mordokel issued swift instructions, and Elifel's body was dragged out. Two additional guards remained, with weapons held ready.

'Marin,' Tyrun said. Marin found his head jerked up as though attached to a line.

'Yes, Divine One?'

'Your god thanks you for your efforts to keep Him from harm,' Tyrun said, and His smile spread warmth through Marin's soul. 'He will remember your devotion.'

Marin felt his cheeks heat, and he looked down again.

'Now begone, all of you,' Mordokel instructed, stepping forward, and eyeing Marin with an expression that he found hard to read. 'The Divine One—'

'Mordokel,' Tyrun interrupted, and his priest instantly fell silent. 'This god has not yet finished meeting His new followers.'

Marin saw Mordokel's mouth open to frame an objection, but the bald man clearly thought better of it, and simply bowed instead. Tyrun, apparently unperturbed by the attempt on His life, resumed his position. 'And what is your name?'

'Adal, Divine One,' Bones replied, and he was weeping, Marin noticed. 'Divine One, this servant begs your forgiveness! He knows he's wronged you!'

Tyrun raised His eyebrows again. 'Indeed?'

'Divine One, Elifel and this servant were sent here by Livnya the Knife of Idramar,' Bones blurted out. 'We were to kill you if we could, because she thought you were a fraud, but this servant sees that you're not! He knows you know his heart isn't pure, but he wanted to say it for himself before you sentence him!'

Marin exchanged a glance with Laz. The Livnya they'd met in Kiburu ce Alaba, and who'd shared the voyage back to Idramar with them on the *Light of Fortune*, had never confirmed that she was indeed Livnya the Knife, but Marin would have taken a bet against his life that she had been. Who else would have been addressed so respectfully by the ship's captain, despite not obviously being an actual noblewoman? To learn she had sent knives to try to assassinate the God-King, the *actual* God-King, even if she'd thought he was a fraud . . .

Well, Marin was glad he hadn't pushed trying to make her admit her identity on board that ship. Otherwise, they might not be here now.

The spearmen had turned their attention to Bones, who was kneeling bolt upright with his eyes shut and tears tracking down his cheeks, but Tyrun raised his hand to halt His minions.

'Adal,' He said softly. 'Look at your god.'

Adal did so, blinking his eyes open fearfully.

'You know your god is true?'

'This servant does, Divine One!'

'And do you swear to serve Him truly?'

'This servant does, Divine One!'

Tyrun nodded. 'Then be welcome here, Adal.' The spearmen stood back again, but Tyrun turned to Mordokel. 'Be at ease.'

'This servant said nothing, Divine One,' Mordokel replied, bowing low.

'You didn't need to say it, Mordokel,' Tyrun replied with a faint smile, and Marin suppressed a smile at the momentary expression of mortification that crossed the priest's features. 'Adal's heart is pure enough, as are all those here. You may go,' He added, turning back to them. 'Go forth, mingle with your brethren, and be welcome. Because you are all welcome.'

Marin realised that he had no idea how you withdrew from the presence of a god. They managed it as a group by backing away and bowing until they reached the tent's entrance. Outside, there was no sign of Elifel's body. Whatever had been done to him, he clearly hadn't been kept around as an object lesson.

'What do we do now?' Channa asked, her expression slightly dazed.

'We find somewhere to sleep,' Laz replied, looking around. 'Somewhere on the edges, this sar reckons.'

'Sleep?!' Adal exclaimed. 'We just met our god! How can we sleep after that?'

'This sar can sleep after just about anything,' Laz told him dryly. 'You don't have to, but we'll be no use to the Divine One's cause in the morning if we haven't slept.'

'Can't believe it about Elifel,' Gershan muttered.

'Never did trust him,' Kenan replied to his brother, casting a quick glance at Adal. 'Always thought they seemed a bit too eager for no good reason, those city lads.'

'Stow it,' Channa snapped. 'The Divine One's declared his heart's pure enough, so you get no say in it.'

'S'man wasn't saying that—'

'Are you well?' Marin muttered to Ravi as Laz started shouldering his way through the crowd and they fell in behind him. 'You seemed a little overawed in there. Which isn't surprising,' he added hastily, 'but it seemed to affect you more than the rest of us.'

'S'woman's well,' Ravi said, without looking at him. She was staring straight ahead, but Marin wasn't sure she was really seeking what was in front of her eyes. 'She's well. She's pure of heart,' she added wonderingly. 'Pure of heart.'

'As are we all,' Marin agreed, resisting the urge to add something self-deprecating afterwards. He was probably the least-qualified to judge about the state of his own heart, after all.

'Have you . . . ' Ravi shook her head. 'Have you lived with a fear your whole life?'

Marin looked at her. 'S'man doesn't imagine you're talking about spiders.'

'No.' Ravi snorted, and a little of her old manner returned. 'No, she's not. Have you lived with a fear your whole life, bone-deep since you were a child, to the point you have to try to forget it at every moment, because if you remember it then it will stop you where you stand?'

'No,' Marin replied honestly. 'S'man hasn't.'

'Imagine that you have,' Ravi said to him. 'Imagine that, and then imagine that one day you learned it was untrue. That you could just . . . ignore it.'

Marin frowned. 'S'man's not sure he can imagine that.'

'Well, when you can,' Ravi told him, 'you'll get an idea of how s'woman feels today.'

Marin did not press further. He walked alongside her instead, and behind his husband, until they found a fire going with people sitting around it who had enough space for newcomers to join them under the summer sky. And then, after they'd eaten some of the food that was being shared around and had talked for a while, and while Laz drifted off and began gently snoring, Marin lay on his back looking up at the sky and thought of the placid-faced young god, and his deep, calm eyes, and wondered what he was supposed to do.

JEYA

NO ONE REALLY knew how Ngaiyu had come to own thëir house, or even by what standards thëy actually owned it, if thëy had at all. But when thëir funeral had taken place – which was not a pauper's funeral, although no one knew who had paid for the priest, and the worshippers, and the flowers – and the mourners had disappeared, it became clear that no one was claiming to be Ngaiyu's child. That meant there was a house in East Harbour with no one living in it, and that was not a state of affairs that would continue for long.

If it was left for many days, someone looking for a place of their own would claim it: and perhaps that was how Ngaiyu had come by it in the first place, for the Hierarchs' tax collectors were the only people who would keep track of who lived where, and they would not ask questions about where someone came from so long as they approved of the amount of money that was handed over. It wasn't as though Jeya begrudged anyone else use of the house, because shé knew well enough what it was like to have nowhere to sleep, but shé worried that whoever ended up living there wouldn't take the same attitude to the street children as Ngaiyu had.

So it was that, slightly before the mourning garlands had properly wilted, Bulang the scribe's assistant – and possible descendant of a god – and Jeya the thief moved into Ngaiyu's place. In theory, given the flowers still held some life, Ngaiyu's ghost could freely visit them. However, Jeya had no fear of Ngaiyu, ghost or otherwise, and shé was sure that if Ngaiyu did visit, thëy would approve. No one else wanted to risk it yet, but Jeya had made it clear that as soon as the garlands had wilted the house would be open on the same basis as it had been before: you paid a few coppers for a space to sleep and a meal from the pot, and you didn't make trouble.

Shé scrubbed the house down, making sure to get rid of any hint of the old bloodstain left from where Ngaiyu had been murdered by Nabanda. The rocking chair was gone, as well: some things were so personal to the departed that they could not be passed on. The big pot was still there, though, as well as Ngaiyu's smaller pans, and the cut crystal on the wall. Shé and Bulang had got a few items of their own together, now Bulang was earning a few coins from Skhetul for the work thëy were doing there. They each had a hammock now, hanging from the ceiling beams, and as someone who had spent most of hér life sleeping on hard floors or street corners, it seemed to Jeya something akin to a gift from the gods themselves.

They were not in their hammocks at the moment, however. They were sitting together on the floor and watching the shadows lengthen and deepen as the sun began to dip behind the peak to the west. Jeya wondered if this time of day would always remind hér of that desperate fight against Nabanda, when shé had realised all hér fears were true and hér best, longest-standing friend had truly betrayed hér, but there was nothing to be done about that. Perhaps it was best to remember it: to remember that this life made people take hard decisions. Shé could never forgive Nabanda, never, but shé could understand the first choices hê had made that had led hîm down that path.

'Are yóu happy?' Bulang asked. Thëir fingers were twined through Jeya's, and shé realised that shé could answer the question immediately and honestly.

'Yes,' shé said. 'Í'm sad too, Í'm really sad. Í miss Ngaiyu, and Damau, and Í miss the friend Í thought Nabanda was. Or the friend hê actually was, for most of my life. But Í have yöu, and we have this house, and we're going to be able to do for other people what Ngaiyu did for mé, and Nabanda, and Damau, and M'bana, and Lihambo, and all the others. And Í really like that.'

'Í like it too,' Bulang replied. 'Although if the house is full every night, that might be a shame.' Thëir fingers tightened on Jeya's, and when shé looked at thëm, thëir eyes seemed exceptionally large, even given how close they were to each other.

'Well,' shé managed, through a mouth that was suddenly clumsy, 'the house doesn't always need to be full. You know, if it looks like it's going to be a dry night, or something.'

Bulang raised thëir free hand and traced one fingertip along the line of Jeya's jaw, and it seemed to Jeya that a line of fire followed in its wake. 'Well, a dry night doesn't sound like fun.'

Jeya felt hér cheeks heat instantly, and shé must have made some visible reaction as well, because Bulang actually laughed quietly.

'Did you just—?' shé demanded disbelievingly, but the rest of hér question was lost as Bulang leaned in and kissed hér.

Within a moment, Jeya was lost in hér lover's lips. Long, deep, searching kisses turned into a line of them being tracked down Jeya's neck and making hér shiver, and then shé was fumbling at Bulang's maijhi, and this time Bulang didn't freeze or withdraw, but shucked thëir shoulders to allow Jeya to pull the garment off. Jeya made an involuntary noise deep in the back of hér throat and leaned back in, putting hér right hand on Bulang's chest and reaching up with hér left to the back of thëir head to thread hér fingers through thëir long, dark hair—

Someone hammered on the front door so violently that both of them yelped. Jeya pulled away immediately and scrabbled for hér knife, while Bulang grabbed for thëir maijhi and fought thëir way back into it.

'*We know you're in there. Open the door.*'

The voice was low, but pitched to carry. Jeya's breath was coming fast, and not just because of the after-effects of arousal. What was going on? Had someone decided they wanted Ngaiyu's house, and were prepared to take it by force despite the presence of the mourning garlands?

'*Open the door, or we'll open it for you.*'

To illustrate the point, something heavy thumped against the door, causing it to rattle in its frame. It had to be a big body to manage that; bigger than Jeya fancied tangling with.

'Out the back!' she mouthed to Bulang, who nodded. They scrambled for the back door, pulled back the bar and wrenched it open—

—only to come face-to-face with two long knives, held by the pair of large toughs waiting for them.

Jeya backed up instinctively, pushing Bulang behind hér and waving hér knife, looking for an opening, but the toughs made no move to attack. They followed hér into the house, though, and behind them came another person: much shorter, barely even Jeya's height, and not richly dressed, but who walked with the air of someone used to telling others what to do.

'Open the front door,' they instructed Jeya. 'My people will break it down, otherwise. I only want to talk. At the moment.'

Jeya swallowed nervously, but hér options seemed limited. The front door *thumped* again, and shé wasn't confident it would hold for much longer. It seemed better not to antagonise this person and their muscle, so shé edged to the front door and pulled back the bar, then moved hurriedly back to Bulang's side. Three more people quickly made their way in, each one of them with the air of brawlers.

The same air that Nabanda had possessed, when hê'd been dealing with people other than hér.

'Hello, little ones,' the person who was clearly in charge addressed them both. They smiled, very wide and not at all friendly. 'I am Kurumaya.'

'Is that supposed to mean something to us?' Bulang demanded, but Jeya had frozen. Shé'd heard of Kurumaya: who hadn't, when you'd spent your life on the streets of East Harbour? Kurumaya was a Shark, and one of the most dangerous. Shé hadn't known anyone who would have been able to put a face to the name, but—

Oh, but what if shé had?

'I never knew Ngaiyu,' Kurumaya said looking around at the house. 'But I know people who did. Thëy were a good person. Nabanda shouldn't have done what they did. That's my fault, in part. I pressured Nabanda to do what they'd told me they could do, and they clearly got reckless. Indiscriminate. I don't like that.' They sighed. 'I paid for the funeral costs, and the flowers, and the garlands you've left hanging outside. It's not much, but perhaps it helped a few people who'd lost someone they valued.'

'Nabanda was working for you?' Jeya asked, the words coming out clipped and half-formed thanks to the fear freezing hér throat.

'Yes,' Kurumaya nodded. 'And the last thing they were supposed to do for me . . . '

Their gaze settled on Bulang.

' . . . was to kill you.'

'Why?' Bulang asked, and Jeya could tell from thëir voice that thëy were just as scared as shé was, but were doing thëir best to hide it. 'Who do you think I am?'

'Well, that's the question, isn't it?' Kurumaya said. 'Someone paid me to have you and your family killed, and they didn't blink at my price. I even made it higher than usual, because they were Naridan, and how should a Naridan know how much a life is worth in East Harbour?' They sighed. 'Then I thought I learned who that Naridan was, and so I pressed Nabanda to finish what they started, because this was not someone whom I wished to disappoint.'

'You're a Shark,' Jeya said without thinking. 'What do you have to be scared of?'

'Even sharks swim carefully when a new predator is in the

water,' Kurumaya said, with a mirthless grin. 'But then Nabanda failed me, thanks to what I have to admit was a very good scheme cooked up by the pair of you. Unfortunately for you, you made a lot of noise when you persuaded your friends to take on Nabanda's crew, and you did it quite close to where I have eyes and ears. I could have sent someone else after you immediately, and finished the job. But then I did what I should have done earlier, and started thinking.'

They moved closer, and looked Bulang up and down. 'Someone rich and powerful wants you dead, and wants it badly enough to come here themselves and pay me to do the deed. That's no short trip, from Idramar. So tell me, little one: why are you so dangerous to rich and powerful Naridans?'

'You killed my family,' Bulang spat at them. 'I owe you nothing.'

'You don't,' Kurumaya conceded. 'But what about this city? Do you owe *it* anything?'

Bulang's laugh was a snort of derision. 'No.'

Kurumaya's face lit up.

'*And nor do I.*'

Jeya blinked. What?

'This city,' Kurumaya continued, 'is still bringing my blood in from our home, and selling them as slaves while the Hierarchs grow fat off the shore taxes.'

Jeya found herself nodding slightly in understanding. Kurumaya did have the look of the folk she'd seen who hailed from the Fishing Islands to the south. A child of a slave, then, since the law said no one born in the City of Islands could be a slave? Or one who'd escaped?

'You seem to matter to important people,' Kurumaya told Bulang. 'Perhaps I should be clever. It could be that you are someone, or that you know something, that could help my cause. Tell me why, and who, and perhaps you don't need to die.'

Bulang hesitated. Jeya's chest was so tight she could barely breathe.

'What do you want?' Bulang asked quietly.

'I've freed slaves,' Kurumaya snarled. 'I've bought them from the rich and let them go; I took over the fighting pits and freed all those who fought there under duress, and replaced them with willing participants eager to earn coin, but *it is not enough*. I want,' they continued, biting down on every word, 'to tear this city down until everyone who views other people as property is crying blood on the street corners.'

'Including the Hierarchs?'

'*Especially* the Hierarchs.'

Bulang swallowed. Jeya shut hér eyes. Shé knew what was about to happen, and shé couldn't stop it. Nor was shé sure shé wanted to. The alternative, if Bulang kept thëir mouth shut, was that both of them were knifed to death in this house, just like Ngaiyu had been before them, because they weren't of any use to this person who claimed they didn't want people to be treated as property.

But shé still did not think that this was going to be the easy choice.

Bulang exhaled.

'I'm the Splinter King.'

EPILOGUE

THERE WAS ONLY *the ocean.*

As wide as the sky, as deep as the night, as old as time itself, perpetually in motion yet never changing. Seared by the sun as it climbed the northern skies, chilled by snow and sleet and torrential rain, whipped up into spray by howling gales as the sun fled below the horizon and the only light from above was the intermittent, twisting curtains of ghost fire. The ocean endured, and was eternal.

Land, though . . . land is not eternal.

Mere specks in the water, points of rigid darkness, away from where the krayk sing their ancient, sharp-toothed songs to each other and the leviathans blow steam towards the sky with each breath. The ocean swarms around these specks, battering at them with waves, cracking their dark rocks and drowning their shores again and again as the long moon and the short moon pull bulges of water in the elliptical rhythm of the tides. The land will not last: one day the ocean will overwhelm it and it will be reclaimed.

This will not solely be the ocean's doing, however.

The largest speck of land is insignificant next to the ocean, but might still be considered big by other measures. Fumes billow around its tallest points: not the fine white steam of a leviathan's breath, but the dark grey smoke of something bigger, older and infinitely more furious.

The land splits, and the spirits claw their way free.

The noise is beyond comprehension. It shakes the sky above, it even shakes the ocean as the very rock itself is torn asunder. The spirits vomit out ash, but that onrushing, obliterating cloud is backlit by the incandescent fire of their bodies.

The land will die. It will be suffocated, it will be buried and it will be burned. Nothing will survive.

The shockwave of the spirits' birth sends a mighty pulse through the waters of the ocean. In the deeps, it is nothing more than a mild swell that passes unnoticed: even beneath the hundreds of ships that escaped the land before it died, led by the dreams of the golden-masked thing that stares unblinking towards the western horizon.

When the pulse nears the shore, however, the shallows will not be able to contain its fury.

ACKNOWLEDGEMENTS

THE FIRST THANKS for *The Splinter King* goes to my manager Sarah Cottrell, who has always been very supportive of my "second career", and agreed to my request to take a twelve-month career break from my role to concentrate on my writing, even though she did not have to do any such thing. She also kept telling me she expected thanks for it in my books, but I don't think she thought she'd actually get any. But she is. Joke's on you, Sarah!

(Also, I ended up not going back. It remains to be seen who, if anyone, *that* joke is on.)

Thanks are also due to my first agent, Robert Dinsdale, for getting me this far; and to my new agent, Alexander Cochran, for taking it on from there. Having a good agent is so important for any writer, and I cannot recommend it enough.

Publishing timelines are strange, particularly when pandemics occur. I'm writing the acknowledgements for *The Splinter King* before I've even seen a physical copy of *The Black Coast*. However, I still need to throw out a thanks to the teams at both Orbit and Solaris, even though at time of writing I haven't actually seen the full results of their efforts, because I *know* the results are going to be exciting, and quite frankly it seems rude not to. Particular thanks go to Nazia, who even in the early stages has been exactly the sort of publicist any author would hope for, and to my editors

Jenni and Michael for their helpful, incisive feedback on how best to shape this novel and curb the "idiosyncracies" in my writing that I wasn't even aware of.

Huge thanks once again to Nye Redman-White, for truly invaluable assistance with language-bothering as I attempted to make things sound vaguely cohesive.

I must thank my beta readers, Jamie and Stewart, who are both wonderful people to bounce ideas off. Thanks also go out to the UK writing/convention folk (hopefully conventions are A Thing again by the time anyone reads this), who make it such a delight to go to random hotels and talk for a few days about making stuff up. It's an important part of making us feel like a community, and you're a strange bunch of vaguely co-workers, but I like you.

Thanks also to everyone else I've missed, out of my own negligence or forgetfulness (such as Kristina Amuan for me pointers on architecture, and Stefan Harrison for advice on names for metal hats, whom I *should* have thanked in the acknowledgements of *The Black Coast*. Belated thanks to both of you).

Lastly, and most importantly, thanks to my wife Janine, for being amenable to suggestions like "Why don't I stop going to work for a year so I can write a novel?" and "Why don't I give up work entirely so I can write novels?", and also for sharing her life with me and making mine so very much better as a result.

I'm not thanking my cats, because to be honest I've not heard a word of encouragement out of either of them.

FIND US ONLINE!

www.rebellionpublishing.com

/rebellionpub   /rebellionpublishing /rebellionpublishing

SIGN UP TO OUR NEWSLETTER!

rebellionpublishing.com/newsletter

YOUR REVIEWS MATTER!

Enjoy this book? Got something to say?

Leave a review on Amazon, GoodReads or with your favourite bookseller and let the world know!

"Vibrant and intricate worldbuilding"
Matthew Ward, author
of *Legacy of Ash*

BOOK 1 OF
THE GOD-KING
CHRONICLES

THE BLACK COAST

MIKE BROOKS

SOLARISBOOKS.COM